THE KEEPERS OF HOAME

Thomas Cross

ISBN: 1519342586
ISBN 13: 9781519342584

CHAPTER ONE

"A solution must be found," said the dark figure as he laid his hands on the table, "the problem will not go away."

The Autarch's Council Chamber was richly furnished with delicately carved wooden panelling and leather-upholstered chairs. It was a gloomy room, sunlight only allowed in through four, small, oblong windows high on one side. Swirling particles of dust danced in the shafts of light well above the men round the table.

Count Zastein stood upright as he addressed the other members of the seven-strong Inner Council. A tall man, he cast an imposing figure with his long, greying hair and black robes. The jagged scar on his left cheek showed above his beard, reminder of an adventurous youth many years previously.

"My Lord Autarch," he continued, "can we not consider promoting a worthy family to the rank of Despot?"

At the head of the table sat the Autarch, whose diminutive figure was in sharp contrast with the Count's broad frame. His eyes, deep set within a small, wrinkled face, moved to the man on the opposite side of the table from where Zastein was standing.

"Baron Schail?" he asked.

The slightly younger man with a pronounced chin stood up. "My Lord Autarch, Zastein," he began, "I am not sure the people are ready for the radical step the Count has suggested. I agree the difficulty appears intractable. It is now almost three years since Rattinger died and there is no sign of an heir materialising."

"What we need is fresh blood," cut in Zastein, still standing.

"Yes," agreed Schail, "but it would set a dangerous precedent to promote an ordinary black. We must protect the existing order."

"There won't be an existing order at the present rate," interrupted one of the other Council members.

"Too much in-breeding," said another.

Baron Schail continued, "That the problem is genetic is well understood. I am chiefly concerned with keeping our credibility if we promote a "worthy" family as the good Count suggested."

"I did not actually *suggest* it," Count Zastein gently corrected his friend, "I merely put it forward as a possible solution. Let us consider the options: if we do not bring in some fresh blood soon the situation will only get worse; I think I can say with confidence we are unanimous in that. So what options are we left with? If not a loyal and healthy black family then it will have to be someone from outside, but a credibility gap will have to be faced with either option."

The figures round the table nodded in agreement. Zastein finally sat down and when it was clear no one had anything further to add, the Autarch spoke. The council members listened intently to every word from his frail voice.

"The matter is of great concern to us and there is obviously no easy answer. I feel it has been useful to have an airing of views, but I don't think we should be rushed into anything. That is why I am going to ask you, Count Zastein," he turned to his right, "to head a committee to look into this whole matter. I also suggest Baron Schail be your deputy."

"Of course," said the Count, making a quick deferential nod of the head to his leader.

"Good, in that case I declare the meeting closed."

A hum of conversation arose as the members shuffled out of the chamber and down the adjoining passage. Gradually the group split up as councillors each went their own way. Schail and Zastein walked together out of the double doors at the end of the passage. They carried along the path by the extensive formal gardens that surrounded the Autarch's Palace. The snow had not long gone and the first few flowers had begun to show. The sun was quite bright as it broke from behind a cloud. After being inside the sunlight made Baron Schail sneeze.

"Oh dear," he said with a smile once his sneezing had finished, "that's better. Now, what did you think of the meeting?"

"Not wholly unsatisfactory, far from it in fact. At least the situation is being faced. There seems at last to be a will within the Council to come up with a solution, that's the main achievement. Goodness knows it's taken long enough. I'm sure you and I will be able to work something out and get the Autarch's agreement. Right now though I could do with a rest. I shall be off to the country to spend a while simply relaxing.

Apart from anything else I'll be able to think clearly about this and without interruptions."

"Good idea, I think I'll follow suit. Now the weather has cleared I'd like to see how the old estate is shaping up."

As he spoke a large dragonfly winged its way close by. Birds in the nearby trees sang loudly as they approached.

Schail went on, "Besides, I'm sure they can manage without us for a while, things are pretty quiet at present."

"Yes," agreed a thoughtful Zastein, not really concentrating on the conversation as his mind wandered, "Yes things are pretty quiet."

The birds, uncomfortable now at the close proximity of the men, changed their tune as they burst forth from the trees, soaring skywards.

CHAPTER TWO

The star cruiser "Cassandra" slipped silently through the void. In the ship's lounge an unequal conversation was taking place.

"Yeah, I tell you Scales, you've never seen anything like it," declared an overweight and overpowering traveller to the latest victim of his memoirs. "Everything about the place was fantastic – the scenery, the food, the women; the *women*! I tell you a guy hasn't lived 'till he's been to Tryon-Alpha Three. Now that reminds me, did I ever recount the first time I went through the Crab Nebula? Yeah I was only a young buck at the time, eager for adventure and eager to get in on a really big deal. We hadn't been long gone outta Station Six when I began to realise the potential of that part of the galaxy. I said to myself, "Boz my young fellow, you'd better seize this opportunity before it's taken away from you." And you know what? I set out straightaway...."

On and on he went, his double chin quivering as words cascaded from his mouth. Scales, the unfortunate recipient of this barrage, kept eye contact while grunting the odd word of acknowledgement so as not to seem too impolite. However, he looked up every time someone entered the lounge for a person he knew. Surely someone would come soon who he could drag in and so extricate himself from this garrulous bore.

As fate would have it one of the few other passengers that Scales had spoken with on the journey was getting ready to go into the lounge. Frank Thorn was in his cabin and had just finished a welcome nap. He studied himself in the mirror and noticed his eyes were still red. What he preferred not to notice was his rather plump appearance as he began to enter middle age. His slightly shorter than average stature and the drab, one-piece tunic he wore accentuated this, but then Frank was not someone who normally dressed conspicuously.

After having a good stretch he took the smaller of the two books by his bunk, left the cabin and made his way to the lounge. The corridors were dimly lit being on their nighttime cycle, but judging from the din coming from the lounge as he approached there were plenty of travellers choosing to stay up and socialise. In fact as he entered the room he was momentarily stunned by the bright, multicoloured lights beaming down and the wall of sound created by the noisy throng. He scanned the scene, taking it all in. The place was crowded with people talking loudly, most of whom were standing. Wine appeared to be flowing freely. Some others were on the short, colourful sofas arranged in little groups near the walls.......... was that someone trying to catch his eye?

'That's Scales,' he thought as he recognised the beckoning man, 'the individual with the greasy hair from the cabin next to mine. Odd that he should be calling me over, we've hardly said three words together the whole journey so far. Nice of him to make me feel welcome.'

He walked across the room and noticed the large, bald man lounging on the sofa opposite who stopped talking and turned as he approached. He found it amusing to see the lights playing on the man's glistening head.

"Hello there!" exclaimed Scales with exaggerated cordiality, then turning to his colleague, "This is Frank Thorn, the guy in the cabin next up to mine."

"Yeah, come and join us, my name's Boz. You must want a drink."

"Pleased to meet you. No drink for me thank you, I'm not thirsty right now."

Boz was puzzled by this answer and while he mulled it over, Frank sat down next to Scales who seized the initiative.

I haven't seen you in here before," he said, still striking a welcoming note.

"I did have a glance in here when we first started off twelve days ago, but I haven't been here since. Normally I prefer to stay in my cabin."

Scales looked interested.

"Twelve days since we left New Delos is it? I find it hard to keep track of days and nights out here in space. It's all very well dimming the lights in the corridor every now and then, but I find my body finds its own cycle."

"So does mine. I've just had a short sleep in fact. Thought I'd come here for a change. By the way have you noticed how few and far between the stars are around here?"

Boz cut in, "That's right, very few worlds out here on the perimeter. So what brings you to this remote corner of the galaxy?"

"A wealthy book collector on one of the moons circling the planet Phelis if you really want to know. I've been assured of some good sales to make the journey worthwhile."

"Book?" shouted Boz with a surprised tone in his voice as Scales mumbled an excuse and left their company, "you an antique dealer then?"

"Yes, but I specialise in books. I don't think I'm a particularly good dealer though, I get too attached to the merchandise," he smiled.

The other man pressed a couple of buttons on the dispenser at the end of the sofa and a fresh drink popped up. He took an eager sip before responding.

"Yeah, but who needs books? They became obsolete centuries ago. I've never learned to read or write and I've got on just fine."

The noise in the room grew louder as a group on the other side burst into raucous laughter.

"If there's anything I need to know I just ask my TRAC," the man continued as he indicated to the computer on his wrist.

Frank gripped the book on his lap.

"Indeed, but that's not quite the point. Anyway, this man I'm travelling to see sounds quite a character, he actually *owns* the moon he lives on. He's a recluse and has only a handful of people there with him, most of the work is done by robots."

"Robotics, now there's a good subject! When I was a boy I always loved those stories of robot armies during the Second War. In fact during this latest one I found it very profitable supplying both sides with robotic spares as well as ion converters. You know I started that company up with a partner named….. Chang or Cheng, something like that, it doesn't matter now he's long dead. He and I both wanted to expand our business in the three solar systems forming the Wasaki Empire. They were a big market, but were only just coming out of two centuries of isolation. A strange, proud people that had to be handled delicately, but I knew I could make a good deal there. You see Frank I know how to handle these primitive peoples and with my new partner's knowledge of the sector we'd soon have it sown up. Once I get the scent of a healthy profit I don't let go. The smell of money gets my adrenaline going! First I set about the pooling of our financial resources in the most efficient way...."

Frank was annoyed. 'What a bore; only interested in himself,' he thought, 'no wonder Scales slid off as soon as he could. I felt he was a slippery customer; he only called me over to get away! Look at this fat slob, he's still rambling on about himself. No, you mustn't be uncharitable Francis; forget the fact you wanted to read your book and listen to him. Poor fellow, he's probably lonely.'

"....So I used this process to ossify a bone structure to make a platform for the more vulnerable skin tissue. They were the best androids this side of Ursa Major."

He had actually stopped talking, so in his most interested voice Frank said, "Really, how fascinating. So what are you doing here, light-years from civilization?!

Boz suddenly became coy.

"Ah, I'm not sure I should say; business security and all that."

Frank gave an understanding smile.

'As if I could care less!' he thought, 'Now come on Francis, you're only annoyed because he's a bibliophobe.'

The background chatter continues at a high volume. A young woman in a brightly coloured, silky dress sat down briefly on the other end of Frank's sofa. She then saw someone she knew and moved away again without saying a word.

"Lots of people on board," Frank observed.

"Yeah,"

"Didn't expect that in this part of the galaxy."

"This book business," said Boz, reverting back to an earlier point in their conversation, "You say there's not much money in it."

"Well there could be I suppose. Some of the books I've sold have fetched quite a premium, but I'm not likely to make a mint, because of the way I choose to go about things. Since I left my home planet a few years ago I've preferred to move around with my wares. I generally go for the wealthy clients dotted about the place. It's not the most economic method with fares being what they are (most of the would-be profits go on travelling), but this way I get to travel and see interesting places as well as indulge in my hobby. I feel it's more of a hobby that pays for itself more than anything else. I don't consider money-making to be too important.

The other appeared quite horrified at this heresy. He whistled quietly through his teeth and fell silent for a while. Then he regained himself and took a gulp of his drink.

"Yeah I guess I'd better be getting along," he said, forcing a smile before downing the last of his drink. "I've got some work which I've got to get finished before we arrive."

He stood up and they shook hands.

"It's been nice talkin' with you Frank, I'll see you around."

As his large frame headed for the door it was eventually swallowed from sight by the mass of people still enjoying themselves in the crowded room.

'Hmm, that's one way to end a conversation,' Frank smiled to himself. 'My telling him I was not interested in profit had about the same effect as if I'd said I had bubonic plague. Oh well.'

Sighing, he settled more comfortably into his seat. He opened his book at last, but found it difficult to concentrate with all the racket in the lounge. It then became impossible when a group of young people came and sat down on the two sofas where he was and started talking in loud, exited voices. He gathered from what they were saying that this was a special party in progress and that virtually all the passengers were there. Frank did not remember being informed of it in advance, but then he had chosen to spend almost the entire journey by himself in his cabin. He had just happened to choose this time to try out the lounge.

Deciding enough was enough; he closed his book again and made his way out through the revellers. Just before he got to the door he heard a distinctive voice again and glancing to his left noticed Boz had not left, but had attached himself to someone else and was telling one of his stories. Frank did not stop, but pushed his way out into the empty corridor and began heading back towards his cabin.

'More than a bit foolish to think I'd be able to read in there,' he thought.

He found his ears ringing as the noise from the lounge receded into the distance. A couple of people walked past him in the opposite direction. Gradually his eyes became accustomed to the soft lighting and he turned a corner to find himself alone in a narrow passageway.

'Yes Francis,' he told himself, 'I guess you're just not a sociable creature.'

He walked on for a while and stopped at a view-port. The ship was crossing empty space between two arms of the spiral galaxy and from this vantage point no stars at all were visible. In fact it looked as if it was simply a jet-black area on the wall. It still held a fascination though and Frank found himself staring into the darkness.

"We'll soon be getting in amongst the stars again!"

The sudden, close interruption made him jump. Finding no one else present other than the speaker, a scrawny-looking character with strange, bulbous eyes. "How d'yer like being a pioneer then?"

Frank recovered quickly from the surprise to reply, "We're not true trailblazers you know. People have been across here before. Even before the military men made their way the Duo-Schonnen system had been re-populated, surely you know that?"

"Where's your sense of adventure man?" the intruder asked, only half-mockingly, adding with enthusiasm, "this is the first commercial cruise of modern times! Fine, so a few pioneers and eccentrics are out there, but you can't count them. Where we go today, others will follow."

"Hmm, that's what's planned – further flights. I certainly hope so, 'cos I'm not going all the way this time, I'm being dropped with instructions for the next cruise to pick me up; certainly hope they don't decide to cancel!"

"No worries!" the other returned, "this ship was way over-subscribed – I tell you, we are the first in a long line on this route. The rings 'round Duo-Climon are one of the wonders of the modern universe, there'll be no shortage of takers."

The man moved off again repeating, "No worries!" as he disappeared round a corner.

Alone once more, Frank settled back down at the view-port. Slowly his eyes re-adjusted to the blackness of space and he was once more absorbed in his own thoughts.

'Well God, you certainly ran out of material when you came to do this part of the universe didn't you.'

His prayer became more earnest.

'I'm sorry Lord I was anti-social back in the lounge. It's dreadful to think I'd rather be by myself than with other people. And I wasn't fair with that poor Boz; I'm just as bad as he is, wanting to talk about myself and things which interest me. I promise I'll go back there again tomorrow and try a lot harder.'

Once his eyes were fully accustomed to the scene he found if he peered hard enough he could make out just a few pinpricks of light in the darkness. It would be a fair while before the ship began to enter the next spiral arm and the screen become peppered with twinkling stars hosting untold solar systems.

Eventually Frank wandered back to his cabin. Sitting down on the bed he put the small book back where it had come from. It knocked his personal computer onto the floor and he stretched out a hand to pick it up when…BANG! The whole ship was rocked by a violent force and he was thrown right across his cabin.

He found himself lying on the floor by one of the walls. The room was in total darkness. Dazed, but otherwise unhurt, he got up and groped to the telescreen. He tried to activate it, but the equipment was dead. He felt his way round the wall towards the door, kicking clothes, books and furniture on the way.

'At least the artificial gravity has not packed in.'

When he got to the door it opened normally, so it was definitely a limited power-failure. But he wondered whatever had caused the violent jolt to the ship. He found the corridor was also pitch-black with no sign of life. There was an uneasy stillness. He strained to hear, but there was nothing.

Standing in the doorway for a few seconds, he tried to clear his head and gather himself. Then suddenly a loud, two-tone alarm started up, shattering the silence. At the same time red, emergency lighting came on in both corridor and room, while an electronic, pre-recorded message began over the tannoy. It was in a soft, female voice, totally calm: "We regret evacuation is necessary. Please follow the directional arrows to your life-support evacuation modules. Thank you. We regret evacuation is…."

Quickly darting back into his cabin, Frank glanced round before picking up a large, thick book off the floor. He then jumped back into the corridor and started running as fast as he could in the direction of the large, red, three-dimensional arrows that had appeared on the walls. Holographic images, they appeared to stand out from the bare metal.

As he ran a million and one thoughts flashed through his mind.

'Whatever must have happened? I don't want to die just yet, I've got unfinished business; the voice on this pre-recorded message sounds ludicrously calm in the circumstances.'

Then he found he was laughing to himself, 'As if they'd have some computer-produced message in a panicky voice screaming, "Get the hell out of here, she's gonna blow up!"'

He ran on, panting hard, down stairs as the arrows indicated. Presumably the lifts were out. Had not noticed the stairs before. Still no other soul around. After the stairs he charged down the last, short corridor, badly out of breath by now. He found himself in what was clearly the launching bay for the life-support evacuation modules, or escape pods as they were more commonly known. The alarm was not quite so loud here. By the look of things he was the first one there.

The pods were neatly lined up. There were several very large ones intended for passengers in times such as these. However Frank wanted to get away quickly and headed for one of the individual, tubular ones. Several androids were there on hand to supervise the evacuation.

'900 series,' he observed, 'a pretty basic model as they're stuck here in the bowels of the ship.

"We are here to assist you," the nearest one told him in measured tones.

"Good," the man replied, "I'm going in this one."

The pod's stabilizing fins for use in an atmosphere were folded up. It housed advanced tracking equipment and looked immaculate in its glossy gunmetal finish with silver nose. Wasting no time he climbed in hurriedly, at the same time realising he was shaking like a leaf.

'Hurry up,' he thought to himself as the android made sure the fittings were secure. It seemed to move slowly in the circumstances, but its unhurried and deliberate movements were, in fact, far more efficient than a rushing human would have been. The gentleness of its touch was most impressive. The last thing the android did before the lid moved across was to insert the intravenous feed-line neatly into his arm.

As soon as the lid was secure, gas began filling the compartment and the sealed escape pod moved into the ejection chamber. Frank felt his heart pounding and was still breathing heavily.

'These pods are really very complex life-support machines, I should be all right. Please God help me now!'

His mind was racing until the gas took effect and his consciousness left him. Nothing was felt by the time the module was catapulted from the stricken ship into the void.

CHAPTER THREE

A new day had broken over the planet Molten. It was a
beautiful spring that year and this particular day seemed
to encapsulate all the beauty of Mother Nature. The dawn had
just passed and the endlessly repeating daytime drama was beginning to unfold throughout the woodland scene.

Soft, early morning sunlight filtered through the trees
down to the leafy floor of the wood. Life in all its multiplicity
of forms was emerging, heralding the start of another busy day.
Small mammals scuttled through the loose undergrowth while
birds' song resounded from the branches high above. A large
beetle ran along a dead branch then stopped to feed.

Two young women entered the wood together searching for
firewood. Both were dressed simply and carried large, wicker
baskets for the task. They chatted eagerly to each other as they
walked along the familiar path, unconcerned about the wildlife that scattered as they approached.

"The pots sold well at the fairground again this year," said
one.

The speaker was called Rachael, an industrious member of the nearby village. She was heavy with child and walked rather awkwardly. Her snow-white hair was long and hung free, blowing in the slight breeze.

"People see your pots for what they are: good value for money," said Tamar, her slightly younger companion.

She too had strikingly white hair, but in a shorter style. Her attractive face was in contrast with the plain-looking Rachael.

"I like to think our pots are good quality. The extra money we got there is going to help for when the little one comes along."

"Of course."

"Paul is good with our money, though. He works it out so conscientiously I don't have to worry."

"I know what you mean."

Rachael brushed aside her hair, which had blown across her face.

"I notice Stephen's been up to his old tricks again," she remarked, changing the subject.

"What, using short weights again on the people from Asattan?"

"Yes, he's a total fool."

"The man's asking for trouble."

"That's it. Everyone around here knows what he's up to. Sooner or later he's going to get caught."

Tamar nodded in agreement and they continued deeper into the wood. They soon came to an area where the tall deciduous trees allowed much less sunlight to reach the floor. It did not seem too gloomy on this bright day though. Rachael felt a stone in her shoe and leant with one hand against a large trunk as she tried to get it out. The grey bark felt smooth and she had to be careful to avoid treading on its massive, twisting roots. Her companion stood patiently by.

Tamar was idly looking up at the treetops when she noticed something strange. Some of the branches high up were broken. A couple of beech trees seemed to have suffered extensive damage as if caught in a violent storm, but there had been no bad winds lately.

"Rachael?" she said as the other put her shoe back on, "look over there."

Together they peered in the direction Tamar was pointing.

"What, the trees?"

"Yes; seems very odd."

"Let's go and take a look."

The two of them walked over to the damaged beeches, still carrying their baskets. Their feet made a swishing noise through the leaves now as they moved off the path. A trail of destruction led them further on. Neither spoke as they climbed to the top of a small ridge. Rachael did not find the going easy in her condition. On the other side the ground fell away quite sharply forming a natural crater about a hundred metres in diameter. In it was a mass of tangled undergrowth, brambles and...

"What's that?" asked Rachael.

Without answering, Tamar put her basket to one side and slid down the wall of the crater towards the object of the question. It was a rounded, charred metal canister, black and dented.

"It's a container of some sort, come down and have a look. Never seen anything like it."

"No I don't think I should," Rachael replied with her hand on her large front.

Tamar scrutinised the container intensely, trying to find an opening. She was fascinated by this mysterious object that appeared from its trail of havoc to have come from the sky, passed through the trees and landed here in the undergrowth. She gently moved a bramble out of the way to inspect more closely a panel on top.

Suddenly the lid opened with a sharp hiss as some gas escaped. They both gasped and Tamar leapt back. Then, with feline curiosity, she slowly crept forward once more, leaning to see inside.

"It's a coffin!" she exclaimed.

"What!?"

"There's a dead body in it."

"I'm coming to have a look."

Carefully she descended towards her colleague, every movement deliberate. Tamar left the container to give her a hand.

"I don't know how I'm going to get back up there again."

"Come and have a look. There's a dead man inside."

As the couple peered over the edge Frank Thorn weakly forced his eyes open.

The women both gave a little scream, but stayed put where they were. Then Rachael announced the obvious, "He's alive!"

Nothing more was said for some time. They just stared as the emaciated figure with unkempt beard gradually closed his eyes again and lost consciousness. Rachael put her hand in and touched the body and was surprised to find it quite so cold. Without knowing what she was doing she took out the tube that was sticking in his arm and felt around for a while before deciding on a plan of action.

"Now listen, this is what I want you to do. Run back and get Paul and tell him what we've found. Tell him to bring something to put this poor soul in. I'll stay here."

"If you're sure you'll be okay. I'll be back as soon as I can," replied her younger companion before starting to scramble up out of the crater and heading back to their village.

After watching her go Rachael turned back to the container with the pale, sleeping figure in it. Soon her knees began to ache, but she found she could hitch herself up to sit on top of the mysterious object. There she waited.

This was a part of the wood she had not been to for a while. Assorted fungi adorned an old, rotten log not far away and a deep mass of brambles covered the far side of this dip in the wood's floor. For the first time that day she noticed the birds singing.

Some time passed and nothing happened. She began to wonder if she had killed this strange, thin figure in the coffin from the sky when she had pulled the tube from his arms. No, there was a faint heartbeat. Also, was it her imagination or was his skin really a little warmer to the touch?

The swishing sound of leaves was getting nearer, mixed with familiar voices. Their words could not be made out at first, then the two figures she had been waiting for appeared in sight.

"Hello my darling, are you all right?" called out Paul.

"Fine, thank you," answered his wife, cautiously slipping down off the canister to the ground.

Paul and Tamar had come with an old wooden barrow. It had large wheels and sturdy sides; an assortment of blankets had been placed inside. They left it as near to the crater as possible before sliding down towards where Rachael was waiting.

"So what's all this about?" asked the newcomer as he picked his way through the undergrowth.

They did not reply to his rhetorical question and Paul began a close examination of the alien vessel and its contents. A short, slightly-built man, he had the same snow-white hair as the other pair. He had a kind-looking face which had well-proportioned features and soft, brown eyes.

"I didn't know what to make of what Tamar told me, but she was so insistent I dropped everything and came immediately like she said." He hesitated to inspect further then continued,

" Well well, I still don't know what to make of it. Let's try to get him out and take him back. He looks in very poor shape, but we can't leave him here."

Paul and Tamar, with Rachael in support, eased the unconscious body out as carefully as possible. The book, which had been resting on the incumbent's chest, fell back into the container. Slowly they carried him in the direction of the barrow. Climbing up the edge of the crater proved awkward, for the leaves had by now mostly gone and the muddy ground was slippery. Tamar slid onto her bottom, but managed still to support the man's body.

"Whoops, careful!" exclaimed Rachael.

"Easy does it," said Paul.

They managed to get up and put the limp, thin figure into the barrow. Tamar put an arm under the man's knees and gently shifted his weight to one side, tugging a couple of blankets free, she spread them over him. She arranged another as a pillow; it would be a bumpy ride.

Meanwhile Paul helped his wife and once ready they started their journey home. He took charge of the barrow while the women walked either side, trying to keep the invalid as comfortable as possible. On the way the three speculated as to what this all meant. None of them had ever known such a thing as a coffin that fell from the sky. Paul charged the other two not to tell anyone about it.

"I think it best we keep this to ourselves, after all he is not one of us."

The women gave him a knowing look. Rachael re-arranged the pillow that was beginning to slip as the vehicle jolted along the path.

Paul continued, "His Excellency is coming to stay soon, we shall tell him all we know."

They nodded. Before long, the village was in sight. The huts were of wattle and daub construction, mostly quite small in size. There were very few people to be seen that morning.

Pushing the barrow before him, Paul headed for his and Rachael's hut on the near edge of the village. The fire had kept in as was witnessed by the thin column of smoke appearing from a chimney sticking through a hole in the thatched roof. There was an annex built onto the hut where the animals and fodder were kept. Another fenced-off and sheltered area was used for general storage. They managed to push him in here and out of sight without being noticed.

Inside the hut itself it was fairly gloomy. There was only the one large, square room with a thin layer of straw covering the floor. In the middle was the fire. It had a chimney formed out of a hollow trunk of a bota tree, covered in fireproof glaze. Not all the huts in the village had chimneys like this; it was a status symbol of the more successful families. Various cooking utensils hung near the fire on nails driven into the wood, a table for food preparation was to one side of the hearth. There were two beds of straw, each within a low, wooden framework, also a sizable carved chest and some stools with woven seats. Apart from this there was no other furniture.

Frank's limp body was taken from the barrow and placed on the bed nearest the door. Wasting no time Rachael began preparing a broth to feed their mysterious new arrival. Tamar decided to go back out to collect the firewood they needed. Paul stood watching his wife.

"If I can't be of any more help here I think I'll get my wheel out."

"You do that darling; if I need you I'll let you know."

While the broth was heating up Rachael tried giving Frank some water. She found it awkward to prop him up at first and wished her husband had not left. Putting the water down she hitched the whole, emaciated body so she could use the wall for support. She held the pewter mug to his cracked lips, but found most of it trickled down his beard. A spoon proved more successful.

With some water finding its way down his throat, Rachael noticed the man's swollen tongue beginning to move and eyes flicker.

"Come on, come on."

Gradually, weekly, the eyes opened. She put the mug down and fetched the broth to feed him.

After an aeon of sleep, consciousness was returning to him. His first impression was of a pale face with unnaturally white hair, clearly an angel. But why did the angel not wear white garments? Why was there a stale smell and why did he feel so weak?

Frank opened his mouth and received a small portion of the broth. He felt the hot food go down his throat as his eyes became better focused.

'A large woman,' he thought, 'why did she have a Latin cross tattooed on her forehead?'

"That's right, Master, you eat up. It'll do you the power of good."

The invalid swallowed then tried to speak, but did not have the strength. Well at least he was alive; he had to be, no one could feel this lousy in Heaven.

"No, Master, don't try to talk, just eat. You need it."

'I can understand her – civilisation! Thank God. Funny accent though..."

He felt himself slipping away once more and had not the strength to fight it. Back he went into dreamless sleep and Rachael decided to leave the food for now. She would try again in a little while when, she hoped, this most strange of newcomers would be more receptive.

More receptive he was, as slowly but surely Frank began to regain his strength. Many days went by, as gradually he was able to speak and move. His muscles were at first pitifully weak through lack of use. With advice from the village physician they helped him with repeated exercises to build up tonicity. It would be a long while before he could start to walk again though. How long he had spent in the escape pod he had absolutely no idea, except that it must have been far longer than the equipment was designed for.

Indeed the escape pod's feed line must have run out long before the machine had landed on this planet. It was only after he had begun to recover that he looked down on this skinny frame and realised quite how close to death he must have come. As time passed and he regained weight he still found himself feeling very tired. He felt certain that the days here were longer and the gravity slightly greater than the Earth standard worked to upon the ship and his body took some time adjusting to them. Still, he was alive and it was not all bad news: the new, slimmed-down Frank Thorn was pleased with his transformed figure once he reached a reasonable weight and resolved to keep it that way.

His hosts Paul and Rachael turned out to be the gentlest, kindest, most generous people he had ever known. Nothing was too much trouble for them, although they seemed unable to answer his questions as to the name of the planet or whether there were any other known survivors from the '*Cassandra*'. Indeed they did not appear to have any knowledge of space travel at all. It quickly became obvious that he had landed amongst a primitive culture, so it was not too surprising they did not know of such things, It did not bode well for his early resettlement within the galaxy's mainstream civilization.

He gathered that Paul, while an artisan, was a highly respected member of the village, His younger sister Tamar lived in the next hut by herself. She was due to be married soon. Paul was a potter by trade, renowned for his craftsmanship. He was also the deputy Head of the village; a post appointed by "His Excellency" Frank was informed. As to who "His Excellency" was Frank could only guess at this stage, because his hosts were not very forthcoming when he questioned them on the subject. From the way they spoke of him he got the impression they were more in awe of him than actually afraid, which was a relief.

Inevitably it was not long before the other villagers found out about the potter's new guest. Although curious they did not, to their credit, pry at all. The village Head was an old man with failing sight. He came to visit once to find out what all the fuss was about, but left after only a brief stay, reassured that Paul and Rachael had everything in hand.

"So you'll speak to His Excellency as soon as he arrives back from the Capital?" asked the Head of the village standing by the lintel as he was leaving.

"Yes, I'll do that," Paul gave his promise again.

He recognised that the old man was seeking reassurance; he had just told him twice.

"Good," said the visitor, "I shall leave the matter in your hands."

Soon after he began to recover from his ordeal, they moved Frank to a small extension to their hut that Paul quickly built with the help of some of the other villagers. Here he was able to enjoy some privacy while happy in the knowledge that he was not depriving others of theirs.

Rachael gave birth around the time that Frank began to walk again. They named their healthy baby Catherine. Paul came into Frank's room after daybreak to tell him the news.

"Both mother and baby are doing fine, Master," said the proud father with an unrestrained smile across his face.

"That's wonderful news, I'm so glad."

"The Lord be praised! Tamar is still with her and the midwife has just left. It's nice to have you with us to share the good news so early in the morning, Master."

Frank thought he had let a certain matter go on too long, now was as good a time as any to bring it up.

"Paul," he began awkwardly, "I wish you would call me by my name: "Frank" rather than "Master" the whole time. After all I'd like to think of us as friends."

His host looked uneasy.

"I'm sorry master, I don't think it would be proper for me to do that."

Then he perked up a bit.

"His Excellency will be here soon. He will explain everything to you. That would be best."

Frank decided not to press the point. He did not want to make Paul feel any more uncomfortable on this, his most happy of days.

"Alright I'll do that," he said, managing a smile, "May I see the baby?"

"I should think so, if we just have a quick peep."

As the potter leaned forward to help his guest to his feet he said, "I thank the Lord Jesus that he has been so kind to grant us this great blessing of a daughter. Also that Rachael has come through the birth so well."

Although he had realised it from very early on, only now did Frank wonder as to the significance of this forgotten planet having Christianity. Had missionaries brought it along with the language? Or were these people descendants of a lost expedition or colonising mission, which had set out before the Second War?

He had learned that their religion was the reason why they all had a cross tattooed in the middle of their foreheads, but it was not a custom he had come across elsewhere.

Every seventh day all villagers went off to a large meeting hall on the other side of the community. Frank had never been invited; he presumed they did not know he shared their faith, not having the mark on his forehead. He was not bothered, however, because he preferred to worship by himself.

"Can you manage, Master?" asked Paul interrupting his thoughts.

"I could do with some support," confessed the other as he held his arm out. Together they went through to take a glimpse at mother and child.

Time passed and Frank's walking improved. Now that he could get about better he was able to help around the home more effectively, which pleased him. Rachael seemed afraid to let him at first, but he had insisted.

The temperate climate was most agreeable; he was not one for extremes of temperature. Too many of the planets he had visited had them. In fact just to be able to live outside was a novelty; the majority of populated planets being only inhabitable within great domes or underground complexes. The climate was reminiscent of his home planet, but here the nights were far darker, inky black due to there being no moon and so few stars visible.

Having left his chronometer on board the ship he found himself frequently wondering what the time was. To his astonishment the natives of this land appeared to have no equipment to measure time, even though their technology was quite advanced in other fields such as furniture and metalwork. He knew better than to expect intricate timepieces, but there were not even the crudest of chronometers, water clocks or the like. Their lives revolved by the light of the single sun of their system and seemed none the worse for it. It took the space-traveller a lot of getting used to, however. He worked out that the new

Earth-year must have been seen in: 'I bet 2602 has a few more surprises up her sleeve yet,' he mused.

The domestic animals, fauna and flora originated on Earth, as was the case on thousands of colonised worlds throughout the known universe. No surprises there.

One thing he missed more than anything else was the absence of books. From a conversation with Rachael he was led to understand there was none in the village, which he found hard to believe. He could do without advanced technology, he had never been a great fan of it anyway, preferring the simple life, but he did miss a good read.

The other villagers were always courteous, but tended to keep their distance and seemed somewhat wary of the stranger within their midst. There was one striking thing about them all and that was their hair. Young and old, male and female, they all had the same pure white, cool-like hair. He felt it was rude to ask about this, but he had never seen humans quite like it before. With his own dark hair he stood out as dramatically different and it was this, perhaps, which made the people cautious of him. He could not complain about his treatment for one moment though. They had enthusiastically helped with the construction of his room and were polite to the point of subservience.

'But where the heck am I?' he wondered.

His hosts were so kind, but always evaded the issue when he tried to find out where this planet was. In fact they clammed up completely and looked most uncomfortable if he so much as mentioned space travel or where he was from. As far as he could tell they had not heard of any other survivors from the '*Cassandra*'. He did not want to embarrass them with persistent questions, because they had been so good to him. Although having limited means they had housed him, nursed, fed and clothed him, all totally ungrudgingly. In fact they appeared to find great joy in helping him and seemed genuine enough. Maybe they were fattening him up for the ritual cannibalistic feast at the end of the year. He hoped not.

He dismissed this fanciful notion with a laugh, thinking, 'No, they put the inhabitants of my so-called Christian home planet to shame.'

Frank was acutely conscious that after all this time he was still not pulling his weight. Collecting wood and keeping the fire going were not much compensation for all the food, clothing and shelter he was still receiving after all these weeks. His lack of knowledge about most of the villagers' basic skills annoyed him, but did not seem to perturb his hosts. The only time they appeared bothered was when he questioned them about matters outside village routine. The best answer to his probing he ever got was that "His Excellency" would be able to give him all the answers when he came.

Late one evening he was considering this problem as he stood outside the hut extension built for him. He leaned against a fence and stroked his beard, peering into the crepuscular sky watching the few stars come out. Due to his poor eyesight he had to squint to see any at all. He had not shaved since arriving and had got used to having a beard. Although all the village men were beardless he had never seen any of them shave, they simply did not grow facial hair it seemed.

A wind was getting up and the gathering clouds were quickly swallowing up the sparse crop of stars that had been visible. Even on a cloudless night the celestial lights were scarce compared with all previous planets he had been on.

'I was never particularly interested in star charts, which is a pity, because I might have been able to work out where I am. Mind you, if only I had not taken off my wrist computer on board ship, that would have told me....if the damn thing wasn't on the blink that is.

'Wonder who this "Excellency" fellow is. I've read of primitive tribes worshipping computers or robots or even monsters. Yes, but Francis these people are Christians and clearly more advanced than that. He must be quite an awesome character judging from the way people refer to him. I wonder when he'll come; they keep saying he's going to. It will probably be pure bathos, some little old man like the village Head. Well if it *is* a man there's one thing certain: he'll have white hair.

He heard someone approaching and turned to see who it was.

"It feels like rain, Master."

It was Paul.

"Yes, I was just contemplating the stars."

The potter joined him by the fence and they stood silently together for a while. Then Frank spoke.

"Actually there is something I've been meaning to ask you about. When you first discovered me did you happen to notice a book in the escape pod?"

"I'm sorry, a what?"

"A book."

"Sorry, Master, I don't understand."

Frank frowned in disbelief. He knew this culture was too backward for the more advanced modes of data capture, but surely they could read. He made signs with his hands to indicate how a book opened.

"A book, which people read; surely as you're Christians you must have a Bible."

"Ah yes, books. Of course, I'm sorry, Master. *We* do not have them, only the blacks, but I know what you mean. I did not notice a book in the er.... Where we found you, but there could be one there. I can ask Rachael and Tamar if they found one."

"Good, failing that can you take me to where you found me?"

"Certainly, Master, I can take you tomorrow morning if they have not got it."

"Excellent. Thank you."

Frank thought he would seize the opportunity while he had the initiative.

"I'd welcome the chance to have a good nose round the escape pod. Remarkable machines you know, able to travel extraordinary distances. Have you heard of any other ones landing near here?"

"No, Master I haven't. It would be best for you to speak to His Excellency when he arrives. He will tell you everything you need to know."

'I'm sure he will,' thought Frank wryly, 'that was the inevitable answer.'

He looked up again at the black sky and felt the first few drops of rain on his face.

CHAPTER FOUR

It rained hard throughout the night and Frank found it difficult to get to sleep. Water trickled through the roof in two or three places, but fortunately these were away from the bed. Considering the ferocity of the downpour the hut stood up to it surprisingly well. Some time passed and he did drop off and go into a deep sleep. This would have continued well into the morning had he not been roused by the sound of people approaching quickly, splashing through the puddles. His sub-conscious was trying to fit the noise into a dream when the sharp click of the latch woke him. Coming to, he became aware of a group of men hurriedly piling into the room out of the rain.

"I'm sorry, Master," announced Paul, "but their Excellencies have arrived and want to see you straightaway."

"Eh....what?"

He sat up in bed to see what this intrusion was all about. It was a grey dawn and Paul lit the candle on the stool by the bed. Frank could see fairly clearly the two men the potter had brought in with him. They took their oilskin capes and hats and handed them to Paul who placed them carefully at the foot of the bed. Paul exchanged a few whispers with the men before going out leaving the two imposing figures who turned to face Frank.

He used the few seconds before they spoke to take in their appearance. The one on the right was broad and wore black robes, trousers and knee-length boots. He must have been around sixty to sixty-five Earth years with greying hair, beard and a long scar on his left cheek. He was having to stoop to avoid his head hitting the roof of the hut.

The other man was around ten years younger and had a pronounced chin. He was bald at the top of his head, but had dark hair on either side. 'Wait; they have not got the white hair of the others!'

"My name is Count Zastein," announced the one on the right. "This is Baron Schail, you will address us each as "Your Excellency"."

He spoke in a stern, authoritative voice, his countenance was forbidding.

"Yes, Your Excellency."

Frank recognised a powerful man when he saw one, now was not the time to antagonise such a person.

"Tell us who you are and where you have come from."

Ever since he had arrived he had wanted to explain this to his hosts, but they seemed too afraid to listen. Now someone was actually asking him he suddenly became cautious and thought twice about telling the truth. He briefly considered making something up, but the villagers would probably already have passed on to these men what he had told them.

"Well, my name is Frank Thorn and I was on board a space-craft when something happened…"

He began falteringly in order to gauge what sort of reaction he was getting. There was none.

"….I'm not sure what it was, a meteorite perhaps…. Unlikely, but…. Anyway, I managed to get into an escape pod and the next thing I knew I was here on this planet."

Still no reaction. The two men were frozen like statues, studying him like a specimen under a microscope. He began to feel rather embarrassed sitting up in bed and wondering whether to ask them if he could get up or get stools for them to sit down on.

Then another thought burst into his mind and he asked, "Do you know of any other survivors?"

"No," answered Zastein abruptly. He then modified his tone to ask, "How many were there on this spaceship?"

"Oh, about three hundred passengers plus crew I think."

His interrogator raised his eyebrows in alarm.

'Well that got a reaction!' thought Frank who felt some reassurance was in order.

"But many of these were in the lounge some way away from the escape hatches. I fear there may have been very few survivors; I could be the only one. After all I have been here some time now and no others have turned up it seems."

That did the trick, they both looked much relieved. The next question came from the man on the left, Baron Schail.

"Have you discussed this at length with the villagers?"

"No, not really, they seemed afraid when I mentioned it at first so I haven't said anything for a long time."

Frank wondered if he had just dug a hole for himself. If there were no other survivors and he had not said much to the villagers they could probably dispose of this intrusion into their world without any fuss. As the question and answer session progressed, however, he began to get the impression that they were genuinely interested and he began to relax a little. The pair quizzed him about space travel (a phenomenon they appeared to be aware of), where he was from, what sort of social structure his home planet had, even whether his hair was its natural colour! He felt it was high time to get some of his own back.

"Can you tell me where I am please?"

"Hoame," the Count answered.

"Home? There's no place like home!"

To say Frank's quip was not fully appreciated by his audience would be an understatement. The two stone-like faces continued to bear down on him and he again felt uneasy as he sat up in bed in his night attire. It was too late to say anything about it now.

"This is the planet Molt, or Molten if you prefer," informed Baron Schail. "You are in the Autocracy of Hoame, in the district known as Ephamon."

"I see, thank you, Your Excellency," Frank returned politely while thinking ironically, 'So now I know everything!'

Their questioning went on for some time. The emphasis shifted to Frank Thorn the man: his beliefs, politics, ambitions and such-like. He answered as honestly as possible; not knowing what sort of answers his interrogators wanted to hear. He got no feedback from their faces, set like flint as they were.

He shifted his position in bed as it was by now feeling most uncomfortable. The two tall men turned away and whispered to each other inside the door. It was a small room, but with the rain still pouring down outside Frank did not catch a word of what was being said. He had just opened his mouth to ask if he could get up when they turned back and Count Zastein addressed him.

"Mister Thorn, I am a busy man and cannot devote the time to you that I would like to. It would have been preferable by far to have arranged an interview in greater depth tomorrow. As it is I have not got the opportunity. Regretfully, therefore, we will have to settle your case here and now. I shall come straight to the proposal I wish to make.

"This planet has been cut off from all contact with the rest of the universe for a very long time. It was by chance you landed here, but for your own good I strongly advise you to give up all hope of ever getting back to your former life again."

The large seal ring on Zastein's left hand flashed as it reflected the candlelight. Frank stared up at his dark frame, what was the man leading up to? He did not have to wait much longer to find out.

"On behalf of the Autarch of all Hoame I am giving you two options as to your future: you can either go into permanent exile, in which case you will have complete freedom to say whatever you wish as far as we are concerned. Or else you may take up the administration on our behalf of one of the districts of this country. If you accept the latter course you shall have a fair degree of autonomy, but will have to abide by certain rules. We have got this society ordered the way we want it and do not take kindly to radical change. You would have to accept a fresh identity and never mention your previous life or space travel again. No mention at all of even the possibility of life beyond this planet. This post would initially be for a trial period, full training would be provided and you would be directly responsible to me."

This certainly was not what Frank was expecting; he was stunned. He managed a quick, "I see," when the Count paused before continuing.

"I realise that the decision you make will affect your entire future, but I would prefer it if you make your mind up in the next few days. I shall arrange for a man to come here this afternoon and give you further details."

"I can probably give you an answer now, but can you tell me why? I haven't had any experience in administration."

"A clerk will be provided who will brief you on such things should you accept."

Frank thought, 'Fine, but that doesn't answer my question.'

The visitors turned to go, but Frank finally got out of bed and stood in his nightgown facing them. He was confused and flustered about the puzzling offer just been put to him, the last thing he was expecting. He must get a proper answer to one more question before they left.

"But, but what's the catch? There must be something terrible about the post for you to be offering it to a complete stranger! Er…Your Excellency."

It was Baron Schail who replied this time. The man double-backed to lay a firm hand on Frank's shoulder, looked him in the face and smiled. There was warmth in his eyes.

"No there is no "catch". Thyatira is in need of a leader and no one else is suitable. Should you accept you will be well briefed and given expert administration advice. You need not worry.

"You have not had this put on to you in ideal circumstances we realise. We were hoping to be able to spend a great deal more time with you – and in more salubrious surroundings," he added scanning the mean interior with an expression of sorrow. "Unfortunately the Count and I have been called back to the Capital earlier than anticipated.

"If you feel you have not enough information with which to make a decision the clerk will answer all reasonable questions you have."

They were putting their capes back on while Frank stood there with his mind working nineteen to the dozen.

'They cannot be leaving just yet, I've got so much more I want to find out and I don't want to wait. If those are the only two choices I've got then there is surely only one conclusion to come to. I hate leaving things up in the air, I'd rather tell them now and get it over and done with.'

"I accept the post, thank you Your Excellency."

"Good," said Count Zastein. "I shall send my clerk Offa to brief you this afternoon. You shall have the rank of Junior Despot."

They put their hats on and Schail opened the door for his superior. The rain had eased off considerably and the sky was brightening up.

Before stepping out Zastein turned round and added in a stern voice, "We have a well ordered society in Hoame and it must remain that way. Bear that in mind at all times, plus the fact you are responsible to me."

Then he concluded in a slightly lighter tone, "Offa is a good man, he will tell you everything that is required of you. Listen to him; he will guide you well. I shall look forward to our next meeting Despot Thorn, I hope to spend more time with you then."

"Thank you Your Excellency."

They were gone, leaving Frank feeling bemused, standing in the middle of the hut in his nightclothes staring at the shut door. He shuffled back to his bed to lie there and think for a while. On his way a large drop of water fell from the ceiling and went down his back, which made him shiver.

'They were a pretty intimidating pair. I wouldn't like to meet them on a dark night! Why do they need me if they can spare someone who is an expert on administration? There must be something wrong about it. The whole thing is baffling Francis, but I don't see that I had any real choice. At least this way I'll have a job and presumably food and shelter. The best thing to do is to see how it goes and make my mind up later.

'I've got so used to seeing the white-haired villagers that the sight of those dark-haired "Excellencies" seemed strange. They didn't have the crosses on their foreheads either. What's more to the point is they were not surprised at the mention of space travel. Perhaps they have spacecraft, but the ordinary people do not – that Zastein character said about they have their society just the way they wanted it. Ah, but why then did he also say this planet is cut off? I don't know.

'Heavenly Father you certainly do work in mysterious ways. I wonder what you've got lined up for me on this primitive planet.'

'My book! If this clerk, or whatever he is, is coming this afternoon I don't want to waste any time getting to see my escape pod, I might not get the chance later.'

The storm had completely passed now and it was easily bright enough for him to extinguish the candle. Next to the candle stand were the remains of the apple he had eaten the night. It had taken some time to get used to the fact that the apples here were not core-less. Hurriedly he dressed and left the hut, stepping out straight into a large puddle. He gave a curse then glanced about to see if anyone was watching him. It seemed not; good.

Round the corner came a pair of the local priest's assistants, they were making preparations for a wedding soon to be held in the village. Tamar had carefully explained to Frank how important the institution was for her people. She told him it was for life and any violator of its sacredness would face ostracism by the community, although adultery was not actually an offence in law. He had been pleased to hear the Christian ideal of marriage being upheld here, on all too many planets it was abused, not taken seriously or even ignored altogether.

The priesthood was, of course, one of the most highly regarded occupations. It was on a par with the village Head and his deputy. The teachers were not far behind in this hierarchy, education being valued greatly. He had not visited the school, but gathered the main subjects taught were various art forms, Bible stories, plus their society's social and moral codes.

He made his way to the main hut where Paul, Rachael and Tamar sat flushed with excitement. Baby Catherine lay fast asleep in her crib. They greeted him enthusiastically when he entered and Rachael fetched his breakfast, which he sat down to eat.

"Thank you, Rachael."

"It is a pleasure, Master, or rather I should address you as "My Lord" from now on."

"Is that the way a Junior Despot is addressed?"

She nodded, "Yes, My Lord, all Despots."

"Does this mean I shall be in charge of you?"

"No, My Lord, this is Ephamon which is under the direct control of His Excellency. Thyatira is a long way from here."

"Does that mean His Excellency Count Zastein is a despot, a senior one?"

"Oh no, he is a member of the Inner Council, a Keeper, he has the Autarch's ear.

'About time he gave it back,' thought Frank, who by now knew better than to say it out loud.

As he began to tuck into his meal, a ginning Paul came forward with a leather purse that he was shaking to indicate its contents.

"His Excellency was pleased with us for having looked after you, he gave us this: thirty silver stens. He gave Tamar another thirty for discovering you."

Frank ate on as the short, fair man pulled a silver coin from the purse and held it out to show him.

'Thirty pieces of silver,' considered the new appointee, 'an ominous sum.'

"I'm pleased he has rewarded you for your help and kindness towards me. I only wish I had something to give you myself. As it is, I have another favour to ask you Paul."

"Yes, Mast...My Lord."

"The book I spoke about last night."

"Ah yes, Tamar thinks she might have seen it the day she found you."

"That's right, My Lord," confirmed his sister, "Although I can't be absolutely sure. It could still be there."

Frank said, "Let's hope so. Can one of you take me to where I landed? If it's not too inconvenient I'd very much like to go when I've finished breakfast."

Both Paul and Tamar volunteered and as soon as their guest was ready, the three of them set off together.

Although it was no longer raining, the leafy path was sodden with some very muddy areas. The trees in the wood were saturated and large drops of water fell intermittently off them. It took a while for them to locate the hollow where the escape pod had laid to rest; Tamar led them past it at first. When Frank caught sight of the machine that had saved his life, it struck him how different it looked from when he had first seen it on board the '*Cassandra*'. Instead of the immaculate grey with a silver nose cone it was charred and dirty. The surface was heavily pockmarked, the effect of interstellar dust particles at high velocity. Most stabilizing fins had been ripped off on its way through the trees and there were some bad dents and scratches down its entire length. Leaves and even moss covered the once-gleaming machine.

'But it did its job, got me to an inhabitable planet safely.'

"I must see inside," he informed them.

He was beginning to have nasty visions of finding his beloved book all sodden and warped. To his relief the lid had shut automatically again after he had been rescued, so if it was inside it should be in good condition. Their only problem was that the lid had jammed tight and would not open.

Frank found the control panel was no longer operational and tried to force the lid open with a piece of wood nearby. After much exertion it opened.

His heart sank, "Oh no, it's not there."

Climbing in to take a better look he exclaimed, "Ah there it is! It's fallen down the nearside."

There was his beloved tome, well fingered, but in fine condition. He thumbed it as the other two looked on.

"I was given this for my seventeenth birthday," he explained. "It was all I could grab when I got away. Gosh it's nice to have this back again."

Paul and Tamar showed no real interest in his discovery and even seemed disappointed as to what all the fuss was about. Frank finally realised they were not going to ask about his book so he tucked it under one arm and tried to find if there was anything else of use to be had from the pod.

'I thought there'd be at least one gun and a survival kit, but there's nothing of the sort,' he wondered as he rummaged about the interior of the machine.

All he could find was a first-aid kit with a broken lid. Considering this was better than nothing, he brought it out and together the trio left the escape pod for the last time.

On the way back, Frank studied the trees. They were mainly beech trees in that part of the wood, he recognised those. There were others he was not certain about, possible genetic modifications, but then he was no botanist.

That afternoon the clerk named Offa came as promised. The weather had cleared considerably and Frank, sitting inside the door of his room, saw him coming from a distance. The first impression he got was of a large, rotund figure with a bad limp. As he got closer he saw a middle-aged man with short, black hair and stumpy legs who was clearly over-weight. He had a cheerful, rounded face with a pale complexion.

Frank went out to meet him and as he did a beaming smile came over the man's plump face.

"Offa, I presume."

"Yes, Sir," he replied still smiling, "you're the new despot that I'm taking to Thyatira."

"Oh you're actually going with me."

"Why yes, Sir, the Count told me to deliver you safely…"

"Here, do sit down."

They took their seats inside the door as Offer continued.

"Thank you…. To your new domain and help you run the despotate until I think you're able to manage on your own."

He smiled again and Frank, finding it infectious, smiled back.

"I see; well that's good, because I'm sure I'll need all the help I can get. What sort of place is it, I mean how big for a start?"

"Thyatira is the smallest of all the despotates with only two villages plus the castle and its surrounds…"

'A castle!' thought Frank, 'sounds medieval.'

"….but strategically it is, in fact, quite important. But I don't want to get too heavily involved in the detail now, Sir; we will have plenty of time on the journey for me to tell you about that. I must admit, however, that Thyatira is the only one of the eleven despotates I have never been to. But we shall not be travelling alone."

"No?"

"No, Sir, the Miner Triplets will be travelling with us. They are natives of where we are going, so I'm sure they'll be happy to fill in the fine details."

"Good."

"Yes, and there'll be a wagon and six to take us there. The journey takes us through Bynar, at the dakks' speed it won't take us less than five days for sure."

'Dakks,' thought Frank, 'I haven't seen a dakk for a good while: "the Frontiersman's Friend." One of the few genetic experiment success stories.'

A completely artificial creature, it was created a genera-tion before a storm of popular sentiment saw inter-planetary legislation banning fresh research. Used in a thousand solar systems, the dakk was not a particularly efficient beast of bur-den. A quadruped, it looked something like the cross between a horse and a camel, though smaller than both. It had propor-tionately longer front legs than the other two animals and did not have nearly the same strength or carrying ability. It could bear a man for a short distance, but then quickly got fatigued. It was more efficient when pulling wheeled vehicles in teams, but only then at slow speeds.

Where the dakk scored over its rivals was its ability to survive. For a mammal it could operate at remarkable ex-tremes of temperature, both hot and cold. It had too the extraordinary ability to breathe in and utilise either oxygen or, for a short while, carbon dioxide. Dakks also stood up to incarceration within the suspended animation chambers of spaceships for long distances far better than either horses or camels could. They bred readily and were easy to feed. Not for nothing were they beloved of colonists the galaxy over. Their presence in a temperate climate like Molton's suggest-ed to Frank that such colonists probably brought them here long ago and further that there were unlikely to be either horses or camels here, because they would soon make dakks redundant in this environment. Then he had only seen a tiny fraction of the planet since he landed, so he quizzed Offa on this point.

"Sorry, Sir," came the answer. "I've never heard of such ani-mals for sure. The dakks will get us there without any trouble."

The clerk gave a little chuckle before continuing.

"I've arranged for some good clothes to be delivered to you this afternoon, I think you'll like them."

"That's very kind."

"Not at all, Sir. The Count asked me to get you some, er... more suitable clothes for your new station in life."

He gave that disarming smile again. When he did so his whole face lit up and Frank considered that a journey with him as company should be most pleasant. Not that Frank usually went by first impressions, but his guide-to-be's eyes told him here was a man without guile.

There was one important point he felt he must raise now. He spoke just above a whisper, "Count Zastein said something about my having to change my identity, is that right? If so, why?"

"It is for the best, Sir. Only a small group know anything about space travel and it would be a shame to worry the whites unnecessarily."

"You obviously have heard about it."

"I have been in the employ of Count Zastein since I was a youth Sir, he knows he can trust me not to say anything."

"Am I going to be given a new name then?"

"No need to change your name, Sir, but I've been asked to spread the news that you are in fact a member of the ruling class of Oonimari."

"Where!?"

"Oonimari, it's a country a great distance away. Most people haven't been outside Hoame and nobody from this country has been there in living memory; it's taken on a mythical quality in fact. Only another despot would ask you about it, Sir, I suggest you do not say too much if quizzed."

"You *will* tell me more about Ooni... whatever on our journey I hope."

"Yes, Sir, there'll be plenty of time for that."

Frank laughed to himself. What a strange people these were; what a lot he still had to learn about them. It was clear though that here was a society ruled by a few who knew the truth about the universe and the many who did not. The latter did not appear oppressed or unhappy in their plight He would have felt it at least some of the time over the past weeks.

For some strange reason, he was being initiated into the few. Frank would have been delighted with food and shelter until a rescue ship arrived to take him back to civilization. If in the meantime they wanted to make him some sort of petty, regional ruler where was the harm in that? He would try to make his subjects' lot as pleasant as possible while he was here, but he was not going to go against the system. There was no point in rocking the boat and ending up in some dungeon or whatever these people did.

"So are you saying not even the other despots know there are thousands of inhabited planets out there?"

"No they don't, Sir, only the Keepers, that is the Member of the Autarch's Inner Council. To the best of our knowledge the other countries are ignorant of these things also. The Keepers of Hoame are powerful men."

Thought Frank, 'Well that old cliché about knowledge equals power certainly works around here. I wonder what other things they know...'

Offa continued, "Of course despots and the rest of us are privy to some things the whites do not know."

Frank was about to say something when Offa called out of the door, "Over here!"

He got up and with his heavy limp moved out to meet two villagers who had arrived with a laden dakk. The beast seemed a little restless and of its handlers had to keep a tight grip on its reins as he stood in front of it. Frank stepped out of the door to watch the scene. The buff-coloured animal was breathing heavily through its nostrils while the clothes forming the load were taken from its back and into the hut. A considerable wardrobe was being delivered. The clerk exchanged some words with the villagers who had by now largely managed to calm the dakk.

Offa and Frank went back indoors to inspect what had been brought while the villagers waited outside.

"How about this, Sir?"

He held a black leather jerkin, which was heavily studied.

"Phew that looks imposing!"

"Try it on, Sir."

He did, a surprisingly good fit. Who had estimated his size for these clothes he wondered; they had probably asked Tamar. After the light, woven clothes he had worn since his arrival, this new outfit seemed very heavy. There were a number of entire sets of clothing plus a wooden chest into which the garments fitted. They were exquisitely made and must have cost a great deal.

"Try the trousers on, Sir."

"Right. Did you say you had bought them?"

"That's right, with directions and finance from the Count."

"They must have set him back a bit."

"I think he can bear it," returned the clerk with his smile. "Besides he sees you as an investment."

Frank did not reply, but took his time sifting through and trying on the clothes given him. There was a wide selection from the weighty jerkins to silken gowns. He looked up from buckling a belt, the trousers had turned out a fraction long and Offa took them back.

"Do you like the outfits, Sir?"

"They're amazing! Yes thank you very much, Offa."

"I'll get these brought up a fraction this evening and bring them along tomorrow morning so you can wear a pair for our journey. It's quite a long way, so I was hoping it would not be inconvenient if we started off early tomorrow morning."

"Fine."

"Good, I'll make sure we get to you shortly after daybreak, Sir. There'll be the five of us: we two plus the triplets. We'll use the journey for me to fill you in on any points I can. I gather your hosts here will not have told you very much."

"No, they weren't very forthcoming."

"We have always instructed them to leave any explanations to us. The Count did reward them for the way they handled things. Good people are Paul and Rachael. I really should call in on them before I go back, to see their little baby."

"Yes, she's beautiful."

"So I hear. Anyway, Sir, we can have a good chat on the journey and I'll tell you all I can."

He lowered his voice and leaned forward before continuing.

"And I'd also like to hear about where you come from; I'd find that most interesting."

Sitting up again he gave another chuckle before calling the villagers with the dakk to collect the trousers and prepare to leave. He got up heavily and as he limped out Frank felt pity, for it was clearly a painful experience having to move his large frame.

They said farewell and Offa went next door to visit the baby as he had said, then he departed with his entourage. A group of children had gathered to watch them go. The obese man seemed to be popular with them. Frank went back to his room and sat down on the bed.

'So tomorrow things really begin. Villages and a castle, sounds like Earth a couple of thousand years ago!'

He felt himself getting quite excited at the prospect; can their world be so like another one an aeon ago? He could not see why not.

'I wish I'd paid more attention to…. Was it Brown's or Rebacker's theories about parallel development of planets? Always did get those two mixed up, don't know why – probably because their names were so similar.

'Well it won't be long now until I get to see the real task the Good Lord has given me on this planet. I only hope that with his help I'm up to it.'

CHAPTER FIVE

Frank found his mind very active that night and did not sleep well at all. He was wide-awake when the dawn came and he decided to get up. There were some spare clothes to put in his new wooden chest and he tidied his room as best he could. Then he sat on his bed and waited. He did not feel like reading.

Noises came from the main hut and after what seemed like an age Paul came to see if he was up. He invited Frank to have his final breakfast with him and his wife. They sat together in the quietness of the morning. Not a great deal was said in the expectant atmosphere as they waited for Offa and his assistants. It reminded Frank of waiting for his parents the first time he took a spaceship off their home planet many years previously. He ate little and watched as Rachael put baby Catherine down again when she kept falling asleep rather than suck. All the while smoke climbed lazily from the small fire in the centre of the room.

After finishing the meal the three of them sat there in silence, while the orange disc of Molten's sun began rising above the horizon.

Then they came. The harsh "coughing" noise of the dakks reverberated through the stillness. When the group was nearer Frank went out to meet them, closely followed by Paul and Rachael. Tamar too had come out of her hut to wish them farewell.

There were half a dozen dakks pulling a heavily laden four-wheeled wagon. It was an open-topped vehicle of wooden construction with large, spoked wheels. A small section at the back was partitioned off from the load where two seats were fixed facing each other. One seat was unoccupied; Offa sat in the other. The driver was a young, strongly built man with long, white hair in plats. He had a rounded face with small, blue eyes.

As they drew near he put the break on the wagon and jumped off to help the clerk get down from the back. Another two young men appeared from behind as the dakks stood there quite still, occasionally shuffling their feet – a lot calmer than the one the day before.

Offa greeted the small assemblage with his beaming smile; how could he be so cheerful this early in the morning?

"Good morning, Sir! Should be a fine day."

"Morning, Offa."

The clerk hailed his crew so he could parade them front of Frank. He shuffled uneasily up to the driver and put his hand on his shoulder and began the introductions.

"This is Rodd, the athlete of the family."

"Hello Rodd."

"My Lord."

Frank studied the other two. Their faces appeared exactly the same as Rodd's, obviously identical triplets. Fortunately their hairstyles were radically different or else he would never have told them apart. The one in the middle Offa introduced as Bodd had neck-length, bobbed hair and the one at the other end had hardly any hair at all, it was cut only about five millimetres from his head all round.

"And this is Tsodd."

"I'm sorry?"

"This is Tsodd."

"Tsodd?"

"That's right."

'Poor sod with a name like that!' thought Frank.

"Can I take your luggage?" asked Bodd.

"Thank you, it's in there by the door."

Tsodd handed Frank the shortened trousers and he quickly went in and changed once his things had been put into the wagon. Then he came out to say goodbye to the people who had looked after him ever since he had fallen from the sky what seemed like ages ago. First Tamar, who by now had been joined by her fiancé Axon.

"I hope your wedding all goes well.... Will you continue to live here?"

"No, My Lord, Axon has a big new place on the other side of the village, we plan to make that our home."

"That's lovely. Thank you for all your help since I came here, most of all for finding me!"

They smiled and he moved on.

"Paul, all you've done for me..."

"It was a pleasure to be of service, My Lord."

"You'll have some extra room now I'm going!"

Frank's laugh quickly died when he saw Rachael. She stood with tears in her eyes, her long, white hair cascading over her shoulders.

"We will miss you, My Lord."

He wondered at how easily emotion overcame people upon parting, he himself feeling a lump in his throat.

"What can I say, Rachael? All the hospitality you've shown me, the patience you've had. All those meals you have cooked me and jobs you've done for me with never a complaint. I've done precious little in return."

She held out a small, round pottery container with a stop in the neck.

"Please take this to remember us by."

It was a bottle of perfume, which Frank tried. It smelled exquisite and he thanks them warmly for it, giving Rachael a kiss on the cheek. He took a last glance at the sleeping baby then it was time to go.

Offa indicated to a seat opposite his at the back of the wagon and they got up. All three brothers assisted the clerk in this exercise and even then it was still a struggle getting his huge body up there.

Meanwhile a small crowd had gathered to see them off, many children among them. Rodd vaulted up into the driver's seat and after getting himself ready they slowly moved off, Bodd and Tsodd walking beside the dakks. They waved and called out as they departed. Frank watched his fingers until a bend in the street took them out of view. The children were running about and screaming playfully, but they too fell behind once the wagon left the village. Finally they were alone.

For a while nothing was said. Offa could tell his ward's mind was elsewhere, guessing correctly that he was recalling the time he had spent in the place they had just left. An assortment of sounds assailed their ears: the creaking of the wagon, the groaning of its wheels plus the ratting of some of the luggage which, from where they were sitting, drowned out all sound of the dakks' hoofs.

As the village passed over the horizon the scene before them was very flat. Spinneys were dotted about, but otherwise the countryside was largely grassland. The dusty road was well supplied with potholes, which Rodd was manoeuvring to avoid as best he could. A stream ran beside. It was immediately apparent that this part of the planet at least was sparsely populated, for there were no habitations whatsoever in sight.

The wagon lumbered sluggishly along while the sun rose in the sky warming the travellers. Offa felt he had better break the silence and pulled out a map to show his fellow passenger.

"This is where we are, Sir," he said spreading it across Frank's knees, "Ephamon. It should take us about a day to reach the border with the district of Bynar and another three across Bynar itself."

"I see."

"For much of our journey we should be able to see a wall of mountains to our right which mark the border with Ladosa. When we get to the district border of your new home, Thyatira, it will take us the best part of a day to get to the castle."

He indicated the places on the map with his fat, stubby finger. Frank nodded as he continued.

"We will not be going through any sizable villages. There are not too many in this part of the country. The whites like to live in communities; mostly villages and a few towns, a gregarious lot. It is possible we could come across some Bynarian soldiers trekking to or from the mountains, because they always have a fair-sized presence on the border."

"I see. Does this plain continue all the way?" the Despotelect asked, observing the flat landscape around them.

"For most of Bynar it does, Sir, then the land gets more undulating nearer the district border with Thyatira. Thyatira itself is a lot more heavily wooded from what I've heard."

After they had studied the map for a while, Offa put it away and again silence reigned. Frank looked round at his travelling companions.

'Now,' he thought to himself, 'Rodd is the muscular one driving who has long hair, Bodd is the one with the shorter hair and poor Tsodd has hardly any. That's right.'

He turned back and spoke to Offa quietly.

"It's most convenient the way the triplets…"

"Sorry Sir, I can't hear you."

The noise of the wagon as it crawled along the dirt road had drowned out his words, so he had to speak up. The truth was there was no danger of the brothers overhearing him from where they were. As the wagon progressed along the uneven surface the pots and pans hung on its side were rattling, making more than enough din to shroud his words.

"I said it's most convenient the way the triplets have got such different hairstyles, I'd never be able to tell them apart otherwise."

"No, that's why they were told to have their hair like that."

"Told to! Who told them that?"

"Oh I don't know, Sir, a black."

"A black? What's a black?"

"You are Sir, and myself. People with dark hair."

"I heard you mention "whites" a couple of times as well. Please explain what this is all about."

"Our society is divided between the ruling class, the blacks, and the common people, the whites. I beg your pardon, Sir, this is so fundamental I automatically thought you'd know."

'He's being serious!' thought Frank.

The clerk continued, he was indeed serious, his familiar broad smile was absent for a change.

"The whites are a simple people, they are not up to being rulers in Hoame. It is the system which has worked here for generations; and it does work."

"Forgive me, Offa, but are you saying that if God had given me fair hair instead of dark that I would not be here now, but stuck in the village as a labourer or something?"

"Please Sir, you mustn't think of it like that. It is what works for us. The other countries do not work our way, but it is our tradition, our system which has helped to keep our independence over the years."

"Why don't the whites revolt?"

Offa sighed, he had not realised his ward was completely ignorant of these basic matters.

"It is not like that. Blacks and whites are brothers, all of us one country and people. It's simply our way of doing things. The whites are proud to be part of Hoame, they don't consider themselves down-trodden."

"You mentioned other countries, what about the whites there?"

"There are no whites outside of Hoame."

"I see," said Frank conceding the argument for the time being. He did not wish to press the absurdity of what he had just been told at this juncture, there would be nothing gained by antagonising his guide. The matter could always be raised again later. What a strange twist of fate it was, maybe he should thank the Lord for giving him dark hair! What would they do with a bald person he wondered.

"All right," said Frank after a pause, "but why me? Why not another "black" like yourself for instance?"

"The despots form a tightly-knit group of families. As a result there has been much inter-marriage over the years. Many fewer children are being born to these unions, I am not sure if it is connected. The position with male heirs is particularly acute. There is no precedent in recent times for upgrading an ordinary black family and the Keepers, that is the Autarch, sees a danger in setting such a precedent as it would devalue the rank of despot. Indeed it would be bad for our entire social structure. It was fortuitous that you came along when you did."

Frank nodded to show he understood and Offa felt relieved that he was not going to become involved in a full-scale argument having to justify his country's traditions.

"Not that your arrival completely solves this chronic problem, not by any means. There are eleven despotates in Hoame and only eight despots, with no male heirs on the horizon. No male children out of infancy anyway and only a couple of those that I'm aware of.

"Three are currently without a despot: Gistenau in the south, Ephamon that is under the direct control of Count Zastein for the time being, plus Thyatira where we are heading. The previous despot there died a couple of years ago without an heir. He never re-married after his wife died, but I don't know a great deal about him; Rattinger was his name.

"The Count has told me to find you a wife from one of the despot houses in order that you can have many offspring and inject new blood into…. Whoops!"

The wagon had hit a big rut and very nearly thrown the pair from their seats.

"Sorry Master Offa!" shouted Rodd from the front.

Offa indicated they were still in one piece. Once they had settled down again Frank voiced his concern.

"I hope I'm going to have a say in all this."

"Oh yes, there are a number of eligible young dessans – daughters of despots – to choose from. I won't force some monster on you."

He laughed and during the break in conversation that followed Frank considered all he had just learned.

'Well Francis, so much for you being a confirmed bachelor! I may as well play along for now; see what happens. Never know, he might find me the woman of my dreams. All I know is she won't be a blond.'

They talked on about this strange, rigid social system where a man's fate was decided by the colour of his hair. He learned that the Hoame people did not intermix with the countries around them, although there was a fair amount of trade taking place between border disputes. There was also no question of blacks and whites intermarrying apparently.

The journey continued, the only wildlife observed being the occasional bird, but then the noise of the wagon was enough to chase most things off. They did pass one or two flocks of sheep, their shepherds taking advantage of the better pastures away from the villages.

Thought Frank, 'This planet brings a whole new meaning to the expression "the black sheep of the family".'

Further on the ground became noticeably less fertile. Grass became sparser and turned a yellow colour. Craggy outcrops of rock dotted the landscape. The long morning continued and Offa managed to get the conversation round to ask Frank about his origins.

"I come from the planet Eden which is probably more than a thousand light-years from here. I think of it as my home-planet although it was not where I was actually born. I've spent virtually all my adult life there. It is a Christian planet, so I was pleased to see you are believers here."

"Only the whites, Sir."

"Really?"

"Yes, Sir, I don't know of a black who is a Christian. Not that they couldn't be, but please tell me more about where you come from and space travel and all that. I'd love to know more about that."

"Well anyway," he paused to take in what he had just heard before continuing, "I'm afraid "Eden" has become a somewhat ironic title the last few decades. It all started a coupled of hundred years ago Earth time when some Christian colonists fist landed there. They set about making a model planet; a society based on love, which would be an example to the galaxy. But as far as I can see that's all turned sour now.

"I was newly converted twenty-three Earth-years ago when, still a youth, I was drawn to the planet. I wanted to worship God "in spirit and in truth" as Jesus said. I developed a lot in the following years and I hope became a better person as my ideas and beliefs matured.

"Then things became so political with various factions fighting for power. Disputes about doctrine and forms of worship began splitting the world apart. People don't like to compromise when the stakes are salvation itself – who'd have thought it in this day and age? A fine example we had become!"

"Did you have a civil war?"

"Oh no, they were much too sophisticated for that, it was all done in committees and votes at synod, as if Truth can be discerned by a show of hands!

"I was, I still am a member of a group called the Primary Radicals, part of the "Back to Basics" movement. Some said it stood for "Back to the Book." It's a group dedicated to the original, ancient forms of worship and doctrine. We were small in number, but dedicated to our ideals. About three years ago we at last found the guts to break away and form our own church. I was all in favour of that, 'cos it seemed the only way to preserve the true faith. We were just being swamped otherwise."

"Were you the leader?"

"Er no, not really, but I made sure my voice was heard in favour of the secession. Then we were betrayed. Within a year of the break people began losing their nerve and were drifting back into the fold. I was disgusted and fed up with the lot of them by that time and decided to get out. The enemy – for that's what they were – used every underhand tactic they could to break our people's resolve. Then when the tide swung back in their favour they called it God's will! Made me sick.

"So I pooled my resources and set off round the Galaxy making my way as a dealer in rare books. I've always loved books and had accumulated a fair collection already. There are plenty of wealthy collectors who prize these articles enough to make it a viable proposition. I don't think I've been brilliant at it, but I've made one or two good deals and with the proceeds I've done a lot of travelling from planet to planet the last couple of Earth-years."

"What are these "Earth-years" Sir?"

"You've heard of Earth, the mother planet?"

"I'm not sure," Offa frowned, "I feel I should though."

"It was the planet from which, according to the theories, all life started. Its location was lost over three hundred years ago during the Second Galactic War, but we still use E.y.s to measure time. I am forty Earth-years old for instance, but we don't usually use the full expression "Earth-years". Throughout the known Galaxy we use E.G.s or Earth Gravity to measure a planet's pull. For instance Eden had an E.G of point nine-five. I've definitely felt heavier here on Molten and the days are noticeably longer here too."

"You say Earth has been lost."

"Yes, I'm surprised you don't know about it. I heard people here telling the old Bible stories – do they think they all happened on this planet?

"I'm not sure, I suppose so."

"I don't suppose you know about the Galactic Wars either."

Offer shook his head.

"Well there have been three. The last one ended only a couple of years ago. In fact I have heard rumours (call them reports if you will) that there are still some the Alliance's deep-penetration squadrons operating even after their home-planets have surrendered.

"My brother has been heavily involved in the conflict. He was in one of the regular armies before becoming a mercenary. I have no idea where he is now it's sad to say. Last time I heard from him he was some sort of a bodyguard for a rich house or guild caught up in the fighting.

"It's probably true about some units of the Alliance fighting on, their cause always did attract fanatics of one kind or another and there are plenty of hiding places – remote corners of the Milky Way. Mind you, this latest conflict was nothing compared with the Second War that lasted over half a century. Then hardly any part of the Galaxy was unaffected. Whole planets were destroyed; they had armies of clones and androids – all sorts of things...

"It was a long time ago now. The reasons for that war are shrouded in obscurity, besides they seemed to have changed as it went along. Fresh alliances were made and broken, empires and entire civilizations collapsed. It's argued that we've never fully recovered. We are told one of the major protagonists were neo-nihilists who destroyed data banks and libraries as a matter of course on thousands of planets. They were a most thorough people it's sad to say; so much was lost.

"Much of the technology has been banned ever since those times, that in turn has been the cause of further minor wars. There is an intergalactic body – the Dycon Inspectorate – that has enormous powers to search and investigate anyone suspected of breaking those ancient laws that banned much of the cybernetics work. The Inspectorate itself became pretty corrupt and there's been a big shake-up of it following the Tangeot Dispute, which sparked the latest conflict. That's usually called the Third Galactic War, but it was on nothing like the scale of the other two, especially the Second."

"Amazing."

"Yes it was catastrophic that the known universe shrunk right back, we are only now starting to make up the lost ground. I talk about moving from planet to planet, but really it's nothing like back in history when so much of the galaxy was inhabited. The cruise I was on, it was hoped, would be the forerunner of a regular run – that's received a set-back!"

"Have I understood you correctly, Sir, your people are <u>re</u>-discovering places?"

"Absolutely, though on board the '*Cassandra*' there was a man boasting about visiting regions he could not possibly have been to. The modern, mapped universe is tiny in galactic terms. All right so there are plenty of planets there, but the solar systems are bunched close together. A man can visit a hundred planets without having to travel very far in relative terms.

"Anyway, I think I seem to be straying from the point. Most astronomers agree on the Earth theory on the origin of life. According to legend it was the most beautiful planet in the Galaxy with swirling white blue patterns as one approached it. I suppose they would try to romanticise it, but the Bible was written on Earth and the psalmist speaks of the great beauty of the place."

"Forgive me, Sir, but if this planet was lost generations ago how can you still compare other planets' gravity with it? And how can you be certain about Earth's time when it has been missing for so long?"

"Well I suppose they must have taken accurate readings from their scientific instruments when they left, although I must admit you do have a good point – they haven't been able to check them recently have they!" Frank smiled then added, "I just take their word for it, all sounds reasonable to me anyway."

The two men never stopped talking while the wagon rolled on over the monotonous, flat scenery. Bodd had taken over the driving from his brother in a quick change. They approached the time for the midday meal, but before they stopped there was something Offa was keen to find out.

"What would happen, Sir, if one of your space-vehicles come here, say to look for you or other survivors? It could cause panic among the whites, we would not want to see them unsettled."

"Hmm, I'm not sure I can see them coming here, the back of beyond. The ship I was on was well away from the usual routes, plus I have no idea how far my pod travelled. I was surprised how many people were on board the ship, but it's a guess as to how many other survivors there were – if any! It's most unlikely, I'd have thought, that any effort will be made to search for them. They wouldn't know where to start looking, plus there'd be no profit in it. No, I've told myself to give up hope after all this time. In any event I shouldn't worry; nowadays they are under strict orders not to interfere with er...." (mustn't say primitive) "....less advanced cultures."

"Do you know how to build a spaceship?"

Frank laughed, "No of course not. Even if I had the materials and facilities I wouldn't even know how to begin. If there were a ship standing there all ready to go I wouldn't know how to start it. No, I only use them."

Offa leaned back and scanned the horizon for a while before focussing back onto his alien master. He had wondered what to expect when first informed of his assignment by the Count, but was pleased at how easy it was proving to build up a rapport with this man.

"No sign of the mountains yet, Sir. We will be stopping shortly for lunch if that is not against your wishes."

"Fine."

"I expect, Tsodd could do with a rest having walked all morning."

Frank realised to his horror that he had been so busy talking he had not thought about the two brothers walking. Both Rodd and Bodd had sat at the front of the wagon directing the dakks for half the long morning, but Tsodd had walked the entire way. He watched the triplets, but they did not seem bothered at all. Rodd was to the right of the animals with his eyes on the road. Frank saw him point out to Bodd a large pothole the wagon was approaching and helped avoid it by taking hold of one of the leading dakk's bridles.

Meanwhile on the other side of the road Tsodd had picked some flowers from the bank of a small stream that ran close by. He was oblivious to the rest of the world.

"Shouldn't we give them a ride with us up here?" asked Frank. "If we rearrange some of this load I'm sure there would be room for them."

"Better not, Sir," advised the clerk looking concerned, "It might seem harsh to someone such as yourself, Sir, who is unfamiliar with our ways, but it would be unthinkable for a white to travel together with a black, let alone with a despot. If you did ask them they would only be embarrassed. It is in everyone's interests that the status quo is not upset," he hesitated before finishing the sentence briskly, "so people know where they stand."

"Yes, of course, I understand."

'Yes, Francis, I think you do at last understand. There is a gulf between these "whites" and "blacks" which must not be bridged unless I'm going to upset things and make powerful enemies. When in Rome...'

"Bodd!" Offa called out, "we'll stop for our meal now."

"Yes, Master Offa."

The wagon halted and they got down to stretch their legs. Frank went to relieve himself behind a nearby thicket while the brothers began preparing the food. Baked mascas and beans - a traditional dish eaten throughout Hoame, Offa informed him upon his return.

During the meal the triplets were quite boisterous, laughing and joking between themselves. The clerk smiled as he explained to Frank the reason.

"They have just finished a season working in the tin mines in Ephamon. Got a nice tidy sum to take home with them and are looking forward to spending it."

"I see. I take it there are no tin mines in Thyatira."

"No, their main export is hulffan by-products. In Ephamon there are extensive deposits of lead as well as tin, all of which is a great help to our country."

He regarded the trio once more, giving his little chuckle.

"Rodd is getting betrothed. He told me yesterday that the betrothal ceremony will take place as soon as they get home, so they have another cause for celebration."

"More beans, My Lord? Master Offa?" asked Tsodd as he came round with the extras.

Soon they had finished the meal and it was time to be on the move again. It was Tsodd's turn to drive once they had cleaned the cooking utensils in the stream and packed everything away. He gave rein to the dakks after they had all helped the obese clerk back into the wagon.

"There doesn't seem to be much in the way of wildlife here on the plain," Frank observed when they were once more lumbering along.

"Isn't there?" replied Offa. "If you want an expert on wildlife, Sir, you should talk to Tsodd. He's very knowledgeable about all sorts of animals and plants. He even collects tiny insects to scrutinise. A simple soul our Tsodd, but he knows more about wildlife than anyone I've ever met."

"Really. What about his brothers?"

"Rodd's main interest in life is running and physical exercise, I don't know why he doesn't join the guard – probably likes his freedom too much Sir. Still, that will soon change when he gets married."

Offa's smile was cut short by something he noticed behind Frank.

"Over there Sir, the mountains in the distance."

Frank turned round and peered hard at the horizon for a while before spotting the tips of the peaks.

"I hadn't realised how bad my eyes were getting. I've been meaning to have an operation to put them right, but I kept on putting it off. It takes no time at all to have it done. I'm just last though. There's a pill one can take which corrects the sight, but it's only temporary, lasts about half a year. I've been taking those instead of bothering to have it done permanently which turns out to have been a bit foolish of me."

"A bit short-sighted of you, Sir."

"Indeed," he laughed.

As they progressed further the mountain range loomed bigger and provided a screen in the distance on their right-hand side. The guide informed him that it stretched for a hundred kilometres or more.

"The only break is at the Mitas Gap as it's known, not that much passes through there, Despot Hista makes sure of that."

The party crossed the regional border into Hista's Bynar despotate early evening. The only indication that a border was there being an obelisk twice a man's height with a worn inscription on it. They passed straight on, but did not travel much further before setting up camp for the night by a small wood that lay by the banks of a stream.

The triplets served a filling supper before they prepared to bed down. Dakks were un-harnessed and ate their full from the leafy trees about. It was a mild spring night and two modest tents were produced from the great pile of equipment for Offa and Frank to sleep in. It did not take the brothers long to erect them for their masters. They, the blacks, slept on dakk-hair mattresses under cover while the white-haired triplets slept on the ground outside.

Frank considered this as he lay in the darkness, having finished his prayers.

'If I'm going to get along here I'm just going to have to see things in black and white.'

The long day's travelling had been tiring and any prick of conscience he might have had was not enough to spoil a good night's sleep.

CHAPTER SIX

No time was wasted the following morning. With their bodies refreshed by sleep and food, the tents and other equipment packed away, the dakks re-harnessed, they were back on the road early. It was still Tsodd's turn as driver.

The spinney by which they had spent the night was soon in the distance as they continued to cross the plain. Still the mountain range formed a curtain to the northeast while the rest of the view was flat, infertile wilderness, dotted about with the odd trees and bushes.

Offa was studying the map again; they traversed one of the large number of streams that crossed the area as the waters made their way down from the mountains. Only close to these rivers was the ground good enough to support plants and trees on any scale.

"Good," said the large man putting the map away.

"May I see?"

"Certainly, Sir."

The clerk retrieved the map and, turning it round so his superior could read it, spread it over his knees. He sat on the edge of his seat opposite Frank and indicated with his stubby finger.

"Here we are, Sir, only a fraction over the border into Bynar. Still a long way to go yet."

"Mmm, this is a fairly large-scale map. What's this to the north of Hoame and what is south of this map?

"This is Ladosa to the north. I happen to know that where we are going the people refer to the country as "Laodicia", which apparently has some significance that escapes me."

"What, you mean they are the same place?"

"Precisely Sir, the terms "Ladosa" and "Laodicia" are interchangeable you might say. I use the former, because that is the proper name.

"Right. Your despotate, Thyatira, has two borders with foreign powers: Ladosa to the north and Rabeth-Mephar to the west. At the very far north of Ladosa they say there is a vast expanse of salty water which no one has ever crossed."

"And to the south?"

"To the south and over here to the east are the other despotates of Hoame. There are various small, passive states around the border there. Oonimari is right over in the far east somewhere."

"Ah yes, Oonimari."

"At the far south there is a desert of sand as impenetrable as the salt sea in the north. Both of these regions are too cold for life."

"So are you saying there is a strip of inhabitable land running like a belt along the equator of this planet?

"That is one theory, Sir. They say that if you were given a fresh dakk each half day it would still take a hundred days to cover the distance from the desert in the very south to the cold sea in the north. Not that anyone has ever made such a journey to the best of my knowledge."

They came to another stream and halted there to rest the animals. Offa and Frank remained in the wagon while the triplets watered the beasts. The brothers then went downstream in the hope of catching some river-snails, a tasty delicacy with which to supplement their diet.

"Pleasant weather," Frank commented, feeling the warmth of the sun on his back.

"Yes, Sir, the spring is my favourite season. I find the cold, damp winter days depressing…and they make my joints hurt. There is always too much snow and then flooding in many areas if the thaw comes too quickly. I understand that parts of where we are heading suffer from that."

There was no birdsong, only the gentle gurgling of the stream. After a while a young black man riding a dakk cam alongside the wagon and introduced himself.

"Greetings, my name is Fitz Wanhelm, mind if I join you on the road?"

They indicated they did not, so the man tied his beast to the rear of the wagon while a space was hastily prepared for him. He clambered on and made himself as comfortable as he could in the cramped area. The newcomer had a sickly pale complexion. Frank guessed his age to be in the early twenties and was struck by his jewel-encrusted rings and long fingernails. His attire consisted of a brown, studded jacket and material trousers with a check pattern.

He told them he was travelling along the road for about ten more kilometres before he would turn westwards to get to his father's estate.

"I am much obliged to you," he declared, "It will be good to give my mount a rest and enjoy some company."

The three blacks completed introductions and Fitz glanced around the chattels piled high about him. They chatted for some time on general topics, the trio sitting up high without another soul in sight. Then Offa, not wanting to lose valuable instruction time, raised an important subject with his charge.

"When we get to our destination we will have to concern ourselves with our near neighbours. There have not been any reports from the area recently, but relations with the foreigners have not always been good."

"Haven't they?"

"No Sir. There have not been any major conflicts for almost a generation now, but this can be a warlike planet I'm afraid."

"Can't say I'm surprised with humans around."

"It is Ladosa which is perceived as the greatest long-term threat by the Keepers. I'll never forget the Count sternly telling me that there would be a showdown one day.

"Ladosa has a strange political system whereby the common people decide who is to run their country."

"A democracy," Frank interjected.

"You are familiar with political science, Sir, that's good. Yes, the main effect of it is much infighting and wrangling from what I can gather, but sometimes they turn this constant belligerence on their neighbours – and they are a large and powerful country."

"That's interesting. In my experience round about I've also found many of the most belligerent powers have been democracies. It seems to be a rule by the lowest herd instincts at times."

Fitz had been listening to the progress of the conversation with increasing annoyance. Finally he could contain himself no longer and broke in.

"I'm sorry gentlemen, but if you don't mind me saying so, I cannot agree."

This comment certainly brought the attention he required. The other pair broke off and stared at him in astonishment, waiting for him to justify his remark. This he proceeded to do.

"Democracy takes account of the feelings of the common people. It is a safeguard against tyranny and oppression when the leaders are accountable to the masses. They cannot do anything too unpopular, because they will be voted out of office at the following election, such elections having to be held at regular intervals. No system is perfect, but democracy is undoubtedly the fairest there is."

These ideas seemed highly amusing to Frank and Offa who both laughed.

The latter enquired, "What about Thyatira then? When the Despot and myself get there we shall be the only two blacks there. Not much point in having an election when only two men can vote."

"Oh no," said Fitz, "Not only the blacks. Everyone should have the vote, not just an elite few. That is true democracy."

"That's absurd!" declared the clerk, "let the whites vote the Despot in and out of power? Have you lost your senses?"

Frank chipped in, "He'll be wanting to allow women to vote next!"

The pale man scowled as the other two grinned at the suggestion.

"That would not be an immediate aim," he replied seriously, "but in the course of time, why not? The great democracies of history allowed for that."

"Preposterous!" Offa exclaimed, "wherever did you get such an idea?"

"I have a friend, no – more than one – who are Ladosans," announced the young man proudly. "We have discussed these theories and honed them to the point of perfection. I am not ashamed of them."

"You *should* be ashamed of them. Have you no sense of decency? Have you no sense of the history of your own country and its institutions, so thoughtfully devised by the Inner Council?"

"We both know that is not true, the villagers were a lot better off before the (I hate to use the term) blacks arrived on the scene. We have changed everything for the worse. I care nothing for your institutions. It is the will of the common people which should count, like it does in Ladosa."

Offa was not normally given to arguing, but he was horrified at what he saw as dangerous, even treacherous heresy.

"Ladosa is hardly an example to set before sane men. It is plain you are a nihilist. If you had your way you would pull down everything that good men have built up over centuries. Men like you would sell them the rope we would all be hanged with! Our whites are not ready for decision-making; they are neither informed nor wise enough to have a say in the running of the country. Then how could they ever be ready for a system that is a Utopian fantasy? In fact it's worse than that, because it puts subversive ideas into impressionable minds.

"The Keepers, meanwhile, know what is right and have the best interests of all Hoamen at heart. I hope, young man, your views will mature as you get a bit of experience in life. In the meantime, if you go around spreading such ideas you will find yourself in serious trouble!"

"I see: you have to resort to threats! Okay, so Ladosa is not the best advertisement for such a political system as I am advocating, but it would have to be worked on. They are not a proper democracy anyway. In a proper democracy everyone is politically aware and knows precisely what the issues are. The common people would have to be given careful political education to make them fit to vote. Those who refused would be disenfranchised. We would make the population as a whole worthy to run the country and not leave it to an unrepresentative minority. Freedom can only come to everyone when power is in their hands.

"And why should we not aim for Utopia? We must aim for a perfect system and for all we know we could get it given time."

The large man shook his head in disagreement.

"This is an unrealistic dream. No wonder, because Utopia means "not a place". From your mouth comes a stream of nonsense."

Fitz's pale face suddenly turned red and he shouted, Oh to hell with you if you're not going to listen! I'm not going to stay here in the company of a couple of narrow-minded bigots. I'd rather be with my friends who understand what life is all about."

With that he jumped down from the wagon and leapt on his still tired dakk. He pulled the rein sharply in his anger and the beast nearly threw him before he got it under control and tore off down the track.

No further words had been spoken and Frank, who had remained silent for most of the argument, noticed his companion was holding his chest and breathing heavily.

"Oh dear Sir," he exclaimed, "I'm not used to this. What a thoroughly disagreeable young man. He's probably lived a secluded life on his father's estate and doesn't know his left hand from his right."

He took another sharp breath before continuing, "He's been developing his silly ideas from his ivory tower; not having any insight into what life is really about."

Sighing once more he mopped his brow with a handkerchief. It was then that the triplets returned. They had given up the hunt for the river-snails upon hearing the shouting, but had remained a way off until Fitz was gone. Now they returned

Offa tried to act as if nothing had happened, although he felt a tightening of his chest that took a while to subside. Upon learning that the snail hunt had been fruitless he told them to depart from that place without further delay. Soon the wagon was lumbering towards their destination once more.

Conversation was slow for a time. The guide explained that fortunately men with views like Fitz Wanhelm were very few and far between.

"Such a *wicked* doctrine to spread," he declared in a slightly calmer voice than before, trying not to let the brothers overhear. "I've got a good mind to report him to the Inner Council. I am sorry about all this, Sir, I don't think I've ever had such a thoroughly distasteful argument in all my life. I'm only glad he is one of a tiny minority – there are very few blacks that label themselves as "intellectuals" I believe – there's no popular movement for their subversive nonsense.

"We should encounter no such problems in Thyatira thank goodness. Once we're established there though we want to encourage more black families to join us – but good, respectable families, not subversives. I do not envisage any great difficulties; most people are more level-headed than our Master Wanhelm."

Things were then quiet for a while before the clerk felt he should return to the subject of Ladosa.

"From what I hear there has been little communication of late, like I said, but there is a chronic mistrust and dislike between our two countries. The Ladosans tend to be unpredictable. There is a particular cycle of madness that manifests itself during the period known as "election time." Then the warring parties promise all sorts of things they cannot possibly deliver. Or alternatively the group currently in power might cause trouble with us, or another of their neighbours, to stir up popular chauvinism and hence popularity for their particular faction at the next election."

"I see. Although to be fair I've hear of that sort of thing being done in dictatorships to draw attention away from trouble at home."

"Hmm yes," Offa conceded, "I suppose that might happen, although the Autarch and Keepers are far too responsible to resort to such tactics."

On they moved at a steady walking pace. Rodd and Bodd were helping their brother steer the dakks through a particularly rough stretch of road before the surface gradually improved. The wagon clattered and groaned as it progressed.

Dark clouds came over threatening rain, but did not come to anything. Further on the ground appeared more fertile with lush grass and a profusion of small pink and yellow flowers that the man from Eden did not recognise. They still saw little wildlife and no further people, although the triplets did point out the smoke on the left horizon, which was almost certainly a village.

"Do the people often get to see the Autarch?" asked Frank resuming the conversation.

"He only rarely appears in public, Sir, although I have seen him often inside the Citadel in respect of my work. On many occasions I have had cause to speak with him; he is not a recluse."

"What does he look like?"

Offa smiled and quickly glanced round to make certain they were not being overheard before he replied.

"He's a funny old man to tell the truth. Don't tell anyone I said that, please Sir. It's easy to…"

He suddenly stopped, realising he had gone too far and was relieved to see Rodd coming running back to address Frank.

"Please excuse me, My Lord, but would it be in order for us to stop here for a while and pick some berries? By the looks of them there are enough for a couple of large helpings all round."

Frank turned to the clerk who nodded. At this they halted to gather the abundant purple berries on the bushes either side of the road. Tsodd applied the brake to secure the wagon then climbed down. Then he and his brothers produced some large containers and began stripping the bushes of their plentiful, ripe fruit. Frank jumped down at the back and offered up both hands, but the big man declined saying it was not worth the effort of getting up again. So he went for a quick walk behind some trees before emerging to help the brothers with the berries, much to their surprise and Offa's amazement. He struck up a conversation with Tsodd who explained that this particular fruit produced crops twice a year, springtime and autumn.

The expression on his guide's face was a picture when he returned.

"It is extremely unwise to associate so closely with the whites Sir, most unwise."

"I know I know," Frank said as he got back into the wagon. "I'm sure it won't hurt to help them gather the crop in though. Besides I wanted to see what the berries were like."

The clerk bit his tongue. Such familiarity with whites was definitely not to be encouraged, but he thought it best not to make too big an issue of it now the others were so close. Rodd took up the reins and they moved off again.

"Do you want one?" Frank asked, holding out his hand with a couple of berries on his palm.

"No thank you."

"Are you angry with me for helping them? I'm sure it won't hurt just this once."

He popped the fruit into his mouth. The whites were back out of earshot if they kept their voices down, so following a sigh Offa said, "I do have your best interests at heart, Sir."

"Yes I'm sure you do. Well it won't happen again. I'm sorry."

Frank's smile was reciprocated and the tension dissolved. He reflected on the power of the word "sorry." As a boy he had had issues with an uncontrolled temper and it was drummed into him to apologise whenever it was called for. He knew he was still occasionally inclined to fly off the handle and hoped that one day he would be able to control himself better, so that no apology would be necessary. 'Well I've been all right since I came here,' he mused.

"Lovely emerald-green colour, the grass here," observed the new despot changing the subject.

"It is, Sir, they must have had a great amount of rain here of late. It is always a wonder how localised the storms can be."

"I remember one planet I was on which was covered in a bright red grass. I don't know what had happened to make it that colour. So many of the other worlds you're cooped up in domes, it's nice to get out into the open air like you could there – or here for that matter. Anyway, this red grass really hit you. It was absolutely beautiful at first, so spectacular. Only thing was, after a while it got too much until you were fed up of seeing red before your eyes. I'd wake up in the morning and peek out the window and remember where I was. "Oh no, not all that red again!" I'd say. I was having great difficulty in getting to see the client I was hoping to make a sale to. Kept me hanging on for days and all that red grass. When the time came to move on I couldn't get away quickly enough."

"You made your sale though."

"No! He messed me about with delays then said I hadn't got anything that interested him. Some people…"

Before long they found themselves passing nearby a sizable village that, Frank observed, appeared very much like the one he had stayed in with Paul and Rachael. Was it really only yesterday morning he had left there he wondered.

Men and women were working in the fields outside a wooden stockade that encircled the habitations. A few women came out to meet the party with homemade ornaments to sell, but under Offa's instructions the triplets waived them away. He warned Frank of the danger of drawing too much attention to themselves.

"We do not want word of us to get back to Despot Hista until we are safely ensconced in your new home", he advised. "He'd probably invite us to his capital, or his country home, and we'd get delayed for days. He's a poor old man, worries a lot. That's probably why of all the despots he keeps the largest standing army. Gives him a feeling of security which he needs having the longest common border with Ladosa. Anyhow, there will be plenty of time for us to meet Despot Hista and the other major black families of Bynar."

"Are there many blacks in Thyatira?"

"Ah no there aren't, Sir, not at the moment. There never have been many black families there and under Despot Rattinger the last of them moved out. He was a very moody person, not at all popular. I only met him on a couple of occasions myself, and they were both brief. Still, there'll be two of us when we arrive and if we can get you a good wife and organise things... who knows, we might attract some black families back to Thyatira and make it prosper. That's the plan anyway. It has all the potential."

"What you're saying is that this place I'm being asked to govern is in the back of beyond, with ruthless enemies on the borders and no one within that I'll be allowed to mix with!"

Offa laughed, "Oh no, Sir, it's not that bad."

"So who runs the place at the moment, with no despot or other "blacks"?"

"I understand the steward has been doing an excellent caretaker role the last couple of years."

"What's his name?"

"I don't know, Sir, but from what I hear he has done a sterling job, probably with the aid of the drones."

"The drones?"

Offer lowered his voice and Frank had to strain his ears to catch the answer.

"I'm surprised you haven't heard about drones since you came here Sir, but then I suppose the village where you stayed *is* rather insular. Drones are the illegal offspring of a union between a white woman and a black man. It is all highly irregular, because it should never happen, but sometimes it does and they are the result. The trouble is they have no place in our society and often lead a totally pointless existence, being neither one thing nor the other."

"Oh."

"Yes, tragic I suppose, but it's not something one thinks about. They could go to other countries to live (in theory), but I've never heard of it happening. We are an insular people, as you will learn if you have not already. You yourself are a unique experiment if I may say so, Sir."

The unique experiment chuckled and let the man continue.

"Blacks could go abroad too in theory, it sometimes happens for a particular reason. Not the whites of course, they would stick out so much. They are *different* you know?"

The mentor's last comment was made with a knowing look that was completely lost on his charge who asked, "Are there many drones in Thyatira?"

"No no, only a couple or so I believe. Some despotates have many more than others. Where they do exist they usually live among the black community. There are strict rules governing their behaviour, for instance they are not allowed to breed under penalty of death,"

'They pay for the sins of the father,' thought Frank.

"Some of them learn to read and write, going on to careers in administration either in one of the regional capitals or Asattan itself."

"I gather from that not many people can read here."

"No, Sir, less than half the blacks and a very few whites are taught for doing the accounts for instance. Strictly speaking the whites should not be allowed to."

"Can you read?"

"Of course, Sir."

"What do you read?"

"I am merely concerned with my job: official documents, treaties and the like, I do not read for pleasure."

"Are there many books around though?"

"No, Sir."

"I wasn't able to salvage any books in the disaster other than my Bible, but then that's by far the most important."

They stopped for a meal, using some of their supply of salted meat. It was not long before they were moving again and the pair had progressed to the subject of marriage, discovering they both had bachelorhood in common.

"Only the despot class go in for arranged marriages. Personally speaking I must admit, Sir I could have taken my pick in my youth, but I always gave my work priority. Then one day I looked about and saw my admirers had gone elsewhere. It was about that time I began to develop this."

He slapped his enormous belly and gave a quick grin before continuing.

"Yes marriage is taken very seriously here, especially among the whites where it has religious connotations. With us it is more a political thing, but of value nevertheless. Not so in Ladosa. They do not believe in lifelong marriage, but each have a string of relationships from what I can gather, none of which last for very long apparently. No wonder they are such an unsettled and brutal people. They are total barbarians in fact, especially in the way they treat their womenfolk. There is no respect for motherhood and they make them work outside the home! In fact there are even some women among their rulers."

"Shocking!" agreed Frank, "Reminds me of one or two dreadful places I have had the misfortune to visit."

"Does it Sir? In Ladosa there *are* a few more enlightened souls, but not enough. It is part of our national policy to give support to these progressive elements within their country, but on the whole they are a most cruel and primitive people."

""The city whose name is Licence, oppression is rampant within her"," quoted Frank to the nodding of his colleague.

He considered how well it was he landed in civilized Hoame and not barbaric Ladosa, clearly God's will. He also considered what a fine fellow this Offa was,

'How clear his perception is. Yet he has not been granted faith. I will have to work on that – with the good Lord's help of course.'

They had continued to make good progress throughout the day and were almost half way through the despotate of Bynar by dusk. Without much difficulty a suitable place was found to set up camp for the night. As usual a site near a stream was chosen so there was easy access to water. The wagon jolted to a halt and a couple of rabbits, taken by surprise, panicked and hopped off in opposite directions. Frank and Rodd helped Offa down at the back; he was puffing heavily.

The big man retired early that evening saying he needed a good rest. Frank stayed up for a while with the triplets round the fire and managed to engage them in some conversation. The trio were reticent at first, but soon thawed out.

They had recently entered a more densely populated part of the despotate and the four of them discussed the villages they had passed late afternoon. These groups of habitations all seemed to be built to a pattern. Also mentioned were the Bynarian troops they had witnessed and the apparent indifference everyone had shown them. The brothers knew the road fairly well and told their despot that all the good scenery was still to come.

The light had failed and the few stars in the sky did little to illuminate the blackness. Frank had never known a planet with as few stars visible as this one. A planet so remote. He said goodnight and walked to his tent by the light of the fire. The mattress felt soft and inviting; he did not stay awake for long.

"My Lord, My Lord, please wake up, My Lord!"

It was Bodd.

'Have I overslept?' Frank asked himself, quickly coming to. Bodd's expression showed it was something more serious.

"What's the matter?"

"It's Master Offa, My Lord, he's dead!"

'Nothing like breaking bad news to a man gently,' thought Frank, "What do you mean?" he asked, rubbing his eyes. Even as he said it he wondered how he could ask such a daft question, the message could not have been put clearer.

"We heard him making noises My Lord and went to his aid. Tsodd and I tried to wake you at the time, but couldn't, so we went back to see Rodd with Master Offa."

Frank was fully awake now.

"All right; just give me a little time and I'll get dressed and be out there."

Bodd disappeared and Frank quickly got up. He suspended thought as he hurriedly dressed and went outside. Throwing back the flap and walking over to the other tent he saw it was barely dawn; Bodd was standing by the entrance and followed him as he ducked inside to where the other two brothers were kneeling over the body. He addressed Rodd.

"What happened exactly? Bodd told me you heard voices."

Rodd opened his mouth to speak, but it was Bodd who chipped in.

"I think it must have been a heart attack My Lord, he was complaining about a terrible pain here."

He indicated to his chest.

"I see. Well I suppose we'll have to turn round and take his body back to Ephamon."

"Actually My Lord," continued Bodd, "before he died he did say it would be the Count's wish that we travel on to Thyatira."

"Did he?"

"Yes, My Lord. May I suggest we bury his body here? We have our picks and shovels from the mining, it won't take long."

"Yes, yes of course. Was there anything else he said?"

Bodd again, "He was most concerned about your arrangements when he got home. He suggested you report to the steward – that'll be Natias – until such time as a new black man to guide you can be sent."

Thought Frank, 'Good old Offa, the faithful and efficient clerk to the end!'

They buried him there as had been suggested. Fortunately the ground was not hard, In spite of his large bulk Bodd was proved right: with the three fit young men on the job the grave was quickly dug. They then held an impromptu service. The fact that he had not been a Christian did not seem to matter one bit. He had been well liked and this was the best way they had of showing their respect. Frank would have liked to have read a Bible passage or two, but his book was hidden under half the wagon's load. He did say a couple of prayers out loud though. The brothers were surprised at hearing a black saying prayers and joining in Christian worship, this was going to be a most unusual despot they concluded.

Once they were under way Frank had time to consider the implications for himself of Offa's untimely demise as he sat staring at the empty seat in front of him. Things were going to be ten times more difficult without the clerk as a guide. He would now have to rely on some of the "whites" to help him run things. These were the people from whom he was separated by a chasm erected by this society's strange customs.

'I was just getting to know Offa. Now I find myself on this forsaken planet with no one I even begin to know. Paul, Rachael and Tamar are now far away and Offa has died.

'He never told me about Oonimari! If someone asks me I won't know at all what to say...'

So it was a melancholic despot feeling sorry for himself who rode alone in the back of the wagon that day. There was not much said lunchtime, nor in the afternoon which saw them pressing on through Bynar. That evening, however, they did manage to get a conversation going over supper.

"Can't wait to get home," declared Tsodd as he took a piece of gristle from his mouth and threw it into the fire, which gave a loud hiss.

"I understand Thyatira is the smallest of the administrative districts," said Frank.

It was Bodd who responded.

"That's right My Lord, there's just two villages plus the castle. When we get to the border we'll cross up-river from where the Lower Village is. We're from the Upper Village, which is nearer the castle. It's twice as big as the Lower one."

"More like three-times," corrected Rodd.

"Yeah I suppose it is now," concluded his brother before continuing. "The Lower Village is quite near the swamp which is why they suffer bad floods in the spring thaw each year. It also probably accounts for the high incidence of disease there. It's not the healthiest place to be in mid-summer either. Everyone knows that, but no one does anything about it.

"I wanted to be a doctor at one time. Seems ages ago now.... but I didn't get on at all well with Laffaxe – he's the castle physician My Lord, he was teaching me."

"He's a silly old fool!" put in Rodd helpfully before getting up to go and inspect the dakks. He took a lantern and disappeared into the dark while Tsodd made an important announcement.

"Hey I know what I'm going to do," he said licking his fingers, "with the money I've saved I'm going to buy the materials to build myself an aviary."

"You've already got one."

"Ah yes, but this is going to be bigger, a lot bigger. I know where I'm going to put it: down by the sawmill, past the piggery. There's a piece of wasteland there which would be ideal. There's not enough room where the present one is to expand much further. I thought if I can build a really big one I can have a second door at the entrance and be able to walk into it."

"That's a good idea," said Bodd.

Frank joined in, "I haven't seen many birds on this planet. I mean in this country."

"You'd be surprised My Lord!" exclaimed Tsodd who had not noticed his new despot's slip of the tongue. "There are at least two dozen species of bird in Thyatira alone, even if that does include three different types of sparrow. There is the palwing, the ulna, the trumpet bird, the..."

Bodd interrupted his brother's catalogue.

"I'm sure his Lordship doesn't want to know the name of every blooming bird in existence thank you!"

Tsodd was quiet.

"No, that's all right," assured Frank, "I was told you are a great authority on wildlife around here."

The triplet blushed and went all modest.

"Oh I wouldn't say, that My Lord, but I do take a keen interest in the subject. Did you know, for instance, there are almost a thousand different types of insect in this country? That includes two hundred different species of beetle."

Frank tried to look suitably awe inspired. He was no expert, but knew that the figures quoted were absolutely tiny for the average planet of this type. He did not know if there really were comparatively few creatures on Molten, or whether the identification techniques for the differentiation of species were not sophisticated enough yet. Either way Tsodd seemed to think the numbers impressive.

He continued, "Apart from building the aviary my biggest ambition is to catch one of the giant dragonfly found in the southern marsh. They're getting increasingly rare these days. I've seen some quite large ones, but reliable witnesses have reported seeing them with a wingspan of over a metre and a half! Imagine that My Lord, they must be absolutely massive!"

Frank agreed.

"…But I think I'll concentrate on the aviary first. I've already planned in my mind how I want it – planned in great detail. I used to think it all out while I was working at the lode."

"Yes I was told you were all miners."

It was Bodd who replied for them.

"The reality, My Lord, is it is simply something we have done in the spring the last three years. In fact we haven't spent so long at it this year. It's dangerous work. The money is very good and we can earn a lot in a short time. I know my brothers especially don't like being away from home, but it's worth it for the money."

"What do you do the rest of the year?"

"We're hulffan croppers My Lord. That's the main industry back home. Of course things were different before the Keepers."

Just then Rodd returned and reported that the dakks were all in good shape.

"I don't know why you don't leave the animals alone," said Bodd, "They'll be okay. They breed like rabbits anyway."

An earnest sounding Tsodd came to the other brother's defence.

"Rodd's absolutely right. If you want fit and healthy animals you must give them lots of care and attention, dakks are no exception."

Bodd changed the subject.

"Anyway, we all know what Rodd is going to do when he gets back."

"See his fiancé?" suggested Frank.

"Yes My Lord," he confirmed, the gleam in his eye caught by the light of the fire.

"What's her name Rodd?"

"Leah, My Lord. It will be lovely to see her again. Then I suppose one of us will have to look in on cousin Katrina and give her back the money she invested." He explained, "Our cousin is rather eccentric, My Lord. She is independent minded which does not become a woman."

"Quite."

"She can be very forceful at times and it doesn't do to cross her. It's sad though, 'cos I believe her husband knocks her about quite a bit. He's in the Guard; don't like him much. Katrina's all right, she's just strong-willed."

"I see. Actually there is one thing I was wondering: the castle I'll be going to, has it got a name?"

"A name, My Lord?"

"What do you call it?"

He was thinking of *"Camelot"*, or some other romantic sounding name.

"It's just called "The Castle" My Lord," replied a rather puzzled Bodd.

Then a terrible thought struck Frank. Was it going to be as he imagined it? He now realised that although he had been anticipating a fine, stone structure in the Norman style, in reality all the buildings he had seen so far on this planet were of wattle and daub. What if this castle was a pathetic, flimsy building? This time when he asked the brothers there was no anti-climax, however. They assured him it was a fine, tall construction made of large stone blocks with high towers and a spacious courtyard. That was a relief!

There was one other point he wanted to clear up. His curiosity overcoming his tact he asked Bodd, "Your names, are they abbreviations of longer ones?"

With a reaction that took Frank by surprise the young man looked quite shocked at the suggestion and said that they were indeed their full names, explaining, "Being the names given at our baptism it is unthinkable that we would allow anyone to shorten them. Only a heathen who doesn't have a Christian name would do such a thing My Lord!"

It was a new convention to Francis, but he decided against any further questions that evening.

The following day's travelling was uneventful, but Frank's melancholy mood returned and developed into a deep depression as he considered that there was now no one he could discuss his former life with, or anything beyond this tiny, insignificant and backward planet.

The terrain became more undulating and heavily wooded. Unfortunately Frank was not in the right state of mind to appreciate the scenery. When they set up camp that evening, the mountains were no longer in view, but blocked by the tall, leafy trees. The brothers slept together in what had been Offa's tent. Frank, meanwhile, alone in his tent, lay awake most of the night. For much of the time it was deathly quiet, with only the occasional creature rustling in the undergrowth. He presumed there were no dangerous animals or other threats in the vicinity from the total lack of concern being shown.

Next morning they forded the river that marked the regional border with Thyatira. It was far wider than any of the numerous streams they had crossed in Bynar, but the triplets steered them through the shallows successfully. Even so, the river was rather swollen and on one or two occasions water threatened to flood the wagon.

During the afternoon Frank began to feel unwell and wondered if it was something he had eaten. The truth was his black mood had begun to affect his health. Smoke from a fire wafted across in a slight breeze. Some woodsmen were sawing up logs nearby, little realising that their new leader was passing by.

The light was failing as the travellers approached the castle. How quickly it became dark on this planet! Slowly the wagon lumbered into the courtyard and as it stopped Rodd, who had been driving, vaulted down and came round the back. It was difficult to see much in the darkness, but they had stopped by an external staircase, which led up to a side entrance. Torches of fire on either side illuminated the door at the top. Bodd went up to the guard there and explained who had arrived. The latter disappeared through the door and returned soon afterwards with another man. As they approached Frank told himself to buck up in spite of the way he was feeling. He got down from the back of the wagon and addressed Rodd.

"You can bring my things over in the morning, you'll never find them amongst that lot in the dark."

"Certainly My Lord, we'll do that."

At that moment the guard arrived with the other man who introduced himself.

"Gweetings My Lawd," said the man with a severe lisp, "my name is Natias, I am the steward."

Frank returned the greetings and tried to get a good look at this Natias in the flickering blaze of the torches. All he could discern was that the man was mature and had a thickset face with a very prominent nose – or was the latter a trick of the light? Either way, the steward spoke again.

"We had been told to expect the new Despot Thorn fwom a messenger only a few days ago. It will be good to have a pwoper leader once more My Lawd."

"From what I hear you've been doing a sterling job."

They ascended the staircase and passed through the door at the top. Natias explained that the main entrance was closed night times, "Although we would of course have opened it for your Lawdship had the guards known it was you." He went on to ask the whereabouts of Offa and Frank had to explain what had happened.

Apart from the man's obvious inability to pronounce his "r"s he made a long, exaggerated and ultimately not very successful attempt at "Lord" each time.

After going down the stairs on the other side they had to cross what seemed to be another courtyard and climb further steps to the large, open door of what was clearly the castle proper. This door was of solid botawood, very hard in itself, but reinforced with metal bars and studs. Only rarely was this heavy construction closed. The group passed through the entrance into a large, oblong hall with bare stone walls.

"You must have had a tiwing journey My Lawd, would you care for a spot of supper and a dwink?"

Thank you no, I do feel rather tired, I'd just like to go to bed I think."

"Of course, I will lead the way."

In fact Frank felt not so much tired as terrible, hot one moment and cold the next. Natias took a couple of candles, carefully lit them and handed one to his new master before leading him along the edge of the hall and up some steps to a wooden balcony. There was a small group of half a dozen or so men sitting at one end of the hall's long tables having what looked like a wild party or drinking session. They were quite clearly drunk from the way they shouted and jeered at each other. When one particularly loud guffaw erupted as he passed Frank wondered for an instant if they were laughing at him. The unsmiling steward ignored them as if they were not there. The two of them went up yet more steps and along a corridor until eventually stopping at what was announced as the Despot's suite of living rooms.

The guide opened a door and then went in. It was a large, square bedroom, well furnished and with fine tapestries on the walls. Natias began explaining about the wardrobe that the fresh despot had inherited and the special feature of a personal convenience en suite, but the only thing Frank was interested in was the bed.

Natias, remembering his master was very tired, said, but I can tell you all this in the morning, I expect you will want to catch up on your sleep now."

"Yes, thank you, that's most kind."

"I shall see you in the morning, My Lawd."

"Fine, yes, thank you."

He was gone.

"Hell I feel ill!" said Frank to himself.

Some bedclothes had been left on a stool, which he changed into with what seemed like his last bit of strength. His daytime clothes were strewn on the floor. He got into bed, blew out the candle and lay there with his teeth chattering.

The steward retraced his steps and descended to the balcony overlooking the hall. A girl of about sixteen appeared from the shadows and addressed him.

"Well, what's he like then?"

Natias frowned at this intrusion and replied in an irritated voice, "Tired!"

He made to move on, but the girl tugged at his sleeve.

"Come on, you know what I mean!"

"He has only just awwived and went stwaight to his wooms. I have not had a chance to speak with him pwoperly yet."

"But you must've got a first impression, I mean what does he look like?"

"Don't be a silly girl, you will see him for yourself in the morning and be able to make your own mind up. You have been impossible these last few days, have you not got anything better to do?"

"C'mon Natias, I only want to know what he's like for pity's sake."

"Illianeth," he replied trying to control his temper, "I do not know what he is like; I have only just met him. You will just have to wait until tomowow like other folk."

The girl's look of disappointment turned to anger as the steward added a barbed comment before departing.

"Why do you not go back to your fwiends?" he asked, indicating to the drunken men still carrying on in the hall. He left, not waiting for an answer.

"Oooh!" she exclaimed, "You, you...pig!"

But he was already out of earshot and the girl found herself fuming alone.

CHAPTER SEVEN

"I think you should go up there. This is getting ridiculous!"
"Yes, you are wight," replied Natias, "but I will leave it a while longer, he was vewy tired last night."

The steward was talking to Japhses, the Captain of the Thyatiran Guard. Japhses was a muscular giant of a man about forty, ten years Natias' junior. With his great mane of white hair that reached down his back he made a striking appearance. It was late morning and the two men were standing in the hall debating what to do about the non-emergence of their new Despot. After a brief silence Natias spoke again.

"As you wish then. I will go up there, are you coming?"
"Right."

Earlier that morning Frank had woken up to find the whole room was spinning round and round. Shutting his eyes did not help, if anything it felt worse! First day in his new position, he just had to get up. Gritting his teeth he left common sense behind, pulled back the bed covers and swung his legs round.

As soon as he put his weight on his legs he felt he was about to faint and dropped back into bed to let the blood return to his head. It was no good, he concluded, so he got back in and waited.

After what seemed like a lifetime he heard soft footsteps approaching and there was a gentle knock on the door.

"Come in."

Slowly the door opened and the face of the steward emerged.

"I beg your pardon, My Lawd, but I wondered if you would like some bweakfast. I could organise some food bwought up here if My Lawd…"

"No…no thank you, er Natias. I'm sorry, but I don't feel at all well this morning."

"Oh I see," said the steward finding he had to reassess the situation. "I shall fetch the castle physician at once. I shall not be long, My Lawd."

Without waiting for a further response from his master he closed the door and went back down the corridor a little way to where Japhses was waiting.

"Was he still asleep?"

"No, he has some kind of affliction; he looked as white as a sheet. I am going to fetch Laffaxe."

The two men continued down the stairs.

"Is that necessary?"

"I am not sure, but it is pwobably best to be on the safe side."

As they stepped from the balcony back into the hall there were several servants working busily. One girl made to go up the stairs with a tray full of food and drink, but Natias held out his arm to stop her.

"Where are you taking that?"

"Crispin ordered it, Sir."

"Put it down on the table over there for now. I would like you to wun an ewwand for me first."

The girl hesitated.

"But Master Crispin won't be pleased if…"

"Never mind Master Cwispin. Put it down there and go and fetch Laffaxe the physician."

While the servant girl obediently deposited the tray Natias added, "Tell him the new Lawdship is unwell and wequires attention in his wooms immediately. You take that lot up to "Master Cwispin" when you weturn."

"Yes, Sir."

When she had gone Japhses commented, "I wonder what Despot Thorn will do with the drones - if he chooses to do anything that is. We'd do well to get him on our side."

"Yes my fwiend, you are wight. I wish I knew more about him; I am not sure what to expect."

The servant sped across the bailey to the physician's house, which was up against the curtain wall of the castle. He was inside working with a mortar and pestle when she arrived.

"Excuse me please, Laffaxe, but you're wanted in the castle. His Lordship is ill and Natias told me to ask you to come."

"Did he indeed? And what's wrong with his Lordship?"

"I don't know, Sir."

"Humph, of course you don't," he snorted, annoyed at the interruption. He put the utensils down with a bang on the side and waived the girl away.

"All right you run along girl, I'll be there presently."

Natias and Japhses were still in the hall talking, but when Laffaxe arrived the Captain of the Guard decided it was time to leave.

"I'd best be getting along now," he said making for the entrance, "Morning, Laffaxe!"

"Morning," replied the physician mechanically before reaching the steward. "Well Natias, let's see the sickly Lord."

Frank had slipped back into a doze when he was woken by the sound of the latch. He saw Natias enter with another man carrying a small, light trunk that he correctly assumed to be the physician.

"My Lawd," began Natias, "if you please this is the castle physician Laffaxe."

"Thank you," replied the invalid, then turning to the other, "I'm sure I'll be fine, it's just a sickness and I'm all dizzy."

"Hmm, let me be the judge," mumbled Laffaxe pulling up a stool to put his trunk on.

He was a fairly elderly man Frank noticed as he came nearer, his drawn face wearing a permanent frown. This distorted the ubiquitous cross on his forehead under his un-kempt, snow-white hair. He put a monocle on as he leaned over to examine his patient, which made him appear even more severe. He asked Frank when his last meal had been.

"Well I haven't had anything today, but then I really don't feel like I could eat a thing."

"Hmm," was all the response he got from this statement.

While the examination continued Natias stood inside the door with his arms folded. Once it was over Laffaxe announced that all that was needed for the Despot was hot food inside him. He did up his trunk and left without another word. Natias was rather thrown by the suddenness of his departure and was not sure what to say.

"Er...er yes. Wight. I will ensure some food is bwought up stwaight away My Lawd."

He hurried off to the kitchens to organise a belated breakfast for his new master. There he found one servant who was a
willing volunteer. Illianeth was still eager to see the new arrival
and made sure she got the job of taking the soup to him. Natias
saw no danger in it.

'The girl is a nuisance at times,' he thought to himself, 'but
basically she is merely capricious. She gets bored so easily and
could do with a proper interest in life.'

Meanwhile Frank was wondering if he was feeling a mite
better. At least the room had not spun round for a while. The
door opened softly and in came a teenage girl with his soup.
She stood before him. He knew by now to expect another
"white" and he was not disappointed. She wore her hair long in
a similar style to Rachael's.

"I've brought you the soup you ordered, My Lord."

"Thank you; and what's your name?"

"Illianeth, My Lord."

"Illianeth," he repeated slowly, "that's a pretty name."

She blushed. He sat up in bed in order to take the dish and
was rather amused by the girl's curiosity as she gazed around
the room. The soup was hot and tasted good. He concluded he
must be recovering if he could appreciate it. Whatever his ail-
ment had been, it was not chronic.

"This is really nice, did you make it?" he asked the girl who
was standing watching.

"No, My Lord, but I shall fetch you some more when you
have finished if you like."

"That's very kind, but I'd best not overdo it for now."

Just then Natias returned and indicated to the girl to leave
which she did reluctantly.

"How are you feeling, My Lawd?"

"A little better actually. This soup is delicious, I was just telling the girl who brought it. I'm not sure I'm well enough to get up though."

"You had best spend the west of the day in bed, I am sure you will feel better tomowwow morning."

"Let's hope so. I feel so silly arriving here and going down like this. Actually there is something on my mind: my baggage, have the triplets left it in the castle for me?"

"I do not know, My Lawd. I will find out."

"Thanks. Also I want to send a letter to Count Zastein and tell him what has happened to Master Offa. I suppose we can do that tomowwow."

"Certainly My Lawd. If My Lawd wishes it I shall show you the castle and its gwounds tomowwow, if you are felling well enough; and go thwough the accounts and the daily woutine."

Frank handed him the empty soup plate.

"Good, I'd like that a lot. Er, what time do you get up in the morning by the way?"

"First light."

"Yes, well I think I'd prefer a call a little later than that."

"Certainly, My Lawd."

The next day he did indeed feel much better. He woke up with a letter to Zastein formulating in his mind and thought it would be a good idea to get it down in writing. There was a desk in the corner of the room with a large quantity of fine quality paper in it. He wondered where such a backward people would get such paper, the desk also seemed to be a more modern design than he expected in the surroundings. He took some time surveying the rest of the room. The large bed up against the far wall, its robust wooden frame held together with neat wooden joints and wooden pins, dominated it. The headboard had a modest amount of carving in it, nothing very ornate. The important thing though was that the dakk-hair mattress was comfortable. The rest of the room was fairly cluttered with furniture of varying styles.

'Anyway,' he told himself dipping a quill pen into the inkwell, 'you can't worry about that, Francis, you want to get this letter written.'

In it he told Count Zastein about Offa's untimely demise and the decision to go on to their destination. He went on to write that the steward would show him the ropes until such time as the Count could arrange for another black to come and act as advisor.

Frank found he had finished the letter before anyone had come to give him a call, so he decided to wander down to the hall by himself. He had a hunt through the wardrobe; what a rich selection of clothes he had inherited! Trying on one of the less outlandish ones he found the fit was not at all bad. Hoping he had chosen suitable attire he left the room.

Unsure of the way he turned right towards a small window at the end of the corridor. Looking out, the castle wall and one of the corner towers were clearly visible. He seemed to be at a dead end, but tried the door on his left. Gradually he opened it and, sticking his head round, found revealed a metal, spiral staircase. He began descending. One floor down and it appeared much like the previous one, so he continued his descent until he found himself in the great hall. It took him a while to recognise it, but soon concluded correctly that this was the same hall into which he had first entered the main castle building. Light streamed in an open doorway and there was also a small window high up at the opposite end that helped illuminate the place.

A dozen or so people were sitting eating; they all got up as he entered the room. He thought they must have decided to leave until belatedly realising they were standing for him.

"Oh please don't stop on my account! Carry on eating, please."

While the others obeyed, the steward remained standing so he could be seen easily and indicated to the chair at the end of the long table for the Despot to sit. He said he had been just about to send a servant to give him a call, but Frank replied that it was perfectly all right; he had merely woken earlier than he had anticipated.

"Please meet my wife Eko," said Natias as the small, frail-looking woman next to him stood up and bowed.

Frank was also introduced to the other people at the table who were all servants and co-workers in and around the castle. A short while later he realised he could not remember a single one of their names other than Natias and his wife Eko. He did, however, have his appetite back and enjoyed a large breakfast.

The steward made conversation while his master ate, telling him that the triplets had delivered his baggage and that he had organised it to be delivered to his suite.

"Excellent," said Frank. "I have also written a letter to Count Zastein; I take it you will arrange a messenger to send it."

"Yes of course, My Lawd."

During their conversation Frank studied Natias' face. As well as having a sizable nose he had two large warts on his chin. He was no oil paining. His lisp always present, he spoke slowly as if trying to pronounce each word carefully, most noticeably his strange way of saying "Lawd."

Finishing his meal Frank reminded his new right-hand man about his offer of a guided tour of the castle. The response was enthusiastic.

"We can start stwaightaway if you wish. May I suggest we start at the gwound and work our way up to the battlements? We could look outside after that."

"Fine."

"Although I am not sure there is much to see downstairs."

"Oh yes, don't miss anything out."

So further they went down the spiral staircase to a dark, smoky world whose smell took some getting used to. Natias swore when he found that the torch, which was usually at the entrance of this subterranean level, was missing. Almost immediately though the only permanent occupant of this level met them: Crag the jailer who was holding a lamp. He bowed so low when Natias announced who had come to visit him that Frank thought at first that he was a hunchback. When the man straightened up he turned out to be quite tall.

"So this is where your dungeon is, is it?"

"We call it a jail My Lawd."

"Oh," said a disappointed Frank. About the only thing he thought he knew concerning castles was that they each had a dungeon. That would teach him for trying to be clever.

Feeling like Orpheus entering the Underworld he followed through the dark corridors, the lamp casting fantastic shadows on the wet, stone walls. Crag showed him the storerooms and armoury first. The air was cold and dank, a dreadful place to be cooped up in. When the jailer turned his face into the light of the lamp Frank had quite a start, for the man had a most ugly appearance. One eye was straight ahead while the other looked up at a sharp angle. His shoulder-length hair was greasy and matted, he was the only "white" the newcomer had seen who did not look like one.

They progressed to the jail, which was merely a few compounds cordoned off by bars, with no furniture other than a low bench in each compartment. Theses cells seemed quite well stocked with occupants, but Crag assured the Despot that there were currently only a dozen prisoners.

"What are they here for?"

"Mostly robbery My Lord, Steward Natias here keeps the exact records though if you want to see them."

"Well, later thank you."

He witnessed with horror the pathetic creatures the other side of the bars in the shadowy gloom. They sat there not making a sound, staring up at the visitors. Frank swore there and then that he was going to do something for these men, but it was best to think about it before running headlong into a course of action.

There was silence as Natias led the way back up the staircase and back into the light of the hall. Once there they stopped and the guide spoke as their eyes adjusted to the relative brilliance.

"Cwag is an excellent man for that unpleasant job; he does what is wequired of him."

"The prisoners, I mean are they given enough to eat?"

"Yes I am sure they are, My Lawd."

"And exercise?"

The steward looked puzzled, which in itself answered the question. Frank change tack.

"Well never mind. Tell me about the legal system, who decides on punishment and so on? Shall we sit down? I'd like to discuss this before we go any further if you don't mind."

"Anything My Lawd wishes," replied Natias, taking up the nearest chairs for them.

A servant was sweeping the floor nearby as he began his explanation. A member of the Guard came through the entrance and marched briskly past them to go up the spiral staircase. Frank got the impression this hall was very much the centre of the castle's activities.

"The letter we weceived fwom Count Zastein told us you were of the governing class of Oonimawi and would be unfamiliar with our ways. We have no pwoper judges here, like they do in most despotates. Largely the two village leaders take over the work here, although serious cases are weferred to the Castle. Since Despot Wattinger's death these have been dealt with by myself or occasionally by one of the dwones. . There is no fixed "legal system" that you asked about: now we have you here the Despot's word is law, although there are guidelines pwovided in the big, old books kept over there."

He pointed to a large, wooden chest over the other side of the hall. Frank made a mental note to look there later. Normally he would have jumped at the mention of the word "books", but he was too stunned by what he had just seen.

"In pwactice I find I need to wefer to them vewy warely. I have been Steward now for thirteen years and one builds up quite an expertise in that time."

"I can imagine."

"I usually know what is wequired. If you do not feel insulted at the suggestion I shall willingly advise on any cases weferred to yourself fwom now on, My Lawd."

"Thank you, I'm sure I'll need to rely on your experience."

"You shall soon learn what punishment is appwopiate, My Lawd. Mostly a good whipping or a fine, but as you can see a few jailings. The odd execution."

"Execution! Do you have many of those?"

"Oh no, My Lawd. In fact we have not had once since Despot Wattinger died thwee years ago,"

"I see.,. well that's all very interesting. I'm sure I will be needing your help. Shall we move on?"

He was shown the rest of that floor: the small Throne Room used for receiving foreign delegates and the like, the well and the kitchens, all of which adjoined the Great Hall. He was introduced to Matthew, the head of the kitchen, a man of stocky build, who was busy organising the preparation of dinner when they called in.

"Bweakfast is the most important meal of course."

"Oh, why's that?"

"It is the only one where nearly evewyone is pwesent My Lawd. Natuwally you may not desire to eat with us whites, but we find it is a useful time to talk over the business of the coming day. It is essentially a business meal."

"I see."

Illianeth was also working hard in the kitchen Frank exchanged greetings with her.

"She is a vewy impweshionable girl," his guide explained as they ascended the stairs of the wooden balcony on the opposite end to the spiral staircase.

"Illianeth was owphaned at a vewy young age. In fact Eko and I helped bwing her up for a while as we have no childwen of our own. That was until one of the women fwom the Upper Village took over. She now lives by herself in the servants' quarters within the bailey. She is so easily led though and mixes with bad company too often for my liking."

"I see. This building is quite amazing, how old is it?"

"It was finished the year my gwandfather was born. I am not sure exactly how many years ago that is, a long time certainly. Of course it was different before the Keepers."

Frank did a quick calculation and reckoned that if these whites had similar longevity and procreation habits to normal humans – there was nothing to suggest they did not – then this building was only about a hundred and twenty-five years old. The original castles on Earth, that this one seemed to be a reproduction of, were already over a thousand years old at the outbreak of the Second Galactic War when that planet, and probably Molten as well, were lost to outside civilization.

"As you may alweady know all the castles of Hoame are built to a pattern laid down by the Inner Council," continued the steward once they had reached the next floor.

"Really?"

"Oh yes My Lawd. Many are bigger than this one and some have far more gwandiose intewiors, lots of gold and silver, but they are all to the same basic layout."

"Have you visited many others yourself?"

Only the one in Aggepawii My Lawd."

"I see."

Meanwhile Saul, the Upper Village Head, was having to arbitrate in an increasingly heated dispute. Sitting at one end of the large Community Hut he looked across at the protagonists and their supporters. In spite of its size the hut was crowded while the atmosphere was close to boiling point.

"I'm afraid you're wrong," said Hanson, the rather smug-looking man on Saul's left, "we agreed on a price of six hundred stens and you are now telling me you are unwilling to pay it, so you simply won't get the land, nor your deposit back."

"You lying frass!" shouted the plaintiff from across the table in the centre of the room.

He would have hurled more abuse had not the Village Head quickly asserted his authority.

"Tsodd, I will not have talk like that in here! It will not help your case at all."

"Okay, but my brothers were with me when we struck the deal: four hundred stens for the four kabs of land down by the sawmill."

Rodd and Bodd both nodded as they stood by their brother, but Hanson, the normally reclusive landowner, had been waiting for this and laughed.

"They're bound to back you up aren't they!" he counter-attacked, not even trying to hide his contempt. "He's a simple youth Saul, he doesn't understand the intricacies of a business deal."

A howl of protest came from Tsodd's supporters who out-numbered their opposition by more than two to one. Rodd was about to stride over and confront Hanson, but his brother Bodd held him back with a firm hand and called out in a clear voice which cut straight through the din.

"If Tsodd doesn't understand the intricacies of a business deal why did you enter into one with him?"

The howls turned to cheers and Hanson looked uncomfortable for the first time.

"That was a nice one," said Rodd relaxing a bit.

Tsodd kept up the momentum by shouting, "We agreed one hundred stens a kab and you know it!"

"That's enough, enough; enough!" declared Saul in a successful bid to quieten the proceedings a degree. "Thank you. My judgement is a compromise."

Tsodd gave a small groan, as did some of his supporters. When the noise died down sufficiently the Village Head continued.

"Hanson will sell the four kabs to Tsodd for four hundred and fifty stens."

There were mixed reactions from the assembly. Tsodd looked at his brothers with disappointment, but Bodd's expression said it could have been worse.

"In that case I won't sell," Hanson announced.

"Oh yes you will!" retorted the tall, lanky Saul glaring down at him. "My judgement is that you must sell at the price stipulated. Of course you can always take up your case with the new Despot."

Hanson was silent and the people began filing out of the hut now that the show was over.

"That's damn annoying!" cried Tsodd to his brothers, "Why should he get another fifty stens for lying?"

Bodd replied, "I know, but at least the compromise was in your favour."

"Yes, but why does it always have to be a compromise? Fifty stens is a lot of money."

"Agreed, but you've got it. And you've got the land and that's what matters. If you take my advice though you'll steer clear of Hanson for a good time; he's a powerful man and not one to be on the wrong side of. He must have thought this important to turn up in person; you know how rare it is to see him. Keep away from him Tsodd and don't brag, let it all die down – that's what I say.

"Come on now, look on the bright side, you'll have the best aviary in Hoame."

"You're right I should. I've worked and saved hard the last three years and I'm damned if I'm going to let a dakk's turd like Hanson stop me enjoying myself. Oh and thanks you two – thanks for your help."

Back at the Castle Natias had just shown the new Despot the second floor.

"So if we were attacked men would fire arrows out of these."

"The awwow slit, yes My Lawd, the glass is hinged like this to come away..."

He demonstrated.

"...so the bowmen can fire down like this,"

Natias replaced the glass while Frank looked on very interested.

"I find this all quite amazing. I just can't get over how thick the walls are!"

"The walls are even thicker in the floors below. Do you not have castles like this in Oonimawi?

"Indeed we do not."

They moved on.

"And you have been in charge of all this the last few years," said Frank as he began to ascend the spiral staircase again.

"In all matters domestic, yes, My Lawd, with help. Japhses has been in charge of secuwity and defence. All in the absence of a despot or other black of course. It is good to see the natuwal order being westored at last."

"That was his room we just peeped in."

"That's wight, the Captain of the Guard."

"He wasn't at the breakfast table this morning was he?"

"Oh no, My Lawd, he was out early. He will pwobably be awound this afternoon and you can meet him then. A fine man Japhses, he will be a worthy advisor for you."

A glowing recommendation then. They had reached the next floor and went over to the Despot's suite of rooms that was ornate and luxurious by comparison, in sharp contrast with the rest of the Castle. Natias explained that a couple of rooms had been used for the visits of important guests during the reign of Despot Rattinger, but this part of the Castle had been virtually untouched since his death.

"I'm most impressed," was Frank's verdict.

"I am pleased, My Lawd, it is designed to be worthy of our wuler. In the old days when there were blacks here they occupied the second floor and I lived in what is now the physician's house. The Captain lived with the others in the guardwoom."

Before they left his bedroom Frank handed over the letter for delivery to Count Zastein. The last place in the Despot's suite for them to look at was the instrument room. This was next to the main bedroom and had no window. Natias produced a lighted candle seemingly out of nowhere and held it up so they could see the contents. Stacked high, and not at all neatly was every kind of musical instrument. Flutes in racks, drums on the floor, violins and guitars in glass cases on the walls, in fact everything from a triangle to a grand piano. It was all covered in a thick layer of dust and had clearly not seen the light for many a day.

"This was Despot Wattinger's gweat love in life. They used to be all over the Castle, then when he was dying he ordered all of them to be placed in here, I do not know why. Are you intewesting in music My Lawd?"

Before he answered he gazed in amazement at a broken part lying on the floor. There was no doubt; it was definitely a fragment of a frequency oscillator from a hologramatic entertainment centre. He knew, because he had had one as a child. For some reason he felt it best not to draw attention to it, he could always return later. He turned to leave.

"Not this type, Natias. Where I come from we did chant, which had no musical accompaniment, although other people there used them. They were generally synthesised though."

The steward appeared puzzled.

"I have not heard of them."

"No? Well I'm afraid I won't be using these, but I could give permission for others to if they're interested."

Moving away from the room and its heaped-up contents they went through a door out of his suite of rooms and into another corridor, which led back to the spiral staircase.

Passing some more rooms on the way Natias said, "These are where the dwones live, it was them you saw in the hall when you first awwived."

There was a note of distain in his voice and his pace quickened. Frank felt he must ask about them.

"How many drones live here?"

"Thwee My Lawd. Only two here at pwesent, it was them you saw with their dwinking fwiends. Alan is out of the countwy at the moment."

Once more they went up the staircase, this time stepping out onto the flat roof. It was easy to see the square layout of the keep up here, with a small tower at each corner. Battlements bordered the area while in the centre sat a large, wooden catapult machine with a small supply of stone ball ammunition. It looked as if it had not been used for a long time; much of the structure was green with algae.

Nearby were two skylights of unequal size. These let the light into the two central "visitors" rooms of the Despot's suite. Frank had not noticed them when inspecting the rooms, but now realised he should have, because these rooms were internal without the possibility of side windows. Both skylights were fitted with heavy, concertina shutters, drawn back at present.

"Natias, will you detail someone to come up and clean these, they're so filthy I'm surprised they let any light through!"

"Yes, My Lawd. It was vewy wemiss of me to overlook them, it is because I so warely..."

"That's all right, I'm not blaming you or anyone, I just think they could do with a good clean.

"Right. Let's take in the view from up here."

As they surveyed the Castle from this vantage point Natias explained the layout. There was an outer wall, then a courtyard divided by a curtain wall from the bailey. The keep where they stood was inside the bailey, as were the dakks' stables, the servants' quarters and physician's house. In the courtyard was the market, which operated for six days of the week. Natias explained that having the Sabbath off was a contentious issue in some despotates, but that Rattinger had allowed it. Frank confirmed that he was more than happy to let this continue.

Beyond the Castle lay the road from Bynar along which the Despot had come. This was pointed out to him, also the way on towards the Upper Village. To the north was a smaller track.

"That leads to the border with Laodicia," Natias explained. "The guardsmen who patrol the border use it, as well as the occasional twader. You can see the border where those mountains are."

Pointing now in a westerly direction he continued.

"A fwaction beyond the howizon, My Lawd, is the wiver that marks our border with Wabeth-Mephar. In all other diwections the countwy is yours for a good distance further than the eye can see."

'That's not very far!' chuckled Frank to himself as he squinted at the blurred, tree-lined horizon.

"I expect you must have owned much more land as a Pwince of Oonimawi, My Lawd."

"No, I didn't," replied Frank simply. His mind was beginning to wonder off as he regarded the domain that had been handed to him on a plate.

'Francis Thorn, Despot of Thyatira, how grand it sounds!' he considered. 'It may be a primitive society, but it'll be a big responsibility being in charge of all this. It amazes me these people have managed to build such an impressive structure as this Castle. What about the oscillator part? What was that doing there? What other bits of advanced technology exist in these regions? I seem to remember hearing that a modified version of the same thing exists in certain weapons; no this wasn't from that. What a place of contrasts: quill pens and hologramic hardware all on the same day! I wonder what other surprises this planet has in store.'

A great many people could be seen scurrying about below, each going about his business.

'In fact I think the scale of the task I've been given is only just beginning to hit me. A strange twist of fate for a man who was once on the verge of retreating into a life of contemplation and prayer, away from all worldly cares. Now the Lord has given me this land and people to administer. A life of relative opulence by the look of my suite, plus servants at my beck and call – ha this is ridiculous! Always remind yourself Francis that life is but a dream and that one day you will wake up and be called to account for it.'

As he lent over the battlements he quoted to the breeze: "To the man who is given much, much will be expected of him."

"I beg your pardon, My Lawd."

Frank faced the steward.

"Nothing. Shall we go back down?"

CHAPTER EIGHT

"You should be ashamed of yourselves with all this superstitious rubbish! I have seen with my own eyes people wearing a rabbit's foot or lagua's tooth on a string around their neck. I've also seen idiots kissing the oskan tree and known people to worry about the number thirteen saying it's "unlucky! What sort of nonsense is this?"

A short distance from the Upper Village in a field the itinerant preacher Zadok was addressing a crowd of about two hundred people. He stood on a makeshift platform with his penetrating voice booming out to his listeners. An elderly man, Zadok's voice had lost none of its power, and with a lifetime of preaching behind him he spoke with a note of authority.

On this Sabbath, like so many others, his audience was attentively listening to his words.

"And that most pernicious of superstitions, fortune-telling, is once more gathering strength among you so I hear.

"If God had intended you to be able to look into the future he would have given us all that gift as a matter of course. He gave it to the prophets of old and they often found it most burdensome, hardly a gift at all. Do not wish it upon yourselves.

"My children, what poor trust you show in the Lord! Do you think he does not care about you? Do you think he will not look after your future? The Lord Jesus Christ bid you live for today and not to worry about what will happen tomorrow, for you cannot do anything about it. Your faith must be *now*, not some other vague time. This is the truth behind the saying, "tomorrow never comes." The Devil tries to make you resolve to be better *tomorrow*, in this tomorrow that never comes. Do not fall into the trap! There are three elements of time: what has gone, *now* and what might happen; only *now* is any good to us. It is *now* that touches eternity.

"Trying to see the future in the stars is a foolish enterprise. Each of the fifty stars is part of God's creation and he certainly did not put them there for you to involve yourselves in idle speculations - horoscopes. Don't let them take your mind off the present moment and how you can best employ yourself.

"Be good *now*, let love reign in your hearts *now* and let superstitions and the future look after themselves."

There was a brief pause before the crowd broke out into enthusiastic shouts and cheers. This lasted a little while and then they burst forth into a song of praise. When this was finished the crowd began to disperse and go back home. Most people stopped to put some coins into the small, wooden chest held by a tall, handsome youth by the side of the platform. This was Eleazar, the priest's assistant who was hopeful that one day he would follow in his master's footsteps.

Some of the congregation stayed behind to talk together and Zadok came down from the platform to join them. One of this group, a middle-aged woman, stepped up to ask the priest a question.

"Is it true what the miner triplets say, that the new Despot is a believer?"

"I haven't met him yet, so I can't say for sure, but I too have heard what the triplets said. I don't know what to make of it though; it would be marvellous news if it were true."

"Yes," agreed a man with a weather-beaten face, "it seems almost too good to be true, to have a black believer – and a despot as well!"

The woman nodded, "I've heard he is from Oonimari originally, perhaps things are different there."

Just then another woman squeezed her way to the front of the crowd by the platform.

"Zadok, you know what you were saying about horoscopes, how would you answer someone who said that horoscopes were just a bit of fun and not meant to be taken seriously?"

The priest's eyes flashed.

"I would say that that person was extremely foolish! To dabble in things they do not understand and then say they are no harm is the logic of an idiot. If they invoke powers in an attempt to see into the future they show a great lack of trust in God. If it is for "fun" it is at very best an extreme form of vanity. Either way no good can come of it."

The woman who had asked gave a nervous smile in response; then hurriedly left to join the people streaming back to the village.

It was the man with the weather-beaten face who resumed the former conversation.

"So you think Despot Thorn could be good for us."

"That remains to be seen," replied Zadok, "but I pray so. I look forward to our meeting; I hope it will be soon."

Following the guided tour of the Castle, Frank chose to have a couple of quiet days getting used to his new home. Thinking he had not allowed enough time for prayer since he left Paul and Rachael's, he spent a good while in his rooms re-charging his spiritual batteries. His Bible had been delivered along with his other possessions and it felt good to be back to some serious studying. He had his meals brought up by Illianeth, but saw nothing of the rest of the Castle population during this time.

"A bloody strange way to run things!" complained Japhses to a tight-lipped Natias.

Frank guessed there would be such criticism, but decided to begin as he intended to go on.

'God must come first in my life,' he told himself, 'if I am right with him all else will slip into place.'

After lunch on the second day he sought the steward out and had him go through much of the detail of the day-to-day administration. Natias explained that the previous despot had delegated authority to him to deal with most problems, only the more serious needing to be referred. This suited Frank perfectly.

While they were talking in the hall a tall man with a flowing white mane entered the building and Natias introduced the Captain of the Guard.

"Ah yes, Japhses," exclaimed Frank cordially, "I have been told all about you by Natias here. I would like to talk to you at length about your duties some time in the near future."

"I am, of course, always at your disposal, My Lord."

"Oh and by the way, when was the catapult on the top of the keep last tested? It looks in a bit of a poor state."

Japhses was quite taken aback.

"Um, not for quite a while My Lord. The previous despot banned test-firing after a stray shot landed on one of the bee-hives outside the wall."

Frank gave a little laugh.

"I see. Well may I suggest you clear a field of fire and give it a few goes? Not much point in having it if it's just rotting away up there. It needs maintaining surely."

"Yes, My Lord."

"Good. Well I'll see you later, Japhses."

While the Captain left and he resumed his conversation with Natias he thought to himself, 'Damn, that wasn't the way to get off on the right foot with one of your key men, Francis! You just said the first thing that came into your head.'

He spoke to Natias.

"What we were talking about, I'm happy to leave the day-to-day running in your hands, but I'd like to have a weekly meeting with you – and Japhses of course – to know how things are going."

They went out to the bustling market in the courtyard and wondered around the stalls. Frank was aware of some people staring at him, but fortunately most were too busy going about their business to stop. Much money seemed to be changing hands and he wanted to recap on what he had been taught.

"Now the basic unit of currency is the sten, right? And a thousand of them equal one grend."

"That's wight, My Lawd, a lot of money is a gwend. There were in fact several cuwwencies owiginally in Hoame, each of the despots stwuck his own coins. It got so out of hand though that the Inner Council decided to scwap all that and began a standardised unit of cuwwency: the sten. We collect taxes fwom the villages twice a year."

Going outside the walls Natias showed him the vegetable gardens and the bee-hives.

'I wouldn't be surprised if Japhses lobbed a few stones in my direction!' thought Frank to himself.

On the way back to the keep the steward explained that they also had winemaking as one of the castle industries. He pointed out the stables and alongside them the blacksmith's and sword-smith's premises. As they passed the physician's house he remarked, "There is Laffaxe's house. He might be a bit cwotchety, but he is wenouned for his skill. He was taught in his youth by the Ma'hol My Lawd."

"Wabeth-Maphar, yes My Lawd."

The two men entered the hall and saw a couple of people sitting at the near table chatting away while they picked at a piece of honeycomb. Frank noticed they did not have the brilliant white hair everyone else seemed to and guessed correctly that these were two of the three drones in Thyatira. He laughed to himself that he was now as conditioned as any of them at looking for the colour of peoples' hair before anything else! Natias spoke.

"I had better intwoduce our dwone fwiends to you, he said in a tone which did little to disguise his loathing, "Despot Thorn, meet Cwispin and Adwian."

Frank was surprised to find they were both men. The one on the right, Crispin, looked like a woman with his hair in a pigtail and smooth features. The Despot held out his hand, which they just looked at – obviously not the custom here. As he withdrew it again Adrian opened his mouth.

"Hello Despot Thawn," he called out in a mocking voice, clearly he was making fun of Natias' lisp, "What's your first name then?"

After getting used to being called "Master" for several weeks, and lately "My Lord", both the question and the tone in which it had been delivered threw him completely.

"Um, er, Frank."

"Welcome to Thyatira, Frank!" Adrian continued in the same tone, "I hope you like it here in our far-flung corner, and that you like cold winters!"

Crispin laughed in a high-pitched whinny to his colleague's remarks and Frank, still shocked at this reception by the drones, just stood and studied them at close range for a few moments. 'Adrian must be in his late twenties,' he concluded. The drone had cropped, fair hair and wore clothes of all different, bright colours, which clashed horribly. Crispin was a little older and very effeminate, although they both had quite high-pitched voices. Frank decided he needed to know more before he tackled them, so he beat a retreat for now.

"Thank you, Adrian, I will see you both later no doubt."

With that he marched quickly from the hall with the steward in tow. He trotted up the stairs by the balcony and as soon as he arrived at the next floor he turned round to quiz Natias.

"Are they always like that?"

"Wude and diswespectful? Yes, My Lawd."

"What do they do all day?"

"Nothing My Lawd, except eat, dwink and be thowoughly obnoxious. I have no authowity over the dwones or else I would have done something about it. In most despotates they are pawasites, but Despot Wattinger, if you do not mind me saying, gave the dwones too much fwee wein and since his death they have been uncontwollable. They get villagers in for dwinking sessions, plus some of the more impwessionable staff."

"I see, so I have authority over them?"

Natias paused.

"Yes, My Lawd."

Frank gave a big sigh before asking another question.

"Does everyone have two names? I've only ever heard the first name of people 'round here."

"Only the blacks have two names, that is how they knew."

"And what did that remark about cold winters mean?"

"I do not know, My Lawd, they are no worse than in the west of northern Hoame."

"The west?"

"No, the west, My Lawd."

"Oh, I see. Well, we'll have to think about what to do with them. I'm going back to my rooms for now, please arrange for my meals to be brought up. Thanks for showing me around again today. Will you take me to the villages soon? I'd like to see them."

"Of course My Lawd."

Back in his room Frank had plenty to think about.

'That'll teach me for getting used to all this subservience! There is certainly a lesson to be learned here: I mustn't become pompous.

'If I were a half-decent Christian I would humbly accept being laughed at and not worry how it looked in front of others. Pride, the deadliest of the sins! And yet, it would be nice if I could get rid of those drones.'

He sat down to read his Bible and it fell open at Isaiah:

"I, the Lord, have called you with righteous purpose
And taken you by the hand;
I have formed you and appointed you
To be a light to all peoples,
A beacon for the nations,
To open eyes that are blind,
To bring captives out of prison,
Out of the dungeons where they lie in darkness."

'That's it! I'll order an amnesty for the prisoners. It will be like the heralding of a new age of mercy in Thyatira; well, something like that...'

"So what's so special about this dragonfly then? Asked Rodd as he trudged along a path towards the marshes with his biologist brother.

"I have told you before," Tsodd replied.

"All right, but tell me again."

"Its rarity for one thing, the green electra is only known to inhabit these marshes and very few people have ever seen one. I'm one of the lucky ones of course. I suspect their life cycle is very short.

We're better equipped than when I came here by myself last year. I didn't get to within striking distance, but if I had, my net wouldn't have been big enough. Now with these I reckon we'll stand a good chance, if we can just get close enough."

He indicated to the long pole with netting wrapped round it that he carried over his shoulder and the metre-and-a-half long pointed wooden pole that Rodd held.

They progressed between assorted deciduous trees, which were then superseded by tall, smooth torkups with their green bark and gangling, thick roots which came out of the trunks two metres above the current ground level. The path began to narrow.

"I can't understand why you don't wait until you've got the aviary built," said Rodd.

Tsodd gave a quick sigh.

"You don't listen do you! I can't finish the aviary until I've had the planks of halku wood delivered."

"Oh yes, sorry."

"Meanwhile it's an ideal opportunity for us to try and catch a green electra."

Rodd found it hard to share his brother's enthusiasm. He could think of plenty of other things he would rather be doing, but thought he may as well go along this time to help out.

"At the risk of having my head bitten off, it's not like you to want to have a dead specimen, it's a pity we can't try to catch one alive."

"Hardly! Its sting is reputed to be able to burn a man quite severely. The most reliable reports say that it will sting you wherever you touch it on its body, also that the sting travels up a metal weapon, that's why we've got the stake.

"Their reproductive system may be similar to the blue, where the eggs are carried on the body. I may be able to pre-serve these, or hatch some out. My theory is that they only live a very short time in the full-grown form before they die and then their bodies rot very quickly. That's why I want to kill it ourselves..."

"Why don't we use a crossbow?"

"No, that's not nearly accurate enough. When I bet it you stick that thing in where I showed you on the drawing, but don't touch the dragonfly itself! When it's dead its sting no longer works. I want to take it back and take out all its insides, then stuff in..."

"Yeah okay, I get the idea. I'd rather not have the details thank you."

The talking died down as they got nearer the heart of the marsh. The path was single file and raised by now. Tsodd indicated that they should tread as quietly as possible.

After a while they found a nest to sit in, formed by the twisting roots of two torkup trees. There they sat as the sun approached midday and waited.

They waited and waited. It was quite interesting at first, even a little exciting sitting there with the netting laid out and the wooden stake ready. The brothers scanned the horizon waiting to spot their quarry, tense in expectation, fully prepared to pounce on their unsuspecting prey.

As time went by, Rodd found himself more and more uncomfortable and shifted first onto one buttock, then the other. He tried squatting to give his bottom a rest, but soon found it to be an awkward position with his feet at odd angles and his shoes unable to grip the slippery bark properly. Either his feet were forced painfully to the end of his shoes or they went to sleep and he suffered from pins and needles. He started thinking how better off he would have been staying at home, or better still going for a walk with his girlfriend. There were a thousand better places to be than this. Nothing was happening, nor would it; they would go home exhausted at dusk after squatting here all day for nothing. What a waste of time. They had not even brought any food – not that he was hungry, but it would relieve the monotony. Again he shifted his position, annoyed that his brother had a better perch than he did.

"Ssssh!" hissed Tsodd at the constant fidgeting.

Rodd sat back again, more uncomfortable than ever and wondering why he had ever come here. Still nothing happened. It was as quiet as the grave with only the odd tiny flying insect in the unmoving air.

Then Tsodd saw it, two hundred metres away and following a zigzag path towards them as the creature hunted for flies.

'Yes it's a green electra alright,' he thought, feeling body tense as his fingers tightened their grip around the net pole.

It was closing in on them.

'What a monster!' marvelled the biologist to himself, hardly daring to draw breath, let alone turn round to see Rodd getting ready to pounce for the kill. 'That's right, come on my beauty… must be at least a metre and three-quarters long, and those wings!…yes come on…nearly there…nearly there…'

"I'm bored!"

The startled dragonfly spun up and away in an instant. Tsodd's head spun round. Far from being poised to go in for the kill, Rodd was leaning up against the tree looking in the opposite direction.

"You blithering idiot!" shouted Tsodd in a croaky voice. Clearing his throat he laid into his brother: "Why weren't you paying attention? We almost had one then and you weren't even looking! You're useless! It was there, another moment and it would have been within our grasp and what were you doing? Looking the other way and moaning! How can you be so…?"

"Yeah, well we might just as well go home now," the other announced, getting up stiffly and flexing his arms and legs.

Rodd started off back down the path and Tsodd called after him.

"Don't leave, there might be another one."

"I've had enough!"

Tsodd quickly gathered his net and ran to catch up.

"Thanks a lot; you completely ruined our chances of catching it. What were you playing at?"

His tirade continued, but it was no use as Rodd was past caring. It took a long time for Tsodd to calm down, but at some stage before they reached the Upper Village he learned to see the funny side of it.

Wondering to himself he said out loud, "I don't reckon it would have fitted in well with my bird collection when I really think about it."

"No, who wants a silly old dragonfly anyway?"

"Yeah!" Tsodd laughed.

Arm in arm the two brothers walked back home together.

Two days later Frank was in the hall of the Castle with Natias and Japhses, organising the release of the prisoners. Also present was Japhses' lieutenant Uriah with a handful of guardsmen. The Despot was speaking.

"So as a magnanimous gesture on my accession I thought it would be a good idea to release the prisoners and give them a fresh start in life; just this once you understand."

"My Lord," said Japhses, "I feel it is my duty to point out these men for the most-part are dangerous, habitual criminals. You would only be releasing them so that they can go out and commit more crimes."

"Thank you Japhses, I'm sure you mean well, but I always feel we should try to see the best in people and give them every opportunity to mend their ways. Anyway enough said, I'd like them brought to me one at a time so that I can talk to them before each is released."

"Here, My Lawd?"

"Yes."

"Would not the thwone woom be more suitable?"

"Oh I find that room claustrophobic. No, there isn't much going on in here for a change; this'll be fine."

Seeing that his master's mind was set on a course of action, Natias meekly obeyed. Uriah went down to the jail with two of the guard to fetch the first prisoner. They returned with a small, shifty-looking individual who was blinking and scanning round with wondering eyes. He was feeling his wrists now that his chains had been removed. His partially opened mouth revealed a row of blackened teeth. Frank was by now strategically placed in a chair away from the end of one of the long tables, flanked by his subordinates.

Uriah informed the Despot that Crag the jailer had been worried he was going to lose his livelihood now all the prisoners were going to be released.

"I see, well when you next go down please put his mind at rest and tell him we'll put him on paid leave."

Japhses had to turn his head away for fear of bursting out laughing.

'I don't believe this!' he said to himself, 'now we're sending the jailer on holiday because all the criminals are having one too!'

"Well, my man," began Frank addressing the prisoner, "and what crime did you commit?"

The prisoner just gave a puzzled look and Japhses answered for him.

"The man is an habitual thief, My Lord."

"I see," said Frank, still staring at the prisoner with his most serious expression, "what is your name then?"

"Simon, My Lord," he replied, beginning to get his bearings.

"All right, Simon, now I'm going to give you a new start in life and I don't want you to abuse it. Thieving is a most despicable crime and there must be no place for it in this despotate. Just image how upset *you* would be if you found someone had stolen a cherished possession of yours, or one you had worked hard to get..."

As he continued Frank became aware that a couple of extra people had come into the hall and had sat down halfway along one of the tables. A quick glance told him who they were; their hair was so different from everyone else's. It was not long before he could hear sniggering coming from their direction.

Frank concluded his long speech.

"...And so I want you to be a model citizen and give up this foolishness of yours. If you can't find an honest job I'm sure we can get you work here at the Castle. Now Simon, do you resolve to mend your ways if I release you?"

For some time the prisoner had seen his opportunity for freedom. It had seemed too good to be true he had thought when first brought up to the hall, but now this crazy black really was offering to release him.

"Yes, yes, My Lord," he answered eagerly, "I will do all that and never steal again, I swear it."

"Good, well remember this when temptation comes your way. All right, Uriah you may release him now."

Simon shot out of the Castle like an arrow before the Despot could change his mind.

Far from doing that, Frank was sitting there feeling very pleased with himself for showing such compassion. In fact he fought hard to resist giving Japhses a smug look. He managed to resist the urge, but there was a note of triumph in his voice when he made the next command.

"Bring the next prisoner in."

The second man was called Hakka, Japhses informed him, an altogether more serious offender, having been a member of a gang of robbers. Frank began a similar speech to the one Simon received, but soon got the impression from the glazed expression on Hakka's face that it was going in one ear and out the other. So he ventured a change of technique.

"What village do you come from?"

"Lower."

"Have you a family there?"

"No."

Natias cut in, "No, *My Lawd!*"

"No, My Lord," repeated the prisoner mechanically.

This one was not going well and Frank could hear the drones' constant giggling up the hall. If only he had taken the steward's advise and held the interviews in the Throne Room.

Deciding to cut his losses with this Hakka, he gave him what he believed was a stern ticking off and, after warning him about his future conduct, released him.

'Surely the rest can't be as irredeemable as that case!' he hoped, 'no, I must think positively.'

"All right, bring in the next one."

Off went Uriah and his guardsmen again and returned with a third candidate for freedom.

"Another member of the same gang," announced Japhses, "It took us a lot of effort to track them down last year."

'Point taken,' thought Frank, 'I wish someone would silence those damned drones!'

The new prisoner looked a real hard case. Dishabille and caked with dirt, he smelt atrocious as he stood defiantly, glaring at the Despot and his lieutenants. It was clear he had not understood that he was about to be released.

Faced with this uncompromising character and following the last debacle Frank decided to try a different approach.

"Well my man, in view of what I have just been told about you, give me one good reason why you should be included in the amnesty."

The prisoner was silent.

"I am offering to release you if you can convince me it would be a good idea."

"Go t'hell."

Japhses leaped forward, "Soab scum, I'll…"

"Thank you, Japhses," Frank called out, "That won't be necessary."

The Captain of the Guard slowly lowered his arm and retreated back to his former position, without once taking his fiery eyes off the prisoner.

Frank decided to try just once more.

"What's wrong with you, man? I am offering you freedom if you will change your ways!"

The man's expression changed as at last he began to take in what the situation was.

"Whataya mean, er M'Lord?"

"I mean that I have just given your colleague his freedom after promising to give up his crimes and lead an honest life. I want to give you the same chance."

It was almost possible to hear the cogs turning in the prisoner's brain as the light dawned.

"Yeah, I mean, yeah I fink that'll be possible M'Lord, yeah…I fink I can change m'ways…"

'Bloody hell what a sham!' thought Japhses, 'I know the Despot will dismiss my protest, but I'm going to have one last go at getting him to see sense.'

"My Lord,"

"Yes, Japhses."

"May I say something?"

"Certainly."

I realise of course that it is entirely your decision, My Lord, but I feel I really must advise most strongly against letting this man go,"

To his surprise, Frank said nothing and allowed him to continue.

"I've got more intention of becoming a Laodician than he has of turning away from robbery. He was responsible for the murder of an elderly man and his wife. He has never shown any remorse. I am totally convinced he would carry on terrorising people and robbing them as soon as he was released. I implore you, My Lord, not to let any more of them go."

Silence reigned. Even the drones were straining to catch the Despot's response. Frank sat there deep in thought.

"'To be a light for the peoples and release the prisoners who lie in darkness of the dungeons" may sound a good idea, but I feel sure Japhses is right. This man has no intention whatsoever of repentance and shows a complete absence of genuine remorse.

'How many bad decisions have not been reversed because of a fear of not losing face? Francis you must do what is right and not worry what men might think.'

"Natias, what is *your* honest opinion?"

"I agwee one hundwed per cent with Japhses, My Lawd."

"Hmm. Are the remaining three prisoners all robbers like him?"

It was Uriah who answered.

"There are only two left, My Lord, the other one was released yesterday having completed his sentence. One of the two is of the same gang. The last is there for something else."

"What's that?"

Japhses cut in, "Like the scum before you he would have been executed if a black had been here, My Lord. The man raped a little girl, a despicable act!"

Frank was shocked.

"Outrageous! Send this one back, there'll be no more releasing of prisoners today."

The guards held firmly onto the prisoner and dragged him back towards the cells as he began to hurl abuse in all directions. Frank told the Captain he could dismiss his soldiers once the prisoner was safely locked up again. Turning his head he saw the drones get up and walk out now that the entertainment was over. Crispin's dreadful laugh echoed round the hall as they left. Frank signalled Natias and Japhses to sit.

"Well my trusty lieutenants," he said managing a semblance of a smile, "That didn't work out very well did it! I want to apologise for not listening to you both sooner and going headstrong into my plan."

The other pair were both embarrassed.

"My Lawd, that is not necessary."

"Thank you, but I think it is. It was ill conceived, I didn't look into it deeply enough first, nor properly listen to my advisors."

Japhses was amazed.

'This Oonimarian Prince is not short of surprises,' he thought, 'I admire him for being able to apologise, no other blacks would.'

"Do you want me to send some of the Guard after Hakka and bring him back My Lord?"

"Er no, I don't think so thank you, that would be unkind. We'll just have to hope he does mend his ways, maybe we can keep a close eye on him.

"Natias I'd like a written report on each of the prisoners – their background, their crimes, when they were sentenced and how long for, that sort of thing, all right?"

"Yes, My Lawd."

"Good. And I'd be honoured if you'd both accompany me on a visit to the villages tomorrow morning, so I can get to know my area better."

While the two whites nodded their agreement, Frank's attention was drawn to a woman in the hall that he had not seen before. She was by the spiral staircase talking animatedly with Uriah. He found he had to squint to see her at all clearly.

'Must be in her early thirties,' he concluded, 'what a lovely slim figure; and what an enchanting manner.'

Snow-white hair fell in ringlets around her face, they danced as she spoke. Frank could not make out what she was saying, but noticed she used her hands a great deal to illustrate what was evidently a funny story from the way she was laughing.

"Who is that woman please?" he asked Natias.

"It is Giella, My Lawd, Uriah's wife."

"I see."

'Phew! She must be the most beautiful woman I've ever seen in my life...'

Jasphses broke his thoughts up by asking, "Is there anything else, My Lord?"

"Oh no, no thank you, nothing else for now."

CHAPTER NINE

Daybreak in Thyatira found the Castle a hive of activity. Matthew, the head of the kitchen, had been up a good while already, making bread and generally organising things in his fussy manner. The duty guard was being changed and the courtyard entrance opened to let in some market traders keen to set up their stalls early.

After a while the hall began to fill up as breakfast was served. Towards the balcony-end of the middle table Natias and Eko were eating with Japhses. Around them children were playing, screaming as they chased each other round the large room. The steward's wife was speaking.

"I hear the crop is well forward thanks to the mild weather."

"That's right," the Captain agreed, "although when I spoke to Reuben yesterday he seemed reluctant to admit it."

"Hey hey hey!" Natias cried out as he caught the arm of one of the children as she ran past where they were sitting. "Come on now, settle down. Better still go outside and play – and take your fwiends with you, there is plenty of space out there and you will not be disturbing anyone. Go on."

The little girl led her playmates out of the door and down the stairs to the inner bailey. As they left Frank arrived to have his breakfast. The others all stood up.

"Good mawning, My Lawd."

"Morning everyone."

"Illianeth was about to bwing you your bweakfast up...ah here she is."

Frank sat down at the head of the table as the servant presented his meal with a smile and a greeting.

"There you are, My Lord."

"Thank you, Illianeth. That's a pretty dress you've got on this morning."

"That's very kind, My Lord," she said blushing heavily.

As she left them Frank decided to get down straightaway to the business of the day.

"I'm looking forward to our visit round the villages. Which do you think we should go to first, Natias?"

"I suggest, My Lawd we go to the Upper Village first. Riding our dakks it should not take us too long. We can have our lunch there and then turn southward to come back via the Lower Village. We should be able to manage that comfortably in a day."

"Did you say *riding* our dakks? Could we not go in a wagon?"

"That would be far too slow, My Lawd. The woad thwough the forest to the Lower Village is vewy poor; it would be tedious and difficult by cart. Some people do use it for such, but weally the woad could do with a lot of maintenance."

"I see, well you'll have to teach me to ride one of those beasts, 'cos I've never ridden."

"Try again My Lord!" cried the stable-master enthusiastically.

Frank was holding onto the dakk's mane with one foot in the stirrup and hopping about on the other foot as the animal chose to go round in circles. A stable-hand came forward to offer a steadying hand and Frank was at last able to swing his leg over and sit in the saddle.

"You promise this is a placid example," he said as he looked for reassurance.

The stable-hand laughed.

"Alsi? She's the quietest dakk on Molt M'Lord."

Frank led her round the inner bailey as he got a feel for riding. They were not large animals, but he felt high off the ground as he looked around him.

'Oh no, there's one of those drones!'

Crispin was standing on the steps of the keep looking down. He was dressed up to the nines that morning with a toga-like outfit that was made out of a bright, silky material. His fingers were covered in jewel-encrusted rings.

"Very good, Frank, very good," he called out in his usual mocking tone.

"Haven't you got anything better to do?" Frank snapped back as he wheeled the dakk round (quite professionally he thought) to face the main entrance. He called out to Natias and Japhses who were mounted up ready.

"Come on, let's go."

They went through the large open gates with guards in attendance and out into the road leading to the Upper Village. The pace was steady, but slow enough for the Despot to manage his dakk without any real difficulty. With a clear road ahead of them the three men rode abreast, Frank in the middle.

"Don't Crispin and Adrian ever do anything useful?" he asked.

"No, My Lawd, they waste their time wather than help at all; and they waste our money on their twinkets and outlandish fashions."

"Really? When we were at the treasury you said the finances would be in a poor state until the taxes were due to be collected again, is that because of them?"

"It is. They were bad enough when Despot Wattinger was alive, but lately they have been dwaining our wesources with their pwofligacy and we have been powerless to stop them."

Frank looked round at Japhses who expressed his agreement to what was being said.

"Right," said Frank, "*that* is going to change!"

As they progressed he found himself pleasantly surprised at how easy it was to ride one of these creatures. Just as he was beginning to relax, however, Japhses announced that they had better dismount and walk for a while. Looking puzzled Frank followed suit, but asked why.

"To preserve the dakks' energy," the Captain explained, remembering that things must be very different in Oonimari.

So they continued for a time on foot. The road was relatively empty, although they did pass a few people travelling towards the Castle, Each of these stopped to give a little bow to their new despot before continuing on their way.

"Not as many people going to market as usual," Japhses observed.

There was no immediate response to this remark, but it had set Frank thinking.

"Exactly how many people *are* there in Thyatira? Do they all live in just the two villages?"

"Yes My Lawd, plus some at the Castle of course. I am not sure of the pwecise figures, although the tax weturns do show the numbers of adults there are. In wound figures there are woughly thwee and a half thousand people. The population had been declining for some time, but I believe it has picked up a bit the last couple of years. I hope now that we have a despot again it will encouwage more people fwom the other despotates to move in permanently.

"At the moment though there are awound twenty-four hundwed people living in the Upper Village and about a third as many, possibly slightly more, in the Lower Village. The Castle staff number a hundwed, plus the guard."

"Yes the guard, how many of them are there, Japhses?"

"A hundred and fifty fully trained and active members, My Lord. In times of peace only half are on duty at any one time, around thirty-five at the Castle and forty on border patrol. We do sometimes have a higher proportion on duty, for instance twice a year when some accompany Natias to collect the taxes."

'Such small numbers!' thought Frank, 'there were five-point six million people on Eden and some planets have many times that. Legend had it Earth had a population running into billions, but then those old stories do tend to get exaggerated.'

"My Lawd, there is one matter I have been waiting to waise."

"What's that?"

"The matter of land pwices. You may not be aware of how our laws work, but basically all land outside the villages belongs to the despot. When a village wants to expand, the despot weleases some for people to buy. It is a good method of taking excess money out of the economy and can be an additional source of wevanue for the Castle, that is, yourself.

"Not having had a despot the last few years there has been no land welease while the demand has gwown. This is because some people have wanted to expand their holdings, or newly married couples have wanted a place of their own. The wesult has been land pwices soaring up out of contwol, meaning the few people with land to spare making wediculous profits. Just the other day one of the miner twiplets bought some land at a hundwed stens a kab, twice what it would have fetched a few years ago…and now no one is willing to sell at under a hund-wed and fifty!"

"Ah yes, the miner triplets, I know them."

"But most people simply cannot afford such pwices. Would it be in order for you to welease some land wound the Upper Village My Lawd? If you agwee to a hundwed and sixty kabs being weleased at a fair pwice of, say, forty or fifty stens a kab, depending on the quality and situation of the land, we could see how that went before deciding further action."

"Is that a lot of land?"

"Enough for about fifty or sixty dwellings, not vewy much."

"Well sure. You go ahead and organise it, Natias, you obviously know what you're doing. You go ahead. Let me know how it goes, whether more land needs to be released in a second phase or not."

'Natias obviously knows what he's talking about,' he thought. 'I've got to trust him, got no choice. Still, he seems a trustworthy person, well organised – plus he was highly recommended to me…'

"Thank you, My Lawd, I will draw up the papers when I have enough time. The wevanue too will help pay off some of the Castle debts. I take it I may inform the dwones that they cannot take any more money fwom the tweasuwy without first seeing yourself."

It was time for them to mount up again and Frank said a quick prayer for help before doing so successfully on the first attempt. They travelled on for a short way before passing a man standing by the side of the road with his heavily laden dakk. He was inspecting the beast's shoes. He had dark brown skin, long black hair and wore a hat with yellow plumes in it. A long rope led from the load to a baby dakk that was crying out to its mother carrying the load. The man swore at it to keep quiet to no effect.

Japhses called out to the man asking if he needed any help, but the answer was in the negative.

"Wasn't he a black?" inquired Frank as soon as they were out of earshot.

"Oh no, My Lawd, he is a foweigner, he does not count. He is merely a trwader, although I am not sure where he is fwom."

"Am I not a foreigner?"

"Oh no," replied Natias gaily, "The Autarch has pwonounced you a Hoamen,"

"I think the trader's from Sarnice," Japhses put in.

"Where's that please?"

"North of here, My Lawd, to the west of Laodicia. It's a long way away, we don't often see their sort here."

"I see. Is there much trade with the outside world generally?"

"Oh yes, My Lawd, a great deal."

"Tell me about it."

"There is a vewy healthy twade with our neighbouring despotates in Hoame: we get non-pwecious metalwork fwom Bynar – and weapons. Fwom Aggepawii the main imports are fwuit, nuts and cloth. In fact our twade pact with Aggepawii is cuwwently being we-negotiated."

"And what do we send them in return?"

Our main exports are wood, both worked and unworked, pottewy and of course the hulffan dewivatives."

"Hulffan?"

"Our main crop," explained Japhses. "We'll soon be passing some fields of it, My Lord. It's a most versatile plant and has saved us from ruin during hard times. It is fortunate for us it likes our soil, for it is very fussy about where it will grow. It is, in fact, illegal to take hulffan seeds out of Thyatira without a licence. It's still early in the season now, but later on it can grow to great heights, almost twice as high as a man in fact, but its wonder is its versatility. It has a fibrous stalk, which is used to make rope, the fruit is edible and the husks of the fruit are melted down and a gooey substance extracted which sets hard when cooled. It is used as mortar for stone buildings and for road surfaces."

"Is it used on the Castle?"

"With certain additives, yes My Lord. Depending on how it is mixed it can have a certain amount of play in it. The streets of the capital use hulffan extract between the stones. Unfortunately it's not used on the roads here, because the money from exports is so good. Ironic really."

"You certainly know a great deal about it."

"Yes, My Lord, my father was a hulffan cropper and his brother, my uncle, used to go on trade runs to the capital until his health gave way fairly recently."

"Actually a proportion of Thyatira's taxes to the Autarch is usually paid in Hulffan-tar."

"I see. And do we do much trade with our neighbours outside Hoame?"

Again the Captain answered, "Occasional trade with Rabeth-Mephar yes, My Lord. We get things such as spices, rare herbs, salt and precious metals from them."

"Surely salt is more fwom Sarnice," Natias corrected.

"Yes of course you're right. Trade is virtually non-existent with Laodicia, although I suppose we do sometimes get paper from there, but then with all these countries it's more a matter of individual traders using their initiative. In the past one or two of our drones have been known to travel afar. They can be a useful source of intelligence in fact."

"It's Laodicia which is seen as the main external threat I understand," said Frank.

"Not lately, My Lord," Japhses corrected, "it has all been quiet with the Laodicians for a long time in fact. I think they're always squabbling amongst themselves. They call it debate apparently, but it sounds like a lot of hot air to me. We do still keep the border patrols up, of course, and like I said glean what information we can from traders.

"No, it's the Ma'hol I'm most concerned about right now. Our long-standing border dispute with Rabeth-Mephar could start to get nasty I fear."

"What's that all about?"

"Oh three small islands in the river which marks the border. They're not inhabited or anything, but they are *strategic* significance.

"The trouble is there are certain elements in the Mehtar's Court..."

"He's their ruler," said Frank wanting confirmation.

"Yes, My Lord, some of his cronies are pursuing a propaganda war, trying to stir up trouble over the islands. From my spies I get the impression the Mehtar himself is not taken in by all the chauvinistic rhetoric, but I don't like it."

"Can we not write a conciliatory letter to the Mehtar to try and settle the matter peacefully?"

"Oh no My Lord, that would be seen as a sign of weakness."

As they progressed they began passing enclosed fields with small herds of pigs in them. The occasional flock of sheep could be seen, shepherds in attendance, beyond these compounds. No hulffan in sight yet.

"Why haven't I been told about this before?"

"I'm sorry My Lord, but it seems to've quietened down lately. With a bit of luck it will all die a death. These things do have a habit of bubbling up for a while before settling back down again. I mean there's been no war between them and us in... goodness knows how many years.

"That having been said, I have got one concern, My Lord."

"Yes?"

"The armoury store under the Castle is not conducive to keeping them in good condition. I would like to commission a new, purpose-built armoury within the bailey. I have a place in mind. I believe this is urgent, My Lord."

"Fine, I'm happy to look at this back at the castle at an early opportunity, if you will take on the responsibility once we have agreed on a site. We'll find the money from somewhere"

"Thank you, My Lord. I would like to get this done quickly, even if I believe the Ma'hol matter should come to nothing."

"Right. Now this is the sort of intelligence I will expect you to share with me at our weekly meetings."

"Yes, My Lord."

"Who has control of the islands at the moment."

"We do."

"Hmm, well let's hope your feelings on the matter turn out to be correct."

They came over a ridge to see hulffan crops spreading out either side of the road and the Upper Village in the distance. The sun was shining brightly in the cloudless sky and Natias remarked how unseasonably warm it was. The three men dismounted once more to walk the final stage. Frank had a good look at the hulffan. It was at that time only around a metre high. The thick stalks were a pale yellow colour with speckles of black. With their strangely shaped inceptive fruit they were unlike anything he had seen before. Natias told him that when mature and ready for harvesting they looked quite different: tall with long, light-brown leaves and dark husks in a clump near the top.

A short way further on some archers were practising on a strip of waste ground. Japhses explained that bows were used for hunting as well as sport. In times of war archers would be used in support of the guard.

When they arrived at the village it reminded Frank strongly of the one he had stayed in when he had first arrived on this planet. It had the same wattle and daub huts with small industries such as pottery and woodwork very much in evidence.

As they began to pass some of the dwellings two men came up to them saying that Saul, the Village Head, would be along shortly to offer his greetings, Natias entrusted the dakks to one of the men and with the other messenger leading the way the Castle delegation wondered along the main road of the village.

A little way up a young woman was working on a loom outside her hut under a wickerwork awning. There were several children round the woman playing quietly for a change. When she saw the men coming she put her work down and stepped out to greet them, shielding her eyes from the sun as she did so.

"This is Kim, My Lawd," Natias said introducing her. "Kim is the sister of Giella who was in the Castle yesterday."

Frank tried to sound as nonchalant as possible, "Oh yes, I remember."

'How could I forget?' he asked himself, 'she was gorgeous. Yes I can see Kim's got a bit of a resemblance, but she's not a patch on her sister.'

"Welcome to the village My Lord," said Kim, "this is your first visit isn't it?"

"Thank you, yes it is. You're busy I see,"

She smiled and opened her mouth to answer when two of her children began fighting and she turned to them.

"Jonathan! Peter! Stop that immediately!"

As she went over to break the boys up, Natias told her they had better be getting along. They moved off down the road once more. After pulling the protagonists apart Kim managed a quick wave and wished them a good journey.

Walking on, Frank considered how very welcome he had been made to feel, so unlike some of the planets he had been on. Like Syner for instance, where under the guise of egalitarianism the main preoccupation of the population seemed to be making everyone else's life a misery, or New Sweden from which he was expelled for speaking out against the tele-screen broadcasts for sexual deviants. They had objected to him referring to the place as New Sodom.

"My Lawd, this is Saul."

"Oh…yes, I've been looking forward to meeting you Saul."

The tall Upper Village Head there greeted him in the middle of the street. A small group of the other important villagers was also introduced. They exchanged banalities as they walked to the community hut and once inside they sat down to more serious business. Things took a while to settle down though as the three visitors each got involved in separate conversations to begin with.

One of the group, whose name escaped Frank, told him that Zadok the priest was extending an invitation to the new Despot to have his midday meal with him.

"That sounds pleasant. Does he live near here?"

"No, My Lord, he is an itinerant preacher, but he has asked to meet you on the pad afterwards.

Frank's blank expression prompted the speaker to explain.

"A piece of community land in the middle of the village."

"Oh I see, well I'm sure that'll be okay."

Saul was trying to get some quiet.

"Gentlemen, please! I'm sorry, My Lord, we have the place of honour reserved for you up here."

Frank was still not used to this treatment. As Saul apologised for the lack of organisation, the guest of honour took up his place with the village head on his right and Natias on his left. Japhses was with the rest of the important men from the village facing Thyatira's leader.

Saul asked permission before starting.

"Today we welcome Despot Thorn on his first visit to our village. We are extremely pleased to have him with us, but as some of you know there has been a serious development in the three-islands dispute. Before daybreak this morning a small group of Ma'hol tried to land on the southern-most island. Our brave guard reacted boldly and repelled the invaders. One Ma'hol was killed and several injured; there were no guard casualties. I'm sure our ruler would like to say a few words on how we are to deal with this worrying development."

Frank sat there for a moment waiting for the next speaker to start when he realised the Village Head had meant him! Seized by a sudden panic he thought it was just as well Japhses had mentioned something about this on their way here. He was just about to start a makeshift speech when the Captain of the Guard came to his rescue.

"My Lord, may I make a suggestion?" Japhses said as he stood up. "As your adviser on matters of defence may I suggest we increase the number of men on the islands and step up patrols along our border with Rabeth-Mephar? We can cancel all leave as well."

"Thank you, Japhses," replied the Despot, who had recovered himself by now. "I think it's a good idea to increase our presence along the border, we can discuss numbers afterwards. I wouldn't have thought we needed to cancel all leave at this stage. If it is only a small group, as the reports suggest, we do not want to over-react. At the same time though we can send a strongly worded letter of protest to them; Natias, may I leave you in charge of that?

"We must keep up our vigilance and not show any signs of weakness. I want all intelligence reports brought up to the Castle as quickly as possible. Japhses, I want you to make extra sure we are prepared for anything they might do.

"Men of Thyatira, rest assured that all precautions to protect our land from these foreigners will be taken. Constant alertness will be necessary; we will not shirk from the task."

The Despot's quick dash of rhetoric had gone down well and the assembly felt reassured. While the rest of the meeting turned to more mundane topics such as land prices, how the main crop was doing and the weather. Frank could not help but wonder what he was getting into. The last thing he wanted was for their letter to provoke the people he knew nothing about, but Japhses had earlier indicated that a show of toughness was the best policy with the Ma'hol.

By the end of the assembly it was clear that the village leaders had used the visit as a business meeting rather than a social call. It seemed despots did not often visit the villages and they had seized the opportunity to get some matters sorted out. They seemed pleased with they way that the border crisis was being dealt with and the decision to release more land was popular too.

As the meeting dispersed Saul said goodbye and instructed his servants to escort the visitors to Zadok the priest. It was noticeably warmer outside as midday approached. On the way Japhses began to apologise for being wrong in his assessment of the border dispute.

"That's all right," Frank reassured him, "it's not always easy to predict how other people will react. But tell me, what are these Ma'hol really like? You said if we talked of peace to them it would be seen as a sign of weakness."

"They are barbarians My Lord, the only way to deal with them is to be tough. A show of strength is the one language they understand."

"But from what I've heard today we haven't actually been involved in a war with them for generations and very little contact in the meantime."

Natias joined in.

"Japhses is wight, My Lawd. They are a vicious, cwuel people. They deal in slaves and some of our white ancestors are amongst them I'm afwaid. Their population and army are much bigger than ours, so as you wightly said in the meeting, we must be pwepared."

"I see. Well when you draft the letter of complaint to their leader I want to have a look at it before it's sent, okay?"

"To the Mehtar, yes, My Lawd."

"Oh and Japhses, I'd like a full report on this skirmish this morning to know exactly what scale it was on and what happened exactly."

"Certainly, My Lord, I will get one of the soldiers involved in the fight to come to the Castle and give you the first-hand account."

"Sad news indeed!" said Baron Schail as he put the letter down. "Offa was a favourite of yours wasn't he."

Count Zastein nodded as he sat upright at his large, torkupwood desk.

"Yes he was. What is worse is the fact that he was just the man for the job: knowledgeable, discreet and very able in his duties. Now he had died I am at a loss as to whom to send as a replacement. There are very few men I could trust with such a mission and with all that's going on right now It's the worst possible time to lose a top civil servant."

"There's Schmitt in the general office," suggested the Baron, "he's always willing to please."

"The man's a talker. I wouldn't trust him with the information I'd have to give him."

"Have you considered Landorff, he's trustworthy surely."

"We can't spare him. His expertise will be needed here, especially if the Autarch doesn't recover."

"You think his attack could be worse than the physicians have indicated."

"I'm convinced of it," Zastein replied. "They said he was asleep when I went to visit him this morning, but from what I hear from elsewhere he's slipped into a coma. I think he's dying, Otto."

There was silence. The Count got up slowly and turned to look out the long bay window. The Citadel was high above the rest of Asattan, capital of Hoame. From there he had a panoramic view of the city. He stared out at the busy scene below on this exceptionally warm spring day.

Schail decided now was the time to ask the burning question.

"When will you make your move?"

Zastein looked up at the cloudless sky and, without moving, said in a grave voice, "The moment I have it confirmed the Autarch is dead."

He turned round to face his companion.

"Yes, my friend, we must not hesitate or the moment will be lost. If those fools think they can set Drakin up as some sort of a puppet and pull the strings themselves they're going to have another thing coming!

"No, looking at it rationally we *should* have enough votes in the Council to swing it, but you and I are going to have to lobby the waverers, the weak-willed. Men such as Mallinberg who turn like a weather-vane in the wind."

Baron Schail rubbed his large chin. He reckoned that now was as good a time for a constitutional crisis as ever.

"I know what you mean, but surely there is a good chance of success. You know where the main threat comes from. It is men such as Deistenau that you will have to be wary of, of course."

"Of course," echoed Zastein. "The good Baron is typical of his sort whose main preoccupation in life is the attainment of power."

He went back to the window and looked out at the view as he continued.

"I have been on the Council for most of my life, like my father before me. I was *born* into power, Otto, it holds no fascination for me, more a burden it's my duty to carry.

"I dread to think what a mess Deistenau would make, pulling on Autarch Drakin's strings. While I still have breath I will do everything in my power to thwart them. I simply don't want to see our country ruined."

He turned to face Schail once more.

"You of all people know my motives."

"Yes and what's best for Hoame. It would be a tragic waste to see all our efforts nullified."

"Indeed. Especially now things are looking up again, what with Despotess Wonstein giving birth to a healthy black heir and our "Oonimarian Prince" Despot Thorn. Which brings us back to where we started.

"Are you going to send another clerk to help him?"

"I can't, there's simply no one suitable to spare right now. We can't just send anyone. He's a little strange perhaps, but I believe he's intelligent enough and he knows what's expected of him. He has this efficient steward to help him from what we know – plus Alan of course; we mustn't forget that!

"Write to him and tell him another black cannot be spared for the time being.

"We'll get reports on his progress anyway and we can visit there ourselves one day, once the present crisis is resolved and our position is secure. It's been a while since we went to Thyatira."

Baron Schail looked up from making some notes on a piece of paper.

"Right, I shall inform him. For the foreseeable future our protégé Despot Thorn will have to fend for himself."

CHAPTER TEN

While Zastein and Schail were in the capital discussing him, Frank was fending for himself quite pleasantly on the Upper Village Pad. Sitting in the shade of a willow tree with his lieutenants, they were being well hosted by Zadok the priest and his assistant Eleazar. A couple of servants were in attendance.

A picnic had been provided and Frank found it quite novel sitting on the grass as he ate a cold chicken leg. He could not help noting the irony of it. During all his years on Eden he had been a strict vegetarian, but after he had begun his nomadic life among the planets he found himself in places where he had a choice of eating meat or starving. He had chosen the former course of action. Principals are all very well, but not much use if you are dead he told himself. It was not as if there was a Biblical injunction against eating meat. It had tasted like cardboard to him at first, but gradually he had grown to like it and was thoroughly enjoying the chicken meal as he sat there talking with the priest.

Zadok had not wasted much time before raising the topics uppermost in his mind. Yes, the Despot assured him, he was a Christian even though he did not have a cross on his forehead. No, the believers did not have such a mark when he came from. Yes, he would allow the priest to hold a service in the castle courtyard the coming Sabbath. No, he did not have any objections to the people building a church in the Upper Village.

As the meal drew to a close, Frank wondered at the formidable man before him.

'He's certainly in the driving seat right now!'

The priest looked thoughtful. He slowly scratched the side of his face, then ran his fingers down the lines of his chin as he spoke again in his booming voice.

"Thank you, My Lord, it has long been my ambition to have a purpose-built place here, but the previous despots would never allow it, because they were not believers. It is God's doing, bringing you here.

"May I ask that you donate the land for the site? The congregation shall of course provide the timbers and other materials."

Frank readily agreed to donate the land for such a worthy project and instructed Natias to make up the deeds. He also asked to see some plans of the proposed building before work began.

"I'd like to see what type of construction you have in mind," he explained. "Have you thought of building it in stone?"

"That would take too long My Lord," Zadok replied.

The steward came in: "Also the construction laws, My Lawd. All buildings made of stone or bwick for whites have first to be passed by the government in Asattan. It always takes a long time for such wequests to be gwanted. The Castle is the only stone building in Thyatira.

"Not being believers, the blacks that run the civil service pwobably would not look kindly on such a suggestion. Besides we would have to employ the services of an external architect."

Undeterred by this, Frank answered enthusiastically, "I see, well let's go ahead with the wooden church for now and in the meantime we can think about what a stone one would look like. We can get various opinions from different people. You can organise that please Natias; another job for you."

"Yes, My Lawd."

The conversation progressed as the servants cleared away following the meal, helped by Eleazar. Zadok explained to Frank that he was teaching his current assistant all the old stories of the faith, just as he had his previous disciples.

"There is so much for me to teach him still: Noah and the ark, Samson and Delilah, King David and most importantly, of course, the life and teachings of Our Lord. Eleazar here is a good learner though, he already has many of the stories from Genesis and Exodus memorised – and The Sermon on the Mount."

Frank was puzzled.

"Don't you have a Bible? All the history and teachings written down?"

"That is not our way, My Lord. Our tradition is the spoken word. Eleazar is the twelfth assistant I have taught the Word to in my life. He is comparatively early in his long apprenticeship. He will know the outline of the stories from school, of course, but as a priest he is required to know them word for word."

The youth smiled nervously. He had hardly said a word the whole time. Japhses too had been rather quiet; Frank noticed he was starting to get restless. The priest continued talking.

"My former pupils are now scattered to the four winds with none currently in this despotate, although one or two do come here on occasional visits. Most are serving in the other regions of Hoame, but some have chosen a missionary life in foreign countries. I don't know if any have reached Oonimari, My Lord.

"I don't get about nearly as much as I used to."

He looked at his walking stick on the grass and was quiet for a short while as his mind began to wonder. Then he suddenly looked up again and spoke in lighter vein.

"It would be an honour if you would grace one of our meetings with your presence. We have much singing and dancing, rejoicing in our worship of the Lord. Many people attend. I usually give a short address."

Was that an involuntary raising of the eyebrows Frank noticed on Eleazar's face when he heard that last comment?

"The honour would be mine," the Despot answered, "it sounds a joyous occasion, although very different from what I'm used to. Back home when we met for worship it was usually in very small groups. The only type of singing we did was in formal chants, many in an ancient language of power."

"How interesting," said Zadok who did not begin to understand what the Despot was talking about.

'What a strange manner he has when talking about such a straightforward subjects such as worship. Then I should not be surprised at his odd ways for it is unheard of for a black to be a Christian at all. I suppose it stands to reason that black Christianity is different.

'I will leave the issue with God. I am certainly not going to argue while he lets me preach at the Castle and gives permission for a church building. These are real breakthroughs in Thyatira.'

Natias broke the silence by asking the priest what he thought of the current three-islands crisis with the Ma'hol.

"Those pagans must be kept out! We must keep those uncivilized wretches away from there whatever it takes!"

He turned to Frank.

"You see, My Lord, the river is of great importance to the Church. For many generations our baptisms have been performed there, just near to the islands. In fact we have several times held services on Telar, the largest and southern-most island. It would be intolerable if those savages got control of the islands and thence the river."

"I can assure you, Zadok, that in the meeting I had here in the Upper Village with Saul, Japhses here and the rest, I made it very clear the commitment I have to hold onto the islands. Patrols are being increased and other steps taken to ensure our sovereignty is maintained."

"Good, I am glad to hear of it."

"Excuse me, My Lord."

"Yes, Japhses."

"In connection with this, would you mind if I were excused so that I can get on with organising the guard and checking our defensive measures?

"I am sure you will be fine going to the Lower Village with just Natias."

"An excellent idea! You go ahead, Japhses."

Natias chipped in.

"Actually, My Lawd, we weally should be on our way if we are going to have a look at the Lower Village and get home before it is dark."

So the party split up. Japhses went first before Frank and Natias thanked the priest for his hospitality and left the Pad. Their dakks were brought to them and the two men rode out of the village on the road south.

Passing more fields of hulffan, Frank noticed a flock of small birds fly overhead. It was by far the largest number of birds he had seen at one time since landing on Molten. A few settled on the yellow hulffan stalks nearby. They were round, grey birds with white and red marks in their tale feathers.

A little further on a group of people could be seen among the crop with hoes. Men, women and children all took part in the heat of the day.

The road was quite good at first, but as they entered a wood it deteriorated quickly. Before long they dismounted and led their dakks between the tall trees.

"Quite a formidable old boy that Zadok," Frank remarked.

"Yes, My Lawd, a forceful character. Despot Wattinger and he did not see eye to eye at all and he was never allowed to pweach at the Castle."

"Do you think I shouldn't have given permission?"

"No no, the whites in the Castle will weally appweciate the pwiest conducting a meeting there. Mind you, I hope the *dwones* don't turn up, because Zadok has no time for them and an argument could ensue."

"Didn't you tell me there's a third drone, on top of Adrian and Crispin?"

"Alan, yes, My Lawd, he is away at pwesent…"

Suddenly a small mammal scuttled across the path making Natias' dakk shy up. Skilfully the steward brought his animal under control without much difficulty.

"What was that!" Frank exclaimed.

"It was just a fwass," explained Natias as he began walking again. "A small carnivore that lives in the undergrowth."

Frank commented, "Moved quickly didn't he!"

"Over short distances they can. Useful cweatures though, the only natuwal pweditor for wabbits. They keep their population down quite effectively."

"I see."

The path narrowed and it got noticeably damper under foot as they neared the Lower Village. The travellers steered their dakks over the tangled torkup roots across the path. They exchanged greetings with a group going in the opposite direction. Natias remarked again that there seemed to be little activity on the road that day.

On they went. Frank spotted a ramshackle shelter amongst the trees, a lone man squatting in front. He was dressed simply and appeared to be cooking something over a fire. Natias noticed the interest being shown and explained, "We occasionally get one or two weligious hermits in these parts, My Lawd."

"Oh yes?"

"Yes, My Lawd. I am not an expert in these things, but I understand they usually make vows before going off to live a solitawy life. For example one might make a vow never to speak to a woman."

"What a good idea!"

Natias was not at all sure whether his master was joking or not and abandoned any further explanation; they progressed in silence.

It was mid-afternoon by the time they reached their destination and the sky had begun to cloud over. When the Lower Village came into view it gave Frank quite a shock. It looked completely different from the other villages he had seen. It was a mass of irregularly spaced small, square wooden huts, which were on stilts to prevent flooding. What shocked him though was the dilapidated state they all appeared to be in. Planks were missing, moss and fungi grew on the walls and some of the huts had collapsed altogether and lay abandoned.

The main street was more of a channel of wet mud than anything else. A couple of children ran past laughing, splashing it up with their bare feet as they went. The fact they were dressed in rags did not bother them.

After taking in the scene for a short while, Frank and Natias mounted up and steered their dakks slowly between the houses.

"It was in the autumn when I was last here, My Lawd. I normally like to get to both villages a lot more wegularly, but it is not easy twavelling in the winter time and I have been so busy in the Castle as of late. I am sowwy it looks in such a bad state of wepair. It has never been as pwosperous as its neighbour, but I have never seen it look quite as bad as this. I suppose there has been a lot of wain up until a week ago, it only dwains away vewy slowly in this gwound."

A man came across their path walking on short stilts to avoid the quagmire.

"Hello Master, are you looking for someone?"

"This is Despot Thawn," Natias said sharply, "where is the weception party to gweet us?"

"I'm sorry, My Lord," the man hurriedly said to Frank before turning to answer the steward, "not sure there is a reception party, Sir. I'll lead you to Gideon's house though, that'll be best."

They made their way up the road, the dakks' hoofs squelching in the mud as they went. Natias was busy apologising.

"I am sowwy about all this, My Lawd. I sent details of our itinewary to Gideon so he would have a good idea as to when to expect us. He is the Lower Village Head. I can't understand what has happened..."

"Oh well, never mind. We won't make a fuss, just see what turns up."

When they got to the Village Head's house the man on stilts called up and after a while Gideon's wife stuck her head out. He explained the situation to her and she bid the visitors come up.

Frank was first. He moved carefully from the dakk onto the ladder leading up to the hut, making sure he did not slip down into the brown, sticky mess below. Once safely on the ladder he turned to thank the man on stilts before climbing. He waited for Natias in a small annex before the woman ushered through the two of them. She introduced Frank to her husband.

Gideon was a tall, broad-shouldered man of almost sixty Earth years with a long, drawn face and a permanent frown. He spoke in a deep, slow voice.

"I did not receive your message Natias. I had no idea you were coming."

He suggested they wait and he sent one of his sons out to collect the village elders. Sitting there in the quiet, biding their time, Frank considered that this house at least looked cosier inside than out. This room appeared to be a lounge with its couch and padded chairs. When he looked closely though, most of the furniture was in a poor state of repair. The seams on the couch were splitting and there were patches sown onto the material that covered the chair he was sitting on.

Not a word was spoken for a long time. Gideon just sat staring into thin air. Eventually some of the village elders began arriving and were introduced to their special visitor one at a time.

What seemed like an age later, Gideon announced that there were enough people there to hold a meeting of the Lower Village Council and invited the Despot to speak. Frank cleared his throat.

"Thank you, Gideon. As you know I am Despot Thorn, your new leader appointed by the Inner Council. I'm very pleased to be here to meet you all in the Lower Village. The purpose of this meeting is to get to know you and hear any problems you might have, so that we can sort them out…"

As he spoke, Frank found he could not help remembering a rather smarmy politician he had heard speak on Ridal Three. He thought he must be sounding just like him.

Not a great deal came from the meeting. There was not the same land shortage issue and they did not seem too interested in the border dispute with Rabeth-Mephar either. Natias pressed the village's leader.

"You know it could come to a fight and all your men could be called upon to join in!"

"We'll be there!" Gideon replied raising his voice.

He was clearly annoyed at Natias and frowned even deeper than before.

The atmosphere settled down again quite quickly though as they moved on to other topics. Frank wanted to bring up the poor state of the houses and whether a restoration scheme could be started. He wanted to do so tactfully and decided the best way might be to start with a mention of the poor drainage.

"Natias tells me you have had a lot of rain in recent weeks."

"That we have," returned Gideon in a deep, slow voice.

"And that the drainage here isn't all that it could be."

"No, My Lord, it's far damper here all year round than at the Upper Village, being near the marsh. As a result we can't grow the hulffan here, which is a pity. We have to rely on our rafts such as pottery and saddle making – and most importantly, the working of wood.

"Have you seen our craftsmen in action, My Lord?"

"Er, no."

"I don't think there's any more points to be raised," Gideon stated, looking at the village elders, "I'll show you round a couple of our factories before you go."

They did indeed visit some of the "factories" of the Lower Village that consisted of even smaller huts with one or two craftsmen or women in each, carving wood for export. It made Frank wonder how they could produce such fine woodwork while their own wooden houses were in such a sorry state.

He put this to Natias when they were finally on their way back home.

"Most of their efforts go into exports to exchange for food and other essentials, My Lawd. The Lower Village, as you have seen for yourself, is much poower than the Upper. It's always been that way, but the gap appears to be widening."

Frank shifted his position on the dakk; he was getting saddle sore.

"Is there resentment at that fact?"

"I have not noticed it, My Lawd, at least among the older genewation. There are a few "hot heads" as Gideon calls them among the youth who behave in a genewally anti-social way, which may be because of a lack of pwide in the state of their village."

"Well we'll have to think what we can do."

Together they rode back home to the Castle.

That evening Rodd was out walking in the Upper Village with his fiancée Leah. As dusk took its grip they stopped outside the smithy, beyond which lay hulffan fields. Matters between them had not felt right since his return and they had finally come to a head.

"I'm sorry Rodd, but I simply can't see what you're getting at."

"No, so I've noticed! You've been acting funny ever since I got back from Ephamon. I just don't know what's got into you."

"I have not. *You're* the one who's been acting funny, if anyone around here has: flying off the handle the whole time at the least possible excuse. You're so different from how you used to be."

"Okay then, why were you not there to greet me that first morning after I got back and why did you take Hanson's side against Tsodd over that piece of land?"

"I didn't!"

"Yes you did!"

No, I did not, I merely said I thought he had a case too; after all it is his land, or rather was. Aren't I allowed to have my own opinion now?"

"Not when it's against my brother in the community hut with lots of other people about, no."

"I didn't say it in the community hut if you must know. I told Marie on the way home."

"Anyway, I thought it showed a lack of loyalty."

"Ha!"

A stalemate had been reached and they stood mutely at the edge of the village in the rapidly fading light. Rodd had wanted to get his resentment out into the open, but it had not gone at all as he had wished. Leah was hurt and confused; not understanding why the young man she loved was acting so uncharitably.

After a while Rodd broke the silence.

"Anyway, you won't need to worry about me, 'cos I've decided to join the guard."

Leah showed no reaction, so he continued.

"Japhses was saying he needed more volunteers with this Ma'hol dispute and I'm going to be one of them. I'll go tomorrow."

Without looking at him, Leah replied, "I hope you come back in a better frame of mind."

'That didn't go according to plan!' thought Rodd, 'but I can't go soft and lose face now.'

So they parted on a bitter note that neither of them wished for that evening. Leah did not want him to see the tears welling up in her eyes. She announced that she was going home and strode off quickly, not once glancing back.

Rodd made as if to catch her up, but thought better of it and she disappeared into the blackness. Too many acrimonious words had just been passed to make up so soon.

They would have to rely on time to heal the rift torn between them that night. Time to bring about an understanding of each other's views.

The next six days were busy ones in Thyatira. Frank started to get into the Castle routine and find his way around. He was given the first-hand account of the skirmish that he had been promised. The impression he got was that it had indeed been on a very small scale with less than a dozen men on each side.

Japhses was busier than anyone. On the one hand he got a new, purpose-built armoury under way. A simple, but adequate structure was designed to go next to the stables and construction began in record time. An urgent overhaul of the equipment to go into it was delegated to Uriah to organise. The Captain also set about reorganising the border defences by stepping up patrols and enlarging the garrison on Telar, the biggest of the islands at the centre of the dispute.

To most people's surprise, however, nothing further was seen or heard of the Ma'hol. A lack of intelligence reports was worrying to both Japhses and Frank. There were currently no Hoamen traders across the border and no one was keen to cross it at present. With the Despot's blessing the Captain's strategy for the time being was to keep up the increased presence along there and wait and see. The letter of complaint to the Mehtar was first delayed, then shelved for fear of provoking trouble when the whole matter seemed to be fading away of its own accord.

Rodd did join the guard, which pleased Japhses who at once recognised his leadership qualities and decided, due to a lack of suitable candidates, to put him in charge of a squad straightaway.

Zadok duly held his meeting at the Castle. He preached a stirring sermon in the courtyard on the subject of persistence in prayer. Frank watched and listened from a distance, he was quite intrigued by it all. This brand of Christianity was so different from anything he had encountered. The dancing and singing seemed even more abandoned than the most enthusiastic group on Eden and a total contrast with the very reserved community he had been in. It was not for him, he decided, but if the people enjoyed it – they certainly seemed to – then he was all in favour of it. The gospel message was not being watered down and that was the fundamentally important thing. He gave the priest leave to preach at the Castle regularly in the future if he so desired. Zadok replied it would depend on where the Spirit directed him to be.

Following the exceptionally warm spell that spring the weather turned colder with a vengeance. One morning Frank was entering the hall with Natias. The steward had some large, rolled up maps tucked under his arm as they descended the stairs by the balcony.

"It's nippy down here!" the Despot exclaimed, "I'm glad I put an extra layer on today. Can't we have that entrance shut for a change?"

"It makes it vewy gloomy in here, My Lawd, may I suggest we go into the thwone woom, it is not so susceptible to dwafts in there."

"Good idea. You know it might be worth considering putting in a false ceiling in the hall, there's no need for it to be so high as it is. Must take an age to warm up in the winter..."

As they crossed the floor, the sound of a furious argument arose from the kitchen. Matthew then appeared leading Illianeth by the arm. When they had got into the hall he pushed her away and shouted at her.

"Don't come back until you are in a better state!"

He looked up and saw Frank and Natias who had stopped to see what all the commotion was about.

"Can't you control your protégée, Natias?" the chef called out, "If you spent more time with her she wouldn't have to hang around with the drones."

Looking over at Illianeth one glance was enough to see she was terribly drunk. In fact she could hardly stand up she was so bad. In a drunken stupor she staggered over to the nearest table for support. It was not a pretty sight.

"Now just a moment!" replied the steward, "I'm not having you…"

Frank quickly interrupted to cut the argument short. He did not want to have a slanging match between two of his senior staff in public.

"All right that's enough! Right. Matthew what's going on around here? And leave Natias out of it, that sort of talk isn't going to get us anywhere. Now come one, what's this all about?"

The kitchen head took a deep breath before explaining.

"That stupid girl, My Lord," he said pointing to the pathetic sight now in a chair, "rolls in here totally legless after spending a drinking session all night with Adrian and Crispin! I'm short staffed enough as it is without having to put up with this."

"Yes, I'm sure," Frank replied, "Well you get on then and we'll sort the girl out."

"Humph!" was all Matthew managed by way of an answer. He disappeared back into the kitchen.

As Frank turned to Natias the steward said, "Just give me a moment My Lawd, I will get Eko to see to her."

"I think I'm going to be sick" Illianeth declared.

It did not take long to find a couple of guardsmen to take the paralytic girl up to Natias' room with a message for his wife to look after her.

Frank waited patiently until Natias was ready, then they went together to the Throne Room. It was a small, poorly lit room with a large chair up one end on a stage. There was little else by way of other furniture apart from an oval table in the middle and chairs round it. The table was well proportioned for the size of what was essentially an audience chamber. Natias laid the maps down on the table and lit a lantern in a not very successful attempt to improve the light.

The other's mind was still on Illianeth.

"I shall have to lecture that girl on the evils of drink once she has recuperated. I can't tolerate that sort of behaviour around here."

"I should think not, My Lawd, only I would ask you not to be too harsh on her, because fwom what Matthew was saying the dwones were wesponsible. I cannot say I am supwised."

"Be that at it may, she is of an age when she really aught to be responsible for her own actions," he then softened his tone, "but all right, I won't be too harsh on her."

They studied one of the large maps laid out on the table. It began curling up and Natias placed the lantern at one end and a lead weight at the other to prevent this happening.

"Fascinating," Frank said as he studied the layout of his despotate. The quality of the map was far better than he had been anticipating. "There's the Castle, the Upper Village, oh yes and I suppose those are the islands there was all that fuss about."

"That is wight, My Lawd."

"Yeah, I wish I'd seen this before our trip out last week, but at least I can now fix it all in my mind...ah, I see, there's the Lower Village."

"I must apologise, but I completely forgot about these maps, they have not been out for a vewy long time. They pwe-date Despot Wattinger in fact."

"Has much changed since then?"

"Not weally My Lawd. The Upper Village has got bigger... and I suppose the Lower Village is smaller than it once was."

"You know that's one thing I find funny about this place. Where I come from they always give place names other than "The Castle", or "The Upper Village" and nobody here even shortens the names."

"My Lawd?" said the steward looking puzzled.

"Well, I don't know, "Uppersville" or something like that."

"Uppersville, My Lawd?"

"Yes well, perhaps not that. I'm not criticising, I'm just saying you're a very precise people who er... well you know."

He was getting himself tied up and was starting to worry lest he offend his steward. Natias though was far from being offended, he realised the new Despot was still learning their ways.

"No you see, My Lawd, the names were given by the Keepers before the Inner Council became what it did. The people follow their example."

"Oh," was all Frank replied, knowing he was not going to get a better explanation.

'If the Keepers decreed it that is an end to it,' he laughed to himself.

"What about the Autarch of the time?" he asked.

"That was before the office of Autarch had been instituted, many genewations ago."

They got back to studying the map of Thyatira. Frank explained that he was so shocked at the miserable state of the Lower Village that he had spent the time since considering what to do about it. His radical idea was to re-locate the entire village further north.

"It will get it away from the marsh and the appalling ground conditions there. If we move it up into this area the lines of communication with both the Upper Village and the Castle will be shorter and therefore faster. In fact we could place it on the edge of the wood here, yes. It would then be on the main road to Bynar, which I'm told is in a far better condition than the present one they've got. It would be about the same distance to the Upper Village then, but a lot nearer the Castle."

Somewhat to Frank's surprise, his conservative steward did not try to dismiss the idea as unworkable straightway. He gazed down at the map showing great interest.

"A wevolutionawy step, My Lawd. A bold move if I may say so, but a good one. I would stwongly suggest we twy to sell it to Gideon and the other village elders there, but the benefits would be enoawmous. A huge task, but well worth the undertaking."

"Good, excellent! Would this land by the new site be suitable for growing hulffan?"

"Certainly worth a twy. However, if that was successful it might not be a good idea to export too much, or else the pwice would dwop on the open market and we would end up doing more for the same income."

"Yes, but I was thinking of domestic consumption. From what you said it would help feed us and we could use some of the tar for road building here in Thyatira. I'd like to see a new road from the Upper Village to the new site. What do you think?"

"It would be the biggest shake up for genwations and there are major financial considewations of course, but I like the idea a gweat deal, My Lawd. It has much to commend it. The only thing is the very scale of the task. As well as hulffan, some extwa wheat fields would be essential. The land will have to be prepared..." his voice trailed off before resuming once more as he considered the map. "The higher gwound here will cut down the likelihood of spwing floods. That will be good.

"We cannot expect the people there to build seventy or so huts themselves though, it would take a lifetime. We would have to contwact in men fwom the other despotates which would be expensive and might be wesented by the Lower Village member."

"I was thinking of drafting in the guard to help. Japhses said half are on leave at any one time, we could get them involved for extra money, or additional land right. I think it would help the economy greatly in the long run. If there was any trouble on the border they would have to be released immediately, of course."

They continued to discuss the project at length and Frank was delighted to see the enthusiasm with which his steward embraced his idea. Natias did again stress the need to sell it to Gideon and his companions. He warned that this might not be such a simple matter as it seemed, because they were notorious for their dislike of change.

The maps were rolled up again once they concluded. Frank said, "So we'll ask Gideon up here for a chat, plus his elders. We can put a good meal inside them first, that should help. I'll leave you to arrange it."

"Yes, My Lawd. We will have to think about a plan of the new Lower Village, how the dwellings and factowies are laid out and such like."

'Good,' thought Frank, 'having the people behind me will help this plan to have a better chance of success. I don't want another fiasco like the release of the prisoners. With God's help we shall improve the lot of those poor villagers.'

CHAPTER ELEVEN

Buoyed up by his ideas for a new Lower Village, Frank left the Throne Room, followed by Natias.

The hall was its usual hive of activity. A servant with a bucket and mop passed them as they made their way to the balcony. Two guardsmen started up the spiral staircase. At the end of the middle table, Adrian and Crispin sat drinking, making snide remarks as they watched people pass.

'That's all they've been doing since I arrived here,' thought Frank, 'just lazing around annoying everyone with their stupid comments.'

"Look at them," Natias hissed, " sitting there as bold as brass!"

"Leave the talking to me," Frank replied in a quiet, but stern voice.

He had disliked the drones at first sight, but wondered if he had given them a fair chance to be involved in some useful work. It was clear that Natias and Japhses did not like them, so perhaps he had been biased against them from the start. He decided not to harangue them with a condemnation of their getting Illianeth drunk, but to try a positive approach.

As they got close though it was Adrian who got the first comment in.

"Hello there, Fwank." He called out, imitating the steward's lisp. "And how are we today?"

Frank noticed they were not drunk themselves. Adrian smiled up at him waiting for a response while Crispin was stuffing his mouth with some green fruit, the contents of a bowl in front of them.

"Fine thank you, Adrian," he replied in a cheerful voice, not letting himself be provoked, "and how are you this morning?"

"Super," said the drone before nodding to the maps, "going somewhere are we?"

"No, in actual fact we're thinking of moving the Lower Village to a different site."

Even as the words came from his mouth, Frank realised he really should not have said anything to them until after he had seen Gideon and company, but he was wanting to seize the opportunity to get the drones involved in doing something positive for a change, so he continued.

"I wondered if you might be interested in lending a hand. I don't know where your talents lie: whether you'd like to work on a layout design for the new site, or even helping with the construction when it begins."

"Dear dear Frank!" Adrian responded with mock concern, "I'm afraid you've got us all wrong. *Us* work, when we can enjoy ourselves here? No no no, that's not our style at all – perish the thought!"

He put his hand to his forehead as he pretended to be fatigued. Crispin enjoyed the display and let out a loud guffaw. As he did so, half-chewed fruit splattered across the table, one or two bits hitting his fellow drone who turned to him.

"Crispin dear, watch where you're spitting next time will you?"

Frank sighed. As he did so he noticed Natias tense up out of the corner of his eye. Given half a chance, he felt, his steward would have attacked the two young men at the table there and then. He looked Adrian straight in the eye, he was not going to give in just yet.

"Why don't you involve yourselves in something worthwhile instead of just lazing around all day achieving nothing? I'm giving you a chance."

"You really don't listen do you, Frank, we're not interested in your little schemes. Can't you stop being so boring?"

Natias started to speak, but his master held out his hand, indicating for him to stop, and said, "How would you like it if I had you expelled from Thyatira?"

"Don't be so petty," returned the drone, apparently unconcerned at the threat.

"I'll do it."

"Ha, you can't. We got Despot Rattinger's guarantee for life."

"So you're not going to help then."

"No, we're not," replied Adrian who then burst into loud, uncontrollable laughter, which was immediately copied by his colleague.

The Despot shook his head and looked round to his fuming steward.

"Come on, Natias," he said in a quiet voice, "Let's go."

They went up the balcony stairs without saying a word. The sound of the drones' manic laughter slowly faded away as they reached the landing on the second floor. Just then a figure stepped out of the guardroom.

"Ah, Japhses, just the man!"

"My Lord?"

"Can we go into your room for a quick chat, the three of us?"

"Of course."

They slipped inside the pleasantly furnished room and Japhses speedily arranged the chairs for them to sit on as he wondered what this sudden, impromptu meeting was all about.

"Right," said Frank, "I want to establish some facts. Natias, I am in total command here, correct?"

"Yes, My Lawd."

"And the drones are not an exception."

"No, My Lawd."

"So if I wanted to I can chuck them out, expel them from Thyatira."

"You can."

"Even if they had a guarantee from my predecessor."

"Yes, My L…"

"Great idea," Japhses interrupted, "It's high time they were shown the door. They were well in with the previous despot, why I'll never know – Rattinger wasn't a homosexual. Since he died they've got even worse, but we've never had the authority to get rid of them. You just give the command, My Lord, and I'll get my men to eject the scum."

Frank told them he could not understand the attitude that the drones adopted. They had not taken the threat of eviction seriously. Japhses concluded their false sense of security was the result of a lifetime of ease with no one willing or able to get rid of them.

"Not a soul would be sorry to see them leave."

"What do you say, Natias?"

"It would be the cause of much wejoicing if they were sent packing, My Lawd, no one will be sowwy to see them go as Japhses says. Let them go back to Gistenau where they came fwom, if they are misguided enough to take them back.

"May I suggest that their jewels be confiscated as well? That will help our finances, they've been dwaining us for years."

"Excellent idea, but why didn't you tell me I could get rid of them before?"

"I am sowwy My Lawd, I did not feel it was up to me to suggest you exile people I dislike."

Frank laughed.

"I see your point. Well there's no time like the present: Japhses, kindly get together the men you need and get them out of here – and tell them never to come back to Thyatira again!"

"Yes, My Lord!" exclaimed the Captain with relish.

He got up and marched out, eager to obey. Frank turned to Natias as he got up.

"Did he say the drones are homosexual?"

"Yes, My Lawd."

"That's disgusting! I don't want their sort around here."

Natias replied quietly, "It may be a force of circumstance: they are denied a means to expwess their sexuality in the conventional manner. Perhaps it is not surpwising they turn that way."

"I suppose not. But tell me: are there likely to be any political repercussions? From the black parents of these drones I mean. Do they have friends in high places?"

"Not these, My Lawd, you are quite safe. Do you mind if I go and watch them thwown out? I have taken a lot of cheek fwom them over the years and do not want to miss this for all the hulffan in Molt."

"No no, go ahead. You lead on, I'll follow."

Natias left to see the spectacle. Frank hesitated briefly as a thought flashed into his brain.

'What about Alan, the third drone, still on some sort of a trip or something? I'd have liked to've thrown them all out at once and get it over and done with. Oh well, I'll deal with Alan when he gets back!'

"Right, Natias, let's go and watch the fun."

"Where do you want this bag put?" asked Bodd.

Tsodd turned round.

"Oh just down there will be fine."

"Right. I see you've finished the base."

"Just about."

Bodd was helping his brother carrying tools to where the aviary was being built. As he rightly observed, the stone base was almost completed. Round the perimeter tall planks of wood pointed upwards, waiting for the horizontal sections to be nailed into place.

"Is that your wire netting over there?"

"Yeah that's going to go right over here so that the birds can have maximum room to fly around inside and people will be able to see them. The entrance will be here… and there'll be a further door a little way in, so that none of the specimens will be able to escape."

"What'll you do if a bird gets through the first door and is flying around in that space in-between?"

"Do you mean one I don't want you? I'd just shoo it out again."

"It might help if instead of having a proper door for the inside one you simply hand strips of thick hulffan fibres down from a beam. That way there wouldn't be any space for the birds to get through when you moved in and out. Plus it would be simpler and cheaper of course."

"What a good idea, Yes I think I'll do that. Reuben is making the doors for me, I'll have to tell him I only want one."

They began arranging the planks of halku wood that were to form the lower walls.

Bodd remarked, "I wish the weather would brighten up again. By the way, have you heard the rumour that the Despot is going to release some more land around the village at the old price of fifty a kab?"

"No!"

"That's what I've heard. A bit ironic considering the amount you had to pay for this."

"Damn! If he does do that I'm going to see if he'll compensate me for the difference, or get Hanson to. It's not fair me having to pay twice the price just 'cos I bought at the wrong time."

"It's worth a try, after all he does know us personally. We'll have to see if it really does happen or not first."

"Yeah. Pass those nails will you?"

Tsodd hammered away as his aviary slowly took shape. The final design was not quite as big as he had originally intended, but it still took up three-quarters of the land he had purchased. There was nothing comparable in Thyatira, probably not the whole of Hoame.

Bodd was having a sneezing fit.

"Oh dear, that's better," he exclaimed when it was over. "You've heard Rodd's been put in charge of a squad by Japhses I suppose."

"No, what already?"

"Yeah, that's a pretty good start isn't it? I'm not sure where he's gone off to now. I think Japhses wants him to stay in the guard permanently, which I'm sure isn't Rodd's intention, or at least it wasn't when he first joined."

"What? You think it was just to prove his independence from Leah you mean?"

"Something like that. So silly those two, it's so obvious they are meant for each other. I just hope they can sort themselves out."

"That's right. Can you move another plank up here?"

"Of course. Sorry, I'm not paying attention."

Early one morning Frank was kneeling by his bed praying. Or rather he had been. His mind was wondering as he could not help but go over the last week's events.

The drones had squealed like pigs going to slaughter as the guards dragged them out. Soon a sizable crowd had gathered to watch the spectacle as they – and the belongings they were allowed to keep – were bundled onto a cart and driven under escort from the castle forecourt. The taunts and jeers were all aimed against them for a change. Natias had watched with much satisfaction, feeling that the humiliation the drones were suffering was their just desserts for years of torment they had inflicted on others. He might have a pang of pity later, but he wanted to enjoy their expulsion at the time. Frank. In the end, had chosen not to observe it for himself.

Gideon and the Lower Village elders had been duly dined at the Castle. A clear majority were in favour of the proposed move, although some had reservations. Two had argued vehemently against the scheme, saying it was against all their tradition and that the residents should at least have a choice whether to move or not. The majority, however, who did not want to see a remnant left behind, overruled them. They would rather see a clean break with the past than a small community left behind to die a lingering death. A new beginning at the more favourable site caught their imaginations. The elders agreed with the proposition put to them that the old site be destroyed as soon as the move was completed.

The decision was taken back to the villagers themselves. With a few exceptions the people saw things the same way as their elders. In fact so keen were some to get the project underway that building work had already started. Frank had not been pleased to hear this, because it was before a proper set of plans for the new village had been drawn up.

Only one other event of note had occurred and that was his receiving a letter from Baron Schail. It had not beaten about the bush: no suitable black could be spared to guide him so he was on his own, at least for the time being.

'Well at least I know where I stand,' he told himself.

The letter had also contained a rather obscure reference to him finding a wife, which he supposed was to do with the need for black heirs that Offa had talked about. That would have to wait.

Frank shuffled to a new part of the cushion he was kneeling on to get more comfortable. He realised his mind had been wondering badly and he grasped his hands together tightly as he tried to concentrate once more.

"Dear Heavenly Father, please help me to be good today. Please help me not to say anything tactless, but always to think before I open my mouth.

"Thank you, dear Lord, for all the blessings heaped upon me. I want to make myself worthy of them and to use the power you have given me to help these people."

He glanced round at his window to see the bright morning sky. The cold snap was well over.

"And thank you, Lord, for a beautiful day and for everything. Amen."

He got up and rubbed his knees, then put the cushion back. He stopped to look at himself in the mirror before leaving the room.

'Yes I quite like the beard Francis; you look very grand. Especially since you got that tailor to adjust Mister Rattinger's trousers so that they fit properly. I've got that new pair to wear as well…'

Feeling light on his feet he started off down the corridor, soon to meet his personal servant heading for his suite.

"Morning, Illianeth. Lovely morning!"

"Yes, My Lord. Did you enjoy your breakfast?"

"Very much thank you. You'll find the tray on a chair I believe."

Down he swept into the hall where the usual bustle was in progress. Lots of people were walking hurriedly about their business. He found his steward peering over some papers on the table nearest the door. The only other person sitting down was Laffaxe, eating a late breakfast further up the same table. It was unusual for the physician to eat in the hall; he usually had his meals sent to his home.

Frank saw the two white-haired men each separately pre-occupied and decided it would be Natias' world he would invade.

"Good morning; and how are you this beautiful day?"

"My Lawd," he said rising, "Nice to see you, you look well this morning if you do not mind me saying so."

"Very kind, and what are you up to?"

"I am looking at the tax assessments, My Lawd, it will soon be time to collect them again."

"I see. Any news on the new village? I'm not at all keen on building work starting before the thing's been properly laid out. These things require careful planning first."

"Yes, My Lawd. Actually Gideon did call in first thing before going to the site. He said the fields were being laid out. They have finished dwawing up the plans for where the huts are going to be situated and who will live where. I have not actually got them here at the moment, but I think you will be pleased with them. I am not sure where I put them."

He scanned the papers on the table and began peering underneath it when he remembered.

"Ah yes, that is wight, he took them back with him. I will make sure you see them today.

"No hurry, not if you're pleased with them."

"I think it is a good layout, My Lawd."

"And what about the site, is it getting properly organised now?"

"John, that is Gideon's son….John is taking command of the building of the new village. The guard have been mobilized as you commanded My Lawd and Uriah is in charge of the soldiers doing the building. There are even some volunteers from the Upper Village who are joining in. The new village should begin to take form quite quickly now."

"Well I hope it's not going to end up being called the "New Village" the whole time, we should think up a name for it."

"Newville, My Lawd?"

It took a moment for Frank to realise his steward was making a joke; it was unlike him.

"Thank you, Natias," he replied with a smile, "but I think… what was that?"

A sudden roar of people outside had stopped him completing his sentence. Everyone present seemed to stop and prick up their ears at the sound. A couple of servants made for the entrance to investigate when a youth who had run up the external staircase of the keep popped his head round the door and called out.

"Alan is back!"

With one accord the people in the hall left what they were doing and headed for the entrance. Frank noticed their excited expressions with puzzlement. Even Laffaxe left his meal muttering to himself.

"Hope he's got my chemicals."

Natias was looking up, it was clear he wanted to go out too.

"What's happening?" asked Frank.

"Alan has wetuwned fwom Aggeparii My Lawd. Let us go out to see, then I can intwoduce him to you."

People were scrambling to get out, but made way for their leader. Frank and Natias stood at the top of the staircase and looked down at the scene below. The inner bailey seemed full with people. All those from the market in the courtyard next door had come through to join the throng.

In the centre of it all was a young man at the head of a procession of heavily laden dakks. He was sitting on the lead animal, a particularly large specimen. His fair hair, as opposed to snow white, singled him out as a drone, but unlike Adrian and Crispin he was roughly dressed. Alan was twenty-five Earth years old and of average build. He sat there handing out sweetmeats and trinkets from pouches round his saddle to the sea of outstretched hands around him. More people were milling around the other dakks, each of which had a member of the guard in attendance standing to attention. The loads were tightly packed and the people could not easily see what goods had been brought. The attending guardsmen stood there stoically, ignoring the eager multitude.

After a while Alan looked up and noticed Frank and Natias watching him. He called out something to the thronging mass, did up the pouches on his dakk, then casually dismounted. He was almost lost in the push of the excited people as he made his way towards the keep.

"Quite a reception!" Frank exclaimed to Natias as the newcomer progressed through the crowd.

Some people began filtering back into the keep.

"Yes, he appears to have bwought a gweat deal with him."

"Didn't you tell me he had gone to one of our neighbouring despotates - Aggeparii?"

"That is wight My Lawd, he was we-negotiating a twade tweaty with them."

'I rather like the thought of a "twade tweaty"' Frank smiled to himself.

Alan had got through the press and ascended the stairs towards them. When he got to the top he slapped Natias on the side of the arm.

"Hello, old friend!" he called out jovially, "I didn't expect to be away quite so long."

He then focussed on the only black present and said, "Hello, you must be Frank Thorn, the new Despot; I'm very pleased to meet you."

"Hello," returned Frank, cold and polite. Before Alan had arrived he had been planning on expelling him as he had the other drones. Now with this extraordinary reception and all the loaded dakks arriving he did not know what to think. He would dearly have loved to have got his steward on one side and get him to explain everything to him.

Natias seemed to be caught up in the excitement as he said to Alan, "Where have you been? You cannot have been in Aggeparii all this time."

"You're right," the drone replied cheerfully, "but let's go in and sit down first."

He glanced down at the crowds still milling in the bailey before stepping into the hall.

"Blue-green ones what a home-coming! When things settle down a bit the men will make sure the dakks are stabled and the supplies brought in. Ah, Crag, you dirty old sod, how ya doin'?"

Frank was shocked at this greeting, but the jailer (making only a rare appearance in the daytime) seemed to love it. As he shuffled along he put his head on one side to look up with his one good eye and gave a big grin.

"Fine Master Alan, just fine."

Frank had never seen the jailer so animated. Alan started leading Despot and steward towards the balcony staircase, but got stopped by enthusiastic people every few metres.

"Welcome home, Alan!"

"Hello my lovely," he replied to Illianeth as he took hold of her waist and lifted her up with ease.

'He's quite short,' thought Frank, 'but a lot stronger than he looks.'

"Put me down!" Illianeth shouted out, although obviously enjoying every moment.

"Certainly."

As he obliged Laffaxe came up and asked in a civil manner unusual for him, "I wonder, Alan, have you got those chemicals I asked you to try and get."

"Yeah sure. Suggest you have a word with Solly, he'll know where they are."

"Thank you very much. Oh and welcome back by the way."

"Glad to be back, "Alan replied, then turning to Frank and Natias he said, "Sorry about this! Let's hurry up and go to my room where we can get some peace."

He led the way up the stairs two at a time.

"A popular man, "remarked Frank so Alan could hear.

"It's not always like this," the drone responded, "it's only 'cos I've been away a long time and brought back lots of goods people want. That's what they're really after. They'll quickly settle down and you'd never know they'd been like this."

"The taxes have not been collected yet," Natias said.

Alan laughed, "Afraid they'll spend all their money first and have more left? Good old Natias."

A young servant girl was walking along the corridor just outside his room.

"Ah, Sarah isn't it? I thought I recognised you. Listen: could you be an angel and bring us three large glasses of wine up to my room? That's lovely."

He opened the door to his room and went in. As Frank followed he paused to have a quiet word with the servant.

Make that two, I'll have a glass of water."

"Phew! It's a bit musty in here isn't it, Natias? I'll open the windows."

"We did not know when you would weturn. The windows were shut duwing the wecent cold spell and have not been opened since, as you can see."

"That's better," Alan said to himself as he swung the window open and let the fresh air in. He looked down at the bailey.

"Things seem to be calming down a bit now. Right, do sit down both of you. How are you settling in then, Frank?"

The Despot had been in a good mood until Alan's arrival had completely unnerved him.

"All right thank you," he announced being deliberately cagey.

He did not want to open himself up to this popular newcomer. As time went on though he realised that this drone was going to show him due respect and not be a threat to him. He began to relax.

Alan began an account of his journey just completed. The cheerful presence of the man was quite electrifying. Effortlessly he had everyone eating out of the palm of his hand, or at least that was the impression he gave Frank.

'The man is totally relaxed and confident while everyone else runs round like worker ants.'

He did not *want* to like this invader to his cosy new world. In his mind he tried increasingly desperately to resent this intruder into his life, but failed totally as the day progressed. While the three of them chatted away over their drinks Frank found he simply could not help but like him.

'There's no pretension in him whatsoever, I admire his straightforwardness.'

They ended up having their midday meal brought up to the room and the conversation flowed into the long afternoon, never once flagging. Alan wanted to hear all the news from Thyatira and seemed genuinely interested in Frank's carefully amended version of how he had come to be there. He had spoken of the place so many times he was almost beginning to believe he really did come from Oonimari! He wondered if he would get his comeuppance one day when someone who actually knew the place turned up. He was not going to let the prospect worry him now though.

Alan told them at length of his latest travels. He had gone much further than he had originally intended, going as far as the capital. He had spent a comparatively small proportion of the time on his chief objective, a fresh trade agreement with their neighbours in the despotate of Aggeparii.

"Wait until you meet Despot Kagel and family, Frank, then you'll know why I didn't want to hang about. I think you'll be glad with the terms of the agreement though.

"I don't know if Natias has told you much about our trade. This treaty is a three summers one that will give us some stability, help us know where we are. I haven't actually got the invoices on me, but our main imports from Aggeparii are normally cloth, nuts, fruit – dried yackoes, scrabs, that sort of thing. I got the usual odds and ends: baubles, lockets, giveaways. Also this time I've managed to secure some glass bottles of dye, which I thought were a bit of a novelty, pus some dakks – good breeders – for the stables here

To pay for all that I've had to increase out timber quota by fifty per cent, but that shouldn't present too much of a problem. It'll create extra employment. On top of that they want a modest quantity of hulffan tar, which makes me wonder if we should plant some more fields of the stuff, 'cos that's what everyone seems to be keen on these days.

I'm afraid they weren't interested in trading some of our pottery which was a shame, but you can't win 'em all."

"You've done a magnificent job!" Natias enthused. He lent forward in his chair before continuing, "Talking of new hulffan fields Alan, His Lawdship here is hoping to develop some of the land by the new village. That would be a help."

"I heard about the Lower Village being moved earlier today. Great idea, but have the Keepers approved it?"

This was something that had not occurred to Frank, but when he looked round his steward was ready to answer.

"I checked the deeds and there is a specific clause giving the despot of the day the wight to authowise new dwellings without the permission of the Inner Council. I weasoned that a new village is weally a collection of new dwellings."

"Rich! I like it," Alan exclaimed as he got to his feet. "I'm just going out to answer the call of nature; I'll be back."

As he headed for the door Natias said to him, "You must admit my logic was good."

"Very good," Alan laughed, "who does?"

As he disappeared from the room Frank looked puzzled.

"What did he mean by "Who does"?"

"Oh that is just one of Alan's expwessions, My Lawd, I would not wowwy about it, he has sevewal."

"I just wondered what it meant."

"I do not think it is intended to mean anything in particular."

"I see, or at least I think I do. Anyway, what I want to know is why you've never told me about him before? I thought he'd be just another drone like the other two; I was going to have him thrown out too!"

Natias guffawed at the idea, then apologised for laughing at what His Lawdship had said.

"No no, My Lawd. Alan is a dwone yes, but he is not like the other two. He has been a gweat help to me wunning the Castle and villages in a black's absence. If I may be so bold you would be wise to include him on the weekly meetings with Japhses, he will be a gweat asset to you.

I should have told you about him before....... I thought I had, but obviously not."

"You definitely never said anything to me. Still, I suppose it doesn't matter now – as long as there aren't any further surprises you've got lined up, I'm just glad he isn't like the other two were. He's very popular isn't he. Does he always get this sort of reception?"

"Alan has the ability to get on with the highest and the lowest in the land. I've never heard anyone say a bad word about him. But no he does not always get the weception you saw, only when he bwings in a major delivewy of merchandise like today.

"May I suggest you keep him in charge of our twade with other despotate, My Lawd? He is the best man for the job."

"Yes, of course."

They then sat in silence until Alan returned. The conversation resumed on the topic of trade and he explained that in his past journeys he had found it impossible to get formal trade pacts with their foreign neighbours.

"in spite of being different from each other in so many ways both the Ma'hol and the Laodicians seem to prefer to rely on a small number of freelance traders wandering between countries at irregular intervals. I haven't been to either country lately though."

The latest on the border dispute with the Ma'hol was then explained to Alan and they also filled him in on the details of their meeting with the Lower Village elders. During the afternoon they covered such varied subjects as traditional dress, woodcarvings and the contrasting drinking habits in different parts of the country.

Time seemed to fly past and Frank found himself recalling the few really close friends he had known in his life. In each case the sense of companionship had grown gradually and there had not been an instant liking or feeling of affinity on their first meeting. With this Alan, it was different. It was only late afternoon and he felt they had known each other a hundred years. The magnetism he felt surely must be mutual.

Conversation flowed and it was as if there were only the three men in the world when out of the blue Alan enquired, "Where's Crispin and Adrian?"

Frank immediately went bright red. 'What will he think of his fellow drones being thrown out the way they were?'

However when Natias told him what had happened Alan laughed and said, "I would have done exactly the same if I'd had the power. Good for you – and good for Thyatira!"

'That's a relief!'

Natias left as evening drew on, leaving the other two discussing childhood anecdotes. It was getting late and Frank realised he really must be going soon. Alan was finishing one of his humorous stories of Despot Rattinger's reign about when a trader tricked the late ruler into buying a dagger with a diamond-encrusted hilt, only for him to discover it was really glass.

"He was livid! The trader was never caught; got clean away with it. We didn't dare go near Ratty for a week after, he was in such a foul temper."

Frank laughed, "Oh dear, I bet you found it funny."

He paused and watched the candle flame flicker and move the shadows on the walls.

"Well I've really enjoyed meeting you, Alan," he said as he started to get up, "it's going to be good to have you around. From what Natias says you'll be a great asset."

"He is prone to exaggerate, but after all the travelling I've done lately it'll be nice to have a good rest at home for a while. I like the fresh ideas you've got for Thyatira. It has been a bit of a backwards place up until now. I guess I'm as guilty as anyone of getting used to the status quo. Not that being away from the hub of things is altogether bad – I can't stand the vulgarity of the capital – but there are some major changes needed here."

"Yes, we'll have to see what we can do to improve things. I'd better be going off to bed now I think, it's getting late."

"Okay. See you in the morning. Maybe we can go and see the site of the new village, yeah and you can tell me about Oonimari, that's one country I haven't been to."

'Yes and just as well,' thought Frank as he said, "Of course, if that's what you'd like. See you in the morning."

He wondered back to his own room holding a lamp, going over in his mind all that had been said that day. It was not long before he got to bed and fell into a deep sleep.

Dreams had just begun when a loud knocking at the door woke him with a start.

"What is it? Who's there?"

"Natias, My Lawd."

Frank was not someone who took a long time to come round. He sat up in bed and struck a light to his candle and called out, "Come in, what's the matter?"

"Sowwy to disturb you, My Lawd, but it's the new village. There appears to have been an arson attack, it has all been burnt down!"

CHAPTER TWELVE

Frank sat up in bed and looked at his steward in the candle-light. The memory of their first meeting flashed through his mind: a similar flickering light, his being struck by the size of the man's nose.

"Do we know who's responsible?"

"Not yet, My Lawd, the weports are vewy sketchy at the moment."

The Despot yawned and did a large stretch.

"Urgh! It must be ages before daybreak. We can't do any-thing now surely, what about if we all go back to bed and in-spect the damage in the morning?"

"I thought My Lawd would want to know what has happened as soon as possible."

"Yes, thank you," Frank replied, "I'm most grateful, but I don't actually think there's anything we can do until morning. If you organise an early breakfast and have me woken just be-fore daybreak we can go along there nice and early and see what's what. How's that for an idea?"

So shortly before dawn Frank received another call and this time he got up and, trying to stifle his yawns, went down to the hall to have something to eat. Approaching the table he was surprised to see Alan sitting next to Natias.

"Good morning everyone, please be seated. You're not usually up this early are you, Alan?"

The drone laughed, unlike Frank he did not look at all sleepy.

"Hell no! but I thought I'd rather take a ride out with you to see the damage – if you don't object."

"No, of course not," then addressing Natias, "Do we know any more about this fire? Was it definitely deliberate?"

A servant arrived with his breakfast of hamble cakes in milk. Alan asked her to pack a midday meal for them to have out.

"It seems so," Natias replied, "but there are conflicting weports as to how much damage has been done."

"I wouldn't have thought that a great deal would've been built yet; they haven't been at it very long."

"It is a couple of days since I was there My Lawd, one hut was nearing completion and a number more had been started. They are quite quick to constwuct, but there were large stocks of timber piled up to be used. If those have been destwoyed it is a severe setback."

"But who would do such a thing? What's the point?"

Alan said, "I hear not all the Lower Villagers were in agreement with your plan, they must be the obvious candidates."

"I suppose so."

"You must wemember, My Lawd, how vocifewously some of the elders argued against the idea. I know who they were, I can have them wounded up and bwought here to the Castle for intewegation."

"Well I don't want to jump into anything just yet, let's go and have a look first. I can't understand why they would be so against progress, it's for their benefit."

"What did you expect, gratitude?" asked Alan with an ironic smile.

Frank raised his eyebrows.

"I don't know, I really don't know."

It was starting to get light. The Despot was stifling yet another yawn when Natias spoke to him again.

"My Lawd, Japhses has already left for the new village with a few guards. Uriah will be escorting us down there with some more soldiers. They will meet us in the inner bailey."

"I see. Some more water please, girl!"

Once the meal was over they made their way down to the site., taking the journey in riding and walking stages as is usual with dakks. On the way Frank tried to have a chat with Uriah, but found his monosyllabic responses unconducive to good conversation. He thought it must be because it was so early in the morning, but afterwards both Alan and Natias told him the Lieutenant was generally uncommunicative, which made Frank wonder how the man had ever got to such a position of authority in the guard.

By the time they were approaching their destination the sun was rising and large groups of men were arriving to report for the construction work. Or was it going to be reconstruction that morning?

As was normal the Despot and entourage made sure they rode in for the last leg of the journey. A large smouldering pile of blackened timbers that had once been a hut greeted them. The wind was in the opposite direction so they did not smell it until they were quite near.

"That's a mess," Frank remarked to Alan.

"Yeah, but the other ones look okay, not as bad as we were led to expect."

Japhses was standing by the smoking debris with a couple of guards directing the inquisitive workers to stop staring and get on with their tasks. The Captain's tall, broad frame towered over those around him as he called out orders.

The damage was a lot less than the initial reports had suggested. The one hut that had been completed was totally gutted, but none of the other, partially constructed buildings had been burnt too severely, although several nearby had scorch marks. Most importantly the huge timber stockpiles not far away were unscathed.

Drawing near, Frank noticed Japhses had his right hand on the shoulder of a young man whose clothes appeared singed and whose face and hair were grimy and black with smoke. So he had caught the culprit.

"Good morning, My Lord," Japhses boomed as the other dismounted. "Not a pretty sight is it?"

"No, but very well done," Frank replied, delighted that the man responsible was under arrest.

"Not me, My Lord, I've only been organising things the little while since I arrived. This is who has done well."

With a grin he gave a hard slap on the back of the young man at his side. The Despot frowned and waited for the explanation that was soon forthcoming.

"This is Cragoop, he has saved the day. He was in the vicinity when he saw some men starting a fire and he…. ah you tell his Lordship man."

The young man was obviously shy, but gained in confidence as he told his tale.

"Er…yus M'Lud. I was just passin' M'Lud when, er… when I sees these men acting suspicious by the timber pile um. An' I goes up to 'em and I says, "What're you doin'? Um… an' they run off…"

"How many were there?" asked Frank.

"Er, I couldn't rightly see M'Lud, bein' so dark an' all that, but I reckon there was about three or four."

"I see – Japhses have any suspects been caught?"

"Not yet, My Lord," the Captain answered brushing his long hair back with his hand.

"Hmm. Please continue er…"

Frank hesitated and Natias whispered the man's name.

"…Cragoop," Frank repeated loudly.

"Uus M'Lud. When these men run away I sees they have piled up stuff for a fire um…you sees I lit a lamp to see. An' then I sees a small fire the other side of the timber pile so I put that out um."

"What about the hut that burnt down, when was that set fire to? Was that later on?"

"Er no, M'Lud. I looks up from puttin' this small fire out an' I sees the hut 'as caught alight. It was burning quite brightly by the time I came to it. I could not put that one out um."

Japhses decided to finish the story of Cragoop's endeavours for him, as he plainly did not enjoy speaking in front of all these important men.

"But he did a grand job, My Lord. He single-handed moved the nearest beams in the stockpile away from the burning hut. He did a lot to prevent it from spreading. Eventually some more people from the Lower Village saw the glow in the distance and came over. When they arrived Cragoop was beating out the flames that were catching on the partially constructed hut next door. Fortunately they had not been built too close together.

Together with the reinforcements they managed to get the fire under control and stop it engulfing the rest of the site. A courageous display on the part of this young man I think, My Lord."

"Yes excellent. Well done, Cragoop. You're from the Lower Village then?"

"Yus M'Lud, but my father works with you up at the Castle."

"Really?"

Natias explained.

"He means Crag the jailer, this is his son."

"How interesting," Frank replied, surprised to hear the old hunchback had a son, let alone a fine young man as this.

"Natias I want you to make sure he gets a suitable reward for his endeavours, and perhaps a smaller one for the men who came to help. In the meantime what are we going to do about all this?"

As Japhses and Uriah organised the resumption of the construction work, Frank held an impromptu meeting with Natias and Alan about the immediate future of the site.

"May I suggest," said a serious-sounding Alan, "that we leave the issue as to who was responsible for the fire, we'd be so unlikely to catch them. If we ensure the building is carried on, with a guard posted night and day, it will soon be completed and the old village pulled down, then there will be no going back. Besides, as the dissenters see the new village taking shape they will see the great benefits of starting afresh."

This was the other side to the boisterous Alan that Frank was seeing for the first time, Alan the advisor. He wanted to press the drone on one issue though.

"Are you saying we shouldn't even try to catch the villains who tried to burn it all down? Surely justice must be seen to be done."

"Yeah and if I thought there was one chance in a thousand of the culprits being caught I'd say try with all the means at our disposal, but I don't think there is. I feel the most positive approach is as I've recommended."

The three men discussed it a while longer until Frank had come round to Alan's way of thinking. He refused another request from Natias to have the suspects rounded up and questioned, mainly because there were so many of them. Apart from the dissenting elders there could be any number of ordinary villagers responsible. Without descriptions of the men to go on, he felt it was unfair to drag them all in; he did not want to increase resentment. The steward reluctantly agreed and so Alan's approach was adopted, although Natias said he would have a word with Gideon and ask him to make some low-key investigations and see if they came to anything.

That evening a small contingent of the guard stayed on to ensure the safety of the site and this became the pattern from then on. With the foundations of several huts already completed, the next week saw buildings springing up quickly as the new village began to take shape.

Back at the Upper Village the triplets' cousin Katrina was lowering a bucket into the well. No one else was present and she worked purposefully without looking up.

Most of the inhabitants obtained their water from the local streams, but this newly renovated well served the north-end of the village. A fine thatched roof has been built over the hole and a fresh winding mechanism installed.

Katrina's face was grave, but then it was rare to see her smile. Her experience of life in twenty-four Earth years had been mostly struggle. Orphaned while still a baby, she had been brought up by her grandparents who had shown little love. Throughout her childhood she had been picked on because she was different: she had a deep, husky voice which made her sound more like a man, but worst of all there was a grey streak in her white hair. How she would have loved to have cut it out, but the taboo against such action was all-powerful.

The last few years of her life had been spent in a loveless marriage to a guardsman called Hatt. She blamed herself for allowing him to fool her into the lifelong contract. He had changed immediately the bond was sealed and made her life a living hell. Often drunk, he beat her regularly as a matter of course.

Since childhood she had built a wall around her inner self, a sanctuary which no one else could reach. With a face of flint set to the outside world she preserved her independent spirit deep within her.

Another young woman arrived at the well; it was Leah.

"Is that you Katrina? I haven't seen you lately."

Before replying she heaved the bucket to the side of the well. "Oh it's you," came the uninviting reply.

Leah tried unsuccessfully to engage her in general chitchat. After noticing Katrina's black eye she tried to steer her eyes away from it, but they kept going back. The younger woman soon ran out of things to say. By this time Katrina's vessels were full and she was leaning against a roof support. At last she offered some conversation herself. In a lazy, expressionless tone she said, "I hear you and Rodd have split up."

"Not so," Leah responded defensively, "we're going to get married soon."

"Shame. Thought you'd seen what he's really like."

Starting to wind her full bucket upwards, Leah flushed with indignity and responded, "Rodd's a fine young man, I shall be proud to be his wife. You should not talk unkindly about him, if your name is mentioned he always springs to your defence, as do his brothers."

Katrina saw she had wounded an ally. Anyway it would be pointless trying to give the love struck benefit of her experience. She lowered her barriers for a moment, long enough to apologise for her remark and wish Leah happiness for the future. She would have left then had the other not suddenly have taken it upon herself to invite her round for a meal that evening. A moment's hesitation preceded a decline of the offer.

"My ever-loving husband left on patrol yesterday morning. Shouldn't be back for some days which would be nice, but I'd better not just in case he comes back early. It was kind of you to offer though."

Resuming her burden, Katrina departed alone. Leah found a trio of older women had joined her.

"That girl been botherin' you?" asked the first one, indicating towards the disappearing figure.

Leah ignored the question, but could not keep her cool when the second woman referred to Katrina as a "miserable drone", snapping, "She's not a drone as you well know!"

The third woman laughed, "You don't deny she's a miserable bugger though!"

"If she is it's 'cos people like you make her life a misery. I'm going now if you'll excuse me."

Strutting off with her load Leah prepared herself for some jeering, but was pleasantly surprised when none came. She did not look back.

'This is what Katrina has to put up with day in, day out. No one gives her a chance. If it was me I'd run away from here and never come back.'

Three days later Frank was strolling through the Castle courtyard with Natias. It was a warm afternoon and from the relatively few people at market, business appeared slack. The steward was just finishing an explanation of the weights and measures control it was his job to administer.

"We make sure we keep the stall holders on their toes, My Lawd,"

"Very wise."

"And soon it will be time for the next tax collection. I will need to take some of the guard fwom the site for that."

"Fine. I'll leave you to discuss that with Japhses. Who's that?"

He nodded in the direction of a young man who was sitting on a stool next to one of the market stalls. He was slowly and deliberately picking the stuffing out of a rag doll and letting the breeze take it out of his hand. He watched it twist its way down to the ground.

"That is Bwogg," Natias answered in a quiet voice. "He is the son of Weuben, one of the hulffan cwoppers fwom the Upper Village. A sad case weally is Bwogg, simple you know, but he is much loved by his family and gives a gweat deal of love in weturn."

They left Brogg to his studying and passed out of the courtyard, through the inner bailey and made their way towards the keep.

Frank announced, "I've been thinking. With both Adrian's and Crispin's rooms unused at present I'd like to have one converted into a private chapel. Probably Crispin's, 'cos that's at the end, by the spiral staircase. What used to be Adrian's can still be a guest room when the need arises."

"How about, My Lawd, if you have the visitors' woom opposite your lounge as the chapel? That way your chapel will be within your suite. I pwesume you have not got any other plans for that woom."

"No, I haven't. That's an excellent idea! We can move some of the good furniture there into Crispin's room and have my chapel as part of my suite as you said. Thank you, Natias. Yes I'll want to plan the décor and trappings myself.

"The form of Christianity I'm used to has mainly private devotions and prayers in it. We only met for communal worship on special feast days. There was a strong monastic tradition on the plan...I mean the place I come from. I was very keen to take up the religious life myself, but it seems God directed otherwise."

The two men began ascending the outer staircase of the keep and exchanged greetings with Laffaxe on his way down. Natias continued their conversation.

"I am afwaid I do not get to go to as many meetings as I should. The Castle seems as busy on the Sabbath as the west of the week and if it is not there are always accounts, inventowies or other matters to be taken care of. I say to Eko that she goes for both of us.

Cwispin's woom needs a good sorting out. Since he and Adwian left their wooms have been used as a dumping ground, especially Cwispin's. There are boxes and things all piled up."

Entering the hall they were met by a chubby man with an emerald cape who bowed low upon seeing the Despot. From his multi-coloured hair he was obviously a foreigner.

"My Lord Thorn, I am honoured to meet you. I have travelled a great distance with my assistants," he indicated to two young non-white girls behind him, "to offer you my much sought-after services."

'Why,' thought Frank, 'was he travelling such great distances to perform his service if it was that sought-after?' I'll resist the urge to ask him that though, I don't want to make him look silly.'

"And what is this service?"

"We do a complete body-care service My Lord," he said, again bowing as he spoke, "the cutting of your hair, trimming the beard, manicure, chiropody, a body massage if this is desired.

"We have come from Bynar where Despot Hista spoke highly of our services. We number Despot Wonstein and Baron Mallinburg among our clients My Lord, it really is an exclusive service."

"I see. Well I don't really fancy a body massage I must admit, but a haircut and manicure…"

As he trailed off a frowning Natias came straight to the point.

"How much?"

"For our supreme service less body massage a mere fifteen stens, a small price to pay for such expertise and professional care.."

"Daylight wobbewy!"

"I must protest! We do have overheads and have travelled a long way to offer our professional expertise."

His tone of wounded pride softened as he turned back to the Desport.

"My Lord, I tell you what I'll do. I'll offer you the complete service – less body massage of course – for a trial price of a mere seven and a half stens: half price! On the understanding that if you find our service nothing short of the ultimate in body maintenance you become one of my regular, exclusive clients at the full price in the future. If you are less than totally satisfied we will never bother you again. A most generous offer, My Lord."

As he bowed yet again Frank found himself amused by this character.

'Anyone who grovels this much to me can't be all bad!' he thought.

"I accept. Did you want to do it this afternoon?"

Before he could answer, a servant announced that Zadok the priest had arrived wanting to see the Despot.

"Oh I see," said Frank, then continued talking to the foreigner, "well can you stay the night and do me in the morning?"

Receiving an affirmative answer, Frank asked Natias to see to accommodation while he went to have a word with Zadok. He found him outside, leaning on his stick while stroking his long, white beard thoughtfully with his free hand.

"Hello, Zadok, nice to see you again. Pleasant weather we're having"

"Good afternoon My Lord, pleasant weather indeed."

Once the niceties were over they decided to sit on the bench outside Laffaxe's home. Nearby the finishing touches were being done to the new armoury with men on the roof fitting the tiles. Stable-hands were exercising the dakks within the inner bailey and the two men watched them as they chatted.

Zadok soon stated the reason for his visit.

"From what I hear there was a "little local difficulty" the other night at the site of the new village. I thought I might be able to help you."

Not knowing quite what he meant Frank remained silent and let him make his point.

"Some of the Lower villagers do not see the benefits of starting afresh. I have seen enough marsh diseases in my time to know that your idea of moving the whole village is a masterful one. In fact, My Lord, I am impressed by your concern for their welfare. Very Christian of you. The mere scale of the operation! It must be using considerable resources. Best to do it now while you are still new here, before you find yourself accepting the status quo.

"I am offering to use my influence to bring those who need influencing … to help them see that the new village will be of great benefit to them. I am not certain the issues have been explained fully enough to them, nor have their worries and feelings been entirely taken into consideration. Most of the Lower villager families have been there for generations and in spite of the sorry state of it, still feel affection for the place. After all, it is the only home they have ever known. Moving them into a clinical new environment is bound to cause objection and resentment. The new village will not have a character of its own yet; that is something that will grow slowly after the people have moved in.

"It is just that I am not satisfied that the peoples' sensibilities have been taken properly into account, My Lord."

Frank had been listening patiently, he now sighed.

"I see what you mean. I suppose I've been thinking it's such a good thing for them I have not concerned myself enough with their legitimate feelings."

The old man gave a knowing smile. He might seem resolute and determined in his sermons, but from his eyes Frank could tell this priest had a softer, compassionate side.

Zadok continued, "I believe you are doing the right thing in going ahead with the new village, even with the destruction of the old, but I feel it should be explained to the ordinary people better."

"What do you suggest?"

"That on the next Sabbath we hold a meeting in the Lower Village and that both your Lordship and myself give an address to the people, laying out the benefits of the enterprise, plus our hopes for the future."

Frank was not slow to see the merits of the idea. The thought crossed his mind that Zadok might know the identity of the arsonists, but let it pass. The priest's plan was accepted and after discussing details the conversation moved on.

"My Lord, at the meeting there will be a celebration of the Lord's Supper. I would very much like you to attend, because I understand you have not done so since your arrival here."

"Hmm. Where I come from we only celebrate the Eucharist twice a year, an awesome ceremony of colour and splendour.

Very different from many of the other groups there. But yes, Zadok, yes, I would love to join you for the Lord's Supper. It's a long time since I last received it. I've got a few days to prepare myself.

"Where is Eleazar incidentally?"

"He is visiting a couple of sick people in the Upper Village."

"Nothing serious I hope."

"Oh no, just the usual minor sicknesses. A fine young man is Eleazar, if a trifle over-sensitive at times.

"Going back to the new village, is there going to be another church building, as in the Upper Village?"

"I really don't know, you'd have to ask either John or Uriah, they should have the plans. I'm happy to authorise one if there's not. How's the one at the Upper coming on?"

"We had only just started it, My Lord. All the available people have gone down to the new Lower Village site to help their brethren there, so I think it will be a while before work is resumed."

"I must say I'm impressed with the community spirit here in Thyatira, with so many volunteers for the building work on top of the guard drafted there. It's heartening to see."

Zadok agreed, "That it is. A true Christian spirit to help their neighbours."

The early morning mist was lifting, heralding another fine day as spring began to give way to summer. Frank looked out on the panoramic view from the Castle roof. Many shades of green were spread out below, although everyone was saying the ground was dry for the time of year. The orange sun rose slowly in the sky on this beautiful, lazy day.

He felt he was settling well into his role on this planet and rarely thought about getting back to civilization.

'But I've always had that feeling in the back of my mind that one day I would ride the stars again,' he told himself. 'Until that time comes, I'm more than happy here.'

It was a week since Zadok's visit. Frank felt the talk he had given at the old Lower Village had gone quite well, but it had probably sounded a bit weak following the priest's fine oration. His was a hard act to follow. The important thing was it had cleared the air. Building at the site was progressing well now. The investigations to find the arsonists had come to a dead end and no one seemed keen to pursue it. Frank felt a bit guilty for not having explained the new village to the common people earlier and was not sad to see the matter dropped.

The Eucharist had been completely different from any he had known, but then all the worship here seemed to be. In spite of all the singing and jumping about it had been nice to share it with so many believers.

'Yes and my private chapel is taking shape too, that is where I will really feel at home. To be able to go and…I wonder what he's up to.'

A lone figure was running as fast as he could along the road from the Upper Village.

'It breaks the tranquillity of the morning to go around like that,' Frank thought as he squinted down at the scene before moving to a fresh vantage point from which he could see the Ladosan mountain range.

'I must keep going!' the runner told himself as his feet pounded the dry road kicking up dust.

His hands clenched and his mouth wide open as he fought to get oxygen into his fatigued body.

'Not much further now. Good, the entrance is already open.'

Bak bak bak bak bak bak! The monotonous sound as his sandals hit the hard clay. Machine-like, his running was now on automatic.

At last the main entrance to the Castle. Without changing pace he dashed past the guardsmen on the gate. They looked, but did not try to stop him. They merely watched as he crossed the bailey and carried on up the steps of the keep.

Inside the hall Natias, Japhses and Alan were sitting together. They had finished breakfast and were talking lazily to each other.

The runner burst in, shattering the tranquil scene. Singling out the Captain of the Guard, he called out in a breathless voice.

"Japhses....terrible news!"

'Well I'd better be getting down I suppose,' Frank told himself.

He glanced at the skylights to his two internal rooms, one now his chapel. They had made a good job of cleaning those up.

Starting down the spiral staircase he went all the way down to the hall. As he entered, the atmosphere could be cut with a knife. His three most senior aides were standing in a huddle near the entrance talking in worried tones. Another white was sitting in a chair with Illianeth by him. He took a cup of water and poured it straight over his head.

Everyone looked at their Despot with worried faces. Before he could ask what the matter was Japhses stepped up and announced solemnly, "My Lord, I have disgraced my office, I wish to resign and fight as an ordinary guardsman."

"Just hold on, what are you talking about, what's happened?"

"My Lord, the Ma'hol have seized Telar and I am to blame. By a lack of judgement I put a new recruit in charge of this island – Rodd whom you first travelled here with – the soab has let us down! But I accept full responsibility, because he was my choice and I am the Captain of the Guard. Please give Uriah the post and let me go back to the ranks."

The big man bowed his head as he finished talking.

"Right, let's get one thing straight!" Frank said, his voice firm, "the last thing we need right now is your resignation. All right, you've made an error of judgement, but we can all do that. Let's together try to put things right. We'll go to the Throne Room to discuss strategy; Natias can you bring the maps?"

Frank led the way into the small room, followed by Japhses and Alan. They left the messenger who was starting to recover as he sat up straight, his face still red. Illianeth had gone to get him some sustenance.

"What details do you know?" Frank asked once they were inside. It was Alan who replied.

"The messenger has come all the way from the river. He rode his dakk into the ground and then ran the rest of the way. He said that Rodd had chosen not to fight, but had withdrawn the garrison of around twenty to twenty-five men when an overwhelming force of Ma'hol had started crossing the stream towards the island. There were no casualties. The enemy were showing no signs of crossing onto the mainland. Our soldiers are keeping observation from high ground up from the river."

"Gave up without a fight!" exclaimed Japhses. "What an example; I'll have him scourged!"

Frank held up his hand.

"I want to hear his side before any judgement is made. I want that understood. Right now we've got to…ah good, Natias, the maps."

"Here we are, My Lawd."

He dumped them onto the table.

"If My Lawdship does not mind, I would pwefer to get on with my other duties. I do not pwofess to know a gweat deal about warfare stwategy...."

Thought Frank, 'You might not know much – I'm a rank amateur!'

".... but if I may be so bold I understand that it is usual to include the Village Heads in a Council of War. That is what I was told, although we have not had one since I was a boy, If you wish, My Lawd, I can send for Saul and Gideon. Oh and I will wequire some guardsmen to help with tax collection the next couple of days."

Frank hesitated.

"Do you think that war is now inevitable? Is there not some way we could negotiate over these islands?"

The other three stared at him in disbelief as if only a mad-man could have asked such a question.

"Well I just thought I'd ask. All right, Natias, you are excused and yes, please do send for the Village Heads to come here this evening. In the meantime gentlemen I suppose we'd better discuss tactics."

Together with Alan and Japhses he laid out the maps to help them consider their best course of action. He once more had to convince his Captain it was in their country's best interests for him not to resign. This achieved they got down to business.

It would be several days before a counter-attack could be mounted. The Guard, who would form the backbone of the army, would have to be assembled and got into a state of battle readiness. A small contingent would have to stay on the Ladosan frontier, but trouble from that quarter was thought highly improbable at present. Hardly any of them had ever seen action of any description, but Japhses assured his Despot that they were well trained and that both discipline and morale were high. Much of their battle equipment was stored at the Castle and had been the subject of overhaul the last couple of weeks.

The Captain also wanted a few days in which to drill the ordinary men folk of Thyatira who would form the militia. These would be the largest element of their army with slightly over five hundred and fifty men compared with the one hundred and fifty Guard.

The catapult on the Castle roof had already been renovated and was ready for action in the unfortunate event of a siege. Many more boulders would have to be taken up to the roof for ammunition.

Alan told Frank that Rabeth-Mephar was a far bigger country than their single, small despotate and that if they were to stand a chance they would need sizable contingents from their neighbours. Accordingly messengers were dispatched later in the day to both Aggeparii and Bynar asking for large numbers of soldiers to "help their fellow Hoamen in their just cause."

At the end of the fruitful meeting they arranged to meet again for a further discussion that evening in the Castle. Then it would be the full Council of War including the village representatives.

Japhses left to spend the rest of the day organising his troops. After lunch Frank spoke to Alan alone in his room. He wanted to question him about the Ma'hol, because he was the only person he knew who had ever been to Rabeth-Mephar.

"I followed your advice to send messengers to our immediate neighbours requesting reinforcements, but I must say I was a bit surprised. From what I hear of the Ma'hol they are a bunch of savages. Surely well-trained troops would be more than a match for them."

"Blue-green ones!" exclaimed the drone with one of his unique expressions, "Who told you about the Ma'hol, Natias?"

"And Zadok the priest."

Alan laughed.

"Yes I'm sure. With all due respect to them neither has ever been to Rabeth and they don't know what they're talking about. The Ma'hol are a highly civilized people, skilled in architecture and medicine…. and also warfare," he added with a twinkle in his eye.

"Do you think it is unwise for us to pick a fight with them then?"

"We didn't pick it, Frank. No, something Japhses said rang true about not to fight now would be a sign of weakness."

"I've heard him use that argument before, earlier in the dispute."

"We are past the point of no return."

"I don't think I've handled it well. We should have had proper negotiations when there was that earlier skirmish, sorted the problem out then when we were in a position of strength, not let is get out of hand."

Alan lounged back in his chair and crossed his legs. He seemed remarkably relaxed about the whole affair Frank thought. Presumably drones did not fight.

"Not great ones for negotiations, the Ma'hol. They usually set their minds on a course of action and go about carrying it out. I must say I'm a bit surprised about this islands dispute though; it's not their usual style. Why seize the island and leave it there when they know the conflict will escalate? I suppose it's been a thorn in their side so long they've decided to end it once and for all, but without a full-scale invasion it seems a little odd."

"You don't think they will invade?"

"Why give advance warning by taking the islands then just sit there?" They could be plotting an elaborate trap, but the Mehtar has always tried to foster….if not good, then reasonable relations with us. Generally it's been a policy of "I'll leave you alone if you do likewise"."

"Ah yes, the Mehtar, their leader, Japhses mentioned him."

"Yeah? He's been in charge since he was knee-high. I saw him from a distance on one of my two visits there."

"Tell me about him."

"Arumah-Ru, Grand Mehtar of all Rabeth-Mephar. He's a pretty imposing figure in his purple turban and cloak. Put it this way, he doesn't have to raise his voice for people to jump!"

"How old is he?"

"Hmm….dunno, probably a little older than yourself. He's been Mehtar nearly all his life, under a guardian until he reached maturity. He is seen somewhat as an elder statesman there."

Franks said, "Japhses said he thought this Mehtar might not be in favour of a fight, that there's a faction within his court trying to stir things up."

"Pure speculation. The truth is we simply don't know enough about them. I can't see them acting without his say-so."

"They're clearly not much loved around here, all the people seem delighted at the prospect of a crack at the Ma'hol."

"Ha! People who have never witnessed a battlefield I'll be bound!" retorted Alan dismissively. "Yes the whites are a pretty xenophobic lot; but then the fact that the Ma'hol have some whites amongst their slaves doesn't exactly endear them."

"Really? I didn't know that!"

Frank's tone then changed from surprise to irony.

"I suppose all the Ma'hol have got *red* hair."

"It's funny you should say that…"

"Oh no!"

"No seriously, the Mehtar and his son both *do* have red hair, although the Ma'hol in general have all different coloured hair: some dark, some lighter.... They're not a pure race like most Hoamen, more mongrel like me!"

'He can laugh at himself,' observed Frank, 'I wonder if I would in his position.'

Alan continued.

"Far from being savages the Ma'hol are very accomplished in the arts. Laffaxe learned his trade there you know.

"The Mehtar's palace is built of an unusual smooth, cold stone. Very hard, quite magnificent with its white and grey patterns in its grain which swirl round."

He illustrated in the air with his hand.

"I'm sorry, but it puts this place to shame. It's got a sophisticated heating system for the winter too, whereby they pipe hot water round the building. If anyone are the savages it's us.

"They're very keen on their god Vorg-hally-something. I can't quite remember it, some long name. They've got a "holy book" as well."

"Were you joking when you said they were renowned fighters?"

"Not exactly, but their reputation is probably a little dated come to think of it. They did give Sarnice a bloody nose in a brief campaign, but that was some years ago now. So like us they haven't tasted war for a while."

"That's a shame."

Alan frowned at this remark so Frank explained.

"Well from my knowledge of history when countries haven't experience warfare for a long time they get far too enthusiastic at the prospect. If it does come to it this could be a long drawn-out conflict which ends up changing a lot of things around here, you mark my words."

CHAPTER THIRTEEN

"Right, forward! Stick together. Don't get all strung out, stick together! That's better, come on..."

A little over a kilometre to the south of the Castle ran a stream. Here Japhses was busy training their forces in preparation from what now seemed to be the inevitable fight. The Council of War had decided the best strategy was a fast crossing of the river using the ford just south of the largest island Telar. They would then wheel round to cut off the three islands, all of which were occupied by the enemy now. Then the assault would come in from both directions. Meanwhile this stream south of the Castle provided a useful training ground.

The Captain of the Guard looked most formidable with his broad frame under breastplate and chain mail. He stood on a small rise with Uriah at his side, armour glistening in the sun. His sword was sheathed and he pointed with a thin stick as he barked the orders out.

Contingents of both Guard and Militia were being taught how to function together as a fighting force. The Guard were uniformly armoured like their Captain, some carrying swords and some long axes. The Militia, meanwhile, were very lightly armoured on the whole, but wore an assortment of outfits and had various weapons, of which a light bow and short sword were most popular.

Hearing a noise close behind him, Japhses turned to see Alan approaching with a dakk in tow. Roughly dressed, he was chewing nuts as he drew up to the big man.

"Hi there, Japhses, how's it goin'?"

The Captain ordered Uriah to take over for a while so he could chat with Alan.

"Not bad, not bad."

"I could hear you shouting from right over there."

As Alan indicated with his hand, Japhses smiled.

"Yes, I'm getting a bit hoarse. But they're doing pretty well in the circumstances. They're all so enthusiastic, that's the main thing. If we can discipline and channel that enthusiasm we'll be there.

Let's sit down for a bit."

They spread themselves on the dry grass while the dakk foraged a short way off. Uriah could be heard calling out directions to the troops.

Alan shoved some more nuts into his mouth and asked, "Was that Rodd I saw in the thick of it with the Guard?"

"Yes," sighed Japhses, "I was going to have him posted to the Laodician border where he couldn't do any harm, but the Despot asked me to give him a chance to prove himself in the fight. To be fair he did make it plain it was a request and not an order, leaving the final decision to me, but I was hardly going to go against his wishes."

"He's not the only one being given a second chance."

The big man looked uncomfortable.

"I must admit I hadn't thought of that, but I suppose you're right."

"What do you make of the Despot?"

"Strictly between you and me he's a bit funny in some ways, but I suppose that's to be expected of a foreigner. That having been said, he's not bad, at least he hasn't been afraid to make decisions. Then he was a ruler in his own country and must be used to exercising power. He's a bit funny like I said, but he could be a lot worse."

"Could be a Kagel!" joked Alan, downing the last of his nuts and wiping his hand on the grass.

"Yes at least we're spared that. No, he's very good in some ways, but has some odd ideas. Some of the things we take for granted completely baffle him. For instance I was wanting to kit him out in his armour, see if Despot Rattinger's suit needed adjusting, but he would have none of it. Said they didn't have wars where he came from and he'd be no good in it. I gather he wants to lead us into battle from behind!"

"Most strange," agreed Alan raising his eyebrows, "but then Oonimari is more noted for its philosophers than its generals. Still he seems to be making the right decisions regarding the Ma'hol – and listening to our advise which is good!

"I must admit I've taken to him, I feel he's someone I can trust."

"Yeah, but you got on well with Rattinger who couldn't have been more different."

"I know which one Zadok prefers, never seen so much of him around the Castle; and Natias is always happy as long as he's allowed to go about day to day without having someone looking over his shoulder."

"Don't mention Natias to me right now! Him and his bloody tax collection! It's a job he really enjoys doing and nothing must get in the way, not even the small matter of an impending war. Oh no, we must get the Despot and Autarch their money straightaway. He's commandeered some of our wagons, made villagers hang around at home rather than come here and be trained…"

Alan, who did not much like talking about Natias behind his back, seized upon the gap in Japhses' list of complaints to change the subject.

"So those wagons I brought back from Aggeparii are proving useful then, the ones Natias is not using I mean."

"Yes. As Natias shows no interest I've got Saul in charge of logistics. You know we're thinking in terms of a lightening raid into Rabeth after the islands have been recovered, not a long campaign. Even so, the supplies needed are enormous: wagons for victuals, dishes, tents, tools…whole wagonloads of arrows. They're making supplies of them all day long in the villages, got the women on that. The master-fletcher tells me they're helping him produce them much quicker.

"Laffaxe and his assistants are hoping to use a few of the wagons as ambulances, would you believe. Says the Ma'hol do this do they can treat their wounded on the battlefield. Sounds like a good idea if you think about it, cut down on fatal wounds with a bit of luck."

"And a morale factor, knowing if you're injured you're not going to be left in the field for ages.

"I've seen all kinds of activity going on around the Castle …… and I visited the Lower Village yesterday where Gideon's got a production line going making new pikes amongst other stuff.

"I wonder when our reinforcements will turn up. Of course Frank's never met either Hista or Kagel, I can't see either of them wanting to hand over command of their troops to a complete stranger."

"No," Japhses agreed.

"I just hope they turn up in time though, that's all that matters right now!"

Frank could not help feeling that there was an air of unreality about the whole situation. While archers practised outside the Castle and guardsmen using pulleys hauled large stones up to the roof of the keep, he still found it hard to believe he was about to start a war with a yet unseen enemy. He knew that all around thought him a foreign prince, born to lead. Nothing could have been further from the truth. He was living on his wits, helped by some ideas from his knowledge of history. This must all be a bad dream.

It had seemed real enough the other evening when the full Council of War had met in the council. Preparations, commands and an overall strategy were decided upon:

seizing and then fortifying the islands was to be top priority, with a raid into enemy territory an option left open. The mood was still one of enthusiasm for the venture. Alan made it plain he would fight along with the whites for the defence of the country. Frank insisted, however, that if the main Ma'hol army were encountered before the Aggeparii and Bynar reinforcements arrived, it would be engaged only if absolutely necessary. They were reliant on a speedy response from the neighbouring despotates, Thyatira's individual resources being far too small.

A system of scouts and messengers was set up, although the suggestion of reconnaissance patrols into Rabeth-Mephar before the attack was not taken up on the grounds that it could give their plans away. Frank was still unsure as to the wisdom of that decision; they were desperately short of reliable intelligence while the rumours were getting wilder every day.

Ever since the morning after the meeting though, he found the prospect of war incredible. He had never been near a war, let alone commanded an army of primitive warriors! Surely things would settle down to their routine again soon and the moving of the Lower Village be completed.

Natias had not helped this air of unreality about the impending conflict. He seemed to ignore it all as he gaily set off with his posse of guardsmen to collect the taxes that were due. It apparently took priority over everything else and had disrupted Japhses' training schedule. The two men were starting to fall out.

One afternoon, with the tax collection finally completed, the steward was explaining the finances to his Despot in the hall. Various ledgers and papers were spread across the tables; they were making the most of the available space.

"So this figure My Lawd, down the bottom, shows a total income of just over twenty gwend, the first time it has topped twenty in fact; the sign of a healthy economy."

Frank nodded.

"I see, but from what you've said I wonder if we're not taxing our people too much. It takes the spirit of enterprise away and causes resentment. I've seen it on other planets."

'Aagh what have I said!' thought Frank blushing heavily.

Natias was so caught up in his favourite subject he did not notice the Despot's gaff.

"With the impending conflict My Lawd we will need every sten we can get. I hate to think what our neighbours will demand in payment for their help!"

Frank agreed, he was simply relieved his extraterrestrial reference had not been taken in. Natias continued.

"We also have many debts to pay off. All told these amount to four and half gwend. Some people have waited a long time for payment, I suggest it is only fair if we pay them off stwaightaway."

He stopped at the sight of Japhses entering the hall. The Captain was in full armour with his helmet under his left arm.

Frank thought what an awesome figure he cut, but was struck by how like the knights of the early medieval period he looked. Surely this was too much of a coincidence.

"Excuse me, My Lord. I've come to enquire whether the Steward has finished collecting the taxes yet."

Frank noticed his frosty tone and that he had deliberately avoided using Natias' name.

"Yes, we have," replied Natias, "and yes your guardsmen *have* been paid."

"Good. *Now* perhaps I'll be able to train the whole army together for a couple of days before we move out."

Natias snorted, "They usually go on a binge after they have got their money."

He looked at Frank as he spoke, but it was clear who the remark was aimed it.

"I'm perfectly confident discipline will be maintained!" said Japhses controlling himself quite well in the circumstances.

"Yes," Natias came back, determined to have the last word, "I suppose they are all keyed up at the moment."

The big man was close to exploding, but stopped himself because his Despot was present. Instead he gave Natias a piercing glance and stalked off.

"I don't like you two getting at each other."

"It was nothing, My Lawd, he has just been a bit silly about the tax collection of late."

"Listen, I don't want you two falling out. I thought your tone just now was a lot less then charitable. Please make an effort, this is going to be a testing time for us all."

"I apologise, My Lawd, I will twy."

"All right," said Frank. Having made his point there was nothing to be gained by dwelling on it. "Now what were you saying about these taxes?"

"Later today a special squad of guardsmen will set off for the Capital with the full levy for the Autarch. We can then welax until next time. I suppose with the Autarch being terminally ill, it will be a new man by then."

"Oh he's ill is he? Nice for someone to tell me!"

People were coming and going from the hall the whole time as usual. Just then one particular woman entered and spoke to a passing servant. He had only seen her once before and that had been briefly more than three weeks previously, but Frank recognised the interlocutrix immediately. It as Giella, Uriah's wife. The servant she spoke to was unable to help and she looked round the room, searching for someone.

"Excuse me a moment Natias," Frank said and moved across to the visitor.

"Can I help you?" Are you looking for Uriah?"

"Oh hello," she said with a smile that lit up her face. "Actually I'm looking for Japhses, do you know where he is?"

Her clear, blue eyes were piercing and her hair so immaculately fashioned. She had perfect skin, smooth and unblemished. Frank was stunned by the beauty before him and eager to assist her if at all possible.

"He was here only a short while ago. I believe he went out that way. I'll help you look for him."

"It's nothing important, My Lord, I'll find him."

He feasted his eyes on her for the final second as she smiled again before disappearing as quickly as she had first appeared.

'Phew, I can't believe anyone can be that beautiful! I got a really good look at her close up this time. Even her voice is so pretty and the way she moves.... Oh I'd better get back to Natias.'

Natias, large nose and warts, was waiting patiently for his master to come back across the room to resume their conversation.

"There are a few more matters, My Lawd, I would like to discuss."

"Er yes," began Frank coming down from cloud nine rather quicker than he would have liked, "What are those?"

"The documents are now weady for the land-welease pwog-wamme in the Upper Village, plus I have some ideas for a stone church building to submit to the authowities in the Capital. You wanted to have a look at them first."

Frank snapped, "Hell I can't think of things like that at a time like this! Don't you know there's a war on?"

His tone mellowed a bit.

"Sorry, Natias, but honestly I can't get into those right now. Kindly put them on ice for the time being and I'll look at them later, all right?"

"Yes, My Lawd," Natias replied as he thought, "'Put them on ice" – what a funny expression, I have not heard that one before.'

"Is there anything else pressing?" Frank asked.

"No, My Lawd."

"Good. Ah Alan, there you are! I was just about to go up to the roof, do you want to come along?"

"Sure, why not?" asked the drone who had only just arrived back at the Castle.

It was difficult holding a conversation whilst going up the spiral staircase, so they climbed in silence. As Frank led the way he found himself trying to visualise Giella's face in detail.

'No, I shouldn't,' he told himself, 'she's a married woman! How could such a beautiful creature like that end up with such a dry old stick like Uriah? She looks so full of life, while he only comes into his own when he's commanding the Guard. The rest of the time it's almost impossible to get two words out of him.'

Emerging from the staircase they were greeted by a sea of boulders covering almost the entire roof with just a few narrow channels in-between for the guardsmen to walk along. The air out there was stiflingly humid after the cool of the hall. A small group of soldiers were busy working a hoist pulling up yet another large stone for the catapult.

"Blue-green ones!" exclaimed Alan when he stepped out, "what a mess!"

Frank called over the squad leader, a short young man called Jonathan.

"What the hell's going on around here, this mess is totally unnecessary, why haven't you stacked this ammunition like any sensible man would have done? If an attack came now you wouldn't be able to move or man the walls with these things all over the place!"

Jonathan was right to look concerned as he tried an explanation, the Despot was furious. The other soldiers had stopped working and were looking on from the other side of the roof.

"We...we were going to pile them up better once we'd got the full supply up here My Lord, it's taken rather longer than we thought it would."

"Well I'm sure you've got plenty to keep you going now. Stack them up neatly so there's room to walk around...what idiot put that there!"

He had spotted one of the potential projectiles resting on the glass of a skylight, the heavy shutters still being open. Thick glass though it was, it was a miracle it had not gone through or even cracked.

"Get that off there immediately! If that glass is broken you will pay for a replacement. I will come up here again before sunset; I want the place looking a lot better by then."

"Yes, My Lord."

"Come on, Alan, let's go back down."

"Okay," the drone replied, but hesitated to have a quick word with the guardsman. "Jonathan, use your common sense and close the shutters of the skylights."

"Yes, Alan," the soldier replied sheepishly.

Frank led the way back down to his suite. Going into the lounge he took his large Bible off a comfortable chair that he offered to his friend. He rounded up some papers and put them with the book on a side cabinet. Getting himself a glass of water from a covered jug we kept there, he also poured some wine from a decanter and passed it to Alan.

"Thanks, it's so muggy today, this is welcome. What was it you wanted to look at from the roof with me?"

"Just the scenery, thought it would be a good place to look out and have a chat. I didn't fancy rock climbing though.

"I wanted to talk to you about how our preparations are going – not very well if those twits on the roof are anything to go by!"

"Don't be too harsh on Jonathan, he's not normally that daft. The squad leaders are picked for brains as well as fighting ability. He's generally pretty good is Jonathan. And as for Rodd, I'm sure he did the right thing in withdrawing from the islands, in spite of what Japhses thinks. There was no point in sacrificing themselves as a noble gesture."

"I understand you visited our men on surveillance near the islands, what's the situation there?"

"Surely you get regular reports from the runners."

"Yes, but I wanted to hear what you made of the situation."

"Okay, but there's not a lot to report. Our men have got a good vantage point there: after the flat piece of land on our side of the river it rises to a small ridge with a copse on it. That's where Hal's squad is stationed. They have a double-lens for seeing far-off things close up.

"It couldn't be more quiet at the moment. Every now and then there is a rush of activity as certain members of the islands' garrisons are relieved. They appear jumpy, on edge as you'd expect. When they leave they disappear into a large wood about a kilometre into Rabeth-Mephar. The rest of the time they're very quiet. So there's not a great deal to report in fact; they're regular troops, not the Imperial Guard."

"I see," Frank replies thoughtfully.

He fingered the glass in his hands nervously and took another sip before speaking again, this time in a more lively tone.

"I hear you've also been to see how our soldiers are getting on with their training."

"Yeah. Confidence is certainly high which is good, but Japhses reckons they'll need at least another week to prepare. That'll give time for the reinforcements to arrive too."

The conversation progressed, but although lighter topics were mentioned they found it difficult to keep away from the subject of the war preparations. It was on the minds of all in Thyatira at present and there was a pervading air of anticipation that the present calm would soon be broken. Frank still hoped in the back of his mind it would not come to a fight, but as time progressed the unreality of the situation was fading, leaving a few stark facts which looked very real indeed. The Ma'hol were showing no signs of leaving the islands and with the mood of expectancy in his despotate growing, war seemed more and more inevitable.

He asked Alan about the battle-armour the Guard wore, saying it reminded him of some illustrations he had seen a long time ago.

"Does it? There's no mystery, all the specifications were laid down by the Keepers a long time ago, they haven't changed."

"But where did they get their ideas from?" Frank asked, leaning forward with an expression on his face.

"No idea," Alan replied as he crossed his legs, "but I do know I've got my new suit ready."

"Oh," came the surprised response.

"It's only just been completed. I tried it on this morning, I'll have to show you."

"Have you been training with Japhses and the men?"

The answer came casually.

"Can't say I have, but I know how to fight."

Alan knew the foreigner would not have heard of Sarcan the great swordmaster, but then he was not given to boasting. He joked instead.

"My armour might be new, but perhaps I am myself a little rusty. I'll see if I can help train the men myself tomorrow. Before we get off the subject of armour, I've been told you've refused to try on Ratty's old suit. It would be a boost to the men, they'll want to see their leader all dressed up to fight."

"Well I don't know, "Frank began awkwardly, "I'd be no good."

He realised how pathetic he was sounding. It had been easy to say no to a white like Japhses, but it was different with Alan who was outside the otherwise strict social ladder of Hoame. He considered it a reflection on how quickly he had become conditioned to think as everyone else did there, in terms of black and white.

"I gather you're not used to wars in Oonimari, you're lucky. It's true we've been at peace for a long time, but this is still a warlike part of the world and certain things are expected. If you are not up to fighting at least lead us to the battle in your armour, even if you then stand off and don't actually fight."

Frank looked into space and shrugged.

"Alright," he said slowly, I'll think about it."

As events turned out there was no time to think about it. That evening a Sarnician trader arrived claiming to have important news. He said he had just crossed from Rabeth-Mephar and that the Ma'hol were forming an army a short distance inside their border. Frank immediately summoned the Council of War. Gideon did not trust the trader, believing it to be a trap. They all agreed that they could not afford to ignore it though and decided to march on the islands the next day, before the supposed Ma'hol army had time to strike first.

Following the Council's advise the Sarnician was placed under arrest. He was put in the not uncomfortable room that had once belonged to Adrian and left in no doubt as to where his fate lay. If his information was proved to be correct he would be awarded with two hundred and fifty sten and released unharmed. Should it turn out to be a trap his head would form the first projectile launched by the catapult. Frank watched his eyes as he was told this, but the trader took it well saying he fully understood their suspicion and was happy with the deal.

The Council members went to bed late that night, hoping that dawn would reveal the banners of their allies approaching.

"My Lord, it is morning, you wanted an early call."

"Uh? Oh thanks, Illianeth," responded Frank sitting up.

He had laid awake for much of the night, then when he had got to sleep at long last it was time to get up. Swinging his legs out of the bed he remembered what was in store for that day and immediately became alert with a rush of adrenaline inside him. He heard heavy rain falling, the tail-end of the night's storm.

Meanwhile in the kitchen Matthew was fussing as usual in his efforts to get the food prepared. Soon the hall began to fill up with people for breakfast, many more than on a usual day.

Frank was seated at the top of the main table with Natias, Japhses and Alan. The tension between his two white lieutenants appeared to have totally gone as they discussed last minute preparations. The steward was to stay at the Castle with a handful of guardsmen. It had earlier been decided not to evacuate the women and children from the villages into the castle at this stage. Frank now questioned whether the villages might not be overrun before they had time to escape. Japhses explained his reasons for not wanting an immediate evacuation.

"It could be see by the army as a lack of confidence in them which would be harmful to morale. I have a large supply of boys to go with us as runners. I will make sure the villagers are kept up to date with developments as required. With the network of scouts operating as well, communications will be most efficient."

Frank would be guided by his Captain in this matter, the man certainly sounded confident enough. They were still talking when a guardsman arrived from the roof of the keep to report that there was still no sign of their reinforcements. He was sent back up to his post.

The despot forced some food inside of him, but he felt no hunger. His stomach felt knotted as raw fear refused to be banished from his mind. When he drank he noticed his hand was shaking.

At the end of the meal prayers were said, then they dispersed to prepare for the march. Frank had been stung by Alan's words into trying some armour on the previous evening. The later coat of mail worn by Despot Rattinger had been loose and uncomfortable, but in the storerooms they found an earlier one in pristine condition which fitted well. It had been packed in harco-bean shells to preserve it. Frank admired himself in front of the mirror. The black metal and over-tunic looked awesome he felt, a pity it was more for decoration than use in his case.

The Guard assembled in the Castle bailey. The Despot was at the head of the column with the Captain of the Guard and Alan the drone. Partial armour only was worn for the relatively short march to the border, the heavy bits being transported there in some of the wagons. They stood by their dakks which could only carry a man in armour for a final charge at the enemy. As they slowly advanced, the bulk of the men formed a column behind them. The wagons followed, each pulled by eight or ten dakks, while Uriah and the rest of the guardsmen formed a rearguard. Without talking they went through the gate and took to the road. Their armour clanked and the wagons groaned, while the dakks made funny high-pitched snorting noises.

The night's storm had made the ground soft under foot, but the air was fresher. As the column spread out along the road to the Upper Village the men began to sing.

At the front they were quiet. Frank found himself shivering and knew it was from fear and not the chilly morning.

'How in Heaven's name did I find myself in this mess?" he asked himself. 'Why didn't I pursue diplomacy and get the matter sorted out that way? I should've taken a lead. Instead we've just dithered about, slipping inexorably to war without even trying to stop it!

'If my opponents on Eden saw me now... those devils trying to wreck the Church with their practices. They cared nothing for God, but everything for what the other planets thought of us. If they were so keen on emulating the other planets why didn't they go and stay there? And that Hurdam was the worst of the lot. He compromised his faith so much I don't know why he bothered to call himself a Christian! If you took out of the Creed what he found unacceptable you'd only be left with, "I believe in Amen"! The arrogance of the man. He was the only one who had ever thought out the problems of the Faith of course, all the rest of us just blindly followed......... well that's what you'd think to hear him talk...

'Here I am about to meet my death in the middle of nowhere, on an uncharted planet amongst a primitive people millenniums behind the civilized universe. What a strange grave!

'We don't stand a chance against this enemy without the re-inforcements. I can't understand the pride of these people, they really would have death than dishonour when it comes to their homeland...

'It would be difficult for me to run away from the battle-field with this chain mail on. This dakk could only take me a few hundred metres. Besides, if I succeeded in escaping where would I go? Try my luck with another country on this planet? I doubt if they'd give me a district to administer. And Hoame is the only Christian country from what I gather. No, Francis, you simply must accept that your future is inexorably tied up with that of the Thyatirans. Besides, why did God put you here?'

Slightly happier after reaching this conclusion he pursed his lips and took in a couple of deep breaths to try and stop himself from shaking.

"All right?" asked Alan looking across, the first words he had spoken since they left the Castle.

"Fine."

Nearby a startled blackbird flew up making its warning cry. They spotted several rabbits on the way, hopping through the wet grass.

Shortly before they reached the Upper Village they were joined by the militia from both villages, swelling their numbers greatly. Their place in the column was swiftly organised and to-gether they slowly marched on, the wagons dictating the pace.

In spite of the early hour the reception received from the Upper Villagers was tremendous. The women, children and old men waved their hands and shouted encouragement and cheers as their army passed through. Frank looked for any faces he might recognise. Kim was there with her children, all were shouting enthusiastically. Alan pointed out Hanson whom, he said, was supposed to have a bad leg and could not fight. He did not sound convinced.

Zadok stood just in front of the crowd and blessed them as they went by, His arms moved up and down in large, exaggerated movements as he shouted out assurances above the cheering crowd that the Lord would bring them victory over the heathens. There were petals in his hair from the flowers thrown by the crowd. The sight of the elderly priest blessing them set Frank's mind wondering again.

'Why ever would the Creator of the entire Universe care less about this petty little conflict? I'm sure He's got greater things on His plate.

'Mind you, I suppose the marvellous thing is He *does* care about each individual. He knows each sparrow that falls from the sky and leaves the ninety-nine sheep to find one that has been lost. So maybe Zadok's right.

Dear Heavenly Father, please protect us this day if it be your Holy Will. Keep us safe and bring us through this time of trial.'

Frank became conscious of the roaring crowd once more. As he looked at the cheering white masses the words written by Thucydides thousands of years previously came to mind: "At the beginning of a conflict the enthusiasm is always greatest. There were great numbers of young men who had never seen a war and were consequently far from unwilling to join in this one." How little people had changed. But where was Giella?

Just when he was giving up hope he spotted her by a wicker fence on the edge of the village, holding the hand of a young man who, from his uncoordinated actions and general appearance was mentally retarded.

Alan noticed the Despot staring at the couple.

"That's Brogg, one of the cropper's sons."

"Oh yes, I've had him pointed out to me before. Hello, Giella!"

She returned the greeting amid the roaring crowd.

Further back in the column Rodd's two militia brothers caught up with him.

"Hi lads. I can't see Leah."

"No," replied Bodd, "She isn't here. She said she couldn't face seeing us – well, *you* really, going off to war. She did ask us to convey her love to you though, and said she wants to marry you when you come back."

Rodd visibly brightened upon hearing this news. His brothers stayed with him among the Guard as they left the village.

The countryside they entered now was deserted and the earlier singing had stopped. The clang and clatter of armour, plus the groaning, creaking wagons were the permanent sounds once more. Frank found himself shivering again.

Scouts and runners were sent out in all directions; whatever happened they did not want to be taken by surprise. The ground here was undulating, dotted about with trees in pairs and spinneys. Thick gorse bushes could be seen to their right. Everywhere was still wet from the rain.

Japhses spoke.

"I've posted a unit at the stone bridge north of the islands as a precaution, but I can't really see an attempted crossing there, 'cos it's so narrow. I thought they might try a raiding party."

Frank let in a deep intake of air.

"Good, we've got to be prepared for everything. How much further 'till the ford?"

"Only about two kilometres My Lord."

While he still spoke a scout riding a dakk came scurrying over the rise in front of them.

"My Lord!" exclaimed the rider as he drew close, "The enemy has been spotted!"

Japhses ordered a halt to the column. The scout, a boy wearing a brown cape and baggy, mottled green trousers, collected himself to give a full report.

"They are coming out of the wood on the other side of the river and are preparing to cross over."

"How many?" Japhses asked.

Several hundred sir, with wagons carrying equipment. It was impossible to say when I left exactly how many."

"What types of soldiers were they?"

"I'm sorry sir, I don't know."

Japhses' face was impassive as he heard the answers. He turned to his leader.

"My Lord, we must make all speed and try to catch them before they can get into proper battle formation on our side of the river. Our wagons can follow as best they can. We should armour-up immediately and engage as quickly as possible.

"Right," said the Despot decisively, "order the men to prepare for battle!"

There would be no going back now.

⊰⊱

CHAPTER FOURTEEN

The column advanced quickly now. Frank was beginning to get out of breath when Japhses suggested they mount up and go ahead to see the situation for themselves. Alan came too and the three dakks trotted off up the rise to the ridge overlooking the river where the observation squad was keeping a close eye on Ma'hol troop movements

A young guardsman came forward to hold the panting dakks as the Despot and his lieutenants dismounted. Hunched forward as they came to the crest of the rise Frank could see what a good vantage-point among the bushes his men had. They were greeted by the squad-leader who handed his Commander a small telescope. Laying down in the wet grass they got their first look at the army of Rabeth-Mephar.

The scene before them was chaotic. The river was greatly swollen by the night's sharp storm and the only wagon to have attempted a crossing in what is usually the shallows had overturned. A large number of men were wading chest-deep around it, but no coordinated action was being taken. Some were trying to salvage the load, but only succeeded in getting in the way of other men trying to release the desperately struggling dakks in the fast-flowing river. Others still were holding onto the wagon trying to stop the entire structure from being carried away.

"They're skirmishers crossing," observed Japhses.

A thin file of men were entering the deep water and attempting to wade across. Frank honed his telescope on the men on the far bank waiting their turn. The skirmishers' only armour was a hardened leather breast / back-plate plus a simple iron helmet devoid of decoration. Each man carried a small shield and had a short, fat scabbard containing a sword.

As he observed the proceedings Frank found his heart beating furiously and his mouth bone-dry. He had to clamp his teeth together to stop them chattering.

Just then a loud cry went up from the Ma'hol ranks as the wagon stranded in the river turned over twice, trapping some men underneath. More soldiers jumped into the swirling water in a vain attempt to help. Now that the wagon was away from the shallowest point greater numbers of the skirmishers began to cross. They waded gingerly across the fast current and most made it, although a few were swept away. Those that did reach the Hoame bank crawled up and stood dripping as they looked round, apparently unaware that their every move was being observed.

"Mustn't let too many get across before we attack," Alan told Frank. "These are just the skirmishers, the regular troops are those further back."

"Look!" Japhses cried out, "Look there, Imperial Guard!"

Frank trained his telescope back to the soldiers crossing the river. As he did so the wagon was eventually carried away downstream, dakks, load and all. In the middle of the crossing skirmishers was a small group, less than ten strong, of much more elaborately armoured men. Only their top halves were visible as they waded across, but these tall men were clearly a lot more formidable than the lightly-armoured skirmishers. For one thing they had proper metal armour, their breastplates were elaborately patterned. These Imperial Guardsmen also wore highly ornate helmets with nose pieces and different coloured plumes for decoration.

One of the Imperial Guard had a man beside him to hold his helmet and shield as he crossed. His features could be seen so clearly through the telescope that Frank was frightened he would be spotted. The man had a striking appearance with a shock of red hair. He had a protruding forehead and angrily shouted at the others, apparently telling them to hurry across. There was an air of authority about him.

Alan exclaimed, "Blue-green ones! That's Sil! Down there, the one without the helmet."

Japhses frowned.

"Keep your voice down!"

Alan turned to explain to Frank, this time in calmer tones.

"That one directing the crossing is Sil Qua'moth-Ri. He's the Menmahuna of Rabeth, a sort of prince I suppose. He's the Mehtar's son, a right arrogant bastard!"

The Thyatiran force had now arrived and was being lined up behind the ridge by Saul and Gideon, out of sight of the enemy.

"They're so disorganised," Japhses said quietly at the jostling muddle that was the Ma'hol army below them.

The squad leader agreed, saying, "Yeah, what amazed us was they 'adn't any reconnaissance. They come up 'ere as a crowded rabble an' just charge into the river with no patrols nor nothin'."

Alan remarked, "They must still think they've got the element of surprise. What strikes me as odd though is that there is only that handful of Imperials, and Sil among them."

Meanwhile the two village leaders were doing a most efficient job at organising the guardsmen and militia, although some men were temporarily breaking ranks to hurriedly urinate in the bushes nearby. They quickly ran back into line. The supply wagons were now visible in the distance.

Forty Ma'hol skirmishers plus the half-dozen or so Imperials had now reached the near bank. Others were still struggling across the fast-flowing river while a few hundred regular troops waited their turn. Despite his shouted commands their leader was not able to install much discipline. They pushed and jostled each other to get to the water in one large crowd rather than the neatly ordered ranks of their adversaries now awaiting the command to attack. Japhses felt proud as he compared the two armies.

Alan could not contain himself any longer.

"We must attack *now* Frank, before more of them can cross. If we can cut off and annihilate those who have made it, including their leader, the rest will turn tail and run. Just look how disorganised they are!"

"No," cut in Japhses, "We must wait until more of them are over here, then attack with every man we've got. There's no point in having an indecisive battle, it would only mean a prolonged war which would be disastrous for us."

Alan shook his head as the Captain spoke. As soon as there was a gap he jumped in again.

"But look! This force is only a diversionary tactic – it's far too small to be the main army and there are only a handful of Imperials."

"What? The Mehtar's son in command of a mere diversionary force? I find that..."

Frank interrupted.

"Enough! We attack immediately. I want half our men to attack that way, the other half that way," he indicated with his hands a pincer movement from north and south of their position. "Oh and I'd better have a small reserve here where I'll make my base."

"Yes, My Lord," Japhses replied quickly, glad that the Despot was sounding decisive, even if he had adopted Alan's idea of attacking now. "I'll take half the Guard and attack from the north and Uriah will come from the south; he can take Gideon's militia with him. I'll have the Upper-villagemen with me," he continued as he began slipping back to their assembled army, "so you'll have about fifty militia in reserve with you, My Lord, if that's acceptable."

"Fine!"

As the big man trotted back to his men Alan looked undecided as to what to do.

Frank asked, "Do you want to go with him?"

"Do you mind?"

"No no, you go ahead,"

Turning back to study the enemy, Frank was surprised at the drone's apparent eagerness to join the battle, but then he found it difficult to think of anyone actually wanting to fight his fellow man.

'But then I'm in a minority of one around here,' he thought to himself. 'Yes it's too easy for me with such a different experience of life from these people. I mustn't judge by unfair standards.'

The Thyatiran force was being grouped ready for the assault. Frank and the squad of guardsmen still laying among the bushes at the top of the ridge found the fifty reserve militia marching up towards them. They stopped on the slope and sat down to wait until they were required. The commander was a Guard squad leader who came up the rise to introduce himself.

"My Lord, I am James, in command of the reserve. I have told them to rest until they are needed."

"Fine," Frank replied, then turned back to look through the telescope again. "Look at this lot, they can't seem to get their act together."

While more skirmishers were attempting the crossing there seemed to be arguments breaking out amongst the troops near the bank. One section appeared to be moving away, back where they had come from. No more wagons had entered the water.

Close on a hundred men were now on Thyatiran soil, all skirmishers apart from the small group of Imperials and a similar number of regulars. They came out of the water with their cloaks and trousers clinging and dripping. Their commander Sil was starting to get them organised. He instructed one of his Imperial Guard to take half a dozen men up the ridge for a belated reconnaissance.

"Oh no!" Frank whispered to himself as the men approached.

Just then loud shouting and yelling erupted as down both ends of the near riverbank the Thyatirans charged. Their loud Kassiahorn sounded the attack command and its note pierced the air. The Ma'hol stood frozen like statues for what seemed an age, but in reality could only have been a moment. Then desperate orders were shouted as they rallied round their leader.

"Defence formation," observed James as the men who had been climbing the ridge ran back to join their colleagues.

'What a relief!' thought Frank.

His heart was still pounding as the battle commenced. The small Ma'hol force which had crossed the river hastily formed a circle round their leader. This was just in position when the Thyatirans, led by the Guard, hit them from both sides. A shock-wave went through the Ma'hol ranks as they absorbed the impact. Then vicious hacking and thrusting began on both sides. Some militia forced themselves between the skirmishers and riverbank to cut off their line of retreat.

The immediate response of the regular troops on the far bank was to throw themselves into the water in greater numbers to reinforce their comrades. Some entered where the river was deeper and were swept downstream. The others found themselves under a hail of arrows from the Thyatiran militia. They tried to protect themselves with their shields, but casualties were high with the archers controlling the entire Hoame riverbank. Militiamen were lined up along the water's edge pouring in their missiles from different angles. They could not accurately reach the far bank, but those trying to cross were at their mercy. The attempts at reinforcement had finally to be abandoned and a few survivors struggled back up the far bank. There the regular Ma'hol soldiers stood forlornly watching the unequal struggle without being able to do anything to help. They did not appear to have any archers, at least any who could reach across the river.

The encircled Ma'hol force on Hoame soil fought on. Encircled and cut off from the rest of their army, their plight was desperate. They were greatly outnumbered and the skirmishers, who formed their bulk, were armoured far lighter than the Thyatiran Guard.

The two sides continued to slash and cut into each other and the roar of battle could be heard a long way away. At the Thyatiran rear the wagons had arrived and a stream of boys began ferrying supplies of arrows to the archers on the riverbank.

Meanwhile in the hand-to-hand combat, the protagonists were now so bunched together that only rarely did anyone get a full swing with their sword. Japhses, however, managed to bring his sword down with full force on one of the Imperials. The Ma'hol soldier just managed to parry the blow in time with his own fat sword. Sparks flew as metal struck metal. Skilfully Japhses quickly twisted his wrist and aimed a sudden thrust at his enemy's throat. The other was caught off-balance and could not move in time. The sword severed his jugular and blood spurted from his throat as he collapsed to the ground.

It was an uneven contest and despite their best efforts, the ring of defenders slowly contracted and the Thyatirans advanced over the dead bodies of the Ma'hol.

"Just a matter of time now," remarked the squad leader James gleefully as he watched from the ridge.

Frank looked over at him and frowned. The speaker had not been expecting this reaction and wiped the smile from his face, adding, "Until all the enemy there are dead."

The Despot jumped to his feet and the other soldiers on the ridge, taken by surprise, scrambled up hurriedly.

"We must take prisoners, not slaughter them all!" he cried.

The puzzled expression on the squad leaders' faces told him all he needed to know. He quickly glanced over at the fighting and realised if he did not act straight away it would soon all be over.

"You!" he barked at James, "Get down there immediately and tell Japhses to disengage the men."

"B-but..."

"Move!"

The young man flew down the ridge towards the conflict as fast as his legs could carry him. In fact they almost ran away with him at one stage and he did well not to fall over. The Captain of the Guard was still in the thick of it and not an easy man to contact. Using his initiative James ran over to the man with the Kassiahorn and ordered him to sound the retreat.

Its shrill note could be heard even in the midst of the fighting. The Thyatirans in the thick of it, in spite of the onset of fatigue, groaned at the thought of having to give up their quarry. It then struck Japhses that this could mean another Ma'hol army was approaching from behind, so he began to pull back while shouting to those around him to disengage.

The fight continued in some quarters for a time, but gradually the Thyatirans extracted themselves and retreated to form a wider circle thirty or so metres away from the remaining huddle of battered and exhausted Ma'hol and the piles of bodies around them.

"Stay here," Frank ordered the other squad leader with his men on the ridge.

The horn kept on sounding as he made his way gingerly down the slope. A panting Japhses had just reached James and was starting to ask him what was going on when the Despot arrived. Frank was startled to see his Captain covered in blood and earnestly enquired whether he was hurt.

"I'm all right, but why sound the retreat? Have more enemy crossed upstream?"

"No they haven't."

The true answer to the question was that Frank simply could not bear to watch the slaughter any longer, but he gave an answer he hoped his listeners would find acceptable.

"I prefer to take these men prisoners, they will be more use to us alive than dead, especially with a few Imperials left. They can be held for ransom and the money distributed among our men."

He no longer had the telescope, but in the blur that the remaining Ma'hol were to him he thought he could make out some of the Imperials' plumes.

The opposing armies stood and stared at each other as a deadly hush descended on the battlefield. Apart from the groaning of the wounded, their conversation was the only sound to break the silence. Frank knew his future reputation hung in the balance and called down frantic, desperate prayers for help even as he spoke. He noticed Alan joining them as Japhses, his adrenaline still high, replied.

"But it's not like that here, My Lord, we don't take prisoners in this part of the world; it's a fight to the death!"

"What about the whites the Ma'hol have as slaves that I hear about then?"

'Nice one Francis!' he congratulated himself, "keep it up.'

"Ah yes, but that's different," Japhses faltered.

Frank pressed his advantage.

"No it isn't, we can take these men and hold them for an exchange of our own men."

He found himself speaking the thoughts that came into his head. Japhses was despairing though, he did not want to be seen arguing with his leader in front of the men, but he had to make him see sense.

"But they're not like that, My Lord. These Ma'hol would rather kill themselves than surrender, and even if they did the Mehtar would sooner see them rot than lose face in some sort of exchange."

"He's right," Alan chipped in.

"Well I'm going to bloody well try! Tell them that if they lay down their weapons and surrender they will not be harmed."

He had nailed his colours to the mast. Japhses and Alan glanced at each other, both knowing that there would be no further discussion. The latter volunteered to parley with the Ma'hol, he being one of only a few who knew their language.

The drone stepped forward and called out to the small group of survivors bunched up tightly together in their strange tongue. Silence returned when he finished speaking; the Ma'hol just stared at him. Japhses was starting to cool down now and became aware of the sticky blood congealing on his face. He tried wiping some of it off. Generally men were starting to get their breath back and began to feel their wounds. It would not be so easy to re-start the fight if the enemy did not heed the call to surrender.

Stepping back, Alan spoke softly to Frank.

"I told them what you said."

"Hmm thanks, I didn't really expect an immediate response."

Amid the groaning of the other wounded one Ma'hol kept calling out what sounded like, "Narfu, narfu...." Without any emotion Alan gave a translation.

"Calling out for his mother."

The temperature rose as the sun climbed higher. Men felt uncomfortable in their armour while the armies stood staring at each other. On the other side of the river the main Ma'hol army was equally as statuesque. A few Thyatirans began talking, but there was a deathly hush in the enemy ranks.

"Try again please, Alan."

Uncomplaining at doing something he felt unlikely to succeed the drone again went forward and called on them to surrender. The response, or rather the lack of it, was the same.

'Please Heavenly Father make them surrender!' thought Frank before he went to join Alan.

"Tell them I want no more bloodshed; if they throw down their weapons they will not be killed and we'll treat them well."

Alan's voice rang out once more, again to be met with a deafening silence.

Then it happened. After glancing both ways one skirmisher threw down his sword which landed with an undramatic thud on a small patch of ground between the bodies in front of him. A few others nearby followed, then to Frank's immense relief the rest followed suit. Only two Imperials were left standing, one of whom was their commander Menmahunate Sil. He tried to bring himself to stop his men from surrendering, but found himself unable to do so. He knew he was paying the price for his own folly and felt unable to call on them to sacrifice their lives needlessly when he had brought them to this end. He dropped his sword to the ground and the last few men around him followed suit. Their defeat was complete.

Huge cheers erupted from the victors.

"Well I never..." exclaimed an astonished Japhses who then went forward to join Frank and Alan.

The drone was equally surprised at the Ma'hol surrender.

"I'll be a blue-green one! Never thought they'd actually do it. Now what are we going to do?"

Frank ordered the Captain to get a squad to extract those Ma'hol who could still walk. The prisoners were herded a short way away and placed under guard where they were searched for any concealed weapons and ordered to take their armour off. Some of their captors took the opportunity to release them of any valuables they could find.

Meanwhile Laffaxe and his team began their work of tending the wounded. The physician set about the task with his usual abrupt efficiency. There were comparatively few Thyatiran casualties and once these were attended to they began seeing if there were any of the Ma'hol wounded who could be saved.

The remainder of the would-be invasion force were still rooted on the far river bank, watching events unfold. They were still mainly standing in silence, although some started shouting obscenities across the river. Scores of them had left the scene while the conflict was still in progress, now more and more turned away. They left the battlefield in at least as disorganised a state as they had arrived. Soon the last of them had departed with their wagons in tow.

A few Thyatirans suggested they be pursued, but found little support for the idea. Some cheered their departure, however the Captain warned Frank that the war had only just begun.

"This has earned us a breathing space, My Lord, but we will still need the reinforcements from Bynar and Aggeparii for when the fighting really starts."

While the Despot went over to Laffaxe, Japhses continued talking to Alan, saying, "I don't like to say "I told you so", but I did warn of the dangers of an indecisive battle. The majority of their army is still in tact and we don't know where they will strike next."

Alan raised his eyebrows.

"They don't look like they could strike a rabbit right now! Their morale's been shattered."

"Ah, but where is their main army? These were only inferior troops. Put it this way, we'll have to remain on our guard and I'd like to get some effective reconnaissance going. With the Despot's blessing I'd like to send some scouts into Rabeth."

"What about the islands?" Alan then asked, "After all they were the original reason for us being here."

Japhses looked upstream towards Telar and waved some flies away from his face.

"Damn things! The enemy still hold them as far as I know, but the latest report I've had said there was no visible activity on them. The channel's deep on our side; the current there's strong and will be a lot worse after the rain we've had. We can't attempt to land there until the water level goes down."

Frank finished seeing Laffaxe and came over for a meeting with his lieutenants. It was agreed the army would tent down a short way back from the river. First they would have to do a body count. The stripping and burying of the dead was a high priority in the heat, but would take at least a couple of days. Frank would not agree with the prisoners helping with this because he wanted to get them away from the border area. For the same reason their interrogation would have to wait. Instead he ordered that those who could walk be taken under guard back to the Castle straight away. After overhearing some soldiers laughing at the hostile reception these captives would receive as they were processed through the Upper Village, he insisted the escort was directed along a cross-country route away from habitation. It would serve no purpose to have them humiliated any further. Japhses shrugged his shoulders, he was beginning to accept that his foreign despot possessed a strange compassionate streak.

Frank was himself quite keen to get back to the relative comfort of the Castle. The sight of a man having his arm amputated by some of Laffaxe's aides had made him feel nauseous too. He just wanted to get away for now and opted to go with the prisoners and their escort. Japhses did not mind, because he would be left in charge of the army. The Captain felt his pride fully restored now, thanks to the day's events.

Alan decided to stay and helped carry the movable wounded into the wagons to be taken to the Upper Village.

A sizeable escort made up chiefly of militia was organised for the prisoners who had their hands tied together. Frank requested of Japhses that the squad leader James be in charge. An interpreter named Falla, a militiaman, was also arranged. A couple of soldiers assisted the Despot in taking off his armour before they left. It was loaded onto a couple of dakks.

The Ma'hol deemed fit enough to make the journey were counted, then they were marched off eastwards. There were thirty-three including the Mehtar's son and one other member of the Imperial Guard. Menmahuna Sil looked a broken man as he shuffled along, face down with the other captives. He turned down Frank's offer of a dakk for part of the journey.

Once the column had left the battlefield, Japhses felt free to organise things as he wanted. Everyone was kept busy: a fortified camp was to be constructed, patrols set up and the dead to be seen to amongst other tasks. The men were quite relieved when a meal-break came.

Soon after setting off Frank realised how his jaw was aching from him clamping his teeth together for long period to stop them from chattering earlier in the day. James seemed to be on a high after finding he had survived the battle, not disappointed at all that he had not in fact laid a blow during the conflict. He chatted away incessantly, even to the point of admitting he had fouled himself at one stage of the proceedings.

Fortunately for Frank the squad leader was soon having to see that his men stayed in line and that there were no stragglers.

'Well, Francis, you survived the opening move of the war,' he pondered now that he was left to his own thoughts. 'They'll be more wary next time. It wasn't really a proper battle, more a skirmish, hardly lasted any time...'

He looked up at the sun and took a drink of water from an animal-skin water bottle. It was lovely to feel unrestricted out of all that armour.

'To think it's still only morning, it seems like a fortnight ago I got out of bed... I wonder what our casualties were. Is there anyone I know dead or badly hurt? Saul, Gideon, the miner triplets? Why didn't I find out earlier?

'I hope Japhses is wrong about the value of these prisoners – surely the Mehtar's son...'

He focused on a middle-aged militiaman walking beside him minding his own business.

"I say, has the Mehtar got any other sons apart from this one?"

The man was taken by surprise and spluttered a response.

"Um er, I'm sorry, My Lord I have no idea, My Lord."

"Oh well never mind."

The journey was uneventful. The militiamen were in good spirits and sang psalms as they went:

"We neither trust in our bows
Nor in our swords to save us,
But you have saved us from our enemies
And defeated those who hate us.
We will always praise you
And give thanks to you for ever."

The route chosen took them well to the north of the Upper Village. It passed through some rugged countryside where some of the walking-wounded prisoners struggled. A few were helped along by their comrades. Their demoralised state and the presence of so many armed militia ensured no one attempted an escape. The interpreter did not find his services called upon during the journey.

Eventually they hit the track leading to Ladosa and turned south towards the Castle. It was mid-afternoon and Frank had long got over his nausea, but his feet were beginning to ache.

Messengers were sent on ahead to announce their coming and a delegation led by Natias came out a short distance to greet them.

"My Lawd, a splendid victowy I hear, congwatulations. Now the islands are secure again!"

Frank was tired, but managed a smile.

"Thank you, Natias. It seems ages ago I last saw you. Yes the way has been cleared to re-take the islands, but the Ma'hol will probably have another fling according to Japhses. Any news of our allies?"

"The weinforcements? Not a thing, My Lawd. Glad to hear Japhses is well though."

The other was glad that their little feud had been forgotten. Together they walked back for the final few hundred metres.

The remaining Castle population turned out in its entirety to cheer their triumphant Despot and accompanying troops. They seemed relieved as much as pleased at the news of an easy victory and their attitude towards the Ma'hol was more one of curiosity than anything else.

It was immediately apparent that there was insufficient space in the dungeons for them to go there. Besides Frank intensely disliked having to leave anyone languishing in the depths of the Castle and had a long-term plan to build an alternative jail. So the foreign captives were herded into an area within the bailey which was hurriedly cordoned off.

"Not him," Frank declared indicating towards Sil, "Bring him here. Where's Falla?"

"Here My Lord."

The interpreter shuffled towards him while the Mehtar's son was brought over.

"Please tell him that he will be held in a separate room more fitting for his status. Meanwhile his men will be handled humanely."

Sil's face was emotionless as the message was conveyed. His long red hair was windswept and tangled. Blood had congealed from a small cut on his cheek. Being above average height he looked down morosely at the shorter Frank, who estimated his age to be around twenty-three earth years.

The young man had nothing to say in reply, he just stood there utterly dejected. His shoulders were slumped and out of his armour he cut a somewhat pathetic figure compared with the warrior leader he had been earlier that day.

"All right," Frank said to a couple of militiamen, "Take him with one of the castle guard to Adrian's room and... you there, Jonathan isn't it?"

The squad leader ran from the bottom of the keep steps, three of his soldiers in tow.

"Yes, My Lord, how can I help?"

"This prisoner is the Mehtar's son. It is most important that he be kept safe and well. Take him with your men to Adrian's room. It may need some tidying up first, these militiamen will help.

"Now I don't need to emphasise the importance of keeping this man secure do I? I want at least three guards at his door at all times and to check that he is all right at regular intervals. Falla here will act as translator. Any problems come to me straight away, is that understood?"

"Yes, My Lord."

"Good. Now until Alan returns I want you, Falla, to stay here at the Castle. I think the room next to where Sil is going to be put will be free, have a word with Natias."

The place was busy once more. He turned again to Jonathan while women, stable-hands and militiamen hurried by in all directions.

"Right off you go... oh wait a moment. Did you tidy that roof up? I never got to check it last night."

"Yes, My Lord, all is in order now."

"Fine."

They left with their charges. Amid all the activity Natias' wife Eko went by carrying a bucket of water. As she passed she called out, "Blessings upon you, My Lord, for bringing us victory over the heathens! I always told them you could do it."

Frank thanked her as she went on her way, then told himself off for accepting praise which he felt he did not rightfully deserve.

Natias appeared again and said there were no spare tents for the prisoners and only a couple of awnings available. He had sent to the New Village site to see if any could be borrowed from there.

"...And another thing: James told me he wants to start intewegating the pwisoners as soon as possible – Japhses' orders. He will need Falla for that."

"I'm sure he can do that when he's finished helping get Sil established in his room if you can't find anyone else.

"But tell James I don't want the prisoners mishandled at all – he will be held personally responsible."

"I will make that cwystal clear to him, My Lawd."

"Good; and please organise some food and water for them."

"Alweady done My Lawd. Does our victowy mean we can welease the Sarnician?"

"Oh what the informer? I'd forgotten about him. Yes certainly. He was right with his information, give him a big reward."

"Two hundwed and fifty stens was the sum agweed I believe, My Lawd."

"Of course, not like you to forget something like that."

That evening Frank had a hot bath in his suite. As he lay there in the tub soaking his aching body he decided not to worry as to the future outcome of the war, tomorrow would look after itself.

Instead his mind wondered to a story he had heard as a boy, about a doomed planet during the Second Inter-Galactic War, the year 2277 to be precise, always an easy date to remember. The planet only had limited numbers of spaceships with which to evacuate the people and although it was nowhere near the fighting at that time, none of the other solar systems agreed to spare craft to help. As a result only about ten per cent of the population could be saved. So what did they do, save the brilliant scientists, artists, or even their leaders? No, because their philosophy was one of 'equality' they held a lottery! They must have been a society drunk on gambling! There were various prizes, from a single passage up to the top prize of being able to take a hundred people (ninety-nine plus oneself) of one's choice on the ships away from the impending cataclysm.

So instead of carefully picked people of the right age and abilities, who went? All sorts: the old and infirm, delinquents, prostitutes and sexual deviants, magicians and fortune tellers plus other dregs of society!

No wonder the whole operation was a disaster with some ships either hijacked or destroyed in rioting. No wonder so many of the ships that did get off were turned away by planet after planet who wanted nothing to do with a band of wandering undesirables. Those who did make it to other worlds had little to offer their new homes...

What foolish people! A well-ordered society is an unequal one in which people know their place, like the blacks and whites here.'

In his evening prayers he thanked God for the victory and for his men's preservation. It did not occur to him that night to offer thanks for being born with dark hair.

⪥⪤

CHAPTER FIFTEEN

The Mehtar's palace in Krabel-Haan, capital of Rabeth-Mephar, was the architectural wonder of his country. It stood on an artificial mound in the centre of the city, dominating the scene. Built almost entirely of white marble, its rounded features and soaring towers made it a wondrous sight. When Alan had visited the country for the first time he could not help contrasting this sophisticated structure with the stark, functional, stone castles of Hoame.

Within the outer wall the colonnades and small temples had skilfully carved designs in coloured marble. Immaculately-kept herb gardens, with slaves in attendance, bordered the walkways. The panelled rooms were inlaid with gold and silver motifs while rich frescos covered the ceilings. There were several courtyards within the complex, the largest of which covered four hectares. Within this fountains played, shooting up different coloured water jets towards the pale sky.

Leading from this courtyard was the Phalabine or main hall. The Phalabine was the focal point of the palace, a long rectangular room where the Mehtar's court convened. It was breathtaking in its magnificence, with high ceiling, tall crystal windows and intricately patterned walls of gold leaf inlaid with semi-precious stones. At one end the floor was raised by several steps to form a stage, upon which the absolute ruler sat on his golden throne looking down on his assembled courtiers. The main body of the Phalabine was unusually packed with people for the important meeting currently taking place. Imperial Guardsmen stood at regular intervals along an aisle down the middle of the hall. This area was devoid of people apart from one lonely man.

The Prime Minister's world had collapsed in ruins around him the last few days. He knew his life depended on his current speech and it was not going well on this hot afternoon. It was rare for the Mehtar to be moved to anger, but right now he looked more furious than the Prime Minister had ever seen him.

Mehtar Arumah-Ru sat bolt upright on his throne. Dressed in the most exquisite silks and sporting a green turban, he did not move a muscle. He was usually a man of few words and, on this occasion was listening without responding. However, to observers he seemed about to explode at any moment! He sat frowning down at the orator, white knuckles gripping the throne's jewel-encrusted arms. The slightly smaller seat to his left was currently unoccupied, while a large fan suspended from the ceiling was being operated rhythmically by a burly slave on the edge of the stage. It was going to take more than that to cool his master down.

"...And and so I w-was deliberately kept in the dark by the conspirators, Oh Glorious One."

As the Prime Minister spoke he glanced at the third person on the stage. The small bundle near the Mehtar's right foot was Rorka the fool. An opportune word or two from that deformed creature might save his life, but Rorka was silent.

'I've deliberately tried to keep on the right side of him all these years,' thought the desperate man, 'Now he just sits there sucking a dried root!'

His speech was interrupted by the arrival in the Phalabine of the Mehtar's favourite wife.

"Her Effulgent Majesty Shalara'tu!" rang the announcement as the most powerful woman in Rabeth-Mephar swept into the room, head held high. She floated down the aisle, female hand-slave in tow.

All the courtiers bowed low as she passed. Making a point of ignoring the Prime Minister, the tall slim figure instead put her hand to an attendant who escorted her to the vacant throne. Once seated she enquired of her husband how the proceedings were going.

"Our Prime Minister is just telling us how he was kept ignorant of all that was going on, weren't you, Prime Minister?"

"Um, that I was the victim of a conspiracy Oh Shining One."

Shalara'tu had never been keen on this man and knew this day held a good opportunity to get rid of him and clear the way for someone she preferred. She let the man continue his vain attempt to extricate himself from his impossible position for a while longer before butting in.

"Let us execute him, he has failed badly and made us look foolish and ineffective."

"And the unit commander?"

"Surely beloved there can be no doubt, they have asked for death." Her voice changed to a whisper as she leant across to her husband, "People laugh at you because of what they did!"

The Mehtar did not move, his face set like flint. There was a deathly hush in the room as his courtiers waited for his judgement. Were the years of the Prime Minister's loyal service not to be held to his credit? Had Shalara'tu made her move too early? He began slowly, his voice one of measured control.

"Bring the unit commanders in."

A sorry group of around ten men were led silently in, their eyes to the ground. They were all dressed alike in brown sackcloth. Imperial Guard lined them up with the Prime Minister in front of the thrones. Once they were assembled their ruler continued.

"So these are my renegade commanders, this pathetic rabble. By Vorg, your bungling perfidiousness has ruined everything! How can any of..."

"Blaming others for your own indulgence!"

A high-pitched voice had cut into the air like a knife. Some courtiers gasped, others visibly shrank and tried to make themselves smaller. The atmosphere was electric, a pin dropping would have deafened. Such a dissenting heckle would mean instant death to anyone. Anyone that is except one person.

"If you had not given your son so much free-rein," continued Rorka in the same tone, "none of this would have happened."

In a supreme effort of self-control the Mehtar checked his temper.

"One more word out of you fool; no, one more letter, and your tongue will be fed to the frasses!"

He hesitated to take in breath. As he did so he nodded to himself and a wry smile broke out on his face for a brief moment. His wife opened her mouth to speak, but the Mehtar resumed first.

"Ha! As usual around here the fool makes more sense than anyone."

He pursed his lips and expelled some air slowly.

"I am too angry to be sure of a just sentence now; lock them up so I can pass judgement when my mind is clear."

He waived his hand and the men were led off, including the Prime Minister, grateful for a temporary reprieve at least.

Shalara'tu lent across and hissed, "You are too lenient, my husband, they…"

"Quiet."

He silenced her with one word as he watched the men led out of the Phalabine. His tone then mellowed a fraction.

"There is no wisdom in a judgement in the heat of the moment."

Rorka's barbs had hit their target he knew; and not for the first time.

He thought, 'That pile of rags has far more sense than the rest of my obsequious councillors put together. Fool? He is not the fool.'

"Oh Glorious One!"

The speaker was an Imperial Officer. A nod from the Mehtar told him to continue.

"A messenger has just arrived from the barbarians. He is one of our men, a prisoner freed with a proposal from their leader."

"A day full of surprises! Escort him to the annex; we will see him there in private.

"Well my dear," he continued to his wife who was still frowning from not getting her own ambitious way, "let us go and see what this unheralded herald has to say. We certainly cannot complain that life is dull at present."

Some days earlier, on the evening of the day of battle, the Thyatirans finished the body count. On top of those drowned and swept away in the swollen river there were forty-three dead Ma'hol left in the field. Fifty-four had been taken prisoner, of which over a third were badly wounded. Some of these would be added to the final death toll in the coming days.

By comparison, Thyatiran casualties were very light: seven dead and sixteen men with serious wounds. After his immediate work on the battlefield Laffaxe set up a temporary hospital in the community hut of the Upper Village. As Ma'hol wounded recovered enough to be moved, they were escorted to their comrades held prisoner at the Castle.

There was no more rain for the time being and the water level fell rapidly. Allowing an easy crossing to the islands. As suspected, they found them deserted and so, ironically, were re-taken without a fight. In fact there was no sign at all of the Ma'hol, in spite of short-range reconnaissance into Rabeth-Mephar itself.

One evening, Japhses was standing on the edge of their camp, a kilometre from the river. The area had been declared a "military zone" and villagers who were not actual militiamen were not allowed to go near there for now. The mid-summer sky was still light and the birds were singing their final chorus before going to sleep. Alan was sitting nearby on a barrel with a dagger in his hand. He felt its point of balance before throwing it up and catching it several times.

"Fine work of art this," he commented, "better than anything we could make."

"Yes," agreed Japhses as he stifled a yawn.

"And those Imperials' breastplates are quite something – interesting to see them close too."

No reply.

"Something on your mind?" the drone asked.

"Sorry, Alan, I was just thinking about the patrols. I fancy sending one deeper into Rabeth, bring back a prisoner if possible – find out what's going on. It's all too quiet for my liking."

"Good idea; why not let Rodd lead it? He did well in the fight."

"So everyone keeps telling me," the big man looked annoyed. "I'll say one thing for Rodd: he must have lots of friends, they keep on putting in 'good words' to me about him."

"Give him a chance then, no one's going to be more motivated to succeed. He's desperate to get back into your good books."

Japhses shrugged and scratched his forehead where his cross tattoo was.

"Okay, but I'll send some more experienced men with him. Nobody will be happier to see the boy succeed in this more than I will be."

Eleazar, meanwhile, had been given the unenviable job of informing the next of kin of the death of their loved ones. He had one last visit to make, but he suspected it would be the most difficult. Growing up in the Lower Village the priest's assistant did not know Katrina at all well. He had been introduced to her at one gathering and met briefly at a religious festival earlier that year, but they had never held a proper conversation. Now he was on his way to tell the unfortunate woman her husband had been killed.

Tales about Katrina were rife: she had some drone's blood in her, she practised witchcraft... just about every slander that could be levelled had been. Eleazar did not like being party to gossip, but he could not fail to overhear certain stories. He tried to blot them from his mind, but it was with trepidation that he approached.

She was at the side of her hut chopping wood for kindling with a hatchet. Putting his trust in God, Eleazar took a deep breath and went up close.

"Good day Katrina. Eleazar, we've met before..." he paused briefly as she suspended her work and raised her head, before continuing, "I wonder if I may have a word with you in private."

"If you like," she replied, no expression in her gruff voice. Hatchet in hand, she walked to the hut entrance.

Eleazar had to lower his head to avoid hitting the lintel. There was relatively good furniture in the living space: wooden frame chairs, a solid chest. From the ceiling hung a lantern and a small wire cage housing a little grey bird, silent in its confinement.

Once settled, and nothing more having been said, she looked straight at him expecting him to proceed. Eleazar felt this woman would not appreciate a roundabout approach, so he tried to be as direct as he could.

"I have come from the river where the battle has just been fought. Now all the...er, casualties have been identified I've been asked to go round the relatives...I'm afraid there is some terrible news..."

Unlike the others he had visited there was no feedback whatsoever. Her face was not blank, she was taking it all in, but she was not making it at all easy for him. He would have to come straight out with it.

"...Your husband has been killed."

Silence, then, "Are you certain it was him?"

"I'm afraid so."

"There couldn't be any mistake."

"No, there is no doubt. They were..."

"Good."

The woman's voice had such a ring of triumph there was no mistaking what she meant, even so Eleazar found himself asking, "I'm sorry?"

"I said "good"," she stared right at him, "that's the best thing that's ever happened to me."

He had been warned that Katrina was unconventional, but he was taken aback by this response. 'Even if she means it,' he thought, 'she shouldn't say it out loud.' He spluttered, "Um, er, surely we should not, I mean we should be more charitable towards..."

"Forget the sermon, I don't need it," she interrupted. Her tone was not aggressive, but she just did not want words wasted on what she should say or feel about her now dead husband. 'What empty words these priests use,' she thought looking at the young man squirming in his seat, 'I hated his guts and am delighted he is dead – that's all there is to it. They can condemn me for many things, but hypocrisy is not among them.'

Eleazar's worst nightmares were coming true; he wondered how the situation might be redeemed. In a token effort he suggested they might pray together for Hatt's soul. Once more she turned him down, again with a note of confidence which did not require aggression. Then just as he began praying in his head to be a thousand kilometres away she offered him a drink.

By the time she handed him a cup of refreshing practil juice he had had a chance to collect his thoughts. About the only conclusion he had reached was to tell Zadok as little as possible about this encounter. This was reinforced when Katrina sat back down and announced in a matter-of -fact way that she had no confidence in priests.

"No priest has ever done anything to help me in my life," adding with fire, "I won't need help now. I'm going to leave here and make a fresh start, nothing here to make me stay!"

A metamorphosis had occurred, she had suddenly discovered she possessed wings and could fly. Leaving him fumbling for a reply she excitedly shared the possibilities her new found freedom bought.

"Hanson's been sniffing over this place for some time now, but Hatt wouldn't sell to him – that'll please the neighbours, she added ironically. "I'll go to Aggeparii, I'll have enough money to look after myself. You won't ever see me again."

The priest's assistant managed to mumble something incoherent. On the one hand he could not condone her being so happy at the death of her husband, nor her anti-clerical remarks, but he knew something of the woman's sufferings and felt a welling-up of pity for her. In his heart of hearts he hoped she would find a better life in Aggeparii, or wherever she ended up. He would tell no one the details of this meeting, how Katrina reacted to the news he had brought. It would only fuel the gossip against her. He concluded that some good prayers were called for: requests to God that something good would come from all this, that this really would be a new and better beginning in her life. After all, he knew God worked in ways no man could fathom.

He was still musing when, without warning, she shot out of her chair and strode up to the bird cage.

"I've been wanting to do this for a long time!"

Rough fingers fumbled for a moment before the cage door opened. The bird hopped up onto the perch, took one jump to the door, then was off. Tiny wings flapping franticly it flew quickly out of the open doorway, chattering as it went.

"There you little bastard," Katrina said watching it disappear, and don't let yourself get caught again!"

Back at the Castle there was rising uncertainty in the days following the battle. There was still no news of the hoped-for reinforcements and the reports from Japhses told of an enemy that had evaporated. The interrogation of the prisoners was handled by the guard squad leaders, James and Jonathan. Restrained from using violence or threats by the Despot they found the Ma'hol either too stubborn or too afraid to talk.

The Mehtar's son appeared to be in a deep depression, staring out his window all day and eating very little. Frank tried questioning him through an interpreter, but could not get a word out of him.

Then on the fourth day two events happened to make the situation somewhat clearer. The first was a breakthrough with

The Keepers of Hoame

the interrogations. Whether threats or violence were used Frank was never informed, he was just grateful to hear they were talking at last. Once one had told the story it was quickly corroborated by others. A picture was soon built up which helped to explain some of the bizarre events on the day of the battle.

It first of all transpired that Sil was in fact the Mehtar's eldest son. For some time he had been a member of the party advocating more radical action against the Thyatirans in the three islands dispute. His father had been uncharacteristically lax in dealing with these dissenting voices, because his cherished son was involved. Encouraged by this, it was a group of Sil's army supporters that had executed the coup of taking the islands when Rodd had been in command of the garrison.

Drunk on this success and the Mehtar's inaction they plotted a far more ambitious project behind his back: the lightning conquest of Thyatira itself before the rest of Hoame could come to their aid. When the ruler went on a visit to another part of his domain Sil and the other leading conspirators seized the opportunity and hastily assembled an army. The plan was to have a successful conquest as a fait accompli by the time the Mehtar returned, so he would be delighted at his heir's triumph and daring.

That was when things started to go disastrously wrong. Certain unit commanders refused to go along with the unauthorised venture and the force which did set out was lop-sided in its make-up, having very few Imperial Guard and being almost devoid of archers. The boats intended to help for a fast crossing never turned up, while there were unforeseen delays in assembling the various army units which did eventually march out of Krabel-Haan.

In the rush to catch up on the time-table reconnaissance had been all but forgotten. The interrogators were alarmed, however, when it was claimed that shortly before the invasion one pair of scouts had crossed the river and got as far as the Upper Village without being detected. They had reported back to their commander that there was no sign of military activity.

Some units had gone along under protest and it appeared that this was the cause of the internal fighting witnessed in the Ma'hol ranks during the battle. All in all not a lot had gone right for them. It had been such a comedy of errors that Frank found he was starting to feel sorry for them until he reminded himself what their aim had been.

The second event that helped illumine the situation a bit was the return of the envoy sent to Bynar. He came empty-handed, saying the despot there had turned down the request for reinforcements. Frank and Natias interviewed the messenger in the privacy of the Throne Room.

"On what gwounds?" snapped the steward.

"He said he was not prepared to commit his troops on the strength of a white envoy sir. He wanted a black."

"Did you explain we have no black families here, only our despot?"

"Yes sir, but I don't think he believed me. He seemed very preoccupied and worried about something. I tried my hardest, but I just couldn't get through to him."

"I will give him preoccupied! Here we are fighting for our vewy existence... I am sowwy My Lawd, I should not speak about a black so, but..."

"Perfectly all right!" replied Frank before addressing the messenger, "but why did you take so long? I've been told you could've been there and back three times in the time it took you."

"I was kept waiting for days before I could get to see Despot Hista, My Lord. No one would take me seriously because I am a white! I tried my best, I really did."

"Oh well it can't be helped now. Do you know what has happened to the envoy we sent to Aggeparii? We haven't heard from him either."

The message gave a negative answer and was dismissed.

"Well, Natias I wish I knew where all this leaves us. How is this Mehtar going to react when he gets back, lead his whole army against us? From what we've learned he wasn't in favour of a war to start with, but he might feel committed now."

"He would be wishing his son's life away."

"Of course, but he still might. What I want to do is send a conciliatory note saying we'll let him have his men back in return for the settlement of the border dispute in our favour and a peace pact.

"I suppose we'll leave the question of the reinforcements for now, but I wish I knew what our Aggeparii envoy is up to. I wish Alan was here."

"I shall send for him if you like, My Lawd. I do not pwofess to know a gweat deal about international diplomacy, but people say the best way to deal with the Ma'hol is to be tough. I'm not so sure of the wisdom of that wight now.... but I would have thought if we are sending one... the sooner we get a conciliatory message there the better."

"You're right, we won't delay. We can compose something and get a note sent today. In the meantime yes, please do send for Alan, I need him here. We'll send one of the prisoners with our message; I don't want to risk one of our own men."

"Fwom what I have heard fwom Jonathan they could be too fwightened to weturn."

"The lure of freedom must help surely; anyway we won't give him any option."

Together they drafted a letter which they hoped struck the right balance between offering peace on the one hand and showing firmness on the other. A prisoner was given his instructions and escorted across the border. Now all they could do was sit back and hope the message would get to its destination and be well received.

Next morning, Frank felt restless and took a walk by himself just outside the Castle wall. The bee-keepers were inspecting their hives while the grass was being cut by a team of women. Already quite warm, it was going to be another hot day.

Just then a lone figure came down the road from the Upper Village. Eleazar the priest's assistant was wearing a light grey habit and walked barefoot along the hard road.

"Good morning, My Lord, is everything well?"

"Fine," replied the Despot unthinkingly, "but I haven't seen you around lately. Your absence was noted when Zadok led the thanksgiving prayers here the day before yesterday."

The young man suddenly looked uncomfortable.

"No, My Lord, I chose not to be there."

"Oh, why was that?"

Eleazar hesitated a moment before asking, "May I talk frankly, My Lord?"

"Of course, please do."

"Between just ourselves, My Lord, my mentor and I do not quite see eye-to-eye on the whole question of war."

"Oh?"

"I'm sorry, My Lord, I do not wish to presume to push my views forward, for I do not think you would agree with them."

Frank laughed.

"Where I come from, the youth do nothing but push their opinions forward! They don't give a damn for their elders with more experience; they despise the older generation rather than respect it. It's rather funny to hear one afraid to speak his mind for fear of upsetting me. No, Eleazar, if you've got a strongly-held view you argue your case, I'll respect you for it."

So Eleazar began his apology.

"It is just that Zadok and I cannot agree about this war, or about any war actually. He says that we are morally right to fight if our cause is just. I cannot believe that that is true. I believe that as Christians we should try to put into practise what The Christ taught in the Sermon on the Mount. He was not talking figuratively when he said "Love your enemy". He didn't say, "Love your enemy until you feel threatened."

"Yes, but is it practical?"

"It was practical enough for The Christ. When He was himself threatened and beaten he did exactly what he preached. He set the example for us all."

"All right, in individual cases yes, but if we all took that line an aggressor – say the Ma'hol in this instance – could just walk in and take us all over. Then the Christians would be taken over by the heathens and the cause of Right would hardly be advanced."

"Ah but My Lord, if I may say so the "if everybody did it" argument is self-defeating, because if *everyone* chose not to *fight* – the Ma'hol and ourselves – then there could be no war."

"But why would the Ma'hol chose not to fight? They are not believers and as far as I know don't have any injunction to turn the other cheek. To advocate pacifism in these circumstances is to bring what could be unnecessary suffering on the women and children because the men chose not to fight the aggressor. Surely that is not acting responsibly."

Eleazar was trying to collect his thoughts and did not respond immediately, so Frank continued, but this time on a lighter note.

"Listen, Christians have been arguing this one for thousands of years. We're not going to settle it in a morning. I know how you feel, no Christian enjoys the idea of war..."

As he spoke he remembered the excited, eager, smiling faces in the Upper Village when the army had marched to war. He dismissed the image.

"...But sometimes we have to fight to prevent a greater evil. Life would be so easy if it was always a choice between good and bad (though all too often we choose the bad even then!), but God tests us by putting us in a situation where the choice is between two evils.

"During the Third War there were Charkons who were annihilating whole populations with impunity. Had the allies not got together to stop them they would have wiped the whole Web System out. I've been drawn to pacifism myself, but that incident convinced me that sometimes, not always by any means, it is right to take up arms against a foe."

There was a pause before Eleazar asked, "Were there many black Christians where you came from, My Lord?"

"Yes there were, or *are* I should say."

"Do none of them have crosses on their foreheads?"

"No that's not our way."

"Do you have speaking in tongues like in the time of the Early Church?"

"Not where I was, but I did meet other believers who claimed to do so, although I never witnessed it myself. What about here?"

"We have increasingly been blessed with the gift of tongues My Lord. The Spirit has seen fit to give me the gift of interpretation at some of our meetings, although I am not worthy."

"Who is?" replied Frank in a matter-of-fact tone of voice before asking another question. "How are you getting on with Zadok teaching you the scriptures, is that going well?"

"We have taken a break from that for the time being. Instead we are going through the legends of how the Hoamen first arrived here. It is hard work remembering it all."

"Now that does sound interesting!"

Before he had time to say any more a voice nearby called out a greeting. Looking up he saw Alan riding a dakk.

"Hi there, I hope you've been missing me."

"Hello, Alan, I'm glad you've returned."

Alan grinned.

"Hi there Eleazar; see, I'm only away a few days and he misses me. Hey Frank, can we go inside? I need a drink."

He jumped down from the animal and the priest's assistant said he had better be on his way as he had some bereaved parents to re-visit. Before he took the fork to the courtyard entrance, he left a statement with his Despot.

"Thank you for our talk, My Lord. It was interesting, but I cannot say you have convinced me you are right."

"I see," was all the response a surprised Frank could think of making at the time.

"What was that all about?"

"Oh nothing. Tell me how's it going at the camp. Any sign of more enemy yet?"

"None at all," Alan replied as they began making for the main Castle entrance, "we thought it was too quiet until yesterday when we heard what your interrogations had come up with. All very revealing."

"Wanted to keep you informed. What do you make of it though?"

"Hard to say."

They acknowledged the guardsmen at the gate. Alan continued.

"The Mehtar's not usually one for taking rash decisions. Mind you, if he's away like they said, he might not even know what has happened yet. Some of the conspirators could have got hold of the messenger, 'cos it's not in their interests to calm things down. Or the man might have got second thoughts about delivering it; we won't know for a while."

"Great! That makes me feel really good hearing that."

Crossing the bailey they passed the Ma'hol prisoners who were being served a meal by the guards. They stood sullenly in line, each waiting his turn – bowl in one hand, spoon in the other. One or two looked around nervously, but most just stared ahead. Their eyes told of men with broken spirits, fearing for their fate.

Frank said, "How strange they always eat standing up."

"Yeah."

"They spend quite a lot of time prostrating themselves and praying to their god. Keeps them out of mischief; in fact they're no bother really."

The pair continued their conversation as they went up the stairs and entered the hall where Alan was given the drink he needed.

"Where's Natias?" he asked Frank, "and where's my favourite Illianeth?"

"Not sure. Natias has been keeping things running with precision as usual (we've needed a lot of extra supplies with all the prisoners); don't know what I'd do without him.

"As for Illianeth, she's in disgrace again I'm afraid. She's been shirking off her work lately and Natias had to have another word with her. Can't seem to stay out of trouble that girl. In answer to your question, I don't know where she is right now.

"Let's go up to my rooms, it's more comfortable there."

Once established in the finer surroundings of the Despot's suite, Alan returned to the subject of the prisoners of war.

"I think I should tell you that there are grumblings amongst the whites about the fact the Ma'hol are in tents while their own prisoner are still in the old jail in the basement."

"That's not fair," began the other defensively. "There are currently only three men held in jail and Crag's under instructions to let them out under escort twice a day now, so they get some fresh air and light. Besides, there isn't enough room down there for all the Ma'hol to go."

"Yeah I agree, but I just thought you should know what people are saying."

"I'd like to see them come and run things better!"

Frank was clearly stung by the criticism. He sat and mumbled to himself. The drone offered some friendly advice.

"You should realise in a position of power, you'll never please everyone. Whatever you do you will upset someone! Besides, you are right not to have "pleasing people" as your top priority: you do what you think's best. Not that you shouldn't listen to advice, of course, but whining complaints never helped anyone. For what it's worth I can't see how you've got any option right now but to do what you're doing."

"I am hoping to get a more humane jail constructed anyway."

"Sure, don't worry about it."

Frank ran his fingers over the carved pattern on the armrest of his chair.

'What right had those critics to say those things?' he thought. 'At least Alan understands the problems.'

Brightened by his companion's support he said, "At least we've learned one very useful thing: Sil's the Mehtar's eldest son and heir; that must increase his value."

"I could've told you that. He's got another son and five daughters."

"Five daughters?"

"Yeah, not very many for a man with three wives. The daughters are all younger than Sil... how is he by the way?"

"Still as sullen and uncommunicative as ever. At least he's eating rather better now. He is going to be the key to all this; I hope so anyway."

"The soldiers are expecting a large ransom to be paid for him so they can all have a reward."

Frank was surprised.

"That's not my intention. I just want to bring peace to the country so we can get back to normal. Plus get back the white prisoners held by the Ma'hol."

Alan considered pointing out this would not be as popular as the money with the guard and militia, but remembering the touchy mood the Despot was in he picked up another point.

"Some of the whites held by them are second or third generation captives. They've never known anything else and have never set foot in Hoame."

Frank was warming to this theme and sat on the edge of his chair with an excited expression.

"Really? How marvellous, it'll be like the Children of Israel coming out of bondage in Egypt. They'll know freedom for the very first time! How many of them are there?"

"No idea, not very many. I wouldn't get too carried away thought Frank, we haven't even had a response from the Mehtar yet, for all we know he's probably leading an army against us right now."

"Hmm I suppose you're right. Yes, I must keep my feet on the ground. I'm just hoping that because this initial battle didn't have his official sanction that he himself doesn't want a war."

There was a time of silence before he continued.

"You know it's funny, when I was on my way here, Offa told me Ladosa was the country to beware of. I find myself at war with my other foreign neighbour!"

"We haven't heard anything out of Laodicia for ages, which is probably just as well, 'cos they're a pretty rotten lot. They're usually too divided to cause us trouble to tell the truth, but it's best to be on our guard I guess."

"What about the reinforcements from Aggeparii though, do you think we should press for them?"

Alan finished his drink before answering positively.

"Dead right, we well might still need them. I don't know what Despot Kagel of Bynar's up to either, but then he can be exasperating at times. I wouldn't put it past him not to agree to send their army 'cos he doesn't know you, but at least you'd have thought he'd let us know. I don't know what he thinks he's doing holding on to our envoy like this.

"Both Kagel and Hista's reactions have been unforgivable; we're part of the same country for pity's sake! Thyatira may be small compared with them, but strategically it's very important.

"If you want to send someone who'll carry more clout than a white, you can send me if you want, I've met the Kagels."

The offer was tempting, but Frank needed his confidant with him.

"Thanks, but no. I think I'll send another white messenger. I can't say I'm over-impressed with the level of cooperation between the despotates, strikes me it's non-existent!"

"Hooray! Good old Bodd," exclaimed Tsodd as the skittles went flying under the impact of the large, black ball.

"Set them up, set them up, come on!" shouted another excited observer.

The monotony of the last week in the camp had been temporarily set aside by the game. Chalfon mats had been laid down on some flat ground to provide a reasonable playing surface. A large group of men, mainly militia, were gathered round watching and cheering as the climax of the final approached. Bodd's score was marked up on a makeshift board as a couple of men dashed out and rearranged the skittles. The other contestant came forward and mimed a few bowls as he prepared himself mentally.

"Do it Solly, you can get eight," called out one of his supporters.

"Aim slightly to the left," another proffered belated advice to the finalist.

"Thank you," the wagon driver acknowledged under his breath as he lined himself up for his last go.

"Ssshh!" The crowd quietened and tensed itself for the finale. Solly's face was a model of concentration, eyes fixed on the centre skittle. Arm back, crouched slightly then he tossed the ball.

"No," he said with a note of resignation.

As soon as it left his hand he knew it was a poor throw. He had over-compensated and the ball skewed to the left over the mats. It swung back at the last moment and hit the skittles. A cheer went up, but it was not good enough.

"Five!" called out John who was acting as judge, "Bodd wins by two skittles!"

A short distance from the resultant roar, John's father was discussing the situation with the Captain of the Guard. Gideon's face was grave as usual.

"We have been hanging around here for almost a week now Japhses and my militia are getting fed up. They want to finish the new village and get all their things moved. Not to mention seeing their loved ones."

"They don't appear too fed up right now."

"A brief diversion. The truth is they are tired of all this waiting about."

"What's this?"

A guardsman from one of the outposts by the river came jogging up with another white beside him. The Captain and Lower Village Head both moved forward to meet them.

"Sir," began the guardsman, "This is..."

"I can see who it is. Peter, what can I say? How long has it been? How did you get caught?"

The new arrival was a short, middle-aged man with a small face and rounded shoulders. He stood there, legs apart. Amongst all the soldiers he looked rather comical in his navy-blue smock and short cropped hair.

"Hello Japhses, good to see a face I recognise. It was the year of the Great Storm, we were on a rustling raid when we suddenly found ourselves surrounded by about a hundred and fifty Ma'hol soldiers no less! They were out on manoeuvres, couldn't believe our bad luck. But I'll have to tell you all about it later, right now I've got to deliver this to the Despot."

He held up a sealed canister.

"Ah the Mehtar's reply," Japhses guessed correctly. "I'll get an escort arranged immediately; you won't have met Despot Thorn."

"Do you know what the message says?" asked Gideon.

"No idea."

The newcomer recognised the questioner, but did not warm to him. He and Gideon had never got on well together and his view had not changed during his years of captivity. Japhses, however, was full of smiles at what must surely be a good omen. He jovially put his large hand on Peter's small shoulder and said, "Dying to catch up on all the news; on second thoughts we can get someone else to deliver the Mehtar's reply."

"I'm sorry, but I've given my word I will deliver it in person."

The big man nodded, it was a matter of honour then.

"If that's the case I'll get an escort to go with you."

With the help of their dakks they quickly made it to the Castle, but entered the hall only to find they had to wait. The second envoy to Aggeparii had returned already and was being de-briefed in the Throne Room. A guardsman knocked at the door to announce the new arrival. Alan opened it a crack and they exchanged a few whispered words so as not to interrupt the current interview. The door was then closed again.

Inside the envoy was explaining a gruesome discovery, saying, "The place where I found the body was very close to the border, My Lord."

"I see. No wonder Despot Kagel never replied, he never got the message!"

"It was fate that I found it in the thick undergrowth," the envoy continued. "Do you wish me to set off for Aggeparii again, My Lord?"

Alan spoke.

"Would you believe we've had a response from the Mehtar already? A messenger's waiting outside."

"Oh, well send him in," Frank ordered as he sat up straight. He replied to the envoy, "Best wait outside for a moment. We'll know very soon if the reinforcements are required or not."

CHAPTER SIXTEEN

"Shocking thing," Frank said as the messenger left the throne Room, "a murder only a few kilometres from here. Who would have done such a thing?"

"Fwom the sound of it they must have been wobbers, My Lawd: multiple stab wounds and all his possessions taken."

"Surely he wouldn't have been carrying much."

"There are bands of wobbers who woam about and kill for next to nothing, but he was carrying a document with your seal My Lawd, that would be worth a lot of money to the "wight" person. They could use it to counterfeit a legal document for instance. The culpwits will be long gone by now My Lawd, no chance of catching them."

"I see. So Despot Kagel has never received our request for reinforcements."

"No, My Lawd, the second envoy weturned here immediately he discovered the body near the border."

"Oh well, we'd better see what the Mehtar has to say."

Upon receiving the signal to enter, Peter came in and discharged his duty by handing the canister to the Despot. He glanced round and saw the steward whom he noticed had not aged one iota during the time of his enforced absence. Natias was sitting at the table with Alan. No sign of the other drones about, but then they never did take an interest in anything serious. The new Despot was speaking.

"Thank you, Peter, for your brave efforts in bringing this to us. Were you treated well in captivity?"

"Not particularly," curtly replied Peter, whose first impression of the new leader was that he was too pompous for his liking. "May I go now, M'Lord? I want some food."

"Ah yes, refreshments! Of course, you go ahead... and thank you again for delivering this."

Peter had gone.

"Funny little character," Frank said, more to himself than the other two as he struggled to get the canister open.

The thought flashed across his mind that it could be an elaborate booby-trap containing an explosive device or something, but he dismissed the idea remembering the technology of this planet was still at an early stage.

"Can I help?" Alan enquired.

By way of an answer Frank tossed the cannister over to him. In an instant it was open and the drone fished out an imposing-looking document.

"It's in High Manuhol script, their official language. Do you want to fetch for Falla to translate it?"

"Can't you?"

"I can try."

He began reading it to himself, paused, took a deep breath, then began:

"'To the Despot of Thyatira, Hoame: these are the words of Mehtar Arumah Ru, Imperial Master of the Seven Lands, Holder of the Great Orb'.......what a load of rubbish!"

"He doesn't say that does he?"

They all laughed.

"I'll try to find the message buried in this garbage....'Our Serene Highness... we acknowledge receipt of your communication and it is our hakta (that's a decision) to consider....'"

He paused to read the rest to himself. The other men present watched in silence. When he had read the whole letter he gave a paraphrase.

"Yeah what he's saying is that there is a basis for discussion. He has ordered his army not to attack in the meantime and asks you to do the same. I gather he would like to know what our precise demands are. I'll try a full written translation for you if you like, Frank, but that's the gist for now."

"Excellent!" declared the Despot slapping the armrest of the throne. "A positive response; I knew he'd see reason. Now we can make progress."

The trio discussed the implications: was it a trick, could it be taken at face value, or did the truth lie somewhere in-between? Alan's counsel was to proceed with caution and not to let their guard down and this was accepted.

Much of the rest of the day was spent ironing out between the three of them what their demands should be. Frank was less keen than the other two to ask for a large sum of money. He was more concerned with securing peace and having the islands as part of that peace plan so that he would have a solid achievement to show for his leadership. A return of the few white slaves held by the Ma'hol would be a bonus. As for the money, Thyatira's economy was going quite nicely at this time and Frank was not the sort of person who liked making what he felt to be greedy demands.

Again the argument about not appearing weak was used against this and under pressure he eventually agreed to include a demand for money worth the equivalent of ten grend, a sizeable sum without being too prohibitive. Natias pointed out this could always be an area for concessions while Alan argued that the Mehtar might feel insulted if they only demanded a small sum in return for his oldest son.

With the reduction in tension, the militia was disbanded for now and allowed to go home, leaving the guard still encamped near the border. The men from the Lower Village recommenced the construction at the new site. Some of their families had already moved into the dwellings which were nearing completion. With the help of a large contingent of volunteers from the Upper Village they soon had enough buildings finished to affect the migration from the old site, which was dismantled and the wood, much of which was rotting and riddled with woodworm, stockpiled for burning during the long winter nights. A squad of guardsmen was spared from the camp to ensure the last families reluctant to move were persuaded to do so and the few remaining ruins completely destroyed.

Zadok ceremonially blessed the New Village as it was now unofficially called. There were still a fair number of finishing touches to be done before it would be truly completed, but life there was beginning to settle into a daily routine. Frank was still insisting on at least two reports each day from Japhses' camp, and that the patrols be kept up. The Despot's greatest concern was that he should be well informed of the current situation. He was not pleased, however, when a triumphant message was received telling how Rodd's long-distance raid had resulted in the capture of an Imperial officer whom they had interrogated. The up-to-date picture of the enemy camp was most useful, but Frank was fearful this could upset the negotiations and ordered such raids to stop forthwith.

Meanwhile the Mehtar's son was beginning to get his spirits back. He began by demanding a servant to wait on him and Frank allowed one of the skirmishers to do so within his rooms. No point in making an issue of it. He then began complaining about his food. Matthew went up to remonstrate and ended up having a meal thrown all over him and the translator. Frank needed all his powers of diplomacy to persuade the highly-strung Matthew to continue catering for the heir to the Ma'hol throne. Then with the help of Falla, the Despot gave Sil a proper dressing down, telling him that if he did not behave in a civilized manner he would find himself in the dungeon.

In spite of the greater part of the guard still being encamped near the river, a sense of normality was returning to the despotate. The number of traders going to and forth – both within Hoame and internationally – increased noticeably and tales of Thyatiran victory and daring soon spread abroad.

Laffaxe returned to the Castle with the last three of the long-term wounded, all Ma'hol. These he billeted in his house within the Castle walls.

One day Frank was in the hall with Alan. They had spent much of the morning there going through the budget and trade considerations with Natias, who had just popped out when Falla came running down the spiral staircase from the third floor. The translator had enjoyed a quiet few days following the ultimatum given to Sil. The respite was over.

"Excuse me My Lord, but Sil is complaining that someone has stolen his book. He calls it his 'holy book'!"

"What, the Vorg-elin't?" put in Alan.

"That's it. He's getting real mad about it!"

Asked Frank, "Is there not another copy we could give him? Do the other prisoners have any copies?"

"Several, My Lord, but he is insisting on his actual book being returned. I couldn't find it anywhere in his room; not that he would allow me to have a good search."

Frank lifted his eyes to Heaven and shook his head before saying, "He's just being damned awkward! I'm not going to take any more nonsense from him. Give him a book from one of the other prisoners and tell him that's all he's getting. I'm not going to have a ridiculous hunt for who might have stolen his silly book! Besides, he probably has hidden it himself deliberately to kick up another fuss.

"All right, Falla, carry on."

"Straight away, My Lord, I'm sorry for the interruption."

When he had left them, Frank remarked, "I preferred it when our hostage friend was all melancholy and depressed. The sooner we get him back where he belongs the better."

"Yeah. Interesting book the Vorg-elin't though. It traces the legends of their god Vorg-habiethmonan."

"How do you remember all these names?"

Without answering Alan continued, "And it has platitudes in abundance and useful advice. There's one of my favourite which does something like, 'Haraga fan foshure lab'ne, syco fan polog'da han' which roughly translated is, 'He who fights and runs away lives to fight another day'."

Frank guffawed, "Any book which gives advice as sound as that can't be bad! I bet Sil's regretting not taking it.

"Natias, you're back, we've just about finished with the finances for now haven't we?"

"Yes, My Lawd," agreed the steward who had entered the room carrying a bundle of documents. He shut the door and re-took his seat, "I am sure a major weason for the impwovement is the banishment of those two hooligans. Adwian and Cwispin were a severe dwain on our wesources for years, but I had never wealised quite how much."

Frank squinted across the room to study Alan's face and see if he resented his fellow drones being talked about like this. His only expression though was a faint, relaxed smile; he clearly did not associate himself with them. Natias continued.

"There is one other welated matter I would like to clear up, My Lawd."

He got up and began showing some of the papers to Frank.

"These are the documents I have dwawn up for the welease of extra land in the Upper Village as we discussed a while ago. I twust you will find them all in order."

"Ah yes," Frank replied and gave the papers a quick scan, "I'm sure these are fine. So the net effect of this should be to expand the village a little and bring in some extra revenue, correct?"

"Fwom our point of view, yes, My Lawd. It will mean less cwowded accommodation for a lot of people and ease congestion. It should also drop the market pwice of any spare land owned by villagers, which will be a good thing because they have become wediculously inflated of late. If there is further pwessure I will wecommend we welease more land. I have made extwa plans for where the new dwellings should be situated, having discussed it with Saul. There will be plenty of space so they are not all over each other like they are starting to get in one or two distwicts. Here they are."

Alan came over and together they approved the plans, to Natias' delight. The man took a great pride in his work and liked it when his ideas were accepted without alteration.

A knock came at the door, it was Illianeth with drinks. It was very noticeable the different ways with which she approached them.

"My Lord," she announced formally as she handed Frank his water.

"Here you are, Alan," she said with a smile, placing the wine glass gently in his hand.

"Natias!" her manner suddenly rude, firmly banging the glass down on the table in front of him. The only reason no wine was spilt was that it was only half full. He stared at its lack of content in surprise, not knowing quite how to react. The servant turned to go, but Alan called to her in a measured voice.

"Illianeth, my lovely, why have you given our illustrious steward only half a glass?"

"Oh yes," she said stiffly, looking at Natias, "Eko wants to see you, she said you promised to help her move the furniture in your room today. I didn't think you'd want to hang around drinking too long."

With that she was gone. The three men looked at each other and smiled. Frank shook his head and uttered what they were all thinking.

"What are we going to do with that girl?"

Not long after this, a message was received from Despot Hista of Bynar. In it he apologised for the "misunderstanding" over the request for reinforcements and that he understood that none were required now anyway. He also claimed to have caught the murderers of Thyatira's envoy to Aggeparii. They had apparently been found trying to sell stolen goods and " to save him the trouble" had already been tried and executed. By way of proof, Hista returned Frank's letter to Aggeparii, complete with Despot's seal. Frank sent a reply thanking him for his action and saying he might need reinforcements at short notice if the negotiations with the Ma'hol broke down.

A possible resumption of hostilities was the last thing on ordinary peoples' minds at that time. One result of the increased trade and high confidence in the Thyatiran economy was a booming market in the castle courtyard. All sorts of new and interesting goods were finding their way onto the stalls and there appeared to be no shortfall in the demand.

Frank, making one of his rare visits to the market, was struck by the variety of items on offer. There seemed to be more stalls than ever before too. He ambled between them, amid the noisy, jostling crowd, feeling glad that most people were too busy to notice their ruler wandering past. Hawkers bawled out their wares, competing with garrulous stallholders.

Markets are the same the galaxy over. He remembered one in particular on Columbus which was grandiose in its scale. Strange planet, its atmosphere was thin and the off-worlders had to take their oxygen tablets at regular intervals during waking hours if they did not want to wear a space suit. The man in the room next door had had a leak in his oxygen pump and had almost suffocated to death in his sleep. The natives, it had been discovered, all suffered from an incurable disease in their bloodstream. The extraordinary thing was that it lay dormant until exposed to what was for them a higher than normal level of oxygen. As a result they could only travel off-planet if they were permanently in a suit or gas tent...

A particularly loud cry from a greengrocer brought Frank back to the present.

"Lovely scrabs," the Sarnician yelled, "quarter a kilo!"

Frank had not seen so many foreigners at the Castle before; they stuck out easily with their dark hair of various shades. Trying to recognise some of the faces of the whites he spotted Kim, Giella's sister. She was surrounded by children as usual and busily serving at her stall. One of her offspring, a boy of about ten, was helping another customer.

Moving on a little, he observed Reuben, one of the hulffan croppers, having a lively discussion with someone behind the next stall. As the other conversationalist came into view Frank's heart leapt. There she was, in all her loveliness!

'Come away, let them be,' part of him said, but the thought was quickly brushed aside as he intruded on the couple.

"Hello, Giella."

He found he had to pause to let in some air.

"Another lovely day."

"Nice to see you, My Lord," she replied with a flash of her beautiful eyes.

Reuben quickly excused himself, saying he had other things to attend to and Frank was left alone with her.

"Market's busy today," Frank started off cheerfully on a neutral topic.

"I've been hearing all about you, My Lord: your quick decisions on the day of battle. Japhses said he was most impressed. You've saved us all from a terrible fate."

"Thank you," he replied, trying to be modest.

He wondered what to say next and paused for a moment. She had a knowing smile on her face, but it was impossible to guess what was going on in her mind. The comment about Japhses had taken a while to sink in.

"So you've seen Japhses since the battle? Ah of course, you've been to the camp to see Uriah."

"Er, yes that's right," his composure seemed to waiver for a moment before returning. "Is it true what they say, My Lord, that you are holding the Ma'hol Prince to ransom?"

"I hope to establish a lasting peace between our two nations; he is an important factor in our deliberations."

Giella swept the ringlets of her white hair back and repeated in mock seriousness, "'An important factor in our deliberations,' you're not always this earnest I hope."

"No, no," assured frank, feeling himself blush.

Her tone changed again. Playfully she announced, "I'm going to give the prisoners a performance on my flute, I hear they're great ones for music."

"Oh yes? When's this going to be?"

"No idea, My Lord, I've only just thought of it. I like to act on impulse, don't you ever?"

They chatted for a long time and to him it seemed like they were the only two people on the planet. The hustle and bustle of the market around them was completely blocked out of his consciousness.

One thing he was afraid of though was that he might outstay his welcome, although she did seem interested in what he had to say. Eventually he tore himself away, saying he really should be getting back to the Castle - "Affairs of state you know."

Gliding back across the bailey he went over every piece of their conversation in detail.

'...and she described how she learnt to play the musical instruments (I could show her my cupboard stuffed full of the things) and how she and Uriah had been married eight years, and about the market place... I think she enjoyed my company, I just hope I didn't seem too serious for her liking... she is such an exciting person to be with... many fine qualities: charming, accomplished, intelligent... I can't help being attracted to her yes, but I'm not in love with her; I *like* her very much, and respect her...'

Back he floated to his room, oblivious to the world around him.

The following Sabbath important news arrived from the Capital. Almost a week after the event word reached them that the Autarch had died. It had been known for some time that he had been in poor health, so no great surprise was expressed. What was unusual, however, indeed unprecedented in living memory, was the announcement which had immediately followed his death. To a packed crowd outside the citadel Baron Schail had declared the office of Autarch abolished and that from now on, the Inner Council would run the country by itself. Also that Baron Deistenau had resigned from the Council "to devote more time to the running of his estate."

Alan told Frank that without a doubt this meant that Count Zastein was now in complete control. Apparently he preferred to pull the strings from behind the scenes.

"The Keepers of Hoame are once more back in complete control of the country," the drone declared. "This coup should not affect Thyatira at all."

"Well I suppose it's good news," remarked Frank, "the Count was my sponsor when I first landed here."

The Castle hall fell silent again, the messenger from the Capital had left a while ago and they were the only two there. The main worship meetings of the day were over and the people gone home. Frank had attended one held at the Castle and had wondered back to the hall to have a browse at the legal books when the news had arrived. There was no sign now of the staff, or guardsmen around. A warm, sleepy Sabbath.

Alan decided to go back to his room leaving Frank by himself looking through the legal tomes which turned out to be a lot less interesting than he had hoped. Everything was peaceful for a while until Natias appeared at the outer door with company.

After scanning round the hall he indicated to his two companions to stay where they were and walked across to where Frank was sitting.

"I am sowwy to disturb you, My Lawd, but I wonder if I might have a word."

"That's all right, go ahead. These books seem just to contain lots of lists, not half as helpful as I thought they might be. What can I do for you?"

"I have Tsodd waiting outside to see you with his brother, Bodd. They want to petition you for compensation for the overpwiced land they bought."

"Oh?"

"But weally it is not our pwoblem, we cannot give money to evewyone who thinks they got a bad deal. I must wecommend most stwongly My Lawd not to give way on this."

"I see," Frank replied sitting up straight in his chair and arranging the books on the table in front of him more neatly, "All right, show them in. I may as well see them here, there's no one else about."

Outside, Tsodd was talking to his brother in a loud whisper, "Come on, Bodd, you said you'd do the talking, that's why I asked for you to come with me."

"I thought it was just to lend moral support."

"Don't be like that. I can't talk to the Despot on legal matters. You're the intelligent one around here. Don't come all this way and then not help me!"

Natias arrived back, "You may go in now."

Tsodd gave a desperate look at Bodd as they entered. The other mouthed, "Leave it to me," as they made their way across to stand at the table, the other side of Frank. Natias took up a position just behind and to the right of his master.

They exchanged greeting, and through Frank's mind darted memories of the journey from Ephamon with Offa and the triplets. He agreed to let Bodd put their case.

"I am not sure how much you are already aware of, My Lord, so I will start at the beginning if you will forgive me for repeating anything you already know."

"That's all right, please go on," said Frank as he pondered how well some of the whites spoke considering their simple education.

"Thank you My Lord. As I'm sure you are aware, all land outside the villages belongs to yourself. If some is to be bought by the villagers it can only be released for sale by the Despot. Now here in Thyatira we were unfortunate enough to go for a long time without a proper black ruler. Natias here could not release any land for sale after the death of Despot Rattinger and so only now has it been done. In the meantime, prices have soared due to demand outstripping supply.

"Before we left on our last mining job Tsodd arranged to buy some land off a farmer called Hanson. After we had come back with yourself, My Lord, he demanded more money and indeed he succeeded to some extent. We bought the land, or rather Tsodd did, at what worked out to be a hundred and twelve-fifty a kab, almost three times what the price has dropped to now.

"Had we known earlier that a new Despot was on the way, My Lord, Tsodd would have waited and bought at the current price."

"I see. What is the current price please?"

"Forty-five a kab My Lord."

Natias intervened.

"The land you have weleased, My Lawd, has been sold at fifty a kab."

Frank bid the petitioner continue.

"The thing is, My Lord, we have been very unlucky with our timing. Had we waited a season we could have bought at a much lower price. Tsodd has been the victim of market forces beyond his control."

He rested his case and Frank asked offhandedly, "What do you expect me to do about it?"

Bodd was taken aback, he had expected the Despot to be sympathetic, or at the very least not to be quite so blunt.

"We were hoping for compensation, My Lord."

"On what grounds? Surely it was a private deal between you and the farmer."

"But, My Lord," Bodd continued, sounding hurt, "Surely you must have released the land now because you knew the market price had got out of hand. You can't think it's right that Tsodd had to pay the inflated price?"

Frank did feel sorry for the brother. He remembered how they had been his fellow travellers with him and had put up with his dark mood when he felt so down after Offa's death. But the steward was right, it had been a private deal and to compensate them would set a precedent without limit. It was tempting to hide behind Natias and say, "I must support my steward's decision," but he decided he should stand up for himself.

"I'm sorry Bodd, I *do* sympathise, but this really isn't the subject of compensation. It was a private agreement; if I gave way on this case I'd be bailing out every person who thinks someone has got the better of them in a deal. Don't you see that? I admit you were most unfortunate with your timing, but that does not alter the principle."

At last Tsodd himself spoke up.

"It wasn't as if I even needed the land, My Lord. It was for the aviary. I wasn't going to hold onto it to see later at a higher price like some folk have been doing."

"I'm sorry Tsodd," came the reply, but that doesn't change a thing. There really isn't anything I can do."

The pair finally realised their case was lost. Tsodd mumbled something and began shuffling out. Bodd thanked the Despot for having seen them before going to catch his brother up.

"It's a pity I can't help," Frank called out to the retreating figures.

He slumped back in his chair. He felt rotten after making the judgement he felt sure was right and looked up at Natias.

"I know, My Lawd, it does seem a shame in a way, but I am confident it was the wight decision. They are not exactly short of money you know, they will not go hungwy this winter."

His words were already starting to have the desired effect and Frank did not feel quite so bad.

"Well that's good to hear at least."

Natias wanted to raise another topic, but was not certain his timing was right. He decided to test the water.

"Would My Lawdship like to be left alone, or may I bwing something to show you?"

The response was more enthusiastic that he had expected.

"No that's all right, what have you got to show me?"

"It is just that Zadok has been pwessing me to pass the plans for the stone church building with you in order that we can send them off to the Capital for consideration."

"Oh yes, may as well see them now."

A little while later the plans were spread out on the table and the two men went over them together.

"Most interesting," Frank declared, "what a fascinating design. By the way where is Zadok? He didn't come to the Castle today."

"No, My Lawd, I understand he is spending most of his time at the Upper Village supervising work on the new wooden church being built there. I expect he conducted services near there today."

"All this building work going on!"

"I don't know where they find the time, but evewyone seems to be so busy these days. There is a new spiwit awound here, My Lawd, people are busy six days a week getting things done. The hulffan crop is wipening nicely too; I would not say that to a cwopper though, they are the most superstitious of people and always make out things are worse than they weally are."

Frank smiled as he looked at the plans, but did not answer.

"Still no word fwom the Mehtar I suppose, My Lawd?"

"No, none," he sighed. "Our diplomacy seems to have ground to a halt after its promising start. I just hope it picks up again soon."

Bodd and Tsodd did not delay their return once they got out of the keep. The latter complained bitterly about the failure of their mission.

"...I told you it would be a waste of time, we didn't get anywhere."

"You never said anything of the sort," returned his more level-headed brother, "you said it was worth a try and I agreed. There was nothing to lose."

"Just as well, 'cos we'd probably have lost it if there was!"

"Come on, don't be an old frass. I'm just as sick as you are, but there's no use dwelling on it."

"Hello, you two!" Illianeth called out cheerfully as she passed them going in the opposite direction.

Upon receiving a grunt from Bodd and no response at all from Tsodd she exclaimed, "Bugger you then!" and picked up her stride.

Her destination was Laffaxe's house. She knocked at the door and went in without waiting for a response. The physician was in the main room sitting on a high stool sorting out some dried leaves. The only other occupant of this room was Haqq, a severely-wounded Ma'hol skirmisher. He had received a blow into his lower face from a two-handled axe during the battle and had a horrific injury. Laffaxe had worked miracles to keep him alive that long, but just when it seemed the worst had been passed Haqq took a turn for the worse and now the physician feared his patient was slipping away. He had used the strongest and some of his rarest medicines to dull the pain and help bring about a recovery, but the prognosis was not good. The soldier lay on his bed not moving a muscle, eye staring out above the bandages. His hands were placed on his chest; both they and his forehead were ghostly grey.

"I've got you the honey," the servant announced.

"Over there."

She put it down where he had indicated and stood at the bottom of Haqq's bed.

"Poor lad, he's not getting any better is he."

"I'm not giving up the struggle yet, my girl, but there are not much grounds for optimism I admit. I just wish that those ignoramuses out there composing poems and songs about "sweet victory" would come in and see him, be with him day and night as he suffers. They might not be so keen on the idea of war as a means to an end. The Ma'hol are not savages, they are men like ourselves."

He looked up from his work.

"Don't stand staring, girl! You can go now."

Illianeth knew better than to be offended by Laffaxe's abruptness, but she had not been thanked for her errand so she reminded him.

"I put your honey there on the side."

"Thank you, girl. Bye now."

She stepped out again and the physician took a glance at his dying patient before turning once more to sorting his ingredients.

The negotiations were dragging. Further Ma'hol prisoners were sent out with messages, one at a time. In-between released whites came back with counter-proposals from Rabeth-Mephar. So far these whites had all been Hoamen captured in the last few years, none of whom had ever met the increasingly mythical second or third generation white slaves supposed to exist. The messages they brought were verbose and legalistic, not progressing the negotiations at all. Alan joked that at this rate all the prisoners would be traded off and there would be no need for a formal settlement! In reality there were still forty-five Ma'hol being kept in the inner bailey. Their conditions were reasonable, but not quite so good now there was a prolonged period of heavy rain. At least the "no nonsense" policy towards Sil was working and very little was heard from him.

At the camp Japhses' suggestion to allow a fifth of the men out on short-term leave at any one time had been accepted and this helped to keep spirits from falling too low. The Captain even began a training programme there for new recruits. This was as much to keep himself occupied as it was the need for more guardsmen. Restrictions on villagers' visits were relaxed somewhat too.

In view of his position he felt he had to keep aloof from his troops to a degree. With Alan back at the castle the only person there approaching his status was his lieutenant Uriah. He tried holding conversations with him. Unfortunately it was notoriously difficult to get more than three words out of him, unless it was about warfare, tactics or the like and Japhses found it very hard work. Not a married man, Japhses slipped back to the Upper Village night-times, but nobody knew what he went there to do.

Summer turned to autumn, the time for the hulffan harvest. All building work, indeed just about everything was dropped to help bring the crop in. As predicted it was a bumper harvest which cheered Natias no end when he calculated the revenue. It was also time for another tax collection, so the steward was kept well occupied.

At last there was a breakthrough in the negotiations. A communication was received which differed in style and writing from the others so much that they wondered as to its authenticity at first. The same Mehtar's seal was there, however, and the freed white assured them that it had been handed to him by a high-ranking official. The concise text requested a meeting in person between Despot and Mehtar in three days time to sort out their dispute once and for all. The venue: the old stone bridge upstream from the islands, the main conditions: no weapons and no entourage within half a kilometre of the bridge.

"I'll go!" Frank declared. "I'll need a translator. Will you accompany me, Alan?"

"Of course, to within half a kilometre. You won't need a translator, he speaks our language more fluently than we do. He's also a skilled swordsman..." he saw the other's face drop and laughed, "but I wouldn't worry about that. He has given his word of honour and that is most important to the Ma'hol. I'm certain he can be trusted."

"I'm having to, with my life!" cried Frank, but he was eager to accept in the hope of getting this infernal stalemate broken. No one urged him not to go.

The reply was therefore dispatched agreeing the place, time and conditions for the meeting. For the next three days all Frank could do was wait for the confrontation.

For the wounded Ma'hol, Haqq the waiting was over. That afternoon he lapsed into a coma and died the following day.

CHAPTER SEVENTEEN

The fine autumnal morning was marked with a heavy dew. It showed up the myriad spiders webs adorning the bushes by the track leading to the stone bridge. Leaves on the trees had turned every colour of rust, carmine, yellow and brown, there appeared to be few evergreens in this part of the country. A chill was in the air and the mist hung in the valleys and dips. The sun was a dull, orange disc just above the horizon.

Quietly the Despot of Thyatira and his entourage proceeded along the track. The flanking guardsmen on either side waded through the tall, sodden grass, rabbits fleeing as they advanced.

When they got to a clump of trees roughly the required distance from the rendezvous point Alan, Japhses and the squad of hand-picked men stopped, leaving Frank to go on alone. They watched him descend the long, even slope to the river. The bridge itself was obscured by mist so he was truly alone as the ground levelled out and he stepped onto the first large white stone.

Slowly he made his way towards the middle of the bridge to where their meeting should be. He trod carefully, for the white slabs looked slippery. The river trickled gently between the many supports. The walkway was only a metre and a half above the water. When there was a prolonged downpour as on the eve of the battle, it became submerged.

That day seemed long ago, but its outcome was the reason for him being at the stone bridge now.

Suddenly a figure appeared out of the swirling mist. It made Frank jump a little, but he quickly realised it was the Mehtar waiting for him and his heart settled down a bit.

"Welcome Despot Thorn," the figure called out in a deep, authoritative voice.

An eddy of thick, grey fog came across forcing Frank to squint to get a look at his adversary. He took a measured step forward before returning the greeting.

"Good morning, Mehtar," he replied using the form of address recommended by Alan as respectful but not deferential, "so we get to meet at long last."

"Indeed."

"Not a very pleasant morning," Frank indicated to the mist with a wave of his hand.

The Mehtar realised the other was very nervous and would have smiled had not the life of his eldest son been at stake.

"I had not realised we had come here to discuss the weather," he responded with a glint in his eye before becoming serious. "I was getting tired with all the drivel my civil servants were sending you in the guise of negotiations. I hope we can settle this issue between the two of us."

Frank was starting to relax a bit; at least he had not been attacked and kidnapped yet. A thought crossed his mind, 'I should have left instructions to execute all the Ma'hol prisoners immediately in the event of my being captured, that would stop such an underhand plot from working. On the other hand...'

He stopped his mind from racing away by responding to the Mehtar's last remark.

"Yes I hope we can get a deal sorted out, it's in both our interests. Your son is well, he and his men are being looked after as well as we can."

"And what are your demands for their release?"

"Well...." Frank began falteringly as he wondered at the Mehtar's directness. He knew the man already had the information. Presumably he wanted to start again from scratch. "We were hoping to have all the Hoamen prisoners released back to us and a settlement of the border dispute whereby you acknowledge our sovereignty over the three islands downstream from here..."

He considered the demand for money he was supposed to make, but found himself unable to do so. It felt greedy and unchristian to demand money for the release of the man's son, so he finished by saying, "and most important of all the signing of a peace agreement between our two nations so that our people can live without the threat of war hanging over their heads."

"So! And your countrymen's' raids? Will you guarantee they will end? That if any more take place, the perpetrators will be brought to justice?"

Thinking that the reference was to Rodd's recent exploits Frank replied in an amicable tone, "Oh yes, of course, that's just special wartime conditions you know, the need to gather intelligence."

The Mehtar was totally puzzled by this response. Is the man being deliberately obtuse? Is it possible he does not know? He then remembered what his sources had told him: this man is not a native Hoaman, he has been brought in from far away to govern Thyatira.

Gently the Ma'hol ruler asked, "Why do you think we took the islands by force?"

It was Frank's turn to be perplexed, but he did not hesitate with his answer, "Because there is a border dispute I suppose."

"Do you claim to be in ignorance of the sheep and dakk rustling raids undertaken by your people?"

"Yes," came the honest reply, "I've never heard of such a thing."

The Mehtar shook his head and dispelled the rising tension with a smile.

"It seems your advisers have kept you in the dark as to the cause of our little dispute. The islands were taken because they overlook the shallows and have been used as a staging point for raids in the past."

"From what I heard you were not in favour of taking the islands by force."

The foreign ruler chose not to respond to that particular point, but said the Hoamen were welcome to them if the raids were curtailed. He continued, "We issued everything from threats to pleas to your predecessor and got no response. The last one must have been before you took over, but it was taken for granted you had been informed."

A blushing Frank assured him he was in ignorance of all this and the Mehtar believed him. In fact he found the Despot's straightforward, honest approach quite disarming. It had a certain freshness after the cagey courtiers and diplomats he was used to and he found himself being a lot more open than usually was in an important international negotiation.

As a result progress was swift: the Mehtar conceded the islands (he was not half as keen on owning them as the Hoamen believed) and the release of all their prisoners (again it was not generally known that there was a glut in the Rabeth-Mephar slave market and to have some taken out of circulation would please many slave traders by restoring prices).

He told Frank something of the Hoamen in captivity: "We have none of your 'black' slaves. The 'whites' have always been kept apart in recognition of their consciousness of the purity of their race. That is something us Ma'hol can appreciate, besides slaves work better when well treated and content. They are all owned by the crown and have been mainly used on major capital projects. I must warn you though some have been there for generations and are used to our ways and customs. Some may not even want freedom in a country they have never seen. I do not know."

The Mehtar assured him that all who wanted to go would be allowed to. In return for the concessions the Despot promised to issue an edict banning cross border raids and to bring anyone who disobeyed to justice.

The two leaders were making such good progress they ended up going into further detail. The Mehtar preferred this to letting his notorious civil servants bog the whole process down in a mass of red tape and jargon. Frank too appreciated the opportunity to get things moving swiftly. He was looking forward to being rid of his prisoners-of-war and getting Castle life back to normal.

A peace treaty was felt to be in both their interests and prior to their parting they agreed to have one drafted up.

"Perhaps," the Mehtar remarked, "We should have brought our scribes after all, we have covered a lot of ground today. No matter, I am pleased to find a man I can communicate with, unlike most of your adopted countrymen."

They expressed a mutual desire to increase trade between them before the two men parted. Frank walked back up the slope towards the small group waiting anxiously for him. The sun was a lot more powerful by now and could not be looked at. His black clothes absorbed its heat and he found himself perspiring heavily as he climbed. He was too absorbed in the success of the meeting to mind the discomfort.

He thought, 'A great deal achieved. I secured the islands and the release of our people from slavery. I didn't mention the ransom money, but according to Natias' last report our finances are healthy without that. A treaty to bring a lasting peace, that's far more valuable. Yes, a good day's work! That Mehtar is someone I can see eye to eye with, he even expressed a desire to visit us one day.'

Alan and Japhses appeared from the trees, relief showing on their faces. The former asked, "How did it go then, Frank? You were a long time. Japhses here was starting to get worried, although I must say you look rather pleased with yourself."

"A great success! The Mehtar is someone we can do business with."

He went through the points agreed as they made their return journey. Japhses was less than pleased that no ransom had been included in the deal.

"My Lord! The men have kept their spirits up knowing that a healthy reward for their hard-won fight was to be forthcoming."

Frank saw red.

"Well there isn't going to be a ransom! I had been under the illusion the men had fought because their lives and the lives of their families depended on it, not for money. As for a "hard-fought fight" it was a brief skirmish in which we were very lucky to catch the enemy off balance."

It just then occurred to him that Japhses and his men had actually fought and killed while he had watched, but he was genuinely angry at the mercenary attitude being displayed and was not going to let a detail like that defeat him. He continued.

"There's a bloody obsession around here with money. You should do your duty and be satisfied with that. I've just negotiated a lasting peace between our countries and all you can do is go on about money. Any fool can go around killing people, it takes skill to get a peace-treaty agreed."

Japhses was dumbstruck at the outburst. He went bright red, but kept his mouth shut.

The party walked on, no one daring to speak. After a while Frank started up again, this time he aimed his comments at Alan.

"And why wasn't I told about those cross-border rustling raids by our people? Why did I have to hear about them from a foreign ruler?"

Alan was not so easily shaken. In his usual relaxed manner he replied, "It's those roaming bandits Natias loves to go on about, it's not a deliberate policy of the Upper Village."

"I should still have been told about them," Frank snapped.

"Granted; and admittedly some of their stolen stock finds an outlet there,,,"

"Right! Well I want you to step up border patrols along there on a permanent basis straight away. Japhses, you must stop these raids and arrest any bandit groups encountered."

"Yes, My Lord," came the muted, grudging response.

They continued in silence a short way, then Frank realised he had better let his Captain cut across back to the temporary camp where the Guard was still stationed. He began wondering if he had overstepped the mark with some of his comments in his tirade against Japhses. A voice came ringing into his brain which told him that if an apology was due it must be given now in front of the guardsmen, because they were present during the telling-off. He ordered a halt and turned to the big man.

"Japhses. Thank you for your escort. You can take your men back to the camp and start to dismantle it. Apart from the extra patrols we can begin getting back to a peace-time footing.

"I went a bit over the top with some of my comments a bit earlier. Your contribution and that of your men was outstanding on the day of battle and I was wrong to try and belittle it. I apologise unreservedly."

These comments were appreciated and Japhses explained that he was more concerned for the widows of the dead soldiers than for anybody else. He received an undertaking that they would be given compensation so they would not go without. The Captain was able to lead his men proudly once more back to the camp, but he did wish the Despot would not have these occasional manic outbursts.

Frank carried on back to the Castle with a couple of guardsmen plus Alan, who thought it best to steer the conversation away from money. Instead he enquired as to what had been discovered about the white prisoners held by the Ma'hol.

"Not a great deal to be honest. He did confirm that there are some second generation slaves there, which confirms something we've suspected all along. The messengers have all been taken from the newer arrivals; they're obviously kept apart. I didn't get any ideas as to numbers, but it's probably not very many or he'd have said.

"You know it's funny, on my way here Offa gave me repeated warnings about Laodicia, or Ladosa as he called it, but I'm not sure he ever mentioned the Ma'hol. We're not antagonising our other foreign neighbours with cross-border raids I hope."

"No you can rest easy on that one, Frank," assured Alan. "There are no villages near their side of the border. We have a few small outposts along there for our guardsmen to keep an eye on things. We haven't heard anything out of the Laodicians for some considerable while. There was a trader from there I spoke with...was it late last year or early this? I can't remember. From him I gauged an impression of the usual internal bickering and arguments; life going on as normal."

The picture of internal division and quarrels reminded Frank all too well of Eden. His party, the Primary Radicals (or "Rads" as they were known) was right in the thick of it. It had been a futile struggle, however, with the Synod run by their bitterest opponents. It was anything but the Garden of Eden.

Alan continued, "No white trader is allowed there without a permit from yourself, I think I'd have heard if any had applied."

"No, none," the other confirmed as he stepped over some dead branches left on the track.

"Actually, Frank, it might be an idea to make it known that a permit is available, on the understanding that the recipient is expected to provide whatever intelligence he can glean to the Despot upon his return. Mind you, there are unlikely to be any takers at the moment, they might get trapped there if the snow comes early. It might be a good idea in the spring though."

Frank had heard there was a heavy snowfall each year in this region of the planet. He had only met snow once before and found it fascinating. He was probably the only man on Molten looking forward to the winter.

Changing the subject he asked, "Have you heard anything about Adrian and Crispin since they left here?"

"I haven't. They most likely went down south, back to their roots."

The Castle came into view, standing out from the flat countryside on its man-made mound. Some sheep were being driven through the courtyard to market. The armour of the sentries on the battlements glistened in the sun.

Alan remarked, "I was pleasantly surprised to hear you had got along so well with the Mehtar. When I visited Rabeth the court was terribly stuffy and formal, and they despised us uncivilized "taltons", the inferior people of Hoame."

"Well I don't know, replied Frank scratching his beard, "I rather got the impression of someone fed up with a lot of formality who wanted to cut through all the red-tape he's used to. It was strange, but I felt – or I hope I did – a strong feeling of mutual trust between us right from the start. He struck me as a very dignified man, not the type who'd resort to trickery. You could see it in his eyes. I think ultimately it was that neither of us *wanted* a confrontation, the will to come to an agreement was always there. Maybe I got him on a good day.

They had arrived back home. The guardsmen at the gate saluted them as they entered. Frank was glad for a sit down once he got to his suite. Alan joined him there, but it was a different girl than usual who served them their drinks.

"Where's Illianeth?" Frank enquired of her.

"She is indisposed, My Lord," the girl answered nervously.

After some questioning by Alan it came out that his favourite was drunk again.

Frank let out a despairing sigh. "That girl! Well this time we can't blame Adrian and Crispin."

He looked across at his friend who took a glass of wine as he lolled in a large armchair.

The servant left the room and Frank continued, "If only I could find her an interest in life, I think that would help. I reckon the trouble with Illianeth is that she is bored."

Alan shrugged his shoulders before turning sideways and hooking his knees over one of the arms of the chair. He tipped his glass up to finish the last drop and put it down heavily on a table beside him. He made no reply.

The next few weeks saw the exchange of prisoners take place. This was accomplished following the signing of a peace treaty and a modest trade agreement. The latter was seen as a first step towards increased ties between their two nations. Frank as usual was not being put off by advice that contact with foreigners was not popular with the whites.

The two leaders did not meet again that autumn, but the Mehtar was sent an invitation to stay at the Castle the following year, to which Frank received an acceptance.

So at long last, Mennahuna Sil Qua'moth-Ri and his fellow adventurers were sent back to their native Rabeth-Mephar. A couple had built up close relationships with two white women and were reluctant to go. It was clear that not all whites were against contact with foreigners! However their staying was out of the question for the ructions it would have caused. As it was the revelations of fraternisation did cause a scandal. The young women concerned decided against going with the Ma'hol they had fallen for, but only after much heart-searching. They made a tearful goodbye.

For the most part, the prisoners were delighted to be leaving the muddy, damp, rat-infested tent village within the Castle walls. They would be glad to get back to civilization, especially as an unprecedented act of clemency the Mehtar had declared an amnesty for these men technically guilty of treason. In the event they were herded into Krabel-Haan secretly by night and the next day took pride of place in a large parade celebrating the Ruler's birthday. Such are the ironies of life.

Meanwhile the citizens of Thyatira were in for a big shock. On the designated morning Frank and all his lieutenants stood near the riverbank where the battle was fought to greet the few dozen or so released whites after they had crossed through the shallows. A large crowd of anxious relatives and friends were there also, along with many curious onlookers.

After waiting a while the arranged time passed and nothing happened. Then the first few emerged from the wood on the other side. They were accompanied by carts and wagons loaded high with belongings. No Ma'hol soldiers were visible. More refugees followed, then more until a long column of them began crossing the river.

"I can't believe it!" Saul exclaimed while the others around him stood in stunned silence.

This silence soon disappeared as relatives and friends ran forward to greet their long-lost loved ones. They shouted, hugged and kissed and soon a great celebration was under way. Soon a huge flood of humanity was pouring out of the foreign woods, as if a damn had burst.

These further whites crossing over seemed strangely re-moved from all the jubilation and peered around nervously. Their leader was a squarely-built man with big eyes. He and his followers, who made up by far the greater proportion of the immigrants, wore strange alien garb. Their thin silky clothes were quite out of place among the coarser, thicker garments of the others. Even their complexion was a contrast, having been tanned by the sun.

Frank and his entourage proceeded down the slope towards them. As expected these were the "second generation" prison-ers, but they turned out to be a lot more than that.

"Welcome to Thyatira," the Despot greeted them cheerfully.

The squarely-built man looked around in wonder.

"It is hard to believe it, the land of our forefathers! I never thought in my heart of hearts I would ever touch its soil."

They gave up counting when the total repatriations passed the two-thousand mark. Fifty originated from the Upper Village and were easily settled there, although some more land had to be released for those without homes to go to. A mere handful were from the Lower Village and went to the new site. So the vast majority were the "second generation" liberated slaves.

In fact fifth or sixth generation was more like it. Their ancestors had been taken prisoner in wars long past. There had been a twelfth despotate called Sardis, a small one simi-lar in size to Thyatira. It had been overrun by the Ma'hol and its people led into slavery. The intense national pride of these white Hoamen had kept alive the hope of returning one day, although it had come to be little more than a dream. They had to a large degree managed to keep the racial purity of the whites which was now so vital for them to be accepted back into the fold. This had been helped by the Ma'hol policy of keeping subject peoples contented as much as possible. Freedom of worship and separate communities were the order of the day. The Hoamen had formed their own colony hundreds of kilometres to the south where they harvested salt from the sea.

Now that they had come to settle in Thyatira it was decided after a short debate that the best thing to do was for them to have their own village. Its population would be considerably bigger than the new Lower Village, their numbers having swelled the whole of Thyatira by more than a third. A site in the east of the despotate was chosen, near the Bynar border and a few kilometres from the mountains that led to Ladosa.

"More building work!" some complained, but houses were constructed in record time. The newcomers were not used to building in wood and needed help on a large scale from their hosts. Some houses were put up too hurriedly and lack of care would cause tragedy later. The Despot was keen that the new village should have a proper name and so the name of the old despotate was resurrected.

The inhabitants of Sardis were soon dubbed "Taltons", a Ma'hol word meaning foreigners. The Taltons were keen to show their patriotism and more than a few volunteered for the Guard. Natias appointed guides to help them adapt to the very different lifestyle that they had come to. It was vital that they do adapt, the steward explained, so as to avoid friction with the other whites. Tolerance of foreign ways is often at a premium throughout the universe Frank wryly observed to himself. The Taltons' own leader was officially made Village Head, while Zadok was kept busy ironing out "doctrinal perversions" that had crept in during the long captivity. He spent much of his time that autumn teaching the newcomers.

With many men out of the Upper Village helping in Sardis, the post-harvest hulffan preparation was seriously delayed. As a result all available men and women were called upon to help cut off the fruit of their staple crop for pickling before it went off. This would be their main winter diet. The talk in the stripping sheds was all about the Taltons and the new village under construction.

"Many of them immigrants is living in tents at present, "remarked Reuben as he pulled fibres away from the fruit to get a clean cut, "they'll need t'be out of them 'fore the bad weather."

He sliced the fruit off skilfully with his fasson, the special hulffan-croppers' knife, and picked up the next stalk.

The long shed was a hive of activity as the fruit were cut off, separated from the husks, then carried out to the next building for the pickling process. The husks would be sorted outside for now; there was not the same urgency to melt them down for tar. The fibrous stalks too could wait a while before being utilised for rope-making.

Reuben was a long-established cropper and worked with an economic, rhythmic pattern. He had especially dark eyes for a white, they were set in and close, which together with his narrow mouth gave him a permanent scowl.

Up this end of the table working with him were Mary his wife and their son Brogg. Opposite sat Kim's husband Amos, to whom Reuben's comment about the Taltons had been aimed. Amos was a round, cheerful person with a cheeky sense of humour. He was fond of children; he and Kim added to their clutch each year.

"Living in tents are they?" he replied. "I hear they feel the cold something rotten too. Hate to think what they'll make of the winter."

He looked across when he heard the door latch click and saw his wife enter with their niece Roil.

"Ah refreshments!" He exclaimed, just what we needed."

They downed tools to enjoy a well-earned break. Kim and Roil handed round the hamble cakes and yacko-juice. Amos tucked in heartily.

"Huh, I'd have preferred wine," Reuben complained as he took the cup. He ignored his wife's protests about ingratitude and asked Kim, "Where's Giella?"

Kim had begun speaking to Mary, so he turned to Roil instead.

"Where's your mother?"

A broad smile came across the face of Amos as he ate his cake.

"Probably busy painting her face as usual!" he joked.

Reuben did not seem amused. Kim looked up. "If you must know," she said stiffly as she glared at her husband, "my sister is helping Uriah in their hut. And we don't all want to see the contents of your mouth."

Amos stuffed the rest of the cake in before replying jovially, "You're quite right of course, my darling."

Mary took a sip of juice then asked Kim where her children were.

"Marie's looking after them. Peter's got his first tooth you know..."

Reuben turned back to Amos to resume their previous conversation.

"Yes them Taltons are going to suffer this winter. I hear they're used to a much hotter climate; they won't know what's 'it 'em.

"I've heard it said they built houses from blocks of salt. Have you ever heard of such a stupid thing? They say they don't know the first thing about building a proper 'ouse. An' all this business of giving their village a name like "Sardis" - damn silly I call it."

Amos looked unperturbed, he knew Reuben too well and knew his friend always liked a good moan about something. He replied optimistically, "From what I hear they're doing very well, keen to show their loyalty to the Despot and quick to learn."

"Huh! Given land free, with subsidies and tax exemptions. I'd be keen an' all, I'm tellin' ya"

"How else could they get established?"

"Still not fair."

"Look on the bright side man. They're bringing new skills and expertise to the country which are bound to help."

"Such as?"

Apart from salt extraction I understand they have craftsmen in precious metal and the like. That means we can import metal in rough form and save money by having it finished here. We could even end up exporting ornaments to the rest of Hoame. That's the plan of their leader Quafta-Harl. Kim and I went to the market the other day and one of the other Taltons told us."

"Yeah see, they've even got Ma'hol names!" exclaimed the unconvinced cropper. "I've heard all sorts of things about them: they eat standing up, just like them foreigners do... and there's even a suggestion there's Ma'hol blood in 'em! I've 'eard tell of some with dark streaks in their 'air."

Kim joined in, "What rubbish you talk Reuben! You always listen to the worst gossips who haven't the faintest idea what they're talking about. If you *must* know their leader is changing his name to Luke. See? They're even prepared to adopt Hoame names to demonstrate their commitment. I'm sure they're a good thing. If you and your cronies give the newcomers half a chance you'll find they'll prove their worth."

Her husband laughed, "Prove their *salt* you mean, my dear?"

Lunch time in the hall found the Castle its usual busy self. Frank was at the head of one long table with Alan and Natias sitting to his right and left respectively. He listened to the latest intelligence reports while he ate the last of his stew. These concerned the mood in the neighbouring despotates of Bynar and Aggeparii. Apparently they were concerned at what was seen as a dramatic rise in Thyatira's power. With exaggerated reports of a crushing victory over the Ma'hol, plus the large influx of manpower, both their near neighbours were feeling uneasy, if not threatened.

"That's a bit daft," said Frank, "I thought we were supposed to be parts of the same country."

Alan replied, "We are, but it's not unheard of for jealousies to escalate into conflict."

A group of guardsmen at the other end of the table got up with a noisy clatter having finished their meal. Matthew walked past into the kitchen mumbling to himself. Frank looked thoughtful.

"We'll have to think what we can do to calm their fears; I don't want any more battles if I can help it."

"My Lawd, you could consider inviting Despots Kagel and Hista here to talk with them and let them see things for themselves. That would allay their fears surely; assure them we have no beligewent intent. I would suggest that personal contact is important in these affairs."

"Yes that's an excellent idea!"

Alan shook his head. "For the Kagels that might be okay, but old boy Hista doesn't like to travel out of his region at all nowadays."

"He's the Bynar Despot," Frank said for confirmation.

"Yeah. He's an old widower and lives with his two daughters. Terrible worrier, keeps a large standing army bigger than any of the other despotates. He'll be the one needing reassurance more than anyone, but you'll have to go to see him, Frank."

"No matter. From what you're saying he's a worrier in charge of a lot of warriors."

"Very good, Frank," an ironic Alan replied.

"Thanks, I thought it was. Seriously though, to recap we'll invite Despot Kagel and his family over for a visit, but go to Despot Hista in Bynar ourselves. We will have to see if we can set their minds at rest so that we can concentrate on problems and concerns closer to home.

With both conversation and meal completed he leaned back and studied the hectic comings and goings around them. At times it looked more like a market than the market itself as people went about their business. A group of hired men carrying bundles were being directed down the spiral staircase by Japhses. They were taking newly acquired winter uniforms for the Guard into storage. Eko was arguing with a Sarnician trader who had found his way into the keep and was trying to sell her cheap cosmetics. Laffaxe was sitting a short way away by himself, a little island of silence amid the noisy scenes. Illianeth brought him another drink.

"Ah yes," Frank exclaimed turning to Natias, "how are the reading lessons coming on?"

"Not badly at all, My Lawd, much better than I had dared hope."

Alan asked, "What's this all about?"

"I've asked Natias here to teach Illianeth to read. It will give her a new interest in life and I'd like her to read my Bible to me while I eat my meals. That would be.... nice..."

His sentence trailed off as a quick squint across the large room confirmed that the diminutive figure talking with Japhses was indeed Giella. It seemed ages since their last conversation in the market place. He felt himself drawn by an irresistible magnet over to the other side of the room and suddenly wished Alan and Natias were not there.

"Right! That just about concludes matters for now doesn't it," he said loudly with a note of finality. "I want to discuss something with Japhses, I'll see you both later."

He got up as he spoke and began making his way across the busy room. Alan was a bit surprised at the sudden end to the proceedings, but with a quick shrug of the shoulders he set off for the balcony stairs while the steward nipped into the kitchen to check on things there.

To Frank's delight the Captain concluded his conversation with Giella and set off down the spiral staircase just before he arrived.

"Hello there," he began cheerfully, "How are things? How's Roin?"

She smiled her beautiful smile upon seeing the Despot, but looked puzzled for a moment at his second question.

"Oh you mean Roil," she exclaimed with a chuckle, "she's well thank you My Lord. And how are the affairs of state today?"

He was annoyed with himself for having got her daughter's name wrong, but she clearly did not mind. An enchanting aroma reached him now he was close; it was the subtle fragrance of an expensive perfume.

"They're all right," he replied as he desperately sought something interesting to say. He was struck by her appearance: eyes elaborately made up in a soft purple which matched the colour of her flowing dress. A thin gold chain supported a small jet pendant around her neck. "Did you give the prisoners the flute recital you were hoping to?"

In response she let forth a high-pitched giggle just as the noise-level in the hall momentarily dropped. She put her hand over her mouth playfully before the hubbub returned and the two of them laughed loudly.

"That always happens to me!" she said. "I did play to the prisoners, My Lord. Actually some of the other girls came along, we had a bit of a party. Those Ma'hol weren't bad."

"Talking of instruments Giella, upstairs I've got..."

He stopped because she was trying to speak.

"I'm sorry, My Lord, but I've got to be getting back, they'll be annoyed with me enough as it is."

With that she leaned towards Frank and to his astonishment gave him a kiss on the cheek.

"See you again soon, My Lord," she called out as she headed for the door, leaving him rooted to the spot in a state of shock.

She flitted away like a delicate, purple butterfly. Frank glanced round, but the busy people going about their business were not paying him any attention. In a daze he started up the spiral staircase to his suite.

Giella was so unlike the other whites, especially the women, who held him in awe. She was like a nymph, finding joy in existence itself, in living a free life and not being tied down.

At last his mind conceded what his heart had been telling him from the moment he had first laid eyes on this irresistible woman: he was utterly and helplessly in love with her.

⚔ ⚔

CHAPTER EIGHTEEN

Early the next day Frank was by himself in his bedroom. He had had a terrible night racked by desire for a married woman. He realised he would lose the fight and end up doing something stupid if his thoughts continued the way they were going. For reinforcements he reached for his Bible and thumbed through the index for a relevant quotation. He had been neglecting its study lately and knew that that had been a factor in bringing him to his present sorry state. Turning up the book of Proverbs he read the verses:

"For though the lips of an adulteress drip honey
and her tongue is smoother than oil,
yet in the end she is more bitter than wormwood,
and sharp as a two-edged sword."

He nodded in agreement as he read, but then reminded himself that his state of mind was not Giella's fault. She had just been her normal cheerful, friendly self; it was he who was having unhealthy desires bombarding his mind. As yet another sexual fantasy formed in his brain he read the words of the Master:

"What I tell you is this: If a man looks on a woman with a lustful eye, he has already committed adultery with her in his heart."

Frank was far from being the first man to be in this situation, but he must purge away these lustful passions. He knelt and prayed hard, determined to rid himself of such sinful suggestions and resolving to tackle any such recurring thoughts as soon as they arose in future. He would have nothing to do with her from now on and keep to a routine of regular prayers.

Gradually he brought things under control as this fresh resolve began to have an effect. By the time he went down to breakfast he felt uplifted as he marvelled at the power of prayer. The sexual desires had been quite banished – for the moment.

No time was wasted in the preparations for the visit to Despot Hista of Bynar. On Alan's advice only a small party was to go: the two of them plus James and his squad of a dozen guardsmen.

It was a cold, autumnal morning as they set out. The sun had not yet climbed above the horizon and there was a heavy dew. The party was well wrapped up against the elements, the guardsmen wearing their new winter uniforms for the first time. They had five dakks with them, one each for Frank and Alan to ride while the other three carried provisions and presents for their host.

Setting off southwards from the Castle it began to grow light. "Steam" rose from their breath as they spoke, but little was said on the first leg of their journey.

Seizing the opportunity, they made a slight detour to see how the new village Sardis was progressing. It was still fairly early in the morning when they arrived and called in at the home of Luke (ex-Quafta-Harl). They were greeted by his wife who told them the Village Head had been up since dawn and was helping direct building operations.

"I see," replied the Despot," and how are you finding your new home? Everything all right is it?"

"Yes thank you, My Lord," the woman lied. The weather was cold and damp, the hut was draughty and she did not see nearly as much of her husband as she had done when they lived in Rabeth-Mephar.

"Nice to see you're settling in so well," Frank smiled.

A little girl crept round from the back of her mother's skirt. She looked up at the visitors and announced confidently, "My daddy is the Village Head!"

Alan replied, "Is he indeed? He must be a very important man!"

"Yes, he is."

James crouched down and held his arms out, "What's your name sweety?"

Instead of answering, the girl squirmed back behind the security of her mother who said something to her daughter in Ma'hol.

Frank remarked, "I had not realised you were all bilingual."

"We have always tried to set the example in our family by keeping the Old Language alive, My Lord."

"Very good."

They moved on to where the building work was going on. The activity was quite intensive. A group of dwellings was being worked on and a system had been developed to maximise the labour force. While some men were digging rectangular holes for the sunken floors, others set stakes round those previously prepared. Further men were at the next stage weaving wooden sticks and hulffan fibre between the posts, these were being assisted by a contingent of women.

Alan asked the whereabouts of Luke to a man carrying earth away. He was directed towards one of the partially dug rectangles. There the village leader was busily mucking in, digging for all he was worth with a spade. To have a village head work thus was considered bad form by James and the other guardsmen (original whites to a man, none of the Talton recruits had passed their basic training yet), but when Luke saw the Despot he broke off and climbed out to meet him. Like the rest of the Taltons he was now dressed in the traditional heavier Hoame clothing, far more sensible in the colder climate and it made them stand out less.

"Good morning, My Lord, is everything in order?"

He was breathing heavily and thick clouds of steam came from his mouth.

"Fine, fine," he was reassured, "we were just passing by and wanted to see how things were going; pretty well by the look of it."

"Yes, we haven't got many more homes to do before we reach our target for this year. Most of the workers are Sardis people now, just a few volunteers from the Upper Village are left to help us."

He made a scan of the scene as he spoke, then turned back to continue, "We understand the snows will be upon us soon, My Lord, so we want to get these completed as soon as possible. Following advise we are concentrating now on bringing in large quantities of wood for winter fuel, stockpiling it throughout the village."

Alan was watching the work.

"I wouldn't worry about the snow yet," he said without looking at Luke, "you're safe for a while yet. Even if it is early this year you've got at least twenty-five clear days ahead of you."

"Oh that's nice to know, thank you. It's just that lots of people have warned us how bad it can be."

"Sure," replied the drone, "pretty bad, but not just yet."

They did not stay for long, but long enough for a quick inspection of the development. Private dwellings had been concentrated on for now, but there were many ideas for the future. Community huts and other buildings were planned for the spring, and large gaps had been left for these. They did not want their village to end up an unbroken mass of buildings.

Leaving Sardis, the group crossed over one of the largest streams coming down from the mountains on the border with Ladosa. It would not be long before they were in Bynar. Frank and Alan rode ahead of the others on their dakks along a narrow track through a wood.

"Did you see the state of some of those houses?" Alan asked.

"No, weren't they very good?"

"I'll say! When I first heard how many had already been built I wondered if quality had been sacrificed in favour of quantity. Some of them struck me as looking decidedly rickety."

"Oh I see. Well I suppose they'll have more time once everyone's housed to make improvements."

"Yeah. I suppose they'll be strong enough to survive the winter." the drone remarked as he pulled out his map. "Anyway in case you're interested I reckon we must be in Bynar by now. This wood extends both sides of the border, but we should be coming out of it soon. Then we'll head south, straight down to Vonis the capital. All being well, we should get there by midday tomorrow."

"Excellent. Probably best to say afternoon to be on the safe side, but that'll be all right."

So Frank was back in Bynar, the first time he had been there since the spring. Indeed this was the first time he had been out of Thyatira since taking over the reins of power there. His mind wandered back to Offa and the journey from Ephamon all that time ago. What would the portly civil servant have made of how he was running the despotate? Not bad, Frank hoped, things seemed to be going quite nicely right now. But he must not court disaster by getting complacent. There would be plenty of challenges in the months ahead as the Taltons had to be integrated properly, especially important to get some practical industry going for them as Natias had warned.

'Yes,' thought Frank, 'I don't think Offa would consider I was doing too bad a job.

'Just a moment though Francis! Surely one of the things he was most concerned about was that I get married to a nice black girl and have lots of little black heirs. I'd completely forgotten about that, but then I haven't met any black women since I've been here. I wonder what there is in Bynar...'

Still riding their dakks they emerged from the wood to behold a green plane ahead of them dotted about with bushes and a few trees. As they did so a patrol of Bynarian soldiers suddenly appeared from their left. When the Bynarians saw the guardsmen following the two mounted men they panicked and drew their swords. Some fifty metres separated the two groups.

It was Alan who reacted quickest, shouting, "Wait, wait!" Jumping down from his saddle he took a few paces forward, waving his empty hands in the air and called out, "We're Hoamen! We're from Thyatira, put away your swords!"

The patrol's leader, a black officer, held his hand up to his men who lowered their weapons. The brief, but nasty moment of tension was over. Alan introduced the Despot of Thyatira to the officer, who ordered his men to sheath their swords before going up to address Frank.

"Welcome to Bynar, Sir, I am sorry about the reception you just received, but we had not been told of your visit."

"That's perfectly all right," replied Frank getting down to meet him, "we had not forewarned you. The visit was decided upon only recently and I was advised that it was best not to delay in order for it to proceed before the winter snows come."

The two men spoke some more around the subject and before Frank knew it he found his bodyguard had been swelled by another ten men for his journey to Vonis.

"Are you sure?" Frank asked, "won't that be putting you out of your way?"

"All is in order, Sir. We are told to use our initiative while on patrol and your safe passage must be the most important thing at this particular moment in time. All is quiet along the border."

So after a short break the enlarged party of men headed south. The black officer's name was Anton, and Frank, walking beside his dakk, had a long discussion with him as the journey continued that afternoon. He was from Setty, a large village in the northern area, about ten kilometres from the edge of the woods where they had met. Anton and his troops had been on the first of a standard three-day patrol. Being diverted to the regional capital would probably mean getting back a day late, but he assured Frank no one would worry too much about that. He went on to complain about the despotate's bureaucrats.

"They keep on sending out directives from the regional capital, but once they get out here to the northern province half of them are ignored. The problems are all with the despotate's local government, not much is heard from Asattan. Our Despot keeps a large number of clerks working and they obviously haven't got anything better to do!"

The officer continued talking quite freely, obviously feeling at ease in Frank's presence – he seemed to have that effect on people. Apparently the Oonimari Despot was famous where Anton came from and far from feeling threatened by Thyatira the common folk were pleased to hear of their resurgence. A strong buffer between themselves and the Ma'hol was something they welcomed.

"You will notice a difference in Vonis Sir. The pace of life is much quicker and there are many people around. They're an arrogant lot to tell the truth, think that the sun revolves round the despotate's capital and that us northerners are all ignorant and lazy."

"I see," replied the other before changing the subject, "how long have you been in the army?"

"Ever since I could hold a sword. All able-bodied men outside a few professions are required to spend part of each year in the army, patrolling here, guarding there. Black or white, it doesn't make any difference – although only blacks are officers of course.

"No, I'm a farmer by profession and I'll look forward to getting back to the land when my current term of service expires."

They went on, making good progress. Frank studied the Bynarian soldiers' uniforms, they were very similar to his own guardsmen at a glance. After a while he began to notice subtle differences, for instance in the shape of the helmets and the design of their shields.

They began to encounter villages more frequently and the road itself was of better quality the further south they went. The officer explained how Bynar differed greatly from one region to another in its population density. The route Frank had taken when he had first travelled to Thyatira had taken him through the sparsely-populated north-eastern region.

"Where I come from in the north there are plenty of villages, but it would be easy to avoid them, although I'm surprised you didn't meet more of our patrols."

They were still some twenty kilometres off Vonis when Anton suggested that the small town they were passing through would be a suitable place to stop for the night. As his feet were aching and the dakks in need of a rest, Frank readily agreed.

Anton knew the place well and organised rooms for Frank, Alan and himself at a very pleasant hotel for blacks in the best part of town. It was a stylish building of wooden construction with a tiled roof. Each of them had a separate room, pleasantly furnished and with a comfortable bed. The soldiers meanwhile were billeted in a couple of white inns in a poorer quarter. Frank was relieved that Alan, fair hair and all, was considered an honorary black.

The man from Eden lay in bed that night wondering at the way these social divisions by hair colour were accepted as totally normal by all concerned.

An enormous breakfast met them when the travellers came downstairs in the morning. Frank did not enjoy it, however, because he kept on worrying about the bill. They had not brought a great deal of money with them and he was beginning to regret that decision. When the subject came up at the end of the meal Anton said, "I have to complete a form so that the hotelier can claim money back from the local government in Vonis. We can only do this in certain circumstances, but it's a good system as long as it's not abused."

The black's smile was met by a look of relief on Frank's face. Soon they had met up with their soldiers and together they went on to the regional capital. Frank and Alan were not riding their dakks as Anton did not have one. The two blacks chatted casually as they went. After a while the Bynarian fell back to have a word with his number two and Frank seized the opportunity to quiz Alan about Bynar's despot.

"Sorry I haven't spoken much to you since Anton and his men arrived," he began.

"That's okay," replied the drone completely un-bothered, "I've been taking in some of the scenery. Not long to go now."

"No, that's what I wanted to talk to you about. You said Despot Hista is the one who's most likely to be concerned about our expanding population and all that."

"That's right, old boy Hista is a real barrel of laughs!"

Frank looked worried at the other's ironic tone. "Do you think we should have forewarned him of our arrival? I'm not so sure we should be dropping in unannounced like this."

Alan replied casually, "Nooo. It wouldn't make any difference." A twinkle came into his eye, "You'll just *love* his daughters though, they're big girls! I just hope we catch Paula on a good day."

Just then Anton returned and Frank did not have an opportunity to ask for an explanation before Vonis appeared in front of them as they came over the brow of a hill.

A walled city, Bynar's capital made an impressive sight after an age of wattle and daub huts. Anton led them in through one of the gates, showing his identification papers and explaining who his visitors were to the sentries. He took them through busy, narrow, cobbled streets to the other side of the city. There lay Despot Hista's castle, in the middle of a large, flat open area which was deserted other than a few military personnel going about their business. The ground was mettled with imported hulffan tar and Anton explained that of the whites only the army or those with expressed permission were allowed in this area.

They ventured across and were not challenged until they got to the outer wall of the castle. There Anton spoke with the sentry and, having discharged his duty, he and his men bid the Thyatirans farewell and went on their way. The sentry saw the travellers through to the outer bailey where a black officer of Hista's bodyguard met them.

This officer turned out to be known by Alan and the two of them struck up a hearty conversation. The Thyatiran guardsmen could not venture any further, but Frank was assured they would be well looked after and billeted nearby. There were stables within the walls to house the dakks. Alan mentioned the presents for Despot Hista and the officer instructed some of his own men to bring them.

Despot Tomas Hista was a man of around sixty Earth-years, but he seemed a lot older both in manner and appearance. He had a thin, wrinkled face. The stoop that had developed the last few years did not help either. He was in his council room having a discussion with some advisors when his uninvited guests were ushered in. The officer announced, "The Despot of Thyatira Francis Thorn and his Chief Advisor, the Drone Alan," and the frail man frowned and turned to see what was going on.

Frank began cheerfully, "I'm very pleased to meet you Despot Hista."

The other peered round with a harassed expression.

"Oh dear!" was all he said.

"Well I suppose you did warn me," Frank conceded later in the privacy of the suite of rooms allocated to him.

Alan was sitting on a plush divan, picking through a bowl of assorted nuts on a side table. He looked up with the now familiar glint in his eye, saying, "I think it was the initial shock to 'im. He seemed pleased enough with the presents. We'll get a bit more sense out of him supper time. Remember the only object of our trip is to reassure him we are no threat or destabilizing influence."

"Haven't you seen all these battlements, soldiers and security measures around here? We're hardly a threat to him!"

"Of course I know that, it's what's in the old boy's mind that matters."

"Right. Did you see how his hands were shaking? Poor man's a nervous wreck."

"Yeah, he's deteriorated quite a lot since I last met him."

"Has he? He didn't seem to recognise you."

"I'm not bothered," returned the other putting a large nut into his mouth, "he lives in a dream-world of his...oops!"

The nut flew out of his mouth as he was talking and he caught it in his hand. They both laughed loudly.

"That'll teach me to eat with my mouth full!"

"One thing I wanted to ask," said Frank returning to seriousness, "what was it you said about one of his daughters – Paula was it?"

"Mmm, that I hope we catch her on a good day. She's a real manic depressive, up one day, down the next."

The two of them sat in silence for a while after that. Frank had been interested in the layout of the castle, it was very similar in its general construction to the one in Thyatira. It was better finished and more sumptuously furnished though. The entrance was different as well, with several ante-chambers leading to a similar hall with a polished wooden floor. The room they were in had obviously been a library, with empty shelving round all four walls. But where were all the books now?

A servant came to the door and announced that Dessans Paula and Vanda Hista were desiring to come in and meet the Despot of Thyatira.

"Er, all right, please ask them in," said Frank standing up.

"Speak of the devil," Alan whispered from the divan just before their hostesses burst in.

"Ah hello, Frankie! Fantastic that you're here, I'm Paula," the large lady announced as she swept into the room, her long black hair trailing behind her, "I trust you don't mind me calling you Frankie."

He opened his mouth to answer, but was then overwhelmed by the second Valkyrie storming the suite, just as large and just as ugly.

"Don't be a bore, Paula dear. Hello Frank I'm Vanda, but you can call me Vandi. Are your rooms to your liking?"

She came right up to him as she spoke, deliberately standing in front of her sister. Frank instinctively took a step back, only to find himself up against the back of the divan.

Thoughts flashed through his head: 'Are these women, or men dressed up? I'd rather die than marry one of these! Where's Cinderella?'

"The rooms are fine, thank you very much," he replied, "er, won't you sit down?"

"You can sit with me," Vanda announced, pushing her sister away. She grabbed the visitor's arm in a vice-like grip and pulled him down onto the divan. With her sitting beside him there was no room for anyone else.

Paula had to content herself with a chair, but not to be outdone she drew it right up close. Alan was happy to be ignored, he found another chair and another bowl of nuts and sat a little way off popping them into his mouth, enjoying the spectacle before him.

Vanda held Frank's hand across her lap and spoke excitedly, "We hear such tales of Thyatira nowadays, a big army and new towns being built the whole time, is it true you are the only black there?"

"Never mind that!" exclaimed her sister deciding to launch a counter-offensive for Frank's attention, "We've heard of your bravery in battle, killing lots of Ma'hol and routing their army. Did you kill many yourself?"

Frank did not know where to start. Not wishing to upset either of them he replied that he *was* the only black in Thyatira and that he had not himself killed many men in the battle. The result was both women fired supplementary questions expecting the first answer and he was no better off. In fact he found himself in the middle of a power-struggle which made the Ma'hol battle seem like a piece of cake. Fortunately it was soon meal-time and the woman were a lot more restrained in their father's presence.

It was all so different from Thyatira. Instead of the large hall, a smaller dining room was used. The architecture here was much finer than the cruder, more functional style Frank had grown used to by now. The table was made of dark wood with delicately carved patterns on its sturdy legs. The cutlery and china were of a far superior quality too. About twenty-five people were seated, all blacks apart from a couple of drones. The only whites were the servants coming to and fro with the food and drink. Frank sat at the right hand of Despot Hista while Alan was towards the other end of the table. He turned down the offer of wine and caused a few curious looks when he quietly said grace beginning his meal.

Fortunately Hista's daughters had been placed a few seats down from where Frank was and could not exactly communicate with him. Opposite him sat Bynar's Chancellor and his wife, while the Army Commander sat on his right. These all turned out to be most friendly and as the small talk developed Frank began to feel more relaxed. He thought he should try to bring Hista into the conversation more, as he had said very little up to this point.

"I was curious about the library in my suite, I wondered if you knew where all the books were."

The old-looking man glanced up from his meal and, still chewing, said, "My father had them all burnt years ago, good job too! Full of damn silly ideas."

The conversation died at that end of the table for a while, then to Frank's surprise Hista started it up again.

"You were escorted down here by some northerners I hear, Thorn."

It seemed like a non-sequitur, but his mind had followed a logical pattern as became clear from his follow-up remark.

"They're full of silly ideas those northerners, no respect for authority! Damned unruly lot."

"My escort spoke highly of you, Despot Hista," Frank responded. He had wanted to defend Anton and his men; his lie was so blatant it might just be believed.

It was not.

"Planning rebellion they are, have to keep a strong army," Hista continued more to himself than anyone else.

Frank expected the Army Commander to voice agreement, but instead he spoke about the reports of Thyatiran victory and expansion. This was the opportunity to allay their fears and he spoke at length about the small defence force in Thyatira which was totally unsuited for attacking anyone outside his despotate. At the end of his speech he got another "Oh dear" out of Hista, but this seemed to be merely a habit and the old man did seem a bit more convinced about this than he did over his own northern province.

Frank then remembered the poor response his envoy had got from this man when asked for reinforcements against the Ma'hol, but decided not to raise the grievance and the rest of the meal passed without incident.

That night thoughts of Giella returned to Frank and he found them more difficult to fight them off than he should have. He was glad when morning came.

A guided tour of the city was provided by the Chancellor and his wife the following morning, although Alan stayed at the castle. Frank was relieved that Paula and Vanda did not come along. He wondered where they were, but did not want to talk them up so kept off the subject. He later found that Alan had misdirected them as to his whereabouts. That is what friends are for.

A centre of commerce, Vonis had large financial and market areas. There were many beggars among the milling crowds and Frank insisted on giving at least one coin to each of them, somewhat to the embarrassment of his hosts. His actions only encouraged more begging. He generally got on well with his guides, however, and learned from them something of the sophisticated tax system with incentives for new businesses.

After the midday meal, Frank and Alan said their goodbyes to the Bynarians. They then collected up the guardsmen and dakks before setting off for home.

It was a largely uneventful journey back. They laughed about Hista's daughters and Frank expressed relief that he had managed to avoid them on the second day.

The guardsmen ate their rations on the march. Frank was pleased to hear about a conversation the drone had had that morning.

"My officer friend, the one we met when we first arrived, turned out to be on the staff. He told me that Hista had ordered more outposts to be built on their border with us a short while back. Early this morning he rescinded that order. If that's not convincing proof of the success of our mission then nothing is!"

"Excellent! Don't often get confirmation as neatly as that; made our brief visit well worthwhile."

"Now all we have to do is a similar job on Kagel. He's not as suspicious as old boy Hista I'm glad to say."

"That's good to know. We hadn't got any kind of acceptance from Aggeparii to our invitation when we left..." He looked up to the horizon and saw the wood that marked the border with Thyatira and added, "It'll be good to get back home."

Someone in Aggeparii was trying to carve out a new life for themselves. A lone figure walked through the streets of the regional capital Aggeparii City. Known by all the locals simply as "the city," it was full of narrow cobble streets and dingy alleyways. Evening was falling and the fresh autumnal air was mixed with the distinctive smell of dyes as the woman passed by the factories beside the river.

A hundred days had passed since Katrina had left her home and set off in search of a fresh start in life. She had got a good price for the well-positioned piece of land in the Upper Village. Her journey across the woodland border had been hair-raising. A lone woman passing through notorious bandit country with a large sum of money, she would have been easy pickings if caught. To hire bodyguards would have meant easy detection, even if they were to be trusted. So she had told no one of her journey and had travelled at night.

It was the first time she had been out of her native despotate. One thing that became immediately apparent about the city was the enormous contrast in living conditions between black and white. This was true of Thyatira of course, but there was no abject poverty there, especially since the resettling of the Lower Village. In fact only now did Katrina realise quite how well off the whites there were. The absence of blacks must have been a factor, with whites such as Japhses, Natias and the Village Heads having real positions of authority. Despot Thorn had made no moves to bring in blacks and had expelled two of the three drones.

Aggeparii could not have been more different. The rigid social structure of this, the most populous despotate, was well defined. Despot Kagel and his immediate family formed the top of the pyramid. What they said was law and everyone fawned to them, trying their utmost to curry favour. Next were the other blacks. These lived in the eastern *carto* or part of the city around the Despot's castle. Here the accommodation was good, large stone houses with comfortable interiors. Centred nearby was the district where the drones lived. Far smaller in number, these were nearly all in the direct service of the Despot. Relatively few blacks or drones were in the villages which peppered the rest of Aggeparii, many of which were exclusively white.

The whites, while being at the bottom of the social ladder, had a hierarchy of their own. Those in castle service were considerably better off materially than their colleagues. As a result they felt themselves superior to the masses of other whites living in rows of inferior timber housing that made up so much of the regional capital. Many of these latter worked in clothing factories dotted throughout the city. These in turn knew their lot was preferable to that of the rural whites existing in even more squalid conditions. Many of the villages were run down, their inhabitants on little more than a starvation diet and burdened by hard work and high taxes.

Being white though, it was in their nature to accept the status quo. A favourite theme of the priests was the temporary and illusionary nature of the physical world. The most popular parable was of the white man called Lazarus and the rich black man. When Katrina had first arrived, the people were still gripped by the Fitz Wanhelm scandal. This black democrat had tried to rally popular support among the Aggeparii whites after failing in his native Bynar. To his utter despair he had found complete apathy instead. He now resided in Despot Kagel's dungeon, a dissolutioned and broken man.

Katrina had no time for politicians or revolutionaries of any kind, believing they were all talk and no action. She had dismissed the Wanhelm affair with a shrug when it was recounted to her. The thing that she did take notice of though was the comparatively huge population. There were no towns or cities in Thyatira and it all took some getting used to. The crowded buildings and claustrophobic alleyways were a shock at first. She rarely ventured into the area around the castle, but when she did it was with a sense of fascination that she observed the large numbers of blacks there.

Settling in a hostel in a poorer part of the city meant she could conserve her savings. The room was not too uncomfortable, good by local standards, and reasonable food was provided. She paid the rent on time and no one bothered her, an arrangement which suited landlord and tenant alike.

So how did she use her new-found freedom? She spent every day working for nothing at a church mission for the sick and dying in the neighbouring *carto*. How she laughed at herself: at last she could do whatever she wanted and instead of looking after number one, as she had always imagined she would, she spent all her time helping others. She found it impossible to remember how she had been dragged into it and kept telling herself she could stop the work at any moment if she chose to. The last thing she would do was admit the truth, that she actually enjoyed it and found the work rewarding.

He co-workers were not at all sure what to make of the strange woman with the husky voice and the grey streak in her hair. Her dedication to the suffering would have put most saints to shame, yet she did not attend the daily services and socially kept herself to herself. The priests who ran the mission were sharply divided for and against the newcomer – Katrina had never engendered indifference in her life – but they knew the patients all looked upon her as an angel.

On this particular evening she had worked later than she had intended. In the past she had always stuck to the good advise to get home before it got dark, but now the light was fading fast. She picked up her step.

When night came on Molten it was as black as coal. No moon and few stars ensured this. There were no street lamps in this *carto* and Katrina soon found herself groping her way, aided by memory and pale candlelight escaping from windows along the way.

Fairly confident she was only a couple of blocks away, she rounded a corner and heard something which made her stop in her tracks. What kind of animal made that sort of noise?

It was a moment before she realised the high-pitched whimpering was of human origin. Advancing slowly, Katrina saw the answer crouched down by a wall in the narrow street, dimly lit from a high window opposite. She could not make out the girl's face, but one thing was immediately apparent was that she had no clothes on. She was sobbing pitifully and called out, "No!" when Katrina bent down and touched her.

"It's okay, it's okay."

The gruff voice did nothing at first to allay the girl's fears, but when she realised the newcomer meant her no harm she allowed a comforting arm around her.

"What has happened to you?"

The sobbing continued as she helped the shivering girl up. Katrina could feel the goose pimples along the naked body, the smell of blood was in the air.

"Come on, let's go home."

The mission had to do without their most regular volunteer helper for the next week. Instead Katrina stayed in the hostel and nursed her charge. She had decided that her room was the best place to look after the girl.

Step by step she managed to gain her confidence. It took a great deal of patience, sympathy and sheer perseverance. Fortunately the girl was responsive, her natural resilience helping to pull her through. Her name was Shalee and she had been the victim of a vicious multiple rape. Just fourteen Earthyears old, she had no family and worked in one of the large sweat shops in the city. Returning late that evening a young white man in a military uniform had come up to her and began chatting in a friendly manner. Having met him briefly on a couple of other occasions Shalee was not suspicious of this sudden attention, but rather flattered by it. After a while he had suggested they go to a drinking house together. Shalee had declined, saying she wanted to get home. Then the man suddenly turned nasty and dragged her off to a deserted building where his accomplices were waiting. It was there that the atrocity had taken place.

The girl's face was so badly beaten it swelled up around her eyes and she could not see at all for the first few days. Gradually she got better thanks to Katrina's patient nursing.

"There, you settle down. Tomorrow I'm off to see the magistrate to get him to bring those bastards to justice."

Shalee sat up in bed. Her face was still a sight, but the bruising was at last beginning to subside. She was concerned at Katrina's plan though and told her to let the matter drop.

"What! You said you'd recognise them."

"Yes, but they were from the Despot's bodyguard, I know that. And the officer was a drone, I told you that..."

"Good, so he'll be executed."

"But you won't stand a chance against them."

"Shame! We'll see about that. I'm not not going to see them get away unpunished. I'll make the magistrate's life a misery if I have to, but I'll make those bastards pay!"

It felt good to be back in familiar surroundings. Frank stood on the balcony of the castle hall discussing a subject that resulted from their visit to Bynar.

"You know, Alan, I was most impressed by the interior of the castle there. I wonder if we could get ours done like that. At least talk to an architect and see what possibilities there are."

"We'd need to hire a guild squad. The only place we could get a first rate architect would be Asattan. It's be costly, but worth it in my opinion. Best thing would be to send a messenger to try and hire one, but it should be someone in the know... I'd be happy to go. I've got the contacts and would be able to get the right squad at the right price."

Frank leaned back onto the wooden balcony rail and said, "Let's think about it. 'Cos there's the stone church too. The plans for that have been in the capital for some time now."

Down in the hall, Natias was finishing off a conversation with a young couple making plans for their wedding.

"I am glad all is well between you now. Wight fwom the start I always knew you were made for each other."

"We're both very much in love," replied Rodd squeezing Leah's hand and looking into her eyes, "I knew we could work it out."

"Good, I'm sure you will be vewy happy together. Oh no!" the steward ejaculated suddenly with a look of alarm across his face, "look who is here. Sowwy, I must go."

Into the Castle had strode the Despot of Aggeparii and nobody was there to greet him. The guards at the main entrance were later given a sound ticking-off for not announcing him. He was followed by his wife and daughter. Behind them a sizeable entourage of servants and soldiers trailed from the hall and down the stairs into the inner bailey.

Despot John Kagel was a man of forty-two Earth years, one metre sixty tall and of average build. He had a small beard trimmed to the nearest millimetre and expertly manicured hands. Aggeparii's vast iron ore deposits made his despotate one of the wealthiest and he and his wife were not afraid to show it. They both wore ostentatiously expensive outfits beneath their long coats which their servants were now helping them off with.

Disagreeably the guests stood and scanned the room. The hall was its usual busy self with men and women hurriedly going about the place taking little or no notice of the new arrivals.

They had not been there long, however, before Natias spotted them and quickly came forward. He introduced himself and asked them if they would like to sit down while he fetched Despot Thorn.

"No, I do not!" Kagel replied, frowning at the wooden benches. "Kindly hurry along and fetch your master; I am not accustomed to waiting."

Up on the balcony Frank still had his back to the proceedings and with the general hubbub going on was blissfully unaware of the arrival of his guests.

"If we're going to pay for an architect and his men to come all that way, we may as well try and get our money's worth out of him."

Alan suddenly looked agitated and speeded up the conversation.

"Yeah, right that's settled then. I'll go to Asattan myself. I'll go alone, I'll travel quicker that way."

He slapped Frank on the shoulder then began to move away up the stairs. "I'll get ready and go straight-away," he called out. "See you when I get back. Bye!"

Frank stood there rather bemused at the abrupt curtailment of the conversation. Turning, he squinted down into the hall to try to make out what was going on. Not finding a satisfactory answer in the blur before him he began making his way down the stairs, to be met by a young manservant.

"My Lord, Natias has asked for your presence to meet Despot Kagel and his party."

"Oh right!"

Eagerly he crossed the hall to greet them. After introducing himself, Despot Kagel introduced his womenfolk.

"This is my wife, Despotess Astra..."

A handsome woman just a few Earth-years younger than her husband, she was the same height as him. Her superior expression was accentuated by her hair being swept up and back, revealing a high forehead. With her coat relinquished, a colourful outfit was revealed, be-speckled with semi-precious jewels. She did manage a brief smile to her host before continuing to survey the stark, functional hall with mounting distaste.

"...And my daughter the Dessan Ilga."

Even though the teenager's hair was in a totally different style, short and with a fringe, there was no mistaking whose daughter this was. She had precisely the same superior expression as her mother and was also looking around disapprovingly, just like a baby dakk will imitate its mother.

Kagel completed his piece with the introduction of a couple of his important black officials whose names Frank instantly forgot.

"Well I'm very pleased you all came. I've been looking forward to getting to know my neighbours. You've met Natias my steward, I'll introduce you to Japhses, my Captain of the Guard, when he gets in. We can go up now if you like and see where you will stay."

'Japhses!?' thought Kagel as they ascended the stairs, 'that's another white name!'

Frank personally showed them their rooms. They were relieved to find them a lot more comfortable than they were beginning to expect. While the servants began unpacking the luggage and the rest of the large entourage were being shown their quarters, Kagel and his family went to his suite. The visiting despot was pleased to have this opportunity to get to know this foreigner he had heard so many conflicting stories about.

"I say Thorn, it's many years since I was here last, when that animal Rattinger was still alive, is it true there are now no blacks left in Thyatira other than yourself?"

"That's right. There've been none ever since I got here in the spring."

"Dreadful!" exclaimed the Despotess Astra with a look of horror on her face.

"Not really; the people here are most pleasant, I get on well with them. Well, most of them most of the time at least. I find pers..."

"You don't know anything different I suppose," Despot Kagel butted in. "It really is too bad though, I would have thought the Keepers would have made better provision."

Frank then had to explain about Offa and Kagel shook his head.

"At least you've got the drones," he said, "they're not quite white."

"Well I've got one, I expelled the rest some time ago as disruptive influences."

"One."

"Yes Alan, he's just left on an assignment for us."

The other nodded slowly.

"Yes, I've met Alan of course."

Frank at first got the impression this signalled further disapproval, but Kagel went on to talk about the extensive trade deal he had negotiated with him.

The conversation moved on and before long Frank was able to work in his speech about exaggerated rumours and Thyatira not being a threat to the rest of Hoame.

Kagel laughed at the idea, "I can see now how true that is. A small defence force with its chalky officers isn't exactly going to set the world on fire!"

Thought Frank, 'They kicked the stuffing out of the Ma'hol; my chalky officers would give you a run for your money!' but he bit his tongue.

No insult was intended by Kagel's comments though, this was simply his style. Frank was amazed and more than a little horrified at the way his neighbours despised their fellow human beings simply because of the colour of their hair. No conscious effort was needed by them, they simply "knew" they were superior and would bring their children up with this same "knowledge". For all the infighting on Eden he had never come across quite this disgusting an attitude. Although intensely annoyed at their arrogance he kept quiet. It was important to keep on good terms with these people. He comforted himself with the thought that they would not be staying long.

With the Kagels retired to their quarters to prepare for the evening meal, however, Frank still had it in mind to brazen out his plan of having Natias and Japhses join them upstairs to eat. He felt it only fair to put his steward in the picture and hurried down to have a word, finding him in his room.

"I want to show them I am not ashamed of you both. It is a matter of principal!"

There was compassion in Natias' eyes as he listened to his master's words. "May I speak fweely, My Lawd?"

"Of course."

"Do not think I do not appweciate the thought, but as a man once said: 'when something becomes a matter of pwincipal then common sense flies out the window.' If you had told me of your plan earlier, My Lawd I would have advised stwongly against it. They would never accept eating at the same table as a white. It is simply not worth upsetting them to pwoove a point."

Frank shrugged his shoulders and sighed.

"It was also to be Illianeth's first reading at the table wasn't it?"

By way of an answer Natias quoted scripture, "Do not give what is holy to fwasses, they will only turn and attack you. Do not thwow your pearls to the pigs, they will only twample them underfoot and turn on you"

Frank smiled.

The result was that no lieutenants were present for the dinner in the Despot's quarters. The host was not too pleased at finding himself still outnumbered three to one by his guests, but when not talking about whites, the Kagels' conversation was not too bad.

Matthew had excelled himself; the food was superb and well received. Towards the end of the meal, Despot Kagel came up with an unexpected proposition.

"I would not be doing my duty as a neighbour Thorn if I were not to recommend to certain of my black families that they move to Thyatira. Clearly there are opportunities for them and it will do you good to have black company. What do you say?"

Manifestly it was designed to be a magnanimous offer, to have declined would have been to insult. No choice then but to accept.

"Thank you very much, that's most generous of you," came the reply sounding as sincere as possible.

"Good, that's settled then. I'll get my secretaries to make the necessary arrangements when we get back."

'What have I let myself in for?' Frank asked himself as the meal was being concluded. 'I'm perfectly happy without any "blacks" here. Alan would have been able to've diverted them if he'd been here. He's deserted me when I needed him most! Where are you, Alan?'

⊨+⊨

CHAPTER NINETEEN

Upon noticing the arrival of the Kagels, Alan had decided to make himself scarce. Of course he had known they had been invited, but when he saw them, the thought of having to out up with them was simply too much. The strain of his stay in Aggeparii earlier in the year had been more than enough. During the protracted negotiations he had had to remain sweetness and light towards those arrogant obscurants. He just did not feel he could manage the effort again so soon. So grabbing up some food, money and assorted supplies he crept back down the spiral staircase and out of the Castle.

He rode his dakk hard on the road towards the Bynar border. As he did so, thoughts of regret came to him.

'I shouldn't have left Frank in the lurch like that. It wasn't fair when he's got to put up with the Kagels.

'He'll be okay,' his other side told himself, 'he is a black after all.

'They'll eat him for breakfast, poor man; when has he ever betrayed me like that?

'Oh sod it, he'll be okay. Besides, I've gone too far to turn back now...'

Too far and too hard. The dakk was foaming at the mouth and somewhat belatedly he dismounted to give it a rest. He sat down and had a snack.

A short while later he was listening to the birds singing in the trees as he walked along the track, holding the rein loosely in his right hand. On either side was a grass verge, beyond which tall, straight evergreens pointed up at the sky. It narrowed slightly as the track rounded a bend.

Caught in a daydream he did not notice them until he was almost upon them. Three travellers were sprawled across the track, apparently stopped for some refreshment. Looking round, their conversation stopped as they became aware of his presence.

It took Alan no time at all to sum them up – rough, unsavoury characters. Their dakks were together, grazing on the verge some twenty-five metres back. The man nearest him wore a wide-brimmed hat and got up off his haunches as soon as the newcomer arrived and, chewing slowly, began to advance. The other two began standing up, one had a scar on his face and Alan felt sure he had seen him before, the other looked more nervous.

"Greetings drone," began the man with the hat in a tone which sounded more like a threat than a greeting. It was not a local accent, more a southern Hoame one. "You got any munus root I can 'ave?" he asked as he still came on.

Alan knew this renegade's intentions and, without answering, his hand moved over to his sword.

Realising his intended victim's guard was not going to be lowered by his poor attempt at deception, the man with the hat drew his thirty-centimetre dagger from his belt.

"Come on!" he shouted to his confederates as he sprang.

In a swift couple of moves Alan's sword was parrying the first thrust as he wheeled his dakk in front of the other two robbers.

He knew he had to dispatch their leader before the others could get to him. Skilfully his opponent blocked his first sword thrusts. Alan had to quickly glance round to see where the others were and the man with the hat seized this opportunity to attack. The drone's reactions were much too quick for him though. Dodging the dagger's thrust he flashed his own blade under the man's guard and plunged it into his heart.

He dropped to the ground like a stone, hat rolling to one side. Not that Alan had time to watch this. The body had not even touched the grass before he was crossing swords with the scar-faced second protagonist. The third man held back, much to Alan's surprise and delight. Scar-face was no match for Alan's swordplay, the latter soon evaded the robber's defence and brought his razor-sharp edge down on the man's sword hand. With a cry the weapon fell from his hand. Blood poured from the stumps of three severed fingers.

Scar-face turned and fled in the direction of the dakks, leaving the remaining man to his fate. As the drone advanced towards him, the third would-be robber let go of his weapon and held his empty hands out. Rooted to the spot through fear he did not follow the example of his fleeing compatriot, but babbled a pleas for his life.

"N-n-no no no. P-please don't. It wasn't my idea, I didn't want to go along with it..."

Relentlessly, Alan approached, sword firmly in hand. His adrenalin was running high and he was not in the mood for granting clemency.

"For Jesus' sake don't," the man still gabbled, falling to his knees, "the other drones forced me into it!"

Alan stopped. What on Molt was the man talking about? Drones sponsoring robbers? That made no sense. Holding the sword to the quivering man's throat he said grimly, "I know nothing of Jesus and I'll take your head from your shoulders as easily as breath. Tell me what you mean by 'the other drones'."

The man was not slow in telling all he knew. His assailant's mouth dropped in amazement as the story unfolded. It was far too detailed to have been made up. These three whites had not been casual robbers, but hired as assassins by a pair of drones from southern Ephamon. The intended target had been Despot Thorn, but there was to have been an extra payment for the death of Alan. The prisoner told him that the mission's leader had been, as Alan had surmised, the man with the hat, who like himself was a native of Ephamon. The third man, "scar-face" was from Thyatira and had known the drone before.

"Hakka is his name Sir."

It rang a bell, but Alan could not quite place him. He told the trembling man to continue.

"I... I did not want to go along, Sir. I was in debt and they threatened my family with imprisonment Sir if..."

"Never mind that," his captor interrupted, still holding the sword to the other's throat, "what were the names of the drones?"

Hesitation brought the blade tighter against his flesh.

"Their names!"

"Er, I – I'm not sure Sir, but they're staying in a village: Ekronsberg south of Asattan. I think one was called Adrian."

The blade moved away as the drone let forth a sardonic laugh, "I'm sure he was; and the other one was Crispin...

"Right, up you get. I'll let your other intended victim deal with you. Where's some rope to tie your hands with?"

Together the two of them made for Sardis with the three remaining dakks. There was nothing in all the equipment with which to tie the prisoner up, but with Alan's eye on him the whole time he made no attempt to escape.

The sun was setting by the time they reached the village. The would-be assassin was handed over to Luke who put him under guard. Alan told the Village Head all he knew and was assured the whole story would be conveyed, along with the prisoner, to the Despot in the morning.

So instead of sleeping rough the first night of his journey Alan had the "comfort" of a crude bed plus a roof over his head. He had lost half a day as a result of his little adventure, but that was not to be helped.

The sound of pigs grunting nearby woke him just before dawn. They were being led past his hut by a young swineherd. Pleased to get an early start, Alan made the most of his location by having a good meal before he left. He also re-packed his provisions and other supplies in a more orderly fashion than he had for his hurried departure from the Castle. Now that there was time for attention to detail, a spare dakk was loaded up and rope procured to add to his equipment.

It was during this operation that the identity of the wounded assassin came to mind. Of course he had seen Hakka before, at the trial of this criminal when he was locked away. Alan had been amazed upon his return from Aggeparii to hear of the man's release by Frank. He gave a little laugh to himself at the irony of it. He made sure Luke knew to include this information in his report to the Despot. He said goodbye and led his dakks away. Before long, the village was out of sight and he was back on the trail.

It was on a frosty morning that he entered Asattan, capital of Hoame. By far the biggest city in the country, it had chronic traffic problems. The narrow streets were congested with carts and wagons, drivers swearing at each other, while their dakks stomped restlessly, sending out clouds of steam from their nostrils. Following a route familiar to him, Alan managed to lead his beasts through the maze towards the Citadel, his destination. He glanced up at it, dominating the skyline, while he picked his way along the cobbles. As he approached it the way became steeper and he was glad the heat from the buildings had kept ice from forming.

A final twist of the street brought him out onto a plateau with a large, flat open area. This was a forbidden zone like the one round the castle in Vonis. On the other side of it the mighty Citadel wall arose, fully fifteen metres high, forming part of the greatest structure in all Hoame. A stream of people comprising all from merchants to minstrels made their way to and fro on the cobbled round skirting the zone, but only a few sentries were within it.

Stepping from the cobbles onto the hulffan tar zone Alan, still with dakks in tow, made straight for a gate in the wall. The sentries there watched him advance towards them.

"Show your pass," one of them ordered.

"I have come to see Count Zastein."

The sentry seemed caught a little off balance by the stranger's apparent confidence at wanting to see the most powerful man in the land. He called for an officer.

"So," said the black as he arrived and took in the scene, "you want to see Count Zastein do you?"

His tone was slightly mocking and his men grinned at the spectacle. Then with a straight face the officer said, "If you have any business with the government you are to present yourself at the main gate round there," he pointed along the wall, "and if you're lucky one of the clerks might just have time for you. And walk on the perimeter road, unauthorised personnel are not allowed in the zone."

The visitor stood patiently during this short speech looking up at the stonework. As soon as the officer had finished he cast his eyes back to him and continued as if he had not heard a single word.

"Kindly tell him that Alan is here to see him."

The officer had been reasonably polite until now, but he did not like finding he had been wasting his breath.

"Listen country boy!" he snarled, "I'm not used to repeating myself. Get off the zone now or my men will throw you off!"

Alan was not at all intimidated by the man's aggressive tone. In his usual calm voice he sought to explain himself better.

"I should've said," he responded, "Count Zastein knows me. Please inform him that Alan is here and he will order me let in."

The officer was unnerved by the stranger's casual manner. He had not been stationed at the Citadel a very long time and did not know absolutely everyone, although this stranger did not look important. There would be no harm in checking his story: if the drone was right and was not let in he would have to face the wrath of his superiors when they found out; if it was a bluff he would have the pleasure of ejecting him with impunity. Leaving the gate to personally check Alan's story, the officer emerged a short while later with a far less arrogant demeanour. Trying to save face he announced in his best official manner, "You may enter, His Excellency will see you straight away."

Without a word, or sign of emotion, Alan strolled through the gate, followed by his beasts of burden.

"What are you staring at?" the officer snapped at one of the sentries, "keep alert, man, keep alert!"

Back in Thyatira Frank had received the report about the assassins. While being relieved to hear his friend was unhurt, he was too busy tied up with his guests to reflect on it at any length.

He bid the messenger keep quiet about it and the prisoner was swiftly put into the dungeon. Of course the story would get out before long, but he did not want the Kagels to hear about it.

That day he went out riding with them, but found they were disappointed there was no hunting.

They enjoyed going after wild pigs back home, but no such beasts roamed this part of the country.

Instead they were taken sight-seeing to the north of the Castle, well wrapped up against the cold air. Soon all references to hunting were dropped as the riders enjoyed the scenery. The trees here were mostly deciduous and the dakks trampled through the wet leaves recently fallen.

Under orders to, Natias came along, while several top blacks and their families accompanied the Kagels. Ilga's dakk had taken a dislike to its rider and refused to move.

"Come on you silly dumb thing!" she cried, adding a few expletives as she hit its rear mercilessly with her riding crop. The beast would not budge.

Thought Frank, 'Maybe it's got a dislike of spoilt children,'

More constructively Natias suggested it might be time to change dakks anyway and in spite of this idea coming from a white, it was accepted. Servants came running up with the fresh animals and the sight-seers changed over before proceeding on their jaunt. Fortunately Ilga's new dakk was less sensitive to her aggressive riding style and kept up with the others.

The two despots led the way as the path crossed a shallow stream and began a wide curve to the right. Kagel spoke.

"I hear your sponsor was none other than Count Zastein himself," he said with a measure of awe in his voice before having to duck to avoid a low branch.

"That's right," confirmed Frank, "he and Baron Schail arranged for me to come here."

"I must say I'm impressed; friends in such high places."

A patrol of Thyatiran guardsmen stood aside as the party went by. The soldiers were on their way to relieve one of the border posts.

Eventually the host suggested they turn and head back for the Castle.

"I'd like to get back 'cos it's the Sabbath and I want to attend the meeting there at sunset."

Kagel's eyes went wide in amazement.

"I had heard reports of the religious despot," he said, "but I still find it hard to believe. You know, Thorn, it's not the best of examples to make, to the whites I mean. We're to show ourselves above such superstitions."

Frank had been going along with virtually everything his guest had said until now in order not to rock the boat. This attack on his faith could not be ignored, however.

"There is nothing superstitious about faith in Jesus Christ, on the contrary, it does away with superstitions. I feel sorry for people who do *not* have the knowledge of God's love."

"Hmm, are there many black people like you where you come from?"

"If you mean Christians, then yes, there are," retorted Frank sharply, getting annoyed at the other's superior tone.

Kagel sniggered. "How quaint," he declared, concluding the conversation before adding an affected, "excuse me will you? I must have a word with my wife."

He wheeled his mount back, leaving Frank fuming to himself. 'Self-satisfied, ignorant toad. I'll be glad when they've gone!'

It was only the next day that they did leave. That night though Frank went to the church meeting as planned. These meetings still felt alien to him, but he quite enjoyed this one. It felt good to be amongst fellow believers. At the very least it helped to calm himself down and feel more kindly towards the

Kagels. After all they were only products of their upbringing and were to be pitied that they did not know any better. They did not know the peace, serenity and love which came from the worship of God's only Son. That night he read his Bible at length and quietly recited all the chants he could remember from his previous life on Eden. It was late by the time he went to bed on a spiritual high and slept peacefully.

"A most interesting visit, Thorn," was Kagel's verdict the next day as he and his entourage prepared to leave for home. Frank was all smiles, as indeed were Astra and Ilga now they were going. The womenfolk said goodbye before getting into their covered wagon.

I'll look into those black families for you," announced Kagel as a parting comment.

"Thank you," replied his opposite number thinking, 'Damn, he hasn't forgotten!'

The column wheeled out of the bailey, escorted by soldiers, both mounted and on foot. Natias stood next to his master as they watched the last of the procession disappear through the gate and away. Frank concluded that the visit had been as successful as his own to Bynar. He was glad it was all over though.

"With a bit of luck we can get back to normal now, Natias."

"Yes, My Lawd."

The conversation had moved on to music by the end of lunch in the hall. Their meals were finished and cleared away, and the kitchen staff had come out to eat theirs.

"Despot Wattinger had a gwoup of musicians who used to play to him each night. They were his particular favowites. Soon after he died they moved down south. There they were involved in a tewwible twagedy when they were performing in a building when it collapsed. Such a sad waste of life." He hesitated, "That is stwange My Lawd: that girl over there with Illianeth, I could have sworn she is one of Despot Kagel's personal servants, but what is she still doing here?"

"Strange," agreed Franks, "Let's call Illianeth over and ask her what's going on."

Illianeth was unabashed, "That's Soosha, she was the Despotess' handmaiden."

"Was?"

"She decided not to go back with them, 'cos she'd like to stay here."

"Was it her decision to make?"

The girl did not answer and Natias began remonstrating with her saying the Aggepariians could be offended by this, but Frank decided the hall was not the best place to discuss it.

"Bring her along when you've finished your meal and the four of us'll go into the Throne Room and we'll get to the bottom of all this.

Soosha was a lot younger than he had expected. Close to, she looked only about twelve or thirteen.

Under questioning they discovered she was an orphan. Standing there shyly with her shoulder-length hair, white as snow, and her big green eyes she had such a look of innocence that Frank was half won over before she spoke a word. Having just experienced the Kagels, her story of bullying and unreasonable behaviour by her mistress was not hard to give credence to. Timidly she told a tale of beatings and persecution. With longing in those big eyes she asked if she could stay and serve in Thyatira.

"I'm not sure," began Frank not wanting to cause a diplomatic incident with his neighbours. "If I receive a request from your mistress to return you I shall have to consider it very seriously and probably agree." He sighed. "You can stay here for the time-being anyway."

The two girls' faces lit up at these last words. The Despot continued, "Where do think Soosha should stay for now, Natias?"

Illianeth cut in eagerly, "She could stay with me in my room."

Frank and Natias exchanged glances as the identical thought came to them both: her enthusiasm at taking the younger girl under her wing might give Illianeth more meaning to life and be good for her. There were already signs with the way she had taken to reading that her rebellious phase might have peaked already. Frank mulled this over and had just decided to give his consent when an alternative suggestion came forward.

"May I suggest, My Lawd, that Soosha stay with Eko and myself for the time being. My wife is in need of someone to help her with various tasks. We will make sure she and Illianeth can see each other often."

So Natias was also won over. Frank looked towards Illianeth and was pleased to see she did not seem too disappointed. He agreed Natias' plan and this was happily accepted by all. Indeed the girls' faces shone with joy now this matter was settled to their advantage, but before they left he chose to remind them that the future was not certain.

"As I said before, a request for your return by Despot Kagel would have to be considered most carefully. Let us hope one never arises."

"There we are, you can let go now. How's that?

Bodd was being asked to comment on the new, sloping roof his brother had just completed on his aviary.

"Very good considering you did most of it by yourself."

"I did have practice with the old aviary, of course, but I think I've done a better job this time. Should keep the snow off anyway, that's what matters."

He slapped the interlocking planks hard with his palm and was pleased at the solid feel.

Taking a deep breath, Bodd stretched and peered up at the grey sky. It was mid-afternoon and the light was already beginning to fail.

"Yes, you've got it done just in time. Won't be long before we all have to hibernate for the winter."

"Look at that!" Tsodd exclaimed suddenly, pointing down a metre or so from where they stood.

"What?" asked his brother straining his eyes at the uneven ground, but seeing nothing.

Grabbing a spade Tsodd dug up a clod of earth at the spot where he had pointed. Breaking it up in his fingers he produced a fat worm. It was about fifteen centimetres long and as thick as a man's thumb.

"How about that?" he asked triumphantly as he held up his trophy. He gently squeezed its middle section with his muddy fingers. "Come on my beauty."

"Horrible," was Bodd's verdict. "What amazes me is how you saw it in this light... what are you doing?"

"It's a candle-worm, this should get its light working better. This middle section gives off a light – see?"

"I don't see it."

"Cup it in your hands like this," Tsodd instructed, demonstrating as he held it up to one eye."

"Eeerh, I'm not going to do that!"

"Don't be so silly. Of course it's far easier to see when it's dark," the other continued as he resumed stroking the worm.

A voice a short way off called out, "What are you two playing at?"

Upon seeing that the speaker was Reuben the brothers were tempted to turn back to the worm without replying, but instead they returned an unenthusiastic greeting. The cropper was returning to the Upper Village with a large bundle of brushwood on his back. Deciding to have a rest he eased his load down onto the road and leaned on it as he shouted across to the two younger men.

"Still playing with animals are we? Pity you can't find anything better to do, some of us work to help the community."

The brothers stood and stared, but did not say a word.

"There's a cold wind comin'," Reuben continued with an apparent change of tack. It soon developed into another verbal attack though. "I notice the bushes are teeming with berries this year, thick with fruit they are. They say it's gonna be a bad 'un this winter. Your precious animals won't survive that's for sure. Caged up in that thing, they'll suffocate they will."

He completed his prophecy with a loud belch. It was Bodd who replied.

"That's what I like about you..."

"Nothing!" Tsodd whispered.

",,,You're always so cheerful. It's nice to have someone look on the bright side the whole time."

"It's okay for you not having to work for a living all year like the rest of us. It's okay for you to laugh. At least your brother's joined the guard now, trying to make something of his life; not wasting his time on silly things which don't 'elp none."

With some difficulty he heaved the bundle once more up onto his back and was on his way, but not before a final shot.

"About time you helped the community like the rest of us. Take a leaf out of your brother's book and do something useful for a change."

"Silly old fart!" declared Tsodd once the humped figure was well out of earshot, "he's all twisted inside."

He threw the worm down where it had come from.

"Didn't you want that?"

"Naaa."

They collected up the tools and began putting them away in silence. This was eventually broken by Bodd revealing what was on his mind.

"I pity Reuben, he's old before his time."

"What, him? Nobody listens to him, he moans about everything."

"Yes, but you must admit he's had a hard life. I mean having to bring up a retarded son and all that. It can't be easy."

"Fine, but he doesn't have to take it out on us. Pass us that hammer will you? Let's not think about him, he's not worth it."

After finishing their clearing up they stood back in the failing light to have one last look at their handiwork.

"There, that looks good," Tsodd announced proudly. "You know I want to dig the rest of the plot over in the spring, then have grass or flowers or something – make it look nice."

"Grass would be easier."

They wheeled away to head back to the village. After a while Bodd once more broke the quietness with his concerns.

"I've been wondering what to do with myself next year."

"Oh no! Don't pay any attention to Reuben, it's none of his damn business what we do with our lives."

"I know. It's not really him, I've been thinking about it anyway."

"Listen, if we choose to get off our backsides and go down to Ephamon each spring and get a well-paid job there... then I think we deserve to do what we want the rest of the year. It's none of his business, I'd like to see him as a miner!"

"It's not him, I mean that. I've been wondering about my future for some time. I've found thoughts welling up inside me throughout the autumn.

"Rodd's now in the Guard and'll be getting married next year. Don't see much of him these days. *You* know what you want to be doing with all your animals and such. You've already said you want to give the mines a miss next year. I don't know what to *do* with my life, it's just going nowhere at present."

Tsodd put his hand on his brother's shoulder in a friendly gesture.

"You're the only one of us with any brains! Have you thought of applying for a civil service job in Asattan? I'm sure you'd get in. You could ask the Despot to put in a good word for you; better still Alan, he's the one with connections there."

"I've been wondering whether to see Laffaxe, see whether he'll take me back as an apprentice again."

"Phew! You must be feeling desperate. Tell you what, let's go and have a drink and forget about it for now. You won't be able to do anything during the winter anyway and who knows how you'll feel or what opportunities will come up after that."

"You're right, a drink sounds like a good idea right now."

For all Katrina's persistence the local *Carto's* magistrate could not be persuaded to take up Shalee's case. He claimed there was not enough evidence to pursue it, but what he really meant was a couple of white women stood no chance against men from the Despot's bodyguard, especially when one of those accused was a drone. Katrina tried not to be too disheartened by the magistrate's attitude, saying she should have expected no better from a black. She knew a bribe was the standard procedure in such circumstances, but both sides could play at that game and the defendants' resources would be far greater than her own.

"Oh can't we let the matter drop, *please?*" Shalee whined, tired of all the fruitless trips to see the local official.

"No!" Katrina answered fiercely, adding in exasperation, "it was you they raped and almost killed, or have you forgotten?"

She could be very imposing at times like these, but by now Shalee was simply fed up

"I know, but this isn't getting us anywhere. You've made the magistrate's life a misery as you swore you would, but he shows no sign of budging. You have tried and I'm grateful, but let's give in now."

"Shame! Just you shut up! I'm not going to give in. We'll do direct to the Despot. I know he's another black, but I'll shame him into bringing them to justice."

Day after day Katrina dragged her assumed ward across the city to the castle. Less than half a dozen petition vouchers were issued each morning, so it was essential to get their early. Often they were first in the queue, stamping their feet to keep warm in the frosty air. It did not help. The vouchers went either to blacks, drones, or if there were not enough of them to take all the places, to the occasional white man, usually a castle-worker. A white woman from a hostel stood no chance.

It became more and more frustrating. The situation came to a head when there were fewer would-be petitioners than usual. Katrina and Shalee had been first in the queue again and had once more watched as two blacks, a drone and a white male castle-worker were each given vouchers to approach the Despot. They stood at the entrance to the great stone edifice, keeping moving in the cold. The "queue" now comprised just the two of them. The white guard sat in his booth looking up every now and then.

It was clear he had another voucher available, but kept looking over the heads of the women to see if someone of higher social standing turned up. Time passed. They were usually all given out by midday, but in spite of Katrina's enquiring the guard said the final voucher was not being released just yet. He feared that if a black arrived late (as occasionally one did) his life would not be worth living if he found out a pair of white women had seen the Despot instead of him.

The guard was glad he made this decision, for just as he was about to hand the document to the women a black factory owner turned up late. With a smile he handed the precious piece of paper over while Katrina looked on with horror.

Then she snapped. With Shalee trying to restrain her she let forth a torrent of abuse at the guard. She also shouted at the factory owner who had no idea what it was all about. Bundling the surprised black into the building, the soldier called loudly for reinforcements to deal with the "trouble-makers." Half a dozen guardsmen came running to the rescue, some still putting on their helmets, or fastening sword-belts. Shalee ran away when she first heard the guard call out. It took all seven men to eject the kicking and screaming Katrina from the compound area.

Back in the hostel her ward finally plucked up courage to say she did not want to go through with it any more.

"I've just had enough, I can't go through with it any more. Please let me go home now."

"That's gratitude for you!" said Katrina angrily.

"I'm sorry. I *am* grateful for what you've done, but it's obvious we're not going to get anywhere and today proved it."

"Let's have one last try."

"No, there's no point," the girl whined.

"One more," the other persisted. "If we're unsuccessful after that we'll give in."

"Promise?"

"Yes."

Reluctantly Shalee agreed. At least it would soon be over. It was not as if she did not want her attackers dealt with, but her short life had brought her realism. She was not one for banging her head against a wall.

Katrina was glad to have once last chance. She was going to get justice for Shalee whether the girl liked it or not.

"Good," she said, "one more go. I *will* find a way."

They left it a week before going back to the castle. A week for things to cool down and for the guards to come to the conclusion they had given up.

Katrina found she was worn out by her recent efforts and instead of going back to the mission she stayed in her room to rest and get her strength back. Just once she undertook a reconnaissance to the castle to help formulate a plan. None of the guards who had thrown her out saw her. Back at the hostel she counted her money and found to her alarm it was going down faster than she had anticipated – two mouths had not been as cheap to feed as one.

Single-mindedly she determined to push all other considerations to the back of her mind until her crusade for justice had either succeeded or totally floundered. Shalee went back to work during this time, but kept her part of the bargain by turning up at the hostel early on the pre-arranged day for their final attempt. She had assumed they would once more queue for a petition voucher, but Katrina had something else in mind.

Normality has swiftly returned to Thyatira's Castle following the Kagels departure. No request for Soosha's return was received from Aggeparii and she soon began to settle down to life as Eko's personal servant. Her new mistress was kind and considerate and allowed her enough spare time in which to see Illianeth as Natias had promised. The two girls were inseparable and soon formed a friendship which became the talk of the staff. The steward observed that the younger one, for all her innocent looks, had quite a forceful personality. He gave a wry smile to see her keeping Illianeth in order and concluded this new friendship was doing them both the power of good.

At last the long-awaited snow arrived. Frank awoke one morning to find the light from his windows unusually bright.

Everything was uncannily quiet as well. Looking out he saw a white blanket covering the entire scene. With the eagerness of a young boy he got dressed quickly into his winter-ware and went hurriedly downstairs to experience it for only the second time in his life. Marching past the tables being set for breakfast he put his hood up with his gloved hands before going out, so only the portion of face around his eyes was exposed to the elements.

It was not as cold as he had expected outside and the air was very still. The snow was no longer falling and lay about a third of a metre deep on the ground. Pausing at the top of the external staircase he swept the dry, white, powdery substance off the wall with a sweep of his glove. He watched it slowly fall before he made his way down, broad smile on his face. The guardsmen at the bottom did not recognise the Despot at first and belatedly jumped to attention. Frank bid them stand at ease and explained that he just wanted to go for a walk round the bailey by himself.

"Very good, My Lord!" the guard barked, not knowing how else to respond to this information. The soldier's hands and feet were frozen and he was feeling miserable. Also more than a little puzzled, for he had never known the Despot to go for a walk this early in the morning. Strange weather to start doing it in he thought.

Frank trudged through the knee-deep, virgin snow. He experimented with big steps, then dragged his feet through to form a furrow. What did it matter if guardsmen were watching? They were not going to spoil his fun.

Looking up he had to squint in the brilliant light. He moved further on. There were few tracks at this early hour, but the sound of a couple of boys shouting and laughing could be clearly heard from further round the large building. Excitedly he worked his way along to where they were. Two of the guardsmen's' sons were throwing snowballs at each other as they giggled and screamed. Making up his mind at once to join them he began wading hurriedly towards them. Losing his balance he fell headlong into the snow. He emerged again looking like the snowman the boys had built earlier and which stood a short way off.

They hesitated as he came into view, but when the newcomer began laughing and pitching snowballs in their direction they quickly resumed again, this time in a three-cornered contest. All else was forgotten as they frolicked in a winter scene like a thousand year old Dutch painting. The young pair never guessed the identity of the man who had come to play with them. Even when the snow on his face had melted, exposing his dark eyebrows, they did not notice, because it was in the shadow of his hood. Besides they were too busy avoiding each other's snowballs to see. Most importantly the intruder's presence was not resented as he entered into the spirit of the game, it did not matter who he was.

For his part Frank was having the time of his life. To stop playing the role of leader and just to have fun for its own sake was an exhilarating experience after all this time. After a while he felt his extremities become as cold as ice, but he persisted with the game. Then to his surprise his hands, feet and ears seemed uncannily hot. What strange stuff this snow was.

Puffing and panting he eventually realised he had had enough. He also became aware of the appetite he had built up.

"No More!" he cried, "I'm going in, thanks for the game."

He put up his hand in salute as a couple of snowballs plopped into the whiteness nearby. The other two returned the sign before continuing the game with each other.

Frank was sweating heavily under his layers. He went straight back in his room having ordered a bath. He took this quickly so that he was not very late for breakfast. Sitting with Natias he was in chatty mood and spoke about the strange effects the snow had had on his hands.

"They got really hot out there for a while. Then I suppose they went numb, because when I came in they hurt for a while when the feeling came back!"

"Of course they would, My Lawd."

Natias was puzzled. Something about this man did not fit. He knew from the guardsmen what the Despot had been up to. He had not only reacted to the snow like a child, but did not even seem to know some of the most basic effects of it. Natias knew very little about Oonimari, but up until now had assumed they had snow like everyone else.

The steward's face gave him away. Somewhat belatedly and not very convincingly Frank began talking about not having seen snow for so long had made him forget. The truth was that his one previous experience of it was a light sprinkling of the stuff on a distant planet which had melted away within half a time segment.

"This is only a small amount to start with, My Lawd. There is a gweat deal more up there in the clouds waiting to come down. It will not be long before winter's gwip is upon us pwoperly."

During sunset Frank went up onto the battlements by himself to look out on the white landscape. As predicted the snow was falling once more, large flakes which quickly built up. In the distance a small figure was wading through it waste-deep pulling a branch behind him. It was not clear where he was making for. It made Frank remember the story of Good King Wenceslas and he chuckled to himself at the thought.

His mind moved on to the Ma'hol. There had been no more border incidents reported since the exchange of prisoners which was good, although the hoped-for trade links had been slow in materialising. Some financial incentives to help would-be traders might be the answer, that would have to be considered in the spring.

'I wonder how Giella is,' he mused, 'safe and sound in her home no doubt. She's so beautiful...'

The cold was beginning to penetrate as he stood there, so he shook the worst of the snow off himself and retired indoors. He stamped hard on the stone floor as soon as he was under cover, then jumped up and down to get the rest off.

Descending the spiral staircase he was met by one of the senior male servants as he got to the third floor.

"Ah there you are, My Lord. Master Alan has arrived back, I was asked to inform you."

"Excellent! Thank you Paul. Where is he now?"

"I believe he has finished his meal My Lord and will probably be in his room."

The servant was right as Frank discovered after he had gone back to his suite to leave his coat and change his footwear. He entered his friend's room holding a flickering lamp.

"So the prodigal son returns. Good to have you back again."

Alan smiled.

"Yeah I cut it a bit fine, another day and I'd have been holed up in Sardis right now."

He was sitting on a divan in front of his fire, wrapped in blankets and with his feet in a bowl of hot water. The fire had not been lit very long and its single flame was giving off a poor heat. Frank sat down and put the lamp beside him. It cast its dancing light round the gloomy chamber.

"We were wondering where you'd got to. I got your message about your confrontation with the assassins, I'm glad you were not hurt. The one you caught is in the dungeon. I wanted to wait until your return before deciding what to do about Adrian and Crispin. I'd like to discuss it with you some time, not now, of course."

This last remark was in response to the other's massive yawn.

"Sorry, I am a bit shattered. I don't mind talking about it now, besides I've taken care of them."

His tone was nonchalant, but Frank gasped in horror, "You killed them?!"

"Nooo... the due process of law caught up with them. They've been executed..."

"So they are dead."

"Yes, they're not only executed, they're dead as well. I just made sure the authorities in Asattan knew about it and they were rounded up, tried and beheaded."

"But surely it was your word against theirs."

"Precisely, that's why they were executed."

He laughed and Frank gave a puzzled smile, wondering what to say next. There was a knock at the door and Illianeth came in. She took Alan's feet out of the bowl and dried them before trying to get more life out of the fire. During these operations Frank decided to drop the subject and just be grateful it was all over. Once Illianeth had left, Alan resumed the conversation on the original reason for his journey.

"Architects are in short supply like we thought, but I've managed to secure one. He should be here with his squad early spring. The man's got a good reputation and I think we're lucky to get him. Won't be cheap, but I think he'll be worth it. I've got the contract in my bags, okay if I go through it with you in the morning?"

"Of course, you'll be wanting to get to sleep now I expect. You look absolutely exhausted."

"Thanks! That makes me feel good," Alan replied with a playful expression on his face.

"You know what I mean. Anyway I'm glad your journey was a success and that you've got home in one piece. It's good to have you back."

CHAPTER TWENTY

Snow had begun to fall in Aggeparii City too, but not very much. Small, powdery flakes swirled round in eddies as Katrina led her friend to the main entrance of Kagel's castle. She had not enlightened the girl as to her intentions that morning, but the fact that they were later than before had been noticed.

"We won't get to the front of the queue today."

Her guide's gruff voice came back, "Just wait and see."

There were no restriction on who could attend the outer court, although in practise it was mainly filled with blacks and drones. It was a large, enclosed area with a roof through which the Despot passed at midday on his way to hear the petitions. In most despotates such matters were dealt with by officials, but Despot Kagel liked to keep his hand in. He enjoyed the exercise of power and never tired of the thrill it gave him.

Shalee had not been there before and looked round nervously at the tall people around her. No one took much notice of the two white women. They stood just behind the front row of courtiers who lined up forming a wide channel for the Despot and his entourage to move down. Large double-doors were at the end of this, guardsmen standing on either side. Katrina's heart was pounding, but the courtiers for the most part looked bored and disinterested. They had seen it all before. There was a general chat going on, but this dried up as the Despot approached.

He was hand-in-hand with the Despotess who usually only attended once a week. They looked relaxed and smiled as the courtiers bowed at their passing. Following in their wake was the Chancellor who wore a tall, square hat which was his badge of office, plus a group of ceremonial bodyguards.

They came close and the courtiers around the two whites bowed. Seizing the opportunity, Katrina grabbed her unsuspecting charge's hand and pushed past the genuflecting blacks and into the path of the surprised Despot.

"My Lord, there's been a great injustice done. This girl..."

That was as much as she got out before the bodyguards had got over their initial shock and pounced, bundling the women over. The Kagels were both astonished at the unprecedented intrusion, but their reactions were quite different.

"Get that vermin out of here!" stormed the Despotess, waiving her arms about. "What do they think they're doing?"

"Wait!" her husband commanded. He had relaxed quickly upon realising no threat was intended. Being in a particularly good mood that morning he was intrigued rather than annoyed at the intrusion. All present were spellbound as he ordered the soldiers to release the women and asked Katrina what she was doing.

"Your love of justice is well known My Lord, I am hoping you will grant it to this poor girl."

She had got off to a good start. John Kagel was most responsive to flattery and smiled sympathetically. His wife though was not so easily won over.

"Something wrong with your voice white woman?" she snapped.

The Despot looked round.

"Let her finish my dear. What is your name? And why have you not gone through the usual channels?"

His voice was firm, but with a note of sympathy. There was something about this woman with the gruff voice he found most attractive.

As Katrina recounted the story of the assault on Shalee and their fight for justice more than a few eyebrows were raised. Kagel was caught by a sudden enthusiasm for the case and ordered them all inside to hear it fully in precedence to the others.

Pairs of piercing eyes glanced back at Shalee as she studied the line of assembled drones. They fiercely resented being looked over by the white girl, but could not protest out loud in the Despot's presence. She had thought she could recognise the one in charge of her assailants, but these men all looked alike.

Despot Kagel sat on his throne. Like the rest of the courtiers he was fully caught up in the proceedings. With a deep sigh Shalee turned to him and, apologising, said she did not know which one it was. Before Kagel had a chance to answer Katrina snapped at her, telling her to look again. With a shrug the girl duly obeyed, starting at the top of the line again. Glances were exchanged amongst the courtiers at these highly unusual proceedings, then they froze again in eager anticipation that the girl would point someone out. A sudden movement among these statue-like onlookers caught the corner of Shalee's eye. Two white bodyguards had been trying to slink away undetected and ducked down when the girl's head spun round. Their reactions were far too slow.

"That's them!" cried Shalee pointing as the men made a lunge for the door. Their way was immediately barred by other soldiers and before they knew it they were disarmed and facing the Despot with the white woman at the side of the throne.

"Dorip and Borska!" the Chancellor announced with a note of triumph, "I might have known you two were involved. Where's your drone friend then?"

The two stood tight-lipped. Kagel thundered, "Answer! Who is it?"

The Chancellor pulled his eyes away from the arrested men. "Oh we know *who* it is Sir, that rebel Justin. He's the leader of this gang that have been playing pranks – no not pranks, crimes. This time they have gone too far..."

"You can't convict us on a *woman's* testimony," one of the prisoners called out, receiving a clout round the ear from a black officer guarding him. The other prisoner winced for his colleague, but kept his mouth shut.

"Just watch me!" the Chancellor boomed. "We've got you this time. Rape is a most heinous crime against the weaker sex. You have lowered yourself to the animals. Take them away Squad Leader and report to me afterwards, I will give you the names of the others."

Kagel looked somewhat bemused. "I wish I knew what was going on," he said quietly, "nobody tells me anything, I'm only the Despot."

The Chancellor began to explain in detail, but Kagel gave a pained expression and said it could wait. Instead he addressed the plaintiffs.

"There! Has that helped restore your confidence in our justice?"

"Yes, My Lord," Shalee replied timidly.

Katrina nodded. She had calmed herself by this time and was stunned by the swift nature of the decision. It was clear the Chancellor had been keeping his eye on this particular group and had had no doubt that its members were the guilty ones. She wondered what would happen to them.

Despot Kagel proceeded to interview the two white women at some length in front of all the courtiers. He showed a genuine concern at Shalee's terrible ordeal and expressed his admiration at her bravery in coming forward. He appeared particularly interested in Katrina though, especially when he heard that she had no job. Before she knew what had happened she found he had arranged for her to work in the Castle library at a ridiculously generous salary. Even if she had not needed the money it would have been most unwise to turn down the ruler's offer. She therefore accepted graciously, trying not to notice the Despotess' disapproving frown, or see the glint in her husband's eye.

Still the snow came. The wind got up creating snow drifts up to two metres deep. Frank was assured there was nothing unusual in that winter's persistent blizzards. The view from his windows was a featureless, speckled white mass.

Normal life ground to a standstill as the villagers were cut off. For more than sixty days their life was one of hibernation, but the large stocks of food and fuel built up for this period saw them through. Only on very rare occasions did anyone venture out: a couple of times Tsodd got through to inspect his aviary and Amos struggled all the way to the Castle to see Laffaxe with a tooth abscess after the village medic said he could not help.

At last the storms subsided and a deathlike silence descended on the land. The man from Eden turned away from his window and shut his eyes. A rare flash of his former life came to him, an image of the doomed merrymakers on board the *Cassandra*. That fat man who had talked on and on, the slippery-looking one who had left Frank with him. After almost a year on Molton it seemed so unreal. Do people really travel between the stars? Do they really live in clinical habitation units where the dust is automatically filtered from the air before it has time to settle? It was more like a distant dream. He felt so at home in Hoame now and found himself categorizing people in terms of "black," "white" or "drone" as much as any of the natives did. He wondered at how his life had changed now that the main concerns in it were how trade with Rabeth-Mephar would develop this year and how good the hulffan crop would be.

One thing he was sick of though was snow. The white sheet that had spread itself across the landscape and had looked so beautiful at first was now utterly monotonous to him. None had fallen for some time and it had lost its freshness, developing a crust on top and looking dirty close to. Yet still from his window a panorama of white filled the entire view. It even snowed in his dreams! How he longed to see the green grass again.

Small clouds scudded across the pale sky announcing the coming of spring. Slowly at first the snow began to disappear from the tree tops and bushes. The branches of the evergreens sprung up as the weight was released from them, sending quick showers of white down to the ground. In the villages and Castle the snow retreated from the warmth of the buildings.

The clouds gathered and darkened. All people were delighted when the thaw was accelerated dramatically by two days of torrential rain. The morning after the storm cleared, a sea of fresh emerald grass met their eyes. It was such a pleasant contrast to the ubiquitous white of the season now past, although a few isolated pockets of dirty ice would remain tenaciously in hollows and other sheltered spots for weeks to come.

Fortunately there was remarkably little flooding that Spring, the ground seemed to take it in very efficiently. Certainly the benefits of the new site for the Lower Village were seen by everyone. Life: vegetation, animal and human, burst forth and the roads were thronged as people sought to travel again following their long imprisonment.

With people came news. Sardis in particular had had a terrible time. Unused as the Taltons were to such severe weather many of the older, frailer ones had died of the cold. The autumn sacrifices of solid construction to speed in the buildings had caused several houses to collapse, burying the inhabitants alive under a mountain of snow. On top of these tragedies there was an outbreak of the endemic hrac disease when spring broke and communications recommenced. Although this illness could lie a healthy man low for several days, there was normally no danger of it killing him. In the weakened condition of many of the Taltons it all too soon did prove fatal, however. Their young, talented physician and two of his assistants were numbered among the dead. Laffaxe headed a group of volunteers who went to assist. They helped with everything from tending the sick to building repairs.

The ravages of winter had exacted a heavy toll on Sardis that first winter and it's population fell by almost a tenth.

"Push! Come on push!" yelled the driver as his family tried to free their cart from the sea of sticky mud which had once been the road to the Upper Village.

"What a fool," Alan remarked as he watched with Frank from a distance, "Why doesn't he get off and steer the dakks from the front?"

They stood just inside the courtyard entrance taking in the muddy chaos caused by the recent rains and thaw. Men, women, children, animals all trudged through the deep slough, churning it up all the more. One man with a bad limp walked past into the courtyard. Looking down they saw one of his boots was off, he had lost it in the quagmire. A young pig trotted briskly through the gate, led from behind by a short boy with a stick.

"At least someone is enjoying the conditions," Frank observed, looking down at the animal. Abruptly changing the subject he said, "All this terrible news from Sardis; they've had a rough time of it."

"Blue-green ones, yeah! Those damned poorly-built huts, I saw them with my own eyes when they were being put up. I should've said something!"

"You can't blame yourself Alan. I don't feel like blaming anyone: John, the builders... they were volunteers trying to help out. Everything was so rushed they weren't given sufficient time to do them properly. I feel bad about it too. I'm sure it sounds inadequate, but it was just one of those things. What more can I say?"

The other man replied with a shrug.

At last the cart driver got down and they managed to extricate the vehicle from the mud.

"Hooray!" the drone called out ironically at the sight.

Frank asked, "Shall we wander back?" and the two slowly made their way through the market towards the Castle. There were many fewer stalls than there would be later in the year, but they had a good peruse as they strolled in-between them. One keen coppersmith tried to sell the Despot some of his wares, persisting with his chatter until a glare from his wife told him to cease. Frank strolled on, totally unbothered.

"Well at least there's one good thing," he remarked to his companion, "that hrac outbreak – is that the way you pronounce it?"

Alan nodded.

"...It seems to be under control from the latest reports being received."

"That's good."

"Yes, no deaths at all last week. I really must make a visit there. I'll go tomorrow, coming?"

"Sure."

"After all, quite a few people from the villages are already helping there from what I hear. That's nice actually, the Taltons will know they haven't been deserted; it's how it should be."

They were just about to enter the inner bailey when Frank spotted Kim at her stall.

"Just a moment," he said as he suddenly doubled back to talk to her. His companion shrugged again before following slowly at a distance.

Following an exchange of greetings the Despot asked Kim about her sister.

"Giella has not been well for some time My Lord. She is expecting another baby and it has affected her badly."

"Oh dear."

"Yes, My Lord she's been very sick and has not left her home even now most of the snow has gone. She's feeling very depressed by it all."

"That's not like her surely."

"She is inclined to dark moods at times My Lord. One day she can be up and laughing, the next in the depths of despair. That's my sister for you! I expect she'll get out of her gloom soon. Shall I tell her you were asking about her?"

"Er yes. Thank you. Please tell her I hope she gets better."

He thanked Kim before resuming the walk across the bailey as the rain started again. Alan was smiling.

"Very attractive woman, Giella," he remarked.

Frank agreed with the observation in a matter-of-fact tone, trying to sound as nonchalant as possible. His friend was not so easily fooled.

"If you feel so strongly about her why not take her as your mistress? Rattinger would've."

"Certainly not!" Frank exclaimed, wounded by the suggestion, "I wouldn't dream of doing such a thing."

"I only..."

"No. There is no *question* of my committing such an act. Let that be an end of it – please."

No more was spoken until they entered the hall. On the way Frank conceded to his conscience that he had no right to the moral high ground. It was true he would fight to resist temptations to make advances on her, but as for not dreaming about it? He knew all too well his fantasies concerning Giella and that Alan had struck a nerve by putting into words what part of his own mind was telling him.

When he had been on Eden there was a man, wise beyond his years, whose thoughts and opinions were subtly put and held in high regard by many. One of the sayings which had fallen from his lips had seemed most strange to the young Francis Thorn, but they had always stuck in his mind. Now it came back with uncanny force, as if waiting for this moment in his life: "We always hate those who reveal the emotions we abhor." He knew now the man had meant the revealing of our feelings to ourselves that we try to hide from our conscience.

He did not *hate* Alan, but it was why he had responded angrily to him. Frank felt it important to apologise, but suddenly found himself in the busy hall surrounded by people. His emotions were still running high and when he noticed the amount of mud being trampled into the Castle he exploded.

"What the hell is this filth being brought in here? It's like a pig sty in here!"

Grabbing the nearest guardsman he ordered him to find his squad leader and tell him he had to organise a clean up, and that until further notice the sentry on the door was not to admit anyone until they had scraped the worst of the mud off their footwear.

"Look at it!" he exclaimed to Alan who was still hovering nearby, "they've traipsed it all up the stairs as well."

The drone replied in a quiet voice, "Hey Frank, if I upset you with what I said out there..."

"Oh no forget it. I did react rather heavily and now I'm annoyed with myself for it."

They were still speaking when an elderly figure with a long white beard got up and walked with a limp towards them.

"My Lord," Zadok called out in his loud, penetrating voice, "It has been a long while since we saw you at one of our meetings."

"Yes well it's been winter and I gather you were in the Upper Village. Did you manage to get the timber-frame church finished before the snow came?"

"Thank you, yes My Lord," replied the old man. He frowned before going back to his original point, he was not going to be deflected. "You did not attend any of our meetings in the autumn either when the roads were passable."

Unlike the other whites this one appeared not to care about a man's status.

"Well I was very busy," Frank replied uneasily. Meanwhile Alan slipped off to his room, the subject holding no interest to him. Soosha and Illianeth walked past close by, taken up in their own conversation.

"Were you a white," the priest persisted, "I would cite the parable of the burning log: a man in the congregation of believers is like a log in the fire. Take that log out and it is likely to smoulder and go out – we need each other's support. As it is yourself My Lord I must appeal instead to your sense of duty: being the only Christian despot we look to you as an example both to the believers and the blacks."

Frank did not know how to reply. Christianity here was of a most primitive sort and he knew that some of Zadok's scriptural exegesis were misguided or just plain wrong.

'You can't allow that to be an excuse Francis,' he told himself. 'If you have such a wonderful knowledge of things spiritual why do you allow yourself to be sorely tempted by the most basic of temptations – those of sex? I should be ashamed of myself for not putting what I know into practice. As the Master said, "Much will be required of the man who has much." These people are sincere in their faith, that is what's important. Never mind not enjoying their meetings...'

"My Lord, can we rely on your presence next Sabbath? I hope to hold our first spring meeting here in the castle."

"Yes indeed, I shall be there."

The following week was a busy one for Frank as he conducted a tour of his domain with a posse of guardsmen. He first made his way to Sardis and found their morale higher than he had feared. The worst of the weather was over, plus they were having lots of help from the other Thyatirans. Above all though the Taltons had an ingrained resilience and belief in themselves. If they could make it through generations of captivity it would take more than a winter's setbacks to destroy them.

The Lower Village was certainly in high spirits. Many of them were working on fields which should produce their first hulffan harvest later in the year. It was emphasised to the Despot that there were comparatively few areas of the country where the soil was just right for the crop, but all the signs were it would flourish there in the south of the despotate.

The Upper Village meanwhile was always the most successful and prosperous. Traders were beginning to show up from the other despotates, although no foreign ones had arrived to date. It was felt that the poor state of the roads was the reason for this.

In all three villages people had many weeks worth of pent-up complaints and petitions which they took the opportunity to present to him. The scribes had been busy. In Sardis some relatives wanted compensation for death and injuries caused by negligent building, in the Lower Village an accusation of witchcraft by a married couple was the order of the day, while in the Upper Village a group of residents said they had been swindled out of some money by a landowner. Frank assured them that all petitions would be looked into fully and passed them to Natias to sort out when he got home. The steward was not pleased with the extra work load though.

Days passed and a warmer spell of weather saw the last of the snow finally disappear. Spring came forth at a pace: daffodils and wellabells came out in large numbers, flooding the valleys in yellow and scarlet. Trees were thick with buds. The birds, recently returned from their winter migration, were very much in evidence as they set about building their nests. The rains eased off and the ground began to harden under a sun that was gaining strength each day.

A high-sided, covered wagon was slowly making its way along the road to the Castle. Young rabbits bounded away as the vehicle approached. Pulled by eight shaggy-looking dakks it lurched through the potholes tossing its occupants about. A thick mop of black hair popped between the front curtain screen followed by a spotty face.

"I say, Matty," whined the young man to the white driver, "do be careful with those ruts."

The driver replied with a lazy, "Yes, Master," without even bothering to turn round. It was soon after this brief exchange that he had to pull the dakks to a standstill a short distance from some extensive roadworks in progress. A regiment of labourers were busy levelling, preparing and laying down a mettled surface, completely blocking the way ahead.

"You'll have to go round," the foreman barked at the driver, "the verge there is hard enough t'take ya."

Looking to where the man pointed, the driver saw where the grass had been churned up by other wagons.

"Huh, no worse that the road we've just been on," he said under his breath.

"What's happening?" asked Spotty Face, poking his head out again. "Why have we stopped?"

The foreman looked up again, having to shield his eyes from the low, afternoon sun. Seeing the black in the wagon he changed his tone.

"I regret the inconvenience master, but we are constructing a proper hulffan-tar roadway to the village; help gentlemen such as yourself have a smoother ride. In the meantime I'm afraid I must ask you to direct your driver to go round."

"Of course, my man. Matty, will you do as the man says please. Pity, I had wanted to get to Despot Thorn before evening."

They arrived at the Castle as dusk took its grip. The Despot had retired to his suite early for a bath followed by bed, no one wanted to disturb him. As a result it was the following morning before the new immigrant was presented.

"Karl Vodant at your service, Sir," the same whining voice cut through the air of the Throne Room. "Despot Kagel recommended me to come here, I understand it's a good place for a man to carve out a new life for himself and his family."

"You've brought your family?" enquired Frank from the throne.

"Certainly, Sir, they are waiting outside, my wife and two children."

"Oh bring them in. I'd like to meet them."

Silence reigned in the small room while the family was sent for. Alan, sitting in an upright chair on Frank's right crossed and uncrossed his legs. Natias and Japhses were standing together by the wall opposite. No one spoke, but all four of them watched as the newcomers shuffled silently in. The wife stood there looking nervously down at the floor while the young children clung to her skirts. Their clothes were worn and shabby and they cut a somewhat pathetic sight, but Frank cheerfully greeted them all while Japhses looked down on them and despisingly whispered to Natias, "Poor blacks – that's all we need!"

The Steward did not respond. He was too busy trying to find out what the arrival of this family meant for him, fearful that after years of running things he would suddenly find himself deputy to a black. He had to remind himself how fortunate he had been as a white, he knew of no other in all Hoame with a position of such high office. He was only human though and did not want to lose his status after all this time.

Frank, however, had no intention of transplanting Natias. He was far too aware of what an effective job he did and was prepared to flout convention to keep him there. He had liked only a few of the blacks he had met in his time on the planet and had been quite happy with the way things were, but now these black immigrants had turned up.

Karl Vondant turned out to be most atypical. From the conversation which followed it soon became apparent that he was not the most successful man in the world, a born loser in fact. Reading between the lines it seemed none of Kagel's blacks wanted to come to Thyatira and this one had because his despot made him an offer he could not refuse. Badly in debt, he had been told by Kagel that his slate would be cleaned on the condition he emigrated to this neighbouring region.

The new arrival was not the sort of man who relished authority and so, far from insisting, the last thing he wanted was to be steward of an entire despotate, albeit the smallest one in Hoame. Instead he was more than happy to be Natias' deputy. When offered a room in the Castle he had to explain his claustrophobia and following some discussion it was worked out that he would live in Sardis and come to the Castle early each morning. Japhses thought this particularly odd, but Natias was so delighted at the outcome he could barely contain his joy.

"I feel sure the awwangement will work, Master," he said soberly, mastering his best self control.

The black looked at the two men standing by the wall and said, "You'd best call me Karl; especially if I am to be your deputy, Natias."

A second shattering of convention, but in the far less formal atmosphere of Thyatira Karl knew he would be more at ease if, as the only resident black apart from the Despot, these two white officials called him by his first name.

Alan answered a knocking at the door to be told by a servant that there was a visitor to see him.

"You don't need me any more do you, Frank?"

"No, you go ahead."

The visitor turned out to be Bodd. Nervously at first he explained to Alan his resolve to go to the Capital and seek an opening there in the Civil Service.

"I hope you don't think I'm asking too much, but I was wondering if you might give me a letter of introduction or something. It's just that I don't know my way around there and and..."

His voice trailed away and Alan came to the rescue.

"Of course I'll assist in any way I can," he began cheerfully. It was his nature to help anyone if asked, he took it for granted. With his friends in high places he was uniquely qualified. "Yeah, I can think of at least a couple of men I can put you in touch with; I'll do that with pleasure. Here, sit Bodd, you'll do fine."

"Thank you, I hope your confidence in me is well placed. I do appreciate you helping me like this."

"No trouble."

His fingers moved gently over Giella's smooth arm.

"Oh Frank," she sighed.

In reply he bent his head towards her and their lips met for a long, passionate kiss. His hand slowly travelled down her naked, silvery body. Going over her hips to her thigh before working its way back...

"Bloody hell!" he exclaimed as he sat bolt upright in bed, images of his erotic dream flying away like sparks from a fire. He repeated his expletive and beat his fist into the bed to wake himself fully and halt the return of a wave of desire.

Quickly he jumped out of bed; best to get up as soon as possible. He fumbled at the buttons and clasps, haste only slowing things down. Calming himself, he got on a lot better and was soon down at the breakfast table.

Natias was already eating and straight-away involved the Despot in a conversation about hulffan tar quotas for export.

"My Lawd, going back to what we were discussing the other day: we know we are gambling on a good weturn fwom the Lower Village cwop by using up our stocks for the current woad-building pwoject, but the early signs fwom the young plants are pwomising."

"Are they?"

"Yes, My Lawd, I tool a twip out to see them yesterday. Gideon pwoudly showed me the pwogwess of the best plants, but I made sure I got to see other aweas which are not doing quite so well. Avewage bottom leaf length I estimated at fifteen centimetres, good for this time of year. At least on a par with the Upper Village. No yellow-fly infestation so far either."

"Really?" returned Frank, he knew he should be more interested than he was.

"Yes, My Lawd. The planting zone was well picked, the hard work done in settling this looks like paying off..."

The conversation continued in a similar vein for a while, but Frank's heart was not in it. He knew Alan would be down soon and wanted to ask the steward something before he appeared.

"Excuse me for changing the subject, but have you heard how the woman Giella is getting on?"

Natias did not know, but called over his wife from the women's table and she provided the answer.

"It's so sad, My Lord," Ekp began, "she had a miscarriage a fortnight ago and has been in a terrible depression ever since. I have not seen her myself, but I heard all about it from a friend."

After thanking her Frank waited until Eko had made her way back to the other table before announcing to Natias that he was going that day to see Giella.

"I twust My Lawd had not forgotten his appointments this morning. You were going to judge those two cases Saul has weferred to you..."

"Oh yes."

"...And you did tell me yesterday afternoon that you wished to speak to me about jail conditions some time today."

Frank nodded thoughtfully.

"All right, but I haven't got anything planned for tomorrow have I? I'll go then."

And go he did. After a frustrating day of official duties, which he did not have his mind on properly, he set off extra early the next morning for the Upper Village. Travelling alone he found hardly anybody about. He dismounted and began wondering through the empty streets. Wattle and daub huts lined the way. One villager was entering a small compound to see to his pigs, but generally there was surprisingly little activity that morning. Both pig-man and Despot were too wrapped up in their own thoughts to notice each other. Frank's mind had begun to wander and the conflict within his re-emerged.

'You don't want to visit her, Francis,' said one part of him, 'you'll only end up embarrassing yourself.'

'Of course I do, I want to see her again,' replied the other side.

'Why?'

'To show my concern and support her in her time of sorrow.'

'Pompous claptrap! You're only going because you desire her.'

'Ah, but it's still an act of kindness to take the trouble of coming here...'

The internal debate was cut short by the appearance of a man walking towards him. He realised he had been meandering aimlessly for some time and was not at all sure of his bearings. Holding his dakk's bridle steady he asked the man for directions, as he did so he felt sure he had been introduced to this villager before and really should know his name.

"Oh yes, My Lord," Reuben came to with a start. The last thing he expected on his way to work in the morning was to bump into the Despot wandering by himself. "It's down that way, third on the left after the community hut.

"Thank you, my man," replied Frank as he set off again with more purpose and was soon approaching the home of Uriah and Giella. Once more he was the only person out in the street, but as he drew near the hut he heard a woman's voice raised in anger. He slowed down as he got close and nervously looked round to make sure he was not being observed. The words were easy to make out now.

"Talk to me!" Giella was shouting at the top of her voice. "Just talk to me."

Frank stood frozen outside the hut, not knowing what to do. The voice resumed.

"Is it too much to ask for? I don't know what's wrong with you, but I can't stand it much longer. It's not a lot to want in life..."

Frank stood in the road feeling increasingly embarrassed and uncertain what to do. He was just glad his dakk was such a placid specimen and stood there motionless watching its master. Part of him desperately wanted to see her again, but this was hardly an auspicious time. Undiscovered, he turned round and started back. Fifty metres up the road he hesitated, but then shook his head and mounted up. Shaking the reins he headed once more for the Castle.

Next day Soosha and Illianeth were sweeping a deserted hall together. The former could not help contrasting the atmosphere with that of her previous home.

"It's much nicer here, Illianeth, you get treated like a human being. The Kagels are such snobs, and all those blacks... they were all so bossy and pleased with themselves. Despot Thorn's much nicer."

"You've missed a bit," the older girl pointed to a dirty patch on the floor. "He's not bad – for a black. Alan's my favourite though, he's lovely. Hey this new black Karl Vodant, you said you remembered him from your Aggeparii days didn't you?"

Soosha laughed.

"Do I remember him? He was a running joke! He was so poor his family used to turn up at Court in little better than rags. Sometimes wore outfits completely the wrong size, one day far too small, the next with sleeves down to here," she said illustrating the point with a hand down to her knees. "The word is he came here 'cos Kagel cancelled his debts. I'm not surprised he jumped at the opportunity... but by the state of his clothes that was all Kagel did."

"Thorny's given him a special grant to get some more outfits made for him and his family. I heard from one of the seamstresses from Sardis up here yesterday, I meant to tell you. Thorny usually keeps a much tighter control on the purse-strings than Ratty did. That's why Natias likes him so much, hates to see money "wasted"."

Illianeth took a deep breath to continue, but hesitated when she saw a visitor enter the building. A thin drone, about fifty, elaborately dressed and with a superior air stepped into the room and began surveying it with his eyes as if he was about to put in a bid. He was followed by a group of whites, each dressed in the same grey overalls.

Handing her broom to Soosha she approached the drone and asked if she could help.

"Yes girl, be so kind as to inform the Despot that Damian has arrived with his Guild Squad," he replied in a very high-pitched voice without taking his eyes off the ceiling.

As she went off up the stairs Illianeth angrily asked herself why people from other regions thought they were so superior.

"Blooming castrated soab! Oh hello, My Lord, I was just coming to fetch you."

She had bumped into Frank working his way downstairs with Alan and explained who had arrived.

They sent her on to fetch Natias from his room.

Meanwhile Damian was complaining to his deputy.

"What a god-forsaken dump this is. If it were not for Alan asking me personally I would never have dreamt of coming to this outpost. The poor man must hate having to live in such conditions, he must have been sent here to be as far away from the Citadel as possible."

"I hear Alan likes it here."

Before the architect could reply to his deputy, the topic of their conversation had arrived along with Despot Thorn. Introductions were made.

"It's usually a fairly quiet afternoon on the Sabbath," Frank explained as if apologising for the lack of normal activity. "Let's sit down and discuss details... Alan can you ask Illianeth to organise some food for our guests."

"I just did."

"Ah, good. Very pleased to meet you Damian, your reputation has gone before you. Natias, my steward, will be along any moment, he'll be your main point of contact."

Damian's tone quickly softened and he turned down the offer of food in preference to going though each point of the work they were about to undertake. While his twelve-man squad tucked into their soup on the adjoining table, the architect thrashed out the minutiae with his hosts to make sure they understood each other fully. His enthusiasm waxed as the meeting progressed and was matched by the others, although Frank could not help finding his high-pitched voice amusing.

'It might be a god-forsaken corner of the country,' Damian reminded himself, 'but to be commissioned by so influential a drone as Alan can only help my star to rise still further.'

"So you begin work first thing tomorrow morning in here," concluded Frank.

"Yes, My Lord. With the assistance of the guardsmen you have volunteered we will bring in the scaffolding from the wagons and commence on the ceiling as agreed."

When the meeting broke up, Frank discovered another visitor had arrived who, after some refreshments, was waiting to see him.

"Harot Jeal at your service," the chubby foreigner with a bright emerald cape announced himself and bowed exaggeratedly low.

Frank took a moment to recognise him. When he noticed the two female assistants in the background he remembered.

"Ah, the masseur."

"The complete body-care treatment, My Lord Thorn, at your service."

"Excellent," the Despot replied cordially, "did you want to start now?"

"Just as you wish, My Lord," Jeal replied, "the fee is of course the most reasonable sum of fifteen stens we agreed upon during my previous visit."

"Fine, I understand. Let's go up to my suite."

The manicure was well in progress when a servant intruded with a letter that had just been delivered by special courier. Frank almost asked him to read it out, but remembered just in time that the man was illiterate. Indicating to Jeal's assistants to stop for a moment he took the letter and carefully opened it. The paper was thick and off-white, speckled with impurities from its manufacture. He read its contents with eyebrows raised.

"Please fetch Alan and Natias at once," he ordered.

The servant disappeared and Frank asked Jeal for an adjournment. Natias soon arrived and said Alan had gone out but should return before long.

"Good. Do sit down. This letter has just arrived from the Capital, care to have a read?"

Natias responded with a quick, "My Lawd" as he took the letter and went through it carefully.

"His Excellency Count Zastein coming here! In two days time! My goodness the Castle will look dreadful if we allow the Guild Squad to pwoceed with their work. On the other hand we would have to pay a gweat deal of money for them to be idle. What a dweadful piece of timing!"

━≺╋ ╋≻━

CHAPTER TWENTY ONE

Frank trotted up the stairs into the hall and made for the wooden balcony. All around him was a frenzy of activity. The scaffolding had gone up the day before and the Guild Squad was efficiently, if noisily going about their business. The sound of hammering and sawing was such that it was difficult to think straight. People were dashing to and fro cleaning, polishing and generally tidying up. When he got to the balcony stairs he found them blocked off with a group of women busy waxing and polishing the structure.

"This damn sawdust everywhere!" exclaimed one, "how are we supposed to do a good job in these conditions?"

"There just ain't the time," answered a second, "we've got to do this now or we'll never get it done."

When they saw the Despot they began moving in order to let him past.

"No no, I won't disturb you ladies, you're doing a grand job. I'll use the spiral staircase like everyone else, sorry to bother you."

Leaving the women staring after him he headed for the other side of the hall. On his way he saw Damian discussing the plans with Natias. The latter broke off briefly to report to his leader.

"The work on the courtyard is on schedule, My Lawd."

"Yes, I've just taken a look for myself. I was told it's taken an army of people to clear up where the market usually is, I'm assured it will be ready for this afternoon."

Moving on, Frank wondered why he had allowed himself to be persuaded by Alan so easily that the improvements work should not be delayed, it looked a complete mess in the hall

"We won't be entertaining him in the hall," Alan had said, "and besides, he'll understand."

He had spoken about how the most powerful man in the land would react with such confidence. Typical Alan, always so casual while those around him panicked.

Frank spotted Crag from the kitchen with a parcel. The jailer had recently received a couple of new guests in the form of a pair of robbers caught red-handed by a squad of guardsmen.

Reaching the spiral staircase, Frank took a last glance at the apparent chaos in the Hall before going up.

Natias had told him he could remember the last time Count Zastein had stayed in Thyatira, about seven or eight years ago. That was around the time Rattinger had started to go rapidly downhill and the Count had not stayed for long. That was the year, apparently, when one Manhausen had died, leaving Zastein second only to the Autarch. Shrewd observers had known for many years previously that with his background and natural authority, Zastein was destined for high office. It therefore came as no surprise to them that when the Autarch died he consolidated his hold by abolishing the office and assuming control himself.

The steward had gone on to say that the Count had visited their region more recently, but not to stay.

All the talk in the Castle was about power politics and the characters involved, everyone had become an expert political analyst overnight. Reaching the second floor he overheard two guardsmen in a like mind on the subject.

"You're right," declared one, "Zastein has been running things for years, the Autarch was only a puppet. He was just waiting for the old boy to die to bring the true state of affairs out into the open."

The second guardsman concurred.

"Yes, it's obvious. A powerful and shrewd lot are the Keepers of Hoame."

Unnoticed by the soldiers, he carried on up the stairs. He was somewhat intrigued at what he had heard, but it also filled him with trepidation at the thought of the mighty man coming to see him.

'What will he think about the way things are being run here?' Frank wondered. 'He might not approve of a white remaining steward when blacks had started to immigrate...well, one family so far. What will he think of my trying to foster good relations with the Ma'hol? That's a plus point surely...'

"Ah hello, Japhses, what's the roof looking like?"

The big man slipped on a stair as he came down and put a hand out to Frank to stop himself falling.

"Whoa! I beg your pardon, My Lord. The roof is all swept and tidy now, ready for inspection."

"Oh, that won't be necessary."

"I have extra lookouts posted as you ordered so that we can spot the entourage in good time."

"Fine. Now all we can do is wait."

The market had been temporarily packed off to the Upper Village. At the last moment the cleaning and tidying was declared to be completed and the work ceased, leaving the Castle quiet and expectant. One cart just left before midday, clattering out of the empty courtyard. Inside was Harot Jeal with his assistants and his money, plus the satisfaction of the knowledge of a job well done and a contented customer. One of the guards on lookout watched as the cart disappeared up the road to Aggeparii. Turning back to the south-east he saw a banner appear over the horizon. Soon soldiers on dakks were visible, followed by high-sided wagons.

"It's definitely them," declared the squad leader, "go and tell the Despot, quickly!"

The Leader of the Inner Council of Hoame had brought a comparatively small retinue, comprising his "right hand man" Baron Schail, an exiguous contingent of officials, clerks and personal servants, two-score soldiers plus five despatch riders. They filed through the main entrance into the inner bailey where, in the absence of a proper reception room, Frank stood with all his top men, including the three Village Heads. All the Guard not on patrol duty were lined up there for Count Zastein's arrival.

The tall man had lost none of his imposing presence. He did not smile once as Frank introduced his lieutenants, although he appeared satisfied enough. Schail looked balder than Frank remembered him. He provided the human face of authority with a smile and a "well done" for their reception.

Arrangements had been made for the billeting of the soldiers and the rest of the entourage and while this was under way, the two Keepers were escorted into the Castle. The hall looked like a builder's yard with scaffolding, planks of wood, tools and workmen everywhere. The dozen members of the Guild Squad seemed many more. Working intensely they took no notice of the group entering the room, as they could not hear over the awful din they were making.

"Alan, where's that Damian?" a flushed-looking Frank shouted above the racket, "I told him to stop when our guests were present."

"That will not be necessary," announced Zastein raising his voice to be heard. "You were not thinking of entertaining us in here were you, Despot Thorn?"

"Oh no, Your Excellency," Frank hastily replied, still red in the face, before hurriedly leading the group upstairs to his suite.

One of his rooms was being used as a private dining room. He sat down to a late lunch with five other men: Count Zastein, Baron Schail, Karl Vodant, Alan and the Count's Personal Private Secretary whose name escaped Frank.

He found himself far too tense to enjoy the meal, but was grateful that Matthew had done a light dish. Karl was obviously very nervous too, his hands were shaking visibly and he said not a single word during the whole proceedings.

Alan looked his usual casual self, but he was not full of conversation on this occasion.

"The work in the hall," said Zastein following a long period of silence, "what is being done, may I ask?"

Frank cleared his throat in order to reply.

"Er some general improvements, Your Excellency. The ceiling is unnecessarily high and it takes a lot of heating in the winter. They are putting in a false ceiling to reduce the volume of air to be heated."

"Hmm, very clever," responded the Count slowly before putting another mouthful in. A piece of food fell off the fork and lodged in his greying beard. Frank wanted to mention it to him, but he was too intimidated by the Keeper's presence to say anything. Instead he watched out of the corner of his eye the particle of food go up and down as Zastein chewed.

What Frank really wanted to do was to ask if any more survivors from the *Cassandra* had been located, but would he get the opportunity to speak with Zastein and Schail alone?

The meal ended and the Count wiped his mouth and beard, much to Frank's relief, and asked him about hulffan tar exports, "Because I noticed extensive, obviously fresh plantings near the road on the way here."

By this time Schail had engaged Alan and the Secretary in a tialogue contrasting town and village life; so for the first time there were two conversations going on at the same time.

"Yes, we have extended our hulffan growing quite considerably this year, Your Excellency," Frank confirmed. "The state of some of the roads out here can be very bad, especially when there's been a lot of rain. The extra tar to be extracted from the plants should mean we can build roads here and still fulfil our export orders. I feel it important that the main communication routes be improved.

"Actually we have made a bit of a gamble, because we have gone ahead with the road programme using our reserves and trusting that this year's crop will be a successful one. The signs from both Upper and Lower Village crops are encouraging, so I am reliably informed."

"Splendid. And where are these roads you are constructing?"

"Well it's just one to begin with, Your Excellency, from the Castle to the Upper Village. It's a big job, several kilometres, so we are not expecting to get the entire distance completed this year, but eventually we will."

The concurrent conversation faltered and Zastein asked Schail in what sounded like a slightly humorous voice, "How would you like to see a road constructed, Otto?"

The result was that after a rest they took a trip out that way. The air was warm as they processed out on dakks, the wagons being left behind. Two sets of spare dakks for the officials were brought by the escorting soldiers, although they only travelled at a walking pace. A great deal of work was going on as they arrived.

"Those men in chains," Frank said pointing, "are a work detail from the prison. Instead of sitting round in the dark all day and night they have the opportunity to get out and do some useful work for the community."

"How very humane," complimented Schail as the prisoners toiled with their picks and shovels, sweat pouring off them.

"Thank you, Your Excellency, we do try."

The visitors appeared quite impressed with the entire operation. Alan, who knew more about the work involved than anyone else in the party, explained to the Keepers various of the processes going on. Totally at ease in their company, he told them how the local experts who usually supervised hulffan tar work in the Capital were not needed there at the present time.

"They'll travel down after the next harvest has been collected and begin work there on the Citadel pathways."

He stopped to take a drink from the water-carrier who was running between them.

"Their expertise is much in demand," he continued.

They talked on. Frank was amazed to see the drone actually laughing with Zastein at one stage.

"Some Water, My Lord?"

Frank looked down at the pathetic figure of the water-carrier, one of Count Zastein's retinue. A barefoot lad with a ruddy complexion and ill-fitting clothes.

"No thank you, boy," the Despot answered with a smile. He watched as this lowest of the servants ran off towards the black officers from the Capital. One of them cuffed the boy round the ear for no reason that Frank could make out. Just then he heard Alan's voice addressing him.

"Are you ready to move on?"

They had seen enough and the party went back via the Lower Village where they received an enthusiastic reception. There was a smile on Gideon's usually long, drawn out face, which made a pleasant change. Time was moving on so they did not stay long. As they left, the Count expressed his wish to travel along the northern border the next day, the one with Ladosa. Seeing Zastein again had brought back fond memories of Offa. Although he had only known the clerk a matter of days, Frank had enjoyed his company and learned a lot from him. How different would things have been had he lived?

For that last leg of the journey Frank found himself with Baron Schail. They had just re-mounted a little while ago and were a few metres ahead of the rest of the party with the Castle in sight.

"Do you often get to travel outside Ephamon, Your Excellency?"

A smile broke over the face of Schail.

"Very rarely in fact, it makes a pleasant change. Things are quiet on the diplomatic front at present and besides the Count does take on extra special interest in this despotate. It's very agreeable to be out here with all the trees, grass and peace – we should do it more often perhaps."

He looked about himself before lowering his voice which then took on a more official tone.

"There will be just the three of us for dinner this evening, so that we can discuss...things."

Frank opened his mouth, but had his question answered before he had uttered it.

"The others have been informed."

Half excited, half afraid at the prospect, Frank wondered what he would learn when he was alone with the two Keepers.

'Actually to be able to mention cruises between the stars and people from other planets... I think they must be pleased with how I'm running things here, surely they must think I'm doing a good job. But you never know, will they have liked the way I handled the Ma'hol?'

Questions like this were alive in his mind as they sat down for the meal that evening. Not much was said while the servants were dishing up the food. Pork and mascas cooked to perfection, Matthew really was excelling himself in the kitchen.

The last of the servants left the room and the three men ate in silence for a short while. After what Frank considered to be a reasonable time, he asked the burning question.

"Your Excellency, I was wondering if any more survivors from the ship have been picked up. Do you know of any?"

"No," said the Count gravely, "there have been none."

Frank's face fell and in response Schail said, "I'm sorry none of your friends survived, but I really don't think there can be any hope for them now, we would have heard."

"You are right of course, Your Excellency. They weren't really my *friends* anyway come to think of it. I had only met a few of them and knew none well. But they were fellow travellers and we would have had that in common to talk about. Still, I suppose that episode of my life really is closed now."

The Baron swallowed a mouthful before saying, "There was something I wanted to ask you Thorn: in a couple of the old books it refers to one of the galaxies as the "Yellow Galaxy", do you know anything about that? Is it because the stars take on that hue through a telescope?"

"Oh not at all. It was called that because there was a preponderance of yellow-skinned people of those who migrated there, supposedly in enormous numbers. It was first colonised in the late twenty-second century as I remember. Silly really, but that's how these things get their names I suppose.

"You mentioned old books, may I ask if you have many, Your Excellency?"

Schail took a glance at his senior colleague, the Despot's enthusiasm was plain to see.

"Several books, certainly. We would not wish any to leave the Council's private library, you must understand the implications of them getting into the wrong hands."

Frank nodded as he conceded the point. How he would love to get his hands on those old books though!

"We can't be too careful," the other continued before perking up again and going back to the previous point, "I have never seen anyone with yellow skin, sounds most peculiar."

"I don't think many set out for this corner of the universe. They're not really yellow, not like this," he indicated to a bright yellow patch on the table cloth pattern, "just a slight tinge. I've met them, they've got a fascinating culture going back thousands of years. I suppose they set off together to be... together."

He had finished his sentence abruptly, because it was apparent that Zastein wanted to say something.

"Despot Thorn," he began slowly, "I am satisfied that you have settled down well here in the last year, especially considering the most unfortunately demise of the clerk Offa. I think we can officially say that your trial period is over and that you are now at the rank of Minor rather than Junior Despot. However, we were very much looking forward to meeting your wife on this visit."

Frank had forgotten he was still on trial and was just taking the significance of this in when the comment about the wife totally threw him. Whatever was the man talking about?

"I'm... I'm sorry Your Excellency, I don't understand. I haven't got a wife."

"Precisely. Did not Offa have the opportunity to tell you of the need for male heirs of the Despot class before he died? I find it extraordinary that he did not, it is the most important reason for your being given the post."

Frank wanted to lie and say that Offa had not mentioned the subject, but he could not bring himself to slander the chuckling fat man whose memory he treasured.

"He did mention the subject, but I had no idea of the overriding importance Your Excellency. Perhaps Offa was going to expand on what he said later on in the journey and never got the chance."

"To be honest with you, Thorn the situation is not as critical as it was a year ago," conceded the Count. He spooned up the last of the juice on his plate before continuing. "A couple of male babies have been born in the south since that time. However, it is a chronic problem that will not go away in the foreseeable future. To spell it out, we still require you to get married and father a healthy brood.

"I hear you have met the Dessans Kagel and Hista."

Franks' face dropped, his expression telling Zastein all he needed to know. As a result his tone became more reconciliatory.

"Never mind, there are many more suitable candidates. We shall have to see what we can arrange."

He sat back at the servants arrived to clear up the plates.

"A delicious meal, Thorn, first class. If only we had such cooks back in Asattan, eh Otto?"

Baron Schail smiled in response and as the Keepers sipped their wine Frank took another drink of water. Once the servants had given out the next course and left, Zastein resumed.

"There is another most important we wish to cover, that of relations with your foreign neighbours."

"Yes, Your Excellency, we did have a bit of a run-in with the Ma'hol, but it was mainly a misunderstanding and relations are a lot better now. In fact we were hoping for greatly increased trade links with them, but they do seem to be a bit slow in coming forth."

"You are too modest," declared Schail, "we heard about your battle with the Ma'hol, a skilful piece of manoeuvring by all accounts."

"Thank you, Your Excellency."

Frank knew it had mainly been luck which had brought the Thyatirans Victory. Had they arrived at the river after the whole Ma'hol army had crossed it and deployed... it would have been a very different story. It was hard for Frank to play it down while he was being complimented though.

The conversation continued between the two of them on relations with Rabeth-Mephar, Frank was interested to hear that the Baron too had met the Mehtar. Then Zastein came back into the proceedings.

"What I was really referring to was the Ladosans, how are relations with them?"

"We've heard nothing of them since I arrived Your Excellency. I don't think I've ever met a Ladosan, or Laodician as the people here call them. We have regular patrols along the border, but they never have anything to report."

"Hmm, interesting," the older man said. He looked over the table and fixed his eyes sharply on his protege, "We have had recent news of a more intense political activity in Ladosa. They are such an unstable society with their democracy, we must be on the lookout for the first signs of trouble."

He relaxed a bit.

"We shall go along the border tomorrow, Thorn, and see for ourselves and hear from the border guards."

'Crikey!' thought Frank, I've never been there. I hope they really do proper border patrols and don't spend their time playing dice or something! After the meal I'll arrange for a messenger to forewarn them; should've done that earlier.'

After the meal the topics of drones came up. It was made clear by the Keepers that they approved of his decision to expel Adrian and Crispin.

"They have now been duly dealt with," said the Count referring to their execution. "Their plot against Alan and yourself sealed their fate."

"They made a trap and fell in it themselves," Frank quoted from the Psalms.

This was lost on his visitors, but after a while a thoughtful-looking Schail said, "I understand you still have a white for a steward."

"That's correct, Your Excellency, been in the post several years."

"So I understand. I only mention it because I am always impressed at how promptly your revenue dues are paid. Other regions are much closer, but for a long time Thyatira has been the only one consistently on time. It was true even during the period we were trying to find a replacement for Despot Rattinger. I'd thought it was Alan's doing, but he assured me it was all down to the steward."

"Natias, Your Excellency."

"Really. You know we could do with someone like him at the Citadel, put our lazy clerks in order."

A look of concern came across Frank's face at the prospect of having to give up his steward whom he considered a good friend as well as an efficient administrator. The Baron noticed his expression and quickly added, "Don't worry we won't take him from you, I was only thinking out loud. We could hardly place a white in charge of blacks, not in the Capital anyway."

Frank wondered if this was a veiled criticism of his having placed Karl under Natias, but concluded that he was being too sensitive. Baron Schail appeared an open sort of person, not the sort to resort to subtleties to get any disapproval across.

Later in his room Frank went through the day in his mind and what the two Inner Councillors had said to him. He was surprised that they had not asked him more about the worlds beyond their own. However, he had learned some crucial information himself. No more survivors from the *Cassandra* and no rescue ships. Hoame was definitely going to have to be home. Still, it could have all worked out far worse. He concluded that the Keepers' stay was going quite well so far. The business about finding a wife had been a bit of a shock, he had been so busy on other matters that he had not thought of what Offa had said about that for a long time.

'Zastein had said leave it to him,' thought Frank, 'so I won't actively pursue the matter.'

In his prayers he thanked God that the visit had got off to a good start. His final petition was that the following day's visit to the Ladosan border would go off without a hitch. Having left this in the Almighty's hands he got into bed and slept soundly.

For Katrina it had been the most extraordinary winter and early spring. With metres of snow outside she had been able to roam freely within the large castle of Aggeparii City. While her tasks were not onerous, her salary was ridiculously generous. Anything she wanted, be it clothes, furniture or ornaments for her room, was always provided for her by the Despot's staff. Food was free. As a result her outlays were so minimal she saved all her wages in the bank situated within the castle complex.

Despot Kagel had made the stupid mistake of taking his family to another of his castles in the south of his region early in the winter. No one seemed to know why they had gone. The snow had come as suddenly as it always did and the Kagels were stuck in much inferior accommodation all season.

The Chancellor found himself in charge of the snow-bound City. He did not relish the inevitable thaw, because he was sure to get his master's wrath for allowing him to take the trip, as if the Despot was not in charge of his own actions. The Kagels' absence was not mourned by the castle staff though. They knew the Chancellor's style was generally more easy-going and did not have to put up with Astra and Inga's moods and whims.

Katrina busied herself in the library which was based in the large private wing of the castle. The vast rooms it took up made it second in size only to that in the Citadel in Asattan. Shelf upon shelf piled up with dusty and often battered books, many of which had not been read for a lifetime, if at all. Some corridors were impassable for piles of heavy tomes with crumbling, rotten covers. The air was musty and damp. She had been given no directions before her employer had left and no other official could tell her what was required of her. Few had ever been to the library and as it was the Despot's own domain, they were afraid to interfere.

Fortunately Katrina soon met and befriended Old Paul, who did restoration work within the building on the odd days he felt like working. An ancient, balding figure with a heavily wrinkled face, Paul had worked in the castle for decades and acted as if he had complete freedom to roam around where he liked around the labyrinthine building. These latter years he did not do a great deal, preferring to paw over his favourite books all day rather than do any work. They spent long, candle-lit evenings together as he taught her the alphabet and then to read.

This opened up a whole new dimension to her. She had barely seen a book before going to Aggeparii and had accepted the job in spite of rather than because of what it was. Paul also showed her the round books he had discovered in one of the back rooms. These were not like the normal books, rather they were small, flat, metallic disks within cases. Snappy titles adorned them such as "Advanced Gravitational Reflex Techniques (Holby Drive B)." The disks themselves were smooth and silvery, there was no equipment with which to reveal their content. Katrina slipped the curios back carefully, she never looked at them again.

Old Paul's friendship was genuine. Many other people approached her offering help and company, but Katrina was not so convinced of their intentions, especially when visits to the library from other castle staff increased for a while after the Kagels returned early in the spring.

"Oh you wouldn't mind just mentioning my little problem to the Despot would you?" they would say, or "A word from you in his ear would help justice to be done." Paul advised her to have nothing to do with such people. "You'll only get one side of their dispute, my girl, and besides they're only trying to use you."

The Despot was in ebullient mood upon his return, the Chancellor need not have been so worried. However, Kagel's campaign to get blacks to emigrate to Thyatira soon fell flat. After that, he took a renewed interest in the library. He spent much time with the new librarian as she got on with her mammoth cataloguing and book-mending tasks. He talked at length and while his attention was not exactly welcome it was not too unpleasant or boring.

It took the Kagel womenfolk no time to notice his new interest and Katrina wisely tried to steer clear of them. The Despotess herself for the time being with icy looks, but Dessan Ilga was more inclined to make sarcastic comments if she caught the white woman alone. Then Kagel's visits suddenly became much fewer, doubtless as a result of their discipline.

There was concern in Katrina's mind that once the Despot's interest in her waned these two powerful enemies would have her expelled, or worse. The last thing she felt like doing though was encouraging the black into a more intimate – and illegal – relationship. Even if she had found him attractive, which she certainly did not, it would have been a dangerous game for a dispensable white woman like her to indulge in. She came to feel a comparative safety tucked away in the library and spent more and more time there, even having her meals brought in. Here among the books might be security, but also loneliness as few ventured there. Having prided herself in the past on not needing other people, she missed Paul now, for he hardly ever dared to come near the place for fear of annoying the Despot. One afternoon he plucked up courage to go there when he knew their master was otherwise occupied. Tentatively he poked his head round the door. Katrina was sitting alone at a desk staring out in a daydream. The air was cold and damp like a catacomb. Even with some of the windows open it was still warmer outside on this bright spring day.

"Hello my girl," he said softly.

"Paul!" she called out with an enthusiasm that surprised them both, "oh it's so good to see you.

Come in."

She wiped her eyes as he shut the door behind him and went to sit down opposite her. It was clear she had been crying, so he tactfully went into a long round up of the latest castle gossip.

"...And so the anti-reform party seem to have got their way over changes to magistrates procedures. I can't say I'm surprised."

"Nor'm I," Katrina agreed with a sigh. She moved over to the nearest window and opened it a fraction more. The view was of the Despot's private courtyard, only rarely frequented. Back in her seat she continued, "My fight for Shalee seems a lifetime ago now. I haven't seen her since, and what they did to those young men... I wonder if I did the right thing."

Caught up in her thoughts once again she looked out at the clouds. Paul did not like to see his friend so melancholy and tried giving her words of encouragement."

"You're in a much improved position now. Most women would give their right arm to be the Despot's favourite. You don't seem to appreciate the power and influence at your disposal. If you wanted you could have jewels and perfumes... all kinds of things. The world is there for the taking, just for being able to lie on your back. They're all saying you don't take advan..."

"Is that what you think?" shouted Katrina accusingly. "Is that what you've told your cronies? For your information I would not touch Despot Kagel for all the jewels in Rabeth!"

"But I thought..."

"Just because I'm a woman it doesn't mean I have to act like a whore to survive. I'm my own person and people can either respect that, or...or..."

In her anger she could not think of an ending to her sentence. Paul was stunned by her reaction. Along with most of the other castle staff he had simply assumed she was Kagel's mistress and his elderly mind found difficulty adjusting to a new understanding of the situation.

Calming herself as best she could she took a deep breath and politely asked to be left alone. Paul crept out without a word. Katrina was beyond tears, she put her head in her hands and stared blankly at the table. She left it would not be long before the end came.

So it proved. She spent all the following morning back in the library by herself, managing to busy herself cataloguing. By early afternoon the only person she had seen all day was the kitchen maid who had brought her meal up.

Shelf upon shelf of ageing volumes. What would have been a paradise to Frank Thorn was of no interest to the people of Aggeparii. Even Paul had been unable to say where all the books had come from or who had gathered them together. He only read romance stories, but had a large number to chose from as these made up the greater proportion of the collection. Whole sections of the library were full to the brim with foreign titles no one at all could read. Ancient languages long extinct on Molten. Katrina's restoration work was pretty crude and the overall task that faced her was enormous. Many of the books had deteriorated beyond repair, some disintegrated at first touch. The smell of decay hung in the air.

The door creaked open slowly, she thought it would be Paul. But no, the short, squat figure of Despot John Kagel appeared instead. He was by himself and quietly shut the door behind him before advancing cautiously, looking round each of the shelves in turn. His slippers made no noise on the wooden floor. He wore an exotic purple outfit with silver trimmings, both hands were encrusted with jewellery.

Katrina was observing him from the other end of the library. It was quite gloomy there which was why it took the new arrival some time to spot her.

"Ah Katrina, my dear, there you are. I wanted to see you."

Warily she got up and had to clear her throat before giving him a husky "Yes, My Lord?" She moved over to him and as she got close the smell of his perfumed oils hit her. This, combined with a burst of sunlight through the window started her off sneezing and he had to wait before beginning his speech. He seemed agitated and she noticed him breathing heavily.

"I haven't had the opportunity to see you recently, I thought it was about time we had a little chat..."

Beads of sweat were breaking out on his bow. Katrina found his behaviour unnerving, especially when he moved so close to her she was almost pinned against the bookshelves.

"...And my wife has gone out for the afternoon," he continued. Then the move came. Beside himself with desire he asked her for a kiss and moved his head forward.

"No!" Katrina called out, turning her head and putting her arms out.

"I mean it!" he said trying to grab hold of her, "you drive me insane..."

"Get off!"

"You can't deny me, I'm aagh!"

With her knee going up sharply into his groin he discovered she could indeed deny him. As Kagel bent double in agony with his hands to his vitals she quickly pushed him away and sprinted for all she was worth to the library doors. He was in no fit state to follow her for a while. She locked the big oak doors and, still clutching the key, ran for the stairs. There would be no time to collect the few belongings from her room.

She had been wondering recently whether it was time to be on the move again. 'There's nothing like having your mind made up for you!' she thought as she hurried to collect her money from the bank. Petrified that at any moment half the army of Aggeparii would be out looking for her, she was glad her transaction went through quickly and was soon out on the road.

Sunset saw a lonely figure walking aimlessly down a long straight highway. The few stars were starting to come out and the temperature dropped quickly. The road was bordered by short hedges and fields lay on either side. Where it led she had no idea, she just knew she had to get away. Trudging on, it seemed ages since she had seen anyone. It was a relief there were no army patrols out searching. What she could not know was the furious Despot had still not been missed; all his shouting out of the window went down to the empty courtyard.

For some time she had been conscious of a large covered wagon gaining on her. It was not military so she was not worried, but wondered if it might offer the prospect of a lift. The light had all but failed by the time the vehicle caught up with her. Katrina was exhausted by now and it was with a note of desperation that she asked the driver if he would mind a passenger.

"Why not? Join the party," replied the Sarnician trader in an off-hand manner, "climb on the back."

'A strange response,' thought Katrina as she moved round to the rear of the now stationary wagon. The reason soon became apparent once she was inside and the dakks slowly got the wagon moving again. The trader already had two passengers, a young couple that were eloping.

"Where are you trying to get to?" she quizzed them.

"Nowhere in particular," replied the youthful man, "we just want to get as far away as possible."

Katrina mumbled, "I know the feeling," before asking if they knew which direction they were presently heading.

"Northwards," came the answer, "before the night's out we should be in the northern forest. I'll feel happier then, because it won't be easy for my father's men to catch us after that. I pray to the Supreme God – all praise to His name – that we get out without being detected."

His Deity looked after them that night. Unseen in the darkness, the fugitives slipped away, leaving Aggeparii behind for good.

Bodd had been to Asattan the last three years with his brothers. However, he had only been to the capital city itself once before. Following an uneventful journey he entered through the main gate at midday. The streets were crowded and he allowed himself to be taken by the stream of people heading towards the centre. The backpack he was wearing dug into his shoulders and he tried to shift it away from the place where the straps were hurting. All the time he clutched the piece of paper with the address Alan had given him showing where he was to report to.

Just when he thought he was lost and was about to ask the way, he recognised one of the main thoroughfares. He stopped on the corner to work out which direction he needed to go. Great crowds of people pushed past. Most were whites, but there was no shortage of blacks and a few drones.

There was no shortage of foreigners too. Bodd concluded Asattan was becoming quite a cosmopolitan place as Hoamen laid aside their xenophobia at the altar of commerce.

"Ah, Straight Street," he said to himself looking up at the sign, "now... number 1147."

After a while he crossed over a bisecting road and noticed that most people were turning down there. He continued straight on and shortly found himself coming to a barrier across the street. It was policed by a couple of white men in official-looking uniforms who asked him his business. A while was spent explaining his mission. The security men were officious, but not rude. Eventually they were convinced the visitor was genuine and issued Bodd with a temporary pass which allowed him to enter the prohibited sector.

The high clouds had been burned off and the sun was reaching its zenith. He walked on, the nature of the buildings having changed in this exclusive area. Brick-built houses were such a contrast with the huts of the villages. Each dwelling was tall with glass windows and a tiled, sloping roof. Metal railings divided the small front courtyards from the pavement. Not having ever been near this sector, the man from the countryside was amazed. He stared at these impressive structures as he progressed up the street, conscious that there were hardly any fellow pedestrians here, just the occasional covered wagon moving along the mettled road.

'I never knew such wealth existed,' he mused, 'and to think my brothers and I thought ourselves well off. I hope Alan's given me the right address...'

Checking the numbers again he found he was quite close and in a short while was standing outside the house. A tall, elegant building, each of its windows had a box full of coloured flowers. In the garden stood bushes and trees giving shade on this warm spring day.

Bodd double-checked with the creased paper in his hand, he did not want to make a mistake. No doubt about it. Swallowing hard, the would-be civil servant opened the gate and advanced up the path to the huge front double-doors. Pausing for a moment to adjust the position of his back-pack, he collected himself and knocked twice. No answer. He waited a while before knocking again on the heavy wooden panels, the occupant might have been on their way and he did not want to annoy him.

There was no immediate answer to the second knock and he was just starting to worry that no one was at home when there came the sound of a latch. To Bodd's surprise a far smaller door within the giant doors opened and before him stood a young white woman, probably a couple of years his junior.

"Excuse me, is this Benedict's house?"

The woman answered in a flat tone, her eyes cold and expressionless.

"It is, you are expected, come in."

He stepped forward and quickly took in the scene before him: tall ceiling, tapestries hung on the wall, wide wooden staircase, top quality furniture – such opulence!

The young woman was gorgeous, no other word for it Bodd decided. Shoulder-length white hair, her face was smooth with high cheek bones, her figure tall and slim, she was stunningly good-looking.

'She's way out of my league,' he concluded as she spoke again.

"Follow me," she ordered and set off upstairs at a cracking pace.

Bodd did as he was told, but he was tired by now and having to sprint upstairs his back-pack cut into his shoulders all the more. He was grateful to be able to take it off and lay it down as they reached the bedroom and she swung open the door.

"Here it is," she said, dull and uninterested.

The room was enormous. It was also luxurious with an enormous four-poster bed, velvet curtains and furniture made by the finest craftsmen in the land. The coving was ornately carved into patterns leading the eye to the brightly painted ceiling. Bodd wanted to say it was too grand for him, but he did not want to offend his hostess.

She said, "You can measure up or whatever you have to do," then turned to go.

Bodd was puzzled by the remark, but too awestruck by it all to question the impatient-sounding woman. However, as she began striding away he plucked up the courage to say, "It's very big isn't it."

Stopping suddenly in her tracks, she turned and said petulantly, "If it's beyond your capabilities then kindly do not waste our time. We can always get someone else. As you were recommended to us we were trying you first, but if the job is too big for you..."

"Just a moment, I think there's been a misunderstanding. I'm Bodd from Thyatira, our drone Alan gave me a letter of introduction to give to Benedict, asking that he put me up."

"I thought you were the carpet man come to measure up," she replied humourlessly, obviously not seeing a funny side to the misunderstanding. "You had better come back downstairs and wait for my uncle there." She added to herself, "I should have got the servants to answer the door," before leaving Bodd by himself.

'She may look nice,' he considered, 'but a sourer person I have yet to find. Except Reuben perhaps – yes they'd get on well together.'

The ante-room he had been placed in was filled with strange objet-d'art such as unusual gadgets and the animal skull under glass just next to him. He inspected an inlaid box on a small, oval table in the centre of the room. It contained nothing of interest, just pins with coloured heads. He snapped it shut again with a bang. The place was cluttered with so many varied items, such as the ornate walking sticks in a rack, or the metre-square, twisted metal frame whose use he could not even guess at which hung on a wall. His hostess did not return and he sank into the comfortable chair she had originally directed him to. Before he knew it, he had fallen asleep.

Waking to the sound of voices in the hall he got up and fumbled for the letter of introduction. Sure enough it was the head of the house returning from work. Bodd went out into the hall and explained who he was and why he was there.

Benedict was a fifty year-old drone, one of the top civil servants in Hoame, Alan certainly knew the right connections. He was also a big man physically whose head seemed disproportionately small for his large body. Upon reading the letter, he greeted his new-found guest enthusiastically. His smile and cheerful disposition helped Bodd feel happier after experiencing the curt woman. She came into the hall at that moment and the large man put his arm around her and said, "You've met Anastasia, my niece. She will be glad to have some company other than the servants at last."

'Could have fooled me!' thought Bodd as he noticed the woman was actually smiling for the first time.

"So you want to enter the service, splendid," Benedict continued, "You'll have to work hard for the exams. I'd instruct you myself, only my work is never-ending these days, he indicated to the case on the floor beside him, "but don't fret, I'll arrange a good one to instruct you tomorrow. No I won't, I'll do it now. Anastasia, run along and get Sarka will you? We'll send him along to the tutor I've got in mind."

"Right, uncle."

She went off to get the servant.

"I'll invite him for dinner so that you can meet him, Bodd. The exams are not far off and there'll be no time to lose. We'll make sure you are well looked after. Alan speaks highly of you which is the best recommendation anyone could have. Splendid! Welcome to your new home."

Count Zastein brought his entire retinue along for the inspection of the border with Ladosa. It meant a long, thin column stretched back down the narrow track which headed north from the Castle. They went a few kilometres before the morning drizzle ceased and it brightened up. Several streams were crossed. Soon they were beyond the northern-most point Frank had been. The countryside was heavily wooded.

He need not have worried about the frontier guards. They came across as efficient and alert. He wondered how much of this activity – patrols, telescopic observation, defence maintenance – was due to his warning, he would never know. Intensely he studied the Count's face as the latter quizzed a squad leader.

"No, Your Excellency, we never have any trouble from the Laodicians."

"Yet you appear well prepared."

"Well prepared at all times, Your Excellency, our vigilance will keep the border safe."

'Extra rations for him!' thought Frank.

Zastein moved on, nodding. The Thyatiran positions were amongst the trees at the foot of the mountains, just before open ground that rose sharply towards the majestic, snow-covered peaks far above. Schail asked the officer whether their patrols ever went right up into the mountains.

"Not very often, Your Excellency," came the reply, "there is no precise agreement on where the border lies and we do not want to provoke a confrontation with the foreigners. Also, they are impassable for much of the year and at other times there is the danger of avalanches.

"It is generally very quiet here. If there was increased activity we would investigate it."

"Thank you, well spoken," the Baron said softly before turning to re-join the others.

Zastein's face was unchanged all the way back, but when they arrived at their destination his verdict was positive.

"Impressive Thorn, most impressive. It's interesting to see the whites here taking on more responsibilities in the absence of blacks. That squad leader was articulate... yes, interesting."

The following day the Keepers declared it was time for them to be getting back to the Capital. They first spent the morning in Sardis, however, meeting the Taltons they had heard about. Much building and repair work was still going on there and Luke the Village Head was too ill to receive the important guests. He had a chest infection and was being cared for personally by Laffaxe. The physician had spent much of the previous few weeks in the village due to the number of people ill there with varying ailments. The Taltons had grown fond of him and were more than happy to put up with his grumpy idiosyncrasies as he tended their people and trained replacements for the medics lost in the winter epidemic.

After having a good look, the Inner Council members said farewell to Frank and Alan, then got back into their wagons for the homeward haul. Head held proudly, the officer in charge of the escort ordered the advance and the column moved slowly on its way.

Frank dispelled air through his lips in relief now it was all over. He waited until they were back at the Castle before starting a post-mortem with Alan.

"Well I think that went all right, don't you?" he shouted above the noise in the hall.

The drone nodded in reply and they went upstairs to continue. Frank sighed as he sank into his chair. He took a long drink of water before saying, "You know, I didn't get the significance of the difference between my being a Minor instead of a Junior Despot."

"There is no practical difference here. If you attended a function at the Citadel there would be some procedural differences, but that's about all. The distinctions aren't what they once were."

The other man still required reassurance that the visit had been a success.

"Honestly, Alan, do you think their stay really went as well as it seemed? I mean it's not always easy to know what Count Zastein is thinking, his expression was very grave most of the time."

"Yeah, he was impressed, but then I knew he would be. Besides I'd given him a good report when I saw him last in the Capital."

"What!" exclaimed a surprised Frank, "you met him when you went to Asattan in the autumn?"

The response was very blasé.

"Sure, I was there to arrange the Guild Squad, so I thought I'd call in on him."

It suddenly dawned on Alan, "You don't know do you?"

"Know what?"

"Count Zastein, he's my father."

Franks' jaw dropped, his face was a picture. Then it changed to a smile and the two of them broke into hoots of laughter.

"I never any any idea!" he cried, remembering he had considered throwing Alan out with the other drones before he had actually met him. He also recalled his occasional outbursts against the son of the most powerful man in the land.

"It's not exactly a state secret," Alan was saying, "but I suppose it's not exactly shouted from the rooftops either. When I was at the Citadel that last time I met some guards who clearly didn't know.

"Just goes to show the hypocrisy in our country though: they outlaw the union of a black with a white, then give the offspring status far higher than the whites."

Frank had never heard him speak like this before. He could not contain his curiosity.

"Hope you don't mind me asking, but where is your mother? Does she live in Asattan?"

"My mother died in childbirth having me, I never knew her."

"Oh, I'm sorry."

The drone shook his head, "It's okay, I've always known it. I was brought up in the Citadel amongst all the Council Members vying for power. My father was always busy, but made great effort to spend time with me, I can appreciate that now. He loved my mother very much and he looked after me well after a fashion, but when I could, I got away from all that intrigue. That's why I came here, 'cos it's nice and quiet... and there aren't lots of people plotting against each other the whole time."

"I see, but if it's illegal..."

His question trailed off, but Alan still answered it.

"Whites and blacks coupling is only illegal when it suits the powers that be. The nearer you get to the top the less anyone is likely to complain. If you were an ordinary black without position and you did it... you would be in serious trouble.

"The double-standards people have never cease to amaze me; do you mind if we change the subject?"

They sat in silence. Frank might have been on the planet a year, but he still had a lot to learn about it.

⚒

CHAPTER TWENTY TWO

"King Solomon gave the Queen of Sheba everything she asked for, besides all the other customary gifts that he had given her so generously. After this she and her attendants returned to the land of Sheba."

"Thank you, Illianeth, nicely read, "said Frank wiping his napkin across his mouth, "you may go now."

"May I tell you something, My Lord?"

"Of course."

"I was told that every time we breath we take in three atoms of Solomon's last breath. Had you heard that?"

"Er, I can't say I had," Frank replied trying to keep a straight face, it was clear the girl was being serious. Then curiosity got the better of him and he asked her if she knew what atoms were.

"Not really, My Lord, little bits of air I suppose."

"Yes, well you could be right. Anyway thank you for that – and for the reading, very nice. Goodbye for now."

Lunch had just been completed and he was sitting with his top Castle personnel in the part of his rooms improvised as a dining area. The servants began clearing the table and the men moved to the more comfortable surroundings next door for their weekly business meeting. They sank into the soft chairs and waited for the Despot to start. Natias brushed a piece of cotton off his cuff, while Karl began picking his teeth with his fingernail.

"Right gentlemen, shall we get down to business. There are one or two things I'd like to discuss today, one of which... Karl, do you have to?"

"Oh sorry Sir," the black said taking his finger out of his mouth.

"Thank you. Yes, one thing I want to cover is Natias' tax proposals that were mentioned last week."

He indicated to the steward who began, "My pwoposed tax wefowms are not designed to alter the net weceits to any gweat degwee, but by putting more emphasis on a land wevanue they will shift the burden onto the better off..."

The meeting progressed at a reasonable pace. One of the items arising was a chronic problem of small bands of robbers operating in the border country in the extreme south-west of Thyatira. Japhses told them his guardsmen were increasing their efforts to track them down and there had been some successes, but too often the gangs slipped over the border into Rabeth-Mephar. Actual reports of robberies were well down he said.

When mention was made the Ma'hol traders starting to arrive in greater numbers Frank had an idea.

"So are any of our people going over there to sell our goods?"

"It would seem not, My Lawd. The twouble appears partly with the language bawwier. The Taltons of course do not have this problem, but are reluctant to weturn to the land of their slavewy, which is understandable I would have thought."

"But surely this "language barrier" works both ways, how come their traders can come here to sell their wares?"

"That's right," Alan cut in, "in my experience if a man is keen enough to do trade he won't let the obstacle of language stand in his way. Besides a fair proportion of the higher class Ma'hol speak our language anyway."

"But our people pwefer to have a more formal twading agweement, such as we have with the other despotates in our own countwy."

"Excellent!" declared Frank, "that fits in well with an idea I've had. I was thinking of inviting the Mehtar here for a summit, a bit like King Solomon used to. We can discuss relations, trade and so on, develop our... friendship with him."

The room suddenly became deathly quiet, even Karl stopped sucking his teeth with his tongue. All eyes were on the Despot.

Then Japhses said, "My Lord, I cannot see such a move being popular with the people, the Ma'hol have been our enemy for generations."

"High time that should change then. From the negotiations over the hostages they were very reasonable, I think we can do business with them."

"We had them over a barrel in the matter of the hostages, My Lord, they could not be anything but reasonable. I for one don't trust them."

"I don't see we are putting ourselves in danger by inviting the Mehtar here, Japhses. Besides I gained a good impression of him in our previous meeting on the stone bridge."

"With the greatest of respect, My Lord," the Captain persisted, "you cannot know somebody from one brief encounter."

"Precisely! All the more reason to meet him again and get to know him better."

Karl broke into the conversation, "May I advise, Sir, that a limit on the size of the retinue he brings might be sensible."

"Good idea," Natias called out.

Frank sighed, "Very well, but I insist on our inviting him to the Castle."

After the meeting was over he kept Alan back.

"You didn't say anything, do you think it is a good idea?"

The other shrugged his shoulders, saying, "I really don't know. The whites have had generations of distrust towards the Ma'hol, Japhses was only expressing what a lot of people will feel."

"And I admire him for it! I don't want to be surrounded by a load of "yes" men. But I'm thinking towards the long-term development of good relations with Rabeth-Mephar. The Mehtar is, like I said, a man I feel we can do business with. We found that out with the hostages. Maybe I'm being a bit idealistic, but I can't see how continued confrontation – or distrust at least - can be in either of our best interests. Well I am going to invite him, he can always say no."

Later that day Frank was in the hall. Just a couple of craftsmen were still working on the ceiling, painting the carved designs there. The others had moved to the external staircase where, under Damian's direction, they had begun work on a roof. This was to lead down to a small reception room at the foot of the keep, Frank's bright idea to facilitate an orderly vetting of unexpected guests. It had been cleverly designed to break into sections which could be dismantled in the event of a siege.

Frank was not the only one who had expressed concern at the lack of control over who was coming into the keep. When it was all finished, the guards in the reception area would be under instructions to be flexible in the admittance of people. The nature of life in the Castle was to be maintained, but a certain element of control and security, even in these times of peace, was thought by most to be a good idea.

In the meantime, life went on as normal as large numbers of people made their way up the stairs where the guild squad

members were going about their business. As they picked their
way between the workmen it was clear they were getting in each
other's way. The architect had a long discussion that day with
his hirer and it was agreed to construct a second, temporary,
wooden staircase up to the keep entrance in order that the
guild squad could work with a minimum of interruption.

"My Lord, can I have a word?"

Frank looked down. Standing by one of the large timber
stockpiles temporarily set up in the bailey was the priest Zadok
with his assistant Eleazar.

'Oh dear,' thought Frank, 'What does the old boy want
now?' then he told himself off for having such an uncharitable
thought.

Zadok was in fact inviting him to a special meeting the
Sabbath after next in the Upper Village.

"There is a great movement afoot throughout the country,"
he explained, "a great revival of faith and worship, can you not
feel it? The Spirit is guiding us along the path. This will be an
important event and it is highly desirable that you be there, My
Lord. It will be the preliminary event for a much greater one
later in the year... with your permission, when men and women
of faith will be coming here from all the other despotates for a
wonderful festival of renewal.

"Meetings such as the one in a fortnight's time are being held
in these other regions at the moment. We will be building up a
great wall of prayer and praise, renewing our commitment so
that our faith can take the central part in our lives once more."

Frank felt embarrassed, he did not know why. Indeed he
told himself what a good thing this all was. Back on Eden
though it had been so different. He had happily spent long
periods in a cell alone, studying the scriptures and praying, the
form of communal worship practised by the whites would never
feel right for him.

'I'm sure these people are far better Christians than I,' he told himself with sincerity, 'I should learn from their example of putting God at the centre of their lives. I find myself too busy for God most of the time these days and there is no excuse for that.'

He assured Zadok that he would look forward to being at the meeting, and happy to sanction the big event they had in mind for the future.

"I knew you would," said the old man, obviously delighted. "Oh yes, there is one other thing My Lord. Natias told me you are interested in books. I have in my possession an old book, a 'dictory' I think it's called..."

"A dictionary?"

"...That's right. I wondered if you would like to have it."

"I certainly would be interested in borrowing it, yes please," the bibliophile replied eagerly.

"You can have it My Lord. I have no use for it."

Life was busy and time flew as a result. The next week and a half saw Frank really enjoying life to the full, directing here, making decisions there. An extra supply of tents, imported from Ephamon, had arrived and were stored away. These had been ordered on Japhses' initiative for use by the guard if required. The invitation to the Mehtar was duly sent, a quick reply was not anticipated. The cover for the external staircase was coming on apace. More importantly was the excellent job being made of it.

Before he knew it, the day of the revival meeting was upon him. Unfortunately his good state of mind left him that morning. For no apparent reason he had got a poor night's sleep and began the day with a headache. Feeling lethargic, he just wanted to stay in bed. Rising above such non-constructive thoughts he got up and went down to the hall for breakfast. Many other people were setting off from the Castle, but he travelled alone. When he arrived and got among the crowds he felt even more alone. There were few people he recognised and all seemed too in awe of the Despot to speak to him.

The organisers could not have foreseen the numbers who would attend. A series of tents, some large, some small, had been set up in a fallow field on the edge of the village. A great river of people was still arriving, making the area more and more crowded. It appeared all the whites in the despotate were there, including the Taltons, some of whom still wore their distinctive clothes, although more and more were adopting the local style even for the warmer weather. The usual sprinkling of foreigners was absent and Frank was conscious he stuck out like a sore thumb.

The main event had not yet begun and the people milled in and around the smaller tents. A group of itinerant preachers from the south had come specially and each was attracting much attention as they spouted forth on the Word.

"Hello, My Lord."

A friendly voice! Frank turned amidst the melee and saw Rodd, partly in his guardsman uniform, easing his way through the crush.

"Hello, Rodd, haven't seen you for a long time. How are you? How is Leah?"

The reply was that they were very well. "It's ridiculous setting this all up in such a small field," the soldier declared, "it wasn't necessary." Rodd went on to explain that he had been called to help expel some foreign traders who had set up stalls nearby. "They're trying to take advantage of the influx of people, but we can't have those heathens operating on the Sabbath."

"All right, but don't be too heavy handed," Frank warned, "I don't want anyone hurt."

Rodd disappeared into the crowd and Frank forced his way through the throng to the largest of the tents. A pair of officials were stopping people from entering the structure, but one of them quickly spotted the Despot and helped him inside. There Saul was directing operations as around a dozen people scurried about the finishing touches to what was to be the venue for the main event of the day. Rising from the grass floor at one end of the long, rectangular tent was a wooden stage with many musical instruments laid out on it. Two men were moving a table across it while women arranged flowers around the edge. There were wooden chairs of a basic design in two rows near the stage, the rest of the area was bare, empty grass. A small group of children were playing there, chasing each other across it and doing hand-stands. They were not disturbing anyone.

When he spotted the new arrival, Saul left off shouting instructions and turned to greet him. He apologised for the congestion outside.

"We were hoping to be able to use the adjoining field as well, that would have doubled the space and solved the problem. All the other nearby fields are being used for crops. That devil Hanson demanded a ridiculous fee for the use of that field though, we just couldn't afford it. He's not using it for anything, hasn't done so since he bought it years ago as far as I know. I have no idea what we'll do later on in the year when we've an even bigger meeting planned."

"Surely I can order him to let you have the use of the field for nothing – just for the meeting I mean. That's within my power isn't it?"

Saul's face brightened right up.

"Well within your power, My Lord. That would be wonderful. We could have an overspill area now and make sure some events are held over there."

"Right, you go ahead. If this Hanson character has any complaints he can always come and see me."

"Thank you very much, My Lord, I am most grateful."

He sped off, leaving Frank alone. Not for long, however. Zadok had been on the stage the whole time, unnoticed by the short-sighted Despot. As soon as Saul had left, the priest came down to welcome him. True to his word he had brought the dictionary. Frank eagerly flicked through it, he would have to wait until he got home before having a really good look.

"We must be getting on, My Lord, there is much to do before the meeting starts, I'm sure you understand. Eleazar, please show the Despot to his seat."

Taking his place on the left near the stage, Frank found the chair most uncomfortable. It was as if it had been designed especially to dig into the sitter's back in just the wrong place. He shuffled about as he waited, but he could not get comfortable. Unfortunately he was still not in the best of mental states. Before he set out for the Upper Village, a little voice inside him had told him he did not want to go. It was now telling him with great effect how he would rather be elsewhere.

As he waited, he glanced at the dictionary, but found himself in such a negative mood he was not interested in it for the moment and put it back down at his feet. He sat there for what seemed like an age, during which time nobody approached him. People came and went on and around the stage, providing plenty to look at had he been interested.

Eventually the masses were let in and they flooded the area like a bursting dam. There was much excitement and high spirits. The rest of the chairs were ear-marked for the important families of the village. In the rigid social structure of Hoame these distinctions were all important. The seat next to Frank was reserved for Saul. Subsequently it was left empty, because the Village Head was fully occupied organising the show. His wife sat next along and exchanged a nervous greeting. After that she made sure she was busy looking after their five children so that Frank felt all the more alienated stuck by himself.

Not that he minded particularly in his current mood. He watched expressionless as a small group of men led by Saul took up their positions on the stage and an air of expectancy gripped the crowd. After a brief introduction, everyone stood up and enthusiastically burst into rejoicing with a song he did not know. Musicians with a variety of instruments accompanied it from the stage opposite him. To the right a group of young women were leading the dancing.

As a fresh song began Frank wondered how it was Natias always got out of this type of event while he felt obliged to come. Alan was neither a Christian nor remotely interested in becoming one.

'I really should have tried witnessing my faith to him properly,' he thought rather feebly.

The music ended and one of the visiting preachers got up to speak. He talked at great length on God's Creation and from the elaborate cosmogony put forward, it became apparent that the man firmly believed Molton to be the only inhabited planet in the universe. He then went into an interminable explanation of the Children of Israel's journey through the Wilderness on the other side of the globe. It was at this point that Frank's mind completely wandered off.

'There must be lots of other primitive worlds where the inhabitants believe they are the centre of the universe and therefore unique. Not the strangest set of beliefs I've come come across. There was that terrible Dracoa where they held that children should be taken away from their parents for the first ten Earth-years of their education. Or Cheng Fong where those funny little people were totally given towards commerce. The gross materialism there was quite sickening. Mind you, they did have beautiful sunsets from their twin stars and I made my best ever sale of a book there.

'Then there was that crazy warlike planet with women in charge...'

He noticed the group of musicians on the stage. Some were fidgeting and one young man stifled a yawn. Then a slim woman came and sat on an empty stool right in front of him and silently unpacked her flute. His eyes widened as he realised it was Giella.

"...and now the music group will lead us in some choruses," the preacher announced and everyone stood.

The song was simple and easily learned, the people joined in with great gusto. The large numbers in the tent made the air warm and stale, but no one seemed to mind. Frank had tried to shake his negative thoughts off, but to no avail. He felt alien to the entire proceedings and found himself taking a proud satisfaction from detaching himself from it all. Instead he concentrated on the beauty before his eyes.

Giella was so close even he could see her clearly. She appeared not to notice him. It was a long time since he last saw her, absence had tended to dull the passion rather than make the heart grow fonder. Now that she was there in front of him once more the flame was re-lit with a vengeance. His current mood blocked any signals his higher self might give him and as the meeting wore on all his thoughts were taken up with her.

Other preachers had their turn and further up-tempo songs of praise were sung until at long last the meeting climaxed in an ecstasy of shouting, hugging and kissing. Some people even came up to the Despot and took him into their arms briefly. He found himself freezing like a piece of board, his face a fixed grimace. When this was all over people began to leave, but many stayed behind for a healing ministry. Confusion reigned as, like ants, each member of the congregation appeared to go his own way.

Amid all the bustle Frank climbed onto the stage where the musicians were putting their instruments away.

"Hello My Lord," Giella greeted him, still looking down at her bag as she packed her equipment. She raised her head, "Enjoyed the meeting?"

"It was very interesting," he lied. "I thought you played well."

A crude compliment and she smiled, confidence showing across her face.

"Thank you," she replied, but her whole aura was of self-assurance, even a despot's compliment she would take in her stride.

There was lots of noise going on around them and he had to raise his voice to be heard.

"I...I just wondered how you were getting on – and Roil. Is your husband here?"

"Uriah is on border patrol chasing robber bands," she said picking up her bag as she stood, "but he did manage to get me my own separate changing tent, did you want to speak to me there, My Lord?"

An invitation not to be spurned. Frank's heart pounded as they made their way a short distance across the still crowded field. The tent took up only a small area, but was tall enough for someone to stand up in. Up close he smelt her distinctive perfume. He wondered at how she seemed so cool when he was sure everyone else at the meeting had been running with perspiration. Her face lingered near him and he leaned forward gently to kiss her lips. At the last possible moment before they touched she playfully pulled her head away.

"If you wait here I shall get changed My Lord," she said, merriment in her voice as she moved gracefully behind a screen.

Frank felt acutely embarrassed at the rebuff. In an attempt to hide this he tried to strike up a casual conversation even though his mind was going crazy with desire.

"I didn't know many of the songs at the meeting."

"Uh-huh?"

"No, they were new to me. You play the clarinet as well as the flute I see."

"That's right, and the piano."

"Oh, a piano, I didn't see one there."

"It wasn't there, My Lord, but there is one in the community hut in the village."

"I see."

Giella continued to get dressed out of his sight. After a short while Frank resumed the conversation.

"There's a big store of instruments up at the Castle you know."

"I didn't... but I'm not surprised considering Despot Rattinger's interest."

"Did you play for him?"

"Yes, My Lord."

"Oh," was all his response before he thought of a way he could re-take the initiative. "Would you like to come up to the Castle and have a good look at the instruments stored away there? I'm sure we could let you have one or two."

There was no reply. Then she emerged from behind the screen. Her dress was the lightest possible fabric, silvery with many pastel shades worked into it. From her thigh it went into pointed strips which ended at the knee. As she approached him these waved in the air. He was aching to caress her. This time she moved only closer and soon their bodies were entwined in an ecstasy of kissing. Frank's eyes were shut as he held her tight and pressed his lips hard against hers. Inside his head he screamed, 'I love you!' over and over again. This must be heaven.

After a while he had to come up for air and, opening his eyes as he partially released himself from her embrace, he noticed Giella's expression of mirth as she answered his question.

"I would like to see the instruments with you, My Lord," she said, resting her left hand on his shoulder and running a finger through his hair, "but I shall be busy tonight. Can I come tomorrow evening?"

He swallowed. "Of course, if you..."

Giella, are you in there?" a voice called from just outside.

"Yes Reuben, you can come in," she cried as Frank took a large step away from her. Then she added, "I've got the Despot with me," as the flap of the tent moved.

"Ah, My Lord, I hope you don't mind," the cropper said awkwardly.

Frank thought, 'Damn you! Why did you have to turn up now?'

"No, no that's all right," he said before looking across at Giella, who appeared completely unbothered by the intrusion, and adding, "Well I'll see you soon then."

"See you tomorrow evening, My Lord," she said gaily, "I'll look forward to it."

A despondent Despot picked up his book and left the tent, giving a big sigh once outside. He took a quick squint at the still dispersing crowds then walked in the direction of his dakk to take him back home. All the way back he was taken up in his own thoughts.

'Honestly, I'll never understand her! First she teases me, then makes it plain she wants me, then when Reuben turns up she's still all smiles and "yes you do come in, I'm not doing anything." Then as I go to leave she says how she's looking forward to seeing me tomorrow! She flits about like a butterfly leaving me in a daze. She must know how much I want her and she's coming up to my rooms tomorrow; I will make sure we're not disturbed...'

Alan looked across the table of the Throne Room at Karl Vondant. The black was slumped in his chair, fast asleep, making a whistling noise each time he expelled air.

"No point in waking him, Natias, we may as well carry on without him. He'll feel better for his nap."

They were looking over a map of Sardis and discussing how best to help the Taltons develop their new village.

"You are wight, leave him be. Now, to get back, just about all the volunteers have left now. They have had to get back to tend the hulffan. A gang of pwisoners goes out each day to help, they are cuwwently pulling down this wow of huts here; they were so poorly constwucted they are weally beyond wedemption. Due to the dwop in population the people were wehoused without too much difficulty, but some new homes do now need to be built, plus some other public buildings of course."

He wiped his big nose before concluding, "The Taltons are a hard-working people, but they cannot be expected to develop their own industwies and complete the buildings all by themselves."

"Hmm. What is the row of larger buildings here?"

"They are workshops – leather-work, silver-smithing, that kind of thing."

"Of course. What about the guild squad, can we utilize them? No we can't, can we," Alan answered his own question, "it's not their cup of juice to do that sort of thing, Damian would consider himself above it. I see their getting on well here with the reception room."

"Yes, although they are beyond the owiginal budget. I have just had to order another supply of timber, best quality natuwally."

"Has Frank got any other jobs lined up when the reception room is finished?"

"He was owiginally talking about having one of the wooms in his suite turned into a "chapel" as he called it, but has not said anything about it wecently."

"Blue green ones! What on Molt was that?" Alan exclaimed in response to a sudden high-pitched scream the other side of the door.

The sharp noise had almost woken Karl, but then he went back to his dreams and mumbled something incoherent. It quickly became apparent that it was a baby crying and Natias mentioned that one of Eko's friends were visiting and she had some young children.

"But to weturn to the subject in hand, I cannot see our getting vewy much further with the new village this year."

"Unless... let me tell you, since the end of last winter I've taken a keen interest in Sardis. In short I feel guilty about what happened."

A serious-looking Alan would not entertain the other's protests. "No I'm sorry, but before the snows came I saw those buildings were not safe and I did nothing about it; I do feel bad about that.

"What I'm thinking of doing is financing, up to a grend, a construction project to have men come in and do the necessary work."

"Most kind, of course," Natias laboured the words, "but that is an awful lot of money."

"I've got a small fortune earning interest in the Capital, I never spend any of it..."

"Nor should you have to," the steward interrupted. Extra finance was always welcome, but he did not want his friend to do it out of a sense of guilt.

"But I want to."

"It could cause inflation, that much money suddenly entering the local economy. Besides, you do more than enough for us alweady; there has been something of a boom since that successful twade package with Aggepawii you secured, the people still wemember that. Your bweakthwough after those pwotwacted negotiations has helped all our pwospewity."

"Thank you, my friend," Alan replied with a kind look in his eyes, "I'll help Sardis 'cos I want to, not because I feel I have to. I'll send Solly to Aggeparii to hire skilled labourers, I know contacts and would rather by-pass the official guild squads... can do without the hassle if I want to stay in charge. With Frank's agreement I'll send a squad of guardsmen to Asattan with documents to collect the money. Most of it will eventually find its way back to Aggeparii I expect, let them worry about inflation. We can discuss details another time, let's have a drink."

Natias ended his objections and expressed his appreciation for what the drone was doing. At that juncture their colleague began to wake up and gave a loud grunt.

"Er, oh... where were we?"

Alan looked across at him with amusement.

"We *were* sorting this map out. *Now* we are off to get a well-earned drink, are you coming?"

"When the wicked man turns away from his sins and does God's will he shall save himself."

Red streaks were shot across the sky the following evening, as if to relay evil portents to the mortals below. A vengeful setting sun sent rivers of blood along the underside of the the clouds as it sunk beneath the horizon. Frank was not a superstitious man, but as he knelt in his room and peered out the window he read the massage in the sky.

"Be gracious to me, Oh God, in your great love,

In the fullness of your mercy take away the wrong I have done.

Wash away all my guilt

And cleanse me from my sin."

Away from the heady aroma of Giella's perfume he deeply regretted what he was getting into.

'What depths have I plummeted to Francis? I'd never have believed it of you: besotted like a man drunk out of his mind you have invited a married woman here this evening in order to entice her into your bed! You used to study scripture daily, pray regularly, now you wouldn't recognise the Bible if you tripped over it. Oh God what have I become? I am a worm, not a man!'

This time he would not let his other side have a say. The side which used excuses of loneliness in the past and spoke of love for her was not given a hearing. He flicked over the pages of God's Word to another relevant passage.

"I will go to my Father and say I am not fit to be called your son, please treat me as one of your hired men."

He could not believe his actions of the day before, but now was a time for honesty and not fooling himself by blaming others.

'She has not enticed me, it is entirely my own fault. I have acted like a complete imbecile! The woman's coming here to-night, soon I expect, what shall I do?'

Filled with resolve, he would not let the other side of his personality get a word in.

'I won't listen to any stupid thoughts about loving her – you just want to use her for your sexual appetite. No! I shall be pleasant to her this evening and show the musical instruments, give her a couple if she likes, I don't use them. Then it's good-bye. I must purge her from my mind once and for all, the only way to do that is regular prayer, meetings and scripture read-ings. I will not miss out on these from now on.

'Heavenly Father, I earnestly desire to be a lot better from now on, please give me the strength to carry this out. Especially tonight Lord God, I humbly ask you to help me to be nice to her without succumbing to temptation or leading her astray.'

Somewhat belatedly, he thought, he got ready for Giella's visit. He got changed and made sure his lounge looked respectable – the servants had tidied it earlier in the day – then waited. Sitting in a chair he twiddled his fingers as the time passed, he did not want to start anything as she would be along any moment. Once or twice he went into the corridor and paced up and down there. Belatedly the idea occurred to him that he could have invited someone else to join them as a chaperone – too late now. Back in the lounge he looked out the window, it was getting dark by now.

Unable to contain himself any longer he went down the stairs, through the hall and down the, now covered, external staircase to the new reception room. The men on duty had not had any visitors enter since dusk, only a few fellow guardsmen had passed through. The Despot went back to his suite.

So she was not coming. Good. But what if she came another evening when his resolve was not so strong? He would just have to make sure it was. He said his final prayers at his bedside in the light of a flickering candle. Blowing it out he got into bed.

Outside a frass gave out a shrieking cry into the night air, it had escaped a sprung trap and although it had lost a piece of skin, the animal was free and would be wiser next time.

Left to his own devises in the house, Bodd was writing a letter to his brothers. He had not got word to them since arriving in Asattan and realised he must seize the opportunity given him of letting them know how he was doing:

'Eleazar, I know you will be kind enough to read this to my brothers so they can hear how I am getting on. Please ask them to give Vaskalani a good meal, hospitality and ten stens in payment for his delivering this for me.

Dear brothers, what luck! I got talking with a traveller in a café yesterday who told me he is just about to go to Thyatira. He readily agreed to take my letter and give it to Eleazar if I can get it to him tomorrow morning.

I went to the address Alan gave me, it turns out to be an exclusive part of the Capital where you need a special pass to get in. The owner is a drone called Benedict. He is big in the civil service. Busy man, but he still had time to help me in my studies. Also arranged work experience, but more on that later.

Benedict is also an inventor in what little spare time he has. He experiments with steam under pressure in a special underground room here. I watched once, but I don't want to go again, afraid the thing will explode!

The house here is unbelievable. It is so big – four stories – and so clean. There is an army of servants who spend all day cleaning and tidying the place, I do not even have to put my bed straight, they do it all for me. And the bed is so comfortable. But I must not go on about these things, I will make you jealous!

'The other person here all the time is a girl about our age called Anastasia. She is a sour frass, I do not have much to do with her if I can help it. Benedict calls her his niece, but I cannot work out how a drone can have a white niece.

My exams are over now. I don't think they went too badly. I will have to wait a whole two weeks from today before I know if I will be accepted. I cannot understand why it takes them so long, but then I suppose there were a good many other men taking them. In the meantime, Benedict has arranged for me to work there anyway. I am in his department and enjoy it, but I guess I will get kicked out if my exams are not up to scratch!

There are many nice people where I work in the Citadel. It is such a different life here though, stone buildings all around and a large number of blacks. I quite often see the Keepers, but have not spoken to any yet. Count Zastein has had what used to be the Autarch's Palace turned into offices and storage spaces for files. There are big rooms with files reaching to the ceiling, just the sort of place Natias would feel at home in. Don't tell him I said that! I have been working in the old Citadel offices.

One of the clerks I have become friends with is called Daniel. He entered the service last year and is a real laugh. Another one in my department is known as Willy, he is very cynical about our superiors, says you have to be very selfish to get on and not give a damn about other people. I find this hard to believe about Benedict.

I think you have all my news now. I know not when I shall be able to go back to see you if I am successful in becoming a clerk. So busy here, this is my first evening free for ages. No, Tsodd, I have not found the right girl yet, I usually go out with the lads in the office, they are such a nice bunch. I did not re-alise until I got here that my hair style is the latest fashion here! They were amazed at the country bumpkin being so modern.

Trust you are both doing well. Rodd, I hope all is well with you and Leah. Tsodd I hope your animals are fine, especially the dragonflies! Please thank Vaskalini for the safe delivery of the letter and, if possible, send a reply via him. He is a good Christian soul as I am sure you will find out.

Also please thank Alan for his help and tell him so far so good.

Your ever-loving brother, Bodd.'

Frank felt refreshed after a good night's sleep and before go-ing down to breakfast took a long, dreamy stare out of a win-dow at the hills in the distance. He thought back to those days on Eden. A keen activist in the Primary Radicals it had been the moment in his life when the decision to break away from the mainstream Church was made, the culmination of years of

struggle. Heady days followed – meetings, debates, long passionate arguments – the atmosphere had been electric. The joy
of seeing all he had worked for coming to fruition.

Then the bitter disappointment when things turned bad as
others lost their nerve. It all began to collapse around them. To
go back cap in hand to the arrogant church leaders was just too
much for the idealists in the party still arguing for holding out. He
could still see Nakajima and Patel crying. The shame of it all, the
memory still hurt.

So then he had begun his life of wandering; buying and
selling rare books (he must find time to have a good look at
that dictionary Zadok had given him), travelling through the
galaxy. He had covered a great distance in a short time.

But now breakfast would be ready. Soon he was downstairs
in the hall eating with the regulars. During the meal it was
revealed to Frank that a messenger from Rabeth-Mephar had
arrived late last night. Not wanting to disturb the Despot they
had given the Ma'hol some food and a bed for the night.

"Let's hear what message he has to deliver then," Frank ordered as he took a bite out of his toast.

"Should we not wather wait until after the meal My Lawd?
Then we can weceive him pwoperly in the Thwone Woom,"

"Thank you, but I'd rather hear what he's got to say now."

The foreigner was summoned to their table where he handed over the Mehtar's letter.

"Good, let's see what he has to say. Ah it's in our language
Alan, your translation....." he paused before exclaiming, "excellent, he's coming! Can't make it for another three weeks, but
that gives us time to prepare."

The news put him in good spirits, but he noticed that Natias
was not sharing his enthusiasm one little bit.

When the meal was over Frank made his way over to the
dakk stables in the bailey with Alan, Natias and the Head

Groom. The renovation of the stables was the latest job for the guild squad.

"I have all the figures back in the Castle, My Lawd, we are alweady considerably over budget."

"Right; we'll call it a day after this. I've been thinking about it, the chapel can wait."

A wagon stopped nearby and men began unloading flour for the Castle kitchens.

"It feels like we might have some rain," Frank continued, looking up at the sky as they stood a few metres away from the stables where the work was in progress. In the corner of his eye he noticed a small, bearded figure with a walking stick coming across the bailey towards them.

"Zadok," he called out in a loud voice when the priest was still some way off, "how are you? I wanted to tell you that I'm looking forward to going to the meeting in the Upper Village next Sabbath."

The old man did not answer at first, but kept walking towards them, concerned frown on his face.

'I like that,' thought Frank rather disgruntled, 'he's always trying to get me to go to his meetings, then when I volunteer he says nothing – there's gratitude for you! Or maybe he didn't hear me.'

Before he could repeat himself Zadok spoke.

"Good morning My Lord, everyone. I am pleased you will be coming to the meeting, but I have grave news to tell you."

The others stiffened and focused their attention on him.

"There has been a murder in the Upper Village, it happened last night. Uriah's wife Giella was found this morning dead in her hut. She had been horribly battered to death!"

⇥┼⇤

CHAPTER TWENTY THREE

They were stunned.

"Who found her?" asked Alan, the first to recover himself.

"It was a neighbour," Zadok replied, "just decided to call in on the spur of the moment. Giella's daughter Roil is away staying with relatives, she hasn't been told yet, I'm getting that organised."

'Well this puts an end to my temptations. I do hope it wasn't Uriah jealous of his wife coming to see me.'

Frank suddenly realised how dreadfully selfish and unfeeling his thoughts were and chastised himself, 'For pity's sake stop always thinking about yourself, Francis! This is a terrible thing that's happened.'

Alan was still quizzing the priest.

"So you have no idea at this stage who did it?"

The other shook his head. It was decided they would continue the discussion in the Castle so, leaving the Head Groom behind, Natias, Frank plus the two who had done most of the talking retired to the Throne Room.

"May I suggest, My Lawd, that Alan be given the task of investigating this fwightful twagedy? He has the confidence of all classes of villagers and is, in my opinion, best qualified, therefore, for the task."

Alan indicated that he was willing to undertake some investigations if no one in the room objected, so that was quickly agreed. He immediately went through with Zadok again what details the old man knew. While this was going on, Natias turned towards Frank.

"It is vewy ware for us to have a murder in Thyatira, My Lawd. There have been a few by wobbers in the woods, but actually in a village...

" Ages ago there was an old wise woman they consulted on things like that, but she died in the year of the gweat storm."

"When was that?"

"Oh about thwee years ago. Pwobably longer in fact, you know how time does that; an event one thinks only happened a year ago weally occurred two or thwee. It's like the guests staying with us at pwesent, they have one child that was born the same week that Despot Wattinger died, we worked out..."

The steward went on for some time about his friends, but Frank found the other conversation in the room much more interesting. While looking at and nodding to Natias the whole time, his attention drifted between him and the other two men. The result was that he took in very little of either conversation and when the talking in the room stopped he had to ask Alan what he would be doing.

"Not sure," the drone confessed. "Fortunately we've not been faced with this problem before. I guess I'll have to go and ask a lot of questions, make a nuisance of myself, see what that achieves."

"Well, I wish you luck."

"We should all pray for Alan's success," Zadok announced and before they parted he led them in a series of petitions to

God. These included prayers for Giella's soul and the bereaved. He then headed back to the village while Frank, for whom the news had not properly sunk in, went to the sword-smith's in the bailey to see how the present for the Mehtar was coming along. The other two lingered a while.

"I hear he has agweed to welease a squad of guardsmen to go to Asattan and collect your money, escort it back here."

"Yeah, they're setting off today, get my capital from the Capital!"

"The Taltons weally will be gwateful for what you are doing for them."

"We'll see, but I'm gonna keep a close eye on the work there, make sure a good job is done this time. We owe them that.

"Right now though I've got to think how I'm going to tackle my new assignment..."

Meanwhile Frank was passing Laffaxe's house when the physician came out and remonstrated with him about the work being carried out on the stables.

"The noise is unbearable – constant bang bang bang! Dust they create comes through the windows; I have to have them open to dispel some of the noxious fumes given off by the bahkti compound I'm working on. I am just about at the end of my tether!"

"I'm sorry about the inconvenience, but the urgent need for their renovation was impressed upon me. Anyway, the Head Groom told me earlier this morning that all work should be completed by the end of tomorrow."

"Then what will they start?" snapped Laffaxe before adding, "My Lord," as an afterthought.

"You'll be pleased to know they will be heading back home after that, You will get your peace and quiet at last."

"Hmph! Not a day too soon."

Leaving the irascible physician to stew, Frank moved on. Before he entered the smithy he glanced round and saw him standing outside his house, arms folded and feet apart, obviously still angry at the situation.

'Can't please everyone,' he said to himself as he entered the workshop.

The sword-smith was taking a well-earned rest with a tall glass of fruit-juice. He brewed his own beer, but did not like to drink it during a working day because, he said, it made him feel more thirsty than ever once he started working again. A broad, muscular man, his face was leathery, the skin pitted and marked with no eyebrows. Seeing the Despot, he leapt up, almost spilling his drink.

"M'Lord, 'tis an honour t' see ya. Will be 'bout the foreigner's blade yo' came?"

Frank had not been in here before and took in the scene as he spoke.

"That's right, how's it progressing?"

A young assistant entered by the side-door with a bag of charcoal and was immediately ordered by his master to fetch the sword.

"Here 'tis," the sword-smith declared proudly holding it up. "Am keepin' to the simple pattern on the blade like you said M'Lord. To yer likin' is it?"

The Despot enthused, it really was an impressive work of art.

"'Tis a sixteen hin blade o'course."

"Sorry?"

"The weight, M'Lord, sixteen hin."

"Ah yes, of course, very good," he said, thinking how curious it was that some of the measurements in Hoame were intergalactic while others were clearly parochial. He had not the faintest idea how heavy a "hin" was.

"An' the bindin' to be completed, but we'll have it all finished in good time for yo' t'present it to 'im M'Lord."

Frank expressed his satisfaction at how the sword was progressing and, declining an offer of a drink, returned to the keep. Entering the sunlight again, he was striding across the bailey when Illianeth tagged onto him and told him she had just been to see Laffaxe.

"Poor old boy, all this din's getting him down."

"He told me."

"I was round by the beehives this morning, My Lord," she continued cheerfully, "got chased by a bee half way across a field! Soosha laughed until she cried, there's support for you."

Frank returned the laugh before asking where her friend was. Usually they were so inseparable.

"Oh she's helping in the kitchen, I'd better get back there soon."

They went through the reception room and up the covered stairway to the hall. The devastating news from early came back to Frank's mind and he concluded from the servant's cheerful disposition that she had not found out yet. Strange, Castle gossip was usually a lot more efficient than that. He certainly wasn't going to mention it.

"You know the players have arrived?" Illianeth asked excitedly. In response to a blank expression she continued, "The players are setting up stage in the courtyard, My Lord. Actors and actresses. They are starting their performances this afternoon I think, I hear they're very funny."

Frank looked disturbed and stopped just outside the hall to find out more. "I'm not sure I like the sound of it, Illianeth. Play-acting, I've seen it before; not very morally uplifting, more of a bad influence."

"It's just innocent fun, My Lord, it's not meant to be anything else," she replied before excusing herself and going back to the kitchen. While thinking the Despot's response was strange, she soon dismissed it from her mind. He would soon realise what it was all about she told herself.

He was far from doing anything of the sort, however. A bad influence is a bad influence and the revitalized conscience within him was not going to allow such a thing in his despotate. But he would give it a fair chance. Tomorrow he would go there unannounced and witness one of the performances for himself. He would not make his mind up fully before then.

'Best not jump to conclusions,' he decided as he retired to his suite.

It was a warm, early summer's evening in Asattan. Bodd was relaxing in the garden with Benedict, sprawled out on couches like a couple of ancient Romans. Although he was a big wheel in the machinery of the civil service, Benedict was not a difficult person to relax with. His manner put people at their ease. Besides, Bodd had every reason to feel relaxed: his exam results had come through and he had passed. In fact, he had passed with distinction and had received a commendation from none other than Mallinburg, the Keeper in charge of the entire Service. One bonus he got for passing the exams was a fortnight's paid leave.

As he discussed his plans with Benedict, the beautiful Anastasia sat down silently close by them. This was most unusual, normally she appeared to avoid the house guest like the plague. They had passed very few words at all since his arrival and she pointedly kept herself to herself. Bodd was indifferent to this at first, a feeling which had gradually given way to hurt at the thought she was deliberately being aloof. He had got the impression she felt herself above the country bumpkin whose presence she was having to endure. After a while though, his conception changed once more. She was simply a loner. She never had any friends of either sex call at the house, only rarely did she venture out herself. Instead, Anastasia sat around at home by herself either doing embroidery or playing cards.

Benedict was blissfully unaware of his "niece's" condition, but then when he was not at work, the cheery drone spent much of his time with his experiments in the cellar. Anyway she did talk more to him. Bodd had given up his unsuccessful attempts at conversation. He did not need to make the effort, there were new friends here to go out with. Rarely did he think about her now, when he did, the emotion aroused was more likely to be pity than anything else.

So even though she was remaining silent it still surprised him to see her pull up a chair nearby.

Benedict asked, "This is your brother in the local army getting married?"

"That's right, he's been in the Guard since the war with the Ma'hol last year."

"And does he enjoy it?"

"Oh yes, very much I think."

"Good, splendid; and what does your other brother do? I'm sure you have told me." "Tsodd doesn't have to work for a living. He saved all his money up from the mines and leads a simple life with his animals. They're his first love – animals, birds, insects, worms, anything like that. He bought some land for an aviary, paid over the odds, and I suppose the money will run out eventually. Until then he's just happy living with all his creatures.

"At least they won't talk back like your brother's wife will," laughed Benedict before he finished his drink and put the empty glass down.

Bod raised a smile, but thought it an odd sort of joke for a drone to make.

"So the three of you used to be miners," Benedict resumed after a pause. Where was that?"

"The tin mines here in Ephamon, not that many kilometres from here in fact. It was a bit of a wild time, fun while it lasted – and well paid – but I don't think I'd want to go back."

"Well paid?"

"Yes, but dangerous, there were several accidents and deaths in the three years were were there."

Benedict was interested to hear about the triplets' exploits in the tin mines and got the younger man to talk at length of those days. Bodd, however, had something else on his mind. For several weeks now he had accepted this man's hospitality and had not contributed a sten towards upkeep. The matter had never been raised, but then he did not normally see a great deal of him out of work. His host certainly seemed not to be concerned at all, but it weighed increasingly on Bodd's conscience and he knew it would be best to seize the current rare opportunity to bring it up. So upon completing a few tales of the mines, he decided to change the subject.

"There's something I want to talk to you about," he began, shifting to a seated position. He looked uncomfortable as he explained, "I am most grateful for all the help you have given me since I first arrived: putting me up, feeding me, finding me a tutor and the temporary post..."

He paused while a couple of servants brought fresh drinks.

"...But I was thinking now that I'm due to take up a permanent post after my break, that perhaps it would be more appropriate if I were to move to another sector, get some room there."

Incredulity swept across Benedict's face.

"You're not happy here?"

"No, it's not that!"

"You want to be nearer your friends?" the drone made a second guess in his struggle to understand.

"It's not really that; it's just that you've been so kind to me ever since I came here, but I don't want to outstay my welcome. I mean, I could be here in the Capital for years all being well."

"Nonsense, my young Bodd, we consider you one of the family now!"

There was kindness in his features as he sought to put Bodd's mind at rest. The latter was pleased that at least Benedict had not taken offence. On the contrary, he went forth into a long and hearty speech at how much he had taken to him, looking upon him more as a son than a guest, concluding, "And after your splendid exam results, I want to make sure I keep up my interest in your career. But here at home, it's just nice to have you around, I'm certain Anastasia enjoys the company, don't you, my poppet?"

"Of course, Uncle," she responded with a smile, not looking at Bodd.

How could Bodd refuse? He would just have to get used to this life of luxury. Graciously he thanked Benedict and considered his amazing good fortune at ending up where he was: sumptuous surroundings, no money to pay for lodgings, freedom to come and go when he liked, the benefits were enormous.

This matter settled, the drone then expressed an interest in Bodd's forthcoming visit home.

"I have only travelled out of the Capital on a few occasions and never stepped foot into Bynar, still less Thyatira. What is it like?"

A wry smile spread across Bodd's face.

"It wouldn't be your cup of juice, Benedict! Lots of mud in the autumn and spring, dust in the summer and snow in wintertime. It's a simple life in the villages, the huts there couldn't be in greater contrast with these fine buildings. It was where I was born and brought up though and it'll always have a warm place in my heart. I must say I'm grateful of this chance to go back, especially to be there for Rodd's wedding which I was beginning to think I'd miss."

"I'm sure we wish you a safe journey; will you leave tomorrow?"

"Yes, I hope to."

"Splendid. Just instruct the servants to pack you a good supply of food for the journey."

"May I come?" came a feminine voice opposite them.

Bodd could not believe his eyes or ears. Had Anastasia really just asked to go with him? Surely he must have misheard. He looked up open-mouthed at the young woman, waiting for her to speak again so he could work out what she had really said.

"If it's not too much trouble I would like to come with you."

Before his mind had had time to properly take this in he found his tongue pointing out that he would be walking. Surely, he thought, this refined lady would not want to trek all that way. He was right, but undeterred, Anastasia pointed out that she had a wagon they could travel in.

"We can take a couple of the servant, plus the driver, of course. I'll organise a large supply of food and water for the journey, but I suppose we'll need money for when we run out. You don't think we'll need a guard do you? In case there are robbers, I mean. I've never been north of Ephamon."

Bodd was totally bemused. Normally she hardly said a single word, now she was getting excited like a little girl about to go on a big adventure. What on Molt had got into her?

"The reports of robbers are greatly exaggerated," he assured her, "at least on the route I... er we shall be taking. If you don't mind me asking though, what has brought on this sudden decision to go to the wilds of Thyatira?"

"I don't know," she joyfully admitted, "I've just never been there, I just thought it might be somewhat enlightening."

"Splendid!" Benedict declared, "it'll do the two of you good to go on a holiday. A change is as good as a rest I always say. Mmm, this drink's good," he continued after taking a sip. "Just the accompaniment for a pleasant family confabulation don't you think?"

Back at the Castle, Frank found himself too busy with the preparations for the Mehtar's impending arrival to make the journey to the Upper Village and visit Giella's relatives to offer his condolences. Instead he sent a verbal message to her family.

Before the week was out, he did manage to snatch enough time to view the players, however, striding over to the courtyard in the midday heat. It was uncomfortably humid which did not help his humour.

The stage being set up within the courtyard meant some of the market stalls had had to be moved outside the wall to make way. Some traders moaned about this, but there was no doubt that the entertainment was popular. Frank stood watching the performance from the back of the sizeable crowd, feeling his shirt sticking to his back with perspiration. The audience was exclusively white; apart from himself, it included a large contingent of Aggepariian traders. No one noticed him standing there, taken up as they were with the action.

A crude comedy with bawdy humour was in progress and the crowd loved it. Soon after the Despot arrived, it ended though, and following a short break in the proceedings a completely different kind of play began. It was a drama, of supposedly everyday life in a village. The whites appeared to know who all the various characters were and followed every line eagerly. Indeed it appeared to exert an almost hypnotic spell on the masses there and a pin dropping would have been heard.

The lone black was most surprised and impressed by the standard of acting, but found the play itself most disturbing.

The central plot was of one of the main characters, a woman, being enticed away from her husband by another man. Individuals from within the audience began crying out advise such as "Go on luv, give it to 'im!" as a young man nearby shouted. What appalled Frank was that far from condemning the incipient adultery in the story many in the crowd appeared to be willing it to happen.

'Clearly not a morality play then,' he told himself. 'In fact not an edifying spectacle in any way!'

He hung out to the end of the current episode, after which the players were presented one at a time to a cheering audience. When the actor playing the lover came forth he received the loudest applause of all, which completely baffled Frank who would have thought jeering was far more appropriate. His mind was made up there and then and he hurriedly made his way back to the Castle in the sticky heat.

Entering the reception room he ordered a guardsman to have the steward and a squad leader report to him in the Throne Room immediately. When he got there he found Alan by himself studying the details of a map laid out on the table. Frank did not ask him to leave, but explained briefly why he was there.

After a short while, Natias entered with Jonathan. Both wondered why they had been summoned, but did not have to wait long to find out.

"I'm not at all happy about that band of travelling play-actors performing in the courtyard, I want them ordered out of here straight-away."

It was clear from his tone and manner that this was not a topic being thrown open for discussion. Rather than plead for a change of heart, therefore, Natias pointed out that in view of the group's popularity it would be prudent to have them evicted by night.

"It might also be wise My Lawd if they were paid a fee for their twoubles. They would expect a healthy pwofit from their audiences on a tour like this, so if we are going to avoid any publicity it may be best..."

"Whatever it takes, I'll leave it to you to decide."

The Despot then turned to Jonathan, "Tonight then you will go with Natias and see that they leave once they are paid. And kindly warn them that I do not wish to hear of them setting foot in this region again."

Unlike the more experienced steward, Jonathan did not appreciate his leader's current state of mind. In a casual tone he said, "It does seem a pity My Lord, the players are so popular."

Natias winced as he waited for the explosion. In the event Frank was more snappy than explosive.

"Why does everyone point out their popularity as if that's supposed to change my mind? I don't care how popular they are. God has seen fit to put me here to do what is *right*, not what is popular!"

"Yes, My Lord."

"Right then," Frank said, calming himself down with a deep sigh, "that's settled. That is all gentlemen, thank you."

He then left the room leaving the three men looking at each other with raised eyebrows. Once Jonathan had also gone back to his duties Alan remarked, "I think he's upset about Giella."

"Yes, I do not think he is in a state to be weasoned with."

"You're probably right," the other agreed then, getting up from his maps and heading for the door he added, "I think I'll try and catch him, give him the latest on my investigations."

Finding him still in the hall, they went up together to the roof to talk as it was such a hot day. There the cooling breeze caught them as they looked out on the countryside. Shadows thrown by the few small clouds were moving swiftly across the fields in the middle-ground. A wagon's dakks were kicking up dust as the beasts were driven in the direction of the Upper Village.

Frank was keen to learn what his sleuth had to report, although it soon became apparent that the investigations were at an early stage.

"Yeah from what I've found out it almost certainly happened the day after the religious meeting, the one you went to. That's what Zadok said if you remember. Her body was found early the following morning by the woman next door, so the priest must have rushed straight over to give us the news. From what the neighbour said about the state of the body it had happened quite a while before that – so we're talking about the previous evening. I hope you don't mind me talking like this, I know you were fond of her."

"No go on, I've asked you to investigate."

Alan brushed away a fly hovering round his face as he continued his report in an expressive tone:

"You know it seems incredible. There were so many people around at the time, but no clues as to the murderer have come up yet. I understand it was late afternoon when the meeting broke up, is that right?"

"Yes."

"And also that you left the tent with her, did she say anything about who she was hoping to see later the next day?"

Frank realised he was being interrogated, but could not complain, because Alan was only doing what he had been asked to do.

"No she didn't," he replied managing not to blush at the memory of that encounter, "but she did say she would be busy that evening as I recollect. I left her with one of the villagers – Reuben."

"Yeah I talked to him, didn't tell me much. Some people are being rather cagey when I question them.... not so much about the events around the time of the murder, but generally about the personalities involved. Got to break down the barriers to find the right clue."

"You're finding it frustrating at the moment?"

"Early days yet!" Alan replied enthusiastically.

A small crested bankel flew up to the battlements quite close to them. The bird kept a wary eye on the talkers while it preened itself for a few moments before swooping away once more.

Frank resumed, "You're certain it's definitely murder, she couldn't have fallen over and cracked her head could she?"

"Not unless she fell to the ground about thirty times," Alan replied dryly. "I'm sorry Frank, but there really is no doubt. I saw the body before she was buried, it wasn't a pretty sight. She'd been clubbed repeatedly and with great force."

"Well I suppose that rules out half the human race, it had to be a man."

"More likely to be a man, but not impossible that it was a woman. Could, for example, have been knocked out by a first, surprise blow.

"There was no forced entry, but that doesn't mean anything in a community such as the Upper Village where most people know each other. Nothing was stolen – and there was money lying about. Body was fully-clothed, no sexual motive. Whoever did it just wanted Giella dead, they made damn sure about it too."

"Suspects?"

"None that stand out. Uriah was away in the west with Japhses on the operations being mounted against the robber bands. I've talked to him, didn't get much."

Frank remembered the argument between Giella and her husband that he had overheard, but preferred not to mention it lest it bring further questions as to what he was doing there.

Instead he asked whether Alan thought Uriah was tying to hide anything.

"Not at all. Don't expect more than two words from him at the best of times. He's so undemonstrative you never know what he's thinking, but I learned from Japhses that he was very shocked and upset when he first heard the news.

"That's about all I've got to tell you. If I could establish a *motive* I'd be making progress, but I can't see who'd gain by her death. I'll just keep plugging away."

"Please do that, Alan, you've obviously been very busy at it, thanks for your efforts. I await your next report with interest."

Frank was pleased that his knowledge of his friend's parenthood had not altered their relationship. The drone obviously had great influence throughout the country, but was not a lover of power. Did he know about Frank's origin beyond the few stars in the Molten night sky? If he did, he never hinted at it. Count Zastein had been most insistent that the alien never breath a word of it to anyone and he had stuck to that apart from Offa and he was dead now.

On a lighter vein, Alan reported on the message he had received from Bodd.

"Luckily he found a traveller heading this way to give the message to. That's the trouble with this region, it's such a backwater, you're not likely to pass through it to anywhere. Anyway, it seems he's settling in well there. You haven't met Benedict have you, he never leaves Asattan. A bit eccentric, but always welcoming. It appears he's looking after Bodd well."

"So young Bodd has landed on his feet then."

"Landed on his feet," Alan repeated, "I haven't heard that expression before, but yeah I guess it fits nicely."

Frank peered down over the battlements. A group of boys were kicking a large ball far below. He could not pick out the details in spite of his squinting. Turning back he suggested they go back down.

"...I've got some paperwork Natias wants me to look at."

"Okay. I'd better get back to the Throne Room. Doesn't it seem quiet everywhere now the guild squad has gone back. Damian might have been pompous, but his men have done a good job."

"They have. I'm glad they've finished and packed up before the Mehtar arrives, won't be long now."

"Still over two weeks Frank, no need to panic yet."

One of those two weeks passed by quickly and a quiet afternoon found Tsodd at his favourite pastime, pottering on his piece of land on the outskirts of the Upper Village. Carefully closing the aviary door, he took the spade propped up outside and set about the small area of land next to the road he had not dug before. Thanks to the rainfall of the previous few days it went easily; it had been too hard before that.

After a while he paused and looked up the road. The weather was cooler and fresher since the rain came. The tree-tops swayed gracefully in the breeze, making a gentle rustling sound. The only other noise to be heard was an intermittent tapping of some birds in the aviary.

Scratching the top of his head he brushed away some mud from his closely cropped hair. As he resumed the work, his spade jarred against something hard. More probing followed which suggested it was a large boulder just beneath the surface. He wanted to leave it, but told himself that if he wanted to do a good job he had better get it out. Going back to the task therefore he tried to find the extent of the rock and brushed away some earth.

'That's funny, it's metal. And a man-made object from its shape.'

Intrigued, he spent some time digging round it, at times kneeling with a trowel. After a while he managed to wiggle it up and down slightly, the movement gradually increased with his digging and soil clearing. It appeared to be a metal brick covered with the remains of some brittle paper. By this stage, it had become a challenge and he did not care what it was as long as he got it out.

"It's coming!" he grunted as at last he was able to get enough leverage to pull it from the ground. It was indeed a small, metal brick, some twenty-five centimetres long, ten high and ten wide. Holding it in his left hand he pulled away the remaining flakes of paper. From its weight and colour there was only one sort of metal it could be.

Three-quarters of a kilometre away in the Upper Village Amos was playing cards in his house with Reuben. This was a weekly event neither of them liked to miss. The stakes were tiny, but it added just a bit of extra spice to the game.

"Ah ha, got you!" shouted Reuben as he triumphantly threw down the last card.

"So you have," Amos responded amiably, "well done, that's three-one to you. Like a drink?"

"I'll say I do."

During the pause in the play Reuben reported on something he had heard the day before.

"These two croppers were in the fields when they saw this long, oval-shaped thing move across the sky. Fast it was, leave a sling-shot standing they said. Then all of a sudden it changed direction and was gone. They reckon they ain't never seen anything like it."

Amos made suitable noises in response, he was aware of the other's love of supernatural tales, but was not very impressed himself. He knew it would not be long before

Reuben came forward with a fanciful theory, he was not disappointed.

"'Tis the Crop Demon I tell yer, a bad omen. We had it all before, some years ago: firey crosses in the sky, on more than one occasion! And what happened? The crop was a disaster. You mark my words, it'll be a failure again like it was then."

Shaking his head Amos scoffed, "Crop Demon, load of rubbish!"

There was a knock on the door, but the two men ignored it, caught up in the enjoyment of their friendly argument.

"You do come up with some funny ones Reuben. The hulf-fan has never looked healthier!"

"Ah, but..."

Kim came bursting in from the other room and headed for the door. Glaring at her husband she exclaimed, "If you're not going to answer it then I suppose I'll have to. I am trying to look after the children you know!"

"Sorry my dear," said Amos meekly.

"You're not a bit sorry," Kim snapped as she took up the latch. "Oh hello Tsodd, haven't seen you for a long time."

"Hello there. I wonder if I could have a word with Amos."

Both card players came to the door and were shown the find.

"Gold!" Reuben exclaimed looking at the four bricks in the barrow, "you been raiding Natias' store-house?"

Amos said, "Don't think even he has this much. Is it genuine?"

"As far as I can tell. I'm just not sure what to do with it though. Seeing as it was Hanson's land it's probably his."

A sarcastic laugh came from Reuben upon hearing this, "Ha, you don't want to give it to him."

"But there might be a reward."

"Naa! Not from Hanson, you of all people should know that. If I were you I'd keep it."

Amos could not resist, "Yes, we know *you* would," he said teasing his friend. "I think you should go and see Natias and get a ruling from him. I wouldn't go to Saul, he's too much under Hanson's influence. Don't tell anyone else, but take it to the Castle first thing in the morning, I'll come with you if you need support."

Tsodd decided to take this sound advice as far as taking to the steward in the morning, but he could not resist taking it round to his sister-in-law to be.

Leah lived with her parents who had gone to bed by the time Tsodd came round with his wheelbarrow. He pushed it into the hut. It was not an unpleasant evening, so she ushered him outside, not wanting to disturb the sleepers. After going through the story of the discovery and its implications Tsodd was asked what his plans for the future were if he was allowed to keep the hoard.

"I don't know. I don't like to think about it, 'cos it might not work out that way. Amos was right when he said take it to the Castle. Natias might not have let me have compensation for my land deal with Hanson, but I'm sure he's honest and will do right by me."

The beating of hoofs and the squeaks and groans of a wagon approaching cut into the still air. As it drew near, the conversation stopped and they stared at the superior vehicle coming down the street. It was driven by a short, dwarf-like white whom they had not seen before.

'Must be blacks in a wagon like this,' Tsodd thought to himself as the driver brought it up a few metres away and leaned back to have a conversation with the occupants, 'but what would any black be coming here in the evening? Not even

Despot Thorn has a wagon as good as this, and when he comes to the Village it's on a dakk.'

He did not immediately recognise his brother's head poked through the canvas near the driver. Only when Bodd jumped down while a servant fitted steps for Anastasia to use did he realise who it was. Tsodd and Leah greeted the homecoming with great enthusiasm.

"We're all very grand now are we?" ribbed the brother, "covered wagon and all that!" He moderated his tone when he noticed Bodd's fellow passenger descending, helped by one of the servants. "Phew... who is this?"

She was wearing an expensive fashion dress of a type never seen in those parts. Bodd had warned her of the impracticalities of wearing it on the journey, advice she had chosen to ignore. It looked marked and shabby now compared with when it was on, but it still impressed the villagers.

"This is Anastasia, I'm staying in her home in Asattan."

If before the journey he had hoped her coming would mean better communication between them he was disappointed. In fact it had been a miserable journey, neither she nor her two female servants had shown any inclination for conversation. Now he was home and tired and just wanted to forget the last few days.

Anastasia too was too tired and Leah, taking pity on her, asked if she wanted a hot drink before she went to bed.

"No, thank you very much," replied Anastasia making her tired eyes smile in appreciation of the kindness being shown.

Leah asked Bodd what arrangements had been made for sleeping and, upon receiving the answer there was none, proceeded to organise.

"You can stay with your brother and we'll be able to put Anastasia and her friends up. Are you going to introduce us?"

The thought of a white having servants had never occurred to Leah, but they were duly introduced. The driver announced his intention of sleeping in the wagon and took the vehicle off to park it a short way off. Soon afterwards Bodd, pack on his shoulders, left with his brother.

"What's that you got in the wheelbarrow?"

"I thought you'd never ask..."

Back where they had just left, Anastasia found herself alone with Leah, wanting to talk in spite of being exhausted by the journey. She found male company difficult to handle, even Bodd who was always polite to her. It did not do to talk casually to servants, so she was pleased to have Leah to confide in. So pleased in fact that she completely put to the back of her mind the rough straw bed she was lying on instead of the plush, comfortable mattress she was used to. The pair spoke softly so that their voices did not carry.

"I understand you are shortly to be married to Bodd's other brother?"

"Rodd, that's right. I'm counting the days, only six to go now."

"Do you mind me asking? How did you first meet?"

Leah twisted round to look in the direction of Anastasia, although it was pitch black by now and she could see nothing.

"I don't mind you asking at all. We lived near each other, here in the village. All the children in our area played together, we just grew up knowing each other. I've known the triplets all my life."

"So you like the other two – Bodd, and is it *Sodd*?"

"Tsodd. Sure I like them, but it was always Rodd I was attracted to. He's the athletic one, he could always outrun the rest of us. I don't think he took any interest in me until a couple of years ago."

"What was Bodd like? I mean he always seems more intellectual than athletic."

Somewhat belatedly, Leah realised the other young woman was not so much interested in her reminiscences as in learning more about the man she had travelled with.

"They're each very different. Tsodd was always picking up slugs and things, Rodd was running and climbing trees, but Bodd liked discussions. He used to have long debates with Zadok the priest even when he was a boy. Then he started an apprenticeship under our physician when he was still quite young...Laffaxe taught him how to read and write. Even that grumpy man was amazed at how quickly Bodd caught on. He gave the post up though when the three of them decided to go to the mines for the first time.

"You like him, don't you."

The last sentence caught Anastasia off guard and she found herself admitting she did.

"But I find it so hard to talk to him, or anyone in fact,"

"Any *man*," Leah corrected, on the right wavelength at last. It was late, but with this visitor bearing her soul she wanted to help if possible. She was pleased now the servants had ended up in the barn on the other side of the road, her guest would probably not have shared her troubles had they been present. Her parents were the other side of a wicker partition, but she knew their whispers were unlikely to wake them.

"Am I that easy to read?" Anastasia asked, "I've never admitted it before, but I feel totally lost in men's company. I was orphaned when still very little and brought up by Benedict..."

"Must be a drone, a name like that."

"Yes, he's always been very kind, but I've never had the emotional support I've needed. I feel there's a big, black hole in my life.

"I shouldn't talk like this, I'm sure you're dying to get to sleep and wondering why this idiot doesn't shut up."

"Anastasia, don't say that. If you want to talk, I want to listen. I don't know if I can offer any sensible advice at the end of it, but I'd like to be your friend and hear what you've got to say. I'll help if I can; I'm in no hurry to get to sleep."

Leah's kind words and soothing tone-of-voice brought tears into her visitor's eyes. Sleepiness had completely vanished for the time being and the two lay talking half the night about men, relationships and the meaning of life.

The country girl found that the young, sophisticated lady she had first spied getting down from the covered wagon had an insecure, vulnerable girl inside her.

When they eventually stopped talking, Leah thought about what had been said and hoped the advice she had given was sound.

"Try and open up to Bodd," she had said. "If you have acted the way you said you have you cannot expect him to make the next move without a lot of encouragement from yourself. The initiative lies with you, Anastasia."

CHAPTER TWENTY FOUR

It was time for the weekly work meeting in the Castle. As Frank shuffled into the Throne Room with his lieutenants, he had no idea that this was going to be a long, and in retrospect, significant gathering. Japhses was back from anti-robber operations in the west of the region and sat the opposite end of the table to the Despot planted regally on the throne. To Frank's right and with his back to the door was Natias. Alan then entered and went round the table to sit facing the entrance, waiting for Karl to arrive. For a while the only thing breaking the silence was the steward shuffling his papers on the desk.

"My Lawd, I would wather not wait too long if you do not mind, I believe we have a lot to get thwough this morning."

"All right, close the door then please and we'll start, Karl can always catch up. Did you want to set the ball rolling then, Natias?"

A lengthy financial report then followed, the gist of which was that the higher than expected outgoings had left the treasury dangerously low.

"The hulffan wevanue should be good this year, My Lawd, but that is still some twelve weeks off. The biannual genewal tax on villagers will be due in four weeks, but we only have enough to pay the Guard for this week and possibly next with a squeeze. It is not so much that we do not have the money, but that a lot is owed to us and it will be some time before we can collect."

"I see. Can we go through some of the reasons for the shortfall again. I understand about the guild squad, it did cost us more than we originally budgeted, but we did have that extra work done. I still feel happy about it, 'cos they did a good job and we got value for money. But what's this about gold bars? You rather lost me there; something about the miner Tsodd."

"Yes, My Lawd. This was something we could not have anticipated. . Yesterday mawning the young man came here with a colleague and said he had found four gold bars on his land and could he keep them. I had to consult the legal books; they were most helpful in this instance. If the pwevious owner of the land could pwoove they were his, then they go to him. As Hanson was in the Castle depositing some money, I questioned him."

"I didn't realise we held other peoples' money."

"Oh yes My Lawd, but only a few. Large sums for safe-keeping."

"Do we pay interest? If we do then surely we can use it in the meantime, like the financial houses back from where I come from."

"The law for such a find as this is a different matter My Lawd, as I will explain in a moment.

"I spoke to Hanson, but in spite of his cageyness it was clear he did not know what I was talking about."

Japhses opened his mouth for the first time, "He was the only person in the Village who didn't know. Tsodd's news had travelled like the wind."

"From what I've heard," said Frank, "this Hanson character is not the most popular of men. Not sure if I've met him.
But surely someone must have some idea about this hoard, it
wouldn't be anything to do with my predecessor, would it?"

"I am sure not, My Lawd. There are no markings on the
gold, it seems it had been buried there a vewy long time. That
having been said, it was wrapped in a strange kind of "paper"
which had not completely disintegrated. Presumably the soil
conditions were such as to pweserve it in some way."

"It's all a bit of a mystery then. Sorry, Natias, I diverted you,
please continue."

"My Lawd. So Tsodd gets the benefit of his discovewy. By
law, a gold find on a quantity above half a gwend must go to
the main Tweasury in Asattan. Therefore, we have to pay him
the monetary worth – less a small handling commission – and
it will have to be twansported to the Capital where they will pay
us the going wate, give us our money back in effect. It is all a bit
of a bind weally, and it means a large sum of money is not available to us until we have made the twansfer. I have asked Japhses
to make awwangements for this as soon as possible."

"How much are they worth?" asked the Captain, flicking
back his long white hair over his shoulder with the back of his
hand.

"Two gwend, just a fraction under. Tsodd is now an ext-
wemely wealthy man. I asked him what he was going to do with
it, but he seemed a bit dazed at the time and could not tell me.
He has deposited the entire sum here."

"And no one knows where the gold originated from," Frank
repeated the observation.

"Nobody knows, My Lawd."

"Is there any more?"

Japhses answered, "Half the village were digging round
Tsodd's place yesterday, My Lord, I haven't heard of any finds.

The four bars found are under guard in one of the turrets right now. Would you like to see them before they leave later today?"

"Hmm, might be rather interesting. Yes we can go along after the meeting. Does that conclude the financial report then, Natias?"

Before he could answer, the door opened with a sudden loud clatter, making the steward jump. It was Karl. The black stood, half in the room, holding onto the door and looking up to Frank.

"Apologies Sir," came his whining voice, "but would you mind terribly if I were excused from the meeting this morning? Only I've spilled a great deal of treacle in the reception room and feel it's only fair I help the servants clear it up."

The others started smiling, but Frank gave his blessing to Karl behind a rather blank expression as he thought, 'I wonder what... no Francis, don't ask...'

"Thank you very much, Sir. I'm sure someone can fill me in with any important matters later."

With that he was gone, leaving the room's occupants having a good laugh. Even Natias found himself joining in, aware that it was not right for him and Japhses to laugh about a black.

Drinks were called for and when they had settled down again, Frank asked to what point the meeting had got to.

"I had just completed my financial weport, My Lawd."

"Fine. Well, Japhses, let's hear about your exploits at catching these robber bands."

"Yes, My Lord, about a third of the Guard was used in the operations in the west..."

"How did you get on? Good news or bad?"

"A mixture, My Lord," the big man continued, happy to be centre of attention. His pure-white hair was longer and bushier than ever, cascading over his shoulders and down his back. The act of flicking it back with his hand was becoming a habit. "On the positive side, we uncovered one major camp, plus a few other, smaller hideouts in this extensively forested region. Our biggest success was when we got to the camp. Most of the robbers present at the time escaped, but we caught three who put up a struggle. All of them died in the action while we only suffered minor injuries. I might add, Rodd excelled himself yet again."

"That's good."

"A minor success to be fair, My Lord. To put it into perspective we believe there may be upwards of thirty robbers operating from that area in total. The three who were killed were all native Thyatirans, in fact two were amongst those released by My Lord when he first took office."

"Hmph! Point taken, go on."

Frank had to laugh at himself; he couldn't blame Japhses for that little dig.

"A supply of weapons was seized," the report continued, "plus some stolen articles which are mainly of Ma'hol origin. The trouble is that these renegades scamper across the border into Rabeth when we go after them, only to return when we pull back."

Alan then came into the discussion by pointing out that the visit of the Mehtar provided the ideal opportunity to bring this problem up with the Ma'hol.

"They're obviously suffering at the hands of the robbers as well. We should be able to mount a joint operation; *that* would help trust between us to grow."

Japhses responded, "If such a venture was mounted we would have to ensure the border with Aggeparii was cut off first. Otherwise they would just slip over there. I cannot see Despot Kagel being happy joining a joint operation with the Ma'hol."

"You're right," agreed Alan, "but we should be able to seal the border without too much of a problem I'd've thought."

"Gentlemen, we can go into detail nearer the time if the Mehtar is agreeable to the idea, but I think we should get on now. Japhses, was there anything further you wished to raise?"

"Yes, indeed there is, My Lord, a matter of the greatest importance."

The room fell quiet. When all eyes and ears were firmly upon him the Captain continued.

"My intelligence sources inform me that there has been a General Election in Laodicia. It was a particularly bloody affair with riots and political assassinations; reports vary as to the numbers killed. More importantly it has brought a new gang into power with some silly name, the "Ardent Nationalists" I believe they call themselves. There has been much rhetoric as is usual, but this new lot seem to be particularly vociferous, pouring abuse on Hoame in order to whip up support..."

"Just a moment," interrupted Frank, "how come all this has been happening on our doorstep and we've only just heard about it?"

Japhses explained, "There is virtually no traffic between us and the barbarians. My reports have come from Sarnician traders coming down via Rabeth. It is not easy for news to get across the mountains."

"I think that is part of the reason for their stance," said Alan, "we are a convenient bogey man for them."

Flicking his hair back once more, Japhses agreed and went on, "There are several things which make the reports more worrying than on previous occasions: the unparalleled violence of the election campaign, the group which has come to power and the economic difficulties Laodicia is suffering. They could use long-standing border disputes with us to distract the attention of their people from their own problems."

"Damn border disputes again!" Frank observed.

In the conversation that followed he learned that Ladosa's main grievance concerned an area of strategic high ground held by the Bynar despotate a couple of hundred kilometres south of Thyatira. The only piece of disputed land between *Thyatira* and Ladosa was a small, rather uninteresting strip of mountainous territory. Japhses said that while it was uninhabited it was patrolled by both sides, his guardsmen were under the strictest orders to avoid any confrontation, indeed any action which might be construed as provocative.

Both Natias and Alan advised keeping things in perspective. The Laodicians were always shouting their mouths off and it would probably all blow over after a while. Frank still felt uneasy, however.

"That's what I was advised about the Ma'hol! I'm not sure I like the idea of them vituperating against us. They sound such a volatile people from what you've all been saying, it might not be easy to predict their next move. Can't we send some spies over there and find out what precisely *is* going on?"

"Difficult, Frank; has to be someone we can really trust and any of the whites would be a dead giveaway.

"Of course we could always send Karl," Alan added with a twinkle in his eye. The idea was not meant to be taken seriously and was met with grinning faces. It occurred to Frank that perhaps he should consider it, but dismissed the thought quickly. He also discounted the idea of dying a white's hair for a disguise, he knew that such a taboo suggestion would be considered shocking.

Alan spoke again, "If you really want someone to go, I shall. I'll bring you the up-to-date news."

Japhses looked concerned.

"A dangerous mission," he warned, "I don't think you should go unless their words start to develop into actions."

"But by then..."

"Japhses is wight. The whole matter will pwobably blow over, My Lawd. I must advise we sit tight."

It was time for the Despot to make the decision.

"I don't want to be caught on the hop like we were with the Ma'hol. I think we'll have to give this further consideration. We've got the Mehtar's visit imminent, I'd like to discuss his take on this.

They're not allied with Laodicia are they?"

"No!" the other three said in unison.

"Right, I can ask him what he makes of it. In the meantime Japhses can you try developing your existing contacts, these traders? At least I want you to pass on any intelligence you receive to me straight away."

So it was decided to await any developments. In the meantime a report was to be sent to the Inner Council. Not that they would not already be aware, but all intelligence would be welcome. A further report was to go to Despot Hista of Bynar. Also decided was for the Captain to oversee an increase in forces near that border, an operational priority being secrecy and camouflage in the build up. The big man stressed the unlikelihood of the Ladosans attacking over such terrain, further south into Bynar being far more likely, but was still in favour of the increased border presence.

His commander concluded by saying, "If the worst comes to the worst we might have to reconsider some sort of spying mission into their country, but lets try other means first."

While the long meeting went on, Illianeth and Soosha were washing dishes in the kitchen. The former was enjoying the attentions of her new boyfriend Halatan, one of the Taltons. A tall, handsome lad, who only in the last year had overcome his natural shyness.

"So can anyone go to the wedding celebrations?" he was asking.

"Course they can. If you're ever so lucky you might be able to come along with Soosha and me," Illianeth replied, passing a cheeky look at her girlfriend.

"Next Sabbath you said. Would you like to come with me then?"

He looked hopefully at her. They had been seeing each other increasingly regularly over the past month, but he would not feel secure until he was more certain she wanted him. In reality she was delighted at her catch, but she was not going to let him know that.

"Hmm, I don't know," she teased, "what do you think, Soosha, should we go with him?"

Just then Matthew stalked across the floor to where the trio stood talking.

"What's this?" he demanded, "you looking for a job, my boy?"

Illianeth groaned at the intrusion as Halatan began stuttering an excuse. Matthew was not interested in excuses however.

"This is *my* kitchen and I'm not putting up with disruptive influences putting my staff off their work! Unless you want to help, you'll leave this instant."

The youth made a tactical withdrawal into the hall from where he could still see the girls. Once Matthew had gone back up the far end of the kitchen, Halatan mouthed, "See you later" to Illianeth.

She nodded, whispering, "In the hall after supper," then watched as he left the building.

"Typical Matthew," she grumbled to her friend as they got back to work.

Back at the weekly meeting, Japhses was still holding the floor.

"So our arrangements for the Mehtar's visit are just about complete."

Which brings me to another matter I would like to raise My Lord. There are still not enough Taltons in the Guard. This must be bad for the integration process. There would be more, but we keep on having to turn their volunteers away, because we are currently right up to strength. I could easily have recruited two hundred and fifty of them. I was wondering as we are facing a time of tension whether we should increase our strength. We could recruit another (say) two hundred men and include both Taltons and volunteers from the other villages."

Natias looked agitated, "The cost would be pwohibitive. The extwa uniforms and further wages, at a time when we are unable to pay the men we alweady have."

"Oh yes," said Frank, "what was decided about that?"

He looked over to Alan for the answer, who replied that as far as he could remember no conclusion had been reached, "... But I've got funds newly arrived from the Capital. I'm happy to tide us over until new taxes have been raised; it's only a temporary shortfall.

"As for your recruitment plan, Japhses, I suspect the Laodician situation isn't as bad as some reports suggest. If their previous election campaigns are anything to go by, it will all blow over. Also, if it is as bad as all that, they could have spies here who would interpret a recruitment drive as a provocative act. It's just a thought."

Japhses protested, "We can't just do nothing on a hope it will all go away. My Lord, I feel strongly about this!"

It occurred to Frank the number of occasions he had overruled the Captain of the Guard, such as the debacle releasing of the prisoners alluded to earlier. He was formulating a compromise in his mind when Alan put just such a thing forward.

"I was about to go on to say I recommend we proceed with some extra recruitment, but on a more limited scale, a hundred men should suffice. Their training should be as inconspicuous as possible. We don't want to alarm our own people as much as anything. I'm more than happy to finance their equipment, plus their wages for a limited period. After all, we will be getting all the money for the gold back in due course. If nothing comes of the Laodician threat the training will not have gone to waste. I mean our despotate is expanding in size, note the whites immigrating from the south necessitating extra land being released for the Lower Village a couple of weeks back."

"And the extra uniforms can be stored for future use," Japhses added enthusiastically.

Thus thanks to Alan, a solution was found which left everybody happy. More details were thrashed out before the marathon meeting was drawn to a close. Natias and Japhses filed out of the room, but Alan indicated that he wanted to have a quiet word with Frank.

"A progress report?" the latter asked as the door was closed leaving the two men alone.

"That's it," said the other settling back into his chair.

"Well first I'd like to thank you again for your help in financing the extra recruits. You've come up trumps again."

"Come up trumps? You really do have the funniest expressions.... anyway, to get on with what I've discovered: I *thought* that Reuben's son Brogg was acting funny when I first spoke to him about the murder. I know he is simple, but I can usually communicate with him. I now know why he was acting so coy, he was protecting his father. It turns out Reuben was having an affair with Giella."

"What?" Frank was incredulous, "do you mean committing adultery?"

"Yeah right," Alan continued casually, "I find it amazing, can't see what she saw in him."

"I don't believe you."

Frank's tone was sharp, his face firm-set. Alan realised his friend did not want to believe the news.

"Look I know..."

"I'm sorry, I just don't believe you; you shouldn't listen to idle gossip, that's not the way to investigate."

Alan gave a compassionate look as he said quietly, "Frank, I know you were very fond of her, but I am certain this is true. Reuben admitted it himself and was clearly terrified lest I pass it on to his wife – which I have no intention of doing of course."

"What's the penalty for adultery."

"There is none. None at least in law. There would be disgrace if the facts became public, but what I'm concerned about is how it brings us closer to the murderer."

"Does it?"

"Not in any way *I* can see. I know Reuben well and have no reason to believe he did it. Their relationship had not been severed when the murder took place. He appeared baffled as well as upset."

"A member of his family? Say his wife knew about it all along."

Alan could not suppress a laugh. "She's got a vicious tongue on her, but physically she's frail and tiny. No I can't see it, I don't think she does know and I suspect Brogg only found out since my investigations began. I found him listening to my first interview with his father and I think that's when he added two and two together, remembering Reuben's behaviour over the previous months with Giella.

"So I'm afraid this piece of information, juicy as some people might find it, does not progress us much farther. I've yet to have a real breakthrough, but I'll carry on if you want me to."

It was noticeable that he was starting to get despondent at his lack of progress.

"Of course I do. If people are beginning to talk to you, it's a good sign. You keep going, you're doing a grand job.

"Right now though I'd better see Japhses; he wants to show me that gold."

They got up to leave. The few words of encouragement had lifted Alan's spirit a degree.

"We've got a good Captain in Japhses," he remarked, "good decision maker. Yeah let's see this gold, see what all the fuss is about."

Four days later, Rodd and Leah's wedding took place. The whole of the Upper Village attended the day-long celebrations, with a sizeable contingent coming from the Castle. As hot afternoon turned to a more pleasant warm evening, large numbers still occupied one of the fields on the edge of the village. In fact, it was the same one that had seen all the tents erected for the big religious meeting early in the year. This time a few tents were back up, but most of the people were outside engaging in conversation, drinking, generally milling about and enjoying themselves. Side shows were there with entertainment acts such as singing and dancing displays. Stalls provided hot food and groups of people could be seen round the perimeter eating under the grey sky. Large torches had been set up around the field for when it got dark, the event was to go right through the night.

It struck Frank how well the seemingly uncoordinated event worked so well. Whether it was food one wanted, or drink, entertainment, or just a chat, each was catered for.

"There's something for everyone," he remarked as he strolled round with Alan, "hmm, not quite as crowded as when I was here last."

"Really. Ah, if it isn't the man himself – hi there, Rodd!"

The groom emerged from a large gaggle of well-wishers to greet them.

"Great to see you, Alan. Welcome, My lord, I'm sorry I missed you earlier. We had the place of honour reserved on the platform for the ceremony, but could not find you."

Frank called out with a chuckle, "Nonsense, Rodd! This is your day. Besides we haven't been here long, we had to be at the rehearsal for the Mehtar's visit the day after tomorrow, I don't want anything going wrong on the day.

"Besides don't you think if I'd have been here you'd have spotted me?" he asked indicating towards the sea of whites.

"Oh yes, of course," the groom's face went red.

'What's the world coming to?' thought Frank, 'here I am reminding them about their own prejudices!'

By now there was a circle devoid of people around the three men, the ordinary villagers were nervous of the Despot's presence and preferred to give him a wide berth.

He continued, "Look, Rodd, I don't want to keep you, but I've known you longer than most people here and I'd like to give you something on this happy occasion. Natias tells me the traditional gift from the Despot to a black couple getting married is exemption from tax for a year. I'm happy to extend that to you and Leah, However, it's not very imaginative I felt. So on top of that I hoped you might like this."

Out of his pocket he pulled a chunky metal object about twelve centimetres high. Rodd suppressed a frown as he took it.

"Thank you, My Lord. Er, what is it exactly please?"

"Can't you make it out? It's for a dakk," Frank announced triumphantly. "I saw it on a market stall the other week and just couldn't resist it."

He took the crudely-shaped piece back in order to demonstrate its functions. Rodd and Alan looked on, equally dumbfounded at the enthusiasm being shown for the tasteless object.

"See this lever at the back, that flicks up like this?... there we are. This is for getting stones out of dakks' hooves. Then there's this one..." fumbling fingers brought forth another devise from the back of the figure, "...good, a comb for the dakk's tail. Clever little piece isn't it?"

Rodd, who did not own a dakk, replied as sincerely as possible, "It's most thoughtful of you, My Lord."

"Excellent! Well we'd better not keep you, I'm sure you're in great demand."

He went to depart, but turned back when Alan asked, "Where's the lucky lady?"

"My wife? It sounds funny me saying that. I don't know where she is right now, somewhere among all this lot."

Frank said, "You've certainly got a great number of events organised."

"It was my friends who organised it all, My Lord. I don't know half of what's going on. I understand the travelling players were due to be here though, they left rather suddenly while in the middle of their performances at the Castle."

"Oh really?"

"Yes, My Lord. It was all a bit mysterious. Rumour has it that it was out of respect for Giella's family, because they departed so soon after her death. It was certainly off. The wedding was not postponed because the stars said it was the most auspicious time; don't tell Zadok I said that please!"

Alan glanced up. "Speak of the devil," he said as he spotted the old man approaching them, leaning on his walking stick.

Rodd said goodbye and made his escape while Frank considered that Alan's turn of phrase was perhaps not most suitable for the arrival of the priest.

"Glad you could make it, My Lord. Nice wholesome celebrations."

They talked for a while before Zadok brought up the subject of the dictionary he had given his leader.

"I trust you are enjoying its use."

"Yes, thank you very much," Frank replied.

In truth though he had only found time to look at it on a couple of occasions. It was so unlike him, in days gone by he would have given his right arm to spend an evening with an old volume like that. How his priorities had changed.

'I must have a good look at it when I get home,' he resolved.

"Tell me My Lord, what are the wedding celebrations like in your native land?"

"Sorry, what did you say?" Frank said, buying time in which to think of an answer. Once the question was repeated he replied, "Well they're very similar in fact. Actually would you mind dreadfully if Alan and I excuse ourselves? We have some important matters to discuss back at the Castle; just wanted to make our presence felt."

This was news to Alan, who tried not to look too puzzled as he was pulled away from the nodding priest.

"What important matters?" he enquired once out of earshot.

Frank, glad to have got himself out of a potentially sticky situation, suddenly turned nonchalant, "Oh nothing really, I was just thinking I don't want to be seen spending a disproportionate time in the Upper Village. I think I'll do a tour of the other two – talk to the leaders, see how the Guard recruitment is going, that sort of thing."

They wandered slowly to the exit as he talked, passing such entertainments as an epic story teller and a juggling act, both of which attracted sizeable audiences.

"Is that all you wanted to discuss?" Alan asked.

"How do you mean?"

"I was looking forward to today. I missed the beginning because of the rehearsal, now you want to drag me away as soon as we've got here!"

In his rush to get himself out of a tight spot Frank had not thought about his companion, who now stood looking thoroughly fed up. He laughed, "Hey, you needn't leave now, of course not. I was forgetting you'd like to stay. I just feel out of place at a do like this. I am painfully aware each time a villager goes out of his or her way to avoid me. You stay as long as you like, if there's anything we need to talk about it can wait 'till tomorrow."

In a few brief moments, Alan's emotions moved from indignation through relief to concern for his friend.

"It will be getting dark by the time you get to the Castle, make sure you take the whole squad back with you. I'll probably be here all night and return in the morning."

"All right I'll do that. Bye then, Alan... oh just before I go: you *do* think Rodd enjoyed his present don't you?"

Mustering all his tact the drone replied that he was sure the present had been *most* appreciated. Smiling to himself after they had said their goodbyes once more, he watched as Frank's figure gradually slipped away. The squad of guardsmen that had come with the two of them were sitting just inside the entrance. They had just finished a spicy meal obtained from one of the stalls. Once Alan saw that they were all getting up to escort their Despot back, he turned to enjoy the celebrations, this time to the full.

Bodd was surrounded by a group of friends who were drinking and telling each other tales of the old days. Loud guffaws rose at irregular intervals. He suddenly remembered he really should be more discrete and not risk being detected by Anastasia.

They had been in the Village almost a week now and ever since the first morning, she had been acting very strangely. She would not leave him alone! Fussing over his clothes (they were not meant to be smart, just practical for the help he was giving Tsodd on his land), going on about certain foods being good for him to eat, suggesting he listen to her poetry when he wanted to go for a drink with the lads (he had put his foot down firmly on that one) and generally, well... not letting him *be*. Talk about going from one extreme to the other! It was clear the young woman was now suffering from some sort of obsessional mental disorder which makes people fuss over things. Bodd's theory went something like this: the unfortunate Anastasia had been cooped up so long in the one house in the Capital that the rigours of their journey had turned her mind. Whether this madness was permanent or temporary, he did not know.

After a while the conversation got round to Bodd's travelling companion, his friends were most impressed.

"That's a beauty you've caught there!" exclaimed one.

"You lucky, old frass," declared another.

"Are they all like that in the Capital?" enquired a third.

Bodd put his hands up to halt the barrage.

"Listen, you lot, she just happens to live at the place where I'm staying in Asattan. I don't even know why she has come along here. There's *nothing* between us."

Sceptical voices were raised.

"Oh yeah?"

A couple of men called out that if he was not interested then they certainly would not mind trying their luck.

"Go ahead," Bodd responded, "see if I care. In fact I wish you the best of luck. Now Paul, you were going to tell me about you and Rachael..."

The sun had set and it was getting dark quickly now, so the large torches were lit, casting exotic shadows around the field and beyond. Jabbering conversation was everywhere, while each act seemed to have its own musical accompaniment. The last trace of light from beyond the horizon had gone and celebrations turned more jovial than ever as more alcohol was consumed. It was all good humoured though and the few people really drunk turned to laughter rather than anger.

Throughout the evening Anastasia had received a lot of attention from members of her own sex as well. The bride had left her in the hands of her sister Rebecca and a wide circle of the latter's friends had spent some time with the visitor.

"What is "in" in the Capital this year? Your dress is exquisite! You say you altered the top part yourself? I think Leah's greatly enjoyed your company this last week, helped take her mind off things. I've heard so much about you, I've been dying to meet. You really are as gorgeous as everyone says – I'm green with envy, dear! So you're the one we've all been hearing about..."

For someone who thought she enjoyed being by herself she was having the time of her life. Yes, of course they were particularly interested in her that evening, meeting other people would not always be like this, but it was a sense of *belonging*. This sense went beyond the complimentary words, the flattery and curiosity. She would not have minded being someone else in the crowd, just not to be out of it again with no one to talk to.

What a snob she had been. These were the country girls she would normally have despised and not wish to be seen dead with. What stupid, arbitrary distinctions we make between people. Leah had been so kind the last six days. As if she had not had enough to do with all the wedding preparations! Then her sister Rebecca had taken time away from her uncle's business to show her round and introduce her to various people.

If only Bodd had joined in. He had hardly been subtle in avoiding her these last few days, declining every invitation she had made to do things together. Leah told her to keep trying. She had not caught sight of him tonight, although of course he was here at his brother's wedding celebrations. The journey back started tomorrow, it was going to be a nightmare together she could see.

Another popular figure present was Tsodd. In fact he was concerned that he had become *too* popular since his find. Suddenly everyone wanted to know him, wanted to slap him on

the back and share a drink. Even Reuben was being pleasant
to him and while there was a first time for everything, he was
highly dubious that a genuine friendship was being offered by
the cropper.

Amos, he knew, was a real friend who would stick by him
whether a rich man or pauper. Together these two took their
food and drink and retreated to a dark, remote corner of the
field where they would not be disturbed. The ground was dry,
but not too hard. Here in relative tranquillity they began con-
suming their meal without a word being spoken. From the distance came the jumbled sounds of music, talking and singing,
with the occasional shriek or shout thrown in, never loud enough
to disturb the meal though.

"What *is* that you're eating?" Amos asked after a while.

Tsodd chortled, "Dunno, can't see in this gloom. Tastes
quite good though. I'm just glad to be in the quiet, never was
one for the crowds."

"They were certainly giving you enough attention"

"I wish they'd just leave me alone!" the other complained,
taking a piece of gristle out of his mouth. "If only they would
stop asking me what I'm going to do with all the money. "Go
to the Capital," they say, "that's where all the wealthy men go."
What on Molt do I want to go there for? Just give me a peaceful
life, that's all I ask."

"At the risk of making myself unpopular, may I ask what you
are going to do with your new found wealth?"

Tsodd's grimace was unseen in the dark. "Seeing as it's
you I won't take offence. To be honest, I haven't given it much
thought. It is all safely stored away in the Castle and I'm going
to leave it there untouched for the time being. I can't think
while everybody's going on at me."

After a pause, Tsodd spoke again on a fresh topic.

"Is Kim here this evening?"

"Pardon?"

"I asked if your wife was here."

"Oh yes, somewhere. She wanted to see the wedding."

"How is she now?"

"What, after Giella? I think she's over the initial shock, she's turned more to anger now. She was always so close to her sister she'll never get fully over something like that. Alan's been asking lots of questions, but I don't think he's close to who did it."

"Have *you* any idea?"

"No," Amos replied softly, "but Reuben informs me he's sure who did it. Reckons Uriah was jealous and had his wife murdered, did it while he was away to deflect suspicion."

"You sound sceptical."

"Highly. You know Reuben, always the first to come up with fanciful theories which are never right."

Amos' tone was never condemning, he knew his friend had many faults, but liked him in spite of them.

They finished their meal and Tsodd gave a loud belch of satisfaction before brushing the crumbs off his clothes. Pronouncing himself well pleased with the spread he had helped finance, he went behind a bush to relieve himself.

Back in the throng, the groom had had rather too much to drink and was being propped up on either side by a friend. Bodd was among the group around him, discussing the other triplet.

"Lucky old Tsssssodd!" shouted Rodd and the others struggled to hold him upright, "he won't have to work again."

"That's what he's sick of hearing people saying," said Bodd,

Rodd frowned as he tried to focus his eyes, "Talking of being sick, I feel absolutely terrible."

All the men round him laughed until Leah burst in amongst them accompanied by her own retinue.

"I think, young man, it's about time you and I retired for the evening."

An eruption of whistling and good-natured cat-calling broke forth from the crowd, but ignoring them she then presented Anastasia to Bodd and continued in a forceful manner, "and as for you, you should be ashamed of yourself deliberately avoiding her the way you have been. Why she still cares for you, I'll never know!"

The angry bride snatched up her unprotesting, intoxicated husband and swept from the scene, leaving Bodd and Anastasia staring at each other – alone together in the crowd.

Reuben was one member of that crowd who decided to make himself scarce. "I'd better get home, see how the old hag is," he said as he left.

Anastasia did not know if it was herself or Bodd who was the more embarrassed by the situation into which they had been thrust, but was relieved when he unfroze and suggested they go for a walk together. The torches were dying down and more people began heading for home. Away from the centre, they could talk more freely. It was Bodd who plucked up courage to speak first.

"Leah was right, I haven't been very nice to you since we arrived."

"I asked for it by my behaviour ever since we first met. The truth is, I have grown more and more fond of you the past several weeks, but as time goes on, it has got more difficult to... speak about it. This isn't easy to say..."

She gave a nervous laugh, but he assured her of a sympathetic ear and bid her continue. At length she spoke about her orphaned upbringing, her reticence at meeting people that had turned into snobbery over the years. Finally, she told him in greater detail about her increasing warm feelings for him and her consulting Leah for advice. She had opened her heart to him, if he laughed at her now she would die.

Bodd had listened to her every word with great concentration. He had never entertained the thought that this Venus actually cared for him. As she spoke, his mind was having to do a lot of re-adjusting, but the last thing he felt like doing was laughing at her.

"You say you want a fresh start between us," he recounted, "that's fine by me. Best we try walking before we can run. Let's take things slowly and see how they go."

Relief showed on Anastasia's face.

"Good idea. Oh and Bodd – thank you."

They ended the night with a kiss, and the promise of a new beginning.

About this time, a tired Despot was climbing into bed. His dictionary was with him and with sleepy eyes he opened the book in the middle and peered at the pages. The night was still, the flame from his lamp stood bolt upright, never flickering, the smell of its oil filling his nostrils. His head nodded down as he began to fall asleep. Just in time he raised it again and turned over a page.

What was this? Molt was a similar to mold which was another word for earth. Was he really on the long lost mother planet? That would explain the vegetation and animals being indigenous to old Earth, although they had, of course, been exported right across the galaxy. The atmosphere was consistent.

With these intriguing thoughts filling his head, he finally dropped off to sleep.

CHAPTER TWENTY FIVE

Deep dreamless sleep. By the time Frank awoke, sunlight was streaming into his room. He sat up to take stock of himself, fingers playing with the covers. His mind was still full of last night's discovery, but now doubts had risen from the depths of his unconscious.

'Is this really the Earth? Mother Earth the poets compose their works about? Surely there are not enough species of animals here. I know many became extinct, but there are few insects even. The creatures are all either indigenous to Earth or genetically created ones...

'Ah, and why has this planet no moon? The moon of old Earth must have been large, otherwise the psalmist would not have written about the moon burning him in the night. But then I suppose it might not be visible from this side of the globe. I could have asked the Keepers if they know. Dammit! They were here and I never got them to tell me about Oonimari. How annoying, I forgot.'

He rubbed his eyes and stretched, peering out at the sky. From its brightness he had slept late. His thoughts moved on.

'Then there was Eleazar, he was going to tell me those legends about the origin of the people here. I might learn a lot from them...'

The sound of approaching footsteps halted the flow. They were a female's, probably Illianeth's he guessed.

"Enter," he replied to a knock at the door. He was right.

"Good morning, My Lord," she greeted, "we were wondering if all was well. Would you like your breakfast brought up here?"

"Er yes, um on second thoughts..."

He could not make up his mind, so the servant helped him.

"Natias is keen to have a word with you in the hall, My Lord."

"Right; I shall come down. See you in a little while."

"I'll make sure your breakfast is ready, My Lord. Oh and I'll bring your bowl of warm water in now."

Once washed and dressed he descended to the hall. It seemed gloomy compared with his room, his eyes taking some time to adjust to it. Having the external walkway covered was all very well, but it certainly cut down the light to the large room. Even on a glorious sunny morning such as this, some of the torches on the wall had been lit, although they had absolutely no effect.

"I twust My Lawd slept well?" asked the figure there to greet him at the bottom of the stairs.

"Yes, thanks. You wanted to speak to me I understand. No major problems with tomorrow's visit I hope."

The Despot took his seat at the head of the middle table. Natias stood at his side and waited until his master had begun his meal before replying in a hushed tone.

"Not exactly to do with the visit of the Mehtar, My Lawd, but it might be a pwoblem. We have had a few Laodician wefugees awwive. They are seeking sanctuary fwom the chaos over there." He indicated to the other end of the hall, but this was missed by Frank who was too busy eating. "They have asked us for asylum."

Showing concern Frank asked, "How many?"

"Four My Lawd."

"Is that all? Are we likely to get many more?"

"Fwom what we have leaned it is unlikely."

"Well that's a relief, surely someone in the villages can put them up."

"I am afwaid it is not that simple My Lawd. Fwom what they have said, and fwom what Japhses has found out these are not owdinary wefugees."

"Where *is* Japhses?"

"He is out, My Lawd, I am not sure where."

Frank took another mouthful and chewed it for a little while before throwing more questions.

"All right; what's so special about these refugees then? Where are they anyway? Here... don't stand over me, come and sit down."

The steward took the seat and brought himself close so that he would not have to raise his voice. Once more, he indicated to the huddled figures round the far end of the adjoining long table in the corner of the hall. Taking a squint at them all Frank saw a small group sticking close together in silence. None of their features could he make out, a fact he put down to his short-sightedness and the poor light in the hall.

"Hmm, can't really see them."

"They are wearing capes with the hoods up, My Lawd."

Frank thought that was strange, because it was not that cold in there, but as Natias unfolded their story he realised they were probably in shock.

"...So you see, My Lawd, what with the murders, the wioting and the burning down of their home they have been thwough a howwible ordeal. They are fugitives in their own tewwible land.

"The new government will still look upon them as dangerous it seems, they have been an important family in Laodician politics for a long time."

492

Frank looked despondent.

"Brilliant, this is all we need with the Mehtar arriving to-morrow! I'll put up with having them here – it's our Christian duty not to turn them away – but I'll not have them organising subversion or plots from this despotate. Kindly make that clear to them."

He slid his empty plate away and told the servant that he did not want any more to eat.

"I must be getting on, Natias. I want to track down Japhses and make sure the final preparations are in place."

"May I just tell you bwiefly who each of our wefugees is? Then you will have an idea when I intwoduce you. I feel you should speak to them, My Lawd, they are important people in their own land, coming fwom one of the oldest families there."

"Go on then," replied Frank resigning himself to the delay.

Natias produced a piece of paper and explained he had written down their unusual names, wanting to make sure he got them right. Meanwhile Alan joined them. Taking the chair opposite the speaker he swivelled it round and sat with his elbows on the back. He gave the impression of someone who was not going to stay long.

"The lady on the left My Lawd is Madam Tersha Arpintonax..."

"Blue-green ones, what a mouthful!" Alan exclaimed, making Frank smile.

"...It was her husband who was the party leader and was executed in all the chaos that weigned duwing the election. He had been awwested on twumped up charges I was told.

"On her wight is her daughter, the Pwincess Hannah Unit, she..."

It was Frank's turn to interrupt, "Princess! Come on, Natias, this is the twenty-seventh century, not the middle-ages, princesses belong in fairy tales."

Alan guffawed, but Natias was not amused.

"It might be pwudent if we kept our voices down, My Lawd," the white warned. He was getting irritated with the other two being so light-hearted. "The lady's pwecise title is umpwonouncable, "pwincess" was my own twanslation."

"Ah," Frank responded, becoming serious again, "but I thought we spoke the same language."

"We do My Lawd, more or less. If I may be allowed to finish: The Lady Hannah Unit saw her fiancé killed in a wiot during the election. He had been leading a demonstwation when fighting bwoke out. So both mother and daughter have suffered the same twagedy within a short space of time."

"Who are the other two then?" asked Alan.

"Oh they are merely servants; one a bodyguard, the other is Madam's personal hand servant"

Frank turned his head to sneeze a few times. "Excuse me," he said, then looked back at Natias, "you've done well to find all this out, saved me embarrassing questions anyway. You think I should have a word with them then."

"It might be best, My Lawd. I will organise wooms in the South Tower for them if that is in order. It is a bit cwamped, but weasonably comfortable."

"I'll leave that to you. Alan do you... where's Alan gone?"

"He left suddenly while you were sneezing, My Lawd."

"I see, well I'll speak to them by myself. How do you think I should address them?"

Natias, the great lover of etiquette, had made sure his research had included this information:

"Madam Tersha is usually addressed as "Madam"..."

"That figures."

"...while the prin... her daughter is addressed like a Despotess: "My Lady". Would you like me to intwoduce you now?"

"No, that's all right. Actually on second thoughts, yes, please."

They walked over to the quartet crouched over the end of the table and after introducing them Natias retreated. The Ladosans would have risen for their host, but Frank bid them remain seated.

Putting her hood back, Madam Tersha Arpintonax made herself sit in her usual upright posture as she thanked the Despot for his hospitality. A handsome woman approximately fifty-five Earth years, the lines on her face told of a depth of character and expression. She held herself proudly with her dark hair neatly set up on top. She and her daughter shared the same ebony skin.

Trying not to stare at them too much, Frank performed his duty by welcoming them. He explained that he was busy with the preparations for the visit of an important foreign guest tomorrow.

"Of course we understand," said Madam Tersha.

Frank was about to leave, but it suddenly occurred to him that it would be rude if he ignored the others.

"But before I go, I would very much like to be introduced to your daughter."

"Darling?" Madam Tersha enquired of her progeny who responded by removing her hood and forcing a smile. She was very tired after the journey across the mountains and mentally exhausted from all the anguish and worries she had recently gone through. Her mother completed the introduction.

"Despot Thorn please meet my daughter, the Hurxajta, Hannah Unit."

"Delighted," Frank said mechanically, looking down on the silent, wan figure struggling to keep her smile going. 'Rather plain,' he found himself thinking dismissively as his attention was drawn to the other two members of the party.

The "bodyguard" as Natias had described him, was introduced as Warshazzap, a soldier in the Ladosan army. He stood up as his name was mentioned, a tall, strongly-built young man with a pock-marked face. Madam Tersha spoke highly of him and the invaluable assistance he had given in getting them all safely across the border.

Lastly the handmaid was introduced. A shy girl in her mid-teens, Nooni was short with shoulder-length fawn hair.

"Well I hope you are all made to feel welcome here. I must dash as I said, but Natias, my steward, will look after your needs."

Frank called his lieutenant back to see after their uninvited guests and went off in a hurry to catch Japhses. The smooth-running of the Mehtar's visit was all important, he hoped all thoughts of Laodicians could now be pushed away until it was all over.

That same morning in Sardis, Karl was visiting Luke the Village Head. The black and the Talton had struck up a good friendship, the warmth of which had taken both by surprise. It was helped by the fact that they were both relative newcomers to Thyatira. They knew the natives patronisingly referred to Sardis as "the new village" and the term "Talton" after all meant "foreigner or alien". Karl was constantly aware that as the only black other than the Despot, he stuck out. All these things reinforced the bond between the two men.

Luke, however, was not a healthy man. He had been struck down by the winter epidemic and had never fully recovered. It left him lethargic and weak, he spent long periods in bed. Sometimes he would go to bed of an evening and sleep solidly for a day and a half. Neither Laffaxe nor the other medics had found a remedy; it was small comfort to be told his condition was shared by three others in the village.

On the morning in question, he was alert enough though and sitting in the sun outside his hut. Karl had just arrived and was asking in his usual whining voice what all the excitement was at the new community hut.

"It'll be the silver delivery," he was informed, "were there guardsmen there?"

"That's right, with a wagon."

"Mmm, that'll be it then. It was due today, silver bars we have bought, raw material for the smiths to work with. Keep them happy for a while....we had been running low.

"The new building is quite impressive isn't it? I know we've had this conversation before, but Alan is being good to us getting all these improvements done."

"Our patron!" Karl announced giving a short, high-pitched giggle. "Yes he's a bit of an enigma. In Aggeparii it was so different, *everything* was different. There was a whole class of blacks and socially they kept themselves very much to themselves. The few drones were tolerated, few were given responsibilities, while it just did not do to mix with whites. I feel much happier here, everything is so informal. You can even call me by my first name."

Luke knew that almost everyone laughed about Karl behind his back: about his funny voice, his seeming ineptitude. It appeared ignorance was bliss, the man was happy with his revived fortunes in his new home.

"My people and I are proud to be whites. For generations we struggled to keep ourselves pure when the Ma'hol tried to mix us with other groups. We hold our heads high and are glad now to be contributing to the defence of our new home with so many of our young men volunteering to join the Guard."

In response to this the other pointed out, "You're not happy about the Mehtar coming though here are you."

Luke's face dropped.

"No we're not! I suppose the Despot has to try to be on good relations with our neighbours if possible, but I'm sending a message to the Castle today saying I am not well enough to be there for the presentation of the Village Heads tomorrow. We want nothing to do with any of it."

Another voice joined the conversation, "You are talking about the visit of the Mehtar?"

It was Eleazar, they had not seen him approach. Karl confirmed the topic of conversation and asked the priest's assistant where his teacher was.

"He has gone for a period of quiet meditation in the forest. The work for the Great Revival Meeting has taken it out of him and he needs a rest before the final run up to the big day. It's only three weeks now."

"You're expecting many people?" enquired Luke.

"It could be numbered in the thousands! The response from all over Hoame has been magnificent. We are expecting contingents from all over the country, even as far afield as Gistenau and the south. Some should start arriving before long I should imagine."

Karl was keen to gauge the newcomer's opinion as to the next day's visit and asked him about it.

"I know you are not keen on it," Eleazar began, glancing at Luke, "but I have to say I back Despot Thorn totally in this matter. Anything which helps build up trust and understanding with our neighbours is good. We must have that if we are going to have a lasting peace which is so important. War is abhorrent – he who lives by the sword shall die by the sword – we must have peace at all costs."

"They had their lunch in the tower," Natias said as he stood in the bailey just outside the reception room, "they wish to west there this afternoon, My Lawd."

"Good, so we can get on with business. Now, is Matthew all set up in the kitchen? You said he was complaining about not having enough staff or something."

'When was he *not* complaining?' thought Natias who was too loyal to his staff to criticize out loud.

"That pwoblem has been sorted out, My Lawd. He is we-luctant about having to cook for the Ma'hol, but I managed to bwing him wound."

Frank was indignant.

"I should think so too. Blooming cheek, not up to him to say who he cooks for!"

"No, My Lawd," Natias said submissively.

The Despot shielded the sun from his eyes as he surveyed the activity in the balcony. A file of dakks was being led back to the stables by a pair of young stable-hands. The animal at the rear was in a foul temper, snorting heavily and only moving when the boy tugged hard on its reins. The area beneath the wall was receiving the attentions of some servants with brooms and bags to collect the litter. Over the other side a Guard squad leader was organising his men taking down the archery targets. They had been much in use the last week, but it was felt prudent to have them out of the way for the duration of the visit. A group of children were playing noisily just outside Laffaxe's house; even though they were only a few centimetres away from each other they still communicated at the tops of their voices. Frank laughed to himself as he imagined the physician storming out any moment to tell them to go away.

Becoming aware of another presence he turned to see Uriah standing there holding the ornate box containing the ceremonial sword ready for inspection.

"Ah hello, Uriah, you've brought the Mehtar's present. I've been waiting to see it all finished."

As he reached across to take it Uriah suggested in his dull monotone voice that it would be best to go inside first.

"Of course the dust," said Frank once he had worked out what was meant, "right, inside it is."

They took it to the Throne Room where the box was placed on the table. As the lid was opened Natias' eyes went wide, "It is magnificent is it not, My Lawd? Such a work of art!"

Frank saw the finished article for the first time and was most impressed. The grip was make of hulffan rope dyed red, the hilt encrusted with semi-precious stones, the blade was long and polished to perfection.

"I autherwised the purchase of the turquoise, My Lawd, it is one of the few pwecious stones not readily available in Wabeth-Mephar."

"Fine, fine," the Despot replied with his eyes still fixed on the gift, "the sword-smith has done an excellent job."

Uriah spoke, "It is still a practical weapon My Lord, if the Mehtar wishes to use it as such."

"Really? How paradoxical that something designed to kill people can at the same time be so beautiful. Don't you think so?"

The rhetorical question was left hanging in the air while Uriah closed the lid and they moved out of the small room. Back in the hall, Frank noticed Alan tugging at a lever near the entrance and went over to see what he was up to.

"Opening these shutters Damian had installed," came the explanation as he wrestled with the lever, "it's got a bit stiff... ah there we are. There, that's better isn't it. Silly not to use them don't you think?"

Frank looked up at the sunlight pouring in and agreed. He did not let on his ignorance of their existence.

"Very good. Alan I wanted to have a quick word with you. You know I asked you to suspend your investigations until the visit is over and done with? Well I think it might be a good idea if you were to assist our Captain in escorting the Mehtar from the border tomorrow. So if you don't mind, I'll ask you to liaise with Japhses."

"Good I want to speak to him, he's been rather elusive lately. There's some interesting information concerning him I've been given – I'll tell you more when I know more."

To the people of the Lower Village the coming state visit seemed very remote. The majority of the men were sitting drinking in the community hut that evening, they had other things on their minds.

John, the son of the Village Head, and his friend Cragoop came out of the building to take a walk, or more importantly to be by themselves.

"I just had to get out of there," the former explained once they were certain of being out of earshot, "all those old men ever do is complain!"

"It's a shame," sighed the other.

"Moan, moan, moan, I'm sick of it! Here, let's go down to the river, it's not a bad evening."

John led them through the trees down the steep pathway to the riverbank where they sat down on the dry grass and listened to the sounds of nature. Soon the last streaks of light from the sun left the sky and it became pitch black, broken only by the few lonely stars twinkling to each other across the vastness.

"Of course you're right, mate," Cragoop said quietly so as not to disturb the calm atmosphere, "they do complain a lot. I hoped things might improve once we moved to the new site, but they haven't of course."

Joked John, "You should've let them burn it down, that'll've learned 'em."

"Huh," was all the laugh his colleague could muster, "I dunno, I suppose they've got some good points. I mean we can't deny the old crafts are suffering now so much time is being taken cultivating the hulffan."

"You're a cobbler, you still have time enough for that surely. That reminds me, I need a new pair of shoes, these have had it."

He flicked the loose sole with his finger, but it was too dark to be seen. The jailer's son paused a while before replying.

"I suppose I've been lucky, but I've heard that not nearly so many pots have been made lately and the woodwork factory's nearly empty. Japhses has been complaining that we're not supplying our fair share of recruits to the Guard, but it's hardly surprising is it?"

They stopped to listen when they heard the dead leaves being scrabbled nearby. A frass was on a nocturnal hunt, it quickly moved off when it smelled its company. The river beneath them slid slowly and silently towards its destination, some distance off a night awk was crying.

"Do you think it'll come to a war?" asked John.

"What the Laodician savages? Who knows mate! ... but the arrival of those refugees does make things interesting. It was a stroke of luck my father came from the Castle today, said he got a good look at them. Said they're being put up there 'cos they're important honorary blacks."

"Yeah you told me."

"Anyway the children have made up their minds."

"How do you mean?"

"Haven't you heard? The teacher found none of the boys were at her class this morning. She organised a search and they were found in that field behind the smithy playing war-games. When questioned they said Japhses wanted them as new recruits and they were in training!"

The two young men laughed. Then Cragoop said he had better get back to the community hut and take his father home.

"I shouldn't've left it this long, he'll've 'ad too much to drink and will've got all melancholy about mum."

"Still misses her."

"Yeah. Come on, let's go."

At last the big day arrived. Everyone in the Castle was up early and ready. The guest rooms were spotless, the hall polished from top to bottom and the bailey swept for the last time.

'I could've done with having my hair cut,' thought Frank as he waited, standing in the shade of the Castle with his main officials except Luke who was ill. An interpreter was on hand, but would probably not be needed, because all the top Ma'hol who came were bilingual. Behind the waiting group was a large contingent of guardsmen lined up with their armour polished and bright. The sky was cloudless and the air still.

The training programme had been put on hold for the duration of the visit, the new recruits being given a few days off as all the experienced troops were needed either for the Ladosan border or escorting and ceremonial duties.

It was late morning as Japhses and Alan rode through the gates at the head of the column. Flanked on either side by walking Hoamen guardsmen, the Ma'hol vehicles slowly trundled into the bailey. The first one was a huge chariot (Frank had not seen one before) in which Mehtar Arumah-Ru sat on an elaborate throne-like seat. His colourful, loose-fitting clothing was both dignified and practical for the hot weather. His head sported an emerald green turban. He was shielded from the sun by a gigantic parasol attached to the base. A driver plus two other male slaves accompanied him, each wore a blue satin loincloth and was naked from the waist up. The chariot was drawn by four of the biggest dakks the Hoamen had ever seen. These impressive beasts, pure white with staring pink eyes, were pulling up a few metres before the reception party and the foreign ruler was helped down to the floor of the bailey by his slaves.

Japhses and Alan dismounted and did likewise, their dakks dwarfed by the Mehtar's magnificent specimens. Frank stepped forward to give his guest a warm greeting.

"Welcome to Thyatira! I've been looking forward to our meeting again and the opportunity to strengthen the bonds between us."

Unemotionally the Mehtar replied, "A pity your country-men do not feel likewise. However," he continued on a lighter note, "I thank you for your welcome.

"This is my Prime Minister."

The man he introduced had just hurried from the covered wagon immediately behind the chariot. The new Prime Minister was a young man for the post, Frank observed he had similar red hair to the Mehtar, possibly a relative he guessed. Not being offered a name he welcomed the Prime Minister who responded stiffly. The atmosphere could be cut with a knife and Frank wondered what was wrong. He glanced behind the Ma'hol official to see if there were any other dignitaries about to be presented to him.

The Mehtar had in fact brought few of his top people. His heir Sil Qua'moth-Ri had seen quite enough of the Castle for his liking and had made it perfectly clear from the moment the invitation was received that he did not want to go. Rorka his fool had a summer chill and was in bed being filled with medication. His chief wife, the gorgeous but moody Shalara'tu had thrown a tantrum when it was suggested she might accompany him. "Stay in that pig-sty with those barbarians?" she had shouted, "I would rather die."

So instead he had brought his latest acquisition. As part of a peace-deal with the Frorcenians, who held a long common border on the western side of Rabeth-Mephar, he had been presented with the daughter of their leader. Rasha-Pi'Pi was a petite girl of only thirteen Earth-years. She could hold a good conversation yet was exciting and playful at other times. The Mehtar had grown rather tired of most of his wives, this new one had brought a new quality of life. Her innocence was so refreshing compared with the sophistication of Shalara'tu. One advantage of the latter staying behind is that she and Sil loathed each other. Sil blamed her for his mother's death (quite wrongly in actual fact) while Shalara'tu disliked anyone in court who had their own influence with her husband. So the ruler had departed for this state visit knowing well that any plots being hatched by one would be thwarted by the other.

Frank waited patiently while Rasha-Pi'Pi was helped from her covered wagon and escorted by her chief maid to her husband, three girl-slaves in tow. She wore the most beautiful, flowing dress of feather-light material with delicate patterns all over it. As he was introduced to her Frank was surprised by her obvious tender age, but captivated by the young lady's contagious smile. Her eyes were clear and fresh, she had not come here with any preconceptions.

While this was going on the Despot also noticed Alan trying to attract his attention. So after presenting Karl he got the black to introduce Natias, Gideon and Saul while he grabbed a quick word.

"What is it?" he asked in a hurried whisper.

"We nearly had a riot in the Upper Village! Never should've gone through there. Japhses is in a foul mood..."

"Oh no," Frank moaned, "look I've got to go – fill me in later."

He returned to the introductions and led the Mehtar and his party to the Castle. They made their way up the spiral staircase to the roof. In the vanguard, Karl and Natias made conversation with the Ma'hol while Frank held back with Alan trying to get a fuller account of that morning's events.

It was clear that Japhses had made a near disastrous miscalculation by leading the Mehtar through the Upper Village. The Thyatirans had turned out in force to shout and jeer at the foreign leader. There had been spitting and much abuse hurled and in Alan's estimation it was a miracle it had not turned to physical violence.

"The guardsmen had to get tough with some of the hotheads to hold them back. Blue-green ones what a shambles! I did warn him."

Frank was furious, but more with the villagers than with his Captain whom he felt should be able to accompany a guest of the Despot without receiving that sort of treatment.

"I'm going to have those villagers punished," he declared.

"We'll never identify them."

"Then we'll punish the whole lot, give them a hefty fine or something. Speak to Natias about it and come up with some proposals by tomorrow at the latest."

Alan confirmed he would. He thought the whole episode was unfortunate, but could not disagree with the idea of fining the villagers. They had acted appallingly and it had seemed most had turned out for the event.

The two men had stopped on the second floor to finish their conversation. Now they made haste to catch the others up.

"Japhses is handling the billeting of the Ma'hol soldiers," stated Frank as he went swiftly up the stairs.

"Yeah... and seeing to the wagons. He was just as angry as you about the villagers. Mind you, he is even more angry at me."

"How do you mean?" Frank asked, but by now they were stepping out onto the roof where the guests were waiting. The answer would have to wait.

The Prime Minister was standing to the fore. Puffing up his chest he announced formally "His Glorious Majesty is impressed with the panorama visible from here."

It was all Frank could do not to laugh. Why the Mehtar himself could not have said he liked the view he did not know. Refraining from a flippant response he replied that he was pleased.

He then got Natias to point out some of the landmarks visible at that height. Rasha-Pi'Pi enthused, the events in the Upper Village had not put her out of humour. Being shielded within her wagon she had had very little idea of what was going on outside and no one was going to tell her now. Surveying the scenery over the battlements her husband looked interested, but did not say anything.

While Natias was keeping Rasha and the Prime Minister occupied answering questions Frank seized the opportunity to have a word with the Mehtar.

"I am mortified to hear what happened on your way here, I have just been given an account. The people responsible will not go unpunished."

There was a pause before the Mehtar responded. When he did it was in slow, measured tones.

"It would appear you misjudged the depth of feeling in your own people. I understand no damage was done so we will let the matter drop. It would be a pity to let it spoil our visit."

"Thank you," replied Frank with great relief. Quickly he changed the subject, incidentally, how is your son? It would have been nice to have met him again in more pleasant circumstances."

"I fear the Mennahuna did not share your sentiment. But he is well; I have got him organising a dam construction project at present."

507

He almost added, "It is necessary to keep him well occupied," but managed not to. Instead he tossed the conversation back into the other's court.

"I was somewhat surprised to be introduced to so many of your 'white' men, the reports we get are that you treat them worse than animals…"

Frank did not know if this was a "polite" counter-attack for his oblique reference to his having once imprisoned the Mehtar's son. As the Ma'hol continued, however, he realised the man was merely making observations and no offence was intended.

"…Such reports do get exaggerated of course, but then you are not originally of Hoame are you. They say you came from the east, from a land famous for its philosophers."

"Hmm… shall we go back downstairs now?"

There the exchange of gifts took place. The Mehtar showed animation unusual for him as he studied the sword. Frank was pleased that it was well received after all the hard work that had gone into it. In return he was given a one-metre square model of the main temple to Vorg-habielhmonn in Karabel-Haan. It was carved, he was informed, from the bone of a munsat, a rare an revered animal found only in the remotest regions of their country. The Thyatirans were fascinated by the minute detail of the carving and spent some time admiring the structure.

The result of this and the Mehtar's refusal to take offence at his reception in the Upper Village was that tensions subsided and the whole mood became much more cordial. Something else that helped this process was the presence of Rasha-Pi'Pi. She seemed oblivious to the electric atmosphere at the start and her cheerful disposition and comments with Natias on the roof had certainly helped to break the ice.

The guests were shown their rooms and in the afternoon they were taken on a sight-seeing tour. While still in the hall, the Prime Minister asked if there were any bralaks to hunt, but not even the whites had heard of them.

"Oh so you do not hunt then," said the Prime Minister sounding superior until he received a glare from his leader and promptly shut up. Frank confirmed they did not hunt and moved the conversation along, "Well I hope you will enjoy the scenery Thyatira has to offer anyway."

The Mehtar was surveying the immediate scenery of the hall. No Phalabine this, no jewel-encrusted patterns on the walls, only stark, cold stone. Strangely enough he found himself thinking this crude architecture had a beauty of its own in its naked strength.

As a young boy he had spent nearly all his time in one or other of the palaces dotted about Rabeth-Mephar. His upbringing had been strict, the moral code of the Ma'hol elite installed into him at every turn. He had ascended to the throne before manhood and had had to learn the practical side of governing – so different from the many theories – quickly.

Now that he was older he found himself increasingly trying to fight many of his society's ingrained conventions. Also the immense bureaucratic machine that was his civil service. No one in it dare say a word against him in the open, but he felt sure the very complexity of the organisation was used by some to slow his reforms down. Certain members of his family seemed to spend most of their time scheming too. Shalara'tu he could read like a book and was always a step behind him. The heir Sil was getting more devious every day and had to be watched. The new Prime Minister was an asset though. Despite his faults he was at least beginning to tackle the problems of the civil service. Also he had allied himself too closely to the

Mehtar to ever be accepted by the more obvious enemies such as the High Priest of Vorg.

By comparison, the simple life of the Despot of Thyatira seemed idyllic. 'Forget all the luxury,' he thought as he stepped out into the bright warm sunshine ready to sightsee, 'give me the simple life here any day!' He laughed inside at the way he was becoming more of a rebel as he got older.

The afternoon went pleasantly as the conversation was kept light and the members of both groups began to get to know each other and relax. That evening they sat down to dinner in the Despot's suite. Frank took his place at the head of the table and bid the Mehtar to the place of honour at his right hand. Round the table anti-clockwise from the foreign ruler were Saul, Karl, Japhses, then Alan at the other end, Rasha-Pi'Pi, Gideon, the Ma'hol Prime Minister and on Frank's left, Natias.

"Curious how our customs differ," the Mehtar observed amiably, "if this were our country I would have had to have had to have placed you at the opposite end of the table."

With a chuckle Frank replied, "If you did that all I would see of you to talk to would be a blurred outline! My eyes aren't what they should be."

The Mehtar was intrigued by this confession, but did not say anything. Frank was about to continue, but paused for the arrival of the soup. Illianeth was not on duty that evening, her reading services were not called for on this occasion. A servant girl Frank had not noticed before brought the bowl for the principal guest. She slapped it down on the table so hard it splashed everywhere, not least on the Mehtar himself. Frank was incandescent, he was was not going to stand further insulting behaviour.

"Girl, come here!" he called to the girl, only the presence of his guests stopping him shouting. Red in the face he ordered her to wipe up the mess immediately and come back with a fresh bowl. Seeing his anger the girl promptly burst into tears, but the Mehtar of all people came to her defence, saying he was sure it was just nerves that had caused her mistake. So while Frank bit his lip and tried to calm himself down the Ma'hol Prime Minister sat in amazement at his leader's soft tones. 'People die for less back home,' he thought, somewhat inaccurately, 'never seen him like this before. These barbarians must have something he needs badly, something he doesn't want me to know about yet.'

Truth was the Mehtar was simply feeling well disposed towards his host. He felt strangely relaxed, more so than he had done for years and did not want the atmosphere spoilt if he could prevent it. He could tell how keen his host was to see everything run smoothly.

Frank was indeed anxious that it went well and was most annoyed at the inauspicious start to the meal. Things soon settled down though as the meal got properly under-way.

The conversation up the top of the table soon turned to trade, with Natias and the Prime Minister joining in their leaders' discussions. The latter had to be persuaded that the ill-feeling of the villagers was not universal and there were good prospects for mutually beneficial commerce. Various options were aired and a general agreement was reached on how to increase imports and exports between the two peoples.

While this was in progress, Frank noticed Alan held in lively discussion with Rasha-Pi'Pi. The two of them were falling behind with their food they were talking so intensely and obviously enjoying each other's company.

Gideon found himself in the unenviable position of being in-between two discussions and not really able to join either. So instead he looked across the table and exchanged notes with Saul and Karl on the state of the other villages.

Which left Japhses who was not talking with anyone. This was probably just as well because he well because he was still in a foul mood from the morning's events – the disturbance in the Upper Village and Alan's questioning. The drone did not turn to speak to him once during the meal, it was as if there was a solid barrier between them and each was oblivious to the other's presence.

Japhses had to perk up and join the proceedings, however, when the Prime Minister brought up the subject of the robber bands plaguing them. The Ma'hol, it seemed, suffered a lot worse at their hands.

Explained the Prime Minister, "They are getting bolder every time, terrorising our villages. We receive assurances they are nothing to do with you, yet when our soldiers chase them they disappear over your border."

"The same happens to us," Japhses declared.

Frank concurred, saying, "We were hoping that you would agree to our launching a joint operation to flush them out of their hiding places in the forest on both sides of the border. Settle this thorn in our sides once and for all."

The wisdom of this was quickly seen, but much planning would have to be done before any offensive went ahead. Following a lengthy, but constructive discussion a strategic outline was agreed upon. By the time the meal was over a surprisingly cordial atmosphere surrounded them. Mutual despising was beginning to be laid on one side as each discovered their foreign neighbours to be not so different after all.

Next morning saw another excursion from the Castle. The Mehtar had expressed an interest in seeing the hulffan crop close to and observing some of the techniques involved in its cultivation. Frank secretly sought counsel from his top men, for he knew how jealously their monopoly was guarded. They advised there was no harm in looking, but that not too much in the way of detail be given. That was easy for him as he did not know much himself.

That same morning Japhses set off for the Upper Village with Saul and three squads of guardsmen to inform the villagers of the fine being imposed and enforce it immediately. In view of this it was decided to take the guests to one of the new plantations outside the Lower Village.

Natias was excused the journey to look after affairs in the Castle. Frank stood outside the reception room accompanied by Alan and Gideon waiting for Rasha-Pi'Pi's wagon to be got ready. The Mehtar was standing a few metres off talking quietly with his Prime Minister. Finishing this he turned to the Despot and was about to say something when he noticed the Ladosan refugees returning from their early morning walk.

"Madam Tersha, I had no idea you were here!" he exclaimed.

The Hoamen looked on in surprise as the two sets of foreigners greeted each other like the long-lost friends they were. Hannah Unit greeted the Ma'hol ruler with a large kiss on the cheek which raised a few eyebrows amongst her hosts. She eventually pulled herself away from the melee and explained to Frank that there had for many years been a close relationship between the Mehtar's family and the House of Arpintonax.

She explained, "They knew that we were the voice of reason and a force for moderation and stability in our land."

When the Mehtar confirmed this in similar terms Frank realised that it was true about these being no ordinary refugees. Also that apart from his introduction two days ago, he had completely ignored them. Hastily Madam Tersha and her daughter were invited to join the party on their excursion, but they politely declined saying they needed to rest.

It was then that the Mehtar proposed a conference that afternoon to discuss the Ladosan situation, a suggestion that was well received.

"I was going to raise the subject anyway," he explained gravely, "I have profound concerns about the way events there are shaping up."

CHAPTER TWENTY SIX

'Four hundred and fifty sten times a hundred and fifty men equals sixty-seven and a half grend,' thought Bodd as he tapped the numbers into his machine. He put the calculator to one side, 'Most kind of the Baron to let me use this for my work, "a benefit for having been top of your class," he had said, "one of only five in existence..." Amazes me how it works without having to wind it up – just keep this bit free.' He licked his finger and wiped it across the solar cell.

A window seat afforded the luxury of a good view, high above the city centre in the Citadel offices. Many of his fellow trainees were in cooler underground offices where strong artificial lights hung on the walls, the fuel for which came by means of pipes. For all this technology Bodd was far happier being above ground and in the sunlight, even if it did get rather stifling this time of year. Trainee Fourth Under-Secretary to Baron Schail was a title to be proud of he knew. Certainly Benedict was pleased for him when he had been told of the appointment.

The office in which he worked was really a spacious ante-chamber with rooms leading off on three sides, the fourth being the outside wall with long, rectangular windows. A dozen wooden desks were arranged in no discernible order. Bodd had one by itself which helped him get on with his work rather than natter all day as was so easy to do if given the opportunity. Three corridors converged on this work place and at its busiest there was a buzz of many workers.

Not that day though. Just the occasional person walked past with a bundle of papers under their arm. A few other clerks sat engrossed at their desks up the other end, but all was quiet. The Inner Council was convening in the conference room across the way. He had escorted an important messenger to the meeting which he understood had been called to discuss the news the man brought. That seemed a long time ago now and they were still deliberating.

In the meantime Bodd was working on the figures for the proposed new standing army subsidy to the regions. The way the figures were coming out it did not look like the idea would get off the ground.

Afternoon dragged and the silence, combined with the warm sun on his back, made him drowsy. Instead of working out budget subsidies his mind wandered to thoughts of Anastasia. The holiday they had together back home had been a turning point. He remembered Rodd's wedding, how he had suddenly realised he was enjoying her company. Since then their relationship had gone from strength to strength. Her coldness had evaporated; he had never known anyone to change so. They went out every night, more often than not to dance. Her dancing was a revelation, she said she enjoyed it and it showed. How strange that someone could have all that bottled up inside them for so long...

The sound of the conference door opening and the clatter from within brought him back to the present and he began another calculation.

Footsteps approached, then, "Boy!" It was Bulow's assistant. Bodd was certainly not going to respond to being called that from him. He continued tapping away on the calculator without looking looking up.

"Clerk, your presence is required."

Unfortunately he could not take too much exception to being called a clerk so this time he got up and followed the assistant back to the conference room.

The meeting was breaking up and while most of the men were still seated at the long, oval table others were getting up and milling around. Bodd entered the fray and was directed to the messenger and instructed to take him to the canteen. Above the general babble Zastein's voice came over loud and clear, "Gentlemen, we will let them play into our hands!" he declared ebulliently. As Bodd took the messenger's arm his eyes met Baron Schail's and the Keeper gave him a friendly smile.

Morale boosted by this he swept past Bulow's assistant and took the messenger to get something to eat. On the way there he tried unsuccessfully to find out from the man what was going on, but he was keeping tight-lipped.

'No harm in trying,' thought Bodd justifying himself, 'I'm pretty sure he's from the north... there's something in the air, but I don't know what.'

None the wiser for his probing he left the messenger eating and went back to his desk. It was not long before he was packing up anyway and scurrying down the whites' stairway. The stone steps were cold and narrow, the sun coming through small slit windows at regular intervals lit the way. After a few flights he began descending two at a time until a group of fellow workers held him up for the last part. A hundred and twelve steps, he counted them almost every time.

Out into the brightness he strode. Hope was in his heart and he was not to be disappointed as he arrived at the rendez-vous point.

"Anastasia! Hi, who are your friends?"

The young woman was standing in the shade on a busy street corner, a stream of people rushing by. She was hold-ing a little girl in her arms, while a small boy clutched her dress. Her face was radiant with joy as she saw him. In spite of her hair being untidy and the rough clothes she wore, Bodd thought she looked more beautiful that ever. The mousy-haired children stared worriedly at the newcomer at first, but soon relaxed when he paid more attention to their guardian than to them.

"They're twins," Anastasia explained glancing at her charg-es, "drones as you can see, abandoned by their mother soon after birth. They've spent all their lives in the home. This is Shanti and the boy's called...Thanton?"

She looked at the lad for confirmation and received a nod. Bodd quickly greeted the orphans before giving her a kiss.

He said, "I didn't know you were allowed to take any of them out. Is there something special on today?"

"Not really, I think the owner's just more used to me there now and trusts me to go out with a couple."

She put Shanti down and holding onto a child with each hand entered the flow of passers by, continuing, "But I think we had better get back. It won't be far out of your way."

"Of course I'll come," Bodd called out, walking behind them until they went down a quieter side-street where he was able to come alongside. "I've been there before if you remem-ber, when you first started. That seems ages ago now, but you haven't been there long have you."

Anastasia agreed and looked down affectionately at the twins who remained silent. An empty wagon trundled past at speed, the metal-rimmed wheels making a terrible din on the cobbles. The road was surfaced with hulffan tar a little further up and the noise lessened considerably as the vehicle reached it. Bodd remarked on this before going on to speak about his day.

"...This messenger obviously brought some important news from the way the Keepers reacted. There's been a buzz going round the place all day..."

"I'm sure you shouldn't be telling me this," she reminded him.

"Ah yes, I suppose you have a point there."

"Besides all that politics leaves me cold. I now know what the important things in life are: helping other people – and special friends."

They exchanged another kiss and led the children back to the orphanage.

Conversation died down in the Throne Room, Ma'hol and Hoamen sat round the table quietly waiting for the Ladosan refugees to arrive.

Frank's mind turned back to the previous night when, between his regular prayers for patience and Giella's soul he thanked God that the Mehtar's visit had been rescued from the early disaster in the Upper Village. Now he felt like praying that the meeting about to take place ran smoothly, but he and his lieutenants were secretly unhappy about having to hold it with Laodician women. It just did not do to talk about matters of state with the female sex, that was obvious. It surprised Frank that the Ma'hol, clearly civilized in many ways, had such a backwards attitude to this. They did not appear unduly bothered at the prospect.

The Mehtar came from too pragmatic a people to worry about this. It was all too important to let matters of principal get in the way. Besides he had known the women concerned for many years and as well as being friends he knew Madam Tersha and her daughter to have no mean intellects, able to hold their own in the best company. No, he would not waste energy on that, instead his mind was also going through the events of the previous night.

After bidding his hosts good night he had called the Prime Minister to discuss the Thyatiran ruler. Due to the lack of space Rasha-Pi'Pi was in the same room, up the other end having her nails manicured by a pair of girl-slaves. The Prime Minister avoided looking at her, such a situation would never have arisen back in Krabel-Haan, but his ruler was putting up with many inconveniences to improve relations with these foreigners.

"Has he no wives at all?" the Mehtar had asked.

"No, none," the Prime Minister had confirmed, "from what I could find out he was actively gone out of his way not to take one of the other despots' daughters as is the custom here."

"Is he more interested in men?"

"Not as far as we know. There is the drone Alan living here, but there is no evidence to suggest there is anything more than friendship there."

Rasha-Pi'Pi called out, "You need not concern yourself there. I can assure you they're not like that, a woman can always tell."

The two women looked at each other embarrassed. The Mehtar considered informing her she should not be listening to their conversation, but in the end meekly replied, "Thank you my dear." and concluded with the Prime Minister by saying, "We had better leave it at that for now, we will not offer him a bride this time."

Brought back to the present by the arrival of the Ladosan delegates they settled down to begin the hastily arranged conference. Firstly, however, Madam Tersha wanted to give the Mehtar an explanation.

"I expect you wondered Arumah why we chose to flee here instead of Rabeth-Mephar. The henchmen of the new government were everywhere looking to apprehend us. There were many friends offering to hide us, but we knew it was only a matter of time before we were found so we had to get out of the country altogether. The northern and eastern borders were a great distance so they were out. We heard that they were expecting us to make for you and that extra soldiers had been sent to Sectors A and C as a result. So we finally decided to try and make it across the mountains to Hoame. Fortunately it is summer and were able to make it across without too much difficulty with the help of a guide. He has gone back to see if there are any others he could help to safety.

"Despot Thorn has been most hospitable to us, giving us shelter, we are most grateful to him."

The recipient of this gratitude felt a bit awkward, he had thought of them as an inconvenience. He sought a platitude to respond with, but before he could come up with one, the Mehtar spoke.

"I am sure you are grateful and so am I," he glanced at Frank, "for helping my friends the way you have. As things have worked out I am pleased to have this opportunity for us all to discuss the current situation together and pool our intelligence. Despot Thorn, as host, I am sure you will want to begin."

Frank sat up straight and had a quick scan of the participants before addressing them. His foreign affairs advisors Alan and Japhses were present, along with Karl. The Village Heads would be briefed later.

"Well I'm sure you know a lot more than we do. We had heard of disturbances during the election, then when the ladies here arrived they were able to fill us in with some details. But we have virtually no contact normally with Laodi... I mean Ladosa – no trade, no travellers – therefore we can tell you very little."

The Prime Minister indicated that he wanted to speak and received a nod from his master.

"We were concerned when we began receiving reports of unusually bad unrest during the election and took the opportunity to increase our... shaktons in the country..."

"Sorry?" asked Frank.

"Spies," Alan translated.

"Not exactly spies," corrected the Prime Minister with a frown, "more informers, observers."

Alan and Frank exchanged a wry smile as the speaker continued.

"Anyway we stepped up our intelligence gathering and got first-hand accounts of the terrible bloodshed before the new government assumed power. Information has been difficult to get since then due to travel restrictions. However, in response to the increased presence on their side of the border we have moved more units to the north-east.

"The most recent reports we have received speak of a lowering of tensions and a slight easing of those travel restrictions."

"Ah, yes," Hannah Unit interjected, "but that is only because they have arrested so many of our supporters and now feel more secure."

To the other Hoamen's surprise, Karl then spoke up, "I hope you are not suggesting we should attack your country to put your side back in power."

'Well put!' thought Frank, but Madam Tersha did not think so.

"We are suggesting nothing of the kind, young man," she snapped petulantly, "but it is important that you all understand the current Ladosan situation. The thugs who now form the government have got where they have by whipping up a hitherto latent fear and mistrust of foreigners. Hoame in particular has been their target, because no one knows what it is really like."

Her daughter continued for her, "These groups in our country that have formed this unholy alliance are not natural partners. Sooner or later the unity will break down and the government knows this. In order to keep it going they may be forced to start a war. Their rhetoric has been aimed at this all along, I fear it may have a momentum all of its own. All we are asking is that you be prepared."

"Why did you not say all this when you first arrived?" asked Alan.

"I think mainly because we were too exhausted," Hannah confessed, "but also because you were all so busy preparing for the Mehtar's arrival."

Clearing his throat, Frank said in a loud voice, "Right, now let us not get carried away by all this. There is talk of momentum towards war, I think if we talk too much like this we could be bringing it upon ourselves. Be prepared, yes, but let's not get carried away by too much speculation and rumour. From what has been said it seems the situation there can change rapidly, I see intelligence gathering as of paramount importance, the more we know, the less we will have to speculate."

The conference continued for some time and the generally accepted feeling among Hoamen and Ma'hol was that they should pool any news they received and keep in regular, frequent contact as long as the crisis was perceived to last. Alan commented on the need to keep their neighbouring despotates and the Keepers informed, while Japhses promised the recruitment and training programme of the Guard would not be slackened.

Madam Tersha and her daughter were well pleased with the outcome. "Preparedness, they said, "is the best hope for peace." Hannah pointed out that there were almost certainly Ladosan spies in Thyatira at present, not only traders, but possibly one or two disguised as villagers. This latter suggestion shocked Japhses and Karl, to whom the wigs or hair dye necessary for such deception were the ultimate taboo.

Frank was delighted, because this all helped to seal the relationship of trust it was his aim to build with the Ma'hol. It was especially noticeable how the Prime Minister had loosed up since his arrival. The Mehtar had even made them laugh when he had jocularly referred to the Thyatiran Guard as "odd job men" because they were used on so many other projects other than simply defending their country. Japhses did not find this too hilarious, but forced a smile so as not to show offence.

Winding up the proceedings, the Despot said that he thought the outcome was most satisfactory.

"We all know what to do: await developments while making sure we are prepared for every eventuality. Of course as long as this state of tension lasts, we will have to postpone our operation against the robber bands."

Later that day a reply was received from Despot Hista that they too were receiving disturbing reports from Ladosa. It appeared that he was taking a similar line to that formulated by Frank.

He may have been notorious for worrying the whole time, but Hista had every reason to be concerned on this occasion. Bynar had by far the longest common border with Ladosa and unlike Thyatira, there were breaks in the mountain chain along it. Bynar did have a large standing army though and that was being put on a state of readiness. Frank was still concerned about the possibility of a war being talked up and when he briefed the Village Heads he tried to play down the likelihood of this happening.

The Mehtar too was well pleased with the outcome of their deliberations, although his Prime Minister was concerned they may get caught in this foreign land with hostilities breaking out.

"I feel I must advise a hasty return, Oh Glorious One, so that you can personally oversee preparations. By Vorg, every day, indeed every qualta spent here now represents time lost."

"We are due to leave tomorrow," the Mehtar replied calmly, "I promised a visit and I am glad I did not put it off. Despot Thorn spoke widely concerning the current situation, we must not let our imaginations get the better of us. If it makes you feel happier as soon as we arrive home I shall suspend the dam project and inform Sil he is to step up our preparations.

As you know, I believe in contingency plans and I have an offensive strategy forming in my mind. It will involve a diversionary force advancing across our border with Ladosa while the bulk joins up with the Hoamen. Before we go, remind me to have a word with Despot Thorn concerning permission to move an army across his land."

"Of course, Glorious One, but is it our fight?"

The Mehtar looked surprised at how naïve his Prime Minister was being in this, "Oh yes, believe me it is."

"May I ask about the Arpintonaxes; are they to travel back to civilization with us?"

"Certainly not, that would be an insult to the Despot's hospitality. Do not underestimate these people, you still have much to learn. The Ladosans may be more materially advanced than these, but apart from a few groups within that country (such as the Arpintonaxes) their hearts are dark. Know who your

enemies are and which are a threat to you. The Ladosan government represents both of these, do not doubt this."

In the Upper Village community hut, Reuben had had too
much to drink.

"Bloody Japhses and his bloody Guard; traitors, that's what
they are, bloody traitors!"

Amos looked around nervously, fortunately there were not
many men there that evening to be offended by his friend's
drunken ravings. Reuben's son Brogg sat in the corner nearby
staring into space, a group of farm-hands sat up the opposite
corner playing dice. If only Tsodd would turn up.

"Never had the bloody Ma'hol swagger through 'ere in old
Rattinger's time," the drunk continued, swaying from side to
side on his bench. He reached once more for the almost empty
bottle of wine on the table, but stopped to add, "It's all Thorn's
fault we were fined, that black bastard!"

"Now that really is too much!" Amos exclaimed. "I'm not
going to have you carted off for spouting treason."

Reuben stopped ranting and tried to focus on his colleague.
It was so rare for Amos to raise his voice like that, things must
be bad.

Just then a fresh face appeared at the door.

"Oh Tsodd thank goodness you've come, he's in a terrible
state. Come in, don't just stand there."

When the new arrival advanced, Reuben looked at him and
frowned deeply, "Huh it's okay for you Tsodd. With all your
money you can afford a *hundred* fines. I... I'll... I..."

His eyes went completely glazed and his head bobbed up
and down while he fought unconsciousness. Fought and lost.
Bang went his head on the table making the other two wince.
The bottle fell off the table and landed on the floor via the
bench. To their surprise it did not break, but rolled away

towards the near wall. Amos got up to retrieve it, worried eyes glued to his insensible friend. As he restored the bottle to the table, the sprawled out figure gave a snort. Shortly afterwards he began to snore loudly.

Turning to Tsodd he apologised for the reception he had received. He tried to makes excuses, saying, "I think he's been having some bad rows with his wife again lately, things aren't well between them. Which reminds me I don't want to be out too long tonight...

"He's been going on about the fine imposed by the Despot."

"Oh that. They came round the aviary to tell me about t. I wasn't in the village at the time, but didn't see any point in arguing, so I paid up."

"Have you still not decided what to do with your money?"

"Oh don't start that again," Tsodd replied with a pained expression. When I've decided you'll be the first to know." He looked at Reuben, "See him sleeping like a baby. Never seen anyone go out quite like that, so sudden. He'll be in a bad state in the morning. Best leave him though, he wouldn't thank us for taking him home in this condition."

Amos nodded and shifted his position on the bench. He glanced over at Brogg who had not moved the entire time. A roar went up from the other end of the room where one of the men had just taken the kitty. Tsodd resumed.

"No I still haven't decided what to do with the money, I'm trying not to think about it right now."

"You should get yourself a wife!"

"I don't think so. Not now anyway, it would restrict my freedom. I'm at the aviary and animal pens most of the time these days...

"You going to Zadok's revival meeting?"

"Yes, are you?"

"Yeah, I think I'll go," Tsodd said dreamily.

"Everyone seems to be from what they're saying; still over two weeks to go. Spoke to Eleazar today, he's talking of many hundreds of people coming up from the south."

"Gonna be a big event then."

Amos changed the subject, "Heard from Bodd since he went back?"

"I haven't, but he's probably busy. The cheeky squad leader who came to collect my fine wanted me to pay Bodd's as well! Am I my brother's keeper? I didn't know the man and he he took some convincing that Bodd now lived in the Capital and shouldn't be fined. I think he had heard about the money and was going to pocket it himself. Anyway I argued long and hard and eventually he gave in."

"The cheeky devil!"

"They say the Ma'hol return home tomorrow and'll go through the village again. There'll be more guardsmen this time you can be sure. Everyone I speak to says they're going to keep well out of the way."

"Too right! I'm keeping firmly indoors this time, I'm not going to get caught up in all that again."

The Castle was extra busy the next morning. The Mehtar had wanted an early start and both Ma'hol and Hoamen servants ensured that he got it.

The orange-white sun was still rising in the sky as the foreign ruler mounted his chariot. A final farewell to his hosts before the monster-dakks began moving his vehicle off with a jerk. One hand on the rail, he adjusted the turban on his bright, red hair with the other. His smile was genuine, he had cemented a worthwhile alliance with one of the Hoame despotates, something none of his predecessors had ever done. There would be faceless critics back home, but he was confident most people would see his achievement in a positive light. He knew this alliance currently depended on the personality of Despot Thorn, but if ties were increased then any future Despot would see the benefits of good relations.

Rabeth-Mephar was a large, land-locked country with many neighbours. The more sections of border with friendly neighbours the better. Trust, the Mehtar had learned, can be a rare commodity in politics, whether internal or international. The Sarnicians had made an alliance with him out of fear, following their defeat. The Thyatiran despotate, on the other hand, had made the first peace overture when they were riding high after a victory. Yes they were much smaller than Rabeth-Mephar, but they could have called on the other despotates to come to their aid for any prolonged conflict, but more importantly people show their true character and intentions when they perceive they are in a position of strength, often foolishly so. No, the Thyatiran hierarchy were trustworthy, he hoped they could carry their people with them – especially if it did come to a conflict with Ladosa. If ever there were a people not to be trusted, it was those fickle devils. While the Ladosans had been divided and squabbling amongst each other they were not too much of a threat. Now, however, the Ma'hol ruler could see a real need to crush them before their new-found unity brought disaster on everyone. No use the old Prime Minister saying it was Hoame's problem. As the Mehtar had sacked him, he said that their country would be next on the list if Hoame fell.

This was the other major achievement of his trip: an alliance against Ladosa and permission to move through their territory in the event of hostilities to join the main Hoame forces making one large army. He had seen enough wars not to relish the prospect, but was convinced in this instance that it was the lesser of two evils. Would the Ladosans play it clever though and hold on until they had built up their forces? Intelligence reports suggested Ladosa's army was large, but poorly trained and equipped. So sooner rather than later would suit the allies.

Frank breathed a sigh of relief as the last of the wagons disappeared through the Castle gateway, escorted by an even bigger contingent of guardsmen this time. As was his habit, he weighed up the successes and failures of the visit.

'The strengthened links were an excellent achievement and that the few unfortunate incidents will be forgotten in the long run. I'm especially pleased Japhses had been won over. Trade still needed to be streng...'

"I need to speak with you in private."

Alan had a business-like expression. In a hushed tone Frank replied, "Of course, you want to speak to me about Japhses."

The farewell committee was breaking up. The Arpintonaxes set off dakk-riding on mounts borrowed from the Castle stables. They were joined by their mountain guide who had postponed his return to Ladosa due to a swollen ankle which was only now starting to improve. Natias set about his duties assisted by Karl while the few guardsmen left at the Castle began setting up the archery targets once more.

"Let's go to my suite," said Frank leading the way through the reception room, "I've just realised I haven't had anything to eat today yet, I'm starving!" He continued talking as they ascended the stairway to the hall, "haven't seen much of Laffaxe lately."

"Nor've I," replied Alan, "seems to spend more and more time in Sardis, that's probably why."

Once in the hall they headed for the stairs, but were interrupted by Illianeth who enquired whether her scripture reading services would be required.

"Er, yes it would be good to get back into routine."

When the girl looked so disappointed Frank asked why. She thought she knew her master well enough to tell him straight.

"It's just that a group of friends are going to have a party in the Upper Village this evening and Soosha and I said we'd help set it up today. We didn't realise the Ma'hol were going to leave so early. Matthew has enough cover and said we could go."

"Well that's fine, you go ahead," Frank replied genially. He was not unduly bothered and besides he had a bit of a soft spot for Illianeth, "but there is one thing: before you set off can you organise some food to be brought up to my rooms, haven't had anything to eat today. Just some toast and honey and a drink'll be fine. After that you're free to go."

The relieved servant's face lit up and she thanked him generously. She slipped off and the two men were able to resume. Alan went to the sitting room and expected Frank to follow him. Instead he called out, "I'll be with you in a moment," and disappeared into his bedroom for what seemed like an age. When he did return Alan was perched on the edge of a tall chair, eager to get on and divulge his important news.

"Ah this is comfy!" the Despot announced cheerfully as he sank into the settee. "Sorry about that, I just wanted to look a word up in my dictionary while it was fresh in my mind; something somebody said. Funny how words can change their meanings over the years, often simply because a large enough proportion of the people didn't know the correct meaning in the first place. People often say they'd like to go back in time and visit famous historical events, what they don't appreciate is that the first thing they'd find is everyone speaking in languages they couldn't understand. You wouldn't have to go back that far to find quite significant changes either – not that I'm an expert in the field you understand. I must admit I admire the Ma'hol for learning our language, the upper class I mean.

"Sorry, I'm rambling a bit. After all it was you who wanted to speak to me. Now, what was it you wanted to say?"

At last! But now footsteps were approaching; if Alan did not get it out this instant he'd explode. Not wanting to be overheard he whispered, "I think I've found Giella's kill..."

A knock on the door.

"Ah breakfast, I'm starving – come in!"

Alan was going half crazy by this time. He had kept the information bottled up for days because Frank had been so preoccupied with the Mehtar's visit. Now it was taking second place to breakfast!

As the male servant opened the door Frank lent towards his friend saying, "Sorry about that, you were saying?"

In response Alan simply put up his hand indicating it would wait until the servant had left. Frank turned to see that the man standing in the doorway was not bringing him his food.

"My Lord."

"Don't tell me you've dropped the toast," Frank said flippantly until he saw the man's serious expression. 'Oh no,' he thought, 'not trouble with the Mehtar in the Village again.'

"What is it?"

"A delegation from Laodicia has arrived, they wish to see you, My Lord."

"Oh. Well I suppose we'd better hear what they want. Alan, can your news wait?"

The answer came in the form of a loud guffaw. If he did not laugh he would cry! They got up and headed back downstairs. On the way, Frank's mind soon turned from his friend's strange response to thoughts of what the Laodician delegation wanted. He had to check himself from letting his imagination run riot, he would soon know.

Collecting Natias and Karl on the way they entered the Throne Room. Only after Frank was perched on the throne and his men had taken their places around him were the foreigners ushered through. The chief delegate swaggered in and stood defiantly in the centre of the room. He was a short man with a smooth, round face and small, closely set eyes. His long, faun hair was curled round and set up on the top of his head, a style most extraordinary to the eyes of the Hoamen. He wore a flowing purple cloak and clearly thought he was important. Introducing himself at some length, he did not notice the blank, unimpressed faces staring back across the small room. Eventually he got to state his business, at which point the listeners perked up.

"As the elected Harbinger it is my duty as representative of the Peoples' Assembly to instruct you to return the Arpintonax renegades, plus any other miscreants you many be holding, over to my care. You are to do so immediately."

It would be an understatement to say the chief delegate's arrogance was not well received. Karl looked daggers at him while both Frank and Alan found themselves in a state of stunned silence. The latter sat for a moment with his jaw hanging in amazement, not knowing whether to laugh or shout at the man. There was no such indecision on the part of Natias. He told the Ladosan official in no uncertain terms that it was not for him to dictate to Hoame.

Trying to adopt a conciliatory tone, Frank suggested they sit down and discuss it. "I can't see us allowing you to take our guests away, but it always helps to talk things over."

For some time he made every effort to get a positive dialogue going, but the foreigner's whole attitude meant that this was an impossible task. His entire attitude was quite extraordinary if he really was trying to achieve his stated aim. Any lingering doubts that the Laodicians might have been prepared to listen at all were dispelled when the Harbinger announced, "I trust you are intelligent enough for me not to have to spell it out to you. I'm not here to enter into a debate, I get enough of those back home. Even a..."

"That's enough!" Frank roared, "get out of here, go on, get out!"

The force of this outburst knocked the chief delegate off his stride and his face started to go red. However, he controlled himself well and, holding his ground, began to speak again. Before he got more than a couple of words out Frank shouted an expletive, called the guard and had him ejected.

The foreigner struggled to no avail and called out, "You've got two weeks or you'll be sorry!" as he was dragged out the door.

Karl accompanied the ejection by calling out some assorted insults in his unmistakable voice, the last one of which referred to the departing delegates as "frass' turds." Alan collapsed in laughter at this, so much so he had to wipe the tears from his eyes before saying, "I love all this diplomatic language you blacks have!"

Frank was not laughing though. As the commotion died away the enormity of his action struck him. Had he brought about a war because he was hungry and had had his meal delayed? In spite of their obnoxious manner he should at least have heard them out. Although his stomach was rumbling his appetite had suddenly disappeared.

Natias made sure the door was shut and returned to his seat. All eyes were on the Despot. Quiet descended for a short while on the Throne Room as he thought about what they had just done. However, he soon found the other three were united in their support for the action taken, none appeared to have a single doubt.

As Alan put it, "Think of the alternative, Frank: were we really going to hand over Madam Tersha and her daughter to those creeps? Come off it."

"It's like they were deliberately trying to provoke a confrontation, maybe that was the plan."

"Yeah, it's possible."

"Shouldn't we at least have... oh I don't know. This could mean war, I hope you realise."

"We're not daft, Frank, of course we know that."

From the debate which followed it was clear Alan, Karl and Natias were of one mind. The honour of Hoame dictated there could be no giving in to the Laodician churls. If it meant war, then so be it.

"You acted just right, don't regret it," the drone spoke for all three. "They were deliberately provocative, they never came here to negotiate. Note how quickly they sent their messengers here, they must already be keeping an eye on us. In fact, I really don't know how they were able to do it, the refugees have only been with us three days. I cannot see how word could have got to and from their government in that time, yet they insisted they spoke in that capacity. Come to think of it, if it was not for the corroborating information provided by the Mehtar I might suspect our "refugees" had been planted on us by the Laodicians."

This is something that had not occurred to the others. Karl asked if it could all be part of a huge plot involving the Ma'hol who were double-crossing them. Alan, however, warned against them getting over-suspicious.

"It won't harm to be wary, but I can't really believe that to be the case. The Arpintonaxes appear genuine and I believe the Mehtar is trustworthy."

"So do I," agreed Frank.

"But if the Laodician envoys are typical I don't think much of them. If what we've been told is true the new government there may feel it has to provoke us into a conflict to preserve their shaky unity and keep their hold on the country. If it wasn't this, they'd think up another excuse no doubt. I reckon they've acted too soon, from what our refugee friends have told us they simply aren't prepared for a war. And if it did come to it we wouldn't be alone this time, the other despotates are watching developments and preparing as far as we know. I'd strongly keep them informed of the latest developments – plus the Mehtar and the Keepers of course. Count Zastein will want to co-ordinate a national resistance to the Laodicians.

Frank thought it sad his friend felt obliged to always refer to his father by his title, but saw the wisdom in the advice and asked Natias to draw up some draft letters without delay.

"Yes, My Lawd, as soon as we have finished in here. May I just say that I feel certain the people will be behind your decision to thwow those soabs out. We cannot let them dictate to us."

"Thank you, Natias, but I don't feel too clever right now. Following a long period of peace, I've been here just over a year and we're about to be plunged into war for the second time."

"Now come on, Frank, let's get this into perspective. That scrap with the Ma'hol was all over very quickly and I personally believe a great deal of good has come of it. The situation we are in now has been forced upon us, it was not *your* doing, as indeed the dispute with Rabeth wasn't. Besides, this current business could still end in other ways. It might well be a bluff."

"Do you really think so?" Karl asked sounding surprised at the suggestion.

"No, I don't," Alan admitted, "but no one knows do they! If only we had a better idea of what is going on over there. What we need is a reliable spy of our own, I don't want us to rely on the Mehtar's men."

"We're in the dark!" exclaimed Karl.

This point was agreed by all, but it was decided to discuss ideas as to what they could do about it when Japhses was present. A further special meeting including the Captain was arranged for the following morning. No great sense of urgency was present, they believed that if it did come to war, it would not happen for a while. If it did the Laodicians were highly unlikely to attack across the mountainous Thyatiran frontier.

The refugees were still unaware of this latest development and they were to be kept in ignorance until it suited their hosts, if at all possible.

Frank was feeling a fraction happier now. "Well that's about all we can do for now. Natias, you can get on with those letters. Karl, will you please ensure that those Laodician envoys get escorted quickly out of the country. I'm going to get myself some food right now or else I'll collapse – you coming, Alan?

CHAPTER TWENTY SEVEN

B ack in the Despot's rooms, Alan finally got the chance to
pass on his startling information. When he did so, Frank
would not believe him.

"Japhses? Oh, come off it! This really is too much; you can't
expect me to go along with that."

"That's up to you," replied Alan with a shrug of his shoulders, "but I'll tell you, I got it from the most reliable of sources."

"Yes, but at this rate you'll have me believing Giella was
having affairs with half of Thyatira. I'm sure she wasn't like
that. People just accuse her now 'cos she can't answer back and
they like a bit of scandal. They should have *more* respect for the
dead, not less.

"I don't think we'll ever find her killer now. I must admit
I've been so busy on other projects I'd forgotten you were still
pursuing it. That might not be the most tactful thing to admit,
but it's true. If all we're going to get are stories like this, then I
think it might be just as well to let the whole thing drop, don't
you? I mean it won't bring her back, will it?"

"You've changed your tune, whatever happened to this business of owing it to her to catch her murderer?"

Alan was finding it hard to understand Frank's attitude. Fortunately, he was not easily annoyed though. So in spite of being asked to stop now his hard work was starting to bear fruit, he was more puzzled than anything else.

He said, "When I questioned Japhses, he more or less admitted his affair with Giella..."

"But not in so many words."

"No, but I wanted to speak to you again before we arrested him and extracted the whole story. Blue green ones! I don't like having to say this, I've known him for years. We can't just ignore what I've found out though, we've gone too far for that.

"From what I've learned from another very reliable person is that Giella had just ended the relationship with Japhses and he was most unhappy about it. I mean it fits: him killing her out of jealousy, or having his desires frustrated. Whoever killed her had strength too, a great deal of strength."

"I thought you said a woman could have done it."

"I've changed my mind."

It went quiet. Frank looked most unhappy.

"All right," he said slowly after a while, "I take your point. However – and I know you're not going to like this – however, with all this Laodician thing brewing up I can do without the Captain of the Guard being arrested right now. We don't want these investigations to drag on any longer I know. They've gone on long enough already, too long in fact. That's not intended as a criticism of yourself, but I am not prepared to tackle Japhses until the Laodicians are dealt with one way or the other."

Alan could see the sense in this, "I think you're right. Whatever else he is, he's a damn fine solder and we need all the help we can get at the moment.

"I'm not sure how much he suspects we know. He was damn annoyed with me when I questioned him about Giella; didn't speak to me for the next couple of days. Seems to be okay now, though. Never intended these investigations to go on so long, but these people have been hard to break down. I thought I'd get their confidence, but when they all clam up, you don't even know which ones have got the information you need."

"Well, you've done a good job, Alan, I'm just sad it's reached the conclusion it has. We won't tell a soul until we agree the time is right to make our move; act as if everything's normal with him."

A short while later he found himself alone with the Captain in the Throne Room while the latter gave a report on the progress of the training programme. Far from acting normally, Frank could not help his mind from imagining the man committing the foul deed. Over and over again he could see these strong arms raining down cruel blows on his defenceless victim.

'How could you do it?' he though as the Captain's report droned on unheard. 'How can you act and look so normal? But then what did I expect, Francis, him to have the word "murderer" tattooed across his forehead? No, but...'

"...So my enlarged and intensified training schedule has put us right back on course, My Lord."

"Very good, well done."

"And do you like the enhancements I detailed?"

"Most certainly I do," replied the Despot confidently as he wandered what on Molt the man was talking about. "Keep up the good work, you're doing a grand job."

Japhses would have left at this point, but his master's sudden pained expression stopped him.

"Was there something else, My Lord?"

"Um yes. You're not married are you."

"No, My Lord, like yourself."

There was a further pregnant pause before Frank asked, "And do you live by yourself at present?"

"Yes, My Lord."

"Hmm, I see."

The big man was starting to get embarrassed. He had not been dismissed, but could not see where this faltering conversation was leading. Helpfully he added, "I do hope to be married later this year, My Lord, a young lady in the Upper Village."

"Ah good, good."

"Is that all, My Lord?"

"Yes, of course, thank you for the report."

The sun got out following a brief morning shower. The rain clouds moved swiftly on and with none to take their place the temperature rose steadily. It turned out to be the warmest summer day to date.

It was Madam Tersha's habit to have a sleep after lunch and while she did so, Frank took a walk outside the Castle with Hannah Unit. He thought it might be a welcome distraction. He had been pleased to find out the day before that the Arpintonaxes were Christians, that already put them in a better light in his eyes. Together the pair admired the flowers and watched as the bee-keepers made a quick inspection of one of the hives. Later they went to sit down in the shade of some trees.

"It was a gamble with the unknown to come here," Hannah confessed as she spread out her wide skirt on the grass.

"I suppose it must have been."

Frank took a good look at her at this close range. He was having to sharply re-assess his initial verdict of this woman as "rather plain." When this assessment had been made she was drawn and tired. Now that she had her vitality back and the sparkle back in her eye he began to realise how wrong he had been. Here was a complete contrast with Giella, whose first sight has knocked him sideways. Hannah's was a more subtle beauty. Her skin was quite dark. She had prominent cheek bones and deep brown eyes, around which was just a hint of purple make-up. Frank managed to forestall an internal debate on the vagaries of human attraction and pay attention to what was being said. She was still telling of her decision to escape to Hoame.

"We know the ruling family of Rabeth-Mephar well, but the authorities in our own country were aware of that and expected us to make a move there. That is why we made the difficult decision to come here. You must understand what a gamble it was to go to Hoame, a country we knew very little about. You have been so kind in making us feel welcome."

The leaves fluttered in the gentle breeze. Her voice was soft and restful. She was blissfully unaware of the Ladosan envoy turning up – and the reaction he had received. Frank felt no inclination to tell her either. The refugees would know soon enough and in the meantime he preferred to be one step ahead. The possibility of them being part of an elaborate plot by the foreign power to provoke a war had still not been dismissed. He wanted to keep an open mind and not draw conclusions too hastily. They seemed genuine enough, but then if they were efficient spies, they would do.

A small piece of bark fell into Hannah's lap and she brushed it off gently before asking, "Please tell me how I should address you. Is it "My Lord" as most people do, or "Sir" as Karl (I think this is his name) does?"

"Oh no, by my Christian name: Frank. I'm not sure I like all this hierarchical stuff, but I suppose it works pretty efficiently."

"I am surprised to hear you say that, Frank. Most people leap to the defence of their social structure when talking to people outside it; often when they actually agree with it or not. I admire someone who is not afraid to express his doubts."

Frank felt he should tell her he was not a native of Hoame, but then he would have to talk about coming from Oonimari and he was tired of telling those lies. Instead he offered more doubts, saying, "I'm a funny mixture really; half the time I tell myself how good an authoritarian, feudal system like this is, the rest of it I think how wonderful anarchism would be."

She replied with a smile, "Never underestimate the ability of the same mind to hold together two opposing views!"

"In a true anarchic society all would be working together and no one lording it over others. I used to think about this in the old days. If we are all equal in God's eyes why do us humans make all these artificial distinctions? I'm not necessarily thinking about Hoame now, but in any society there are always the "haves" and the "have-nots". If there was a large group of sincere-minded Christians who could see the sense in all working together... I couldn't try it here, the Keepers would soon have me out of a job. They probably would do if they could hear me now... anyway the whites seem to like the status quo.

"But a Christian anarchism would be the most wonderful place if it could ever be brought about. It's ages since I thought about it. All resources would be pooled: like the first generation Christians in the Bible."

"Ah, but they did have a structure with bishops and deacons in charge, and prophets and so on."

"I suppose so, but that need not be the case. There would be mutual cooperation."

"It would never work surely, people being what they are."

"It would never work because there would be too many people saying it won't work."

They smiled at each other. The pace of the conversation had speeded up and they were both enjoying it. Good times on Eden came flooding back. It was unfortunate perhaps that the realities of Hoame rule were never too far from his mind. More types of government were discussed before Hannah showed her true colours.

"Ah but I'm a democrat," she announced, "*there* is a system which is practical and as fair as any human institution can be."

"Oh dear, not sure I can agree with you on that one. I suppose we are all coloured by our own experiences, but some of the worst societies I've ever come across have been democracies."

"Some of the best I would say," Hannah retorted, before adding, "but then I don't suppose it would be very tactful for me to espouse that cause to a despot like yourself."

A relaxed Frank replied, "I don't mind at all, I'm enjoying our discussion, let's not stop now. Just as long as you don't give my staff any ideas!"

"It's a deal."

They spoke on, Hannah talking at length about her dreams of the ideal democracy. Frank felt a real connection with someone else who liked to aim for the ideal.

"...That is what we were trying to bring about in Ladosa, but there is always an inbuilt danger with democracies, you can let a terrible lot such as the Buffs get in power."

"The Buffs?"

"So called because of the colour of their banners."

"I see, I think. I once lived in a place where there were many different groups vying for power. I didn't like it, people trying to score cheap points off each other all the time."

"Do I gather from what you said that the Buffs have not long been in power?"

"That's right. They won the last election, but many people suspect ballot rigging, while intimidation was rife. The political make-up varies in different parts of the country, but basically there are three main parties. Each are known by their colours. The old guard are the Pinks which formed the governments for many years. Our party's emblem is a yellow star on a purple background. When I was small, we did hold certain government offices alongside the Pinks – my father was an important minister – but it did not work out because there was too much in-fighting."

"So you mean the purple and pink clashed," Frank said flippantly. Not for the first time in his life did his humour fall on barren ground.

"That's right," agreed Hannah earnestly, "and we have been a party of opposition ever since. Our fortunes have not been good lately, I must admit, I think it's because we haven't got our message across to the people properly. Then the Buffs came long with their bully-boy tactics... all the terrible things that have happened since then."

"Yes and our country finds itself being threatened by..."

He had stopped mid-sentence because he had suddenly realised that she was crying. He found himself apologising for being insensitive, but she shook her head.

"No it's not you, Frank," she said wiping the tears away while making determined efforts to stop any more from forming. "I've been so enjoying our discussion, but it has reminded me of similar ones I used to have with my fiancé. He was killed last year by our opponents who are now in power. He was a man of passionate convictions who could argue the hind legs off a dakk. It happened during a demonstration... I should not dwell on the past. He used to say that.

"Let's change the subject, if you don't mind."

With that, the conversation fell flat. They sat quietly and watched the bees go back and forth on their flight-path nearby. He felt a flash of guilt for getting so involved in their discussion that he had not been immediately sensitive to to her feelings. She had shown a vulnerable side that brought out his protective instincts. He wanted to put his arm around her, but restrained. Instead he admonished himself for discussing politics with a woman.

At last Hannah got the conversation going again when she remarked how refreshing it was to find large numbers of Christians in Hoame.

"Back home we are a small minority and far too fragmented for my liking. I belong to the Canusian Church which is small in size, but not in passion. For all my countrymen's democracy I must admit there is much godlessness which is rotting our society to the core. The Christians try to bear up the banners of righteousness," she giggled, adding, "that sounds very grand doesn't it, you know what I mean: trying to get people to live a good life. People just do not care about God at all. I'm reminded of what the prophet Hosea said, "There is no good faith or mutual trust, they break oaths, kill and rob, nothing but adultery and licence. They know nothing of God"."

"That reminds me of Ezekiel: "The country is full of murder and injustice. They think there is no God that sees them.".... is it really that bad?"

"I am impressed," said Hannah, "it is so true, though. Not for nothing do your countrymen change Ladosa for Laodicia! I don't know what is to be done."

The warm afternoon drifted by unnoticed by the two of them sitting among the trees. Conversation ebbed and flowed, but it was never forced. They were enjoying getting to know each other and exchange ideas, finding to their surprise they had many interests in common.

Supper-time they dragged themselves away and emerged from the shade for the walk back, still chatting away.

"I left my mother a message as to who I'd be with. I don't want her to worry if I can help it. The weather always affects her moods, so I'm hoping this beautiful day will have helped."

Changing tone as they entered the bailey she observed, "Your guardsmen appear busy, especially since our meeting with the Mehtar."

"Well we like to be prepared, that's all."

Frank realised he was being cagey and decided to expand a little, "Japhses – that's our Captain of the Guard – is always keen on having our men in tip-top condition. It's not unusual for exercises or tough training sessions to be in progress."

He was still not giving anything away, although by this time any doubts he might have had about +her being genuine had been dispelled. 'This is no double-agent planted on us, I'll stake my life on it.'

Little did the thinker then realise quite how prophetic he was being. Hannah meanwhile was considering how well they had got on in this, their first proper conversation together.

"I usually take a long time to get to know someone. With you though, I feel that we've known each other ages, yet we've only just met."

"Yes," agreed Frank with a smile, "I know exactly what you mean, I feel the same."

"Where's that frango Halaton got to?" Illianeth enquired, more to herself than anyone else.

"He'll be here, don't fret," replied Soosha as she found a place for the plates she was carrying. She set them down on a table already crowded with food and utensils.

The two girls were putting the finishing touches to the party preparations in the Upper Village community hut. The tables were arranged up one end leaving a large area for dancing. Many young people were expected that evening.

"Ah, here he comes," said Illianeth. She bounded to the window only to be disappointed. "No, it's only Zadok and Eleazar."

Soosha continued to carefully arrange the cutlery on the table, Without looking up she said, "I keep telling you don't fret, he'll be along."

Outside the priest and his assistant had plenty to discuss. Eleazar had just got back to the Upper Village after spending a long time in Sardis.

"I noticed a lot of activity around the Castle on the way back Sir, preparations for war. Certain elements seem bent on it, I don't like it at all."

The older man stopped and leaned heavily on his walking stick. He tugged his long beard and replied in his usual loud voice.

"It is not for us to question the decisions of those God has chosen to put in charge. They will be judged according to their deeds like the rest of us, and because the Lord has given them greater responsibilities all the harder will they be judged. I do not envy their task."

Eleazar had grown up a lot in the last year. He was a great deal more confident in his beliefs now and, while he still held Zadok in the greatest esteem, was not afraid to argue a point with him.

"I am certain you are right Sir, that they do indeed have a grave responsibility, but I wonder if the Despot's advisors are not all of the same opinion so there is no proper debate. I do hear things from the Castle staff.

"I remember after the battle with the Ma'hol having to go round the bereaved relatives – it was not a pleasant duty. All that grief was so pitiful, so unnecessary." He hesitated, recalling the scenes.

They were on the edge of the pad by now and sat down on a bench overlooking the green, open, common land. Children played in and out of the trees a few hundred metres away, nearer a carrion bird was feeding off a dead rabbit.

When the priest's assistant resumed, it was with a note of puzzlement. "One of the widows I visited acted most strangely – Katrina, Hatt's wife. She seemed positively pleased he was gone. It was quite dreadful."

"You never told me about that."

"Didn't I Sir? She left soon after that, haven't heard a thing about her since."

Zadok was glad the topic had dried up, he had something much more interesting on his mind.

"Now!" he boomed, "let us discuss the meetings, my boy."

"Of course."

"It isn't long, only two weeks."

"Do not worry Sir, now that I am back I am going to devote my time helping to organise it."

"Good. The villagers have been hard at work on the extra land Despot Thorn has lent us: a veritable village of tents and temporary huts is being set up. An impressive sight by itself. We have had it confirmed that the Rehner brothers will be coming for the entire three days."

"The guest speakers we wanted, that's great! I hear they are filled with the Spirit and very exciting."

A smile flickered across the old man's face.

"I saw them in their early days, they showed a great potential right from the start. From what I have heard, they are just what we need. Now, to go through how the other preparations are proceeding..."

This the priest did, in great detail. It was important that nothing was overlooked: food and accommodation for the large numbers of people expected from the other despotates (Despot Thorn's original grant had been topped up when it was seen more resources would be required), timetable of events, sanitation arrangement, the positioning of the tents where the various groups would be stationed. Meticulously he went through every point. Eleazar was in awe of how Zadok's ageing mind was able to hold so much information and his ability to disseminate it without faltering once. As he ended though, he admitted to his assistant that there was one bit of important news that he had forgotten to mention.

"The plans for the stone church have been approved. Just this morning the news came through that the authorities in Asattan have given us permission to build it."

"Really?" cried Eleazar exuberantly, "I don't believe it!"

Zadok gave a bigger smile this time, "It *is* hard to believe. To be honest I thought they would turn us down. My life-long ambition fulfilled, it will transform this village."

While many of their meetings were held outside, a stone church would mean the luxury of shelter during bad weather. Possibly it might even mean some meetings during deep winter snow. More importantly to the priest and his assistant though was that a stone church would be a symbol of God's authority and a fine structure through which He could be glorified. It was unheard of in their experience for white villagers to be given permission for any stone building, let alone a church. It was only with Despot Thorn's blessing they had considered applying. Most despots would have looked at the project with mistrust and never have sanctioned the application to the Capital, let alone agreed to help fund it as he had. In amongst the huts a large stone church would be a real statement. Its effect could not be over-stated. The pair congratulated themselves on their success.

A group of croppers walked by on their way to tend the hulffan. Tools slung over their shoulders, they carried food and drink in their back-packs. They exchanged greetings with the churchmen.

When the opportunity, arose Eleazar resumed his pacifist grievances.

"I wonder if they are deliberately causing agitation with the foreigners *now* to disrupt our meetings. I know, Sir, we have not always seen eye-to-eye in these matters, but it does make me wonder. After all, they know we have been planning this event for a long time."

The older man was not about to be drawn into another discussion with Eleazar on the subject of war, each knew the other's immovable position. There was, in fact, almost no debate in Thyatira outside the Castle on the prospects for war, with the exception of the tiny anti-war group in Sardis. Virtually all the villagers were of the opinion that their rulers knew best and that if that meant war then so be it. They were well informed though, news of the Laodician envoys' expulsion had soon got out on the whites' grapevine, but it had more of a novelty value than material for serious debate. Zadok had faced these difficult moral questions a long time ago and felt he had arrived at the best answers available. He could not get too worried over Eleazar's strong opinions though, seeing his own youth reflected in his assistant. 'There is still more maturing to be done,' he concluded, 'time will mould him further yet.'

Eleazar persisted, "The Despot is under the influence of those who cry out for bloody conflict. If they can disrupt our revival meetings, it will serve their evil purposes."

Zadok shook his head, he was not going to be drawn in. In contrast to his normally penetrating voice he said quietly, "You still have a lot to learn, boy, the world does not revolve round the likes of us."

Next day the top level meeting was held in the Castle. All the important whites in Thyatira were assembled in the hall. Alan arrived with Karl and announced that the Despot would be along shortly and they should go through to the Throne Room.

Natias went in first, clutching a bundle of papers under his arm. Japhses followed him, his giant mass of white hair streaming down his broad back. Next came the Village Heads: lanky Saul from the Upper Village, the dour Gideon representing the Lower and Luke. The Sardis Head's fluctuating health was on a good day and he found himself quite excited as he sat down on Japhses' right. He was less experienced at this sort of thing and eagerly looked round in a conscious effort to absorb the tense atmosphere.

As Alan went to enter, Karl clumsily bumped into him. What would have been a source of amusement in normal circumstances was instantly dismissed; Alan indicated for the other to go in first.

The delegates sat round the table in the cramped room, expectation in the air as they waited for their leader to arrive. Japhses was leaning across the table, whispering something to Natias, apart from that, quiet prevailed. At least it did until Karl decided the best way to release some tension was to talk. Turning to Gideon on his left he said, "That is a magnificent gift the Ma'hol left us isn't it? The model temple. I was trying to work out how they did it, must be such tiny tools they used. I looked at it afresh just now..."

Gideon's initial reply was a frown and an expression which said, "Are you mad, jabbering on about such trivia?" Belatedly he remembered it was a black addressing him and, clearing his throat, growled, "Yes, Master."

Frank arrived. He let Illianeth in first who had a tray of drinks for the delegates; it was going to be a long meeting.

"Sorry to have kept you waiting gentlemen," he said cheerfully, trying to ease the expectant atmosphere a little.

He ascended the platform to the throne and took his seat overlooking the rest. Illianeth left the room, shutting the door behind her. The light was poor and with his weak eyesight, Frank could not make out the expressions of the men now turned towards him. He was acutely aware that this was the most important meeting he had ever had. On the decisions made now would depend all their futures.

"Right, gentlemen, let us begin. In a moment I will ask Alan to explain the current position in our crisis with Laodicia and what has led to it. I then want a full discussion – do not hold back, feel free to speak your minds – all your opinions so that I know where we all stand. I then want to go on to discuss what our future strategy should be. Thank you. Alan?"

The drone gave a resume of events, mainly for the benefit of the Village Heads. Frank wanted everyone up-to-date with events and his actions understood and, if possible, agreed by all.

Alan concluded, "Our choice was either to hand back the refugees, thereby facing humiliation and a loss of integrity, or face the possibility of a war we do not want."

Frank was pleased his right hand man had expressed himself so admirably. In the initial exchange of views which then took place, the Village Heads quickly fell into line. There was in fact not a dissenting voice in the room against their resisting foreign threats. The village heads had not even met the Arpintonaxes, but felt the honour of Hoame itself was at stake.

Following this success, the Despot breathed a sigh of relief and the conversation moved on, first to training, then to strategy.

"I have increased the patrols on the north-eastern border," said Japhses, "but there has been no upsurge in activity on the enemy's side."

Use of the word "enemy" was, Frank hoped, premature. It was Alan who replied.

"I can't say I'm surprised. The accepted wisdom has always been that if an invasion came it would be further south, through the Mitas Gap into the plains of Bynar."

Frank said, "But surely they will want to isolate Thyatira, not drag the other despotates into it if they can help it. After all, none of the others came to our aid against Rabeth-Mephar."

"Ah, but that was different, Frank. Count Zastein won't let the others sit back this time, not against Laodicia. As soon as our latest message gets to him – oh and by the way it has gone with a good escort to make absolutely sure it gets there – he will galvanise the whole country. This is the moment he has been waiting for. The only trouble is that it will take several weeks to organise and we don't know how long we've got."

Japhses responded by saying, "We don't know, the Laodicians might hope to isolate us. If we are attacked by an overwhelming force before the other Hoamen can come to our aid, I suggest we should hold out for a siege here in the Castle. It would be easier to get the villagers here (I'm thinking mainly of the Upper Village which is nearest the border, of course. The others can withdraw to Aggeparii or Bynar."

"Can we not fortify the villages?" asked Saul, "At least make a go of it. They might be just intending to sack them before retiring to "teach us a lesson." If we put up a resistance, we could prevent it."

At this point, everyone tried to speak. Alan eventually proved the winner and backed Japhses' strategy of withdrawal to the Castle and waiting for relief. After a protracted discussion this was agreed upon and the Captain said he would get Uriah to work out contingency plans.

Finishing the last of his drink, Alan declared, "I still feel it more likely they will attack Bynar if it does come to a war. Not that we shouldn't be preparing for all eventualities. If only we had a better idea of what their plans are. What we need is better intelligence."

"What about the refugees?" asked Gideon, "what has been learnt from them?"

"Not a lot," Alan admitted.

Frank said, "They were more concerned with getting out of their country than intelligence gathering. Besides, as each day goes by, any information they may have had gets more out of date. We have been promised reports from the Mehtar, but none have come through yet – they will take days to get here anyway."

"Pah!" Luke exclaimed at the mention of the Ma'hol leader.

"I would not trust the foreigners, My Lord," warned Japhses.

"Which?" asked Frank, "The Ma'hol or the refugees?"

"Both, My Lord. The Ma'hol are only with us while it suits them. As soon as our back is turned, they will attack us again. As for the refugees, their story does not add up. I would not be surprised if they are all in a plot together, they have admitted knowing each other a long time."

There were nods of approval from the village heads as the Captain finished. He crossed his arms and leaned back on his chair, pleased with the response. Alan and Frank exchanged glances. They knew something about Japhses the others did not and although it should not have clouded their judgement in the present context, in practise it did not help his credibility in their eyes. The Despot spoke.

"I'm sorry, Japhses, but I really cannot go along with this conspiracy theory of yours. You will just have to adjust your mind to realising the Ma'hol are now our allies and the Arpintonaxes our welcome guests."

In order to curtail the uneasy silence that followed, Natias suggested they take a short break. He left the room to order more drinks while Karl nipped out to relieve himself. Japhses sat in a huff. He mumbled under his breath, "Rattinger used to listen to me."

Once the meeting had reassembled, Alan came forward with the suggestion he had been saving for the right moment.

"I think we are all agreed that what we need most is up-to-date information on what the Laodicians are doing. With this in mind I propose undertaking a spying mission across the border. I have sounded out the refugees: Warshazzap is keen to accompany me; his mistress has given her permission. They also told me that their guide is still present."

All attention was focussed on the drone. The delegates were fascinated at the prospect of their respected and admired colleague risking himself in this way. None of the whites had thought of such a plan, partly because each knew they could never go unnoticed outside their native Hoame. It was also due due to their extremely insular outlook on life, it would simply never occur to them. Frank, for all his time on the planet, was still not quite on the same wavelength.

"Aren't you going to take anyone else with you?" he asked.

Alan hesitated and looked across the table, "Although I have not mentioned it to him I was wondering if Karl might like to accompany us."

The black looked horrified at the suggestion.

"I don't want to go!" he whined.

This instant reaction took Alan aback. He thought the man might at least have considered it, but from Karl's face it was clearly not worth pursuing.

"If that's how you feel..." said Alan, trailing his sentence off. He looked up at Frank, "In that case, no, I'm not going to take anyone with me, It'll be just the three of us."

"I'd like to go."

The room suddenly went deathly quiet with everyone facing the Despot. He was joking, was he not?

"I'll go with you," Frank repeated.

From out of the shocked expressions Alan said, "I'm sorry, Frank, but you're needed here. I'll be okay, there'll be no need to endanger you, but thank you for offering."

'A fine time to discover your backbone!' thought Japhses.

"No, I mean it, I'm sure you'd rather have a second Hoaman with you. Besides I've had a sudden urge for some adventure. We won't be gone long, I'm sure; no one's expecting an attack in the next few days."

There was uproar in the room. All were horrified at the thought of their Despot endangering himself in such a way. To lead them into battle was fair enough, but this was so undignified, so unnecessary. Japhses, Natias and Saul each held the floor in turn, giving many good reasons why his place was there, the others threw in their comments at the same time. Their leader was in stubborn mood though. He had not suddenly become brave, but the thought of a little adventure had just caught his imagination. The initial pandemonium that had broken out had surprised him in its intensity, but he thought back to his talk of egalitarianism the previous day with Hannah. Unlike the other men in the room, he knew there was nothing special about him; he was no member of a God-chosen ruling class.

Natias was making an impassioned speech for Frank to change his mind, saying amongst other things that his own job would be untenable if he watched as his master leave on such a dangerous mission.

"I will have to wesign or face disgwace," he concluded.

Trying to calm the proceedings Frank assured him there would be no need to resign and that before he went, he would write out and sign a declaration saying the steward had not wanted him to go but had been overruled.

"And me!" called out several others.

In amongst the hubbub Gideon was urging Karl to change his mind, but the black did not say a word and stared down at the table.

Next it was Japhses' turn to threaten resignation. In a petulant display he brought out a year of accumulated grievances.

"There was the time you released the prisoners from the dungeon so they could rob again, the time when we captured all those Ma'hol after the battle and you would not agree to demand a ransom... you have never listened to my advice, ever since you came here. We will become the ridicule of the world if we let our leader go on a foolhardy mission and get captured or killed."

"So glad to hear you've got confidence in me," Frank said ironically. He put his hands up to restore some order to the proceedings. "Right! Now shut up the lot of you and listen."

"You did ask for opinions," Alan pointed out.

"Yes, but not in this matter I didn't," the Despot replied changing the rules. "Now, Japhses, I have every confidence in you as our Captain of the Guard..." the thought flashed through his mind that he could live to regret those words if the allegations were true... "and I will not accept your resignation. You do an excellent job and I *always* listen to any advice you give. That doesn't mean I'll always agree with it. Often I do, though, more often than you give me credit for. Anyway, I'm not going against *your* advice this time, I'm going against everyone's!"

The room had settled down by now. He continued, "The more you all try to bully me the more I feel I want to go. Maybe that's perverse, but I've made up my mind. I'm sure it'll only take one or two days over there to get an idea of what the position is."

"My Lawd."

"Yes, Natias."

"May I say something?"

The steward had seen this look in his master's face before and knew it indicated his stubborn streak was prevailing. In one last bid to make the Despot see sense he asked if they could go round the table one at a time and ask if the delegates thought it was a good idea for him to go. Frank happily agreed.

Alan, "No, I don't."

Japhses, "No."

Luke, "No, My Lord."

Saul and Gideon, "No."

Karl mumbled something incoherent, then Natias ended the count with, "I agwee with the others My Lawd, for your own safety I do not think you should go."

"It's unanimous then" Frank declared with a smile, "I'll go."

Alan tutted, Natias shook his head while Japhses expelled air through his pursed lips in exasperation. They knew they had lost the argument, or rather failed to make their Despot to see sense. He had always been a bit unconventional, but this sudden urge to go off on a dangerous, clandestine mission seemed out of character. The whites' greatest fear was the humiliation they would face if their leader came to a sticky end this way. They did at least get an assurance that as few people should know about his going as was absolutely necessary. If something did happen they might be able to cover it up.

The final segment of the meeting was a distinct anti-climax. Following the furore that had just passed, no one could find much enthusiasm to discuss other matters such as the permission received for a stone church in the Upper Village.

They drew to a close. Alan by now was resigned to Frank going with him, foolish though he thought the idea. Before they broke up, he told the black he would have a word with Warshazzap about the planned mission and get the guide to accompany them.

"What's all this nonsense!" Despot Kagel growled, thrusting the sheet of paper back at his aide.

"I have you that first, Sir, so that you would see the documents in the correct order," the man explained carefully.

"What do you make of this then, Chancellor?"

Aggeparii's leaders were in an ante-chamber to the main conference room of the castle. Despot, Chancellor, aides and counsellors filled the floor, blacks and drones all with their special duties. Through the windows the first shy stars could be seen appearing as night fell.

Kagel had just come home from a three day hunting expedition. He was in poor mood having not caught a single charider and gained multiple bruises from a couple of nasty falls. To return tired and worn and find himself embroiled in what looked like being a protracted meeting with his advisors did nothing to improve his state of mind.

The Chancellor replied, "I suggest you look at the other communication we have received Sir."

Making a grunt, the Despot put out his hand for the aide to pass it to him.

"Don't see why the hell we should help them," he grumbled, "a religious nut in charge of a whole load of chalkies, or is it the other way round? Oh!"

The letter from the Keepers put rather a different perspective on things. While the others waited, he read through it slowly a second time.

"Why the hell didn't you tell me about this before? This puts a whole different light on things man! This one from the Count is dated before Thorn's; has Zastein got second sight or something?"

Taking a deep breath, the Chancellor explained, "Despot Thorn has been good enough to keep us abreast of the situation, Sir. This is only the latest in a line of reports that have been sent to us. If you remember you told me you were not interested in seeing them. Clearly he has also kept the Inner Council well informed."

A young white servant-girl had been let into the room. Nervously she approached Despot Kagel. Once the Chancellor had finished she quietly said, "My Lord, if it please you, your bath is ready. You asked me to tell you as soon..."

"What?" Kagel shouted, scowling down at the timid girl, "I haven't got time for that now, go away!"

All ignored the servant as she slunk away, tears welling up in her eyes. The Despot asked the Chancellor where their Colonel-in-Chief was.

"He retired to his room early, Sir, with a migraine."

Kagel would have got the man up straight away had not his advisers persuaded him to wait until morning.

"Hmph, I suppose you're right. I want to be woken early tomorrow, this takes preference over everything. I want Justin... where's that drone?"

"He has gone to bed early as well, Sir," an aide explained.

"Not with the Colonel-in-chief I hope."

They all laughed, then Kagel dissolved the assemblage.

"Tomorrow we prepare for mobilization. Now is bath-time. You're all dismissed, where's that damn white girl gone?"

Back in Thyatira there was a day's delay due to the guide's insistence he needed a little more time to be fully fit. Frank sat around his bedroom after lunch on the day following the meeting. He was feeling at a loose end, wanting to get on with it.

That morning he had discussed strategy with Alan and Warshazzap. Ladosa's main city and centre of government was far from the border. In view of this, they had decided to make for the second city Laybbon which would mean being on hostile soil nearer a week than the couple of days originally envisaged. They would try to find out what exactly was going on while attempting to gauge the mood of the people as well.

The bodyguard told them he had never been where they were heading so they would have to rely heavily on their guide. Neither Alan nor Frank had yet met the guide and would in fact not do so until they actually left together. Warshazzap said he had only known him since their flight from Ladosa, but there was no reason to doubt his trustworthiness. The others hoped he was right.

Frank decided to go up to the roof and get full benefit from the warm afternoon sun. The scenery might take his mind off things. He found another person already taking in the view.

"Hannah, hello. I haven't seen you or your mother all day."

"No," she replied, the look on her face belying her stern tone. "My mother thinks you have been deliberately avoiding us."

"Why should I do that?" he asked innocently.

"Why indeed. Just a little matter of an envoy from our country."

"Aah, yes."

Sounding hurt she asked why they had not been told. "We're not children Frank, do we not have a right to know what is being done in our name? We were already acutely aware that we might bring trouble down on your heads, now it seems that is just what is happening! I've half a mind to suggest to mother that we go back of our own accord, get..."

"No no no!" Frank exclaimed, "certainly not. We're not going to let them push us around. You're right, we should have kept you informed. The trouble is we are not at all certain what their next move will be; whether they really will attack us or if it's a bluff. I suppose we should have asked for your opinion, but you yourself told me you cannot predict what these new men in power will do."

"If our party activists have risen up throughout the country they may feel forced to play their "foreign threat" card to stave off internal dissension. One of our contingency plans was for our people to set about widespread strikes and disruption to force the government down. I wonder if this would have the opposite effect now."

"It's very strange hearing you talk like this, it's all so different here, I can't imagine Japhses organising disruption in the villages!"

His guffaw might not have been so genuine had he known of the plans Eleazar's anti-war party were devising. Glancing down to the bailey, he noticed the huge stockpile of arrows being formed in one corner and hoped they would not be required.

Hannah then made reference to the reconnaissance mission being undertaken to her homeland. She knew the identity of three of the participants and he decided to tell her the fourth.

'Rather this,' he thought, 'than face a second charge of keeping them in the dark at a later date. Always supposing I get back that is.'

She was highly flattered and not a little impressed. Frank felt good as she spoke of the bravery he was showing.

"...You're putting your life on the line for us! I feel humbled. There I was earlier haranguing you for not keeping us informed, never realising you were about to risk your life for us. Whatever you do don't let them take you alive. They do not stop at torture and are utterly without pity. They are not always well organised though, so if you remain inconspicuous you do stand a chance.

He winced, "Can't you go back to the bit about bravery? I much preferred that to this "life on the line" business."

They laughed and she squeezed his arm affectionately which took him by surprise.

"I think I'd better start getting ready," he informed her.

Hannah still had a smile on her face and her eyes sparkled as they looked up at him. She moved forward to kiss his lips just as Frank turned to go downstairs. The moment was lost. Down and round the spiral staircase they went. Belatedly he realised what she had tried to do. He cursed himself for being so slow. But it was too late now.

Politely they said goodbye and Frank went to his suite to prepare himself for the dangerous task ahead.

Darkness fell as the travellers assembled in the bailey. Guards held lamps for them as they put on their provision-filled backpacks. Rolled blankets were also strapped on. Karl, Japhses and Natias were there to see them off, but first Warshazzap had some introducing to do.

"Dirkin this is Despot Thorn; this is Dirkin our guide."

"Do I call ya "Despot"?"

Frank was not sure if the man was joking. Remaining serious he suggested they each call him by his Christian name.

"My Lord, may I just say something?"

Japhses looked uneasy. The big man hesitated before saying, "keep safe, My Lord."

In the flickering light of the lamp he had said more with his eyes than his mouth. Frank patted him gently on the arm and assured him he would try his utmost to do so.

The Despot then exchanged goodbyes with Natias who was trying to put a brave face on the situation. His last farewell was with Karl.

"I... I'm sorry Sir that I did not want to go. Only it's my wife, she would have hated it if I had gone. She gets very nervous you see, Sir, brings her out..."

"It's all right Karl, I understand, you don't have to explain. I'm glad you said no," he added cheerfully, "I wanted to go."

They then both went to speak at once and stopped.

"You go first," said Frank.

With a frown Karl replied, "I don't know what I was going to say, Sir... no it's completely gone. It will have to wait."

"Until I get back, you mean."

"That's right, Sir,"

"Good, it's nice to leave on an optimistic note."

Alan by this time had said his goodbyes and the adventurers set out into the night led by Dirkin holding a lamp. As they left the bailey, cold chills went down Franks' spine. He had volunteered for this escapade; if what Hannah said was true he could end up getting more than he bargained for.

None of the four spoke as they hit the trail to the north. The others went as far as the gate and then peered until the blackness swallowed the last flicker of Dirkin's lamp.

CHAPTER TWENTY EIGHT

The four men stuck to the narrow track leading to the Ladosan border. Dirkin led, followed by Warshazzap, then Alan, Frank took up the rear. Soon they were in the forest. It was so dark it was not possible to see a hand in front of one's face, but their guide, using the feeble light from his lamp, never faltered.

They made their way to a guard-post at the edge of a small clearing just inside Hoame territory. A pair of torches burned steadily outside the log construction. A sentry challenged the party in good time and was immediately put at ease by Alan. The drone went inside with Dirkin, while the other pair waited by some trees. Frank did not speak, the last thing he wanted was to be recognised. As far as he was aware his participation in this mission was only known of by a small group of people who would be making every effort to cover up for his absence.

Inside the guard-post squad leader Jonathan informed them it was a quiet evening.

"No activity at all," he reported, our latest patrol just in confirms it."

"Is that unusual?" Alan asked.

"Not at all, quite normal."

Thus reassured, they turned down an offer of an escort and the quartet began trudging up the slope by themselves. The lamp had been extinguished and it was pitch black. This was no-man's land where both countries patrolled. Up and up they went. Although the pass was well below the mountain tops it was still a steep rise from the border. The air turned cooler and Frank was puffing already. His body felt hot while his face and hands were chilled. The weight of his pack felt enormous, but he could not complain, because the rest seemed to be managing comfortably. He loosened his clothing around his collar to let some cold air in.

The pace was kept up and no one talked. No one that is until Frank almost fell. He stumbled badly in the darkness and did not manage to hold his balance. The others had not heard and marched on regardless. Getting up and shifting his pack Frank hurried to catch up.

"How does he manage to see in this?" he asked Alan, "I'm completely blind!"

"Hush! Not now," Dirkin hissed from the front.

The guide was of course right, This was the most crucial part, crossing over the border region. They carried on in silence. After a while a whispered command to hug the left was passed back. Feeling the rock-face with one hand, Frank guessed correctly there was a sharp drop on the other. The sound of shale cascading down on his right side confirmed his fear. They went on like this for what seemed like a lifetime until the pathway widened and the all-clear was given.

The next section of the pass was strewn with boulders, the travellers climbed on all-fours. Frank was struggling. He felt the perspiration on his forehead turn cold and took in great gulps of air. Just when he thought he could take no more, the going levelled off and then began a gentle downwards slope.

It was midnight when they stopped. The guide informed them that they were safely through the border area and that he proposed they halt here for the rest of the night. No one was going to argue. Frank just had enough energy to unfold his blanket and cover himself up. He was asleep before his head had touched the ground.

"C'mon you lot, can't spend all day here!"

Dirkin stood with his hands on his hips surveying the other three as they awoke. Stretches, yawns and groans abounded.

"I thought I was the one not fully fit," he declared, "just look at ya all."

Frank rubbed his eyes and looked about. He felt stiff, but happy that they had made it across the border safely.

"So this is Laodicia," he announced, continuing to survey his immediate surroundings.

They had spent the night in a clump of pine trees. There was a dip in the ground where they lay, so it was not possible to see beyond. Brown pine-needles covered the ground which was naked of vegetation in the immediate area. The sun was rising, its light flickering between the gently swaying branches.

Alan and Warshazzap conducted a quick scout around making sure it was safe. Frank washed his face with a small amount of water from the canteen he had been carrying. He then held up a hand-mirror as he combed his hair. As he did so he observed their guide for the first time.

Dirkin was a small man with a balding head and thick, black eyebrows which met in the middle. With shoulders small and rounded his weak-looking appearance hid great stamina. He speedily unpacked and set up the cooking utensils, glancing up at intervals to see if the others were returning. Every now and then he would hawk and spit into the trees.

"It's fine," reported Alan who had suddenly reappeared, "no one for kilometres… as far as the eye can see, in fact."

The meal was got under way by the guide, who refused Warshazzap's offer of help. Lighting a fire, the sticks cracked loudly and gave off a most distinctive smell. Bean stew, it tasted good. Binsted berries and cream for pudding was a treat, but there was only enough for one helping each. Not much was said as they ate. Frank was not the slightest bit hungry that early in the morning. However he made sure he ate it all up, because they did not plan on having another proper meal until the end of the day. Chewing his last mouthful he felt the small pouch at his side. This contained the tiny gold bars which they planned to exchange for local currency once in town.

We'll be getting' under way soon," the pathfinder warned as he began packing the utensils away again. "I wanna make good progress today y'know."

"How long until we reach Laybbon?" Frank enquired.

Dirkin did not cease packing and tidying up as he replied, "We got three days travellin' ahead of us. I know a cosy place we can head for t'day, with luck we can be in Wesold by the end of t'morrow. Laybbon the day after – y'know?"

Everyone ready, they hitched up their back-packs and set off. Emerging from the trees a flat, yellow-green landscape came to view. The odd few trees were dotted about, but there was no sign of life or habitation. The mountains behind them made a spectacular backdrop as they progressed along the rough track which proved the country was not totally deserted. The pace Dirkin set was steady, but not too fast.

"Big country Ladosa y'know," he explained, "Lotsa people, but not many near the border, specially here in Sector Five."

Alan came alongside him.

"I heard the country was split into sectors, are these administrative areas?"

"S'pose so," the guide answered not sounding very interested.

Instead, Alan turned to Warshazzap.

"Will we be going near where you live?"

"No, not at all. This is Sector Five, and we will travel through Four – Wesold's in Four – on to Two where Laybbon is situated. I'm from Sector Eight over to the west. It borders on Four, but I've never been to Wesold before. Never travelled much at all until a fortnight ago."

A voice from the rear called out. "We could have had our villages called One, Two and Three, that would've been easy to remember!"

Alan returned the grin before turning back to Warshazzap.

"How long have you known the Arpintonaxes?"

"I've known them by sight ever since I was a kid. I became a party member some years back, but I've only been directly in their employ a couple of years. Mind you, they've been eventful years!"

They walked on, the path skirting the occasional spinney. A sharp eye was kept out for signs of life, but no people were spotted at all that morning. By the time the sun had climbed to its zenith the water in their canteens was running low. Dirkin said he was especially concerned that they did not run into any army patrols.

"We ain't sure what these travel restrictions are like, and besides some units can be a rabble, y'know? Rob ya and say it's all for the good of the government. The officers are just as bad as the men."

The words were no sooner out of his mouth than they rounded a bend to find a group of soldiers resting in the shade of some trees. It was too late to double-back. The guide hesitated and glanced round at his party, but none needed telling what to do. Without a word they picked up their step and carried on. The soldiers were lolling around on the ground, they were either finishing, or had just finished their lunch. They took a mild interest as the travellers passed. Several sets of eyes tracked their progress, but nothing was said.

Alan and Frank for their part were fascinated at the first sight of their potential enemy's fighting men, although they tried to observe from the corner of their eye and not stare.

A few men lay back in the sun, their faces soaking up its rays. Most were in the shade either laying down or sitting in other casual positions. Their scruffy apparel matched their lazy demeanour. No armour was apparent, in fact it was hard to discern a uniform. Each was dressed differently, although brown leather trousers appeared a popular theme. Similarly, not many weapons were in evidence, just the odd four-metre pike stuck into the ground. A partially furled-up battle flag lay propped up against a boulder, its orange and yellow colours clearly visible.

Their commander was sitting quite near the path by himself, sucking at what looked like a twig. His outfit was only marginally better than his men's. He too watched in a half-interested manner as the four men went by.

"G'd afternoon," Dirkin greeted him. A grunt was issued in response, but that was fine with the travellers. Once past, they kept up the pace and did not dare look back until they were a good distance away.

"Well they didn't seem too bothered by our presence," said Frank once they were safely out of earshot.

"They didn't," Alan agreed, "maybe things aren't as bad as we've been led to believe."

After that they began to pass a few hamlets and the occasional small village. The houses were of a similar style to those of Hoame, except that the roofs were taller and tended to have exaggeratedly large lintels with much carved decorations. The people smiled and appeared friendly enough, but the travellers pushed on.

"Which part of the country do you come from?" Frank asked their guide.

"Me? I ain't a Ladosan, I'm a Slan y'know."

Warshazzap helped out, "A nomadic tribe that lives more in Sarnice than Ladosa, but there are a fair few in the cold northern regions."

"I see; well what made you come down this way?"

Totally ignoring the question Dirkin spat at the ground and said, "I ain't 'aving us staying in one of the villages y'know. I got a place lined up in some woods further on, but we'll 'ave to walk quicker if we're going to get there 'fore nightfall."

It proved to be as he said. Just as the sun was setting they entered a small wood and were led to a tiny clearing in the heart of it. Dirkin had been here many times before, because it offered privacy and the luxury of a spring. Any water would have tasted good to the thirsty men, but this was sheer nectar. Eagerly they drank.

From his previous visits, he had built a shelter, but the weather was dry, warm and still that night and it was not required. By the light of a camp fire they ate bean stew and rested their feet. Another day's walk would see them in Wesold, they were right on schedule. Frank took his boots off as he settled down for the night, he was pleased at how he was bearing up. Dirkin was older than him, but used to walking great distances. So far he was enjoying the adventure he concluded, falling asleep with a smile on his face.

It was still inky black when Frank awoke, but he felt fully refreshed (if a little stiff) and concluded sunrise could not be far away. Dawn was a quick affair on Molten and before he knew it it was light. Not wanting to disturb the others, he crept out of the camp and went to take the view. Emerging from the trees he noticed how heavy the dew was on the ground. He just caught a glimpse of a young frass which, startled by his presence, bounded into the long grass. In the distance streaks of mist hung just above the ground, soon to be burned off by the rising sun. He gave an enormous stretch and returned to the others.

Back in amongst the trees the others were well awake and breakfast was being prepared. Warshazzap was filling the canteens from the spring while Alan was cleaning the blade of a vicious-looking knife he carried, its blade a good thirty centimetres long.

"Morning everyone, it's a beautiful morning out there, I think it's going to be another sunny day."

Alan looked up from his work and replied in a cheerful voice, "You're really enjoying this trip, aren't you. I think I understand now why you were so bloody determined to come!"

In response, Frank gave an enigmatic face and they sat down to eat together.

Before long all was packed up and they were on the trail again. Following their guide the three chatted amiably as they hiked their way across the foreign land, having the incentive of a proper bed and shelter that evening if they made Wesold. They made a stop midday after having found some shade, but the weather was showing signs of change after the warm morning.

"Starting to cloud over," Warshazzap observed, "could have rain before we finish today."

The Hoamen agreed. Dirkin was too busy coughing up phlegm to join in the conversation on the weather. He gave a big spit and announced with triumph, "That's a good one!" at the result. The others pretended not to notice.

Good progress continued throughout the afternoon and with some time to spare before sundown they passed over a long, high ridge overlooking the small town of Wesold. That day's goal in sight, they began the descent.

"Well the rain held off, Warshazzap."

"Yes, I'm glad I was wrong."

Alan asked Dirkin, "Will we be staying in a hostel?"

"Hell no! Me brother-in-law's place, didn't I tell ya?"

The high street was wide with identical looking shops on either side. These were tall, covered in thin, graitwood slats and again the large, decorated lintels. All were closed for the night. The four of them proceeded through the merchants' quarter, which did not have many people in it early evening. A few hurried past on their way home, while one or two shop-keepers were still securing their premises. Dirkin exchanged a swift greeting with a man who was stacking empty boxes round the side of his shop. The next building was larger than most and had dull-looking flags flying from its roof. Warshazzap sneered at the sight. The foreigners had it explained to them that this was the local Buff party headquarters. They did not slow down.

Streets got narrower and the town's character changed as the men got to the residential area. A brief break in the clouds found the sun low over the roof-tops. Just as fatigue was start-ing to bite, they arrived at their destination and were let into a modest-sized house. Heaving sighs of relief, the visitors sank into cushioned chairs and pulled their boots off.

It turned out that Dirkin's brother-in-law Volatailisus was by himself, his wife and seven children were staying with her mother for a few days. This was giving Vol, as he was known, a welcome break. He did not seen unduly bothered at receiving the unexpected guests, however, seeming to accept the brief explanation of them being "friends from the east." In fact, he was a great talker and they learned some useful information from him that evening in-between listening to a lot of dross.

There being no women present to prepare their meal Frank asked if one could be brought in. He was earnestly informed by his host that this would be "genderism" and while the term meant nothing to the Hoamen, he sat quietly while Dirkin went into the kitchen to do it.

The internal walls were plastered and fairly smooth as a result. They had a clean appearance except for the damp patches starting to show in the corners.

"Mmm, that wasn't bad," said Alan licking his fingers after finishing his pork chop. It was nice to have a change from bean stew.

Dirkin came in and sat down after having cleared everything up. He quickly fell asleep in the corner allowing the others to pump Vol for information without inhibition. Alan and Frank sat at the table chatting to him. Warshazzap sat back a little way off and let them get on with it.

The guide's brother-in-law was also a Slan, although he was now permanently settled in Wesold. A tubby, joyful and loquacious man, he kept a keen interest in events while apparently giving no loyalty to any party.

"I think they're all as bad as each other," he declared. "You've chosen a queer time to visit your friends in Laybbon, but then things have settled down now I suppose. Besides if you arranged this reunion a long time ago you've got to stick to it haven't you. At least you can get around the countryside without too much bother now."

Frank said, "So it's true the travel restrictions have been relaxed."

"Oh yes, there's no need for them now. That's how my wife was able to go and stay in Sector Eleven, she couldn't go before. Funny really, the first day without the little terrors, it was heaven; peace and quiet at last. No more running, fighting, shouting – I was able to get on and do things. They'd only been gone a couple of days though when I began to miss them. Now I'm looking forward to them coming back, place seems empty without them."

"I'm sure it does," agreed Frank. Showing no finesse, he brought the conversation straight back to the part which concerned the mission. "Why have they eased the travel restrictions now? I thought there was supposed to be some sort of a crisis on at present."

"I wouldn't say that. There was some trouble after the election with the purples, they..."

"Ah!" Frank interrupted, "now that's the Arpintonaxes."

"You know about them?"

"Er, not a lot, but we have heard of them."

"They haven't got much of a following around here, but I gather that there was some fuss over in Sector Eight. All that's come to nothing."

Warshazzap's ears pricked up, but he did not say anything. Alan tried to find out what else was common knowledge.

"We heard one rumour that their leaders had fled the country, do you know if that's true?"

"Rumours? Ha ha, there's no shortage of them! This one's probably true 'cos what I've heard people say, the purples have been disbanded. I heard one man saying all their activists are either jailed or scattered to the wind. Probably a good thing to have one less political party, there are so many of them. People say give these Buffs a chance to see what they can do. They're not bad. They've raised taxes now they're in, but they all do that. Can't take their promises at all seriously neither..."

While he spoke Frank considered all that Hannah had told him. All her hopes of a popular uprising seemed to have come to nothing if what this observer said was true. Warshazzap was hunched up in his chair, he was depressed at the news. It would be interesting to see what the people in Laybbon had to say. When the regional capital was mentioned Vol was scornful.

"Huh! That's the *talking* capital. It's a Buff stronghold, they're always having rallies there. Plus debates: they pride themselves on being able to blah-blah all day long. Talk, talk, talk on any subject you care to mention; talk and no action, that's Laybbon."

'You would fit in well,' thought Frank as he asked, "From what you have said it could be a place of influence?"

The tubby man hesitated.

"That *may* be so. The actual seat of government moves around the country. It was just here last week I think it was. Now they've moved on, things have settled down a bit.

"Is that someone at the door?"

The house-owner left the room to see, leaving his guests to urgently speculate.

Alan whispered, "That's how they were able to send their message to us, the government was in the area near the border."

"Yes, I thought that when he said it," Frank concurred.

"There's no sign of impending war," added Warshazzap, "everything seems calm. Should we ask?"

The Hoamen looked less than pleased at the idea, not knowing how far they could trust Vol. He had seemed happy to talk with them up to that point, but they did not want to test their luck with too many sensitive questions and arouse his suspicions. The question hung in the air as the man returned.

"Just a neighbour returning a tool I lent him. What were we talking about? Ah yea, the travelling circus. No, I shouldn't call them that even if they do ask for it at times. They were jabbering on about going to war against that uncivilised rabble south of the mountains. All the fuss and noise they make. Complete nonsense I call it.

"Ah, Dirkin, you're awake. Pull up a chair, I want to show you my new acquisitions."

Taking his would-be interrogators by surprise, Vol then got out a small, wooden chest from a corner of the room and proceeded to show them his extensive collection of shells. He informed them they came from the Great North Sea and contained several rare specimens. With great relish he went through them one by one, showing an in-depth knowledge of the subject. This was in spite of the fact that he had not been further north than the adjoining Sector Two since he was a boy. He had built up his collection mainly through purchases from travellers or dealers and showed such enthusiasm over them that his listeners found themselves taking an interest in spite of themselves. This was apart from Dirkin who had heard most of it before.

So just as Alan, Frank and Warshazzap thought they were getting the vital information they had come for, the moment was lost. Before they settled down for the night in the bedroom allocated them the three managed to have a longer, hushed conversation on what Vol had said. The man's scoffing attitude towards his government, plus the apparent lack of tension made them wonder if they were on a fools' errand. They decided not to draw too many conclusions for now and reserved judgement until after they had explored Laybbon. They got to bed late.

In contrast with the previous morning, they slept in. Frank was still dead to the world after everyone else had surfaced. His eyes were bobbing about in his head as Alan gently shook his shoulder.

"Eh, what? Oh I was right in the middle of a dream!"

He began to sit up and saw Warshazzap doing up the strap of his shoes. The Ladosan had a broad grin across his face as he called out, "How do you know it was the middle of the dream if you never finished it?"

Frank rubbed his eyes and looked distinctly unamused, "Are you always so clever this time in the morning?"

A concerned Alan stared down at his friend with the blood-shot eyes and asked if he was okay.

"Thanks, I'll be fine if you just give me a moment. I just don't like being woken from a dream, middle or otherwise."

"'Cos you've been doing well until now."

"For my age you mean? Thank you," Frank said sarcastically before he caught the other's eye and could not keep a straight face.

Alan laughed, "So this is what Illianeth has to put up with in the mornings! The poor girl."

Frank half-heartedly launched a boot in his direction and missed.

Breakfast was soon over and having packed up their things they said goodbye to Vol, giving him a healthy tip. Before they left the town, Warshazzap successfully exchanged most of their gold for local currency and then hired a cart and eight dakks. That day's journey was only about half the distance they had travelled each of the previous two, but to be able to put their feet up was sheer luxury. Throughout the day, the dakks ambled on. Dirkin held the reins, but as they were merely following the road he did not have a lot to do.

The scenery was little changed, flat grassland and groups of trees. They had not had rain for some time and everything looked faded and dusty. This included the berries in the roadside bushes which they thought about picking before changing their minds. Their first proper stop was soon after midday when they crossed a shallow ford.

Warshazzap read an old, battered sign by the side of the road: "Sector Two. This is the ford Modold on the river Trad, named after the m."

"What's an "em"?" Alan enquired.

"Dunno, the corner's been smashed off, we'll never know."

The dakks plodded through the stream at the bottom of the wide, largely dried-up river bed. Once on the other side, the adventurers halted and got down to fill their canteen and generally stretch their legs. Dirkin and Warshazzap led the unharnessed animals back to the stream for a drink.

A small group of travelling players passed in the opposite direction in a pair of brightly decorated wagons. They exchanged cordial greetings.

"Everyone seems very friendly," remarked Frank to Alan once they had got going again, "Handy that we speak the same language too."

Alan nodded before standing to peer up the road ahead. "Dirkin, is that Laybbon I can see in the distance?"

"It is y'know."

"I thought it must be," he added more quietly sitting back down. "This is what we've waited for eh Frank?"

"Yes, we'll discover if this is all a wild goose chase or not."

Warshazzap said, "This is a funny expression, I haven't heard that one before."

"Yeah, he comes out with them from time to time, I just ignore him now."

Alan gave Frank a friendly shove and they laughed. If nothing else came of this mission the three men in the back would be closer because of it.

Mid-afternoon, they hit busy Laybbon. The foreigners looked around in silence at the scene. They were not sure if it was a special market day or it was always like this. Street vendors abounded, calling out their wares. Some had large stalls selling woven carpets or basket work. People jostled one another in the frenzy.

Their guide knew exactly where to take them and led the cart through the clamorous streets to the inn. It was a tall, wood-frame building with small windows and situated near the centre of town. The ground-floor reception room was dim and small in size, floor space having been given up for extra guest-rooms. The landlord and lady were a young, friendly couple. She was heavily pregnant and walked with a waddle. After introducing themselves, they went through the rules of the house.

"Y'can buy y'drinks here, but y'must either take them upstairs or outside to consume. We haven't the space here as y'can see. There's the Selerm across the road if y'want to drink sociably... or debate, it's known as the wind house. Debta will see to y'cart an' dakks. I'll take you to y'rooms."

They were led to the first floor and two rooms, each with a minimum of furniture and threadbare rug over the floorboards. They were at the back of the building, insulated from the street noises. Frank would naturally have gravitated towards being with Alan, but from the order in which they went upstairs he found himself in with Dirkin.

The four of them got settled, then they had an impromptu parley on what to do next.

Warshazzap said, "Alan and I want to go and have a quick look round the town, see what we can discover. We can all go."

"Ya can go. I'm gonna have a drink y'know? I need a drink. Ya go ahead."

"Frank?"

"Actually I think I'll take a rest. I'll come out this evening when we've had something to eat. You two go by all means, let me know what you find out."

All appeared happy with these arrangements. Once by himself, Frank pulled his boots off and, propping his back up on the wall, lay on the bed. He tried to doze, but found he could not, because he was not particularly tired. After a while, he reached down to his back-pack beside the bed and took out a biscuit to chew. Had he been back at the Castle he would have pulled his large Bible out and begun reading it. In the stillness it dawned on him that he had not said a single prayer since the evening they had set out. It was a terrible thing to admit, but he did not find the time for God these days. He hoped God would find time for him. Finishing his biscuit, he slipped gently off the bed and knelt beside it.

He was still in this position when the door swung open and Dirkin waltzed back in, glass in one hand, half-empty bottle in the other. Frank had not thought the man long gone, but he was well intoxicated.

Upon spying his room-mate the guide let out an enormous belch and offered a drink. Frank declined, alarmed that the man could get drunk so quickly, the security of their entire enterprise might be risked by such a weakness. He got back onto his bed while Dirkin staggered past to his and slumped down onto it.

"What ya lookin' at me like that for?"

Frank flushed and averted his eyes without saying anything.

"Too good for m'company are ya? Mister Despot!"

His whole tone had turned distinctly nasty. Not wanting to antagonise him, Frank remained silent, fixing his stare on the wall over by the door. It did not stop an abusive tirade. Dirkin's animosity towards Hoame came as a shock to his listener. The drink was loosening his tongue and bottled-up resentment poured forth.

"...There ya all go with ya beautifully worked out hierarchy: ya blacks, ya whites, ya drones y'know. Two different peoples existing together an' trying t'make out it's working well for all. Dakk's crap! When ya an' ya kind arrived they saw the whites as easy pickin's an' herded the poor devils t'gether like sheep y'know. Ya use the whites t'... t'... whenever ya want them ya use them. Not even the same species."

'What?!' thought Frank looking round with a puzzled expression. He had tried to turn off without much success. To have walked out would have been to admit defeat, he had wanted to portray an air of superiority to it all.

The drunk man took another swig from the bottle. It was a very gaseous liquid and he gave another loud belch. He carried on at length in a similar vein much to Frank's disgust.

Footsteps. The other two had returned. As they entered the room Frank shot from his bed and stepped up quickly to greet them. In his relief he almost hugged Alan. Quickly assessing the situation, Warshazzap gently took the bottle from the unprotesting Dirkin and led him outside to sober up. Frank was surprised at how meekly he went. It was as if he had finished his protest and had nothing further to say.

Alan asked what had been going on and was given a quick resume. He dismissed it with a shrug and then said what they had discovered.

"Yeah we took a good walk round the town... oh, before I go on I must just mention something the landlady just told us. We can't have a bath, 'cos the water is rationed. Still, it's not as if we're going to be here very long.

"Anyway, there were loads of Buff flags everywhere, much to Warshazzap's disgust! It seems this is indeed a stronghold of the ruling party. The most important thing is that there's going to be a major political rally here in two days time; Warshazzap and I feel we should stay to hear its outcome."

"Fine."

"Found out about this in the "Selerm" across the road. It appears to be a kind of community hut used for drinking and gossiping. Much bigger in scale of course. Clearly this is the place we should frequent if we want to find out information. We were told that long debates take place there most evenings with it getting very crowded. We got in for free just now, but you have to pay then they said. Everyone we spoke to seemed okay, not at all cagey. Best that we take a low profile if we go there, let the Laodicians do the talking and learn from them if we can."

"A low profile, yes that's the best idea, I agree. So you think we've come to the right place to find out what we want."

"As far as I can gather. Ah yes, there was one other important thing I must tell you: they mentioned Hoame and the ultimatum sent there. The people here said it was sent by the *local* government of Sector whatever-it-is, in the hope that the central government would support it."

"Have they?"

"Not certain. From what one man said they will be annoyed, 'cos they didn't want it handled that way. It..."

"That's fantastic! Frank interrupted enthusiastically, "you've found out so much all ready."

Alan was keeping his feet firmly on the ground.

"I'm not sure how much we can trust this information. It had more a feel of idle gossip about it than hard fact. And, if you remember, this contradicts what Vol told us about their government moving about from one town to another."

"Oh yes, you're right. Had they heard of such a thing?"

"No."

They would have to keep their minds open until such time as more reliable information was available. It was all so different from what Frank had expected. Instead of trying to glean snippets it was going to be a sifting exercise from a mass of chatter.

After a while, heavy footsteps approached along the corridor. It was Warshazzap carrying the unconscious Dirkin over his shoulder. He entered the room and heaved his load down on the bed like a sack of hulffan fibre.

"You didn't knock him out, did you?" Frank asked looking concerned.

Warshazzap shook his head as he watched the lifeless figure.

"I didn't have to, his legs collapsed from under him as soon as we got outside. Put him on a bench. Eventually I thought I should bring him in.

"Seen him like this before, wouldn't take what he says too personally. He likes his alcohol, but it has this effect on him. Just leave him, he will sleep it off and be grand afterwards. Oh and if it's like before, he will wake up and remember absolutely nothing."

Alan and Frank decided to follow his advice and together they left to go downstairs for an early evening meal. The room was crammed and the rabbit pie tasted a bit strange, but a delicious desert and the friendly demeanour of the landlord more than made up for this. Frank drank practil juice while the other two shared a bottle of "washti", a local wine with a low alcohol content. By the time it was over, they were keen to get across the road to the Selerm and see what they could find out.

This was Frank's first time to the hub of Laybbon's social life. The building was huge, converted from old warehouses. Whitewashed brick walls and rows of small windows. Customers had to pay a hefty fee at this time of day to get in, but one drink each was included in the price. The main room was massive and had retained the original high ceiling. It had been decorated recently and long, colourful friezes, some of them erotic in theme, stretched across the walls. The ceiling was a dull white and clusters of oil lamps hanged down from long cables.

The would-be spies entered and stood just inside the entrance. A few of the tables dotted about the room had people seated around them, but many were yet to be occupied. There was plenty of space between the tables while a long, empty stage snaked its way down the middle.

Alan said, "There were many more people here earlier."

An employee who over heard the remark guessed correctly that these were strangers and explained that it would soon be getting full.

"We have a break late afternoon," he explained cordially, "this is just the beginning of the evening session, the fashionable time to be here. It'll soon get crowded, so if you want a proper seat you'd be wise to take one now. The bar's over there where you can collect your drinks."

After thanking him, Frank remarked, "Must be a wealthy man who owns all of this."

"It is a woman, in fact, Sir; she built the Salerm up to what it is today. But if you'll excuse me I must be getting on."

They found a table in the centre of the room and settled down there. Warshazzap got the drinks and they sat and watched the trickle of people entering.

"Remember," said Frank, "we must blend in, not give ourselves away."

It was hardly necessary to point this out to his colleagues, but they held their tongues. Glancing at the empty chair at their table, he continued, "I don't suppose Dirkin knows we are here."

"Don't worry about him," advised Warshazzap, "he'll take a good time to sleep that off. Strange man, but indispensable to us at present I'm afraid."

Their table was nearer the wall than the stage upon which a young man was rehearsing a song with the help of another man and a woman. None of the growing number of people entering was paying much attention to the rehearsal.

"This is not like my home sector at all. A few of us used to gather round to discuss farming matters, but there are no entertainment halls like this. This is the sort of silly, idle world the Buffs want to bring about."

Frank was in good spirits. He enthused, "Everyone seems so friendly and sociable, they hardly seem like a people about to go to war. I'm really looking forward to this evening, it's going to be interesting to see what it's like."

As he spoke, a prostitute wondered lazily over to their table. Not as young as she once was she wore a short, tight-fitting dress, the top of which exaggerated her cleavage. Long, nicely-shaped legs ended in red high-heeled shoes. Frank only noticed her as she sat down uninvited in the spare chair at their table.

"Which one of you handsome men is going to buy me a drink?" she enquired.

Alan and Warshazzap stared daggers at her, but with complete innocence, Frank gave her a warm smile and said cheerfully, "I'll be happy to get one for you."

Slowly and deliberately, Alan said, "Go away!"

His tone froze Frank in his tracks as he was reaching for his purse. He was still in this pose when Warshazzap backed up the command to the woman saying, "You heard the man, get lost!"

Weighing up the situation in that instant, she stuck her nose up in the air and left, mumbling a few words of abuse.

A quiet, expectant face looked across at Alan waiting for an explanation.

"You *do* know what she is, don't you?"

Frank thought for a moment then, "Ah, you mean she's an alcoholic!"

The other pair gave a loud groan, then laughed.

"No, you great... she's a prostitute!" Alan hissed, trying not to be too loud.

"Oh!" exclaimed Frank with surprise, "really? How interesting. Well I never knew, I've never really met one before."

A group of female singer/dancers began a sexually provocative act on the stage, some distance away from where they were sitting. The audience close to it were cheering and guffawing, clearly enjoying the performance.

People were now pouring into the Saelerm. The spare chair was commandeered by a large, loud group of youths and young women who landed like a swarm of bees at the large table next to them.

Yet more hoards arrived and sat around on tables and the floor once all the chairs were in use. The employee had been right about it getting crowded. Inevitably, they encroached on the trio, but if they wanted to gauge to mood in Ladosa, they were certainly getting in amongst the people!

The gabble of tongues reached fever pitch, they could neither see nor hear the stage act now. Leaning over and speaking just loud enough to be heard by Alan, Frank said, "We're not going to learn a lot in this din!"

"No," agreed the other, "but let's leave it a while and see."

Alan and Warshazzap sat silently amid the noise fingering their three-quarters empty glasses. Frank, who was nearest the youthful group, turned his chair round to hear more of what was being said. Strange nicknames came forth: "Brooster", "Spike", "Slick" and for the young women "Wandy" and "Cleesa" appeared to be the main protagonists in the debate.

The peripheral chatter died down and he could at last make out what was being said:

Brooster: ...Relationships, we were showing each other our fantasies and the most ludicrous things came to mind. Like when you've had sex and you're waking up some time later having your post-mortem talking about it... you know and these incredible things are coming out, but it's a sharing experience. So there we were fantasising about other people, they were brought into the experience which made it enjoyable for both of us...

Wandy: What, were they people you knew or...?

Brooster: Not necessarily

Cleesa: But do you find it can help, it can help keep you faithful to one partner if you're fantasising about someone else?

Brooster: Yes

Frank was beginning to wish he could *not* hear what they were saying. Maybe they would turn to the political situation in a while.

Spike: I mean, it's just a fantasy.

Brooster: If you're open to it, I think it can help you know. It doesn't matter what sex they are. It's just amazing casting away all our frustrations and inhibitions and that's what makes it worth doing.

You know?

Slick: It's the closest we ever get to being animals, which is what we are.

Spike: Yeah

Warshazzap lent over to Frank, saying, "You're the nearest, what are they talking about?"

"Phew, you don't want to know! Nothing at all useful yet, but it's still early."

The debate was warming up.

Brooster: Essentially we *are* animals.

Wandy: I think that's rubbish, I don't agree at all! For me, and I think Cleesa would agree with me, for me sex is something very civilized, it's...

Slick: It's not new is it!

Wandy: I feel there's... an awful lot of thought that goes into it. It's something I make an art of, or at least I hope to, but I don't think it's got anything to do with getting down and grunting.

They all started speaking together until the one with the most penetrating voice made himself heard.

Brooster: But it's the casting off of any inhibitions

Cleesa: In what way?

Brooster: To be free to explore each other and your emotions together.

The animated discussion had been going on for some time on the same topic before someone mentioned the risk of infection.

Wandy (addressing Slick): You said you live among a community of fifty people who regularly have sex with each other, don't you feel worried about it?

Brooster: It's not very easy to catch, it's been blown out of all proportions.

Slick: Yeah the Christians have used it as a device against us. Maybe there's a degree of paranoia as well.

"That's it!" Frank said angrily, "I've had enough."

He remained seated though, his actions not matching his words. One or two people seated on the floor nearby glanced up at him, but fortunately no one paid him much attention, listening as they were to Brooster and company.

Alan implored him not to leave.

"We agreed we would stay here and try to find something out to our advantage. We can't expect to hear precisely what we want on the first evening, we've been lucky up until now."

There was sense in what he said. Frank sighed and forced himself to relax a little. The conversation next to them had broken down by then anyway. Warshazzap decided to get more drinks and Alan said he would go too, so after all that, Frank stayed where he was while the other two left for a stretch. He watched as they picked their way between the bodies on the floor, unexpectedly finding that the chairs they vacated were left alone.

Soon afterwards there was a change-around at the large table nearby with a number of people leaving the scene. Brooster and Wandy were still there, but some fresh people had arrived. Frank made pet names for them in his mind: "Hang-dog" was a short youth with a hang-dog expression; "Orange" a loudly-dressed young woman with an orange head-band and "Darks" a dark-skinned woman with unkempt hair but a pretty face.

Another young woman was standing up debating with the others, parrying their questions like a solitary soldier facing a dozen blades at once. She frequently waved her hands in the air to express her points. From the conversation, it was quickly apparent that she was a Christian apologist facing an unsympathetic audience, but she was not making a bad job of it:

Brooster: When we came and had a look at one of your meetings it was weird, I mean like you were off your heads, like you were taking drugs, it's horrible, it really does...

Christian: Okay. Let me just say for a start that you seem to be coming from a very biased position. Something taken out of context can seem weird though.

Wandy: Can you answer me: what is baptism of the Spirit? Speaking in tongues as well.

A male voice from the crowd chipped in, "Is it a human language?"

Christian: Let me talk about speaking in another language. God is a supernatural God, so sometimes He does things which are outside our way of thinking, 'cos God is supernatural. That is a fact, see?

Her antagonists voiced agreement in order to allow the argument to progress.

Christian still: When His Holy Spirit comes within us, He brings gifts, and one of these gifts is the ability to speak in another language. Some people describe it as many things, the love language which comes from within to communicate.

Orange: Don't you think it is all reduced to having a wild time? A great way of recruiting people?

Christian: Within a church there's a certain attitude see? There's a time to be with God together and it's a natural expression.

Wandy: Yes, I'm interested in this. Don't you think to expose new members to these supernatural goings-on is dangerous?

Christian: First of all, let me say Christians don't spend all their time in meetings. They spend all the rest of the time in the natural world. But God, He is supernatural.

A large body of people was listening to the dialectic; every piece of floor-space was taken up. Frank was dying to chip in a few words of support, but knew he should not. Besides, the young woman was defending the faith admirably; he doubted he could do better. He glanced back and found the chairs vacated by his friends had at last been taken over. Of Alan and Warshazzap there was no sign, so he concentrated back on the debate.

Wandy: Can I just ask a fundamental question? You seem all happy and satisfied in your beliefs, but what about other people who are happy in theirs? That is what I see as the major hypocrisy about the Christian religion. What about the thousands of people who do not want to be a Christian?

Christian: All right. What is a Christian? It is someone who knows God, who loves God and, therefore, follows God, and follows the way He intended it to be. God intends us in many parts of our life to go in certain directions, to be followers of Jesus. So there are guidelines, see? But when people talk about happiness the way you do it's a transient thing. What we're talking about is *real* issues of sin, eternal life, of death, as God intended things to be. We are followers of Jesus, everybody's got a choice.

Hang-dog: That's fine. You want to see everyone living in harmony.

Christian: Yes, I do.

Hang-dog: But you only want to see it on your terms!

Christian: On my terms? When you take the viewpoint that God is the creator of the universe, God has set aside certain plans for the world. It's *God* that loves people, it's God that wants world harmony...

Hang-dog: Why can't you be happy with people who aren't Christians?

Christian: *My* happiness is neither here nor there. What I'm talking about is God's perspective on the whole thing. That's what...

Orange (interrupting in a loud voice): You talk about having instant access to Heaven. Don't you think that is rather arrogant?

Christian: That's a funny term, "Instant access to Heaven", who on Molt said...

Orange: No, but you go on about talking to God. Don't you think this is terribly arrogant? That you have access to God while some of us don't?

Christian: Right. Some people think that God is some sort of a force up there that has no relevance to me. I think it's wonderful to know that God has said to me, "I want you to know me." And He is saying that to you too, see? I don't find that arrogant, I find that totally humbling that God wants to know me.

The girl continued to give a good account of herself, but Brooster came back to his favourite topic, and a contentious one at that, of sex.

Brooster (concluding)...I mean whatever you do is wrong. How do you cope with sexual frustration when you've got to be celibate for years?

Christian: If you're a Christian then you've chosen a certain life-style and I would say that in your daily talk to God you actually do talk about sexual frustration. He doesn't close His ears, and you can't shock Him, see?

There was a general uproar, it was as if she had touched a raw nerve. Up until this point the discussion had been generally good-natured, even if impassioned in places. All of a sudden several of the protagonists got very heated at the young Christian's words and the atmosphere turned decidedly unpleasant.

Wandy (pointing accusingly): You're talking complete rubbish!

Orange: Listen, I am a sexually liberated woman...

Darks: Sex is a beautiful thing, shouldn't be repressed.

Orange: ... I like to express my sexuality.

"Now who's talking rubbish?" Frank asked in a loud voice, much to the audience's astonishment. He did not like to see them turning on his fellow Christian like a pack of wild animals, it was time to spring to her defence. "So you like to "express your sexuality" indeed! That's pathetic, you're just a slave to your desires. You just wrap it up in high-sounding words, but no one with a sense of right and wrong is fooled for a moment."

Orange was too stunned to reply at first. Before she could counter him, the Christian woman came in again.

"God has given us the institution of marriage to..."

"Marriage, ha!" Orange interjected scornfully.

Brooster was not quite on the same wavelength as his womenfolk. Reflectively he mourned, "When you've had a drink, your morals go out the window."

Frank launched another attack, "What d'you mean? You lot haven't got any morals. If you listened to God like the young lady says, you'd know how to behave. All this rubbish about..."

Orange rose from her seat, indignation across her face. "Just hold on there, hold on!" she bellowed, "who the hell are you?"

In the instant he got ready to reply, Frank heard a familiar voice behind him calmly ask, "Is this your idea of blending in?"

He never did get the chance to reply to Orange. Before he knew it he was being pulled smartly from the scene by his friends, one on each arm.

"Excuse our colleague," said Alan, negotiating between people on the floor, he's had a bit much to drink. I'm sure you understand."

Open-mouthed, Orange found herself nodding as the two men dragged her attacker away into the crowd and beyond.

"Who was he?" Brooster asked.

"Never seen him before," replied Orange.

Outside the sky was dark, lights from the Selerm illuminated the street as they crossed back to their inn. Frank was in repentant mood.

"I'm sorry, that was really silly of me, I know. I just felt it was my duty to help the Christian girl. Not that she needed my help I suppose, she was doing a much better job than I could've most of the time. But I... oh, I don't know."

Alan gave a big sigh as they entered the inn. Going up the stairs he declared he still wanted them to go back again the following evening.

"Only next time we'll not let you out of our sight, plus we'll put a gag on you, okay?"

Frank was glad they were able to laugh it off. He resolved to keep a low profile on their next foray. Going into his room, he noticed Dirkin fast asleep in his bed. He made sure he remembered his prayers that night, the last of which was one from the heart thanking God for good friends.

⊰⊱

CHAPTER TWENTY NINE

Following a lie-in the late breakfast at the inn went down well. Dirkin was subdued, saying very little to anyone. Frank was a bit put out that he did not receive an apology, but the truth was the guide could not remember a single thing from the night before. Towards the end of the meal, he announced, "As ya won't be needing me t'day I'm going out. Be back when I am y'know."

With that he was gone. Once they had finished eating, the three retired to one of the bedrooms to have a more detailed discussion on the night before.

"Well I hope you're not going to go on about me getting embroiled in that argument."

"I don't see the point," said Alan, "what's done is done. You've learned your lesson."

"The truth is I'd only just started speaking when you arrived."

"Forget it. Let's sum up what we've learned. Obviously it is not just political debate at the Salerm, although when we left you we did have a chat with one of the employees who said quite a lot of that takes place. It seems they dissertate on just about any subject without necessarily worrying about conclusions. I'm beginning to understand what Vol said about Laybbon being the talking capital."

Warshazzap said, "I knew it would be different from my home sector, but I never realised quite how different. These Buff supporters see themselves as being so superior and sophisticated, never done an honest day's work in their lives. To be honest with you, it has gone through my mind that perhaps I was being a traitor coming here with you. I feel alien in my own country now. It's a funny feeling I have, or I'm going through, but Ladosa has changed and I no longer feel part of it any more. As for this place, I can't be sure we're going to learn anything worthwhile here."

"Tomorrow is the political rally," Alan reminded them, "let's stick to our plan of staying on for that and seeing if it holds any significance. Today we can look around the town and this evening we may as well go back to the Selerm, we can afford it, can't we?"

It was Warshazzap who was looking after their main funds. He said they had plenty left. Thus confirmed in their strategy, the spies set about the town.

An uneventful morning followed. There was no picturesque part of Laybbon and it all got rather monotonous after a while. Most of the buildings were built to one pattern. At the top of a rise they looked out at rows of identical roof-tops, it was by far the biggest place Frank had seen since landing on the planet. On the skyline was an aqueduct of wooden construction that brought in water from the north. The sight-seers moved back down to the commercial quarter. The shops were functional, selling shoes, crude furniture, groceries and the like. There was nothing of great interest to Frank, although Alan and Warshazzap seemed to quite enjoy to browse. Not too far away was an athletics ground, they could see it from a distance although the road they were on turned away from it without getting close. From what they could see it was not in use on that day.

Early in the afternoon, Frank left the other two looking around and returned to the inn. There he had a sleep on the bed. The Selerm held a particular fascination for him, bringing back as it did memories of debating circles on Eden. He was rather disappointed with his performance the night before though. Due to his despising his opponents he had turned more to abuse rather than positive dialectic. He knew he could do better and was eager at the thought of a second visit. They were there to listen and not get involved, he knew. But he might always get asked his opinion and it would be rude not to answer.

The other pair returned and the trio decided to go across in good time to be sure of a table. There was a short queue to pay their money and go in. Similar to the previous evening the crowds had not yet started to arrive and they had the pick of where to go. Whilst they stood there deciding, a young man came up to them and asked them if they were "Ardents". Frank gave a blank expression, but Alan got rid of him by saying they were not interested in politics.

"What was he talking about?" Frank asked.

"No idea," Alan confessed.

They chose a table near the wall in a different part of the vast room. Warshazzap collected their drinks before the bar got busy and they sat quietly and watched the people arrive.

Again there was a spare chair at their table. Before long, a man carrying a small bundle under his arm came and sat on it. Carefully he began unfurling his load: a patch of green baize with markings on it contained crudely- carved wooden figures, half of which were painted white. As he did so, he asked with great confidence, "Do they gamble where you come from?"

"No!" snapped Warshazzap, "go away."

This stopped the man in his tracks. He hesitated then began rolling his bundle up again.

"If you're going to be like that," he said, sounding offended, "I'll give someone else a chance to win some money."

"You do that," Frank called out as the figure retreated. He was amused at the gambler's tone, as if they were going to miss out. A stranger came over and told them they had done the right thing, saying the proprietress was very strict about gambling and would have had them all thrown out if caught in the act.

"She's not someone you'd want to argue with!" he declared.

Before anyone else arrived Warshazzap took their spare chair and put it at another table. Meantime a music group started up on stage. Playing guitars and percussion, they played catchy instrumentals, mid-Narcassan style; the growing audience received them well.

The evening bore many similarities to the previous one. Large numbers flowed in and filled the available space. The stage acts disappeared and the debates started. This time there *were* some political topics raised, but they appeared to be either historical in nature or to do with petty domestic issues, nothing of interest to the spies.

Around mid-evening Warshazzap started to complain he was feeling unwell. It got worse, the noise and the stuffy atmosphere not helping at all. His face turned a ghostly pale.

"The room's spinning, I'm sorry I can't stay here."

Alan volunteered to take him back to where they were staying. Getting up he said, "I don't see myself coming back this evening, see you back at the inn – tomorrow morning if you're late. Now don't you get carried away!"

So unwisely, Frank was left to his devices once more. Had the dialectics remained on local politics all might have been well, but as fate would have it an entirely different subject came up, one he could not ignore.

With his colleagues gone, the chairs were soon taken over this time. The table he was at became the focus of attention when a fresh group arrived and instigated an intense argument. A large, densely-packed crowd was gathering to listen. Frank remained firmly in his chair, with strangers seemingly not noticing him as, standing up, they pressed in on him from the sides and rear. Fortunately, nobody from the previous night seemed to be present.

Another lone Christian apologist, a youth this time, was fighting a rearguard action against a large, hostile assemblage. The subject: the existence of God. Unfortunately, he was not in the same league as the young woman of faith the evening before:

Apologist: What about if you'd never seen one before and you came across a falsapt. With all its intricate working mechanisms you'd have to conclude it was made by someone; it didn't just happen by coincidence. How much more intricate are we? The products of mere chance? It would be more sensible to believe the Kabra Beta was the result of a rock-fall in the northern mountains!

While some of the terms were unfamiliar to Frank, the gist of the argument was clear enough. He turned to look at the adversaries. On this occasion he had not had time to study them and make up nick-names.

Adversary 1: What about the Padka Horon-scape then? That's just the result of wind eroding the rocks?

Adversary 2: A fasapt is not self-perpetuating, we are. God didn't make the falsapt, bloody people did. One we were set in motion. We could do what we like. Even if God did make us there's no evidence he's around now. Look at the harshness of the world, man – you ever seen the barren ice sheet in the north? There's a godforsaken place if ever there was one!

Apologist: God is called "The Living God" because He is always with us. To redeem us, He came down in the form of a man, Jesus Christ. He...

Adversary 2 (amid jeers aimed at Apologist): Jesus was just a man! A good man perhaps, but it's just bloody childish to say "God came down" and all that crap.

Apologist (having to raise his voice against the animal noises): The Bible teaches us that Jesus was the perfect man, God's only Son. He was without sin, he did not *have* to do it, it is thanks t'....

Adversary 2: You can't bloody *prove* he was perfect. The Bible is obviously biased in his favour, it doesn't record all his actions. Or were you there at the time?

Adversary 3: Jesus never said he was God, his supporters made that up after he died.

The Christian youth went red under a flood of catcalls and shouts. It was proving to be a noisy affair that evening. Frank could restrain himself no longer. 'He could do with a bit of assistance' he told himself, I'll just help out with a few points.' His heart thumped as he chose a lull in the din to come in.

Frank: May I say something?

It rapidly went quiet as they watched the stranger get up and waited to hear what he had to say.

Frank: There's no way the disciples would have disobeyed their master by deifying Him. He did accept worship from Doubting Thomas anyway. Of all the cultures, you wouldn't have expected the ancient Jews to describe a man as God incarnate. Had it been the Greeks or Hindus, you could have understood it. It was something completely new and unexpected for the disciples.

Adversary 3: Yeah, but did he actually say he was God?

Frank: He was not blatant to put it in those words, but for anyone with even a hint of subtlety could understand his great "I am" statements this way. After all "I am" was the Jewish name for God: Jehovah.

Adversary 1: I can accept he was a good man.

Frank: You can't say he was just a good man! Anyone who claims to be God is either mad, a liar.... or God.

Frank sat back down again, flushed with success. He had silenced them and allowed himself a little pride in the achievement. He had put up a constructive argument, much better than the previous evening.

Then from out of the silence a light-hearted woman's voice burst his bubble.

Adversary 4: I think it's nice that someone can say things like Jesus did, it's rather nice to have a few eccentrics. I mean, religion is nice if you enjoy that sort of thing.

Intensely annoyed at what he considered an empty-headed statement, Frank eyes the Christian youth hoping for a response. Unfortunately he was more than willing to let the newcomer hold onto the baton once he had picked it up. It was clearly up to him to respond.

Feeling attack was the best form of defence he turned on the woman who had just spoken.

Frank: That's a pathetic thing to say! These are important issues. If what Jesus said is true then it is our duty, as well as our joy, to worship Him.

Adversary 2: Yeah, but if God really does exist He must be a cruel, spiteful being if he allows people to suffer.

Frank: How could you have a world without suffering? There'd be no responsibility, you wouldn't have to take care, 'cos you'd know nobody could get hurt and therefore suffer.

Adversary 3: Why should innocent people suffer? Like in that building collapsing last week? I could understand it if bad people suffered.

Frank: Again, think it through! Accidents happen. What sort of world would it be if a building collapsed and all the bad people were killed and all the good ones pulled out unharmed? People would try to be good for all the wrong reasons.

The volume around him went up. Frank sensed that his opponents were getting annoyed now they had lost the initiative.

Adversary 1 (amid supporting shouts): You damned Christians, you're just a load of hypocrites making out you're better than everybody else!

Adversary 4 (puzzled): I'm lost, can we start again?

The argument was getting out of hand, more and more noisy as the crowd resorted to jeers and cat-calls.

Frank opened his mouth to continue, but suddenly everything went quiet. Even Frank was not vain enough to think it was for him, besides all eyes were on something behind him.

"You there – come with me!"

He turned to see the origin of this authoritative, earthy voice. Squinting at the source of the command he saw, to his surprise, a short woman with jet-black hair watching him with a stern expression.

'She must be in her early thirties,' Frank guessed. It went against the grain to be seen obeying a woman, but all eyes were on him now and an eerie hush had descended in that part of the room. Concluding correctly that this was the proprietress he resigned himself to being ejected from the Selerm and got up without saying anything more. Muscled bodyguard in front and proprietress behind, he was led through the hushed and staring mass towards the exit. But no; instead of going outside he was directed up to a metal stairway fixed to the internal wall. The sound of their footfalls on the metal steps were soon drowned out as the chatter returned. People turned away as fresh topics were explored, the stranger would soon be forgotten.

Wild thoughts flitted through Frank's mind as they approached an office high up overlooking the vast room. 'Are they going to kill me? Beat me up and throw me out as an example? I shouldn't have provoked them all and got myself into trouble. They might torture me and find out my true identity...'

It was a functional room with all the furniture and paraphernalia one would expect to find in an office several hundred years previously. A large desk was covered with papers while a separate table had what appeared to be ledgers laid out on it. The bodyguard hesitated, then a hand-signal from the woman instructed him to lead the way through to the next room. This was a comfortable living quarter. By Frank's estimate where they now stood was external to the main building, possibly an extension added later.

To his relief, the bodyguard was dismissed and the woman, still in a gravel-voice, asked him to sit down in a far more polite tone than before. He studied the surroundings while she stood studying him. The brown leather armchair he found himself in was of superb quality and most comfortable. Two other identical chairs with low backs adorned the spacious apartment. Heavy fabric curtains were drawn across the windows, their magenta colouring mirrored in the pattern on the carpet. The room was expensively decked-out, but the note of vulgarity had not been entirely eradicated.

The proprietress cleared her throat, forcing his attention from the décor. Before she could speak he enquired as to whether she was suffering from laryngitis. Normally such a question would have annoyed her intensely, but with genuine concern written on his face, she simply informed him that she was not.

"I know who you are," she said.

Across the road in the room at their inn, Warshazzap was sitting up in bed. He had been sick and felt a lot better for it. The symptoms were those of mild food-poisoning, but he had not had anything different to eat than the others. In the end, they gave up the guessing game of trying to work out what had caused it and just felt grateful it seemed to be over. Still feeling weak, he chatted over tales of Ladosan village life with Alan who sat on a chair nearby.

"... And we used to play with an inflated ball, kicking it to each other – we used to form teams. As a boy, though, the highlight was the travelling acrobats who used to come round each spring, I used to love that.

"Then there was a story-teller, an old man who claimed his tales were handed down to him from generations ago. He spoke of a time when people used to fly through the air in machines and speak to each other though they were hundreds of kilometres apart, swore it was all true."

"I've heard of such tales. When I was young, I used to be fascinated by that sort of thing: man-made contraptions which flew through the sky, weapons of unbelievable destructive force. I did not see much of my father as a boy, once I mentioned these things to him he got very angry and told me not to. I've never forgotten that incident. It didn't stop me playing games about them with my friends... but that was a long time ago. No one mentions such stories now, although that could be because I spend most of my time in Thyatira now, their traditions are different. It might be strategically important, but it's the tiniest of the despotates, in case you didn't know... stuck out as we are it's Hoame's backwater."

"You haven't always lived in that part of your country then?"

Alan smiled to himself, "Not by any means. I like being there, though, I've got no desire to leave. There's not the same in-fighting as within most of the other despotates. Frank's been with us a little over a year ago now and I get on well with him, used to his idiosyncrasies. You can only get so close to him though, he leaves a gap. Never likes to talk in any detail about his previous life in Oonimari, changes the subject straight away. It's up to him, of course, but I'm conscious of that gap, I know almost nothing of his past. What I do know is that he takes his morals very seriously."

"Is that not commendable?"

"I'm sure it is. I'm not sure I'd make quite the same song and dance about it though. It's just his way, he's never tried preaching to me."

"I hope he's okay," Warshazzap voiced his concern.

"Yeah if he's got any sense, he won't make the same mistake twice. He was so contrite after last night, I'm sure he'll 'ave kept his head this evening."

Things were not going too badly for Frank, all things being considered. While the proprietress knew who he was, she showed no interest in having him handed over to the authorities when he asked her intentions.

"I presume you're here 'cos of the envoy sent to Hoame, but I really don't care. It must be said I'm more concerned about you upsetting my clients. You won't find anything useful from them, empty-headed lot, you're wasting your time. It's in other Sectors they're having to whip up anti-Hoame feelings. Here they're all Buffs to a man, the fools will do whatever the new government bloody well tells them to."

She decided she had better answer the question his puzzled expression asked.

"My name is Katrina, I used to be one of your serfs. I saw you when you made your first visit to the Upper Village."

The use of the word "serf" was very pointed, Frank had not heard a Hoaman use the term before. 'Must be embittered,' he concluded, 'wonder what she wants from me.'

"You've dyed your hair," he observed.

"How sharp-eyed you are," she responded sarcastically. She certainly was not in awe of her former master, "Yes, I dyed my hair. I wanted to make a complete break with the past, with Hoame. It was only my hatred of the place that kept me going at times. If I live forever I shall always bear a deep scar from my time there."

Frank asked her about her life on Hoame. Katrina gauged from his tone that his interest was not superficial so she obliged. In some depth she went through her childhood in the Upper Village, the girl who was always picked on for being different. She then spoke of her unhappy marriage to Hatt and the feeling of release when he was killed in battle. On to her stay in Aggeparii, the friends and enemies she had made there. Frank was particularly interested to hear of the library, but she had to admit she had only scratched the surface as to its contents.

"Besides," she continued, "after I left, there was a fire in the library and a great deal of it was destroyed..."

"What a tragedy!"

"Mmm, a shame. I heard this quite by chance from a Sarnician trader just a couple of weeks ago."

There was a pause before he asked Katrina to continue her account of her flight from Aggeparii.

"If you like. The trader who took us north skirted through the southern tip of Thyatira then into Rabeth. I left them there and went on alone. I had a few lucky breaks and hitched another ride into Ladosa as it's called here. I reckoned my chances of making it were better here than in Rabeth and so it proved. Ended up here in Laybbon.

"I bought up the Selerm when it was a storehouse, largely disused. Got it for a knock-down price, but even so, it took most of my savings. I'm a great believer in being careful with money, I don't mind saying it. I won't allow gambling on my premises."

"So I hear. What made you buy it?"

"It's a long story. In brief, I saw an opportunity and seized it. All those youngsters meeting outside or in poky rooms needed something better and I provided it. I had teams of volunteers helping me convert the place, seems so long ago now, but it wasn't." The hardness of her features melted away as the fond memories flooded back. Frank felt himself more at ease as she continued, "Even I had miscalculated the demand. I never dreamed it would be as successful as it has been. All the hard work has paid off."

"Yes," agreed Frank, surveying his surroundings once more, "you do not appear to be doing badly for yourself. But right now I'd like to know my status, am I your prisoner?"

It was all very well hearing her life story, but he needed to know what was going to happen to him.

Staring him straight in the face, she replied without emotion, "You're not my prisoner, you can leave whenever you like, I thought..."

"No no no, I just wondered where I stood. I was enjoying hearing about your adventures, if that's the right word."

"I just can't have you upsetting my customers. They're not used to losing an argument, the group you were talking with this evening. Besides, I could hardly believe it really was you and wanted to see you close up." Then she added hastily, "Not that I want to know what you're up to! I really don't. I can guess, but I won't get involved."

He was getting used to her husky voice by now. She really was the strangest of white women, she spoke to him like an equal, without hesitation. She had even taken steps to have the cross on her forehead removed, but close up a trace was still visible.

It appealed to his vanity to hear a third party pronounce him the winner of the argument downstairs. Feeling more confident now that he knew he would not be kept against his will, he decided to tell this woman - a traitor when all was said and done – just what he thought of these Laodicians.

"I didn't think much of their arguing techniques, but their immorality amazes me! They're living fossils with their sodomy and the like, they come from a time that should have died ages ago. Advocating strange sexual practises, abominations for the gratification of abnormal desires, it's just so... old fashioned! Have they been completely by-passed by the moral regeneration of the century just gone?"

Given what she had just told him, he was not unduly surprised when she came to their defence.

"Shame! What about your country? I'll no longer call it mine. You Hoamen bastards may call yourselves moral, but you practise your own kind of "abominations." How many female drones have you drowned at birth? You blacks hate living in the villages with the whites. You impose your Keepers' laws and ways... shame, shame! You've no right to come here and preach to us. Get out of here, I don't want to see your face again."

She pointed to the door. Slowly and deliberately he got up. As he did so he gave her a flicker of a smile and a superior look as if to say, "I've been kicked out of better places than this." Spoken words were unnecessary.

'I'm glad I said what I did,' he told himself, 'you were quite right to stand up for the truth, Francis.'

He took his time going out through the office and down the metal staircase to the exit. There was no sign of her bodyguard. The truth was that the sudden turn in their conversation was unfortunate. While she had been telling him of her life, he had felt genuinely sorry for her; he had even been considering inviting her back to a fresh start in Thyatira. However, it was not to be.

The evening air was fresh as he went back to the inn. He considered taking a stroll up the road then thought better of it. There was much to go over in his mind: some of the things she had said tied in with Dirkin's earlier rant. 'Is it something about this place that makes people have these destructive outbursts?' he asked himself. 'I *cannot* believe the whites back home are that unhappy, they never seem it: Natias and Eko, Illianeth, Japhses – maybe he's a bit touchy sometimes, but he wants to work within the social order – the squad leaders, the village heads, what about Giella? Damn, what about Giella!'

Standing in the empty corridor outside his room, the memories of his infatuation with the white woman came flooding back. He had only spoken with her on a few occasions, but had been totally besotted. Now she was dead and her killer was still free. Poor Giella.

A scuffling sound came from Alan and Warshazzap's room and he stepped softly up and knocked gently before opening. The invalid was sound asleep in bed, while Alan was still sitting on his chair very much awake.

"How is he?" Frank asked in a whisper.

"He's fine, feeling a lot better. I'm sure he'll be as right as rain in the morning. How did your evening go?"

"Very good thank you, I thoroughly enjoyed it."

Alan would have liked to have asked if Frank had got involved in any arguments, while the latter wanted to tell his friend he had won an argument single-handed. In the event both held their tongue. Instead Alan filled in some details of Warshazzap's sickness before asking if anything useful had been learned at the Selerm that night.

"No," replied Frank in an off-hand manner. He felt certain that Katrina would not report them, she was too independently minded for that. So instead he amused himself by echoing her judgement of her clientèle, "They're a pretty empty-headed lot, not worth arguing with. I'm looking forward to getting this political meeting over and done with tomorrow so that we can go back home."

"You're not getting homesick are you?"

"Damn right I am. When we get back I'm going to appreciate every single thing and every person. Hoame sweet home."

There was no sign of Dirkin the next morning, he had not slept in his bed. Warshazzap was fully recovered and went down with the Hoamen to breakfast. They were due to leave that afternoon after the rally. If their guide had not returned by then, they would have to leave without him and make it back as best they could.

"Well we may as well take another stroll round the town this morning," said Frank once they were outside, "we've got some time to kill. If our fund can manage it, we might buy a souvenir of this terrible place."

"What had you got in mind?" Alan enquired.

"I don't know, we can have a look around though."

It was still early as they began their saunter through the alien streets. Finding themselves in a run-down area they came across a colony of down-and-outs who had been sleeping rough around the wooden supports of the aqueduct. A rubbish-strewn wasteland spread out between two disused and decaying warehouses. A beggar approached them, an elderly woman with blackened teeth and dressed in rags. She departed a good deal better off after being handed some coins by Frank.

His eyes turned away from her and up at a dilapidated roof of one of the huge buildings. He exclaimed, "See the state of that!"

The other pair nodded. Warshazzap said, "It might collapse at any moment. Shall we head back for the better part of town?"

Their route took them past the athletics ground which was in use that morning. A low fence by the path was all that separated them from the facilities. A few spectators were there watching the athletes going through their paces. The grass had obviously been watered regularly as it was a rich green and not bone dry like everywhere else. No rationing here, obviously.

Frank squinted hard to watch the runners practising on the track.

"That's funny," he said, "they look like women!"

"They are," Alan and Warshazzap echoed in unison.

"What are they doing?"

"Running, Frank."

"Yes I can see that, but it's not fit to have women running like that. It's not right, not feminine."

His companions did not reply, but continued watching the athletes' progress. Another bystander came up and began extolling the achievements of one of the runners.

"Yes friend, she'll be the Champion of the Games again she will. See her fly round! What a champion."

Frank tried giving the enthusiast a look of contempt, but ended up returning the man's infectious smile.

"They say she's the richest woman in Sector 2. She's earned it all right, she's earned it."

Frank asked, "Why does she put her body through this undignified process if she is so wealthy?"

The enthusiast did not understand the question. With a puzzled expression he replied, "This is how she earns her money, from the games; and lots of it too! Surely you know this, friend."

"Time to go, Frank," Alan urged.

"What, you mean they *pay* people to run round and round?"

"Frank!"

Heeding the voice, he came away. The man meanwhile found someone more on the same wavelength to enthuse to. The spies crossed the road and headed towards the centre of town.

"Honestly what a terrible lot! The more I find out about these Laodicians – present company excepted – the worse I realise they are."

Warshazzap, who thankfully was slow to take offence, responded, "If you think these are bad, I'm sure you wouldn't approve of the bladators – women paid to fight each other!"

"You're incorrigible, Frank," said Alan. "If I didn't know better I'd guess you got yourself into trouble last night as well!"

"What me?" Frank exclaimed innocently before lying, "I was as quiet as a lamb yesterday evening."

A loud "Hmm," and a disbelieving stare later, his friend changed the subject, "Let's find somewhere to have lunch."

The sun hung directly overhead as they arrived at an open-air café. It was situated on the edge of big plaza none of them had discovered before. Similar timber-frame buildings on all four sides faced each other across the square, while arterial roads left from each corner. Only on this, their third day in Laybbon, had they found the true heart of the town. The neatly laid cobbles and the smart buildings offered a pleasant scene for them to eat by after the less salubrious parts the travellers had just come from. In the middle of the plaza were tall statues, some riding stone dakks, and a group of parked, open wagons. These were covered in Buff ribbons and flags, some of which had slogans painted on them. It did not take a genius to work out that the afternoon's political rally was going to take place there.

Not knowing what to choose off the menu they took the waitress' advice and ended up with fried steaks in batter which were very oily. Situated not far from one of the entrances, it was quite interesting to watch the flow of people go by, each with their own concern written on their features.

Unintentionally a cabaret act was being provided in the form of yet another debate. This took place in the square not far away. Unlike in the Selerm, this was a most civilized affair between two individual speakers. They each had a box to stand on which raised them slightly above the small crowd which had gathered to listen. These eristics stood about ten metres apart and spoke in loud voices so that all could hear. The table where Frank and his colleagues sat was close enough for them to catch the proceedings without having to strain. Strain the ears that is, Frank had to strain his eyes to get a good look at them.

The man on the left was the younger of the two. He had a thin face and Frank soon named him "Cassock" in his mind from the brown garment he wore. His appearance was similar to members of one of the religious orders back on Eden. His opponent, while older, seemed more agile in his movements as he expressed a point. A long, grey beard gave him an air of distinction. This one began with an oration about the Age of Aquarius and, not being able to think of anything more fitting, Frank named him after that.

Aquarian: ... I would say, my good man, that you have put the cart before the dakk. We are each a soul which presently has a physical body, not the other way round.

Cassock: That is all very well, Sir, but I find it hard to take seriously a doctrine that says we come back as an animal. I suppose if I'm a naughty boy, I'll be a fly next time around.

Aquarian: With the greatest of respect, that is not what I was saying at all. The modern understanding of reincarnation, and indeed the original ancient teachings, clearly state that once humanity has been attained one can only be reborn as another human being. Thereafter, progress is made and lessons are learned through each life amid better surroundings.

Cassock: What better surroundings do you mean? Having a bigger house and more possessions as a reward for being good? A strangely materialistic concept is it not?

Aquarian: That is not what I meant, my dear fellow. One's circumstances depend entirely upon the lessons needed, learning at any particular time. It would often be pointless for a more advanced soul to be born to utter poverty though and have to spend a life merely trying to keep the body alive.

Cassock: But surely, Sir, progress is possible without returning to Molten.

Aquarian: What wonders what progress is conceived in your Heaven where there is nothing to test the soul. Without any of the multitude of political, commercial and other problems that we have down here with which to sharpen our mental facilities...

Cassock: It is surely vain and arrogant to try to imagine the glorious state that God has in store for us and silly to think of it in terms of a lack of politics and suchlike. Most people would think a world without politics to be Heaven indeed!

The audience laughed and Aquarian too raised a smile. While the debate continued, greater numbers were entering the square and focusing on the platform belatedly erected in the centre. The chanting of political slogans had begun. Many of the people held small, Buff flags being handed out by party officials stationed at the entrances. These all wore black uniforms with buff armbands. The crowds on their way to the rally bypassed the much smaller gathering listening to the debate. It was easy to get the impression that there was no love lost between these two groups.

Cassock: As an unbeliever it is difficult for you to understand the total trust we put in the Lord God. We know He will not let us down. What surely condemns reincarnation is its coldly calculating doctrine leaving no room for Christian forgiveness.

Aquarian: Would you expect the law of gravity to have mercy on you if you jumped off a roof-top?

Cassock: Your law of reincarnation is unnecessary due to the cross of Jesus Christ.

Frank was enjoying the debate on a subject he knew less about, although his friends were starting to get restless and wanting to join the large and swelling crowds of the political rally. A Buff official came over to the debate and warned both speakers that they would soon have to finish.

"Come on Frank, we'd better get going," Alan declared.

"Just want to hear this bit," his friend declared holding his hand up.

Alan and Warshazzap sat uneasily on the edge of their chairs as the debating continued. The arguments went back and forth for a while, Cassock putting forward an impassioned plea for his views. His adversary was not slow in responding though.

Aquarian: Oh, my good man, this is wishful thinking non-sense! It is a marvellous idea, but it is simply not true. Whether you like it or not, these infantile ideas are.....

At this point they were cut off as a large contingent of uni-formed party workers, some carrying clubs, came along to break this fringe meeting up. Roughly they pushed people away and manhandled the speakers from their platforms. Frank and his friends were horrified at the unnecessary violence being used, but powerless against such numbers. In fact they were still recovering from the shock when more Buff bullies ordered the café to close and aggressively instructed the customers to attend the rally.

The spies quickly joined the throng gathering for the po-litical event rather than have their chairs kicked from under them. Immediately they were enveloped in a crowd as more people hurried to join. The atmosphere was tense and expect-ant as a woman stood on the base of one of the statues and harangued the populace. For this purpose she used a crude amplifying device which helped to carry her voice right across the square.

"On with the Freedom Party! On to victory over the foreign disrupters!" she declared.

"On to victory!" the crowd roared back loudly and in great earnest.

Wide-eyed, Frank studied the faces around him. As if mesmerised they all stared unerringly at the woman leading the chants, then to the local party leaders assembling on the platform. He had not had time to absorb the debate he had been following so closely before being hurled into this maelstrom of emotion. He felt as if he was in the jaws of a gigantic monster. The people in the plaza had ceased to be individuals, they acted as one: chanting, clapping, shouting in unison. It was only by great effort that the three travellers were not taken up in the process mentally as well as physically.

"Freedom, freedom! The Old Guard are traitors, the Old Guard are traitors!" ran some of the chants. They had only been partially conscious of the meeting steadily building up while the debate had been in progress. Now they suddenly found themselves in the middle of this mania, the intensity of which was quite extraordinary.

Then after a while, the chanting died down as an important party member began addressing the rally. Frank noticed his hair was curled round and set on the top of his head in the same outlandish fashion displayed by the envoy who had attended the Castle. He began fairly restrained, but soon by degrees was raising his voice as he got the huge crowd going again. He thumped his fist into the palm of his hand as he expressed his points.

"... Are we going to sit here while this goes on? Eh? No, we are democrats, we fight for what we believe it! We always have.

"Look around you at these statues, what do you see? Martyrs I tell you, martyrs" ... pause for cheering... "Yes, men and women of the past who have laid down their lives for the cause we know is right. And are we going to shirk at our duty? Eh! Are we not going to uphold the values these heroes and heroines died for? What do I hear you say? We will fight. Yes we will fight! I say death to the foreigners!"

The crowd screamed back, "Death to the foreigners, death to Hoame!"

"Yes, my people. Within a week our army will be setting off to crush the aggressors. We need volunteers for the militia, every able-bodied man and woman here will be joining."

"Hooray! Death to Hoame," came the response.

All around Frank the people were shouting at the tops of their voices. A woman next to him suddenly broke down in uncontrollable sobs. He tried to move away, but found it difficult in the crush. Hysterical people everywhere were screaming and shouting, the situation was more than a little frightening. Nervously he looked to his right and saw Alan's face a few bodies away trying to catch his eye.

"Let's go!" Alan mouthed. He had to repeat it so his squinting friend could make out what he meant. This second attempt was successful he knew as Frank turned and with strength born of desperation pushed his way through the crush towards him.

"C'mon, we're going," Alan whispered loudly in his ear. Frank did not need any persuading and with Warshazzap leading they forced their way to the edge of the crowd. No one paid them more than fleeting attention, caught up as they were in the frenzy.

"The Buffs, they're not letting anyone out of the square," Warshazzap announced when they had made it to the perimeter.

Spaced out at regular intervals were the uniformed Buff Party activists keeping an eye on the proceedings. They were approximately twenty metres away from the extremity of the crowd and as the bodyguard rightly pointed out they were forbidden from leaving.

Hungrily Alan eyed up the situation. He considered skirting round to try finding a weak link in the chain, but thought this would only draw attention.

"We don't have to leave just yet," Frank pointed out quietly. His heart was not in his words though, he wanted to get away from this madhouse as much as Alan and Warshazzap did. He certainly did not want to be press-ganged into the Laodician army. His friends did not answer him and he noticed Alan fingering the sheath of his knife as he sought a way out.

That they had not already been noticed facing the opposite way to everyone else was because an individual a little to their left was attempting to leave and had begun arguing with the activists. Without warning one of the Buffs raised his club and began beating the protester. This drew the attention of the other activists and, seizing the opportunity, Alan shouted something and ran straight for the nearest one, knife in hand. The youthful-looking Buff took one look at the figure bearing down on him, dropped his club and ran away. Alan burst through the blockade, friends close behind. Taken by surprise a couple of activists set off in pursuit. But shortly gave up the chase when they realised they were not going to catch them.

On they went, Frank had not realised he could run so far so fast. He was bringing up the rear, but was only a short distance behind the others as they rounded a corner. Before he did so himself, Frank glanced behind him and saw that they were no longer being followed. He stopped and bent over, hands on his knees. Between pants he told the others. After collecting their breath they made their way back to the inn without delay.

The streets had few people in them for mid-afternoon, so great were the numbers at the rally. As nonchalantly as possible they approached the inn. To their surprise their cart was sitting in the road outside, fully loaded and with dakks standing silently in harness. Dirkin was in the driver's seat waiting for them. In reply to their expressions he spat into the street and said, "Y'said y'wanted to leave this afternoon y'know. I've packed y'things, all ya got t'do is pay the landlord."

They were delighted their departure had thus been speeded up and marched in to pay the bill. There was a strange feeling of normality here, as if the rally a few blocks away was in fact in another dimension. The landlord was very chatty and it took them some time to drag themselves away. He spoke at length about his future plans which included marrying the heavily expectant landlady, which did not go down at all well with Frank. Just as they thought they could eventually get going the landlady entered the room and announced, "You're going to have another traveller with you on your way back, has he told you?"

The men exchanged nervous glances, what was the woman talking about? She led them out to reveal what she meant.

'A Buff party member? Katrina?' wondered Frank amid even wilder speculations.

She went round the side of the building and brought forth the extra traveller: a baby dakk.

"Yes," said the landlady with a chuckle, "One of your females was even ahead of me" She gave birth this morning. The baby's fine, so no reason why he can't travel with you. Lovely little creature isn't he?"

The adjective "lovely" was not the word most people would have used to describe the oddity she proceeded to tether on a long rope at the rear of the cart. Standing a metre and a quarter at the shoulder, the baby dakk looked curious with its disproportionately large head and long legs. Like all infants of its kind, it had grey speckled markings down its neck and back. As they watched it stamped its hooves playfully while rolling that large head. In comparison with the adult dakks at the other end of the cart it appeared so tiny that Frank asked if it stood a good chance of making Wesold.

"Oh yes," they all chorused and once they had all had a good ogle the travellers got on board the cart and left without further ado. Slowly the vehicle pulled away from the inn and they watched as the landlord and lady went back indoors.

There were still not many people about and no one tried to stop them leaving Laybbon. They passed out of the town and back onto the road they had come in on. The roof-tops gradually slipped from view and they breathed a sigh of relief.

"Glad to be out of there!" Warshazzap said.

"Yeah," agreed Alan, "Hoame here we come."

CHAPTER THIRTY

That summer's drought in Ladosa was plain to see. The ground was baked hard and both plant and animal life were having a difficult time to survive. Lazily the cart was pulled southwards, taking the spies ever closer to home. It travelled so slowly that comparatively little dust was thrown up by the metal-rimmed wheels. This was a blessing for the baby dakk following them on its rope. Its legs had to work much faster than its adult counterparts, but it did not seem to mind as it skipped along quite happily.

The cart went over a large pothole with a bang, shaking up the passengers. Dirkin swore and steered away from the edge now that the road had widened. Frank stared back at the deserted road behind them lost in his thoughts, grateful to be getting away. It was a good thing they were not being pursued, because at that pace they could easily have been caught. Still it was good for them to have their feet up that afternoon, for there would be a lot of foot-slogging to be done the following couple of days.

After a long gap in the conversation, Alan remarked that they never had got a souvenir of Laybbon.

"Apart from memories," replied Warshazzap, "I don't mind telling you it disturbed me. I hate the thought of my home village having to follow that bunch of bullies."

A voice came from the front, "Did y'find out all y'need t'know then? Is the war on?"

Without waiting for an answer Dirkin eased the dakks to a halt and got down from the driver's seat and began relieving himself by the side of the road. As he did so he called over his shoulder, "Well? Are y'going t'war or not?"

Glancing at the other two before replying Warshazzap said, "From what we have learned today, yes there will be one. The government representatives at the rally were hell-bent on whipping up support for war. In fact, he announced that they were going to march on Hoame within a week, so I cannot see how a conflict can be avoided."

"Within a week?" Dirkin repeated incredulously as he mounted the cart again, "you must be joking! Warshazzap you've lived such an isolated life in y'village y'know. Y'd believe anything government told ya! It'll take them far longer than a week t'march. Then there'll be enormous numbers, but mostly poorly or untrained militia y'know.

"Don't y'know this all ready? I call it daft, going t'war without ya sitting down first and working out the odds, whether y'can win or not."

His passengers exchanged more looks, but did not offer a reply. The cart creaked steadily on, dakks straining at the front, baby dakk skipping along behind.

They got back to Wesold that evening. As it was getting late they went straight along to hand the cart and dakks back before going on to Vol's. Dirkin explained that if they returned their transport before the next day the hiring charge would be less.

It occurred to Frank that they might be better off using a cart for the next couple of days travelling. Then he reminded himself that while it might be more tiring, it would be no slower walking and easier to hide if trouble was at hand.

The hirer was a short man who displayed a collection of blackened teeth when he smiled. He was delighted to receive the baby dakk to his stables and gave them a special discount off the hiring fee for its safe delivery. He said he had had no idea its mother was pregnant.

The man's chatter provided some useful information. He said that there had been a big change in the town since a recruiting platoon had been through two days previously. Now all the talk was of war against Hoame.

Said Warshazzap, "In Laybbon they seemed prepared to press-gang people into military service."

"That's Sector Two for you," replied the hirer, "no one here was forced into anything, although many joined and were marched off just this afternoon."

His tone seemed weary and Frank asked him if he was against the idea of war. The hirer answered with some friendly advice.

"Foreigners are best out of the country right now. If you have to stay, don't ask any more questions. You're all right with me, I'm not a native Ladosan myself, even if I have been here for a greater proportion of my life."

He went on to explain that he had been born in a far off country which had been in a state of war for more than five decades.

"I've seen enough of war to know I never want to see any more. Don't know why everyone's so damn enthusiastic about this one."

Frank asked him to tell them more of his home country. Not having any pressing engagements, he obliged.

"In my grandfather's time, when the war began, we held sway over a large track of land. With successive defeats on the battlefield and plague in the main cities our strength was sapped and our territory waned year by year. When I was a boy, we had a roughly rectangular piece of land linking the northern and southern capitals. I'll never forget the day of Fal Haradin, the battle where the enemy broke through our lines in the centre, cutting these two remaining cities from each other. We poured every available soldier in to try to reconnect them, but to no avail. My father was killed in one of the subsequent engagements."

"I'm sorry, I..."

"It was a long time ago, it almost doesn't seem real in a way. We never heard from the northern capital again, don't know if it survived. It's years since I escaped from the siege of Beldat in the south, that could be over-run now for all I know. I've betrayed my country. I broke the blockade to recruit help for the war effort and... and never went back. Looking back I was very naïve and as a result was conned out of the funds I'd been smuggled out with. They should have sent someone more worldly wise..."

It was all riveting stuff to Frank, but he sensed his colleagues were getting restless so after thanking the man he said they must go.

"Look after yourselves," was the hirer's final advice as the quartet departed in the rapidly fading light.

There was no sign of life at Vol's house, but it was not locked so they still went in and slept there for the night. It had been a long and eventful day.

'Thank you for bringing us through safely,' Frank prayed before going to sleep. 'If it be your will, please make tomorrow a lot less exciting.'

There was indeed nothing exciting about the following day, just a long, hard slog. There did not appear to be a heightened level of activity in the villages and the road was largely deserted.

Not a great deal of talking was done, it made sense to save their energy for walking. Their longest discussion that day not surprisingly was on the preparations for war. Many of the signals they had got appeared contradictory: large numbers of people in anything but war, then the rally with a great crowd chanting for Hoame's blood. Warshazzap remarked that he already knew his large country was a place of contrasts and wondered how representative the scenes they had witnessed were. Alan and Frank were convinced they should continue to make every preparation for a conflict. The Arpintonaxes' bodyguard seemed once more beset with doubts as to whether he was doing the right thing in spying on his own country, even if he did not agree with its government. The Hoamen did not try to convince him it was, such a matter of conscience had to be left to the individual concerned.

Dirkin kept well out of the discussion. No one asked him where he had been the last day and a half in Laybbon either. He had, however, re-stocked their food rations, even if he showed a lack of imagination. They were back to bean stew. He had also ensured they had a good supply of water. This was heavy to carry, but they did not complain,   because they knew how parched the land was. The smaller riverbeds had dried up completely and bigger ones were reduced to a tiny trickle.

Night fell and they were still some kilometres short of the guide's shelter amongst the trees. However, he knew of another place at a crossroads next to a stream fed by a spring, so it was an excellent alternative. It did not matter being out in the open, there still being no sign of rain. The travellers were shielded from that night's cool breeze by the tall bank leading up to the roadway.

The rays of the early morning sun crept over a nearby hill and, alighting on Frank's face, woke him up. Lazily he looked around from his vantage point high on the bank. The others were still in the shade, fast asleep.

A parched landscape stretched out into the distance, yellow-brown grass and clumps of trees, some shedding their leaves early. Far away in the distance were the mountains they would have to cross. To a good pair of eyes, they would have appeared sharp and clear against the pale sky.

A butterfly winged its erratic way past. It landed briefly on a wild flower nearby before disappearing up and over the bank. He watched it go, he was in no hurry to move and was interested in it, having seen so few flying insects on this planet other than flies and the bees near the Castle.

The grass was fairly long where he lay and he pulled a stalk off to suck, even though it was bone dry. Then looking up he found to his surprise they were not alone. Sitting nearby on a tree-stump at the crossroads was an elderly man. From what Frank could tell he was unaware there were other people present and sat there quite still, observing the clouds and the slight swaying movement of a young tree struggling to survive in the arid conditions. Almost embarrassingly close he could see the stranger clearly. He was clean shaven with short, grey hair combed closely to his head. His nose was long and he had lines going down from the corners of his mouth. The most striking feature of him though was his eyes. Clear and blue, they had a sharpness extraordinary for his age.

A lone traveller approached along the path. Keeping dead still, Frank watched events unfold from his vantage point.

"Hello, Old Man," the traveller greeted quite cheerfully.

"Hello, Sir," returned the other politely as he turned his piercing eyes on the newcomer.

"I say, nice morning isn't it?"

"Indeed."

"I say, I'm new to these parts, I wonder if you could tell me. I understand there's another village not far up this road, is that right?"

"Yes, Sir."

"What are the people... I mean what are the people like there?"

"May I ask you, Sir, what were the people like in the place you have just come from?"

"Where I've just come from? Oh they were a friendly bunch, so kind, couldn't do enough for me."

"I feel certain, Sir, that you will find the people in the next village much the same."

The traveller thanked the elderly man for this information and set off again with added zest in his step. A while passed and the man resumed his contemplation of nature and Frank continued lying still, feeling pleasantly attuned to nature. He was not going to wake the others, quiet moments like this were few and to be savoured.

Another solitary walker converged on the crossroads travelling in the same direction as the first one. He too greeting the elderly man on the tree stump and asked what the people in the next village were like. This struck Frank as most curious and he sat up to listen.

"And what, Sir, were the people like at the last place you stayed?"

"Urgh! They were a terrible lot: nasty, back-biting, mean – I couldn't get on with them."

"Indeed. I expect, Sir, you will find the people in the next village just the same."

As the second traveller moved on, Frank got to his feet and, scrambling up the top of the bank, walked over to where the elderly man sat. The latter did not seem at all surprised at the sudden appearance of a third stranger. Frank had a quick peer down each of the four roads that converged there. Once satisfied no one else was coming he sat down on the verge next to the tree stump and introduced himself in the cheerful way he found himself that morning.

"A number of people out on the road early this morning," he continued, "I must say I thought your answers to those two were good."

The elderly man said something in a soft voice which was missed. His piercing eyes seemed to search straight into Frank, but they were not frightening in any way. There was wisdom and understanding in those eyes, no hint of condemnation. Frank immediately got a feeling of great compassion, tinged with something else – was it sorrow?

Whatever it was its effect was to make Frank garrulous and he spoke at length about his visit to Laybbon. As he did so he noticed from the corner of his eye his confederates starting to wake up. He continued by talking about the theological arguments he had become embroiled in. He concluded, "It was nice to win that one, I must admit."

The elderly man had been listening with great attention. When the tale ended he paused for a moment before asking, "Why is it important to you that you won?"

"Um, I don't know really," Frank spluttered, "it felt good at the time. I suppose it all sounds a bit petty in the cold light of day...." Following a moment's pause he picked up his thread once more, "No, I'm a Christian. It was my duty to defend the faith against those people. I know I shouldn't take any pride or merit in it, if I won it was because the Holy Spirit was putting the words into my mouth."

"What happens when you identify with an ideology?" asked the other before going on to answer his own question. "Whether it's a political viewpoint, a religion or whatever, you feel an extension of that ideology and when it is threatened then you feel threatened."

"Ah, but I was standing up for the truth."

"Don't you think the truth can stand up for itself?"

"No, I don't!"

"Why do you have to have any beliefs at all? Why cannot things simply *be*?"

The conversation continued for some time. Frank was fascinated in this man's strange way of looking at things. Meanwhile his companions were preparing breakfast – no doubt bean stew again. Alan had noticed him having the conversation and left him to it. The elderly man continued his theme.

"If you are not careful your mind becomes set in its ways, stuck in a groove of your belief-system. Then you are unable to perceive things directly, because you are always using the filter of your habitual thoughts."

'His body may be old,' thought Frank, 'But his mind is sharper than ever!' He said, "But I find my mind flits about the whole time. If I'm saying a prayer, for instance I think I'm concentrating on it, but before I know it my mind has moved on and is thinking of something else. It can be very frustrating at times the way it won't keep still, keeps flitting about."

"Of course it flits about. The mind is apprehensive, chasing the security that lies at the end of the rainbow. It always wants something: building itself up, seeking security, reassurance.... it judges, compares... so it is never still. A never ending futile struggle to find satisfaction. This selfishness is utterly vain."

In a moment of silence, Frank looked up and saw Dirkin had managed to set the dry grass of the bank on fire. He was dashing around madly beating at the flames with a jacket while Warshazzap emptied freshly filled canteens on the ground to dampen it down. Alan was not in sight. Fortunately the blaze was very localised and soon put out, the crisis could have been far more serious. Frank could not avoid a smile at the sight of the guide hopping around like madman as he fought the flames. The whole episode was over very quickly and the guide soon resumed making breakfast and the others got on with their own tasks.

Frank was pleased he had not been required, because he was fascinated by what this man said and did not have time for fire-fighting. He said, "There is so much in what you say, how can it all be avoided? If we cannot conquer selfishness, and all the division and great hurt it causes, what are we to do?"

"You cannot do it by force of will, that is the problem in the first place."

"All right, but surely there must be some way forward!"

"It must not be of the will."

"Not of the will," echoed Frank.

"Indeed, Sir. What is required is action that comes out of direct perception, without the operation of the will."

Alan called out that breakfast was ready. Frank put his hand up and replied that he would not be long. Hurriedly he said, "I have always been a seeker after the truth. This has been so throughout my life, although often worldly cares get in the way. There..."

"Can your mind seek out truth? This mind that is always in conflict with itself? Only by the annihilation of the "me me me" can you appreciate the oneness of life that is all there is."

Joyfully Frank laughed and shook his head.

"There is so much here, I can only begin to take it in." Standing up he asked enthusiastically, "Won't you join us for breakfast? I'd love to hear more."

For the first time the elderly man smiled. It was a gentle smile, full of understanding.

"You are most kind, Sir. However, I must away; I am due in Halipan village by noon. I am well rested and must be off now."

With that he rose and carefully brushed some dust from his trousers' seat. Frank asked him a second time to have a quick bite to eat, but this was once more politely refused. Alan called out to Frank again.

"Be with you in a moment," he shouted back, then quickly turning back to the elderly man asked, "Will you come to Hoame if you get a chance? You're so interesting."

"I have not been to Hoame before. Yes, I will make it when I can if you would like."

"Very much so. I'm... we're from the Thyatiran despotate, just ask for... er, Mister Thorn." He knew he was not being prudent by giving away such information, but he was too caught up in his enthusiasm to care. It was obvious the man wanted to be on his way, but Frank had one more burning question.

"May I ask where you are from, please?"

"Why on Molten that is important to you I cannot tell. However if it helps you I am from Oonimari."

Frank swallowed hard and stood watching as he at last allowed the elderly man to leave. He was only brought back to the present by Alan's voice close by asking, "Who's your friend?"

Together they walked back.

"I don't know, he didn't give his name."

"Seemed like you were enjoying yourself. You could've asked him over to share breakfast, I'm..."

"I did. He declined."

"Oh. Anyway I didn't think you'd want your stew getting all hard and spoilt..." he hesitated, "and I'm afraid we've had a bit of an accident."

"What d'you mean?" Frank asked as they reached the others. He began helping himself to his meal from the pot hung over the smouldering fire. The patch of grass nearby was charred black, with one or two puffs of smoke still rising from the ground in places. The fire had been dowsed with water which was soaking into the hard earth. In answer to Frank's question Alan side-stepped down the bank to near where the other two were still sitting, finishing their food. He held up a jacket, it was badly burnt with great holes. It was Frank's.

The owner put the ladle back in the pot and moved down towards them. When he saw what had happened he went livid.

"Did you do this?" he rounded on Dirkin.

Not sounding too concerned the guide answered, "I had t'use something, that was the nearest thing available y'know."

"You bloody idiot! Look at it, it's ruined!"

"Not a lot I can do about that now is there. I had t'act quickly."

"You're a complete imbecile, I'd hardly worn it and you've completely destroyed it!"

"Right. Well, there ya are."

Frank stepped menacingly towards Dirkin who stood up to protect himself. Alan lunged in-between to prevent a fight. Warshazzap too sprung up, but was not needed.

Had he not been hungry, Frank would have thrown the cook's bean stew in his face. Wisely though, his friend defused the situation by carefully leading him away.

"That devil ruined my jacket on purpose."

"Come on Frank, you know that isn't true. Please bear with him, he was only doing what is best – just think how quickly the fire could have spread, everything being so tinder dry. Besides, I'm as much to blame, I knew it was your jacket and didn't try to stop him."

"Hmm, I suppose you're right."

"Yeah, and remember we need him to get back across the mountains."

After this, Dirkin threatened to leave them and go home. It took all Alan and Warshazzap's diplomatic skills to get him to change his mind. Eventually the quartet got packed up and left together, a stormy silence prevailing.

Step by step the mountains got bigger. Then clouds appeared and rapidly spread across the sky as a wind got up. This kicked up a great deal of loose soil which swirled around and got into their eyes. Unfortunately the wind's predominant direction was against them which cut back their progress.

Then it rained. It poured down and soaked the travellers to the skin. Alan offered his own jacket to Frank who turned that down, but accepted a short blanket the former had been carrying. The dust was quickly settled by the deluge, but the ground was so hard from the prolonged drought that it had difficulty in absorbing the water quickly and they were soon splashing through large puddles in the narrowing road.

None of them felt like having their usual midday break and without a word having been said they carried on throughout the day. The rain eased off in the afternoon and eventually stopped by the evening, but it was a lot cooler than before.

The four exhausted men arrived at the place amongst the trees where they had spent their first night. It was exactly a week since then, but seemed more like a lifetime. Totally fatigued, they collapsed onto the damp ground and, following a quick hardtack supper, lapsed into unconsciousness. Over-tired and with aching muscles, it was not a good night's sleep.

"Wake up Frank, something's wrong."

"Oh dear, what? What is it?"

"Look lively, Dirkin's missing."

Clearing his head Frank sat up and took in his surroundings.

"Where's Warshazzap?" he asked.

"Gone to try and find him. Now, we'd better get packed up, we don't want to get caught here if he's turned..."

A rustle in the undergrowth made him stop. Quick as a flash Alan dived behind a tree, knife firmly in his grip. He realised it was a false alarm when the large shape of the Arpintonaxes' bodyguard entered the clearing. He did not say anything, leaving it to the character following him.

"I only went for a widdle y'know. Can't a man have some privacy?" They breathed a sigh of relief.

When they took stock of the situation it became immediately apparent to them that their plans had gone amiss by a day. They were supposed to have got to that stopping place early evening then have a short rest, holding out until it was dark before embarking on the final short, but tough leg over the mountain pass. Now they would have to hang on for a further day. Their guide was adamant they should not travel during daylight, because there was evidence of increased Ladosan army patrols.

All day long they sat amongst the trees while a constant light drizzle fell. Little was said and there was nothing to do. A small supply of biscuits was the only food left and these were distributed evenly. Large drips of accumulated water fell from the branches at irregular intervals, every now and then one of the travellers would be hit on the head by one and curse. To a man they were fed up and simply wanted to get to their destination. Frank felt filthy and was dying for a hot, steamy bath when he got back. Throughout the long tedious day, a lookout was kept for soldiers and more patrols were indeed spotted, but none particularly close by.

The light failed and at last it was time to move on. Dirkin did not have to remind them about not talking this time. As before, Frank took up the rear. Drained of emotion he walked mechanically, feeling like a space freighter on robot drive. As the ascent began it all seemed like a bad dream: the climbing, stumbling, fatigue, the intense damp and penetrating cold. Then the feeling of elation as the downwards path began.

Sensing the soft grass once more beneath his feet he could have shouted for joy had he the energy. It might be pitch black, but he knew they were in no man's land. In no time at all they would be home, there was even a squad coming out to greet them, their flaming torches bobbing and flickering as they came nearer. Oh Hoame sweet ho...

"Who approaches? In the name of the people declare yourselves!"

"Oh bollocks!" exclaimed Alan to himself. "Quick, Frank, you run, that way- quickly!"

A shove in the back and no further prompting was necessary. As shouts and the clash of cold steel commenced, Frank snapped out of his hypnotic state and ran downhill as fast as his legs could carry him. Arms outstretched in the inky blackness, he took exaggeratedly large strides to help him from stumbling. Even at that critical time it occurred to him that if he had been doing it in daylight he would look quite ridiculous. At that moment though the only thing he cared about was that the first object he ran into was Thyatiran.

Behind him all hell had let loose. There were cries and curses, grunts and screams as more torch-lit figures entered the fray. Sparks flew with the clash of sword against sword.

A young ulna flew onto one of the Castle turrets. It was unusual for this night bird to be out after dawn. It jumped down to the battlements and stood there spying out the land below with its large eyes. A colony of rabbits were playing in the damp grass far below. They were safe from the immature bird with its wingspan of only fifty centimetres. The orange ball in the sky was getting clear of the horizon. The ulna realised it had stayed up long enough and in a single movement hopped off the battlements and swooped for home.

Inside three men were standing by the spiral staircase near the entrance to the Despots' suite.

"I am sowwy Japhses, but I weally do not want to take we-sponsibility for waking his lawdship up. He was particularly tired when he went to bed, and that was well after midnight. He needs his sleep."

"Pah!" the Captain exclaimed in disgust as he began pacing up and down impatiently. "This is just like when he first arrived here. You tell him Laffaxe, we need to know what happened and he's the only one uninjured."

Laffaxe yawned, "It's all very well for you Japhses, you weren't dragged out of bed in the middle of the night." Then in response to the big man's glare he added, "No, you're right, we need to know. We were just too busy last night with our immediate concerns to..."

"See, Natias! For all we know, the entire Laodician army may be coming over the mountain pass this very moment. Let's wake the Despot up and find out what he can tell us."

The steward bowed to peer pressure and led the delegation into the suite. Gently he tapped on the bedroom door. An ex-asperated Japhses was just starting to tell him to knock harder when to his surprise a stentorian, "Come in!" erupted from in-side. They duly entered and stationed themselves around the bed while Frank sat himself up.

"Good morning, everyone. Hello, Japhses, great to see you again. I've just had a dream which woke me up. I'm sure I could go straight back to sleep again, but it's good that you're here. How is everything? It was all so hectic last night I didn't find time to ask before I collapsed." He studied his filthy hands and added as an afterthought, "I didn't have a bath either."

Natias welcomed him back on behalf of the three of them in his strangely formal style. Their leader was a sight: unkempt and dusty hair, skin brown with dirt and eyes still red from not enough sleep. Clearly his spirits were up though, he was delight-ed to be back. He gave a big yawn then, spotting Laffaxe, he looked concerned and asked how Alan and Warshazzap were.

"No reason to worry, My Lord," the physician replied, "Alan's head wound is superficial, in spite of all the blood. He will feel weak for a while and may suffer from headaches, but that is all. The Laodician has a nasty gash on his right arm, but it should heal cleanly given time. They are being well looked after My Lord and both being strong young men with high morale..."

He allowed his sentence to trail off as the Captain jumped in, asking what they had learned from the reconnaissance mission.

"Well that's a good question. We learned that they can talk a lot."

"Talk a lot, My Lord?"

"About everything from sexual perversions to reincarnation! It was a place of contradictions: many people were friendly and seemed totally oblivious to the crisis, while at a rally we attended the crowds were baying for Hoame's blood. All most odd. Their morals were appalling, even the seemingly pleasant people like our landlord and lady. They really were ignorant of the gospel and in need of it. Many others seemed content to debate endlessly the strangest of philosophies while others were calling for war."

"Are they about to attack us, My Lord?"

"I think so. Yes they are, but I'm not sure when. They would have marched for the border there and then on the last day we were in Laybbon... but our guide was adamant that much of their army is made up of poorly-trained militia and that to mobilize them would take weeks rather than days. That reminds me, we don't know what happened to our guide. Dirkin is his name."

The confused events of the night before were still very much in his memory. Frank had managed to get to a Thyatiran guard-post quite quickly and found them hurriedly assembling a probing squad in response to the sounds of fighting near-by. He was able to tell them what was happening before the guardsmen had charged out, flaming torches and swords in hand. Then the wait before anyone had returned – how long it had seemed at the time! He could still see Alan emerging from the dark, supported by two guardsmen, his face covered in blood. Also Warshazzap holding his limp sword arm with his other hand. Frank had left his friends at the guard-post once first-aid had been administered. He returned under escort to the Castle in the knowledge that they were not seriously injured. Natias had been woken up to receive him while Laffaxe had gone to the border with two assistants to see the wounded were treated professionally.

There had been no need to wake Japhses and he had slept through the entire episode. He now said, "There was no sign of your guide, My Lord. We did take several prisoners and suffered no fatalities I am glad to say."

"Yes," Laffaxe confirmed, "I see no reason why all the wounded should not make full recoveries."

"Well, let's thank God for that. But we were betrayed! That horrible little specimen Dirkin sold us to the Laodicians the day before, I'm sure of it now. I want..."

"With all due respect, My Lord," interrupted the Captain, "The preliminary interrogation of the prisoners does not bear that out. According to them it was by mere chance that you walked into one of their patrols. I have no reason to believe they were not telling the truth."

"Oh," replied Frank, surprised at this. He sat silently for a moment taking this in, a vacant expression on his face. When Japhses asked if these prisoners should be housed apart in the old dungeon, he just nodded. His mind was still elsewhere as he belatedly asked his lieutenants if they want to sit down. They declined, remaining standing around the bed.

New life was breathed into the room when Natias mentioned Hannah Unit.

"She asked about you at bweakfast, My Lawd. She said she wealises you are vewy busy, but would vewy much like to see you at the first opportunity."

"Then I shall have to make sure I don't disappoint her. Now, quickly: tell me all that's happened since I've been away.

It had not been an idle week in Thyatira, although there was still no word from Count Zastein. There had, however, been a curious episode some days previously concerning a deputation of high-ranking Laodicians. They had been intercepted as they crossed the border from Rabeth-Mephar soil in the extreme north-west of the despotate. They had come before Natias, Karl and Japhses, only to end up arguing amongst themselves and not being able to come out with any coherent demands. In the end they had been ejected like the previous delegation.

"Yes, well that rings true," said Frank, "they do seem a most confused lot, their left hand not knowing what their right hand is doing."

Preparations for war had continued apace. Production of weapons and ammunition had reached a new peak with many people being drawn out of the fields to help. Close border re-connaissance and training had not let up. Laffaxe was now permanently back at the Castle and with his assistants was preparing large amounts of medicines, bandages and other such items. The physician was also overseeing the conversion of half a dozen wagons to ambulances.

In the Upper Village, Zadok and Eleazar and a band of dedicated helpers were being kept fully occupied with preparations of their own: for the series of religious meetings now only a couple of days away. (In fact Eleazar had been so busy with this, that his small group of pacifists based in Sardis were feeling deserted and dejected, but the Despot's deputies knew nothing of them).

Frank asked, "By the way, where is Karl?"

Japhses answered, "He went out at first light, My Lord, to help organise the Lower Village with Gideon and John. I believe Cragoop the jailer's son has been doing a good job there. I'm due to go down there myself this afternoon, see how preparations are progressing.

"Good."

"The other important thing, My Lord, is that we have been receiving the promised reports from the Mehtar."

"Really?"

"Yes, My Lord, I must admit I may have been wrong about him."

"Never mind, tell me what they say, have you got them here?"

"Er no," replied the big man as he edged towards the door, saying, "I shall go and find them."

Frank put up his hand. "No, don't bother just now, just give me a brief outline of their import. I can read them in full later."

Natias and Japhses smiled at each other before the former began, saying, "The Ma'hol appear as confused as ourselves about the Laodician behaviour, My Lawd. The weports speak of twoops concentwating in certain "Sectors" near their border with Bynar, of some aweas of gweat activity while in others life going on as normal. It appears to be particularly quiet along our common border according to these weports, vewy little movement indeed."

The Captain confirmed, "This links in with our own patrols which have discerned no increase in enemy activity – apart from last night's activity that is. We are, of course, retaining our vigilance."

"Hmm, on our final day in the country we thought we noticed more patrols, but the numbers were not great and there was no sign of a proper concentration of troops. Have you stepped up our patrols?"

"Yes, My Lord."

"Good, good."

Japhses noticed how keenly the Despot was listening to their reports. He asked, "What do you think was achieved by your mission, My Lord?"

'Bugger all!' thought Frank as he suddenly decided to plump up his pillow and rest back into it. He replied, "It gave us great insight into the workings of their society, from which their army is formed. We now know we can expect large elements of their forces to have received only a minimum of training. The equipment we saw on soldiers close to didn't look that brilliant either. Our foray also helps us to confirm the information received from the Ma'hol."

"Yes, My Lord. I will pass on to my squad leaders the information you gave me that they should expect to see more enemy patrols.

Natias told me that Madam Tersha said that you were going to the wrong sectors and would not find much information. Apparently she was put out at not being consulted."

Natias looked uncomfortable at this, annoyed that his colleague had mentioned it. He had not seen the point in doing so, the mission was over and could not be changed now. As it was Frank dismissed the remarks.

"Well, it's too late now. She probably just resents the fact we didn't ask her. Tell me, have we heard from the other despotates?"

"Yes My Lord, we have had a good response. They are mobilizing their forces too and have assured us of their full support."

"So we won't be left on our own this time."

"No, we won't."

"Although, My Lawd, there is nothing implicit in the communications I feel certain the guiding hand of the Inner Council is behind them."

"I see. That being the case, I wouldn't be surprised if we heard from Count Zastein very shortly."

Frank was getting ever more self-conscious of the fact he was conducting the meeting from his bed. The more he thought about it the more absurd it seemed and he became eager to reconvene in more functional surroundings.

The others all wanted to wait until the following morning. Laffaxe pointed out that Alan might be able to attend if he got a good rest before then and besides, each had a busy schedule for the remainder of the day. Also, to get the village heads involved it was felt desirable to give them more notice. Frank was struck by the lack of urgency, but did not overrule them. He would experience far greater frustrations in the coming days.

"Time to get up!" he cried, clapping his hands, "Natias, please instruct the servants to organise a bath for me, I've been waiting for this for a long time."

That same morning, Anastasia returned to her home in the Capital. She had been away visiting friends and while it had been a pleasant change it felt good to be back. Bodd watched from an upstairs window as her tall, elegant figure dismounted gracefully from the covered wagon. How was he going to tell her?

Servants were buzzing round their mistress, unloading the wagon and opening the gate for her. She did not seem to notice them as she glided towards the giant front doors. She was wearing an ankle-length, short-sleeved dress with a purple flower design, her long white hair flowed like a waterfall down her back.

Swallowing hard, Bodd turned from the window and started downstairs to meet her. He tried out a few smiles to take the concerned look off his face. The year was going like a fairytale for the young man from the country. He had been accepted into the civil service and was already highly thought of, his recent promotion – unprecedentedly early – was proof of that. This superb house in the most exclusive part of the city really felt like home now. To top it all, he had recently become engaged to a beautiful heiress with whom he shared a deep, mutual love. It was hard for him to believe they had only met in the spring, he felt like they had known each other a lifetime. He knew now that the cold exterior she had displayed at first had merely been a protective shell, a covering up of a real vulnerability. The trust in him she now felt had released her warm and loving personality. He had overheard tongues at work, saying his attraction was as much to her purse as anything else; how unfair and unkind people could be. He would have wanted her for his bride had she been a destitute villager. The fact that she had access to great wealth was irrelevant to him.

So why when everything was going so perfectly was he going to risk throwing it all away? He concluded he must be mad.

She entered the spacious hall and to her surprise saw him descending the wide staircase.

"Hello my darling, this is unexpected."

"I know, I have taken some leave."

"Oh that's nice, come and give me a big hug!"

They stood embracing while the servants entered silently with her luggage and took it upstairs.

"You look radiant," complimented Bodd, "how as your journey?"

"I don't feel it!" she laughed, "it wasn't a bad journey, but the roads are awfully dusty outside the Capital. Marna's well and so is the baby, the most gorgeous little thing you've ever seen! He's almost sitting up, he has the wickedest smile..."

The couple moved into the ante-room while Anastasia continued talking in some detail about her visit. It was the same room that she had ushered him to wait for Benedict when he had first arrived. Nothing about it had changed, it was still crammed full of ornaments and strange objects. She asked as to the whereabouts of her "uncle" and was told he was at the Citadel.

"Oh of course he is, I was forgetting it was a work-day. Anyhow, tell me my darling what you've been up to while I've been away, behaved yourself I hope."

Bodd found it impossible to return her smile. Swallowing, he said, "Everything is fine at work, the new job is very interesting..."

"Ah the new job, of course..."

"And back here Benedict has invented a new book-binding technique. Says it will protect the spine from wear when a ledger is opened.

"Things are very busy in the Citadel because of the mobilization. There's a tremendous amount to do, all leave has been cancelled... except mine, of course."

"Oh?"

He looked awkward and dug his fingernails into his hand on the side away from her and said, "I'm sorry, you're not going to like this, but I've got to go back to Thyatira for a while – only a little while."

"What for?"

"You must have heard the news, the way the whole country is being threatened by the Laodician menace. My home despotate is right in the thick of it and I want to go there to help out."

"How? What can you do there that you can't here?"

"Fight in the militia. I've..."

"What!" she exploded, "don't be ridiculous, you're far more use to the Keepers here than being bashed over the head on the border."

"I've done it before, when the Ma'hol were invading, I..."

"I don't care. You must be crazy even to consider such a wild adventure." Her eyes flashed like fire before she decided to try a rational argument. "Look: anybody can join the militia, but you are far more valuable here. I know you are being brave, but you don't have to prove anything to me. Benedict told me how well you are doing in the service, it takes real talent to get on there and he says you have it."

All the time, she spoke Bodd was waiting to get back in again. Nothing anyone could have said just then would have changed his mind.

With face set hard he replied, "I'm sorry Anastasia, but I've got to go. I would be letting down my brothers and friends not to."

"But..."

"No, let me finish. Thyatira is only small and it's a tight-knit community. I owe everything to it and the least I can do is return to stand side-by-side with my brothers. It must be so hard for you to understand, the society here in Asattan is so completely different. No matter how much I like living here my roots, my very blood, still belongs there. Don't care if it sounds dumb, if I sat around at my desk at this time I'd just... I just couldn't do it."

The argument continued back and forth. To an outsider it would have been quite apparent that there was no communication involved, neither party actually listening to the other. A final time, Bodd reaffirmed his position adding, "Benedict understands, that's why he's letting me go."

The knowledge that her beloved uncle had sanctioned him leaving came as a blow to Anastasia. She realised that of course he must have, only he could have allowed Bodd leave at such a time. Even he had betrayed her. She had wanted to argue more, even if it was futile, but now she felt a deep emptiness inside and fell silent. She looked miserable in her helplessness.

Bodd felt terrible. Not knowing what to do, he mumbled that he should be going and left to collect his back-pack already in a corner of the hall. He did not want to leave her so upset, but hated even more the embarrassment of the situation. So putting on his pack he forced a weak smile and, softly saying goodbye headed for the door.

Anastasia, with a sudden desperation, implored him to take her along.

"I can help. I've met your friends, they will show me how..."

"No, Anastasia," Bodd was firm, "your uncle would never agree to your going so near to the battle-front. Besides I have not got much time by all accounts and I can travel quicker alone. I'm sorry."

As he moved to open the door, she threw her arms around him sobbing, "Just come back in one piece!"

A long, bitter-sweet kiss later, he glanced into her tear-filled eyes once more before stepping out. "I will," he said.

Alan slept through the morning after arriving back home. It had been a most confusing border skirmish in the dark the previous night. His memory of it was not very good, due no doubt to the clout to the head he had received. Now that he was awake odd glimpses were coming back. He could recall pushing Frank in the direction of safety and then seeing him again later at the guard-post. Someone had been pouring water on his wound and as he had sat with head bowed he had seen a stream of red flowing past his eyes.

The door latch clicked and in crept Frank who, seeing his friend awake, asked how he was.

"Oh, not too bad. There's a dull ache at present, the throbbing comes and goes; it's gone for the moment. Grab a chair, Frank, come and talk to me."

As quietly as possible the other obeyed. There was enough space alongside the bed for him to draw the chair near. He studied the patient at close hand. The top of Alan's head was in bandages, arms lay still at his side while his back and head were supported by a mound of pillows. Alan's eyes were beginning to get their sparkle back, he would not be bed-ridden for long.

"Laffaxe has just been to see me," he informed.

"Yes? What did he say?"

The drone put on a grumpy voice, "Going on bloody silly adventures, you should know better – not surprised you got yourself into this state, lucky it wasn't darn worse!"

"So he was his usual sympathetic self."

"Yeah," laughed Alan before reverting back to his Laffaxe impersonation, "and as for that old man, Thorn, I don't know what he thought he was doing there."

"He didn't say that!" a shocked Frank exclaimed.

"Only joking."

"Huh! Not much wrong with..." he broke off as Alan winced as pain shot through his head. "I'd better let you rest."

"No, don't go. You do the talking, I'll listen."

With that he took a deep breath and closed his eyes for a while. Frank did not say anything at first. One he had collected his thoughts he reflected, "I'm sorry I... insisted on going on the mission to Laodicia. I never should've. I held you up, I put us all in danger by getting myself involved in arguments the whole time. I was more of a liability than an asset. I just couldn't keep my damn mouth shut. I acted like a complete twit!

"It was all completely selfish of me. I thought it would be fun to have a bit of adventure, never... never thinking about all the possible consequences."

Alan's eyes were open again. With a smile he put his hand out and said, "We're back safely aren't we? I'll soon be as right as rain again, it wasn't your fault we bumped into those soldiers in no man's land. Don't be too harsh on yourself, it won't help you to think straight in the coming days. Laffaxe told me Warshazzap's only got a scratch and..."

"Oh, I know," said Frank with a sigh, "anyway what did we really achieve?"

"Blue-green ones! I thought you'd come here to cheer me up, not depress me. Of course we achieved something, a lot. We have a much better idea of what we are up against thanks to our going there. There's no substitute for finding out first hand. Remember how blind we were before we went!

"It's great to be back in a proper bed again. I'm surprised we didn't catch pneumonia out there in the wet."

They exchanged smiles. Alan's optimism was helping to blow the other's gloom-clouds away.

Frank then related about the Ladosan prisoners captured and the reaction of the Arpintonaxes.

"...It's only her mother who's so damned self-opinionated. I'm going to keep out of her way as much as possible.

"You know Warshazzap's up and about. He asked me if he could join the guard. I said yes, but I think he's terribly mixed up inside. Poor boy got told off in no uncertain terms by Natias when he addressed me by my Christian name! Funny how we have to be all formal again now we are back here.

Ah, I've forgotten the most important thing: we received a message from your father late this morning, it almost crossed with another one we were about to send out. The Inner Council is ordering all the other despotates to join in the war effort (many are already preparing from what they've told us) and ordered that we be ready at the Mitas Pass in Bynar in five days from now, that's next Sabbath."

"I've lost track of the days, gives us five days you say?"

"That's right. Should take us a good day and a half to get there I am informed."

"So it's definitely war now."

"I'm afraid so."

The throbbing had returned to Alan's head and he winced again. Frank quickly concluded by mentioning the meeting the next morning which he hoped they could all attend.

"Okay, Frank. I think I'll try and get some more sleep now, build up my strength. All being well, I'll be up tomorrow; be there for the council of war."

The Despot slipped out of the room and stood alone in the corridor for a moment. Council of war, that's what it would be. He shrugged off a cold chill then headed back to his suite.

CHAPTER THIRTY ONE

The Rehner brothers had arrived at the Upper Village. Jeshu and Joseph were to be top of the bill for the immanent series of religious revival meetings. They came from the Ephamon despotate where Frank had first landed and spent most of their time in the southern part of the country. Rehner was the village where they were born and was used as an easy means of identifying them, whites not having surnames as such. This was only their second visit to Thyatira, the first being several years previously and very low key.

Zadok and Eleazar showed their guests round the tent "city" which was now all but complete. It covered two large fields on the outskirts of the village. These adjoined a third in which the open-air meetings were to take place. These had deliberately been left fallow for this major event which had been planned for a long time. Crops of hulffan surrounded the site on three sides, its mustard colour beginning to turn golden in the bright sunshine. Beyond this, the gentle hills rose in the distance.

Pilgrims from all over northern Hoame, especially Aggeparii and Bynar, were now flocking in to take up the temporary accommodation. Quite apart from the spiritual dimension, the boost to the local economy would be enormous, but that was merely a fortunate spin-off.

That particular day the priest was showing the Rehners inside the large group meditation tent while his assistant waited outside.

"Good afternoon, Eleazar," greeted Saul as he approached, "our guests inside here?"

"They are, did you want to go in?" he moved to open the flap for the Village Head, but the latter declined, saying he was only having a look round.

"Not that I haven't been here many times already, but it is heartening to see it start to fill up."

"Yes indeed," agreed Eleazar with a grin, "it's hard to believe it's actually happening after all this time. A lot of planning has gone into this. Zadok is especially delighted, he was telling me that during Despot Rattinger's reign such an event would have been out of the question."

"It's true, but then surely you must remember Despot Rattinger, it was not so many years ago he went to meet his maker."

"But I was only a boy then and had not entered the priesthood. Besides, he hardly ever left the Castle at all."

"Hmm, that's true. That's where I've been summoned to tomorrow; just received the message. I exp..."

"Plotting war while we pray for peace," Eleazar interrupted. His superior voice suddenly annoyed Saul intensely who, looking down on the shorter man snapped, "Take some good advice from me: keep your misguided opinions to yourself! I don't have to justify myself to you, and you'll do well not to criticize the Despot."

With that he marched off, back in the direction of the village. Eleazar always liked to have the last word, but before he could call out to the retreating village head, Zadok appeared out of the tent with his guests. They were busy talking and had not heard Saul's raised tones.

"Hanson is rarely seen in public," the elderly priest was explaining, "he has never wished the church any good. I remember him as a child, he got up to some horrible pranks, I always knew he'd be a bad 'un."

"Brother," replied Jeshu softly, putting his hand on Zadok's shoulder, "we must never give up hope for any of our fellow men, no one is beyond redemption. We will have to pray all the more earnestly for this Hanson character. A personal invitation to our meeting would not be inappropriate I suggest."

Zadok was reproved. Amazed with himself for having succumbed to idle gossip, he grit his teeth in annoyance before apologising, "You are, of course, right. I should know better." His frown disappeared as he added, "The two of you are like a breath of fresh air around here, just what we need."

On a nearby hill, a group of about a dozen croppers were hoeing round the tall hulffan plants. Due to recent rain the weeds came out easily. These men were mostly too old to be included in the militia. A couple of exceptions, however, were Reuben and Amos. The first was too cynical in the ways of the world to join the crusade while Amos had been ordered not to by his wife.

"Those damn fools down there with their religious nonsense," moaned Reuben, "as if God wants all that singing and dancing. If I was God, I'd send down some thunderbolts and shut them all up before it all started!"

His friend was getting acutely embarrassed and hissed, "If you must blaspheme, keep your voice down!"

Reuben shrugged and let out a sigh. "Everyone's turned fanatical all of a sudden. If they're not God-bothering they're trying to drag me off to war. I want none of it. I heard a group of these "pilgrims" go past my hut yesterday evening. They couldn't keep in tune to save their lives. Sounded like a bunch of demented dakks on heat. Everywhere you turn it's the same.

"Even my son's got all excited about Zadok's blooming meetings. He's been hanging round down there for days now helping them all out. I'm sure he's only doing it to annoy me. Brogg turned religious, I ask you! Brainwashing my own flesh and blood. I don't know what..."

"I saw Tsodd yesterday," Amos butt in, changing the subject. He threw some weeds into a nearby barrow as he added, "He's back in the militia for the coming business with the Laodicians."

"Yeah, typical! I think he's a bloody fool, but then you know that. He's got all that money and doesn't do nothing with it. What a waste, I'd be able to spend it. He just wastes all his time on that silly aviary of his. I mean I might hate Hanson, but at least he gets the most from his wealth by getting people to work for him; an' he wouldn't be so stupid as to go off to war when he doesn't have to."

They fell quiet and for a while the only sound was the clicking of metal tools against stones. Then one of the elderly croppers spoke to a colleague just loud enough to be sure Reuben could hear.

"I see all our brave young men are preparing for the coming fight."

"Yes," replied the other, "most of them are brave enough to face up to their duty."

Tensing up visibly, Reuben was still considering a retort when Amos' wife arrived with some food and broke his concentration. Kim had two of her sons in tow who were helping bring the provisions up the hill. Amos and Reuben broke off from their work to greet them and take refreshment. With some food inside him, Reuben cheered up a little and was not so snappy when Kim began talking of the impending conflict.

"I'm worried sick about it," she was saying, "all the mothers and wives will soon be having to say goodbye to their loved ones, off to fight the strange foreigners. This will be a war on a scale unlike anything in our lifetime. The pilgrims from the south I have spoken to all tell of similar preparations under way. They are all praying that bloodshed can be avoided or, failing that, we can have an easy victory."

Thought Reuben, 'If there was a God, I'm sure he'd be confused by such a contradictory set of instructions.' However he said nothing as he munched one of Kim's cakes, but let her continue.

"I miss Giella so. She was always able to see a bright side to anything. I think Alan's given up trying to find her murderer. I can never seem to catch up with him; on the rare occasion I can make it to the Castle he's always at a meeting or away somewhere. Everyone seems to have forgotten my sister, they just don't care anymore."

"They've got a war to care about now," Reuben remarked.

"Before this dreadful affair is over there will be many mothers weeping over the bodies of their dead sons. I am so grateful mine are... Peter! Take your fingers from your nose! ... that mine aren't there. And that you are needed here, my darling."

Her husband looked uncomfortable and began talking about the weather, but Kim brought the subject back by saying, "At least we know we can trust the black, they would not have led us to this point had it not been absolutely necessary."

Reuben would have scoffed, however he did not want to antagonise Kim. She had been very anti-Reuben since her sister's death, but seemed to have forgotten her resentment for the moment. Besides, it would have been unwise for him to have criticised either the Inner Council or Despot in the hearing of the old men still working nearby. "We'll see," was all he said.

A slight mist hung over the ground early the next morning, cutting off the top of the hulffan from view. The orange globe turned yellow as it climbed the sky, it was to be another warm day. A giant deciduous phantillian tree stood by itself some metres away from the edge of a wood near the Lower Village. Its branches reached out as if offering a benediction to the land, as it had done for twenty generations or more. Beneath this mighty specimen, two militiamen were taking a well-earned rest.

Cragoop and John had been up half the night on manoeuvres. It was felt by Captain of the Guard, Japhses, that all men were now fully trained on night tactics. Karl was in command of the schedule for the Lower Village and was not making a bad job of it. At daylight he had ordered a break in the proceedings, but only so they could have a short rest before further manoeuvres.

"That black isn't quite the fool everyone makes him out to be," John remarked.

"He's tough mate! Just a pity he's got such a squeaky voice. I couldn't take him too seriously at first, my aching limbs do now though! I guess sitting in my workshop all day has made me unfit."

John gave a big yawn and stretched his arms. Clearing his throat he said, "My father's going to an important meeting at the Castle later today."

"Yes, I know."

"Says it'll be the last one before we march out. So I wouldn't be surprised if this isn't our final session with Karl before we go out for real."

It was a sobering thought. In the distance pale streaks of magenta cloud stretched out across the sky. They disappeared as quickly as they came while the mist in the middle-distance retreated still further.

"Remember the Ma'hol?" asked John.

"Course I do, mate."

"The long build up – at least it seemed long at the time – then when it came it was over in no time. There was even a sense that it was... er, an anticlimax."

"Right now I wouldn't mind an anticlimax one little bit. I can't believe it's going to be so easy this time."

"It's on a much bigger scale this time. The Keepers themselves are involved, want to break the threat from the north once and for all: that's what the Despot told my father."

"So that's what it's all about," Cragoop replied, "I'm sure the blacks know what they're doing."

"But to talk of more important things: how are you and Lettie doing?"

The other gave a long, "Oh!" before adding, "she said she doesn't want to see me any more. I'm now trying to get off with her sister, might have better luck there."

"Yeah?"

"Mmm. I didn't notice Shalla at first, but I've got to know her being round Lettie's home of course. I think she's cute, not as loud as Lettie."

"You're on to a good thing there, mate," Cragoop enthused, "I reckon Shalla's by far the better looking of the two."

"A bit young though."

"Never mind, mate, you stick to it, you're not in a hurry."

John shifted his seat on the leafy ground. Eyeing the branches above their heads he remarked, "Curious how different they are for sisters, both looks and personalities. I remember the first time I saw her, she..."

His reminiscences were cut short by a messenger running up and informing them they were to re-assemble. Soon the pair were back among their fellow militiamen ready for what they believed would be the final exercise. The Lower Village militia had a variety of clothing, some wore leather breastplates for protection while others had rudimentary armour. In contrast, a group of guardsmen with them looked inspiring in their brightly polished uniforms, chain-mail and coal-scuttle helmets. These professionals were gathering round Karl to hear what was required of them.

The black was magnificent in his full suit of heavy, dark armour. He wore a fuller helmet than the guardsmen, it gave protection to his cheeks and jaw, with slits for his eyes and mouth. It had a short, black plume on the top and was quite fearsome in appearance. While he gave out instructions, it struck more than one subordinate how incongruous Karl's whining voice sounded. It was perhaps a pity he chose to keep his helmet on while disseminating his plans, because it made him very difficult to hear. None of the whites had the courage to ask him to repeat it and immediately after Karl turned his back to take up position, the guardsmen who had been nearest him were quizzed as to what the instructions were.

While this was going on, Cragoop and John were a short way off with a large group of fellow militiamen. These were all getting ready, making last minute adjustments and fixing pieces of armour back on after their rest. There was much chatter going on.

"Am I all twisted at the back? John asked, "It feels a bit funny."

The jailer's son gave a quick tug at his friend's belt and pronounced it just right. He spotted the hulffan in the distance. The crop was taking well to the soil here and Cragoop said as much.

"Yeah, let's hope there are still enough people around to harvest it when the time comes."

"Hey, you're cheerful mate! When do...?"

He was cut off by a guardsman barking orders. "Come along you! Look alive. We're moving out now."

Immediately the talking stopped and the men got into line. The final exercise had begun.

That afternoon the final pre-war meeting at the Castle was to take place. Alan and Frank were in the Throne Room early. As the Despot sat above the raised platform sorting out some papers, Alan noticed a grin on his face.

"Care to share the joke?"

"Oh I was just remembering our little foray into Laodicia. Now we are back safely, I can afford to laugh at it. I was thinking about the sight of Dirkin fighting the flames in the grass."

"With your jacket you mean."

"Yes," Frank nodded with a wry expression, "I was none too pleased when I found that out.

"There was that extraordinary old man there, never did get his name. He told me all sorts of things which were fascinating at the time, but I'm not sure I can remember any of it now. I hope he does come here as we arranged. I'd like to have a much longer chat with him next time."

"What kind of things did he talk about?" asked Alan becoming interested.

"That's just it, I can't remember.... I do remember he said something about letting yourself go, plus how your mind forms patterns of thought."

Alan did not respond, so Frank concluded by adding, "Well it made sense when he said it. I hope he does come here one day.

"Still it's good to be back, have meals other than bean stew!"

Their chuckles died as the door swung open and the delegates came in. The mood was serious and there was no preliminary chatter. The Despot set the tone with his initial speech:

"Gentlemen, we are currently facing the greatest crisis our country has seen for more than a generation. Through the issuing of unreasonable and unacceptable demands, the Laodicians have forced us into a conflict none of us wanted. We have been as conciliatory as any reasonable people can be, but we are faced with an unreasonable opponent. They have displayed a great deal of irrationality, something Alan and I encountered on our very useful foray into that country. We are not dealing with a sane adversary; they have no love of God and His divine laws. They are a primitive, unprincipled people that have allowed us no room with which to find a peaceful settlement.

"Let history judge correctly who is the aggressor in the forthcoming fight: by their love of power and hatred of all that is good, these disgraceful foreigners have brought about the situation entirely themselves. They are totally to blame.

"Now; the current position is this (oh and we received a communication from His Excellency Count Zastein just this morning) the armies of Hoame are on the march! From each and every despotate men are streaming forth to do battle with our enemy. Together we will wipe them off the face of Molt."

"What is the plan, My Lord?" enquired Saul beginning to get impatient for detail.

"I'm coming to that," Frank retorted. He did not like being knocked out of his stride. "The plan is to push through the Mitas Gap into enemy territory."

Karl stated, "I thought that was where we are expecting the Laodicians to head."

"It is. There's a high probability we will meet there according to the most up-to-date intelligence received. The thing the Inner Council is most concerned about is to halt their advance before they get into Bynar and spread out. So we will defeat them and use the gap as our own doorway.

In order to be there in good time, we need to leave here the day after tomorrow. That way we should arrive at our rendezvous point ready for the Sabbath which is the day we are ordered to be there."

"Why the Sabbath?" enquired Luke, concern showing across his face, it does not seem right to organise a battle on the Sabbath."

Frank shrugged his shoulders. "I have no idea, it's probably merely a coincidence. I don't think it ever entered their heads. Anyway that is the day the Council has decided upon. Besides it doesn't necessarily mean that is the day the battle will take place."

At this point, both Gideon and Saul spoke up to raise the series of religious revival meetings about to take place.

"Can't they be postponed?" the Despot asked trying to dismiss what he thought was a minor obstacle. The village heads looked shocked.

"Oh no, My Lord," began Gideon, sounding deadly earnest in his slow, deep voice. "The preparation has taken a very long time, the people have come from all over the country – women mostly, but a good number of men – if the meetings were to be cancelled now, it would have a severe effect on morale."

Saul chipped in, "There is an expectant mood among the population, many see this as part of the overall crisis; the meetings and the war-effort have become inexorably linked in peoples' minds."

As the leader puffed in frustration, the Upper Village Head expanded, "Zadok has done a great deal in helping to whip up popular support for what he calls the crusade against the Laodicians. Apart from anything else, these meetings will boost our soldiers' determination to do well – especially the militia."

It was true, many of the whites were deeply religious and the event was to have a dramatic effect on them. Luke and Japhses each put in words of support for Saul's line. Frank noticed that neither Alan nor Karl said anything. He concluded that not being Christians, they felt unqualified to voice an opinion. Surely they would have said something against the views being expressed if they had felt strongly enough.

This left the steward. He had not said anything either, but he was not a particularly religious man so would not be biased in favour of Zadok's ambition.

"Natias?"

"My Lawd?" he replied clearing his throat.

"Your considered opinion please."

"Ah yes, My Lawd. Either way it is a pity it will be shortly before the corn harvest. The tax collection too will have to wait. As to the question of the meetings, I would say that on the one hand, if the army leaves tomowwow as has been suggested, we would get to the battle on time, but at the expense of ill feeling and arguments. On the other hand if they go the morning after the last meeting takes place, which would be... just under thwee days time, the mood of the twoops would pwobably be much better and, who knows, we may still be in time for the start of the fight."

"That's right My Lord," Japhses added his weight. "Against such a large enemy it will not be over in a day or two. Many of my men are keen to attend the meetings now that the intensive training is being concluded. Their worth must not be underestimated."

'Even the Captain of the Guard in favour of a delay,' Frank mused as he protested, "Surely the Keepers will want every man available right from the start."

"I do not think, My Lord, a couple of days delay on our part will prejudice Hoame's position materially in terms of numbers. In terms of morale, the meetings will be a real benefit."

The Despot glanced at Alan who avoided eye contact. The drone clearly wanted to be kept out of this. Karl too remained silent while the whites presented a united front for holding the rallies before marching. So this was the dilemma: either go against his benefactor's order or antagonise a large section of his people. 'Well,' he reasoned once the talking had died down, 'I am not actually disobeying Count Zastein, merely delaying our arrival one or two days. We might think of some excuse...'

The men waited for his decision. Before announcing it Frank said, "It's funny, I thought religious meetings were to call for peace and reconciliation, they were on... where I come from. You tell me it is more a device for whipping up the people into a... I don't know, "frenzy" seems too extreme a word."

"May I answer?" asked Saul.

"Go ahead."

"The meetings are much more than that, My Lord. I have spent a large amount of time of late with Zadok and the preparations just north of the village. I have also met and spoken with the Rehner brothers who have come to preach.

"Over the years we have become dull in our love for God, worn down by everyday toil and troubles. This series of meetings will redress that by putting fresh life into us. With so many ardent souls coming up from the south it will be a marvellous opportunity to get together, renew old friendships, put right the wrongs of the past."

"And help the Upper Village's economy," whispered Alan, fortunately unheard by the Village Head who continued, "The people are full of expectation, it would be a severe blow to have it all abandoned at the last moment. After all..."

"All right, all right!" Frank called out holding his hands up in surrender. "The meetings go ahead as planned. But I want everything ready so that we can leave at dawn following the last evening of the meetings. We march in three days time.

"Now, if we can return to the strategy involved: as some of you all ready know, our allies the Ma'hol are sending the main body of their army to be with our forces at the Mitas Gap. They will also be conducting a diversionary attack across their border into the west of Laodicia. That should keep the enemy occupied and help prevent any attack over the mountains here they might be contemplating.

"Our information is that the Ma'hol are mobilizing a huge force. I have been informed that they can even spare some to ensure the robber bands to the south-west are firmly pinned-down and will not cause anyone trouble. I have given them permission to pursue any operations against them across the border if they see fit – a necessary measure whilst most of our men are away."

A detailed discussion followed during which the composition of the small defence force being left in Thyatira was ironed out. Also Alan produced some maps and, leaning on his personal experience, described the Mitas area in depth. Frank said a bit about communication channels set up with the Ma'hol, but for much of the proceedings just listened.

He thought back to his past life on Eden. 'What a crazy turn my life has taken: here I am a medieval warlord planning a battle with my warrior chiefs. I will be sending men out to cut and slash at others using equally crude weapons. I suppose it would be no different were I not here, I am merely a figurehead for this tiny clan. Yes, but what happened to this great lover of peace, whatever happened to him?" If my fellows from Eden could see me now... not for the first time I've thought that. Still, God must have inspired the hand that wrote, "for everything there is a time, a time for peace and a time for war," I could not stop it now anyway, no matter what I did.'

Japhses was speaking, "To a man we are ready to die a hero's death!"

"If need be," Frank added, thinking, 'I thought the aim was to kill the opposition!'

"Good, so it's all arranged then. We assemble at dawn on the morning after the last of these revival meetings at the Upper Village which will be held in four days time, right?" he looked across to Saul for confirmation and got it.

The Captain caught the mood of the whites when he called out, "With you at our head, My Lord, Thyatira's warriors will make a worthy contribution in the fight against the foreign devils!"

There was a cheer from the village heads and Frank concluded this was the right time to draw the meeting to a close. As it broke up, he sat thinking further on Japhses' words. Before the big man had left the room he called him over.

"I was wondering... if we're all about to go off to battle I feel I really should be taught how to fight with a sword. You know, just in case."

Japhses was astonished at his Despot's naivety. Picking his words carefully he said, "It is not something that can be taught in a day My Lord. In Hoame the skill is gradually acquired from childhood, especially for blacks."

By this time everyone else had left the room except Alan who was still in his chair, tipping it back onto its hind legs. He seemed absorbed in his own thoughts.

Frank told Japhses he accepted what he said, "But I hoped a few useful hints might go a long way – I know nothing at present. As in the Ma'hol affair I prefer to command from a distance, but I would still appreciate it if you would give me a rudimentary lesson."

"Of course, My Lord!" the man barked as if on the parade ground, "when would you like the lesson?"

"Oh I don't know, when would be the best time for you? We've got several days."

The next morning was agreed upon and the Captain of the Guard was dismissed. Frank had a smile on his face as he began gathering together his papers, unconscious of his friend's presence until he spoke.

"You know he's still our murder suspect."

"Oh damn!" responded Frank, the smile suddenly wiped from his face. "I'd conveniently forgotten about that."

"Again."

"Yes, again, I just don't know," he continued, looking concerned this time, "but I just want to shelve the Giella... um, investigation, until this Laodician crisis is over. We've had this conversation before."

Alan shrugged, "Yeah, we have. Okay if you don't want me to mention it again, I won't."

Feeling awkward Frank replied hesitantly, "It... it might sound callous, but it seems a long time... um, well I just can't in my heart of hearts believe Japhses did it and I don't want to question him in the current... situation. I..."

"Okay, forget I said anything! It's your decision. I'll consider myself relieved of the investigation. If you ever want to revive it though, I suggest you question Japhses about his part."

"I'm sorry Alan, I didn't mean to waste your time, and I know it's immoral of me to stop trying to find her killer, but..."

"Blue-green ones!" the drone interrupted once more, "don't go on. I'm not a lover of "morals" at the best of times and I don't enjoy seeing you get hung up on them." He stopped tipping his chair up and rose to leave, "Just put it to the back of your mind. Men's lives will be at stake in the coming days and they'll be relying on you."

"Keep your guard up. Keep your guard up, My Lord!"

"I'm trying Japhses. This damn thing feels like it weighs a tonne."

With a sigh, the white explained, "Then we shall have to try the fourteen hin if the sixteen is too heavy. Guard! Fetch the Despot a fourteen hin sword."

The lesson was to have taken place in the bailey, but at the last moment they both felt it a little too public and had retired to the Castle roof. With the sun high in the sky there was no shade up there. As Frank waited for the lighter weapon to be brought, he felt the perspiration stream down him. It took longer than expected and he sat on the thick frame of the catapult in his semi-armour, next to a neat stack of projectiles.

Japhses waited expectantly at the entrance. The guardsman who had scuttled off to find the lighter sword eventually emerged with one, only to be castigated by his Captain for taking so long. This was somewhat unfair, because there were not many about, all the guardsmen used the standard, heavier weapon.

They were soon at it again: thrust and parry, the slashing stroke and defence. Frank found the new weapon easier to manage, but once more cursed his poor sight, having a permanent squint to catch the other's moves. By the time he called it a day he was feeling a lot more confident. He had no illusions to being a master swordsman, but felt he had learned enough in the brief time available to hold his own.

"How do you think I did?" he asked innocently while a pair of servants undid the straps of his breastplate.

Japhses peered down at him, flicking his great mane of white hair back across his shoulder. "Not bad, My Lord," he replied, "in the right conditions – against an inexperienced foe, with the element of surprise on your side and a good dose of luck – I would give you a fair chance of staying alive long enough for one of us to come to your rescue."

'Rare praise indeed!' thought Frank, ' a real vote of confidence.'

"My Lord, I think I should mention that a small group of dissenters were caught trying to disrupt the people clearing up the market this morning."

"Oh? I thought we had popular support on our side."

"We do, My Lord. This tiny group comes from Sardis. Fanatics with an evil doctrine of appeasement. Luke has kept a close eye on them for some time. He felt that while they kept themselves to themselves they posed no threat. Personally, I would have had them kicked out anyway, but he is more diplomatic.

"I only mention this in passing, My Lord, there is no cause for concern, the people are with us."

"These were Taltons you say."

"You need not worry about their commitment, My Lord. All reports and observations show the Taltons more than anyone heeding the call to arms. They are a fine people, I will be proud to have their men under me. The dissenters were as a spot on an otherwise healthy body."

"Yet this group still felt strong enough to come out into the open."

"They only numbered seven and were not at all well organised. They had only begun their attempt to poison the minds of the innocent folk in the courtyard when they were arrested. By a stroke of luck, squad leader Jonathan was taking his men past when the trouble started. He acted swiftly and the disruption was contained before most had any idea what was going on."

"Excellent, he needs commending for his swift action."

"I have My Lord. The dissenters are currently in the jail, the old jail."

"Ah you mean the grotty one. Not in with the Laodician border guards I hope, they could influence each other."

"No My Lord," Japhses replied patiently, "they are well segregated."

"Good. Well I suppose they're out of the way for the time being and that's what matters."

The last piece of armour was off and Frank directed the servants to prepare a bath. As he did, so the Captain suggested the "traitors" be executed as an example. Frank was not surprised at the remark. Starting down the spiral staircase he replied, "We don't want to waste any more energy over them. We'll leave them until after we get back, they can't do any harm there if they've got no public sympathy."

Arriving outside his suite, he stopped and thanked Japhses for the sword lesson, "And never fear, I'll direct operations from the rear as much as possible."

Frank came down later feeling much refreshed. It was wonderful how revitalising a good soak could be. Wishing to take a break from the preparations, he set off to find Hannah whom he had hardly seen at all since his return. His search took him to the bailey.

He exited the reception room into the busy outside. Men and women were everywhere hurrying about their business. A wagon nearby was being unloaded, its cargo of salted pork heading for the cool recesses of the Castle. Guardsmen were making an inventory of the munitions wagons now assembled within the walls. A large dakk kicked up dust as it was ridden past in the direction of the stables.

"They were charging forty-six stens," a woman standing by the meat wagon was saying.

"No!" exclaimed her colleague, "that's nothing less than theft my dear, they're not even worth half that."

The observer was starting to get interested and find out what was not worth the money when he heard a voice he knew addressing him.

"My Lord, may I have an urgent word with you. It's about the Pacifist League members you..."

"Good afternoon, Eleazar. I'm looking for Hannah Unit, you haven't seen her have you?"

"No I haven't, My Lord," the priest's assistant said quickly, trying to brush that aside to resume his grievance. With the Despot's eyes at last focused on him, he began again. "Please, I must have an important word with you, where may we speak?"

Lazily, Frank replied, "Here's as good a place as any. What's on your mind?"

A group of stable-hands went by, they were fooling about, shouting loudly to each other. Blocking the noise out, the young man began earnestly, "It is about my colleagues from the Pacifist League, My Lord, they have been arrested. May I ask what you intend to do with them?"

"Nothing," came the offhand response of a man clearly not taking the other's grievance very seriously.

"I'm sorry?"

"I don't intend doing anything with them for the time being. I'm quite happy for them to stay where they are for now."

"What crime have they committed?"

Frank looked amused and gave a short laugh, "I think you know the answer to that. We can't have people undermining our just cause. Fret not, they'll be safe in the dungeon. Crag assures me they're being well looked after."

"I've seen that black pit, these good men and women of conscience do not deserve such a fate. May I ask you a question, My Lord: how can you reconcile Christianity and war?"

Still being flippant, the Despot replied, "Depends what sort of mood I'm in." Then more seriously, "I am beginning to lose my patience with you. Listen: It's easy for you, you've got no responsibilities; well, major ones. You..."

"But if you are serious..."

"Look, I'm not going to argue with you. I'm not having our plans disrupted, I won't put up with it. If I hear you're stirring up trouble, I'll have you joining your friends in the dungeon before you can say "knife". It's no skin off my nose."

Eleazar paused before saying, "That will not be necessary, My Lord, I will not stir up trouble."

Frank was taken aback by this sudden and uncharacteristic climb-down, not like him at all. Surely he was not capable of bluffing? "What's this, a rare attack of pragmatism?"

"I believe I can do more good on the outside, My Lord. I will not cause disruption; you have my word on it."

"Good. Now go away and leave me to get on."

Red-faced, the young man turned sharply and stalked off. The Despot made for the stables, justifying in his mind the stance he had just taken. He was still mulling it over when, level with Laffaxe's home, he turned to see Hannah appear from the reception room. Instantly he perked up and speedily retraced his steps. In her eagerness she ran to meet him and they met with a peck of a kiss. He was tingling all over as she spoke.

"They told me you were looking for me. I've been trying to keep out of your way the last couple of days, 'cos I know you've had so much to do."

"It's great to see you, Hannah. Well I haven't got anything to do right now, let's go to our shady spot outside the walls."

They picked their way through the busy scene towards the tranquillity of the spinney he had referred to. Frank said, "I find I'm not so much a "doer" as a facilitator. I've been un-blocking the obstacles which others find in their way. I don't actually do much of the work as such."

"My father would've said that's the sign of a good leader: delegates to others while remaining available to deal with any difficulties that may arise."

"Well I'm blessed with a good team, men who know their business and what's required."

Arriving at their destination, the pair sat down in the pleasant shade. Following a brief pause they both began to talk at once then stopped and laughed.

"You go first," said Frank.

"No, you."

"All I was going to say was I feel it's important that we keep an overall perspective as much as possible. That's why the meetings with Alan, Japhses and the rest are so important. Anyway, what were you going to say?"

"Oh, I was going to change the subject; I didn't know if you'd heard about Warshazzap."

"No."

"He's decided to go back home, in fact he left this morning."

"But I thought he was going to join the guard – here I mean. That was the last thing I heard."

"Yes he changed his mind, several times in fact. He had great difficulty making it up and I didn't want to influence him too much. In the end he couldn't face the thought of fighting his fellow countrymen in battle, even if he does still believe in our cause."

"I'm glad you said "our", how do you feel about fighting against your fellow countrymen?"

"I'm not actually going to have to look men in the eye as I bonk them over the head with my sword. Warshazzap felt he could be more use as a spy for us back home and I think he's right. He'd be just another soldier here, but of far more use over there."

"Either way you are losing your bodyguard."

"That's the least sacrifice we can make, releasing him. He is heading for Sector Eight, hoping to locate our people there and let them know what is happening. I have sent letters with him. Now I only pray he is not caught."

Frank nodded seriously, "Especially with a knowledge of our plans. I'd have preferred him to've delayed a few days had I been consulted. No denying he's brave though.

"A man of conscience."

"Oh no!"

"What is it? What's funny? She asked, puzzled at his sudden change.

"It's just that I've had enough of "men of conscience" for one day. When I met you just now, I'd moments before sent Eleazar packing. I wasn't in the mood to hear his protestations. I'm convinced we are up against an evil regime hell-bent on destroying us if they can. I'm sorry I speak harshly against your people, but..."

"I understand. I genuinely believe that a defeat for my people in this war, a bad defeat, will be the quickest and surest way of bringing them to their senses. Then they might shake off those grasping men who have seized power for themselves."

He moved off his hip which was starting to go numb. Bright sunshine flickered through the rich green, swaying leaves. Turning back to Hannah, he was acutely aware of her curvaceous body so close to him on the grass. However she was still caught up in the conversation.

"My mother is not taking it very well. She has lost a lot of her drive which is not like her at all. Spends most of her time indoors with only Nooni for company. I've been trying, unsuccessfully, to get her to come out, never had to do that before. Eko has been most supportive which is a blessing."

"Ah yes, Natias' wife. She always strikes me like a mouse. She's always about in the Castle, but you don't notice her most of the time."

"You do say the funniest things sometimes!" Hannah said, contented expression across her face as she edged still closer and stretched herself out on the grass with her arms above her head. "I want a kiss."

This time he was not slow to respond.

"Okay, you can move that one out now, report to Karl at the Castle. Right, you two begin loading this one. Nilo, go to the granary and see what's delaying Hal and his men. Tell him to get a move on. Solly, where's that list?"

Early afternoon in the Upper Village and it was sweltering. Standing in the open directing operations, Alan wiped the sweat from his forehead. Soldiers ran to and fro at his command, but the area was almost devoid of villagers. This was to be the last consignment of supplies shipped to the Castle. If a Ladosan army did manage to cross the mountains to get here, they would find nothing to sustain them.

One young villager who was helping them came up and announced that only one more wagon-load was left in the warehouse.

"Good," declared the drone, "We can move on after this."

Disengaging his eyes from the hurrying figures about him, he saw Kim making towards him. Unusually she was not surrounded by at least some of her many children. Rather she was striding out with a purpose. It was only as she got to him that he guessed what that purpose might be.

"Alan, I want a word."

"Kim, hello, I haven't seen you for a while. Where's the family?"

She was clearly agitated. He hoped the best posture to adopt was a friendly one, but there was no diverting her as she came straight to the point.

"I want to know what is happening about you finding my sister's murderer."

Not wanting to discuss it standing in the middle of the road, Alan told a squad leader present to take over and led Kim round the back of the warehouse into privacy and shade.

He opened his mouth to speak, but she got in first, saying, "I think you're trying to avoid me. It's been weeks since my only sister was butchered and for all I know you have given up trying to discover who did it. Why don't you tell me how the investigation is going as you did at first? Or have you given up trying? What's going on? Why haven't you found them?"

"Okay, now calm down," he said putting his hand on her shoulder as he tried to pacify her.

"But you..."

"Now c'mon, let me say something. Which question shall I answer first? The situation is this: no, I haven't stopped searching for the culprit, but with the war looming it's been very busy lately." He continued quickly when he saw Kim was about to interrupt again, "I am trying my best, I haven't given in. I assure you we will catch them in the end. But you must realise I'm no expert in catching murderers, no matter how much I want to. And it seems several of the people I've spoken to have lied to me about their role and I find myself relying on other peoples' gossip in the absence of hard facts."

"Who lied to you?"

"I don't think I should..."

"Have you interrogated Reuben? I don't like him, it would not surprise me to discover *he's* the murderer."

Still trying to keep the conversation rational, Alan replied, "I have spoken to Reuben. There are several areas of investigation still open, I..."

"You know he was blackmailing her into... doing things? He's disgusting!"

"I've heard stories, but he denies it."

"Of course he denies it!"

"But I don't see what motive he had for killing her."

"You should torture the truth out of him, that's loosen his tongue. Rattinger would've, I suppose Despot Thorn won't let you."

"We never discussed it. Apart from anything else, it's extremely inefficient at arriving at the truth; under torture people say whatever they think you want to hear. I have questioned Reuben, but he is not a prime suspect."

"Who is?"

Alan was still finding himself on the defensive, "I'm not saying we have one."

"So you're no closer to finding Giella's killer," she snapped petulantly.

"We could be, we're not sure at this stage."

Kim began to say something then stopped. Tears suddenly welled up and she put her hand to her eyes to wipe them. "No one cares anymore! My neighbours go about with their own concerns, Amos is always swanning about with that Reuben wretch. Roil has gone into herself. Worst of all is Uriah! You'd think her husband would care, but nobody does." She sobbed.

Not knowing what to say, Alan tentatively put his arm around her and was relieved when the gesture was not rejected. He spent some time making sympathetic overtures, knowing full well that what she really wanted was hard news of his progress. What could he tell her, that he did have a prime suspect but the Despot would not sanction his interrogation until the coming war was over? He thought not. Instead he again promised her the investigation would not be wound up and the hunt for Giella's killer would still continue.

'Blue-green ones! Why did Frank get me involved in this thing?' he moaned to himself, 'I'm not cut out for it. I hate going round listening to villagers back-biting in order to find a lead, but what other way is there? I don't know. I should've turned him down.'

She was calmer now and he took her back to the front of the building and the heat of the blazing sun. The soldiers loading the wagon stopped and stared at the couple, but quickly resumed when Alan flashed a glance in their direction. He asked Kim if he could escort her back home, but she declined.

"No I'll be okay, I'll head back" she said, but stopped for a further comment. "I can see it's not easy for you and I shouldn't have judged you so harshly, I can see that you do care. No one in the village seems to care any more, the only one who's shown any sympathy recently was that simpleton Brogg. Anyway, I'd better be going, bye bye then."

"Take care."

She turned and shuffled back. He watched her for a few moments before turning his attention back to the men. The runner had returned from the granary and was standing patiently waiting to report. When given the signal, he did so.

"Hal's squad will be a while longer. They suffered a broken wheel on one of the wagons. It was almost fixed when I left."

The drone nodded. Just then a large crowd of children came running towards them. Their ages ranged from about three to twelve Earth-years and they were in playful mood. They showed much merriment as they bounded up to form a rough semicircle round the working soldiers. Their spokesman, a young, skinny lad with wispy white hair called out, "Hi Alan, can we watch?"

"Sure," he replied, pushing his thoughts to the back of his mind, "course you can."

The light was falling as the first seizable Hoame force arrived at the Mitas Pass. The First Light Ephamon Regiment was one of many new units formed out of Count Zastein's army reforms two years previously. Since then all the bigger despotates' forces were organised in the traditional way. Thyatira's guard and militia were a drop in the ocean, but the same Count felt it a most important drop, because that smallest of all despotates was providing the excuse for the war he had long felt necessary.

Strangely though, it seemed the initial action would not be fought on Thyatiran soil. Hoame scouts had located two huge, lumbering Ladosan armies still deep inside their own territory, but moving seemingly inexorably towards the only employable mountain pass on their common border. A profound inevitability appeared to have been set into events. It would take an enormous effort to avoid a showdown at Mitas in a few days time. No such effort was being made to stop it.

There was remarkably little tension there thought Commander Schallestein as he led his men onto the western plateau overlooking the flat-bottomed valley that evening. He introduced himself to the junior officer in charge of the reconnaissance unit all ready present.

It is good to see you Commander, I am Lieutenant Berger. I have forty men under me, just under half are here at the Pass right now."

"I want a full briefing as soon as we have eaten."

"Of course, Commander, I am at your disposal."

A small camp had been established there for a fortnight. It was an excellent vantage point looking down to where the action was expected to take place. Hand-picked, they sent out long-range patrols to scan deep into Ladosa for signs of the enemy.

The new arrivals pitched their tents for the night. After he had eaten, Commander Schallestein sent for the reconnaissance officer. He arrived promptly and briefed his superior on the latest position. His superior was surprised at the news that a Ladosan spy had been caught.

"Just a single man?"

"Yes, Commander, we have applied torture, but not got any sense out of him."

"Hmm, not really what I'm here for. Keep him alive and tell the Keepers when they arrive shortly. Continue your report."

The lieutenant did so, concluding, "So everything is very quiet here at present."

"All that will change. More regiments will be arriving throughout tomorrow and many more are expected the following day, including our Ma'hol allies. In two days time you will not recognise this quiet place, the camp fires will stretch to the horizon."

"I was expecting Despot Hista's Bynarians to be here before this; they have the least distance to travel."

"They have deliberately held back for strategic reasons I will not elaborate on. They shall be here in the morning, though."

"It will not be a moment too soon, Commander. Even at their slow pace the main enemy force will be upon us in three days, maybe less."

Concentrating on the map laid out in front of him, Schallestein replied, "Let them come, pigs to the slaughter. Now: you say along this strip the Pass is three-quarters of a kilometre wide?"

"Yes, Commander, the narrowest channel."

"And one and a half long."

"Yes."

"Fine. Now here, here and here," he said pointing at the map, we will be setting up three small, tent-like structures first light. They do not look like ordinary tents, they will be small, but more upright with striped canvas. Now, no unauthorised personnel must go near them, not blacks, not other commanders, not even despots. The only men authorised are crews, who all wear red arm-bands like this," he indicated to the scarlet stripe on his left arm, "or the Members of the Inner Council, the Keepers themselves, is that understood?"

"Yes, Commander," replied Berger, wondering what all this was about. If despots are not allowed near these special tents, this Commander was certainly not going to divulge their contents to him. "I shall inform my men."

"Good. We can talk further tomorrow, I should like to be shown the view from your forward-most observation point. We will have a long day ahead of us, I intend to get some sleep. You are dismissed for now."

"Of course, good night, Commander."

CHAPTER THIRTY TWO

While the Hoame vanguard was retiring for the night at the Mitas Pass, the mood in a neighbouring despotate was markedly different. The first of three nights of religious revival meetings had got under way with a swing. The predominant mood was one of fellowship as the crowds belted out lively songs of worship. Men and women from each part of the country were represented, although the male contingent from outside the host despotate was badly depleted due to the call to arms.

It was a night as black as any other on Molten, but the fields were lit up with hundreds of tiny lights. A gentler hymn was begun and hand-held candles moved slowly from side to side with the swaying bodies. Following on from the warmth of the day the air seemed pleasantly cool. More than one participant felt this somehow only added to the special atmosphere of the occasion.

Earlier that afternoon, the programme had officially been started by the Rehner brothers in a brief ceremony. Several of the fringe events had, in fact, been going on unauthorised for some days. Now that it was evening the star guests took centre stage and spoke in turn to the multitude. Jeshu gave the longer talk and chose Jesus' words to Nicodemus as his theme.

"So what was the Master meaning with this teaching? To turn over a new leaf and try harder? Far more than that. To be born again means just that, it is to enter into a new relationship with God, nothing less. Your body can only be born once, that is obvious. We are all fortunate enough to have had the second birth; the birth of the spirit in communion with the Holy Spirit.

"Entering into this new relationship with God and his Holy Spirit means our future is assured. What a wonderful feeling of security we should all feel being protected in the arms of our Heavenly Father! He will make sure that no matter what we have to go through, our destiny is with Him, He will never turn us away. There will be testing times ahead, but we should all rest easy in the most wonderful assurance..."

Jeshu spoke for some while and his words were well received. He felt a little disappointed though, the magic he had hoped for was not quite there. Deciding not to mention this feeling to his brother he prayed that Joseph's talk the following evening would really set the event alight.

"Good morning everyone!" the cheery Despot greeted as he joined the others for breakfast in the hall. He sat down at the end of the table with Natias to his right and Hannah to his left. Everyone else had long finished and were about their work. At his arrival, servants went quickly to prepare some food and a short while later, Illianeth carefully laid his meal in front of him.

"Thank you, my dear," he said jovially before tucking in.

"With a smile, Hannah inquired if he had enjoyed his lie-in. He noticed the pair sitting with him had just about finished theirs, plus the absence of other people and remarked that he had not realised he had had a lie-in.

"Still," he said, "We are well ahead with the preparations seeing as we will not be able to leave for a couple of days yet."

Natias soon left to go about his business and Frank was able to give Hannah his full attention.

"You're looking lovelier than ever this morning," he commented.

The compliment took her by surprise and she could not contain a blush. Recovering herself she replied, "You're in a good mood this morning, you should have a lie-in more often!"

The hall was unusually quiet, most people being involved in duties outside. The bailey was still a hive of activity where Karl and Laffaxe were in charge of the baggage train of supplies and equipment for the forthcoming march east. Here inside the Castle, the warm morning sun was not penetrating the thick walls and the air was pleasanter.

Illianeth was allowed to clear up their table and then began scrubbing the one alongside. Against this background the couple chatted away in their little oasis of calm.

"Have you heard any reports of how the first meeting went last night?" Frank enquired.

"I have. Eko went. It was spell-binding by her account. She told me she had been keen to get there early and she did just that. There were many side events to consider, she said. She plans to spend most of the next two days up there."

"I see."

"I'm going tonight. It sounds very different from back home, but it could be what I need. It sounds so refreshing after my country. Why don't we go together?"

Frank shook his head. "Sorry, I'm just not in the mood for it. Zadok told me at great length what to expect and it just isn't me."

"But I'd enjoy your company."

"I was afraid you were going to say that. I could lie and say I'm too busy with preparations for the war, but the truth is I'm a bit disillusioned with the whole thing. You could accuse me of being selfish, but... oh I don't know, it just isn't for me all this rhetoric and communal singing."

"I noticed you never come to the Sabbath meetings. When we talked about it before you said something *then* about not liking communal worship which struck me as rather odd, if you don't mind me saying. Surely it gives us all a boost to be able to share our faith together, we can't all be like John the Baptist alone in the Wilderness."

Lifting up his eyes as if seeking inspiration, Frank noticed the lower, false ceiling he had had put in. The guild squad had done a good job of it.

"I don't know that I would model myself on John the Baptist, although I'm rather flattered at the thought. I have never felt at home with this type of worship, where I come from it was so different. Not that I criticise those who practise it, if they find better communion with God that way then that's fine.

"I do think my own beliefs and ideas are shifting further though, I feel a period of change in my mind, I'm not sure where it will end. Have you found that in your life – like the rings of a tree you have a period of growth followed by one of consolidation?"

Hannah nodded more in sympathy than agreement. He continued, "I don't know, it's just that recently I've been questioning the need for priests at all. Should we have a filter between us and God? The church has always had them, but when I return to the source, the Bible, I become increasingly convinced that Jesus wanted to do away with all that and for people to have direct communion with God like he did.

"You remember the story of the woman at the well? When she asked him which was the right place to worship, the Temple or the mountain (both entailing a priestly ritual) he replied that neither was, rather individuals should worship in spirit and in truth."

"Maybe you are a mystic, but for the rest of us, we need our priests!"

Their smiles gradually faded as they sat in silence for a while, then Hannah remarked that she had heard that the whites did not use the Bible, but handed down the stories and sayings by word of mouth.

"I know," said Frank, "It surprised me too, but they don't lack commitment because of it. It's odd though, because it's not as if none of them can read. They are a fascinating people and I admire their religious fervour, I really do."

Hannah grinned, "You like *people* don't you. I can tell."

"Ha, some people perhaps! You're right if you mean I enjoy my life here. But enough of me, how's your mother feeling?"

"Oh far better, thank you. She is helping Laffaxe out with preparation for the field hospital, although she'll be staying here when you march of course."

Their eyes met and for a while they were content with silent communion. Even in the poorly-lit hall Hannah's long, black hair had a sheen to it. Her dark skin looked darker still. She in turn scrutinised his features: his not-so-neatly trimmed beard, the unassuming clothes he had on that day, his eyes. She found great depth in those eyes. They told of many layers of personality, so far she had only scratched the surface.

"So, what'll you be doing today then?" she asked.

"Well I'll be coordinating food supplies this morning here at the Castle. After lunch it's a visit to the Lower Village. Much of the food has been stored underground, below us now. Got to make sure there'll be enough wagons to take it all when we load it shortly before we set off.

"Very important, food. Japhses likes to emphasise ammunition stocks, and while there's nothing wrong in that, we must keep a sense of balance, because a good food supply is just as important in a campaign."

"You obviously know what you're talking about."

Thought Frank, 'It's only what I've read!'

Said Frank, "Well we probably won't be able to live off the land you see, to the north they're had a much drier summer than here, everything's parched as you probably know.

"As for the ammunition wagons in the bailey, they will have to be moved out after lunch. While our army is away, most of the remaining villagers will be sheltering here. Natias is in charge of accommodation arrangements, he's going to set up the tents in the same way as when the Ma'hol prisoners were kept, but on a much larger scale."

"Eko told me she felt guilty in a way, 'cos Natias is staying here while many of her friends' husbands will be off to fight."

"That's not fair; someone has to stay and mind things here and he's by far the best choice."

"I can see how she feels though."

"Hmm," Frank nodded. His fingers played with the edge of the table as he said, "Some guardsmen will have to say goodbye to their families sooner than others. At the meeting we decided to send an advanced party ahead of the main army, a token force to represent our despotate. The truth is our main force will arrive late and this is a measure to placate the Keepers."

At this point, Karl entered from outside and asked the Despot if he could help in the bailey.

"Of course," said Frank getting up. He told Hannah Unit he would see her again soon and left with his black officer.

As they descended the stairs, Karl said in his uniquely strange voice, "The weather has suddenly got hotter Sir, hot and sticky."

"Has it?"

"Yes, Sir, most uncomfortable."

Through the reception room and into the bailey.

"Phew it's like an oven out here!" exclaimed Frank as the heat hit him. "Anyway, tell me – how are the men from the Lower Village shaping up? I hear you have been working them hard which is what we need."

"They are in great shape, Sir. One would never believe they were ordinary villagers, they are a tough bunch. Spirits are high too, they are raring to go."

"Excellent! The sooner we get going the better. From all that I've heard you have been doing a good job down there, thank you, Karl."

The black was pleased to have received a compliment, he had not once got one from Despot Kagel. Opening himself up a bit, he said, "I am so much happier here than I was in Aggeparii. The whole atmosphere is pleasanter, none of the back-biting and behind the scenes manoeuvring that went on there. My family like it here too. It was the best move we ever made."

Resuming his more formal persona, Karl added, "I need to take you through the inventory Sir before we move the wagons outside the walls."

"Of course, carry on."

That afternoon Alan was back at the Castle. He and Frank were together in the courtyard overseeing operations there. Somehow order seemed to be forming out of chaos.

The Despot observed, "The livestock pens are still empty."

"They'll be led up here at the last possible moment with their owners," Alan replied.

A runner came charging up and immediately sought out the Despot. Well out of breath he gasped, "My Lord... the Ma'hol... they are coming through the Upper Village right now!"

"Has there been trouble?" Frank asked, anxious expression on his and Alan's faces.

"No, My Lord," the runner replied, starting now to collect himself, "no trouble, but Japhses thought you should know they are approaching."

In fact trouble was the last thing there had been. The enormous army of Rabeth-Mephar had received a tumultuous welcome as it passed just north of the village. As well as the villagers, people from all over Hoame attending the rallies had poured out to cheer and garland the Ma'hol troops. Wild scenes greeted the soldiers as they marched out to do battle on behalf of their common cause. At their head, the Mehtar stood proudly erect in a light chariot pulled by four dakk abreast. His red hair seemed ablaze in the bright sunshine. A greater contrast there could not have been with the previous time he had been that way. The jeers of that day were replaced by cheers and flowers, in many cases by the exact same people. The irony of it was not lost on the Ma'hol ruler who remained stone-faced throughout.

There was another contrast with that previous occasion. Then it had been a modest force, now the size of the army left the whites breathless. With baggage-train included the column stretched for kilometres. Japhses had sent the runner on his way as soon as the vanguard had begun passing through. As he spoke to the Despot the crowds were still cheering the flow of men and material.

A long formation of Imperial Guard immediately followed the Mehtar. This haughty elite made a fine show in their ostentatious uniforms with long, flowing plumes. They appeared oblivious to the heat.

There was no doubting their allies' commitment. The only contingent of Imperials left in their homeland was a small section Mennahuna Sil would incorporate into his diversionary attack against Western Ladosa.

The runner finished reporting and Frank turned to Alan, saying, "This does make us look bad with our procrastination! The road runs right by here, what do I say to the man?"

"My Lord, am I dismissed?"

"Oh yes," replied the Despot having forgotten the runner's presence, "go and get yourself some water, you look about to collapse."

Alan suggested it might be a good idea for their advanced party to accompany the Ma'hol, an idea which immediately found favour with Frank.

Nearby Uriah was directing a pair of guardsmen carrying some fencing. The Despot called him over.

"Where are the men who will form our expeditionary force?"

"At rest, My Lord," he replied pointing to one of the towers. He was not going to volunteer further information, so Alan added, "They're Rodd and James' squads Frank, they were helping in Sardis this morning."

"I see."

"They were due to depart at sunset, but if the Ma'hol are almost upon us I'm sure they can ready themselves now."

Before he went to inform the men, Uriah volunteered to lead this unit. Alan, however, said Japhses would not thank them for sending his number two without consultation, so they reverted to the original plan of James being in charge as the longer serving of the two squad leaders.

Uriah left them without another word and the pair climbed the battlements to try and spot the approaching allied army. Inside one of the towers it was cooler. Alan peered through the large arrow slit but could see no sign at first, only the heat haze far into the distance. Frank was standing behind and asked, "Would you like me to fetch for my telescope? It's in my rooms somewhere."

Screwing up his face Alan replied, "Naa, not worth it."

"I must remember it when we go."

A guardsman present took over the watch and in a short while announced he could see something.

"Many men, My Lord, just over the horizon. See the sun reflecting?"

So saying he made way for the Despot who, squinting hard, saw the sunshine flashing off golden armour some kilometres off.

They came back down and, with Karl having now joined them, formed a reception committee outside. Standing against the west wall facing the road there was no shade until guardsmen rigged up a canopy for them. Close by was the courtyard entrance, soon out of which the men of the advanced party marched. Having been given permission to take a wagon to carry their armour and supplies the guardsmen themselves travelled lightly. After James and Rodd had reported to the Despot, they lined their men up.

Further along towards the main entrance dozens of wagons lay parked, fully laden and ready for the dakks to be hitched to them.

"We're running out of animals," informed Alan, "with up to seven pairs required to pull the heaviest loads that's a hell of a lot of dakks. I had to order the requisition of all those in private hands, I don't know if you've noticed the extra paddocks on the east side. Hanson was none too pleased when we took his, but with five dozen in his stables it's a handy addition."

Remarked Frank, "I've never met our reclusive Mr Hanson."

"Nor have I," added Karl.

"You haven't missed much," Alan assured them.

They waited. The drone told them that teachers from all three villages had combined to set up a temporary school in the tower near Laffaxe's house. They were particularly well organised apparently.

Still they waited. It was a good time before the Ma'hol soldiers became anything but a blur on the shimmering horizon. Then they seemed to approach much quicker. Before they knew it they could see the Mehtar's chariot easily. This was his war-chariot, a far smaller and lighter machine than the one used for the previous visit. The Imperial Guard followed behind, heads held high as they marched with an air of arrogance. Their plumes and banners were alive with colour if not movement in the humid, still air.

"Look at them," said Frank with a note of amusement in his voice, "strutting like peacocks."

The other two looked puzzled and he had to explain, "Oh, a mythical bird famed for its showy plumage. I don't know what they are looking so superior about, we beat them when it came to a fight."

Neither Alan nor Karl made the obvious point that it was only a tiny fraction of the approaching masses they had defeated, and then in peculiar circumstances. The truth was Frank was feeling very defensive about having to delay their departure; he was dreading some sarcastic remark from the Mehtar.

Perhaps he should have known the Ma'hol leader was not normally given to sarcasm. In any case when he reached the Castle and the welcoming committee, he was so pleased to see the Despot again he jumped down energetically from his chariot and walked across with a spring in his step. An officer behind him barked an order for his men to take a rest.

The greetings were cordial and the Thyatirans were introduced to some senior Ma'hol officers. Not all of them were
bilingual, but Alan and Karl seemed to manage some sort of
agreeable conversation while Frank led his chief guest back to
the keep. It seemed a bit of a trek considering the Mehtar had
said they would only stop briefly, but Frank felt more confident
dealing with him on a one-to-one basis. As they went through
the courtyard whites hurried out to the Ma'hol army with water
for the resting soldiers.

Once ensconced in his sitting room, Frank went into a
lengthy explanation of the reason for the delay in his marching:
the religious meetings, the simple white folk who need that sort
of thing, the moral factor. Mehtar Arumah-Ru sat impassively
in the comfortable chair provided, gently sipping his practil
juice. His host went on to explain about the token expeditionary force and requested they have the honour of travelling with
the Ma'hol army.

The Mehtar spoke softly, "They will be welcome. And we
look forward to seeing you once more when your main force
arrives."

An erubescent Frank thanked him. No sarcasm, just a quiet
noting of the facts. He breathed more easily as the other man
went on to report the latest news from his spies. A gigantic
army had been formed deep in Ladosa and was moving as one,
slow mass in the direction of Bynar. The enemy was putting all
his trust in this one combined effort, no other forces of any size
were apparent elsewhere.

One other development north of Rabeth-Mephar. Sarnice
was mustering an army. At this stage it was not clear whether
this was to be aimed at the Mehtar's homeland or Ladosa, they
were a long-term protagonist of both. He said he did not rate
the Sarnicians as fighters, however, concluding he was confident the Mennahuna could deal with the threat.

"How *is* your son?" Frank enquired.

"Much matured," came the answer. At long last a wiser man was emerging, one his father could put trust in.

"And your wife, is she well?"

"Which one?"

Frank dug deep into his memory and was delighted that he remembered her name quickly, "Rasha-Pi'Pi, the enchanting young bride you brought on your last visit."

"Of course, she is due with our first child in a matter of weeks."

He then enquired about the Arpintonaxes and was told of their good health.

Time was up, no more niceties. The Mehtar set the pace as the two men marched briskly back across bailey and courtyard to the resting soldiers. Upon their arrival more orders were shouted in an unfamiliar language. Lines of men reformed efficiently and the Thyatiran contingent was allocated a place behind the Imperial Guard. The Despot gave them a final blessing, his last words being to the squad leaders, "Make sure Count Zastein sees you!"

"Yes, My Lord!" declared Rodd and James in unison, then exchanged a quick sideways glance before taking their position.

The order was given to march out. Frank retreated beneath the canopy again, rejoining his lieutenants. They watched in awe as rank upon rank of extravagantly dressed fighting men went by. They seemed like a never-ending river. Many of the Castle's inhabitants came out to observe the spectacle. There was the occasional cheer, but mainly they stared in silence, in contrast with their Upper Village brethren a short while earlier.

Karl quizzed Alan about the different types of soldiers: Imperials, skirmishers, regular troops. The drone professed not to know a great deal about the individual units, but when a regiment of men with pink capes and holding long spears passed he exclaimed, "Ah, they're Forecenians, one of their House-carl Legions."

"Are they a special unit?"

"Their significance is they're not Ma'hol, they're from their allies on their western border."

Next were a large contingent of Ma'hol light cavalry, each walked beside his mount, a honas or slave-boy leading the beast.

"An impressive sight," whined Karl, "with this great army on our side victory must surely be ours."

Alan was also impressed by the size of the Ma'hol commitment and said so. He went on to joke, "I don't think we need march after all, let them do the job for us!"

Laughingly Frank agreed. The army they were witnessing could not be much smaller than the entire Hoame one. Count Zastein's ambition to stub out the long-term threat from Ladosa was surely going to be realised..

With the unglamorous baggage-train rolling slowly past the people watching began to melt away.

"I'd better get a move on if I'm to visit the Lower Village this afternoon," Frank said, turning back towards the courtyard entrance.

Just then another messenger arrived. Karl took the baton from him and, opening it, passed the rolled up paper to his Despot. Unfurling it he read in silence for a moment before announcing, "It's from Despot Hista. He says the army of Bynar has moved out... and that we are welcome to cross his land to make our rendezvous. Just as well really, because we were going to do that anyway!"

They all laughed and strolled together through to the courtyard. There Alan took his leave.

The bailey was a lot less cluttered now. Guardsmen were supervising the prison work-detail as they pushed one of the last munition wagons out the main entrance. Chained together, these were the regular criminals, not pacifists nor the Ladosan border guards recently interred. Nearby Madam Tersha and Laffaxe were engaged in a gripping conversation standing in a strip of shade close by the wall. Next to them stood one of the field hospital wagons.

"Sir, you had better take a generous supply of water with you when you visit the village."

"You're right Karl, I'll have a good drink right now as well. It's so damn sticky you almost need a knife to cut through the air. All my clothes are saturated, I shall be glad when this weather passes."

It was still light as the second meeting at the Upper Village got under way in earnest. Soon though the sun was setting while thick banks of cloud came over from the west, resulting in it staying far warmer than the previous night. The humidity, combined with hundreds of dancing people, brought about an entirely different feeling from the previous night. It was far more dynamic and exciting.

Joseph Rehner had been given the Holy Spirit's gift of healing.

"Come up, come up I beseech you. Receive the outpouring of God's Spirit. All who are unwell or troubled in any way. Come up and receive God's gift given freely to you."

In the highly-charged atmosphere many sick people came forward for blessing and more than a few miracles were witnessed to. The meeting also went on far longer than the previous night. It was shortly before dawn when the last members of the congregation retired.

Back-stage, Joseph wiped his face with a damp cloth as he sat down for the first time. A drink was offered and gratefully received.

"Thank you, Jeshu," he said, then yawned heavily, "I suddenly feel really tired... utterly drained." His normally piercing eyes had lost some of their lustre.

"You will soon feel better after a sleep. We have seen the Spirit at work this evening."

"We have, of that there can be no doubt."

Jeshu sat down himself, "I felt the power of God's presence here, I felt it strongly. Through His grace a great many people have been healed, it was a wonderful sight."

"It is so."

Pulling themselves up onto their weary feet, the brothers headed towards their quarters. An equally tired Zadok and Eleazar had been helping clear up out front. Clutching torches they now hurried to join their guests for the walk back.

"Tidying things up slightly," the priest's assistant explained, "a pretty hopeless task by torch-light, we'll wait 'till morning to finish, have more helpers then too."

Joseph said in a concerned voice, "You were waiting for us, you shouldn't have."

Their hosts assured them it was nothing, but Joseph went on to say he felt guilty keeping them up unnecessarily, "We should have told you not to wait for us."

"Nonsense!" Zadok said amiably, "we wanted to see you safely back. Besides, I haven't had the opportunity to tell you properly how wonderful this evening was; the event is proving all I dared hope for – and more!"

"It is so. We were saying a moment ago how God's Spirit was clearly felt among us this night. And tomorrow will be the climax. The theme as you know will be the righteous fight against the unbelievers. We will give our boys a send-off to remember. My brother here will stir the people greater than anything tonight."

So saying he stared at his brother in the light of the flickering torches. He wanted to install more confidence in Jeshu who he knew had not been too pleased at how his talk the night before had gone.

Zadok missed all this, he liked what the man said and was enthusing, "Just what they need, Joseph. We will send them off with fire in their hearts! It will be a wonderful day for God's people!"

Eleazar turned to face the darkness and bit his tongue.

Frank followed up his visit to the Lower Village with one to Sardis the following morning. This was now the last day before the troops would leave for battle. Close on a thousand men would soon be setting out for an uncertain future. Meanwhile the exodus to the Castle was gathering pace with large numbers of villagers arriving to take refuge. Natias was in charge of this operation and had his work cut out.

The sky had a blanket of grey cloud across it now, but the temperature had not dropped at all. The air was hot and heavy, more than a few people complained of headaches. It felt like it must rain soon, by lunch time thunder could be heard in the far distance.

Retreating to the comfort of his suite, Frank was alone with his thoughts. Outside the villagers were already beginning to crowd within the walls. Here he had over half a floor of the keep all to himself, but his mind was on other things. All the preparation that could be done for the forthcoming campaign had been done: the training, the reports, the supplies, everything. On the roof the catapult had been readied and tested successfully. Now all he could do was wait the rest of the day out. How he wished for dawn when they could get on with it. Fingers drummed on the arms of his chair.

Feeling about for something to do he absent-mindedly pulled open the drawers of his bureau one by one to inspect their contents. Nestling in a corner he found the small, round pot containing perfume that Rachael had given him just before he had left to take up his post. Fond memories came back producing a warm smile as he slid the drawer shut again.

He tried reading, but was not in the mood. In the end he sat and contemplated his life, wondering how an obituary would read. This led to a period of prayer. In his current mood he could not bring himself to ask for personal safety, but merely that he should have the courage to accept the divine will. Nothing more to say, it was time for dinner.

The air was alive with static and he got a shock off the door handle. Down towards the hall he could hear the peals of thunder getting closer, but as yet no rain. The meal was slightly earlier than usual to allow participants time to get to the final meeting if they desired.

Squinting from the balcony he saw all the tables were full except his place at the head of the centre one. Natias and Japhses were sitting either side, wanting to report the latest situation. Eko was next to her husband. His other lieutenants were next, Hannah and her mother a long way down. This was to be a business dinner, he would have to catch her late, a final opportunity before they left.

Once he was seated, the Captain launched himself into a detailed report on the readiness of their army to march first thing in the morning. Illianeth came across and when she could get a word in edgeways said to Frank that she presumed her reading services were not required that evening. To everyone's surprise he replied, "On the contrary my dear, that's an excellent idea. You run along to my bedroom and fetch it, you'll find it by the bed."

Before she could leave Eko spoke up. She told the servant she could use the Bible Madam Tersha had given her, "I have it right here."

It was a slim volume, far more manoeuvrable than Frank's weighty tome and the lectern could be dispensed with for once.

The Despot's senior advisers were not the most religious group of men, they decided to get on with their meal while Illianeth asked which passage to read, "We have been working our way through Jeremiah My Lord."

"Yes, one of my favourites...but let me think. Something extra special tonight... let me think..."

Gently he took the book from her and thumbed through the pages for some while before his eyes alighted on a passage he wanted."

"Read this please."

It was from the Gospel of Saint John and she read it well. Natias in particular was impressed at how this once rebellious girl performed. Frank tucked into his food as he concentrated on the words.

"...This is my commandment: that you love each other as I have loved you. There is no greater love a man can show but to lay down his life for his friends."

"Thank you, Illianeth, that was beautiful."

She left. Round the Despot none of the whites wanted to be the first to speak, although plenty of chatter was coming from the other tables. Alan came to their rescue. Speaking for the first time, he reminded Frank that the Captain was half way through his report.

"Ah of course, do carry on."

There was a time when Japhses would have shown his annoyance at what he considered the Despot's eccentric behaviour. His eve of battle report interrupted by a Bible reading! He had almost come to expect it now though. Still he very nearly asked his leader if he wanted to listen to the rest of it. Instead he took a deep breath then carried on, consoled somewhat by the Despot's apparent attention to his words.

"Well that all sounds on target. We agreed at one squad left at the Castle didn't we? Who is in command of that?"

"Natias, My Lord."

"Ah yes, I meant the squad leader."

"Jonathan, My Lord."

Frank hesitated, "Isn't he the one who put the rocks on my skylights last year?"

"He has come a long way since then," Japhses hastened to defend his man, "I have every confidence in him."

Natias backed him up, then went on to talk about the influx of villagers to the Castle. "A fair number have come here alweady to weserve their places. Many are slipping out again to attend the meeting."

"How is chaos to be avoided tomorrow?" Eko asked, "with the remainder of the people trying to get to the Castle, plus the soldiers on the march, surely there could be problems."

Japhses politely assured her this had been foreseen. Guardsmen and militia were to be given priority. "Those from the Upper Village are to get here at first light, the others joining on the way. Once the soldiers have left, the villagers will be free to seek out their Castle refuge."

The main course was finished and servants cleared the plates away. Alan rose to leave saying he was not staying for the next course. Frank took hold of his arm and asked if he was all right, he was concerned by his friend's lack of conversation during the meal.

Speaking quietly he replied, "I'm all right as I can be right now. Just feel like a bit of solitude tonight if you know what I mean."

"I do know what you mean," Frank replied with an understanding look in his eye as he let him go.

The others were still talking. Replying to another point raised by the steward's wife Japhses was saying, "There can be no doubt evacuation is necessary. It is probably inevitable people will compare the current situation with the Ma'hol crisis, but they are quite different. There will still be scouts on the border, I see no reason why the evacuation should not be carried out safely and without disruption."

Natias backed him up, "Fwom tomowwow it will be my wesponsibility my darling, I am confident."

"Nasias?" asked Frank, "are you sure there is nothing further we can do to help? Keep some troops back until it is complete?" He had asked the question before and received the same answer.

The white was sure all who wanted would be within the walls by midday. There had been no known Laodician border incursions, nor other signs of impending invasion, he felt secure enough about the operation. He also did not want to hold up their departure for the front any more than it already had been.

With the topic exhausted no more was said. After the meal, Hannah Unit made a bee-line for him so he did not have to seek her out.

"I'm off to the meeting shortly, but I wanted to see you before you go. You're bound to be pre-occupied tomorrow morning so this will be my last chance."

Up on the roof they got a light show for free. Around the sky spectacular lightning flashed its twisted course to the ground. Still no rain though, but it must surely come that night. They went to hold hands, promptly got an electric shock off each other and said, "Ouch!" in unison, then laughed and put an arm round each other's waists instead.

She said, "I didn't go to the meeting last night 'cos I decided to go tonight instead."

Why she could not have gone to both he did not know, but he listened attentively as she continued, "Looks like I'm going to get soaked for my delay. It's going to be a Catambra of a storm when it comes, and I think it'll be soon."

"A what of a storm?"

"Oh that's Ma'hol; Catambra, the mother of the great god Vorg-habiethmonan. She gave birth to him in the Crystal Sea after forming the seven worlds."

"You're really into Ma'hol mythology aren't you!"

"Not that much, just snippets I've picked up. I'm just showing off, to tell the truth."

They kissed, slowly and warmly.

"Won't see any stars tonight," Hannah remarked staring up at the black sky. The lightning had momentarily stopped.

"You can't see many from here at the best of times."

She looked curiously, "Why, do you think there are more stars up there? Can you see more from your homeland?"

"Many more," he replied dreamily, "the sky is full of them. Just think, my brother could be looking out at them as we speak."

"You have a brother?"

She sounded interested.

"Yes, my only living relative. At least I hope he's still living, I was thinking about him earlier today."

"Do tell me about him, what's his name?"

"John. He's my younger brother. He chose to be a soldier, a mercenary for hire. I didn't, that's why it's so ironic it's *me* about to lead an army into war."

"He's back in Oonimari is he? Are you close?"

"Not as close as I wish we'd been. As for where he is, he could be anywhere, I just hope he's still alive. I wish we'd spent more time together. I do have my regrets over John, I never tried to understand him the way I should've."

He paused and as he did so, there was a tremendous flash-bang very close by. They both jumped.

"Wow, did you see that!" he exclaimed.

"Yes I did! It hit that tree over there."

At that point her handmaiden Nooni appeared at the entrance saying Hannah's mother had sent her. "Madam Tersha wishes to get along without delay."

"Your mother's going to the meeting," Frank stated somewhat surprised.

"She wasn't interested at first," explained Hannah as they began negotiating the spiral staircase down to the next floor, "but she volunteered after I told her you weren't going."

"Oh dear."

Hannah giggled, "No it's not like that! She just changed her mind. I think she's looking forward to it now. If we don't get struck by lightning or drowned by a deluge we'll have a marvellous time."

He loved her sense of humour. As they stood outside his suite entrance he studied her laughing face trying to take in every detail; it would be the last time he saw her before he left. There was a further clap of thunder, but it was muffled by the thick walls.

"Well I hope you enjoy it. I'm going to retire to my rooms now, I need an early night, get my strength up for tomorrow."

With Nooni present they felt restricted in their actions. Hannah felt glad she was there in a way, it helped put a break on their emotions. As she said goodbye to Frank she only now fully realised quite how deeply she was falling for him. Before she disappeared, her final words were a whispered, "Be careful, my love."

How inadequate these words were she thought as she left him. With servant in tow they made their way back to their rooms in the South Tower. There she told Nooni she would be along shortly, but first must be left alone for a while. Once by herself she could contain the emotion no longer, tears fell down her face as she sat helpless in a chair. After losing her father and fiancé to the Buffs she could not bear the thought of

Frank being killed. 'No,' she told herself, 'I must not think of these things, but I feel something dreadful will happen to him. Why does disaster follow where I tread?

'I told myself that my interest in politics was to blame. We ran away here and all we have succeeded in doing is dragging these good people into a conflict. They say they are fighting for a principle, but that principle is the safety of mother and me. How are we going be be able to face the widows and orphans we create?

'Oh God, please keep Frank and his men safe, do not make them suffer because of me and my stupid ambitions. I swear if you keep Frank safe I will give up any ideas for ever returning to rally party members. I will give up all such selfish endeavours, 'cos selfish I know they are. But please keep Frank safe.'

"Thunder's movin' away," Reuben observed sitting with his legs up in Tsodd's living area.

His two friends nodded. Amos was slowly peeling a hulffan fruit, tossing the pith into the empty fire-place.

Tsodd had been contemplating life through the glass window he had recently had installed. Unlike the other pair, he was in the militia and would be marching at first light. Turning back into the room he remarked, "It's heading in the direction of the Castle. I reckon we're the only ones in the village this evening, everyone else is at the meeting."

This was the cue to start Reuben off moaning about the "God-botherers", but instead his outstretched arm touched a metal candle-stand and he received an electric shock, so he swore about that instead.

"You know I was thinking..." Amos began.

"Damn static! What's that you were saying?"

"Um, I don't know, I've forgotten," his friend said vaguely, puzzlement over his face.

"You're mad! Do you know that? They say my son's simple, I think he's the sanest one around here."

"Where *is* Brogg?" Tsodd enquired, "at tonight's meeting?"

"Need you ask? Poor boy's been totally indoctrinated by all this religious nonsense."

"He's a young man now you know."

"Nonsense, he's vulnerable and they know it. Anyway, I don't want to talk about it. Honestly Tsodd you really ought to get some decent furniture. This old chair's..."

He stopped due to a knock on the door. All looked round, but nobody stirred.

"I wonder who that could be," said Tsodd.

"Bloody open it, man!"

At the same time a voice outside asked to be let in. Tsodd jumped up, "It's Bodd!"

Racing to the door he threw it open. It was indeed a heavily-laden Bodd returned from Asattan. The brothers hugged before coming into the room. Amos smiled from ear to ear as he greeted him. Even Reuben looked a bit less sour, but when the visitor explained the reason for his return he flew off the handle.

"Now I'm convinced you're all crazy! You get a well-paid, cushy job in the Capital, then you come back here to get your skull cracked open. I tell you, I just can't understand it."

Tsodd guffawed, telling his brother, "In his own way I think he's trying to tell you he cares."

The other joined in the laughter, even Reuben, shaking his head. He never would understand other people.

Food and wine were lavished on the hungry traveller while Amos and Tsodd listened attentively to news from the Capital and tales of great armies on the march. He asked about Rodd and was told he had gone on ahead with his squad.

"I was afraid you'd *all*'ve gone by the time I got here, I thought I'd left it too late."

After explaining about the religious meetings, Tsodd went on to say, "Almost everyone's coming along for the fight. There's a lot of excitement, most people wouldn't miss it for the world! We're goin' to have to be up early in the morning though. You'd better get a good rest."

Breaking off from his food Bodd noticed the other two had gone very quiet. He guessed correctly that they were among the few villagers not volunteering for the militia. Reuben suddenly decided he had better be getting back. Reaching out to collect his cropper's knife on the table, he got another electric shock and swore once more.

"Wish this bloody storm would hurry up and break." Then collecting himself, but still with a frown on his face, he said, "So, Bodd, you didn't have the gumption to stay away; and I'd have wagered your new woman would have knocked some sense into you. Still, now that you are here, I wish you... you know."

He did not want to be getting sentimental, so he did not finish the sentence. Instead he pointed at Tsodd and cried, "And look after the man with the money!"

The three chorused farewell and he was gone. "Same old Reuben," Bodd said to the others amusement.

Tsodd then became serious and remarked, "You didn't have to come back you know, we'd have understood. Sounds like you're doing important work in the capital."

"Not really. No, I wouldn't miss this for the world. I've seen the soldiers from nearly every despotate assembling, the mood in Asattan is almost manic. Except in the area I live in I suppose, it's always so quiet there nothing could disturb them. Several others in the department I work in are joining the fight too. No one wants to miss out, there's a euphoria in favour of war."

"You wouldn't have have found our training very euphoric; back-breaking more like! Never known anything quite the same.

"It shouldn't be for you though, Bodd, you're the one with the brains, we need stupid people like me to join the militia."

"Don't say that!" Amos protested, "you're both super people with a lot to offer. I should say you are both wasted going off to fight, but the truth is I wish I was going as well. Kim says she needs me as much as ever, but I feel a coward."

It was the others' turn to protest. Bodd in particular came to his defence saying neither he nor his brother had any children, but Amos was needed by his large family. He went on to talk about his own plans.

"I'll settle down when this is all over, marry Anastasia, have some sons. I just want my bit of adventure first, something to tell my grandchildren about." He paused before adding, "Hell I don't know, there's just a lot of excitement and I want to be part of it. Yes I feel patriotic, especially since my home despotate is in the thick of it. It's only natural, but that's not what it's all about. It's about not wanting to let my chums down."

It went quiet and they sat thoughtfully. Wanting to break the atmosphere he had helped create, Bodd declared jovially, "I'm looking forward to getting started, want to catch Rodd up."

Amos got up to leave, "I'd better be off now, want to get home before the storm breaks." He wished the brothers well then left them alone together.

Bodd peered out of the window, but there was nothing to see.

"Better get some sleep," his brother said, "Long day ahead of us."

The final meeting took off where the previous night had left. Zigzagging lightning provided a dramatic backdrop to the proceedings. The threatening downpour was holding off and people felt they were defying the elements to be there. The crowd was enormous and alive with energy, enthusiasm and expectation. The atmosphere was electric in more ways than one. Knowing it to be their final night before they left many more men attended, especially from the Upper Village. It was dark by the time the main event got underway; a score of flaming torches on poles lit the stage area.

Jeshu need not have worried about his speech. He could feel the wave of affection as soon as he stepped out on stage. As a loyal white he felt whole-heartedly in Hoame's cause against the unbelieving Laodicians. In putting the case for war he found an attentive and willing audience. He settled for telling them what they wanted to hear.

"People of Hoame, the Great God Jehovah is calling on you. With his help you will crush the idolatrous Laodicians like our forefathers the Israelites crushed the Midianites and Ammonites. As when Moses led their armies and said, "I have prepared my flashing sword, and set out to administer the Lord's judgement. I will punish my adversaries and take vengeance on my enemies. My arrows and sword shall devour the flesh of the evil ones, the heads of the enemy commanders will roll in their own blood." God has called upon you to administer His judgement, I know you will not be found wanting."

The crowd shouted their appreciation, it was going well. There was one other theme Jeshu wanted to bring out, but the timing was important. Subtly he changed the subject when the opportunity presented itself.

"...We are being called upon by God to rid the world of these devils. For that task we are required to be a holy nation. A righteous people is needed to perform this cleansing, nothing less will do. It is only through each one of us receiving Jesus Christ into our lives as our Saviour and Lord that we can hope to do this. We must turn from our sinful ways, trusting God to forgive us completely because Jesus died for our sins.

"We have all sinned, all fallen short of perfection. But there are no misdeeds too shocking for God."

He paused; was that a spot of rain on his face? He hurried his speech along.

"No matter what you have done, God will wash you clean of your sins. No matter what your iniquities He will wash you whiter than snow. The first step is confession. We must accept our need for God and that we have fallen far short of the standards He has set. Then comes repentance, through repentance the most dreadful of misdeeds are blotted out. There is no limit to his mercy."

More spots of rain, Eleazar and Zadok at the side of the stage looked nervously up at the black sky.

"Repent then! When the wicked man turns away from his wickedness and does what is right, his soul shall be saved. Turn back to the Lord your God, He is gracious and compassionate, long-suffering and ready to..."

It was there that he had to break off. With every moment the rain was coming down harder: drops had turned into a torrent in the space of two sentences. It poured down. The huge crowd began to scatter, even the most devout were heading for the tents. With the force of the thunder storm these would only provide a temporary refuge. Chaos reigned in the rain.

The speaker saw his brother and Eleazar bundling the elderly priest away. People were running every which way. The torches were being extinguished one-by one by the extraordinary deluge. It struck Jeshu as a a bizarre ending to an otherwise successful evening. Turning to flee he was stopped by a plaintiff cry from below the stage. A penetrating, desperate voice was calling his name. A lone young man was advancing towards him, oblivious to the soaking he was receiving. He was obviously in need and there was no question of ignoring him. Abandoning any idea of safety from the storm (he was drenched already) he knelt at the edge of the stage to see what the man wanted.

They were alone in the rain as the man began, shouting to make himself heard in the downpour, "I need to be clean of my sins. I need your help," he implored, "please tell me what I have to do!"

Jeshu noticed immediately the strange, dull look in the supplicant's eyes, the speech with a hint of a slur, but there was no question of him being the worse for drink. The preacher had never tried counselling in anything like these conditions before. He dropped down from the stage upon which the rain was beating hard. Only a couple of torches were still alight now. Their hair and clothes were soaked through and stuck to their skin.

He advised confession as the first step to starting afresh. It was only when the young man took him up on this suggestion that he discovered the full extent of what he was getting involved in.

CHAPTER THIRTY THREE

Frank Thorn opened his eyes and blinked hard. Seeing her master awake, Illianeth quickly set his clothes out ready. He sat up and watched her, not sure he enjoyed witnessing such industriousness so early in the morning. She had lit the candle next to him to give extra light, for nature's efforts were only beginning.

How grateful he was for a good night's sleep. His mind had been very active when he first went to bed and through sheer will-power he had shut it up in order to drop off. It had worked.

The rain had stopped, although excess water was still dripping outside the window. Illianeth made mention of the night's storm then, as she continued getting his things ready, followed it up with one of her amazing facts: "I was with Soosha last night, My Lord, we were watching the rain from one of the windows on this floor. You know Jonathan, one of the guardsmen? Anyway he came along and told us the most amazing fact. He said if you put together all the rain drops from that storm in a long line they would stretch from here to the sun! Did you know that, My Lord?"

"Can't say I did. Are you sure he wasn't having you on?"

She stopped, straining to understand what he meant. It was almost possible to hear her brain working. Eventually she asked him, "How do you mean My Lord? There was an awful lot of rain."

"Um yes, I'm sure there was," he retreated, not wanting to pursue the matter, "are my clothes ready?"

Coming back to the real world she replied, "Oh yes, My Lord. Stephen will of course help you with your under-armour garment after breakfast. Your bath is ready as usual."

"Fine. Thank you."

He waited until she was gone before getting out of bed. The bath was warm, the aroma of herbs rising in the steam, exactly how he liked it. However, time was at a premium, so following a quick dip he was back in his room to get changed. It occurred to him the tremendous effort it was to get him his bath, the water heated downstairs and brought up in wooden buckets.

His reverie was broken by a knock on the door. After obtaining permission, Alan entered, all dressed and ready to march immediately. Warm greetings were exchanged, then as Frank began to get dressed he remarked, "No matter how early I get up, you're always ready before me!" When he noticed his friend's concerned expression he enquired if everything was all right, "Any news of the enemy?"

"Oh nothing like that," Alan put his mind at rest, "but there is something that can't wait. We've found Giella's murderer."

"What?!" Frank stopped in his tracks.

"Yeah, it was Brogg, Reuben's retarded son, he confessed last night at the meeting."

"Are you sure he wasn't making it up? After all, if he's a bit simple..."

"I'm sure all right, he showed me the fasson, all blood-stained still – not a pretty sight! He's kept it neatly wrapped up under his bed since doing the deed.

"After he'd told the preacher they came into the tent where we were sheltering, I had a long ch..."

"Hold on, wait a moment. *You* were at the meeting?" he asked incredulously.

"I went with Hannah."

"Gosh, this morning is full of surprises; and I'm not even dressed yet. I thought you told me last night you wanted to be by yourself."

With difficulty Alan replied, "Er, yeah, but it changed after that."

"Well go on."

Frank speeded up his dressing and listened to the rest of the story. Alan did not disclose why he had gone to the meeting, but go he had with the Arpintonaxes. When the storm came they had taken shelter in one of the tents nearby. This quickly became a mass of steamy bodies as more people sought shelter there. So when Jeshu had brought Brogg in and the latter gave his confession to the Despot's right-hand man the news spread like wildfire.

The full details came out once the rain had abated and Alan, taking charge of the prisoner, decided to walk him to his parents' home. Brogg was on a high following the meeting. Jeshu had pronounced God's forgiveness, but insisted that the due process of law had to be adhered to. Meekly the young man obeyed, fully cooperating – there was no question of his trying to escape. Alan for his part was not quite sure what to do in these extraordinary circumstances and wondered if it might not be best to take him back to the Castle that night for his own protection as much as anything else.

Jeshu left them. Still with Hannah Unit and Madam Tersha in tow, the two men made for Reuben's hut. There, amidst a raging argument between Brogg's parents almost greater in force than the lightning had been, the truth was revealed. The cropper was indeed having an affair with the beautiful Giella. Somehow he had discovered about her and Japhses and, threatening to tell her husband, blackmailed her into having an affair with himself as well. It was not long before his son found out.

Alan explained, "in his mind, Brogg erroneously blamed the flirtatious, but innocent woman for entrapping his father."

"Innocent?"

"Ah, innocent as far as the affair with Reuben went. Anyhow, that was his motivation: in a simplistic way he saw her as the problem and proceeded to get rid of it."

"He clearly was conscious of morals enough to know what he did was wrong."

"Yeah. He showed me his fasson (cropper's knife) he had used, had stashed it away among his keep-sakes."

"The parents' argument subsided when his mother broke down and pleaded with me to let him stay with them one more night."

"What did you do?"

"What could I do? Especially with the other women there with me. Reuben promised me he'd bring him here this morning and surrender him to Natias. On capital offences though, you're the one who'll have to make the judgement."

Frank was almost ready and knew he must not hold everyone up, so slipping on his last boot, he said, "Well, I'm not making a judgement right now, it'll have to wait. What I do want to do is talk with you more about Giella, I still find it all so hard to believe of her, but that'll have to wait. Come on, let's go downstairs.

On their way, they met the steward and his wife, they were arguing.

"I was only twying to help you, my pwecious, you took it the wong way. Oh, good morning, My Lawd."

The foursome went on to the hall together. Frank was not hungry that early in the morning, but forced some food into himself while listening to Natias.

"What do I do with him, My Lawd? You tell me you are not going to pass judgement until your weturn, but in the meantime he must be kept secure, because he has committed a tewwible cwime. Besides, we don't know how other folk will weact. Evewyone knows he is not all there, but folk can be so stwange. However, I would wather not subject him to the dungeon with all the wetwobates there..."

He ended the sentence in the air. It was obvious he would have preferred his master to make a few decisions, but Frank was taken up with greater concerns. Emptying his mouth, he said, "Well I'm sorry, Natias, but it's up to you to work out what to do with him until I get back. I've got other things on my mind right now. Why don't you put him under guard somewhere nicer if that's the way you feel – Laffaxe's house for instance, that's a good idea even if I say so myself. He won't be needing it for now."

"But there will be lots of other families sheltewing in the bailey, My Lawd..."

"Got it!" declared Alan, "He can take my room. There's enough space for his parents as well – if they want to, that is. They weren't on the best of terms last time I saw them.

"Come on, Frank, we've got to get a move on."

No more time was lost. The Despot hurried upstairs where he was helped on with his clansit or under-armour garment.

It was light, but padded, designed to absorb shock and lessen the penetration of a weapon that had pierced the armour. The armour itself was loaded into a wagon with some of the guardsmen's helmets, breast and back-plates. Frank's knowledge of medieval times was limited, but he felt sure that while the armour he was using looked similar to that era, it was both lighter and easier to put on. It was a good day and a half's march and they did not expect any contact with the enemy before the Mitas Gap, so it made sense to travel as light as possible.

Grabbing his small telescope he descended to the bailey through hall and reception room. All the time he kept an eye out for Hannah in case she had come to see him off, but there was no sign of her. He told himself she must still be sleeping after her late night, but secretly he was disappointed not to see her one last time.

Alan was waiting at the reception room door. The sun was still below the outer wall, but it was easily light enough to see the crowded bailey. Together the two walked between lines of tents, avoiding the many puddles as they went. The oily coating on the canvas had kept the tents from leaking, but many were flooded. After many days of muggy weather, the air was fresh, so fresh! It felt good to have in one's lungs.

Frank remarked, "With all these temporary dwellings here, I wonder if we have enough tents for our own men."

"It's all been worked out, we'll be okay."

One final glance back at the tall keep, then out to the waiting troops. Men and wagons stretched back as far as the eye could squint, all waiting patiently for their leader's arrival. The road was narrow and the wagons could not go two abreast. Also, some wagons needed such large teams to pull them that the longest took over forty metres. It was not surprising therefore that it stretched such a long way. A large number of Castle staff and other helpers had been up half the night harnessing the dakks and getting them into position.

Alan and Frank hurried to the front where Japhses was waiting. He was on foot, standing in front of a small cart and four. A short, thin driver sat impassively for them to climb aboard. It had a detachable cover that was currently folded up, resting along its right-hand side. Cushioned seats had been fitted especially for the Despot. Frank went behind and peered inside, he found it amusing that they had gone to such trouble to provide him with a bit of comfort. 'They must think I'm dreadfully soft.'

A large formation of guardsmen stood to attention behind the cart. He did not recognise the squad leader in command, his men standing neatly in rows of four abreast.

"Sorry I've kept you, Japhses," he said, hovering at the entrance to the cart.

The big man was staring into the distance as if searching for something.

"We are men short My Lord, a dozen guardsmen from the Upper Village plus many militia. Uriah has gone back to... ah, here he comes now."

"Chaos, bloody chaos!" Uriah shouted while still fifty metres away. The Captain's deputy was unusually animated as he explained, "The villagers are not holding back as they should be, they're intermingling with the men at the back, pushing past munitions wagons trying to get here early. Our men are held up behind them. Karl's got an impossible task trying..."

"Look!" shouted Alan, pointing up the road in front of them, "the other villagers are coming up this way as well!"

It was true, the agreed procedures were not being adhered to and what had been planned as a smooth operation was rapidly descending into farce.

Frank immediately agreed Japhses' suggestion to get going straight away. The soldiers left behind on the road from the Upper Village would have to catch up. The Despot got in the cart prepared for him, but Alan chose to walk with the Captain at the front. A squad of guardsmen was detailed to go a hundred metres ahead and prepare the way for the advancing column.

Those few kilometres to the rendezvous with the other villages' militias will not go down in the annals as Thyatira's finest hour. The road was full of large puddles, flooded right across in places. Trampling feet and hooves churned up mud on this unmetalled road and the wagons' inertia increased in the sticky mess. Large numbers of militiamen were called upon to push from behind to ease the dakks' burden.

Out front the guardsmen were making no friends as they cleared the way, sometimes quite brutally. Old men and women were shoved unceremoniously onto the waterlogged grass as the soldiers lost patience with them. It seemed to be going on for ever.

Eventually the crossroads near Sardis was reached and the civilian problem evaporated. Luke and Gideon were waiting patiently with their men. Only a little more time was lost as these were incorporated into the column at the prearranged points. While this was going on the missing soldiers from behind were able to catch up.

Frank felt it best to let the professionals get on with the job and he sat observing the spectacle from his perch in the cart. Alan found time to come over and have a word. Standing in the mud he looked up with a big grin, "We must be optimistic, it can only get better from now on." Frank tutted and the drone continued, "Seriously, I think we're getting our act together at last.

"I thought of a coincidence as we left the Castle. Do you remember the morning we left to deal with the Ma'hol? Then too there had been a rain-storm the night before. Let's hope it's a good omen."

"Let's hope so, we could do with one after this debacle!"

They moved on, at long last in good order and the correct formation. At the front Frank had Japhses and Gideon for company in the cart, with the latter's Lower Village militia, and a contingent of guardsmen marching behind. Following them were the first lot of wagons which included Laffaxe and the medical team with their mobile hospital. Next Alan and Luke with the Sardis militia plus guardsmen and wagons, then Uriah, Saul and the Upper Village men, attendant guardsmen and wagons. Bringing up the rear Karl and a squad of hand-picked soldiers under him.

Most of the dakks were being utilised for pulling the carts. A small number of prime animals were being led by hand. Having no load these were being kept fresh for the commanders' use in battle.

The leading cart's driver called out that he had to stop, he was worried one of the dakks was going lame. The animal was quickly inspected and declared fit to continue. Seizing the opportunity, Frank pulled out his telescope and scanned rearwards. The road was straight and narrow, the line of men and materiel stretched so far back he could not make out the end of it. On either side of the road was a wide verge with no trees. It was not yet mid-morning and it was pleasantly warm. While the weather would get hot later on, it would not be the baking, clammy heat of late. With a sudden pull, the cart moved on once more.

The army was still within its home despotate and no enemy units were believed to be in the area. However, in order to play safe – and for good practice – flankers were placed wide on either side. Scouts also went on ahead.

"We will be at our most vulnerable while on the march," Japhses explained to the Despot, "it is essential to make sure we get as much notice as we can in the event of an ambush."

Spirits were high and the guardsmen struck up a song. It was a battle-psalm delivered with gusto:

"Sharpen every fighter's sword,

"String the bow and hold it steady.

"Deadly shafts prepare for war,

"Arrows of fire are at the ready."

Far over to the north, the peaks of the mountain chain bordering Ladosa could be seen, these would gradually get closer as they progressed. They rose majestically from the plain and presented a permanent screen on their left-hand side. They entered a wood near the regional border and the road led down to a ford across a river. Sunlight flickered through the trees and the occasional large drop of accumulated rain fell down from the branches overhead. Scouts ran back to report all clear for the crossing.

"How badly is it swollen?" asked Japhses.

"Hardly at all, Captain," came the reply.

The cart moved on, bumping over exposed tree-roots. Gideon had his dour expression even after hearing the good news of the river. "Can't have rained so hard here," he droned, "or at least not to the north. It will help our progress."

Crossing the river went without incident. Once the whole army was safely into Bynar the order was given to stop for lunch. Frank was pleased to see the meal was far better organised than the exit from the Castle had been. Well refreshed, they were soon on the move again, this time along a drier road. The few small puddles were steaming in the afternoon sun and the Captain relaxed noticeably. Deciding to be nearer his men, he jumped down from the cart and marched with them.

Towards the rear of the procession, Bodd and Tsodd were travelling light. The large contingent of Upper Village militia looked more like a strolling crowd than a fighting force on the march. Their numbers were swelled by some men from the south who had come to attend the religious meetings now over. While the neighbouring guard units marched in semi-armour and carried their weapons, all the militia's arms and (mainly home-made) armour was slung in some wagons provided. Had there been a sudden attack they would have had a mad scramble to get their equipment. Such thoughts had been pushed to the backs of their minds though as they sauntered, chatted and laughed along.

"How are you spending all that money you got?" Bodd enquired.

"Don't you start! That's all I get from Reuben and one or two of the others. I'm beginning to wish I'd never found that gold on my land."

"Are you?"

"Okay that's not strictly true, but some people do go on. For your information, I *am* spending some of it: I had that glass window put in – they don't come cheap – plus I'm organising an expedition when I get back."

"Oh yes?"

"Yeah. Get a properly organised group together that I can take to catch a green electra. Now that would be something worthwhile to come out of my wealth. I'll have to make sure I don't invite Rodd along, but I reckon it'd be the last place on Molt he'd want to visit again."

Bodd had to laugh to himself. Tsodd's fortune was probably not far short of Hanson's, but instead of building himself an impressive house, stockade all round and locking himself inside, his brother was carrying on his simple life much as before. Strange how differently wealth affected people.

"It's great to be back Tsodd, amongst you and all my mates. Dying to see Rodd again. When we get back to the village I

think I'll help out with some of the corn harvest before returning to Asattan. Haven't done that for years.

"Remember when the three of us used to travel south each
year to work in the mines?"

"It was only last year."

"I suppose you're right, seems longer though. I don't miss
it. I quite fancy a go at helping with the harvest though, they'll
need every hand this year I'd have thought."

"What about your woman waiting back at the Capital?"

"I'll send her a message, tell her I'm okay. Good thinking."

For a while they stopped talking and instead listened to the
others. There was much merriment going on with friendly ban-
ter and laughter. One man produced a small bottle of wine and
began passing it round before one of his colleagues told him
to put it away.

"Quickly man! Before Saul sees you, he'd knock your head
off if he saw it, you know the orders."

Seeing that his peers were unimpressed, the wine-owner
took it back and tucked it away again mumbling a few words of
protest.

The chatter re-commenced and the tension of the moment
dissipated. Straight overhead now was the sun, but there was a
slight cooling breeze and the heat seemed gentler than of late.

"What a beautiful day," Bodd announced before a note of
irony entered his speech, "who could think of a better thing to
do on a day such as this than to go off and kill someone you've
never seen before? A beautiful day for a war."

Towards late afternoon, Japhses had re-joined Frank and
Gideon in the leading cart. Unable to get much conversation
out of the Lower Village Head, Frank had begun shouting comments down to the Captain who then felt obliged to get back in.

"Nothing happening then."

"No My Lord. Scouts report all is quiet, which is what we should expect."

By now they had left all recognised roads, but satisfactory progress was being maintained through the grasslands. It was typical scenery for this part of Hoame: gently undulating land with spinneys and isolated thickets dotted about. Not a single habitation had been sighted since they entered Bynar and visible wildlife was scarce.

The following guardsmen had ceased their singing and now marched in silence. Gideon nodded off to sleep thanks to the warm sun and the rhythmic moving of the cart. Occasionally it went over a rough patch and rocked up and down, but even this did not wake him. He frowned in sleep as when awake, an expression well matched by his black clothes. The dark, metallic blue pattern woven into his cloak was most intricate and must have been expensive to produce. Frank studied it carefully, after more than a year among these people he could still be surprised by some of the artifacts. He would have to ask Gideon where he had got it.

Japhses enquired, "Have you considered where we should pitch camp for the night, My Lord?"

"No, I hadn't. You can choose – somewhere you think suitable."

"I strongly recommend we stop at the next stream in that case. We do not want to leave it too late, for we will need to do a longer reconnaissance sweep and get all the tents pitched before nightfall."

The Despot nodded, happy to leave these details to him. In amongst such serenity, it was easy to lose track of what they were there for. It was never far from their mind though. He decided to ease his curiosity by asking his Captain, "What form do you think this battle will take?"

Japhses paused, "I am not sure I understand the question, My Lord."

"Well I'm not sure myself exactly. I mean, do you think there will be a lot of lightning strikes, or stand-offs with the archers ruling the battlefield? I really don't know."

With carefully picked words the other replied, "As far as any of us know there will be two huge armies comprising thousands of men about to clash in a confined area. There will be no room for manoeuvre. It will probably end up one almighty hacking contest, to be won by mere strength and numbers. Casualties in such a contest will be high on both sides. Just a bloodbath. If I may be so bold, My Lord, I would say I do not agree with our overall Commander's tactics – as far as I know them – there will be no room for proper tactics: feints, out-flanking moves, for... for brains, My Lord."

Then with a shrug he added, "Whatever we believe will happen will turn out differently though. It always does in war."

The cart gave another jolt and Frank wished he had not asked the question.

Considering the early difficulties encountered, good progress was made that day. The army camped by one of the many streams coming down from the mountains as recommended by Japhses. It was a river in winter, but greatly reduced now in mid-summer. There was not even a hint of dampness in the grass here, quite the contrary it was dry and brittle. So different from earlier in the day, but as more than one pointed out, storms could be very localised.

Everything seemed to be working more efficiently now, the operation to set up camp went particularly smoothly. All were under military discipline and it was beginning to rub off even onto the Upper Village militia. Most superfluous chatter had stopped while they put their tents up and organised parties to bring firewood in. By dusk the last of the reconnaissance sweeps had returned and reported all quiet. Sentries were posted and the bulk of the army settled round their camp fires to eat.

The senior white officers ate together, Frank had Alan and Karl for company. This trio settled in a small, natural hollow for their meal, although comfortable sleeping quarters for these commanders were being prepared in the hospital wagons. The hollow was surrounded on three sides by binstid bushes and provided some privacy which they appreciated. The guardsmen assigned to them kept a good fire going, for the night was cooler than of late.

Together they ate their harco beans and, as the blanket of darkness fell, watched the candle-worms in the bushes. Little was said until Karl enquired of Alan whether he knew exactly where they were.

"Mmm, north of Setty I'd say. About where I'd hoped we'd be tonight. If we pack up at first light there's every chance we'll get to the Pass by midday tomorrow."

"Good," said Karl, "it's all slipping into place. If you will both excuse me, I will grab an early night."

He slipped off, leaving them chewing their dried yackos. Almost immediately there was a bump and a muffled curse. Returning to collect a torch he explained somewhat unnecessarily that he had fallen over. Again he departed, this time flaming torch held high. As they heard no more they assumed he made it safely to his sleeping quarters.

"Probably burn down the wagon," said Frank with a grin.

For a long time the remaining pair sat in silence. Alan took a piece of husk from his mouth and threw it into the fire. It hissed in the intense heat. He watched the flames dancing while the Despot thanked and dismissed their attendant after the soldier had checked his leaders had everything they needed.

When they did get talking again almost inevitably the topic of the murder came up.

"Huh! Yeah, so much for my investigations. I remember when I first had a word with him I got the feeling he was protecting his father, I never suspected Brogg himself. Last night when he explained to me what he'd done he was quite lucid, not his usual monosyllabic self. He knew such detail there's no doubt he did it himself and isn't covering for his father or anyone else. At least I *think* there's no doubt, I suppose I could be wrong again."

"You did a good job," Frank tried to bolster him, "it was never going to be easy. You would probably have got there in the end."

The drone gave a sarcastic snort then replied slowly, "Frank, put it this way: if we have any more murders, please don't ask me to find the killer."

Frank turned away to study the flames and went quiet. With a sigh Alan recommenced, "Look, I'm not getting at you. You were quite within your rights to ask me to do the investigation. As I recollect, you said I didn't have to do it if I didn't want to. I'm just not at my best this last couple of days. That's why I needed a moment to myself last night."

"Would you rather I left?"

"No don't go now," Alan returned quickly. "If you can put up with me, I'd like your company right now more than anything."

He could not see the tear in Frank's eye as the latter stared across the subsiding fire. Although it meant something slightly different to each of them, their friendship was mutually precious. For either of them to have tried to put it into words at that point would have spoilt the moment. They just knew that what they had was precious.

Seeking to progress the conversation, Frank glanced round before saying softly, "How much of all this does Uriah know?"

"Can't hear you."

He moved closer to repeat the question, adding, "After all, it's a pretty shocking tale."

"I'm as sure as I can be he knows nothing at all, they say he'll be the last to find out. I for one am not gonna tell him. A strange character, I'd think "poor man", but he never shows any emotion. Just gets on with his life saying hardly anything."

"I don't know, he was pretty lively first thing over the mess up with the villagers."

By way of agreement, Alan raised his eyebrows, a gesture barely caught in the light of the fire. Nearby a sudden roar of laughter erupted from another group before dying down again. Frank could not help smiling at the sound. The background chatter resumed as he remarked, "You're right, Uriah is a strange one, can't normally fathom out what he's thinking. Surely Giella was a complete contrast: flighty, flippant and flirtatious."

They laughed at the way this sounded before Alan replied, "They say opposites attract. It's hard to over-emphasise the store whites hold on fidelity, not like the blacks at all. Reuben and Japhses will be held in low esteem once the story has spread. Reuben never was particularly popular, but it could undermine Japhses' position."

"You think so?"

"Not so much amongst the men I suppose, especially now they're all keyed up for the fight. But when this is all over it could get tricky for him if the women-folk decide to ostracise him. I pity his fiancée, she'll be going through it."

"That's right, he told me he was getting married."

"Mmm, a nice girl, can't remember her name for the moment. Many peop-le will be shocked by the revelations, they'll forgive Brogg for murder more easily than Reuben for adultery – strange set of priorities those Christians – the whites I mean," he quickly added.

Frank was deep in thought and did not notice. He had been so infatuated with Giella and bewitched by her flirtatious manner he had imagined she had been going to the Castle to commit adultery with him that fateful day. He had been severely tempted, but he reminded himself he had overcome his desires and resolved not to let it get out of hand. What if she had had no such intentions, but was actually going to the Castle to tell him about the blackmail she was under? Maybe she had been wanting his help and he had misinterpreted it due to her vivacious manner.

'But she had kissed me... such a kiss!' he remembered, but struggled with details of the precise words she had actually spoken on that occasion. Some things would never be explained.

Alan was speaking.

"No, what I wonder is what her sister Kim's going to say. Or rather what she's saying now. Then there's Brogg's fate to consider."

"Well I haven't the faintest idea what I'm going to do with him. I certainly am not going to worry about it now. As I told Natias I've got other things on my mind. I'll worry about it when I get back – if I get back."

A feeling of expectation was in the air early next morning as the camp was roused. Feeding such a sizeable body was no easy matter, but the operation went well. The large quantities consumed meant several dakks' loads would be lighter that day.

"It's going to be another warm one," announced Alan coming back from the stream, naked from the waist up. Japhses nodded as he adjusted his clansit. Near him Uriah was pulling on his boots in silence.

Tents were being collapsed while a further reconnaissance sweep reported no contacts. Like a nest of ants the organisation was not obvious to the untrained eye with men scurrying about in every direction going about their duties. Shouting drivers directed the dakks as they manoeuvred their charges. Cooking equipment and tents were packed away. More than one logistics officer was seen to scratch his head and wonder how they had managed previously to pack it all in. Before too long though everything had been found a home and the column of men, dakks and wagons was being re-established.

An energetic Despot fairly vaulted into the cart to sit opposite Gideon who looked up in surprise. Japhses was still down on the ground directing operations. Once everything was set they moved off once again.

The front of the column recommenced the advance across the grasslands, the scenery was just the same. The length of the line was such that Karl's rearguard only began marching after the men at the front had been going some while.

Wagons creaked, boots thudded, the guardsmen seemed to have given up any ideas of singing that morning. The expectant atmosphere quickly settled down as the prevailing mood changed. Enthusiasm became resignation to another day's slog. They knew it would be some time before anything happened.

Frank's mind floated back to his early days on this planet, fond memories. Back in the present he studied his fellow passenger opposite him. Gideon made an interesting sight with his snow-white hair and jet-black clothes. The man was scanning the view to the south and the ever-vigilant flanking soldiers staying just within view.

"Their uniforms have not changed since the arrival of the Keepers," he said suddenly, making Frank start.

"Oh, what? Sorry?"

"The uniforms, My Lord," the Lower Village Head continued in his deep voice, "my grandfather told me they were introduced when the Keepers arrived. Not that he was around then of course."

"Of course," Frank echoed, not knowing at all what the other was talking about.

He looked around. Japhses was still marching with the leading guardsmen. Progress was slow, but steady. If Gideon was going to be more communicative this morning, he may as well engage him in conversation.

"Do you still have some villagers bemoaning the re-siting of your village?"

"I am glad to say we do not, My Lord. Even the die-hards can see the benefits now. I believe what did it was the spring thaw when there was no flooding. I am also relieved our hulf-fan crop appears so healthy. I do not profess to be an expert you understand. I am Lower Village born and bred, but the men who know about these things tell me it is exceeding their best predictions."

Abruptly his expression became earnest. "May I ask one thing, My Lord? If anything should happen to me in this fight, that you will make my son, John, the new Village Head."

Frank was taken aback by the sudden request which the man proceeded to expand upon by adding, ""If I can know that you will at least seriously consider him for the post. He is mature beyond his years. He will make an excellent leader of men. He has a keen sense of responsibility as I am sure you are aware. He knows the people of the Lower Village and they respect him."

Seeking to brush off the reason for the request the Despot tried to mollify with assurances of their good chances of survival. However now that he had raised the issue Gideon was not to be put off so easily. He pressed the point, "Yes, My Lord, but just in case something should happen to me. I would like to know my future is assured."

'What can I say? I've no idea who his successor would be! I can't have him getting all upset about it though.'

Taking the easy option therefore, he replied with a promise that Gideon's son would be his most likely successor. "But I feel certain such a situation will not arise for a good many years."

It did the trick. The white settled back with only a glimpse of his standard frown. Frank concealed a sigh of relief and with the conversation over, went back to his memories.

'Arides, now there was an interesting planet. Twin suns and a whole cluster of moons. I really should have got more for those novels though. I asked far too little for them. Well you live and learn... I'd've enjoyed my stay there more had it not been for the way they treated the under-class – helots was it? These whites live like kings by comparison...'

Midday was approaching when a wide, shallow stream was reached. It was decided to have their meal once this was crossed. The stream's bed was strewn with large stones and the dakks made heavy going of pulling the cart across. Some of the following guardsmen helped push it under Japhses' direction, but others could not wait and strode past, kicking up spray. Once onto the far bank they sat down to rest and watch. However, the Captain shouted at them to go back and aid the wagons.

Soon the Despot's cart was safely over on dry ground. The driver took the vehicle a further fifty metres before parking it. From his high perch Frank took the whole scene in. Behind them there was a hold up while dakks and soldiers struggled across the stream with a heavily-laden wagon. A few guardsmen surplus to the task were wandering about nearby. In front the way they would take lay before them. It was a grassy vista with the odd clump of trees dotted about to the right. Four hundred metres away on the opposite side was a pair of almost identical, tightly-knit spinneys. They were oval in shape, separated by twenty-five metres and lay about twice that distance from their route. Hazel and bota trees predominated.

Near these, one of the scouts was walking, he was not as far advanced from the main force as usual. Frank did not have anything to do and chose to observe the soldier through his telescope. He had not noticed the scout before, but his short, scarlet cape made him quite distinctive. As he watched the man appeared to fall over which he thought was curious. Peering more intently through the instrument he witnessed to his horror a dozen or so men come bounding out the nearer of the two spinneys and start dancing round their victim. He could see many more figures a little further behind.

He pulled his head away in horror, but he had not been the only one to see what had happened. Before he could speak the cry went up from guardsmen nearby, "Ambush, ambush! Enemy sighted!"

CHAPTER THIRTY FOUR

Frank's mouth was as dry as a bone and he felt momentarily paralysed. Fortunately no such affliction hit Japhses who, sizing up the situation in a flash, immediately abandoned the wagon mid-stream and barked the order to stand to. Guardsmen ran forward to form a defensive line to hold off the assault. One of their number was sent back down the column crying, "Arm yourselves, enemy attacking!" The Kassiahorn sounded loud and clear, cutting through the air.

Squad leaders calmly organised the distribution of equipment to their men. Those in charge of the militia managed to keep a semblance of order as their armour and weapons were handed out. An ecstasy of fumbling as more than a thousand men prepared for battle.

Gideon had hesitated only a brief moment before jumping from the cart and making for his Lower Village militiamen. The cart driver peered round at the frozen figure of the Despot still staring ahead. He wanted to move his vehicle out of the way and in the end called out, "My Lord, I must move back to the stream... we will be in the way here. We..."

He stopped when his commander indicated silence with his hand. Frank then put the telescope back to his eye and said in amazement, "They're not attacking yet."

It was true. While more of the enemy were out in the open between and in front of the two spinneys they were not advancing. Rather they were dancing wildly, jumping up and down, shouting something. The Hoamen at this stage were not too concerned as to what they were shouting, they were making the most of it. With every passing breath another soldier was ready for battle.

"My Lord," said the driver indicating behind the cart, "your adjutant is here."

Looking down Frank saw a guardsman holding his armour. He at last got down from the cart. The soldier showed great proficiency as he helped put the protective layers on his commander.

With more units getting lined up, Japhses eased the congestion by advancing the line and fanning the troops out. A fully armoured Alan ran up, helmet tucked under his arm.

"You almost ready?" he questioned as he saw his friend buckle his belt.

Without waiting for an answer the drone leapt onto the stationary cart to get a better view. He said, "They're still not attacking. The fools. They've lost the element of surprise." He scanned in other directions to see if they were witnessing a feint, but there was no cover to speak of and no sign of more enemy. Flankers stood faithfully in their positions, keeping their eyes peeled.

Militiamen were coming forward in droves by now, the officers' dakks were led across the stream. The cart driver asked once more if he could move his vehicle back and was told not to as it provided a useful observation platform.

The Captain left Uriah to complete organising the battle-formation and came back to report to the Despot who was now ready. Karl also converged on the cart while the village heads saw to their men.

Before they had begun to speak a couple of runners returned from the flankers and reported there was no sighting of the enemy.

"Are we to conclude," asked the Despot of his lieutenants, "that there is only one force of Laodicians there?"

"There's no cover on their flanks," Japhses observed.

"They could be beyond the horizon," said Karl.

"That's true," the black whined.

They quickly decided to throw all their forces into an assault on the enemy concentration they knew of. There was no time to probe how many Ladosans were behind the trees, but they had no option, they had to fight and fight on the ground already chosen for them.

Alan, still on top of the cart, had one ear on the deliberations while he watched the enemy's movements through the telescope. Around fifty were visible between the trees and these were continuing their jeers and taunts while the Hoamen were being neatly lined up stiff and quiet as if on parade. His platform provided an excellent view.

Suddenly the observer exclaimed the foulest of swear words causing Frank and his entourage to look up.

"What on Molt is it, Alan?"

The drone looked sick, "I don't know whether I should tell you or you look yourself." Then making his mind up he said, "Those bastards! They've cut up the body of our scout and are waving the parts about above their heads." Getting down he added, "Wait 'till those devils get a taste of my sword. What are we waiting for?"

A groan went up from the Hoamen lines when they saw what was happening. If any man had needed his resolve building, he no longer did.

Without further thought Frank told his Captain, "I will fight alongside you."

Using a minimum of words, Japhses then outlined an attack plan which was readily agreed by the others. The main force would be in the centre and bear down on the visible enemy in-between the two small woods. This would consist of the larger part of the guard plus a third of the Upper Village and all the Sardis militia and would be led by Despot, Captain, Alan and Luke. While this main assault went into action, two outflanking attacks would act as pincers on either side. Lower Village militia plus guardsmen to the left under Karl and Gideon, the rest of the Upper Village militia plus guardsmen to the right under Uriah and Saul. These two smaller forces were to swing round to attack from flank and rear. One thing commending the plan was that it would require the minimum of reorganisation from the battle formation the Captain had already instructed Uriah to set into place.

They were just leaving to inform the squad leaders and village heads when a pair of guardsmen went by dragging a screaming colleague away from the lines. The man was in a terrible state, crying out and thrashing about. One of the soldiers explained to Japhses, "That's his brother out there," nodding towards the Ladosan lines. The Captain, face grim, marched swiftly to the battle-line.

The officers were still being briefed as Alan and Frank took up their positions next to Luke. Front-centre they stood, dakks' bridles in hand. Along with their army they stood in silence and watched the enemy lines. The Ladosans were making no move to attack, it was clear they thought their defensive position strong. It was worrying, how many soldiers did they have in reserve behind the trees? Their bating continued, exaggerated dancing and holding their grisly trophies aloft.

Briefly scanning to either side, the Despot felt pride in his command. 'A thoroughly professional army, we will show these Laodician devils a thing or two.' His mind flitted about, 'I'm shivering and I'm certainly not cold... hurry up, Japhses. My mouth is so dry! Ah here he is...'

Taking up his place, the Captain declared all was ready, a guardsman handed him the bridle as he spoke. Frank waited, what for? What a strange feeling power could be, more than a thousand men waited upon his word to hurl themselves into a fight to the death.

Clearing his throat he rather feebly instructed Japhses to give the order.

The giant man put on his helmet, the others followed suit. Unlike Karl's the Captain's did not fully enclose his head. But protruding cheek plates gave his face good protection. Indicating with his arm forward he bellowed, "Advance!" at the top of his voice.

The Kassiahorn sounded and a mass of men in tight formation began moving forward at a slow walk. Breathing heavily, Frank felt the inertia of the heavy armour and was concerned about the limited vision he had through his visor. The army advanced as one, shields by their sides. Those guardsmen with axes still had them slung over their shoulders, swords were still sheathed. Three hundred metres to go... two hundred and fifty. Though he could not see them the archers followed behind the main body, bows ready, but not yet taut.

Two hundred metres, the enemy had stopped their dance and were bracing for the attack, it was not easy to make out individuals distinctly, but they were still concentrated between the two groups of trees.

One hundred and fifty metres, on they walked, the tension unbearable. Frank thought his heart was going to pop right out.

"Mount up!" Japhses called and the line halted while the Despot and his lieutenants all did. The Captain unsheathed his sword with the distinctive "zing" and held it high in dramatic fashion. All along the line, weapons were brought out to be held at the ready.

The walk was resumed, slightly faster now, then faster again. One hundred metres from the enemy a pair of probing arrows fell short. Ridiculously the realisation flashed through Frank's mind, 'They're shooting at me!'

Faster, the dakks were trotting now and having trouble not breaking into a canter. When would he give the order?

"Charge!" A thousand tongues responded with a roar that felt it should make the ground tremble. Like a mad dog unleashed the Thyatiran army threw itself forward.

The four mounted men in the centre moved ahead of the main body, dakks at full speed. Arrows whistled overhead, front line soldiers on both sides dropped. With a great crash the two armies met. A mad frenzy of hacking, slashing and spearing began. Men reacted instinctively, no time for thought. The momentum of the charge carried the few on dakks well into the heart of the enemy. Frank saw a short Ladosan aim for him with a single-headed axe and brought his sword down with a swift movement as he passed on. He did not know if he had killed him, but whatever he hit gave way and the man was gone. No time to look, another was on him, a taller figure in chain mail wielding a mace. This assailant was dispatched clinically by Japhses.

Before he knew, it they were clean through the enemy's lines. A quick glance took in the fact there was no second line nor reserves visible. They were in the gap between the two spinneys which stretched back some distance. All four dakkmen were still mounted and in a swift manoeuvre turned their mounts to attack again from the rear. As Frank pulled at the rein he saw his beast was already frothing pink foam from its mouth at the strain. He was less skilful than the others and found himself behind his colleagues who closed up. For the moment he found his beast was wedged in-between the rears of Japhses' and Alan's and was unable to engage the enemy.

The Ladosans had hidden half their force within the trees, but before these could attack the central Hoame formation, they found themselves engaging the superior numbers of the Thyatiran pincers. The battle: screams and shouts, the clang of metal against metal, the dull thump as an arrow hit.

On the left flank, the Hoamen fought on the edge of the trees. With a great thud and a crack Gideon found his shield disintegrate under the force of a two-handed axe. He tried to get at his protagonist with his sword, but another stepped in his way. Desperately the Village Head struggled with his new assailant, he had to dispose of him before that axe could strike again. There was no one to help him, everyone else was engaged in life-struggles of their own. John was nearby, but he was fully taken up with a mace-bearing Ladosan. Gideon grappled against his enemy, feeling a dagger's blade graze his side. Making a feint he dodged the next assault and picking his moment precisely thrust his sword between the man's ribs. He fell, too late. In a fraction of time Gideon saw the axe descend and tried to block it with his sword. Before he could engage weapons, it crashed with full force into his head.

"Father!" cried John as he saw it happen. The lapse of concentration was fatal: an enemy sword thrust into the young man's heart and he collapsed at his father's feet.

Some militia nearby began to lose heart and fall back, but Karl had seen what had happened and came forward with a group of guardsmen. The black looked two metres tall in his full armour, purple plume riding high. With tremendous force his group exploded once more into the enemy line, ferociously chopping and cutting. The Ladosans were overwhelmed by this renewed onslaught and the tide turned in Hoame's favour. Bolstered by this action the militiamen surged forward, finally making their superior numbers tell.

On the right flank, the Upper Village militia's casualties were relatively light and became the first to break through the woods and attack the main body of the enemy in the flank. The central Ladosan force had been split in two early on. Frank found himself surrounded by a deep cordon of his own men. They were so protective of him that he could not get back into the fight. Seeing what a poor state his mount was in he got off and settled for a role as observer.

Although being overwhelmed by a superior force and in danger of being cut off, the Ladosans did not attempt an escape. Instead their diminishing numbers held on bravely in the ferocious battle.

The din was terrible – the cries, the clashes. Japhses led by example, his strength doubled by the memory of the atrocity witnessed when the enemy first came into view. His huge sword cut into the flesh of his protagonists. In order to get a better swing, he stepped onto bodies of his dead and dying victims.

On both sides now, guardsmen and militia broke through. The Despot retreated and watched the remnants of the enemy in their death-throws, now completely surrounded by the far larger Thyatiran army. Karl ran up to report.

"No more..." he paused to suck in breath. "No more resistance on this side, Sir. Permission to take some men back to the wagons... make sure no enemy."

"Go."

He did. The last stage of the battle was in progress. The Thyatiran arrows had long since stopped flying for fear of hitting their own men. A few Ladosans held out to the last, they were all concerned with defence by now, no more Hoame casualties were being taken.

Saul and Uriah joined their commander to witness this final slaughter. Unlike the clash with the Ma'hol Frank felt no inclination to stop it. In fact he felt nothing at all – only a vague thankfulness that he was still alive came through the mists of his mind. Uriah was not talkative at the best of times. He said not a word now.

There was a mere handful of the enemy left standing when the butchering ceased and they lay down their arms. All resistance was at an end, no Ladosans were found attending the baggage train nor anywhere else. The battle was over.

"Can we not change the subject? I am trying not to think about it. It's difficult enough as it is."

"Of course, my dear, how insensitive of me."

Anastasia was entertaining a friend in her lounge. Octavia was another member of the unique white, leisured set in Asattan. Slightly older than her hostess, she was the wife of a senior civil servant in the Capital, one of Benedict's deputies. For all the ingrained prejudice, a white with ability could rise high in that profession, the Keepers not being too particular when talent was needed.

The pair had not stopped talking since Octavia had arrived at midday. It was now mid-afternoon and all the windows were wide open in the glorious weather. Anastasia struggled hard to find a fresh topic of conversation, all her thoughts seemed to converge on the one she had tried to steer clear of. The garden was so quiet, not a bird, not even a fly was making its presence known. Nature was holding her breath. As peaceful as a grave? Maybe, but after a long pause something began to stir, something outside of nature.

"Anna my dear, what is that noise? Can you hear it? A sort of low, throbbing sound. It appears to be getting louder."

Indeed it was, so much so that the floorboards were starting to vibrate. Anastasia knew what it was, but did not have time to speak before there was a muffled explosion from the bowels of the house.

"Uncle!" she cried as, without warning she tore out of the room and headed for the stairs down to the cellar. Lifting her long skirt she descended rapidly and ran along a corridor taking small, fast steps. The vibrating had ceased immediately after the explosion and she could feel water vapour warm on her face.

Rounding the corner of the laboratory she was relieved to see Benedict was unhurt, although he was surrounded by a scene of utter devastation. A large pool of steaming water covered the floor. There were masses of pipes and other twisted metal lengths lying in the middle, while bits of thin wooden slats, jagged splinters for the most part, were spread over the whole scene.

"Ah hello, my darling," the drone said turning round and scratching his head, "A spot of luck I was out of the room when this little lot went off."

"You're okay then," his 'niece' asked to confirm what her eyes already thankfully told her.

"I am, although a mite shaken I must be honest. Must clear this little lot up."

Octavia was at the scene by now and, speechless, gazed wide-eyes at the effect of the explosion. Steam was everywhere.

Pulling Benedict's arm, Anastasia ordered him to go upstairs, "The servants can clear this mess up. You need to have a good sit down and a drink."

A short while later, the obedient civil servant was sitting meekly in the lounge making polite conversation. After covering several items of small-talk, the guest could contain herself no longer and had to ask what on Molt the man had been doing in the cellar.

Anastasia threw in, "I'm sure you wouldn't be interested, Octavia.

"Nonsense, my dear, it looks positively fascinating. Do tell me, Benedict, why are you heating up water in the cellar? Did your experimental bath go wrong?"

Taking this in good humour he told her some details of his experiments with steam power. "...And as you saw for yourself, my reinforced barrel was not strong enough for the job..."

"My goodness!"

"...So I shall have to try something a lot stronger. I have been working on a design for a metal cylinder, but have not progressed beyond drawings until now. Trouble is I shall have to bring in outside help which I am not used to doing."

"You are trying to keep it a secret?" offered Octavia, "you need not worry about me, your secret is safe, I shall not tell a soul."

She seemed to revel in being privy to an exciting secret, but was deflated by the response she got.

"Oh no, not that, several of my colleagues in the Citadel know of my little hobby. I'm sure your husband does. I am used to working by myself, that's all. I will need someone with the necessary expertise for building the cylinder, expertise I do not possess. I will have to ask Bodd, he always knows where to find the right people. Never met anyone so good as he for knowing where the right people are. It isn't even as if he were a native of Ephamon, but he seems to have established lots of connections in a short time. Don't know what I'd do..."

He broke off seeing the mention of her fiancé was having a harrowing effect on his niece.

Octavia told her, "You must pull yourself together my dear, there are many others in your situation, they don't all break down every time their loved-ones' names are mentioned." Then more softly, "You know I am saying this for your own good, my dear, you are no use to anyone in your current state."

"But I'm sure something terrible has happened to him!"

"Pull yourself together, this just won't do. "Think positively" - that's what my mother used to say. If you think positively things will work out for the best.

"We must press on, My Lord, get to the Pass this afternoon."

The Captain was advising his Despot as the latter delayed, spending longer than his subordinate felt strictly necessary with the wounded. They had been loaded onto the back of spare wagons, those conscious seemed to appreciate their leader's gesture. Wispy clouds scudded across the sky, it was a beautiful, warm summer's day. Not a good day to die though, not if you were the youth Halaton. Illianeth's beloved should have had a long life ahead of him, instead it was ebbing away before their eyes.

With remarkable efficiency the battlefield had been cleared and most of the wagons brought across the river before the Thyatirans ate. Their dead had been laid out neatly for all to pay their last respects prior to them being loaded onto wagons to be taken home. Thirty-four of them, much higher casualties than against the Ma'hol. More would join their ranks from the wounded. Frank would never forget the sight, nor the numbness when he saw the frame of Gideon lying dead. Half his head was missing, but from the distinctive clothing there could be no mistake. That distinctive clothing was covered in blood and something else Frank did not recognise. Next to him lay his son John, by contrast no visible wound on him.

'Silly the way poets talk of the dead as being asleep,' Frank had thought at the time, 'these twisted bodies have no semblance of those in slumber. It could have been me lying there, I'm glad it was them instead.'

How he had recoiled in horror as this thought had bobbed up from his own sub-conscious. 'What sort of despicable person am I to think like that?' Then he came to his own defence with the realisation that it is only instinct to feel that way. There was simply a great feeling of relief at still being alive – at least for the time being.

Like a computer, his mind registered the fact that the man he had been chatting with most of the morning was now dead, but it did not sink in on an emotional level. This was obviously unlike Cragoop the jailer's son, weeping bitterly over the body of his close friend, John.

"Sorry Japhses," he said coming to, "what did you say?"

"I advised that we get under way, My Lord, everyone is ready."

"Right, I'll be with you in just a moment," he replied mechanically. Moving on, he found Bodd and Tsodd lying in the end wagon. The former was nearest the end with his head heavily bandaged. He had trouble focussing his eyes on the Despot when addressed.

Forcing a weak grimace he said, "I'll be okay, M'Lord. I'm not going to die, Anastasia'd never forgive me if I did – in fact she'd kill me!"

Frank could not help smiling at the black humour. Taking a glance at Bodd's brother he found him asleep or unconscious. Stepping back he found Laffaxe behind him.

"Are you sure you want me to return with these wounded, My Lord? There may be a greater need of my skills after the main battle yet to come."

"Yes I'm sure. See if you can get back to the Castle as quickly as possible. With this heat you might have to bury the dead on the way – I'm informed you have the tools."

Without waiting for an answer he wished the physician God's protection and crossed back over the stream to where the army was waiting to move out.

So the Thyatiran force was divided, the two parts departing the scene in opposite directions. Laffaxe got his wagons under way with their cargo of dead and seriously wounded. They were escorted by a squad of guardsmen whose other responsibility was the small band of Ladosan prisoners of war. Only a handful of the invaders were left alive and they had not been allowed to give their fallen comrades a decent burial. Instead they had been forced to pile the many bodies, stripped of armour and weapons, into one great pile. There they were left to the frasses and other carrion. It was an ignominious end, but there was no time to bury them and cremation was taboo to Hoamen.

Very little had been learned from the prisoners in the short time available for interrogation. The consistent story that came out was that they had been a unit that had become detached from their main army and had thus avoided the main confrontation they believed to be taking place further to the east. A local herdsman had shown them a narrow pass through the mountains – they maintained there were no other units using it to the best of their knowledge. Much that he abhorred what the prisoners stood for, Frank would not allow torture to be used to extract further information. Along with Alan, he concluded that they had the essence of it: that, in fact, this band of Ladosans had been similar to their own, separated from the bulk of their army and not involved in the main showdown.

Fortunately for the Thyatirans they had held considerable numerical superiority.

The Despot considered these things as his cart led the way across the flat countryside. For now everyone seemed to have become introspective as they considered what had taken place. It was thus a subdued column that continued its advance along the last stretch to the Mitas Gap.

In spite of the warm afternoon sun, Frank felt uncannily cold and wrapped a cloak around himself. Looking across at his Captain he made an involuntary smile, but he found a feeling of great affection welling up for this giant of a soldier. When he thought about it, this was extended towards Alan, Karl and all the others involved in the fight. They had faced death together and came through the ordeal with a greater bond. Nothing was said, but it was there, very tangible.

A long-range scout returned, he had made contact with the main army and what he had to say aroused great interest. He was called into the leading cart so that his report could be given on the move.

"A great victory has been won, My Lord, the enemy has been crushed with enormous casualties!

Most of our forces have gone on in pursuit."

"Did you hear that?" Japhses cried to the squad leader marching behind with his unit. The latter called out the news to his men and there was a great roar. It was quickly disseminated down the line and further cheers went up at intervals.

"How far?" Frank asked the scout, "How far is the pass from here?"

Pausing only briefly, the man replied with a note of certainty, "Five kilometres, My Lord."

"I see. The casualties, no doubt they were very high on both sides."

"No, My Lord," the scout returned with enthusiasm, "ours are comparatively light. One Bynarian told me they had sent down fire into the enemy once they were in the valley in sufficient numbers, burned them all up. There were many thousands caught in the Gap My Lord, a huge force they had. I call it the judgement of God. What's left of them is running away."

Japhses was puzzled as the report progressed. To have had the effect the scout was saying the Hoamen would have had to have had a thousand or more catapults to hurl the burning pitch. He felt sure they did not exist in anything like this number, they could never have been transported or constructed on site in the time available. Neither would there deployment have been practical.

"Did you see many catapults there?" he asked.

"No Sir, I only stopped a short while. The Bynarian I mentioned said they had a new type of weapon to send the fire down, it was up on..."

"Did you see Rodd or James there?" the Despot interrupted, not being too interested in catapults, "our advance party."

"Not to talk to, My Lord, although I was told they are all unharmed. Several members of the Inner Council are there, My Lord, I was told they await your arrival. I saw them from a distance, they appeared in good spirits."

"Hmm. Have you anything further to report?"

"I don't think so, My Lord."

The scout was dismissed and Frank turned to discuss the situation with his Captain.

"In view of the delays it's hardly surprising we missed the main event."

"If I may suggest, My Lord, we have reason to be proud of ourselves. We have destroyed a sizeable Laodician raiding party. If they had been let loose on some of the Bynarian villages (not all have easy access to castles or strongholds) our people would have been massacred."

"You don't buy the theory that they merely became detached from their main force?"

"No, My Lord, it did not ring true."

"So there could be more of them infiltrating behind our lines?"

"But they would be hard to find, the area is so vast."

"I shall have to mention this when we arrive. They may feel it best we patrol back here rather than join up with the other despotates. Yes you're right, I must emphasise the good that's come from our delay. Besides we now know they have beaten the enemy conclusively without our help.

"One thing I don't understand is why the Laodicians did not lie low. If they had watched they could have seen we well outnumbered them. Why attack us? They could have laid low until we were gone, then travel on to attack our lightly-defended villages. Even if the inhabitants are probably evacuated one would have thought the opportunities for plunder and general disruption of our rear to be worthwhile for them."

"The Laodicians showed poor tactics throughout, My Lord. I wondered if they were on drugs."

"That's possible."

"Instead of attacking us while they had the element of surprise they danced about like a bunch of idiots until we were ready. Not that I'm complaining of course..."

"Indeed not!"

"Presumably they felt more confident in defence."

"Yes...did you get a look at the two wounded brothers, Bodd and Tsodd? Do you think they'll be all right?"

"The miner triplets," said Japhses using a term not as frequently applied to the brothers as in the past, "it did not look good for either of them, but you never can tell."

For a while, the two men lapsed into their own worlds until Frank said, "I wonder if we were fortunate not to have more casualties. After all, when one saw how many dead the Laodicians had, the figures were disproportionate. I know we outnumbered them, but even so..."

"Our casualties were highest on our left flank, My Lord, they appear to have put up the stoutest resistance there. Gideon met his fate there – fortunately none of our other commanders was hurt. No, I was unimpressed with the enemy either as fighters or tacticians."

"Everything I have seen of the Laodicians appears confused and contradictory, they are a strange people, as much at odds with themselves as with anyone else."

"Some of their number were women."

"No!"

"Yes, My Lord, among the dead a dozen or so were noted."

"Then these people truly are condemned!" Frank warned, "they can have no respect for women-hood, sending them out into battle like that. The country must be rotten to the core, small wonder our armies are proving victorious."

"I think God must have been playing a joke when He created the Laodicians, My Lord, they are the most ridiculous race ever."

"Well that's one way to look at it, I suppose. I remember where I came from being involved in a debate as to whether God has a sense of humour, I came down on the side which said He does not. I'm having second thoughts now."

Soon after this conversation they reached their destination. The great Hoame encampment came into view. A sea of grey tents spread out before them. These were standing on their side of the pass. On the other side the ground fell away sharply into the huge valley which was the Mitas Gap. This was at first hidden from the view of the newcomers. On the far side of this chasm, more tents were pitched. The mountain chain that had been close to their left flank for more than a day stopped abruptly before resuming afresh a few kilometres further along.

The column did not stop, but changed course slightly to skirt round the northern perimeter of the encampment. There was not a great deal of movement visible in the canvas city that late afternoon. The occasional guard just watched them go by in silence. A few groups of men busied themselves taking down tents and packing them away into wagons. Otherwise it appeared deserted. The only real signs of life were further along the ridge to the north. Here stood half a dozen or so tents of a different type, with vertical walls and multicoloured pennants flying. As they approached, they could see groups of officers and other blacks talking. The Thyatiran column lumbered slowly towards them.

Alan came forward and got into the cart while it was still moving. Frank gave a smile in greeting. "We're heading up there to what appears to be the headquarters," he explained unnecessarily.

"So I see. Ah, we have company."

Frank was referring to the group of soldiers, all blacks, coming down the slope towards them. As a reception committee they lacked both charm and finesse.

"Halt your wagons!" cried the officer, a short man with a thin moustache, "stop now!" The cart's driver was not to be intimidated and eased the dakks to a standstill far gentler than most of their stops had been.

"Your name," the officer demanded, looking Frank straight in the eye with a fierce stare.

Put out by this sudden rudeness he did not reply at first and the officer repeated himself even more aggressively. When eventually the Thyatiran Despot announced himself the man suddenly became all sweetness and light.

"Ah welcome, Sir," he said with a sickly false smile, "his Excellency, Count Zastein, would like to see you, please come with me."

Alan and Frank rose to their feet. As they did so the officer added in a superior voice, "Alone please, Sir, the drone will have to stay with the rest of your men."

Before Frank could protest Alan told him, "Don't worry, it's okay."

"But..."

"It doesn't matter Frank, you go on. I'll stay and see the men are taken care of."

He sat back next to Japhses. Frank's heart went out to the pair of them and before getting down he said quietly, "You two are worth any number of arrogant bastards like him!"

Karl had come up from the rear, "Have we arrived then, Sir?"

"We have. You go and sit in the cart if you like; they'll put you in the picture."

Seeing the Despot striding out purposefully towards him the officer ordered one of his men to look after the remaining Thyatirans. He then accompanied Frank up to the centre of operations. Following a step behind, the new arrival took a keen interest in the activity there. More tents became visible higher up the slope, these being interspersed with shade-giving trees.

A large field hospital was established on the flat area on the top of the truncated ridge. This strip of land was some hundred metres wide before the almost vertical descent into the valley began. The officer led him on a route parallel with, but some distance from the Gap. Skirting the edge of the hospital, Frank witnessed rows of wounded men lined up in the open with makeshift screens to provide an element of shade for most. None of those he saw seemed in any particular discomfort and he concluded they were the less serious cases who had already been ministered to. Orderlies and medics were busying themselves going in and out of the tall, colourful tents. An air of efficiency abounded, but the speed of operations gave an impression of crisis passed.

To eyes used to seeing a preponderance of white people, the lack of them here was striking. Apart from a few drones all here, whether medic or patient, were black.

It was still not possible to get a view of the pass from the route the officer was taking. The off glimpse between tree and tent revealed nothing to one as short-sighted as Frank.

Facing forward again he noticed a lone, white soldier walking in the opposite direction. To his amazement he recognised who it was.

"Rodd, hello there, what are you doing here?" he asked with great enthusiasm, grasping the young man by both shoulders.

The guardsman jumped in surprise. He had grown used to oppressive blacks around him the last couple of days and had not been expecting one to suddenly greet him like a long lost friend. Recovering himself he returned a formal greeting.

"A bit silly asking you why you're here," Frank continued in light-hearted vein, "I ordered you here."

"They've got me running errands, keeping me busy. The rest of us are in the whites' camp, about the only ones still there."

"The rest of our advanced party, yes. So they're keeping you busy."

While this chatter went on the black officer stood nearby with his arms folded and a cross expression on his face. He was most disapproving of whites and blacks conversing in such an informal manner. The interlocutors instinctively turned their backs on him and eagerly caught up on each other's news.

"Were you here for the main battle?"

"The second day, My Lord, it was horrible. I've never seen anything like it, made me sick, physically sick."

Frank was puzzled at this reaction, "Why? You were in the fight against the Ma'hol surely, you've seen war before."

"This wasn't war, My Lord, this was hell! You haven't been told what happened then."

"Um, briefly; the scout said something about fire being hurled down on the enemy from catapults while they were trapped in the valley."

"Not from catapults. I don't know what it was, My Lord, some special magic weapon hidden in tents just burned the Laodicians up like... like I don't know what. All I do know is it was a bloody massacre, nobody deserves to die like that.

"It was on the second day when it was used to full effect, I guess there weren't enough of them in the Gap the day before. Only yesterday, but in a way it seems far longer. I do know I'll never forget the sight of those writhing bodies... one of the tents exploded killing some of our own men – up there on that rock, can you see, My Lord?" he pointed further up the ridge beyond the camp. Frank nodded, but he could not see anything. Obviously affected by what he had seen Rodd continued, "I felt glad, yes glad, I wished the others had gone the same way. You've never ever..."

"Sir!" the black officer interrupted, "the Count awaits your presence."

The Despot realised he must drag himself away and began moving off, "I'll see you later," was all he could think to say to Rodd.

"Yes, My Lord, are my brothers here?"

'Why in Heaven's name did he have to ask that?' "Er, no. I must be getting along now, the others will fill you in on what's been happening to us."

He hurried away, in step with the officer who was glad the interruption was over. Frank began to rebuke himself for not having told Rodd about his brothers when asked. It had been cowardly to leave it to someone else to break the news.

There was no time to dwell on it though, for there forty metres away was Count Zastein with his entourage. These high-ranking blacks were in celebratory mood, standing outside the last tent but one on the ridge. Behind that the flat ground narrowed abruptly and there was just one small tent, beyond which stood a single gnarled tree, then the terrain became rocky and barren.

A story was ending and a burst of laughter came from the group as he arrived. The officer reported to Baron Schail, the Count's ever-present companion.

"Mmm good, hello there, Thorn," the Baron called out stretching forth a hand and patting him on the top of his arm.

Frank had always found the man's presence reassuring, the warm eyes showing his humanity which put people at their ease. All eight were introduced and as usual Frank only took half of them in: "... Despot Schllessenger, Despot Kagel you know, as of course you do, His Excellency, the Count."

"Your Excellency," his protégée said with a deferential nod of the head.

"Ah, Thorn, glad you could make it."

The words sounded sarcastic, however the expression on Zastein's face indicated it was not. Not a man given to joviality as a rule, but he certainly appeared cheerful enough this afternoon. A great weight had been lifted off his shoulders with the success of his plans looking assured.

"We were involved in a battle on the way here," Frank announced.

"Oh yes?"

"We annihilated a Ladosan raiding party several hundred strong."

He then went on to give a concise account of the morning's battle. The other men appeared interested enough and it seemed to lift the Despot of Thyatira's credibility in their eyes.

"Jolly good," was Zastein's verdict.

"Now my young man," he continued, fixing his stare on the not-so-young Despot Thorn, "And what are you doing about obtaining a wife? You turn your nose up at Hista's daughters and now I'm told the lovely daughter of Kagel here is betrothed to another. Am I to decide for you? Nominate a lady of my choice?"

His tone was only mildly chastising, although the message was clear. 'But why now? Frank wandered to himself, 'we're in the middle of an all-out conflict and here he is going on about finding a bride. I suppose I'd better say something he wants to hear though...'

"I can assure you the matter is in hand, Your Excellency; you should not have to wait long."

"Is this so?" asked the imposing figure taking a keen interest in this revelation, "and who is the lucky lady?"

"The Lady Hannah Unit Arpintonax Your Excellency. She..."

"The Ladosan," Kagel interjected.

"..I trust that is not an impediment. She is of good stock."

To Frank's immense relief the Count agreed, stating, "As long as she will accept the proper role of a woman in our society, there can be no objection. Everyone knows of the Arpintonaxes' lineage, she will make an excellent despotess I do not doubt."

'Pity he could not choose a Hoame-grown girl,' he thought, 'but then I should not expect too much of the alien.'

Such was still going through his head when a runner came up with a report for him. With him thus distracted, Frank considered whether he should engage the others in conversation. He was a bit worried about what he had just announced. It would be news to Hannah that she was going to marry him. He did not baulk at the idea himself, but she might not look upon it so favourably even if she had shown him some affection. What if she heard of his remarks before he had a chance to propose? He must get to her first.

He supposed he loved Hannah, but he was finding a deep distrust of that emotion within himself after his experience with Giella. However this was completely different, it was more a meeting of minds than an infatuation. He knew, however, that the game was up. If he did not obtain a wife pretty damn quick he would find himself with one of those dreadful Hista women – and expected to produce heirs!

Kagel spoke up: "If you've this moment arrived you'll not've seen the battlefield. Come, let me show you."

With Zastein still busy cross-examining the messenger the two despots strolled casually in the direction of the valley. For the first time Frank noticed the Aggepariian had his arm in a sling. The man saw him staring and explained the wound was pre-battle.

"...A big fire in the castle, burnt out a whole floor just about, lucky the whole damn building was not gutted. Started in the library, it was near there I got this."

He raised his arm a fraction, it did not appear to be causing him pain.

"Were you trying to save the books?"

"I say no!" Kagel replied, amazed at the very idea, "I had far more important things to do. No I wasn't actually in the library, but close by when a timber came crashing down and I put my arm up to protect myself. I say Thorn, if one good thing came of the affair it was the clearing out of the library. I'll be able to put that floor-space to good use now.

"Here we are!" he added without pause now that they had arrived.

It was almost a sheer drop to the flat bottom of the Mitas Gap. A geological oddity, a complete break in the mountain chain that stretched along the border. The parting of tectonic plates in pre-history could have caused it, or had an impatient giant hewn a path for himself through uneven ground in the days of legend?

Frank stared down into the valley, a sea of colour struck him: yellows and reds in particular, but also purples, blues plus a myriad other hues. It was hard to make out exactly what it was, so he fumbled for his telescope attached to his belt.

"I say," the ebullient Kagel started up again, indicating with his good arm into the valley, "fairly made mincemeat of them, eh? There's only a remnant got away and they're scattered. Our boys are hunting them down now."

Putting the instrument to his eye it somewhat belatedly dawned on Frank what he was witnessing. The scout's report had not prepared him for the scene. An ocean of corpses covered the valley floor. A man could have walked for hundreds of metres standing on nothing but dead flesh. The unsuspecting enemy had been fed into a mincing machine, no wonder Rodd had felt sick. As he watched he noticed small gangs of Hoame soldiers picking their way among the bodies, salvaging any items of interest or worth. This looting of the dead was clearly being organised and was not an unofficial or random action. The bright colours he had first noticed were fallen Ladosan battle flags, many of which were fluttering where they lay like so many shrouds. Their uniforms too were colourful, very different from the drab-looking Ladosans he had encountered earlier in the day.

His escort was still crowing, but Frank did not hear him. He interrupted with a curt, "I'm going back."

He would have liked to have returned to his own men, but knew he had better report back to the Count. He re-entered the group and found that Zastein was keen to tell him something in private and led him away towards the single tent, pitched by itself away from camp and people. A pair of guards stood outside the erection which, the Count explained, had been put up the day before.

The most powerful man in Hoame lowered his voice, his subordinate coming closer to hear as they stopped fifty metres away.

"I have found someone who knows you, Thorn, another man from beyond the stars. He was captured as a Ladosan spy and under interrogation told a story very similar to your own. When I mentioned your name he claimed to know you. I thought you might like to speak with him."

"Yes!" Frank hastily replied, although he could hardly believe his ears.

"He was facing execution, but if you feel he should be spared I will listen. Go to him now."

With that he turned and headed back to his entourage without turning round, leaving Frank in a state of shock.

'It could be John looking for me, he got tangled up in this mess,' he thought as he struggled to come to terms with what he had just been told. 'It's years since he's seen me, he won't know me with my beard.'

Taking a deep breath he advanced to the tent and passed the guards who stood like statues either side of the entrance.

'Well there's only one way to solve this puzzle!' he reasoned as he pulled the flap back and walked in.

There, sitting on a chair, manacled and tied to the centre support pole was... someone he did not recognise!

The small. mousy man with shifty eyes was certainly not his brother, he had no idea who he was.

"Hello Thorn, boy I'm glad you've come."

"Er, um..."

"I'm Scales, had the cabin next to you on the *Cassandra*, remember?"

Yes, Frank did remember, he had left him in the lurch with that terrible bore in the lounge, but what was he doing here?

The man continued, "They're going to kill me if you don't help me. I know you have influence here, they even knew about you in Ladosa. They're going to execute me as a spy if you don't stop them."

"Um, yes of course, I can have a word with Count Zastein. I'm sure he'll agree to allow you into my custody."

"You give me your word?"

The desperation in his eyes was clear, Frank had no reason to want him dead, even if he was not exactly his favourite person.

"Yes, of course. I've seen enough death today. If I can avoid one more I'll do so. Were you really spying?"

"I'm dying of cancer anyway," Scales came back with grim laugh avoiding the question, "but I don't want to go just yet, especially like this."

"All right, you have my word. You're the only other survivor of the *Cassandra* I've come across."

"I'm not surprised, you won't find any more here."

"Are we the only two survivors?" asked Frank looking bewildered.

"You don't know, do you?"

"What?"

Scales laughed. Something was clearly highly amusing, his chains jangled as he moved on the chair. He was relishing the moment he would disseminate the information.

"You evacuated the ship as ordered?"

"Yes."

"I thought so. The order was cancelled as soon as you left, it was a false alarm."

Frank was less than amused at this revelation and did not really believe the man. His face drained and he asked earnestly, "How do you know that? Why are you here then?"

"I knew there were a couple of enforcement agents on board. They were going to arrest me the minute we landed. News of your departure was well known and it gave me the idea. I wasted no time in grabbing a few things and going off myself. I'd rather be free to live out what little time I have left than rot in a prison. The dozy idiots hadn't re-set the robots from emergency mode, they strapped me in! Ha ha... so just think Frank, you needn't have left the ship after all. You could've carried on with the cruise. They're not going to come for you now, you're stuck here mate..."

Frank was no longer listening. He staggered out of there in a daze. To his immense relief, Zastein was nowhere to be seen. His single desire was to be alone. He made for the old tree as far away from everybody as possible and a promise of shade. Glancing round he could not see Schail or the other men either. Good, he would have killed to be alone with his thoughts at that moment.

A large dragonfly winged its way past close by. The tree held a flock of birds which sang loudly as he approached. The sun was still strong although the shadows were lengthening.

Frank Thorn laughed as he walked on. The irony of the situation was not lost on him: 'Serves me right for doubting the Almighty's sense of humour, he's certainly played a massive practical joke on me. Yes, Holy Lord, you don't do things by halves. Oh Supreme God, your Holy Will be done.'

The birds, uncomfortable now at his close proximity, changed their tune as they burst forth from the tree, soaring skywards.

THE END

Characters by Region - The Keepers of Hoame

Frank Thorn	Interstellar antique book salesman
Boz	Fellow traveller
Scales	Fellow traveller

Hoame, Keepers

Autarch	Head of Inner Council
Count Zastein	Inner Council Member
Baron Schail	Inner Council Member
Baron Mallinberg	Inner Council Member
Baron Deistenau	Inner Council Member

Hoame, Despots

Despot Tomas Hista	Bynar
Paula Hista	Dessan, or Despot's daughter
Vanda Hista	Dessan, or Despot's daughter
Despot Jon Kagel	Aggeparri
Astra Kagel	Despotess of Aggeparii
Inga Kagel	Dessan, or Despot's daughter
Soosha	Astra's handmaiden
Despot Wonstein	Gistenau

Hoame, Ephamon

Offa	Black, civil service clerk
Paul	Villager
Rachael	Villager
Tamar	Villager. Paul's wife
Benedict	Drone, civil servant

Anastasia   Benedict's ward

Hoame, Thyatira

Blacks

Karl Vondant

Drones

Adrian
Alan
Crispin

Whites

Castle

Crag   Gaoler
Eko   Natias' wife
Illianeth   Servant
Japhses   Captain of the Guard
Laffaxe   Physician
Matthew   Head of Kitchen
Natias   Steward

Upper Village

Amos   Hulffan cropper

Bodd	Miner, working seasonally in Ephamon
Brogg	Reuben's son
Eleazar	Trainee priest
Giella	Villager, Kim's sister
Hatt	Guardsman
Katrina	Villager
Kim	Villager, Giella's sister
Leah	Villager, Rodd's fiancée
Reuben	Hulffan cropper
Rodd	Miner, working seasonally in Ephamon
Roil	Giella's daughter
Saul	Village Head
Tsodd	Miner, working seasonally in Ephamon
Uriah	Guardsman, Giella's husband
Zadok	Priest

Lower Village

Gideon	Village Head
John	Gideon's son
Cragoop	Cobbler, Crag's son

Rabeth-Mephar - Ma'hol

Mehtar Arumah-Ru	Head of State
Shalara'tu	Wife of Mehtar
Sil Qua'moth Ri	Heir to throne

Ladosans

Madam Tersha Arpintonax	Member of political family
Hannah Unit Arpintonax	Madam Tersha's daughter
Nooni	Hannah's handmaid
Warshazzap	Soldier

Follow Frank's further adventures in the other books in this series:

Secret of the Keepers
The Molten Fire
The Journey Hoame (a prequil)
The Vortajer Plot
Death in the Senate

50281196R20421

Made in the USA
Charleston, SC
22 December 2015